NOW AND THEN, AMEN

Jon Cleary, an Australian whose books are read throughout the world, is the author of many novels including such famous bestsellers as *The Sundowners* and *The High Commissioner*.

Born in 1917, Jon Cleary left school at fifteen to become a commercial artist and film cartoonist – even a laundryman and bushworker. Then his first novel won second prize in Australia's biggest literary contest and launched him on his successful writing career.

Seven of his books have been filmed, and his novel *Peter's Pence* was awarded the American Edgar Allan Poe Prize as the best crime novel of 1974.

Jon Cleary's most recent novels have been *A Very Private War*, *The Golden Sabre*, *The Faraway Drums*, *Spearfield's Daughter*, *The Phoenix Tree*, *The City of Fading Light* and *Dragons at the Party*. He lives in Australia and travels the world researching his novels with his wife Joy.

Available in Fontana by the same author

THE SUNDOWNERS
THE BEAUFORT SISTERS
THE PHOENIX TREE
CLIMATE OF COURAGE
THE LONG PURSUIT
HIGH ROAD TO CHINA
THE HIGH COMMISSIONER
THE CITY OF FADING LIGHT
DRAGONS AT THE PARTY

JON CLEARY

Now and Then, Amen

FONTANA/Collins

First published by William Collins Sons & Co. Ltd 1988
First issued in Fontana Paperbacks 1989

Copyright © Sundowner Productions Pty Ltd 1988

Printed and bound in Great Britain by
William Collins Sons & Co. Ltd, Glasgow

For Hamilton and Gerald,
the oldest of friends

Author's Note

Since the completion of this book the New South Wales Police Department has been re-structured into regional divisions. There is no longer a Homicide Bureau as such. No person, living or dead, is represented in this story. It was all written with mirrors.

J. C.

ONE

I

The murdered nun was found slumped, like an overcome voyeur, on the front veranda of Sydney's classiest brothel.

Scobie Malone was at home in Randwick, trying to catch up on the weekend's newspapers, when the phone rang. It was answered by Claire, his twelve-year-old, who, naturally at that age, thought all phone calls were for her.

'Daddy,' she said resentfully, throwing back her long hair just like an androgynous pop star when things didn't go as she expected. 'It's Sergeant Clements. Don't be long. I'm expecting Darlene to ring me.'

'Find a drain and fall down it,' said Malone, who hoped she wouldn't.

'You talking to me, Inspector?' said Russ Clements, then laughed. Clements was a big untidy man who professed to have a lugubrious view of the world but who couldn't stop laughing at himself. 'Sorry to spoil your day, Scobie. They've just found a dead nun outside the Quality Couch.'

'I'm not in the mood for bad jokes, Russ. It's a wet Sunday.'

'This'll be better than going to church.' Clements was an agnostic, though, like a good many others, he had arrived at that frame of mind more through laziness than determination. Then he apologized: 'Sorry. You've probably already been?'

'Not yet.' Malone was a lip-service Catholic who if he missed Sunday Mass didn't feel he was being singed by the fires of hell. Though he worked in a profession with a high danger factor, he did not expect to die without at least a moment or two for a last-minute deal with The Lord. 'Okay, I'll meet you there in twenty minutes.'

Lisa came into the hallway as he hung up the phone. 'You'll meet whom where?' Lisa was Dutch-born and could sometimes be pedantic about her English. She was meticulous about saying *whom* when it was called for; she also, unlike most Australians, including her husband, knew the difference between *disinterested* and *uninterested* and sometimes sounded like a recorded English lesson. Malone, nonetheless, loved her dearly, grammar and all.

'Russ Clements. There's been a homicide.'

She made a face; she hated the thought of anyone's dying, even the deserving. 'Where?'

'Outside the Quality Couch in Surry Hills. A nun.'

'The brothel? What was she doing there? Demonstrating? Trying to convert the randy? No, I shouldn't joke. How long will you be? We're going to Mother's and Dad's for lunch.'

'Aaaagh!' That was from Maureen, the nine-year-old, and Tom, the five-year-old.

'That's no way to talk about Grandma and Grandpa.'

'But lunch is so *boring*. And Grandpa always wants us to listen to that boring *classical* music.' Maureen was a devotee of rock video clips. 'Let's all go with Daddy to the brothel.'

'What's a brothel?' said Tom, more innocent than his sister.

'No place for a five-year-old,' said his mother. 'Now all of you go in and tidy up your rooms. They look like brothels.'

'Gee, I better have a look!' Tom scampered into his room to broaden his education.

Lisa got Malone's raincoat and umbrella out of the hall closet and handed them to him as he came out of their bedroom pulling on his jacket. She looked at him with love and concern, wondering what their life together would be like if he were not a detective. He was a tall man, an inch over six feet, and he still had the build of the athlete he had once been; he had played cricket for the State as a fast bowler, though she had never seen him play and would not have understood the game if she had. He was not handsome, but he had the sort of face that would not deteriorate with age but might even become better-looking as the bones became more prominent. He had shrewd blue eyes, but she knew that they could just as often be kind and gentle. She worried that his police work would eventually coarsen or embitter him, but so far it hadn't happened.

She kissed him. 'Don't get too wet. And I hope she isn't a real nun. Maybe she's one of those queers who dress up as nuns.'

'Maybe,' said Malone, but he had learned long ago never to have preconceptions about a murder case. There are recipes for killing people, but most murders are pot luck.

When he got into the car, a four-year-old Holden Commodore, in the driveway he looked back at her through the rain as she stood in the front doorway. One year off forty, she was still beautiful and looked younger. She still had some of her pale summer tan that showed off her blonde hair and even in the grey light of the dismal late March day her smile suggested sunshine. There was a composure about her, a serenity that was like a haven to him; he always looked forward to coming home to her. Even their home, a Federation house over seventy years old, was the right background for her; both she and it suggested a permanency in his life. He backed out of the narrow driveway, cursing that murders should happen on a Sunday, supposedly a policeman's as well as everyone else's day of rest.

Randwick was a sprawling suburb five miles from the heart of the city, spread out along the top of a ridge that looked down on the smaller seaside suburb of Coogee. The western side of the ridge sloped down to the famous Randwick racecourse and to the University of New South Wales, built on the site of a former racecourse. It was an area whose few wealthy residents had made their money from racing; some grand old homes survived, though most of them now had been converted into flats. Indeed, most of the area now seemed to be flats, many of them occupied by overseas students; Asian faces were as common as the wizened faces of jockeys and strappers had once been. It was somehow illustrative of the country that the State's largest university and the biggest racecourse should be separated only by a narrow road. Life was a gamble and no one knew it better than the elements in Randwick.

Malone drove in through the steady rain towards the city. Surry Hills had never had any of the wealth that had once been in Randwick. It was an inner-city area, once a circle of low sand-hills that had been built upon and that had been mostly a working-class domain for over a hundred and fifty years. It had also, over the years, been home to countless brothels, some of the locals joining them as workers. None of them had ever been as up-market as the Quality Couch.

It was situated in one of the wider streets on top of a ridge where a few plane trees had survived the city's atmosphere. It occupied two three-storeyed terrace houses that had been converted into one and refurbished at great expense. The houses had been built by middle-class burghers in the 1880s, tight-fisted men who had wanted to stay close to their factories at the bottom of the hill, and were now lying restlessly in their graves and regretting they had invested in softgoods instead of sex. The Quality Couch catered for well-heeled businessmen, many of them visitors from overseas; one girl was said to be able to sing fourteen national anthems in their original tongues. All its girls were expected to be at least bilingual, even if only in shrieks of ecstasy. Many of its clients were professionals, accountants and advertising men and one well-known judge who liked to perform wearing his wig and nothing else. It was also visited by assorted shady characters whose incomes were larger than their reputations for honesty and decorum. Malone had been in a raiding party when he was on the Vice Squad and the brothel had first opened for business; an arrangement had been arrived at with the

Superintendent in charge of the Vice Squad and as far as Malone knew there had been no raids since. Tilly Mosman, the madame, could never be accused of running a disorderly house. Her discreetly worded brochures, claiming the precautions taken to ensure that her girls were free of AIDS, might have been written by the Australian Medical Association, especially since at least half a dozen doctors were amongst her clients.

An ambulance was parked outside the house and with it were three marked police cars, several unmarked ones and the inevitable TV newsreel vans. A dozen or so local residents stood on the opposite pavement, some of them in dressing-gowns, all of them huddled under umbrellas. They looked more melancholy than curious, like mourners who had been called earlier than they had expected.

Malone nodded to some of the uniformed policemen standing around in their glistening slickers and went into the big house through the rather grand front door. The Quality Couch did not encourage its clients to *sneak* in; it prided itself on its open-armed welcome. There was, however, no welcome this morning for the police.

Tilly Mosman was in an expensive négligé and some distress. 'A nun! Jesus Christ, what sick bastard would dump her body on my doorstep?'

'This is Inspector Malone.' Russ Clements looked unhappy, but as he turned his head towards Malone he winked. He was not given to sick jokes, but there was some humour in this. 'Miss Mosman, the owner of the establishment.'

'As if he didn't know!' She looked him up and down, something she had been doing to men since she was fifteen years old. 'Hello, Inspector. You used to be on the Vice Squad, right? I never forget a face.'

'That's all I've ever shown around here,' said Malone and was pleased when he saw a small grin crease her face. Women, and men, were always easier to talk to when their humour improved. 'How was she killed, Russ?'

'A knife or something like it through the heart. The medics say she would have died instantly.'

'Anyone hear anything? A scream?'

'Nothing. Myself, I think she was knifed somewhere else and dumped here. The body's completely stiff, she's been dead a fair while.'

'When was she found? Who found her?'

'I did.' Tilly Mosman sounded more composed now, though she kept casting anxious glances at the police officers who were tramping in and out the front door. She was house-proud to a fault: 'Wipe your feet! This isn't a crummy police station!'

Malone grinned and looked around the entrance hall in which they stood. What looked to be elegantly furnished rooms opened off on either side and a staircase with a highly polished balustrade led to the upper floors. Peach-pink carpet covered the entire ground floor and the stairs and Malone saw the footmarks already beginning to appear on it. 'Careful, fellers. Treat it as you would your own home.'

The police officers stopped in mid-stride, looked at him, raised their eyebrows, then went back outside and wiped their boots again. Malone looked back at Tilly Mosman. 'They're not used to such elegance. On our pay all we can afford is linoleum. How did you find the deceased?'

'The – ? Oh, her. You really do call 'em the deceased?'

'Sometimes we call them a stiff. But never in polite company. How did you find her?'

'When I went out to get the milk.' She pointed to a small wire basket that held four cartons of milk.

There seemed something incongruous and amusing about milk being delivered to the doorstep of a brothel, especially one like this. He wondered what the milkman would get as a Christmas box... He was aware of the atmosphere of the house, despite all its discreet elegance. The most expensive sex in the country, except for that practised by women who married for money, took place under this roof. Milk was too

6

mundane for it: champagne should be poured on the Wheaties, if breakfast was served.

'What time was that?' he said.

'I don't know for sure. About a quarter to eight, I guess. She was just lying in the corner of the front veranda, behind one of my big pots, one of the shrubs. I thought it was some drunk at first. Or a junkie.'

'Had you seen her before? I mean, had she been picketing your place?'

'Why would she do that? Nuns never picket places like mine. They know what men are like.'

'Some men,' said Malone and grinned. She smiled in return; her mood was improving. 'What about any of your girls? Would they know her? Are any of them here?'

She shook her head. 'None of them sleeps on the premises, except those who have all-night clients. But they have to be out by seven.'

'You don't serve them breakfast?' *No champagne on the Wheaties?*

'No. Some of the men don't like it, but I insist. I don't like the place looking like a brothel all day.' Even as she spoke there was a sound of a vacuum cleaner somewhere upstairs.

'My wife feels the same way,' said Malone.

She smiled again. She was a good-looking woman in her late forties; when one looked closely one saw that the years and poundage had started to catch up with her. She had big, innocent-looking eyes, but Malone suspected that if she had a heart of gold she would give none of it away but would wait for the metal prices to rise. She had buried two husbands with no regrets and it would have been surprising, in her calling, if she had had a high opinion of men. She had an equally low opinion of feminists. She was, Malone guessed, a classic madame, a businesswoman with no illusions.

A junior officer came to Malone's elbow. 'They're taking

7

the body to the morgue, Inspector. You want to see it before it goes?'

'*It?*' said Tilly Mosman and shuddered.

'I'd better.' Even after all his years on the force he was still upset when he had to view a corpse. It was not so much the sight of the still, grey body, or even the ghastliness of the wounds of some of them, that affected him; he looked at the stillness of the dead, at the utter irrevocable finality of death, and grieved for the life that had once been there. Even in the most hardened, brutal criminals there had once been some spark of innocence, some hope on someone's part for a better fate. He looked at Clements.

'Have you identified her?'

'Sister Mary Magdalene. Yeah, I know. It sounds like a bad joke, putting her on Tilly's doorstep, and maybe that's what it's meant to be. But that's her name, all right.'

Malone went out and got into the ambulance. The young nun looked as if she were no more than asleep, though the pallor of death had already settled on her; she also looked remarkably young, though he knew that death, perversely, could sometimes do that. If she had suffered any pain when she had been knifed, it had left no mark on her face. She had a handsome rather than a pretty face; she looked as if she might have been strong-willed, though he knew that death-masks could be deceptive. She was dressed in a grey woollen skirt, a grey blouse and a grey raincoat; a narrow-brimmed grey felt hat with a cross on the band lay on the pillow beside her. Malone made a sign of the cross with his thumb on her forehead, then on his own. The Celt in him never left him alone.

He got out of the ambulance into the rain dripping from the plane trees and Clements crowded in beside him under his umbrella. 'You ought to look at her shoes, Inspector.'

Malone frowned, then looked at the smart black walking shoes and the brand stamped inside them. 'Ferragamo? They're –'

'Yeah,' said Clements. 'I dunno much about women's wear, but I know that brand. They're Italian, pretty bloody expensive.'

'What would a nun be doing wearing shoes like that?'

They went back into the house and Malone held out the shoes to Tilly Mosman. 'How much would a pair of shoes like that cost?'

She looked at them, raised an eyebrow. 'Ferragamo? Two hundred and fifty, three hundred dollars. Was *she* wearing them? Jesus, aren't they supposed to take vows of poverty?'

When he was satisfied that Tilly Mosman could offer them no more information, Malone went on into Homicide head-quarters, taking Clements with him.

'There goes my Sunday. Lisa and the kids are going to walk out on me one of these days.'

Clements, damp and rumpled, like a big Airedale that had just fallen in a creek, sat slumped in the car seat. 'Why would they have dumped her body outside a brothel?'

'Had she been raped or anything? Molested?'

'Nothing like that. It's almost as if whoever killed her was looking for publicity.'

Despite the new multi-million-dollar Police Centre which had been opened recently, the New South Wales Police Force still had sections and bureaux spread all round the city. Homicide was on the sixth floor of a leased commercial building, sharing the accommodation with other, more mundane sections. Murderers in custody often rode up in the lifts with clerks and typists from Accounts.

The squad room took up half a floor and had a temporary look about it; Malone sometimes thought it was intended to give heart to the accused. He took off his raincoat and jacket, hung them on a coat-tree that had been 'requisitioned' from a murdered swindler's office, and slumped down in his chair at the battered table that was his desk.

'Righto, what have we got?'

Clements had produced his 'murder box', the crumpled old

cardboard shoe carton which, over the years, had been the repository of all the physical clues on dozens of murder cases. It was like a lottery barrel: some won, some lost. Clements sat down opposite Malone and laid out what he had on the table.

'Rosary beads – pretty expensive ones, by the look of them. The crucifix is solid gold – feel it.' Malone did, weighing it in his hand; it was something worthy of a Renaissance cardinal at least. He thought of his mother's rosary, no heavier than a string of rice grains. 'A handbag with some money in it, forty dollars and a few cents, a comb, a mirror, a key-ring with two keys on it, some tissues – the usual things from a woman's handbag.'

'Nothing else? How did you identify her?'

Clements dropped the items he had named into the 'murder box'; then, with clumsy sleight of hand, he laid a small black notebook on the desk. 'She had this hidden up in her armpit, under her jacket. As if she had been hiding it from whoever did her in.'

Malone picked up the notebook. 'Leather, not vinyl. This nun went in for nothing but the best.'

Inside the cover was her identification: Sister Mary Magdalene, Convent of the Holy Spirit, Randwick. Malone sat up: 'My kids go there! I've never heard Claire or Maureen mention her. I was there at the school concert at Christmas – Lisa and I met all the nuns.'

'Maybe she started in the new school year. When the kids went back in February.'

'Maybe. But Maureen would've mentioned her – she brings home all the school gossip, never misses a thing. She wants to come into Homicide when she grows up. She thinks we work like those fashion dummies in *Miami Vice*.'

'I'd drown any kid of mine who wanted to follow me.' A confirmed bachelor, he was safe from committing infanticide.

Malone went back to the notebook. It was new, perhaps a Christmas present three months before; it had very few entries.

There were three phone numbers and, on a separate page, a note: Check Ballyduff.

The top phone number was marked *Convent* and the other two were marked only with initials B.H. and K.H. Malone dialled the convent number. 'May I speak to Sister Mary Magdalene?'

'I'm sorry,' said a woman's voice. 'Sister won't be back till this evening. Who is this, please?'

Malone hung up. He did not believe in giving bad news over the phone.

2

He and Clements drove out to Randwick. He hated it whenever he was called to a crime in his own neighbourhood; it was as if his family were being endangered. The rain had stopped, but everything looked sodden and limp, particularly the people standing at the bus stops. When he and Clements pulled up at a red light near a bus stop, the five or six people there looked at them resentfully. Because his father could no longer drive, Malone's parents always travelled by public transport and he wondered what they felt towards those who could afford to travel in cars. His father, who still divided the world into 'us' and 'them', the workers and the bosses, probably felt just like those staring at him now. The natives had become surlily envious since the economy had worsened.

The Convent of the Holy Spirit was perched on the highest point of the Randwick ridge, with a magnificent view down to Coogee and the sea. The sun, it seemed, always came up first on the Catholics.

'You ever notice,' said Clements, 'how the Tykes always have the best bit of real estate in the district, no matter where they are?'

Tykes: it was a word for Catholics that had gone out of

fashion. But Clements, like himself, still clung to words from his youth.

'Five of the Twelve Apostles were real estate salesmen.'

'I thought they were all fishermen?'

'Only on Fridays. Anything to make a quid.'

The jokes were poor but they were part of the cement between the two men. They had started together as cadets twenty-two years before and though, over the years, they had been separated into different squads they had never lost touch. For the past three years they had been working in Homicide. Malone had gained a jump in rank, but there had been no jealousy on Clements' part. He was entirely without ambition, a bachelor who saw no point in burdening himself with responsibility in either his private life or his career.

They drove up the winding driveway to the cream buildings, dominated by the convent chapel, on the peak of the ridge. A young novice, looking bewildered and frightened when Malone introduced themselves as police officers, took them to the office of the Mother Superior.

Mother Brendan was a small woman, sharp-beaked, sharp-eyed and sharp-tongued; she believed in discipline, for herself and everyone under her. 'Mr Malone, you're here as a police-man, not a parent?'

'I'm afraid so, Mother.'

'Who's been playing up? One of our girls?'

'None of your students. We're making enquiries about Sister Mary Magdalene.'

She looked at him shrewdly; her bright eyes looked as if they might burn holes in her spectacles. 'So it was you who telephoned earlier? What's happened to her? Is she in trouble?'

'She's dead, Mother. Murdered.'

All the sharpness suddenly went out of her. She turned her face away and, in profile, Malone saw the trembling of her lips. Then she recovered and looked back at him. 'God rest her soul. This is dreadful –' Then she stopped, her bright eyes watering.

As gently as he could, Malone told her what had happened to Sister Mary Magdalene and where she had been found.

'Outside a *brothel*? Will that be in the newspapers? I have to think of our girls ... No, I don't.' She had recovered some of her sharpness, her self-discipline. 'I have to think of Mary Magdalene. Whoever killed her had a sick sense of humour, wouldn't you say? I presume you know who and what the original Mary Magdalene was?'

'Yes.' The town bike: but you didn't say that to a nun. 'Did she ever tell you why she chose that name?'

'She was a rebel. She was quite frank about that. She joined us only two months ago – she'd spent two years in Nicaragua, with our mission schools there. She was a bit of a handful, a radical, if you like, but I put up with it. The senior girls called her Red Ned.'

Red Ned: he had heard Maureen mention her, but he had never asked who Red Ned was. He would have to pay more attention to school gossip in future.

'She never took her politics into the classroom and our girls absolutely adored her. They'll be heartbroken.'

'Her politics?'

'She was something of a Marxist. Not really, not in any party sense. But she had some pretty radical ideas. The young ones, when they come back from working in the missions, are often like that.'

'Were you?'

'I grew up in a different time, Mr Malone. We never questioned anything we were taught. Now I'm sorry that we didn't ...' Then she looked as if she could have bitten her tongue. She turned her sharpness on Malone. 'Well, have you arrested her murderer?'

'No, not yet. So far we haven't got a single lead. Who was she? Where did she come from? Has she any family?'

'As far as we know, no, she had no family. She did her training at our home order in Ireland – we're an Irish order. She said she was born in England and brought up by foster parents – there always seemed to be a bit of a mystery about her. She went straight from Ireland to Nicaragua, then out here. We know very little of her background, but that isn't unusual in our vocation. A nunnery has just as many individuals as ordinary society. We're just less exposed to temptation, that's all. That's all I ever warn our girls against – temptation.'

'That's always been my downfall,' said Clements and looked surprised at the warmth of her smile.

'She had no friends in Sydney?' said Malone.

'Oh yes, she had friends – or one, anyway. Miss O'Keefe. She came here once on a visit. We all liked her and I gave Mary permission to visit her. She was supposed to be spending this weekend with Miss O'Keefe. They were going to the opera last night, I thought.'

'Where does Miss O'Keefe live?'

She looked embarrassed, an expression that sat strangely on her bright face. 'I don't know, exactly. Somewhere in the country. Mary had permission to stay with her last night at the Regent Hotel.'

Malone kept his face in place: the Regent was perhaps the most expensive hotel in the city. He nodded at Clements and the latter produced the items he had taken from the murdered nun and a plastic bag containing her shoes.

'Did Mary Magdalene have any money of her own?'

Mother Brendan shook her head. 'Not as far as I know. I queried her about those shoes and that rosary – they were presents from Miss O'Keefe, she said. I wasn't happy about such extravagance.'

'Can we have a look at her room? Is that what you call it?'

'They do nowadays. I still call it my cell.'

'Does it have bars on it?' he said with a smile.

'Only to keep out the outside world,' she said, but didn't smile. She knew where the dangers, and the temptation, lay.

It was a room bare of all but the essentials. A narrow bed, a small wardrobe, a chest of drawers, a table and chair, a prayer-cushion and a crucifix on the otherwise bare wall: even Ferragamo would have wondered what his shoes were doing in such a cell.

Sister Mary Magdalene's possessions were as meagre. Amongst them, however, were two items that aroused Malone's curiosity: a small photograph and a pocket diary. 'Who's the woman with Sister Mary?'

Mother Brendan looked at the handsome blonde woman in the rather flamboyant trenchcoat, her arm round the young nun. 'That's Miss O'Keefe.'

Malone flipped through the diary. The entries were brief, written with an impatient hand. 'Who is K.H.? There are two entries here. Meet K.H. at Vaucluse, 4 p.m. – that was for last Tuesday. Then there's another for yesterday – Meet K.H. same place 1 p.m. Did you give her permission to leave the convent last Tuesday?'

Mother Brendan frowned. 'She was supposed to have gone to the dentist. She's never lied to me before, not that I know of. She was always almost *too* honest.'

'Who's K.H. then?'

'I have no idea.'

'Let me see that notebook, Russ.' Clements handed over the black leather notebook. 'Here it is – K.H. and a 337 number.'

'That's Vaucluse way.' Clements was a lode of inconsequential information.

'May I use your phone, Mother?' Lisa would have been proud of him: *may*, not *can*. He was afraid that Mother Brendan might be an English teacher.

She led them back to her office, a big room that was obviously furnished to reassure parents that they were not committing their daughters to a prison. Two couches and the window-drapes were in colourful prints, though they didn't quite match. A bright Pro Hart print hung opposite what could have been a Neville Cayley painting of a colourful dove or the Holy Spirit in a fit of apoplexy.

Malone dialled the 337 number and a woman's voice answered. 'The Hourigan residence.'

'I'm sorry, I think I must have the wrong number. Which Hourigan is that?'

'Mr Fingal Hourigan. Or were you wanting Archbishop Hourigan?'

'No. I'm sorry, I do have the wrong number.' He hung up and looked at Clements. 'Fingal Hourigan. And Archbishop Hourigan.'

'K. H. Kerry Hourigan. That's the Archbishop.'

Malone looked at him gratefully and admiringly. 'Is there anything you don't know?'

Mother Brendan said, 'Archbishop Hourigan? His name came up one night at supper and I thought Sister Mary was going to blow her top. She got *so* angry . . . But she wouldn't tell me why. She apologized and just shut up. He's one of *the* Hourigans, isn't he?'

'Yes,' said Malone. 'I think we'll go and see *the* Hourigan himself. Old Man Fingal.'

'Can we claim Mary Magdalene's body? I'd like to bury her with a Mass. Unless we can find Miss O'Keefe, we may be the only mourners.'

'I'll try the Regent,' said Malone.

3

There was no Miss O'Keefe registered at the Regent and no Sister Mary Magdalene. Clements, who had gone in to check, came out and got in beside Malone. It had started to rain again and taxis were banking up in the drive-in entrance to pick up departing guests. One of the bell-boys came along and looked in at Malone.

'The commissionaire says would you mind moving on, sir?'

'In a moment.'

'No, *now*, sir.' He was a bell-boy with ambitions to be a manager.

'Police,' said Malone. 'One of our few perks is parking where we like. We'll be moving on in a moment. G'day.'

The bell-boy thought for a moment, decided he held a losing hand and went away. Malone looked at Clements. 'I don't think Sister Mary Magdalene was as honest as Mother Brendan thought. Do you know where Fingal Hourigan lives?'

'No, but I don't think we'll have any trouble finding it. I've seen his place from the harbour, he built it about twenty years ago. It looks like a cross between a cathedral and a castle. There's probably a moat and a drawbridge on the street side.'

They drove out along the south shore of the harbour. Vaucluse was at the eastern end, rising up towards the cliffs along the coast. New money had moved in over the past couple of decades, but Vaucluse still smelled of old money; some elements were said still to offer pound notes instead of dollars to the local tradesmen. Down in the waterfront homes money probably never made an appearance at all: the rich didn't need it.

The home of the richest of them all had no moat or drawbridge, but it did have a ten-foot-high stone wall. Inset in the wall were tall wooden gates that totally obscured the view from the street. On the gates were welcoming signs that offered the possibility of either life imprisonment or dismemberment by guard dogs. YOU HAVE BEEN WARNED, said a final hospitable note.

Malone spoke into the intercom in a box beside the gate and a woman's voice answered. 'Yes? Who's that?'

'Police,' said Malone. 'We'd like to see Mr Hourigan.'

'Do you have an appointment?'

'Do I need one? I once got in to see the State Premier without an appointment.' He winked and grinned at Clements. It was still raining and they were huddled together under Malone's umbrella like over-sized Siamese twins.

It was two minutes before there was a buzzing noise and

the gates swung open. There were no signs of any guard dogs; presumably they had been called in. The grounds were not large, perhaps no more than two acres; but two acres of harbour frontage would buy fifty to sixty housing lots out in the western suburbs where the dreamers and battlers lived. Malone was apolitical, but lately he had begun to feel anti-capitalist.

The house was built of stone and had ruined the architect's career. Fingal Hourigan had wanted an Irish castle with the sun-catching aspects of a Mediterranean villa; what he had got looked like a drifting hulk in the Bay of Biscay. Cruising ferries on the harbour headed for it with their loads of tourists: it was the comic turn of their guided tours. The Japanese, being polite, didn't laugh but wondered why the Australians made fun of their rich; the Americans smiled indulgently but thought, what the hell, a man could do what he liked with his money; and the British, at least those who bothered to make the cruise, only had their opinions confirmed that the Australians, especially Irish-Australians, had no taste anyway. Fingal Hourigan, never a man to worry about public opinion, least of all British opinion, only kept adding to his castle-villa. The latest addition was a gargoyle brought from a ruined French abbey and now standing on a terrace balustrade and poking its tongue out at the tourists.

Malone had met Fingal Hourigan only once, nineteen years before when he had been temporarily assigned to the Fraud Squad. Hourigan had come out of that investigation smelling of roses, but Malone had only remembered the smell of the fertilizer that had been used. He had seen no money change hands, but three months later a senior officer at Police Head-quarters had a brand-new car.

Hourigan was smaller than he had remembered him, but perhaps that had something to do with his age; he was rumoured to have turned eighty. He had a handsome lean face, spoiled only by a certain foxiness about the pale-blue eyes; his hair was thick and silvery and he obviously took

18

pride in it; and he had a smile that could be read a dozen ways. He was dressed in a dark-blue cashmere suit, a cream silk shirt and a blue silk tie, and he leaned on a solid-silver walking-stick. He was said to be the country's only billionaire, but he was too shrewd to confirm or deny it. There is nothing so frustrating for self-made men than to be kept guessing about another man's riches.

'I was just going to church.' He had a firm, mellow-toned voice, that of a much younger man. 'You're busting in, you know, Inspector.'

Malone apologized, careful of where he trod; another of the rumours about Fingal Hourigan was that he could pull more reins than a race-full of bent jockeys. 'I really wanted to see your son, Archbishop Hourigan.'

Hourigan showed no surprise. 'What about?'

'A murdered nun,' said Malone, hoping for some surprise this time.

There was none; the pale-blue eyes stared back at him. 'That's not a good subject for a Sunday morning. In any event, he's coming with me to say Mass.'

'I won't delay him too long. Perhaps he can say Mass for the dead nun.'

The pale-blue eyes didn't flash; they just seemed to go dead, became pale-blue marbles. He stared at Malone for a long moment, then turned and pressed a button on a table near him. Almost as if she had been waiting poised on one foot for the call, the housekeeper who had admitted Malone and Clements appeared in the doorway. She was middle-aged, plump, matronly and brusque, the sort Malone had seen around presbyteries: she would say the rosary while she shot the butcher for over-charging. She looked at Malone as if he should be shot for intruding on her master.

'Maggie, tell the Archbishop he has a visitor. A police officer.' Malone wondered if his ears were too acute: was there a warning in Hourigan's voice? 'And ring the church, tell them we may be a little late for Mass.'

'Will I tell 'em to be starting the Mass without His Grace?' She had a brogue one could have sliced with a peat-shovel.

'No, they can wait. Ten minutes' waiting won't hurt them.'

The housekeeper went away and Malone wondered what the local parish priest and his congregation would think of being kept waiting. Australians never liked to be kept waiting, not even by the Pope.

While he did his own waiting Malone covertly took note of his surroundings. Hourigan, it seemed, was an eclectic collector; the big drawing-room, one couldn't call it a living-room, looked as if it had been furnished from a museum's left-overs. There were Aboriginal bark paintings, Greek vases, an Egyptian sarcophagus, a Celtic stone cross, a French Impressionist painting and a Streeton landscape. The chairs, tables and couches were dark and heavy, right out of the middle of the worst of the Victorian period. A grand piano stood in one corner, covered with an emerald-green silk shawl; one could imagine a concerto being converted into a lively Irish jig. It was what Malone's mother, who might have been able to afford one of the chairs, would have called a 'nice home'.

Kerry, Archbishop Hourigan, came striding into the room. Malone's first impression was that he would *stride* every-where, even down from the altar to give communion ('Here, take this! Move on! Next!'). He was taller than his father, six feet at least, and heavily built; he gave corporeal meaning to the term 'a solid church man'. He had a plump, blandly handsome face with the long Irish upper lip and eyes only a little darker than his father's. His hair was thick, like his father's, dark-brown and wavy and beautifully cut; he would hate to spoil it by having to cover it with a mitre. He had an air of arrogant authority about him that, Malone guessed, made junior priests and altar boys wish they were Presby-terians. He might question the Pope's infallibility but never his own.

'A police officer to see me?' He had his father's mellow-toned voice, but fruitier and better projected; he would never need a microphone in the pulpit, he would keep awake the dozers in the back pews of even the biggest cathedrals. 'A parking fine or have I crossed against a red light?' He was all smiles; Malone waited for a blessing. Then he sobered: 'No, Inspector, it's more serious than that, isn't it?'

'Much more, Your Grace. We're investigating the murder of a young nun, Sister Mary Magdalene. Your phone number – or rather, your father's – was in her notebook. She also had a date, or so her book said, with you yesterday at four p.m.'

All the colour, even the weight, seemed to go out of Kerry Hourigan's face. He looked at his father and shook his head as if he had been punched. 'Oh no! Not that girl . . .'

'Her?' Fingal Hourigan looked directly at his son; Malone and Clements might as well have not been in the room. 'When they said a murdered nun, I never connected . . . Holy Jesus! We'll have to have a Mass said for her soul!'

Malone was suspicious. How many nuns did Fingal Hourigan know? The Archbishop had collapsed into a chair and Malone, turning away from the old man, looked at him. 'How well did you know her, Your Grace?'

'Eh? Know her? I –' He took out a handkerchief and wiped his nose without blowing it. Malone recognized the ploy, had seen it a hundred times; it was a way of gaining time while the thoughts were put in order. Kerry Hourigan put away the handkerchief, but not before Malone had recognized it as silk. The Catholic religious seemed to be living well these days: Ferragamo shoes, silk handkerchiefs . . . Peter's Pence must be doing well against the devalued Aussie dollar. 'I didn't know her at all. She telephoned me, said she wanted to talk to me about something. She sounded rather – well, uptight, excitable. A lot of these young nuns are very militant these days. They want to change the Church, as if they have some right to take it over. Women are running amok.'

I should have Lisa here with me. Malone turned to Fingal

Hourigan. 'How did you know about her?'

'She came here to see my son and I told her she wasn't welcome. I showed her the door and she left.'

'Just like that? How did you feel about that, Your Grace?'

The Archbishop didn't look at his father. 'I didn't think it was very charitable.'

Hourigan didn't seem put out that his son was criticizing him in front of strangers. 'My son is a very charitable man. Sometimes he has to be protected from himself. Blessed are the meek, but not the militant, I keep telling him. We're sorry to hear of the young girl's death and we'll have a Mass said for her, but she is no business of ours, Inspector.'

Malone wished he were better educated in the Bible; but he could think of no apt quotation to answer Fingal Hourigan. 'So the girl was a complete stranger to you both, you know nothing about her?'

'That's what we just said. Now if you'll excuse us?'

'Inspector –'

Clements' diplomatic cough sounded like a bad attack of croup. Malone looked at him and the sergeant nodded towards the grand piano, at something Malone had missed in his quick survey. On the silk shawl stood a gold-framed photograph of a woman, a handsome blonde woman in what looked like an artist's smock. It was Miss O'Keefe, Mary Magdalene's friend.

Malone kept his surprise to himself, said carefully, 'That lady looks familiar, Mr Hourigan. Who is she?'

It seemed to Malone that Fingal Hourigan was just as careful in his reply; at least he took his time. 'She is my daughter Brigid. I don't know where you would have met her.'

'My mistake,' said Malone. 'I must have been thinking of someone else.' Then he looked at the Archbishop, who was still sitting in his chair. 'I remember reading in the papers that you are only here on a visit. When will you be leaving?'

'I'm leaving on Saturday. I'm going back to Rome.' Kerry

Hourigan stood up, regained some of his authority. 'I take it you won't be needing me again, Inspector?'

'Oh, I can't promise that, Your Grace. Police work is much like religion, I should think – we never know what the sinners are going to do. You won't be going to Rome, will you, Mr Hourigan?'

'If I decide to go, will I have to get your permission?'

'I don't think so. The last thing I want is to bring the Vatican down on my head.'

Fingal Hourigan abruptly smiled; his teeth were expensive and bright, but his smile was charmless, at least at the moment.

'You're Irish, aren't you? I've never known an Irishman yet who was a good copper. It's something in our make-up.'

'Some of us keep trying,' said Malone. He looked at the Archbishop. 'There has never been an Irish Pope, has there? But they must keep trying. Like us Aussies.'

The Hourigans looked at each other. Then Fingal said, 'Goodbye, Inspector. Watch the dogs on your way out.'

But the dogs were not in sight as Malone and Clements walked down the driveway to the tall gates. It was still raining and Malone wondered if they were the sort of guard dogs that only worked in fine weather.

'Like the dockers,' said Clements, who had his prejudices. Then he said, 'Did you notice the chill when you made that crack about an Irish Pope? I thought my balls were going to fall off.'

'I didn't mean anything by it.' As they got into the car the rain suddenly ceased and small patches of blue appeared in the low grey overcast; they were not sunlit and they reminded Malone somehow of Fingal Hourigan's eyes. 'There was a chill, too, when he mentioned his daughter.'

'Miss O'Keefe? I've got the feeling we've been listening to a pack of lies this morning. I wonder how many she'll tell us when we find her?'

'How much do we know about Fingal Hourigan?'

'I only know what I've read in the papers.'

'How much is that?'

Clements thought for a moment. He chewed on his lip, a habit he had had since childhood. Then he shook his head.

'Now you ask,' he said, 'I know bugger-all about him.'

TWO

I

Malone and Clements drove out to see Brigid Hourigan, also known as Miss O'Keefe. They had no trouble in finding where she lived: Malone rang an art critic whom he had met through Lisa.

'Brigid Hourigan? She lives at Stokes Point, got the sort of home no art critic could afford. She's one of the best artists we have, but for some reason she almost never exhibits here in Australia – maybe she thinks she would be trading on her father's name. All her stuff goes overseas and sells for big prices. She's very popular with European collectors. She sort of takes the mickey out of religious art, without being blasphemous, like some of these young smart-alecs who paint naked Christs with big derricks. You and Lisa thinking of buying something of hers?'

'On a cop's pay? Don't be blasphemous.'

As they drove north out of the city the sky had begun to clear and the promise of a beautiful autumn day had begun to assert itself. Malone loved the change of seasons; it was almost as if it gave him the opportunity to change moods. Summer had been a fine season twenty years ago, when he had been playing cricket; but it was not a term in which to be slogging through an investigation; tempers were always cooler in cooler weather. He longed for winter, which was not his season of discontent.

'You think Old Man Hourigan will have phoned Miss O'Keefe?' said Clements.

'If he hasn't, the Archbishop will have. Get the Irish and the Church together and even the confessional holds no secrets. So says *my* old man, a lapsed Irish Tyke.'

'My folks were Congregational. If they lapsed, they never knew.'

Stokes Point was a narrow strip of road and bush-surrounded houses on the eastern side of Pittwater, a wide stretch of yachting water twenty-five miles north of the city. The houses were a mixture, from old fibro weekenders to more expensive abodes by experimental architects. Brigid Hourigan's was the grandest on the point.

The garden surrounding it was lush and semi-tropical; it suggested lassitude, an indolent passion for laziness. It was not well kept; if there was a gardener he believed in letting nature take its course. The house, large and terraced, had a Mediterranean look to it; several marble goddesses stood on the terraces, their hauteur spoiled only by scarves of kookaburra crap. Everything looked slightly run down, like a scratched and faded painting left too long in the open.

A young Italian houseman greeted them at the big teak front door. He was dressed in sandals, black slacks and a white jacket buttoned to the neck. He was belligerently unwelcoming till Malone produced his badge, then he looked suddenly afraid. 'Does Signorina Hourigan know you are coming?'

'Possibly,' said Malone.

The houseman went away, glancing back at them over his shoulder as he went, and Clements said, 'Signorina? Somehow it doesn't go with Hourigan.'

The room in which they stood, though cluttered and untidy, had more taste to it than Fingal Hourigan's drawing-room. There were antique Italian and Spanish tables and sideboards, chairs that might have accommodated the broad bums of *conquistadores* and *condottieri*, heavy figured drapes that

26

suggested castles and *palazzi*. There were small pieces of statuary, but only two paintings, each in a richly carved frame. One was a Goya and the other was a Canaletto, but neither Malone nor Clements knew that. They both liked what they saw: neither painting had been done by a smart-arse.

Brigid Hourigan came into the room, the young Italian trailing her. She was dressed in a bright-red housecoat that threw colour into her face. She was younger-looking than Malone had expected; her photos did not do her justice. She was not strictly beautiful, but strikingly handsome, her thoughts hidden in her wide, heavily-lidded eyes which were much darker than her father's. She was, Malone guessed, a dark-minded Celt, one who would never be sentimental about Gloccamorra or Mother Machree. She held an expensive cut-glass tumbler of whisky in one hand and looked ready to toss it at Malone if he asked the wrong questions.

'I have some bad news, Miss Hourigan –'

'Yes?' She gave nothing away: he might have been telling her it was going to rain again.

'Your friend, Sister Mary Magdalene –' He waited for some reaction, but there was none. Bugger it, he thought, they *haven't* phoned her! What sort of men were Fingal Hourigan and this woman's brother, the Archbishop? He said gently, 'She's been murdered.'

The whisky in the glass shook a little, but that was the only sign that she was upset. 'Where? How?'

'She was killed with a knife. Her body was found outside a brothel in Surry Hills.'

'Oh Jesus God!' Then the reaction did set in; for a moment it looked as if she might collapse. The young Italian moved quickly to her, put his arm round her and led her to a chair. He looked in angry reproach at Malone, as if the latter should not have brought such news, but he said nothing.

Malone waited till Brigid Hourigan had recovered. Through the wide plate-glass doors of the big room he could see out over a broad terrace to the shining expanse of

Pittwater. The Sunday yachts, glad of the break in the weather, were already beating their way up from the yacht club moorings at the south end of the big inlet. A small dinghy went by close inshore, sailed by a couple of teenagers whose shouts and laughter came up clearly, almost derisively. He looked back at Brigid Hourigan, was surprised to find she had been weeping: he hadn't expected that of her.

'How did you know to come here?' She had the family's deep rich voice. A family conversation must have sounded like an oratorio.

'Mother Brendan, at the convent, told us about a Miss O'Keefe. Then we saw your photo in your father's house at Vaucluse. Didn't he phone you we might be coming?'

'My father and I don't communicate regularly.' She took a sip, a long one, of her drink.

'What about your brother, the Archbishop? Do you and he speak to each other?'

'Occasionally.' Then she seemed to realize that this interview might not be as short as she had hoped: 'I'm sorry. Won't you sit down?'

Malone and Clements lowered themselves into the big leather chairs; neither of them looked like a *conquistadore*. Australians can be heroes, but somehow never look heroic. Perhaps they are always afraid of being taken down a peg or two.

'Why the Miss O'Keefe? Did Sister Mary know who you really were?'

She hesitated, then said, 'She always knew. We just thought it better the convent didn't associate me with the Hourigan name.'

Malone wanted to ask why, but decided to leave that till later. 'Were you close friends?'

She nodded. 'I wish we'd have been closer. We might have been, if she'd lived.'

'Did she ever confide in you? Have you any idea why anyone would have wanted to murder her?'

'Not – murder her, no. But not everyone liked her opinions. She felt very strongly about certain things.'

'Such as?'

She looked up at the houseman hovering behind her and said, 'Perhaps the gentlemen would like some coffee or a drink, Michele?'

'Coffee,' said Malone, and Clements nodded.

'Refill that for me,' she said and handed her glass to Michele, who then went out of the room. 'I like my liquor. My brother, the Archbishop, preaches little sermons about it, but I think there are bigger sins. What do think, Sergeant?'

Clements was no authority on sin: 'Inspector Malone tells me you have to be a Catholic to know what sin is all about.'

'How true,' said the Archbishop's sister and looked at Malone. 'I've been surrounded by sin all my life. Or the condemnation of it.'

'Did Sister Mary condemn it?'

'My drinking or sin in general?' She shook her head and all at once looked sad and older. 'Teresa had more understanding than any young girl I've ever met.'

'Teresa?'

'Did I say that?' For a moment she seemed annoyed with herself. 'Yes, Teresa. That was her given name before she went into the convent.'

'What was her surname?'

'She was known in the order as Teresa French.'

Malone sensed the evasion. 'But French wasn't her real name. What was it?'

The Italian houseman came back with a tray on which were two cups of coffee, some biscuits and the refilled whisky glass. When the three had been served, he retreated to a corner of the room and stood there. His mistress made no attempt to dismiss him; she did not seem to think it odd that a servant should remain listening to her being interviewed by the police. But then servants in Australia, even immigrants, have always looked upon themselves as equals of their masters or their mistresses. Jack's as good as his master was part of the national anthem, though Jack was never prepared to accept arbitration on the matter in case the decision went against him.

Brigid Hourigan sipped her drink, then said, 'Hourigan.'

'Pardon?' said Malone, sipping the strong Italian coffee and trying not to make a face.

'Hourigan. That was her surname.'

Malone put down his cup, looked at the strong handsome face, saw the resemblance that had escaped him till now and said, 'She was your daughter?'

She nodded. 'Illegitimate, if you want to be bourgeois about it.' The second glass of whisky was loosening her tongue, though not thickening it; the voice was as rich and deep as ever. At the moment it was also sad and full of love and regret. 'It doesn't matter who her father was – he's dead.' And sounded forgotten. 'He was French – hence her fake surname. She was always religious, even as a child. I don't know why, unless she inherited it from my mother – though she never met my mother. Perhaps she was just atoning for my sins. I've always been a sinner,' she said without coyness or pride.

'Perhaps her uncle influenced her?'

'My brother didn't know she had become a nun till two years ago.'

'Did your father know?'

She shrugged. 'Perhaps. My father seems to know everything.' The tongue certainly was loose.

'Had she been seeing much of your brother? I mean since he got back to Sydney?'

'I don't know. She'd been pestering him – she told me that. And so did he. They didn't see eye to eye on much connected with the Church.'

'Anything specific?'

All at once she looked tired, ready to break. She put down her glass and the whisky splashed on her housecoat. Malone, as so often, felt the sudden hatred of his job. He was continually bruising people, most of them innocent, as if the law compelled him to carry his bunched fist ready to hit them. He was not concerned with justice, that came later from other, supposedly better-educated people; but on the way to justice the law (and society) sometimes expected too much of men like himself and Clements. He glanced at Clements and saw that the big man had turned his head away and was staring out at the distant water.

'I'm sorry, Miss Hourigan –' In normal circumstances, he guessed, she would not bruise easily, if at all. Today, however, she had lost a child, her only one, and she had abruptly realized the depth of her loss.

Then she drew herself together; it was a visible effort. 'Why don't you ask my brother?' she said spitefully. 'The Archbishop has always had great regard for specifics. His sermons are full of them.'

'We'll do that. But we may have to come back . . .'

She nodded and stood up, swaying a little. The Italian houseman hurried forward and took her arm. 'The signorina will have to lie down. Could you please see yourselves out, signori?'

They went slowly out of the room, he now with his arm round her, she with her head on his shoulder. Malone looked at Clements and the latter raised his thick, untidy eyebrows.

'Is that what servants are for?' said Clements softly.

'Why not?' said Malone. 'You miss out on a lot in an egalitarian society.'

'Egalitarian? You been reading the *Times on Sunday* again?'

The shallow joke camouflaged the pity they felt for the woman. It was not something they could confess to each other.

They drove back to the city under a now bright blue sky, against the Sunday morning traffic heading for a last day on the beaches before the weather turned cold. A convoy of three battered cars cruised by them, surfboards strapped to the roofs, fins sticking up like those of cruising sharks. At Brookvale the crowd was already arriving for today's rugby league matches, going into the ground with their club scarves and beanies and flags, like hordes of squires ready to set up the battlefield for their knights.

'Who do you think will win today? I've got twenty bucks on Manly.'

'Russ, is there anything you won't bet on?'

'I've never bet on the outcome of a case,' said Clements, looking sideways at him. 'You thinking of betting on this one?'

'With the Pope as the Archbishop's trainer? But I think we'll go and have another look at his form.'

When they reached the Hourigan mansion they had to go through a repeat routine. 'It's Inspector Malone again. I'd like to see the Archbishop.'

The intercom crackled with disapproval. 'Have you got an appointment with His Grace?'

'Just tell him I want to go to confession.'

There was another wait of a minute or two, then there was the buzz and the gates opened. The housekeeper was waiting for them at the front door, looking as unwelcoming as the first time. Malone had a moment of fantasy in which he saw her as one of the guard dogs, a Doberman with an Irish bark.

'What has a policeman got to confess?' she demanded.

'Where's your sense of humour, Maggie?'

'Mrs Kelly, from you. And I keep me sense of humour to meself.' And she would, like a family secret.

She led them this time not into the big drawing-room but into a library only slightly smaller. Or perhaps it was an office:

on side tables stood a word processor, a computer, a copying machine and a wire basket full of documents. But books lined the walls to the high ceiling and the titles there were as eclectic as the pieces out in the drawing-room. Fingal Hourigan sat behind a magnificent antique desk at which nothing less than a major armistice of war should have been signed. Or a papal bull.

Archbishop Hourigan sat beside the desk in a high-backed chair designed for the hierarchy, either ecclesiastic or commercial. Malone and Clements were motioned towards two lesser chairs. Malone had the sudden feeling that he was in an annexe of the Vatican, that at any moment the Swiss Guards might appear on the terrace outside the big french doors.

'Have you come to tell us you've found the person who murdered Mary Magdalene?'

'No, Your Grace. We're not much more informed than when we left here a couple of hours ago. Except that we've found out she was your niece. And your granddaughter, Mr Hourigan.'

Father and son looked at each other. There was sudden pain in the Archbishop's face, but his father's had no expression at all. Then Kerry Hourigan said, his voice unexpectedly hoarse, 'I suppose we should have told you that. But we were trying to protect my sister.'

'Oh? In what way?'

The Archbishop waved a hand: not helplessly but uncertainly. 'I really don't know. It was instinctive. My father doesn't like publicity ...'

'You've had plenty of publicity, Your Grace. This past month you've been on TV, in the newspapers ... How do you feel about that, Mr Hourigan?'

Fingal was still showing no expression. 'If it helps the Church, I have no objection. My son is a public figure.'

So are you, mate. 'Your daughter also doesn't like publicity.'

33

'So I'm told,' said Fingal, but didn't say who had told him.

Malone looked again at the Archbishop, who now seemed to have regained some of his composure. 'Why did you tell us earlier that you didn't know her?'

'I really don't know. I suppose I was just so shocked by the news. It was stupid –'

'Yes, damned stupid,' said Malone, feeling that for the moment he was in command here. But out of the corner of his eye he could see Fingal Hourigan, who would never let any situation get away from him. 'I understand you and Sister Mary didn't agree on certain Church matters?'

'They were generational differences.'

'What exactly do you do at the Vatican? I've forgotten what the papers said.'

'I'm the Director of the Department for the Defence Against Subversive Religions.'

'Subversive religions being communism, things like that?'

'Not only communism. The new Islamic fundamentalism. Certain other religions.' He had the smug certainty of someone who had got the word direct from Jesus Christ. Malone, a live-and-let-live Christian, the sort who turned the other cheek out of laziness, felt the intolerance he always felt when other people sounded intolerant. But maybe the others were more aware of the dangers ... 'There are enemies, Inspector.'

'Sergeant Clements is a Congregationalist – or was. Would he be part of the enemy?'

The Archbishop glanced at Clements, smiled, raised a hand as if he were about to bless him. 'I'm sure the Congregationalists aren't subversive, Mr Clements. Do they still exist?' His arrogance was going to be a handicap when he got to Heaven, but nobody has proved Heaven is full of humble citizens.

'Was Sister Mary subversive?' said Malone.

'Yes,' said her uncle emphatically. If he and his father felt any grief over her death it had been rapidly submerged.

34

'Did she disagree with anyone else besides you?'

'She would have disagreed with Jesus Christ himself,' said Fingal. He had the look and sound of a man who would have done the same himself, as an equal. 'She was looking for trouble.'

'Jesus Christ!' said Clements, but only Malone heard him.

'So she might have made some enemies?'

'You can be sure of that,' said Fingal, taking over from his son.

'In Nicaragua, maybe?'

'Possibly. There could be some Nicaraguans here. The country's full of people from everywhere these days.' He had been in Australia long enough to consider all late-comers as foreigners. He had the same antipathy towards the Aboriginal Australians, who were too foreign for him to understand. 'Why don't you look there, amongst the Latin Americans?'

'We'll do that,' said Malone. 'Were you ever in Nicaragua, Your Grace?'

The Archbishop nodded after a moment's hesitation. 'Some years ago, before the Sandinista Government took over.'

'And not since then?'

Again there was a slight hesitation, as if he were checking his memory, then he said, 'No.'

Malone looked at both of them, father and son. 'So you have no idea who might have killed her?'

Archbishop Hourigan looked shocked, or tried to look that way. 'Did you really expect us to? Good God, man, we don't know *murderers*!'

I wonder what mortal sins you've heard in the confessional? But Malone didn't ask that question. Whoever had killed Sister Mary Magdalene wouldn't be the sort to ask for absolution.

'No, I suppose not. It's never as easy as that – I mean for us police. Oh, your sister left us before –'

'You've been to see her?' said Fingal.

35

'Of course. Didn't you expect us to?' The look on the old man's face told Malone he had scored a point, but he didn't press it. He went on: 'We didn't have time to tell her the body is in the City Morgue. Mother Brendan, from the convent, was going to claim it, but she didn't know Sister Mary Magdalene was a Hourigan.'

'She was never that,' said Fingal Hourigan.

'Oh yes, she was,' Kerry Hourigan told him. 'She took Brigid's name by deed poll when she came home three months ago. I guess she hadn't told them that at the convent.'

The expression on the old man's face suggested that Teresa Hourigan had introduced AIDS into the family instead of just herself. He stood up and without a word walked out of the room, the silver walking-stick thumping once on the tiled floor of the entrance hall like a rifle shot.

'You must forgive my father,' said the Archbishop, pressing a button on the desk; somewhere at the back of the house a bell rang. 'He is a man of strong feelings.'

'He'll have plenty of practice with them,' said Malone as he and Clements rose. 'I'm sure we'll be back to test them.'

Mrs Kelly, all a-glower, swept them out of the house. 'You had no right coming here! They are decent gentlemen, both of them!'

'Maggie,' said Malone quietly and kindly, 'haven't they told you? Mr Hourigan's granddaughter, the Archbishop's niece, has been murdered.'

'Holy Mother of God!' She was suddenly flattened, turned to a cardboard figure in the frame of the big doorway. Then she frowned, as if she hadn't heard right. 'Who?'

'The young nun who came here yesterday. It was yesterday, wasn't it?'

She blessed herself, mouth trembling in a silent prayer. 'Yes. She came several times ...'

'Maggie!'

Fingal Hourigan stood behind her, a small figure of towering rage. The silver stick quivered like a lightning bolt; for a moment it looked as if he might strike the housekeeper. Then, abruptly, there as an amazing change. The rage disappeared, gone as if a mask had been whipped off him; he smiled at Malone, tapped the floor with the stick as if seeking some rhythm. Mrs Kelly looked over her shoulder at him: she was unafraid of his temper.

'Someone around here should be praying for her, yes,' she said and pushed past him and disappeared into the house.

Malone looked directly at Fingal Hourigan. 'It would seem that someone around here isn't telling the truth.'

Hourigan smiled; but it was a challenge, not a friendly expression. 'The truth is a dangerous weapon, Inspector. It should be prohibited by law. Good-day to you.'

He shut the door in Malone's face.

3

Malone made it home in time that evening to go to six o'clock Mass with Lisa and the children. He sat in a back pew of the Sacred Heart Church in Randwick and listened to Father Joannes, the parish priest, drone on with all the old platitudes that were now brassy with usage. He came from the old school of priests and politicians who taught that everything had to be said thrice, as if the sinners and voters were criminally slow on the uptake. He believed in fear of the Lord and not love of Him. He was followed by a trio twanging guitars and singing a pop hymn whose words were as banal and meaningless as those heard on *Countdown*. Malone sat and wondered what he was doing here in this gathering, which, except for the guitars, might have been the same sort of service his mother had come to fifty years ago. He found himself wondering what Sister Mary Magdalene, the rebel, had thought of it all, she with the mud and misery of Nicaragua on her Ferragamo shoes. If, indeed, she had worn any shoes at all in that racked country.

Going home Lisa said, 'A bad day? You really look down in the dumps.'

'I always am when I have to work on Sundays.'

'Weren't they terrific hymns?' said Maureen, the rock video fan. 'They make Mass *interesting*.'

'Jesus,' said Malone quietly.

'Are you swearing?' said Tom.

'No, I was praying. Who wants to go to McDonald's for supper?'

'I'd rather go to Prunier's,' said Claire, who read the social columns of the *Sun-Herald*.

Malone looked at her. One day she would be beautiful and would probably be featured in the *Sun-Herald* herself; by then, he knew, he would have half-lost her to another man. 'Let's settle for McDonald's tonight.'

They all agreed to, including Lisa, the Dutch gourmet. 'Well, at least I shan't have to cook,' she said defensively. 'I'm like you, I don't like working on Sundays.'

The meal was the best spot of the day for Malone. He munched on his Big Mac and looked at his family and compared it to the Hourigans. We're happy, he thought, and what more can I offer them? Maybe dinner at Prunier's or Berowra Waters, but he was sure happiness wasn't an item on the menu at those restaurants.

They drove home and the children were put to bed. Then he and Lisa settled down to finish off the weekend papers. But first Lisa said, 'Do you want to talk about it?'

He knew what she meant. After fourteen years of marriage nothing had to be spelled out between them, not unless they were arguing and wanted to be defensive. They were compatible, but in the best of ways, by not being too alike. She had a natural patience; he had had to learn to wear his. Being a Celt, he had not been born a listener, but he had learned to be that, too; being Dutch, coming from the crossroads of so much historical trade, she listened to the bid before she made her counter-bid. Invariably she always left him with

38

the feeling that he had lost all their arguments.

Tonight there was no argument. 'I've got a young nun, murdered, and two-thirds of her family don't seem to care a damn.'

'Who's the one-third who does care?'

'Her mother.' He explained the circumstances of the case. 'Old Man Hourigan doesn't worry me – he seems to be just a self-centred rich old bastard. But the Archbishop . . . I could have been telling him Martin Luther was dead, for all he seemed to care.'

'Do you think archbishops are so much different from other men?'

'They're expected to be. A little more charity and compassion . . .'

'You expect too much of people.'

'When did you become so cynical?'

'I'm not. It just hurts me to see you lose your illusions.'

'They were lost years ago, even before I met you.'

She shook her head, leaned across and kissed him. 'You're wrong. They're like your sun cancers – I don't think you'll ever get rid of them.'

Then the phone rang out in the hallway. She got up, went out and came back a moment later looking concerned. 'It's for you.'

'Who is it?'

'He wouldn't say.'

Malone got up, hoping this wasn't another call to duty, went out and picked up the phone. 'This is Inspector Malone. Who's that?'

'It doesn't matter who I am, Inspector.' The man's voice was soft, with a faint accent. 'We'll probably never meet. For your sake, I hope not. Take heed of my warning, Inspector –' The formality of the words brought a small grin to Malone's face, though he knew the man did not mean to sound humorous. 'It will be better for all concerned if you let the Sister Mary Magdalene case just rest. Let it die quietly.'

'Thank you for the warning, Mr –?'

'No names, Inspector.' One could almost see the man smiling at the other end of the line.

'Righto, no names. But no deal, either. I don't drop murder cases, warning or no warning.'

There was a moment's silence; then: 'You will regret your attitude, Inspector. Good-night.'

The phone went dead in Malone's ear. He replaced the receiver and stood staring at the wall in front of him. It was not the first threat he had received; he could be afraid but not alarmed. When such threats were made he thought not of himself but of his family: they would suffer more than he, even if, or especially if, he were killed. But no archbishop would go *that* far... Then he wondered why he had instantly connected Archbishop Hourigan with the threatening stranger.

He went back into the living-room. This was home, his harbour: he felt safe here. The house, an old-fashioned one with gabled roof and decorated eaves, had been built at the turn of the century when houses had been built to last and tradesmen had taken pride in their work. It had survived the climate, termites, burglars, mortgages and the Malone kids. The Malones had bought it cheaply, because of its run-down condition, and Lisa had lovingly restored it. It was no castle, but it was a fort against the woes of the world, political doorknockers, Avon ladies and Jehovah's Witnesses.

But even now, at nine-thirty on a Sunday evening, there was a knock at the door. 'Don't answer it,' said Lisa.

He looked at her, curious at the fear in her voice: she was not normally like this. 'Why not?'

'I don't know,' she said lamely. 'I just feel . . . I don't know.'

This time there was a ring at the front door; whoever it was had found the bell. 'There's someone at the front door!' yelled Maureen, ever helpful.

Malone walked down the hall, switched on the outside light, opened the front door but kept the chain on. Through the screen of the iron-grille security door he saw a dark-haired young man in jeans and brown tweed jacket. He carried a black motor-cyclist's helmet in one hand, like a spare skull.

'Inspector Malone? I'm Father Luis Marquez.' He lifted the collar-peak of his open-necked shirt and showed the small cross he wore there. 'I'd like to talk to you. I'm sorry to break in on you like this –'

'What about?'

'Sister Mary Magdalene.'

Malone hesitated; he hated the intrusion of police work into his home. 'Can't it wait till tomorrow? At Homicide headquarters.'

'Please, Inspector –'

Malone hesitated again; then he unlocked the security door. He led the young priest through into the living-room and knew at once he had done the wrong thing when he saw Lisa's remonstrating frown. 'I'm sorry, darl. This is Father –?'

'Marquez,' said the young man. 'I'm Nicaraguan.'

He was almost as tall as Malone, olive-skinned, with high cheekbones, a flat straight nose and black eyes. His hair, too, was black and lay on his long head like a pelt. He was handsome and on other occasions he might have been aware of it; but tonight he looked only worried, perhaps even afraid. Or worse: a priest who had run out of prayer.

'Would you like a drink?' said Lisa. 'Or coffee?' She prided herself on her coffee, being Dutch; she would offer it even to a Brazilian or a Colombian. 'I make good coffee.'

Marquez smiled; it was a handsome smile, one that would have been devastating in either pulpit or bedroom. 'I haven't had a good cup since I came to Australia.'

'When was that?' said Malone as Lisa went out to the kitchen.

'Well, I'm lying, really. My mother makes a good cup.' Again there was a flash of very white, straight teeth. I'm being worked on, Malone thought. The charm was like a bribe. 'I came here fifteen years ago, when I was sixteen. My father

41

had fought against the Somozas. As a young boy, fourteen years old, he fought with Augusto Cesar Sandino.' He paused, but Malone was unimpressed. He had never heard of Sandino. Then Marquez went on, 'He went on fighting, after Sandino was killed. But finally his luck ran out and we had to leave Nicaragua. We came to Australia. My mother was tired of soldiers everywhere, she said she wanted a quiet country where the sun shone and no one was afraid of the soldiers. It was she who chose Australia.'

'Is your father still alive?' Malone knew nothing of Nicaragua's history other than what he occasionally read in the newspapers. But ignorance of the world is not a crime; if it were, 99 per cent of the world would be behind bars. Ignorance was not bliss, either: not when it was brought home to you in your own living-room. 'Is he mixed up with Sister Mary Magdalene's death?'

'Mother of God, no!' The handsome face was suddenly strained. 'He's dead, he's been dead three years. And my mother – she's not mixed up in it! It's just me – and all because of Mary Magdalene. Well, no, that's not the truth –' He shook his head and his face slackened, seemed to age. 'I think I was just waiting for my conscience to come alive.'

'What parish do you belong to?'

'I don't belong to any, not a church parish. I'm one of the two R.C. chaplains on campus at the University of New South Wales. I'm supposed to look after the ethnic students.'

'Are there any Nicaraguan students there?'

'A couple, I think. There aren't very many of us Central Americans in Sydney. They're mostly *South* Americans – Chileans, Argentines, Uruguayans – most Australians think we all come out of the one pot, anyway. But I look after all of them, including the Mediterranean ethnics. Even the odd Catholic Turk – and they're pretty odd, I can tell you.' He smiled again.

'Have you been home to Nicaragua?'

'Once, a couple of years ago.'

42

'Are you a – what do they call them? A Sandista?' Like most of the natives, when he read a foreign word in a newspaper or book he usually ran all the letters together and came up with his own interpretation. It was a variation on the old English attitude: the foreigners of the world really should Anglicize themselves.

'Sandinistas. They're named after Augusto Cesar Sandino, the man my father fought with. No, I don't belong to them. But I guess you could say I'm sympathetic to them. But I'm not rabid about them, not the way Mary Magdalene was.'

Lisa came back with the coffee, sat down, became part of the interview. Malone didn't mind, not this evening. Normally he tried to keep her well removed from any of his cases, but tonight he was glad she was there.

'How did you meet Mary?'

Father Marquez sipped the coffee, nodded appreciatively. 'Very good.'

'It's Colombian,' said Lisa.

'My mother always uses it. Nicaraguan coffee is pretty terrible. Everything in Nicaragua is pretty terrible these days. That was what Mary was always on about. She spent two years there, you know, up in the mountains. She was captured by the Contras, but managed to get them to release her. She came to the University to talk about it. That was how I met her.'

'How did you know to come here?' said Malone. 'And why?'

'When I saw the news on TV tonight –' He stopped, stared at his hands for a moment. 'I couldn't believe it. Then I rang Mother Brendan at the convent. She said you were in charge of the case. She said your children went to the school and she gave me your address.'

'She had a hide,' said Lisa. 'You'd think private people like nuns would respect other people's privacy.'

'I'm sorry,' said Marquez, acutely embarrassed. 'I should not have come. Mother Brendan was only trying to help.'

Lisa poured herself a second cup of coffee, having drained the first in an angry gulp. She looked at Malone. 'Do you want me to leave?'

He grinned, not annoyed at her intervention; she had said only what he had thought. 'No, stay. If Father Marquez is used to dealing with the odd Catholic Turk, he won't be too upset by you. Now let's get down to brass tacks, Father. Why are you here?'

Marquez put down his coffee cup. 'Because I think I may be next on their list.'

Lisa sat very still and so did Malone; but it was an acquired habit with him, born of long practice in interviews such as this. 'Whose list?'

'I said there aren't very many Nicaraguans in Sydney – that's true. But there are some here, maybe a dozen or more, who are strong Contra supporters. When Mary came on to campus to talk to a group, they turned up out of nowhere and picketed her and abused her. It never got into the papers. Picketing is pretty common on campus and anyway the general public doen't seem very interested these days in what students are on about. But the Contra supporters got pretty nasty.'

'Are you saying they could be her killers?'

'No, not them. But the people behind them – yes.'

'What people?'

'I'm not sure. Two of the top Contra men came into Sydney about three weeks ago, from Miami, I believe. They got here about a week after Archbishop Hourigan arrived. He came from Miami, too.'

'You'd better be careful here, Father. Are you saying the Archbishop is connected with the Contras?'

'I have no proof. But Mary Magdalene was certain he was. I went with her one night to a meeting he was addressing and she stood up and charged him with it.'

'I'm sorry she's dead,' said Lisa, 'but she sounds a real pain in the neck.'

'Most true believers are,' said Father Marquez gently.

'What did Archbishop Hourigan say?' Malone had never been a true believer in anything, though God knew he had tried.

'He just ignored her. He's so – so arrogant – it's impossible to describe –'

'I've met him.' But arrogance, like ignorance, is not a crime. If it were, certain Prime Ministers and State Premiers would have been declared habitual criminals. 'So Mary Magdalene never had any real contact with him?'

'Oh yes, several times. I don't know how –'

'She was his niece.'

Marquez had put forward his cup at Lisa's gesture of more coffee; both of them looked sharply at Malone and the coffee spilled into the saucer. 'She never mentioned that! Mother of God!' Marquez shook his head in wonder. '*That* was how she knew so much about him . . .'

'How much did she know?'

'She never told me everything – she always seemed to be holding something back. I don't think she entirely trusted Australia or Australians. She said we were too smug, too suburban to care passionately about anything. Some of us might care about rain-forests and wetlands and the killing of kangaroos, but we didn't care about *people*.'

'She didn't think of you as a Nicaraguan?'

'She said I'd been here too long, I'd been brainwashed, that the sun and the beer had got to me. She was a bigot, in her own way.'

'I'm beginning to dislike her,' said Lisa.

'No, don't,' said Marquez quickly. 'She was just, I don't know, too *caring*. I go to the convent occasionally, to talk to the classes. The girls in her classes adored her. She just had this, I suppose you'd call it Marxist, thing about Nicaragua.'

'Are you a Marxist?'

'Me? God, no! I've only voted twice in my life and both times for Malcolm Fraser – and I don't think God has forgiven me.' Again there was the smile. The girls at the convent, Lisa thought, might adore him, too. 'No, you can be for the Sandinistas without being a Marxist.'

'What about the Archbishop?'

Marquez laughed. 'He's even further to the right than Pius the Ninth.'

'He was before my time.' Malone had always had difficulty in remembering popes' names and their numbers. 'Did Mary ever mention her grandfather, Fingal Hourigan?'

Marquez shook his head. 'The rich old guy – he's her grandfather? God, he's worth *millions*!'

'He's a billionaire,' said Lisa. 'I'd mention my grandfather if he was in that bracket.'

'No, she never said a word about him. She never said anything about her family at all. I really didn't know her that well at all. I just *liked* her. And I think she liked me.' Then he looked at both of them defensively, as if they might have made the wrong inference. He's aware of his looks and his appeal to women, Lisa thought. 'I don't mean there was anything like *that* . . .'

'Who are the men you think might want to kill you?' said Malone.

Marquez hesitated, then said, 'I don't know who they are, but I'm sure there are some ex-Somoza men here in Sydney. The Somoza dynasty ran Nicaragua as if they owned the whole country – which, I guess, they did in a way. The last President, Anastasio, is dead, but his gang still hang on, running the Contras and trying to raise money wherever they can. Mary thought that was why the two guys came in from Miami. Their names are Paredes Canto and Domecq Cruz.'

Malone jotted down the names, asking for the correct spelling. 'You think they are the ones threatening you?'

'I don't know, to be honest. I've had two phone calls, one last week after I'd been to the Archbishop's talk with Mary, the second one this evening. The man spoke to me in Spanish. He had a Nicaraguan accent like my father's – in Central

46

America the accents are quite distinct. He mentioned my father – he knew all about him. He said they knew about my association with Mary Magdalene and just to forget her or I'd regret it.'

'Are you afraid?' said Malone, testing him.

'Yes,' said Marquez without hesitation or embarrassment. 'I'm not a guerilla fighter, Mr Malone. I was on Mary's side, but I wasn't carrying any gun for her. She knew that and sometimes she couldn't understand it, especially since I was born in Nicaragua and what had happened to my father there. He was tortured by the Somoza National Guard ... But we came out here to start a new life. I became a priest because I wanted to preach peace – I believe in a loving God, not a wrathful one ...'

'Are you asking for police protection? I don't know that I can arrange that, not at this stage. How did you get here tonight?'

'I have a motorbike.'

'Were you followed?'

Marquez looked surprised. 'I don't know. I didn't think to look. I'm not used to this, Inspector –'

'You'd better be more careful, for the time being anyway. You're pretty vulnerable on a motorbike.'

'University chaplains can't afford cars. We're the bottom end of the totem pole – I think we're supposed to be symbols of poverty to the students.' He smiled again, bravely this time, Malone thought. He found himself liking the young priest and didn't blame him for being afraid. Bravado was another form of heart disease.

He showed Marquez to the door. 'I'll want to see you again – I'll call you at the Uni. If you want to get in touch with me, if these blokes call you again, phone me at Homicide.' He lowered his voice. 'Don't phone me here.'

'I understand, Inspector.' Marquez lowered his own voice. 'I'm sorry I intruded. It won't happen again.'

Malone switched off the light in the hallway behind him

and waited while Marquez went out to his motorbike, put on his helmet, started up the bike and rode away with a wave of his hand. Malone waited to see if any car pulled out from the kerb in the quiet street, but none did. He re-locked the security door, closed the front door and went back to the living-room.

Lisa was waiting for him, the tray of coffee cups and the pot ready to be taken out to the kitchen. 'It's got worse, hasn't it?'

'Much worse,' he said, but didn't tell her about the threat he had received just before Father Marquez had arrived.

'How do these things ever start?'

He grinned. 'Original sin,' he said, but he doubted if even Father Marquez or Archbishop Hourigan believed that. 'It may have started yesterday or it may have started years ago.'

THREE

I

It had indeed started years ago, in Chicago in 1929.

Seamus (Jimmy) Mulligan chose a St Valentine's Day card from the rack in the drugstore. Mae, who had the same name as his boss's wife, was a girl who was full of romance; she often told him that, lying on her back under humping customers, she dreamed she was being made love to by John Gilbert or Ronald Colman. It didn't annoy Jimmy that she didn't dream of him. He never dreamed of her.

He pocketed the card and envelope without paying for it and went to the drugstore's pay phone. He dialled a number and while he waited for it to be answered he looked out at the dreary afternoon. Snow was falling, looking as unreal as he always found it; like falling souls, his mother used to describe it and blessed herself with a flurry of fingers. He hated Chicago in the winter, but so far he had never made enough money to go south for the freezing season. He had money in the bank, but he was a careful man: he would never splurge it on a long vacation. Not unless he knew suckers at the vacation spot who would finance it.

The ringing at the other end stopped and a rough voice said, 'Yeah? Who's dat?'

'Jack O'Hare,' said Jimmy, who always used Irish aliases; he was not romantic, but he was superstitious. It was bad luck to deny your heritage: that son-of-a-bitch St Patrick would send the snakes after you. 'Is your boss there?'

There was a grunt at the other end, then Moran came on the line. Jimmy in his mind's eye, which had 20/20 vision, could see the big morose Irishman at the other end. The battered face, as intelligent-looking as a drummer's travel-bag, would be screwed up as its owner tried to concentrate. George 'Bugs' Moran hated talking on the phone, where he couldn't glower at the other man.

'What you got, Jack?'

'Al Brown's had another consignment of booze come in from Detroit. I got it right off the boat.'

'Where's it at?'

'Ah, Mr Moran, you know I never tell you that. I oughtna be telling you where I got it from, only I thought it'd make you feel better.' Moran hated the man from whom the liquor had been hijacked. 'It's all yours, Mr Moran, a whole truck-load for fifty-seven bucks a case. Old Log Cabin label, the best. The Mayor himself drinks it.'

Bugs Moran took his time, as he always did when asked to give any subject some thought. He had inherited the leadership of the Dion O'Banion gang by default. Vincent Drucci, who had taken over from O'Banion himself, who had died of a surfeit of bullets, had suffered that most ignominious death for a gangster: he had been shot by a single policeman, a travesty of justice in gangland's eyes. Moran, with the mantle of leadership thrust upon him, had, like certain Vice Presidents in the same situation, stumbled around in the dark. When he had finally collected his thoughts, which weren't many, he decided that bootleg hijacking would be the best way of using his talent, which was mostly muscle. He chose to hijack the shipments of the Capone gang, a decision that showed his Irish idea of logic.

'Okay, I'll take 'em,' he said at last. 'Bring the truck to the usual place tomorrow morning, ten-thirty.'

'Cash on delivery?'

'Aint it always?' said Moran, who prided himself on certain concessions to honesty.

'You'll be there? I don't wanna deal with any of your stooges, Mr Moran. You know me. It's always between the principals.'

'I'll be there,' growled Moran and hung up.

Jimmy Mulligan turned up the collar of his Irish tweed overcoat, the best that Donegal could weave, pulled down the brim of his grey Borsolino hat and went out into the grey, freezing day. He had never liked Chicago in any season, from the day he had been brought here as a six-months-old baby from Ballyseanduff in County Kerry; for the first five years of his life he had suffered from colds, croup, bronchitis, influenza and a constantly running nose that had earned him the nickname at school of The Drip. But, as his father had told him, Chicago was where the money was to be made, so long as you didn't worry about scruples.

'Only the rich can afford scruples,' Paddy Mulligan had said, 'and they had to be unscrupulous to get rich.'

Paddy Mulligan had come to America in 1890. He had tried to get a job with Tammany Hall in New York, but all the good jobs were already taken in that hive of political patronage. He had come west to Chicago and been taken on by John 'The Bath' Coughlin and Michael 'Hinky Dink' Kenna, two God-fearing, church-going scoundrels who ran the First Ward; he had become a devout Democrat, though he had never bothered himself with the party's national policy or image. He had gone back on a visit to Ireland in 1904, met, courted, married and got pregnant Cathleen O'Farrell. He returned to Chicago and she followed him a year later with young Seamus, already dribbling at the nose.

Jimmy grew up, got over his chest ills, wiped his nose and joined his father in the First Ward. But politics didn't offer enough for an ambitious eighteen-year-old. He began doing odd jobs on the side. He invented the term 'feasibility consultant', putting it under his name on printed business cards, and equally ambitious but minor gang leaders began paying for his advice. He did no killing, never carried a gun; he just

51

advised on the feasibility of an assassination, the risks and potential in a new bootleg territory; he was the forerunner of one of today's flourishing professions. He came to the attention of Dion O'Banion, Hymie Weiss and Vincent Drucci, three wise men looking for a wiser one, but he always remained his own man. Working for men as disparate as those three, he had to be his own man if he was to survive.

Then he had been called in to do a job for the Big Fella himself. Al Capone's liquor was being hijacked; he suspected it was being done by Bugs Moran, but he was not certain. Could Mr Mulligan infiltrate the Moran gang?

'I can give it a try, Mr Capone. Moran don't know me – he never met me when I did a job or two for o'banion. I'll try another name and see what I can do. Is it okay if I lose a consignment of booze, maybe two, just to get the proof?'

'Sure. I'll get it back, one way or the other.'

So he had been working for Capone for a month and every day he was coming to realize that no one remained his own man while working for Capone; or ever would be again. Consultants, more than any other businessmen, should be aware of their own expendability.

So on this February day in 1929 he walked uptown, with the wind behind him, to the Metropole Hotel on South Michigan. Snow covered his shoulders like his mother's shawl; but his expensive hand-made shoes were dark with slush. Winter lashed, poked and scratched at him; the North Pole let him know it was just a suburb of Chicago. He pined for sunshine and warmth, for Florida, which he had never seen, or even for that home of ratbaggery, California, which he had only read about. He would go out there and make love to Billie Dove or Lil Tashman, two classy dames.

He turned in to the Metropole Hotel, glad of its warmth. He walked across the big lobby to one of the private elevators, nodded hello to the house detective who stood outside it, and got the elevator boy to take him up to the second of the two floors occupied by the Capone mob. Each floor was more heavily guarded than the White House; occupancy here was not guaranteed by the voters. In any event, who would be bothered bumping off Herbert Hoover?

Jimmy Mulligan got out of the elevator, looked down at his soaked shoes in disgust; he should have worn his two-toned galoshes. He took off his overcoat and straightened his silk tie against the stiff collar of his Sulka shirt. He had once heard a newspaperman describe him as 'natty' and the description had haunted him ever since.

'Mr Mulligan to see Mr Brown,' he said to the chief guard, two hundredweight of lard and a few dimes' worth of brain.

'Al ain't here.' Capone was still referred to as Al Brown, a *nom de guerre* he had adopted when he had first come west from New York; he was also known as the Big Fella, a compliment he appreciated though he did not like to be addressed as such to his face. He positively hated to be called Scarface, even behind his back. 'He's down to the other place. He expecting you?'

Mulligan nodded, only half-attentive to the big hoodlum. He was always fascinated when he came up here, or to the floor below. Capone rented fifty rooms in the hotel; this was the powerhouse of his empire. Politicians and judges and police officers came here to pay their respects and to be paid off; Sunday morning was pay-day and the supplicants came straight here from Mass, their souls clean if not their hands. The senior ones got in to see the Big Fella himself, in Suite 409–410, where he sat beneath portraits of his three heroes, George Washington, Abraham Lincoln and Mayor Big Bill Thompson. There he burdened them with little homilies on the dangers of being in the limelight, an illumination the politicians couldn't live without, and how he longed for respectability, the dream of every mother for her son. Mrs Capone had raised five sons and four of them had become gangsters; even her only daughter had married a gangster. If Mrs Capone had been praying for respectability for her family, she had been facing the wrong way. The fifth son had left home in 1919, gone out to Nebraska and become a law officer, a blot on the family honour.

Today was a slow day: there were only whores, gamblers and bootleg liquor salesmen on the two floors. But this was Monday and the smell of Sunday's power still lingered; it was like snuff in Jimmy Mulligan's nostrils. Some day he would have power like this, but in a warmer climate.

'Call the other place and tell him I'm coming,' he said, practising authority, and the hoodlum, recognizing someone higher up the brain scale than himself, made a gesture that almost looked like a salute.

Jimmy put his hat and overcoat back on, went out of the hotel into the grey day that now seemed lighter because the snow had settled in thickening banks. He walked two blocks down to 2145 South Michigan, his feet freezing in his soaked shoes. He paused outside the doctor's office, admired the respectability of the name-plate on the door: Dr A. Brown. He pressed the bell-button and was admitted. The Metropole Hotel might be where the power lay, but this was where the money was. And Jimmy Mulligan was as fascinated by money as he was by power.

There were people waiting in the reception room, but none of them, Mulligan knew, would be patients. Not that they were a healthy-looking lot; they had the look of men and women who rarely, if ever, saw sunlight; their livers and lungs would resemble a brown string-bag. The prescriptions they were waiting for were cheques or bills.

Mulligan was admitted at once to the surgery behind the reception room. The back wall was lined with shelves, on which were rows and rows of bottles of various sizes, all containing coloured liquids. These were Dr Brown's medicines, his panaceas and elixirs: samples of all the liquors supplied by the man behind the desk. Who was Dr Al Brown himself, the Big Fella, Alphonse Capone.

'Mr Mulligan –' The relationship between the two men

was always formal. There was very little difference in their ages; each of them had ambitions to be a gentleman. 'You made the arrangement we talked about?'

'It was like selling candy to a sweet-toothed idjit,' said Mulligan. 'The brains in that outfit wouldn't make a decent breakfast. Greed turns intelligence into a headache.'

Capone looked around at the four other men in the surgery. 'Don't you guys wish you had Mr Mulligan's education?'

'I had no education,' said Mulligan modestly. 'An hour a day in the public library, that was all. Emerson on Monday, Thoreau on Tuesday ... I've also read Machiavelli,' he added with touch of his forelock to Mr Capone's Italian heritage.

'I've heard of him,' said Capone, impressed. His four henchmen nodded, thinking he was probably some educated hood from New York or Detroit. 'So Moran is expecting the shipment tomorrow?'

Mulligan gave him the details. At the same time he was observing Capone, as he always did when he met the crime boss. The big jowly face with the two three-inch scars down the left cheek and the thick lips was not a friendly one; the smile could be pleasant, but the dark eyes never seemed to match it. The thick fingers sported diamond rings and the gold watch on the fat wrist was a reminder that time could be expensive. The silk-and-mohair suit was a little flashy for Mulligan's taste and so were the grey spats above the small, almost dainty shoes. But Capone owned an empire and emperors have to have the right clothes. A little vulgarity never hurt, since 99 per cent of the peasants were themselves vulgar.

'What do I owe you, Mr Mulligan?'

Mulligan had already got his payment, though Capone didn't know that. 'I'll leave that to you, Mr Capone. Ours has been a gentleman's agreement.'

Capone smiled: even the eyes seemed to have some mirth in them. 'You trust too much, Mr Mulligan. Ain't you ever been double-crossed?'

'Once.'

'You kill the guy?'

Mulligan shook his head, 'There are other ways, Mr Capone.' He had betrayed the double-crosser to the police; but it would not be politic to tell that to the Big Fella. 'You're not a double-crosser.'

'No, you're right, I ain't.' He had all the assurance of an emperor. 'That's what fucks me about Moran. Two grand for your trouble, Mr Mulligan, that okay?'

'Three, Mr Capone,' said Mulligan and was aware at once of the stiffening attitude of the four henchmen in their chairs against the walls.

But Capone was relaxed, just smiled again. 'They told me you was ambitious. You hoping some day to make the sorta money I make?'

'Maybe.' Mulligan knew he was treading on ice much thinner than that out on the shores of Lake Michigan, but he could not resist the thrill of it. 'I ain't aiming to compete against you, I ain't that dumb. But there are other cities ... I'm fascinated by power, Mr Capone, and you gotta have money to have that.'

Capone nodded, still relaxed: this Irishman would never be a real competitor. 'That's right. I'm king of this city, of the State too, and I only got that because I got the dough. I could be king of America, if it wasn't for the fucking Government.'

'I'm sure we'd all vote for you,' said Mulligan, who hadn't voted in his life.

'Sure,' said Capone, who knew a liar when he sat in front of him. 'Okay, go through to the back room. Mr Guzik will fix you up. You want it in cash, right?'

'Is there any other form of currency?' said Mulligan. 'Good-day, Mr Capone. May your empire increase.'

'It ain't getting any easier,' said the crime boss. 'The fucking Government's starting to take itself seriously.'

'Ain't it always the way? Power corrupts, absolute power corrupts absolutely.'

Capone pondered that for a moment, then nodded. 'Who said that?'

Mulligan could not remember, but he never admitted ignorance. 'Leonardo da Vince.'

'Us Italians,' said Capone, though he always claimed to be 100 per cent American, especially when talking to Immigration. 'We got it all figured out, right?'

'You certainly have,' said Mulligan and thought, But wait till us Irish come into our own.

2

Next morning, St Valentine's Day, at 10.30 Jimmy Mulligan sat in his car fifty yards up the street from the S.M.C. Cartage Company's garage at 2122 Clark Street. His car was a 1928 black Chevrolet tourer, an inconspicuous vehicle that was the opposite of Mulligan's dream, an emerald-green Duesenberg, the sort of car that should be driven only in bright sunlight. The Chevrolet's side curtains were up against the biting wind and Mulligan sat hunched down behind the wheel.

Clark Street was a good site for a massacre, an urban substitute for the Badlands. It was an ugly narrow thoroughfare of small stores, apartment buildings that looked like eroded cliffs, gas stations where only shabby, rundown vehicles stopped, and the occasional narrow-fronted warehouse that hinted at secret stocks behind their locked doors. The street's inhabitants, blue-collared and hopeless, welcomed any sort of excitement as long as they were not harmed personally. On this cold, windy, snow-swept morning the street was virtually deserted.

At a few minutes before eleven o'clock Mulligan sat up as he saw the big black tourer come down the street. It drew in to the kerb just north of the cartage company's garage and five men got out, three of them in police uniform. Wonderful, thought Mulligan. Only an Italian, a Machiavelli, would think of sending killers dressed as cops.

The five men went into the garage. Mulligan waited, face pressed against the micre window in the Chevrolet's side curtain. Then, out of the corner of his eye, he saw the three other watchers on the opposite side of the street. He turned his head slightly, then abruptly slid down in the seat. The three men on the other side of the road were Bugs Moran and two of his bodyguards.

'Holy Jaisus!' said Mulligan, who, like all Irishmen, was given to prayer when in need of help. Holy Jesus had one ear continually turned for yelps for help out of Ireland.

Moran, equally Irish, had been late for his appointment. There was a burst of gunfire from the garage, then silence, then several more shots, as if *coups de grâce* had been effected, though none of those involved or watching would have called them that. The police report would later say that over a hundred bullets had been fired, including fourteen into the body of one man who, as he lay dying, insisted to the police, 'Nobody shot me.'

Mulligan did not bother to count the shots, even if his ear had been sharp enough and his National Cash Register mind nimble enough. He heard only one shot and it seemed to him that it was destined for him, though it might take a day or two to hit. He lifted himself up in the seat and saw the three 'policemen' come out of the garage, herding the two civilians ahead of them with their hands up, a nice pantomime that Mulligan admired even as he felt close to vomiting with shock. The five men got into the Packard tourer and drove off at a sedate speed. He swivelled his gaze to the other side of the street, but Moran and his bodyguards were already gone. They would not have seen him, but that did not matter. They would know who had set up the massacre and that it had been intended Moran should be part of it.

Mulligan started up the Chevrolet and started south, then

east. He finished up on Lake Shore Drive, though later he would not be able to remember how he had got there. He parked the car and sat in the freezing tent of it, while the snow, coming in across Lake Michigan, piled up to obscure the windscreen. It didn't matter that he couldn't see the other side of the street. He could see the future.

He had been too smart, but not smart enough: he hadn't allowed for bad luck, a Celtic fate. Banking on Moran's demise, he had already sold the supposedly hijacked truckload of liquor to a man from Kansas City; if Capone had queried where it had gone, he would have blamed it on the dead Moran. But now ...

He started up the car, got the snow off the windscreen and drove home to his one-bedroom flat just off Prairie Avenue, on the South Side. He lived five blocks from the Capone family home, but he had always kept his private address as private as possible; his business card put him at a downtown hotel, where the day and night clerks took all messages for him. Now he had to find a new address, one far from here.

He packed three suitcases, taking time to pack them neatly; on top of his folded clothes he put the brass-framed photo of his dead mother and father. He had no brothers or sisters; his nearest kin were cousins in Ballyseanduff in County Kerry. As he was going out the door he saw the envelope and card on the table: he had forgotten to send Mae her St Valentine's greeting. He had already written in the card: *To Mae, my favourite hump*. He thought a moment, then he put the card in the envelope and addressed it to Mrs Mae Capone.

On his way out he dropped the envelope in the mail-box on the street corner. Then he put the suitcases in the Chevrolet and drove to his bank. He drew out his entire bank balance, including the 3,000 dollars he had deposited the day before: 28,869 dollars. Then he got back into the car and pondered where he should head. For one moment, out of sentiment for his mother and father, he thought of going back to Bally-seanduff, his birthplace; it would be a good place to hide while he planned his future. But the Winter Country, as its Roman conquerors had called it, was not inviting: he had had enough of winter. He started up the car and drove south, not sure where he was going but knowing that he was not looking for the sun but for safety.

Eight months later he landed in Australia. His name now was Fingal Hourigan and he was determined to found an empire, maybe not as evil as Capone's but just as rich.

He could see the years stretching ahead of him like a golden road. Like all of us, though, he couldn't see those whom he would meet along the way.

FOUR

I

Commissioner John Leeds was the neatest officer in the New South Wales Police Department; Assistant Commissioner Bill Zanuch was the second neatest. Sitting opposite them, hunched down as if he had been flung into his high-backed chair by an Opposition front-bencher, an unlikely political happening, was the untidiest politician in the country, State Premier Hans Vanderberg.

'It's no good turning your good eye to skulbuggery.' He was also an untidy man with a phrase.

'No,' said Zanuch and looked at his chief to see if he had got the meaning of what the Premier had said. Leeds just looked imperturbable, which was the only way to survive a meeting with The Dutchman, as he was called.

'Something's going on and I don't want to know anything about it,' Vanderberg went on.

'Are we talking about Archbishop Hourigan?' Leeds guessed that they still were, but the Premier did have a habit of going off at tangents that might have been lunatic in a less devious man.

'Who else? His old man, Fingal, was on to me first thing this morning, half-way through my porridge. That bugger of yours, Malone, is causing more trouble.'

'He'd only be doing his job.' Leeds hadn't yet read the summaries that were always waiting on his desk for him each morning. He and Zanuch had been here at the State Office

Block for a nine o'clock appointment; Vanderberg, who knew better than any of his ministers how to handle power, was his own Police Minister. 'Is he handling that nun's case, Bill?'

Zanuch nodded. He was a vain, handsome man whose ideal world would have been lined with mirrors; but he was a good policeman and hoped some day to be Commissioner. He looked at the Premier, the man who appointed commissioners. 'I can have him taken off the case.'

'No,' said Leeds. 'I'll talk to him first. What's Fingal Hourigan's complaint, Hans?'

Vanderberg had watched the split-second encounter between the two senior policemen; he got secret enjoyment out of watching the same sort of rivalry in his Cabinet. He believed in a divided world, otherwise politicians wouldn't be necessary. He rolled the end of his creased, twisted tie round one finger; it was a tie that had been presented to him by a country cricket team. He hated cricket, but even cricketers voted and you never knew who counted in marginal seats. Fingal Hourigan certainly counted. Any man who gave $100,000 every year to the Party, even if he didn't vote Labour, had to be counted and listened to. The Dutchman had no scruples, only common sense, a more valuable political gift. He liked to think, however, because politicians like to think there is some good in themselves, that he had one or two more scruples than Fingal.

'Malone has been making a nuisance of himself with the Archbishop. He's been out to the Hourigan place twice.'

'Bill can talk to him, ask him why.' Leeds looked at Zanuch. 'But don't take him off the case. Not yet, anyway. It's no good for morale if we keep interfering.'

Zanuch smoothed down his already smoothly lying tie. It was a Police Force tie, but in silk, not polyester. He was in civilian dress this morning, while Commissioner Leeds was in uniform; somehow, and Zanuch was smugly aware of the impression, the Commissioner looked the odd man out amongst the three of them. Zanuch knew how much politicians disliked uniforms. Nothing catches the eye like medals, braid and bright buttons and politicians hated losing the voters' eye. So he always did his best not to upstage the Premier. Upstaging his own Commissioner was another matter.

'We can't have Malone stirring up another of his hornets' nests. He never knows when to be discreet.'

'I'd have thought that was a good thing in a police officer,' said Leeds, though he didn't believe it. Lately he had found himself wanting to disagree with his senior Assistant Commissioner on anything the latter proposed.

'Discretion never hurt anyone, John,' said Vanderberg, who had hurt more people in more ways than could be counted. 'The Archbishop will be going back to Rome at the end of the week. Just hold off till he's out of town. We don't want to upset the Catholics.'

'I thought you were one,' said Leeds.

'Only on Sundays.' A non-voting day. 'Every other day in the week I'm as ecumenical a bugger as you can find. I was out at a Muslim mosque the other day. Malone should be a Catholic, with a name like that. You'd think he'd back-pedal.'

Leeds stood up. 'I'll talk to him,' he said flatly, neither promising nor denying.

He waited for Zanuch to rise; he wasn't going to let his junior remain with the Premier. Zanuch hesitated, then decided on his own discretion: he stood up. The two police officers nodded to their political boss and went out, Leeds leading the way.

Vanderberg grinned after them. He had come to Australia from Holland immediately after the Second World War; he had mastered local politics but he had never really become Australian. He still saw the locals with a stranger's eye, but a knowing stranger: he was the con man who could make himself sound and look like the natives. He had a European sense of superiority, but he was too wise ever to let it show. He got his way by letting the local elements, the white

Aborigines, try out their superiority on each other.

He reached for his intercom. 'Miss Parsell, get me Fingal Hourigan on the phone. He's waiting to hear from me.'

2

'You're at it again, Scobie,' said John Leeds.

Malone sighed inwardly; he knew the signs. 'Another complaint, sir?'

'I've just come from seeing the Premier. It seems that this time you're harassing the Catholic Church. What's your version?'

Malone told him, briefly. He and the Commissioner had been involved in other cases, though at opposite ends of the totem pole, as Father Marquez would have said, and he knew he could speak frankly, although always with respect. Leeds did not encourage 'mateyness', the national weakness in labour relations. He was a sympathetic boss who protected his men against outside interference; but he was the boss. One who could be talked to: 'Archbishop Hourigan's name just keeps cropping up. I'm beginning to think Sister Mary Magdalene was murdered because she was harassing him.'

'I hope you haven't been making a statement like that to anyone? That's an explosive charge.' He hadn't meant a play on words: on serious matters he was a very serious man.

'I haven't mentioned it to anyone, sir.' Except to Lisa, in bed last night, and she was beyond the Commissioner's authority.

Leeds put his hands flat on the almost-empty top of his desk. Police desks were notorious for their wild fungi of paper; but the Commissioner's could have been that of the abbot of a monastic order, one not given to illumination. 'Do you have enough evidence to bring him in for questioning?'

'No, sir. I have some other leads I want to follow up.'

'Such as?'

'I was threatened over the phone last night. So was Father Marquez.'

Leeds's fingers tensed on the desk top. 'I don't like that sort of thing happening to my officers. Nor to priests,' he added as an ecumenical afterthought. 'That alters my view of the case.'

'This isn't going to be an easy one,' said Malone. 'I'm aware of the clout I'm up against.'

Leeds allowed himself a smile. 'Clout has never worried you before. Just be careful. And don't make any arrest until you've checked with me through the usual channels.'

'If I have to, do I go and see Archbishop Hourigan again?'

Leeds pondered a moment, lifted his hands to form a steeple in front of his chin, emphasizing the image of an abbot. 'Use your discretion. In which, I'm afraid, I have very little faith.'

Malone grinned: there was an empathy between the two men despite the difference in rank. 'I've mellowed, sir.'

'Famous words that didn't last. Good luck.'

Malone went out through the outer office, aware of the stares of the secretaries. Junior officers like himself were rarely called before the Commissioner unless accompanied by a Superintendent or above. There had, however, been two or three cases over the past few years in which the Homicide detective and the Commissioner, had, through political circumstances, worked in closer contact than was normal. The two men shared certain secrets, an intimacy which is always the subject of envy in any organization. The secretaries looked at him, then rang the typing pool, who would make carbon copies of the envy and spread it amongst the Assistant Commissioners and Chief Superintendents, who all had their own secrets but none shared with the Commissioner.

Russ Clements, who destroyed secrets by sharing them with everyone, even some criminals, was waiting when Malone got back from Administrative Headquarters. He sat with his 'murder box' in his lap, looking as if waiting for the manna of clues to fall into it. 'There's not much to go on.'

'There's a little more,' said Malone and told him about Father Marquez's visit last night and the phone threats.

'We can check those guys from Nicaragua. I've got a good contact in Immigration.' He lifted the phone, rang a number, spoke to someone and sat waiting, smiling at Malone with anticipation. 'When computers work, they're a great invention... This is against all the rules, Immigration has a strict code of confidentiality. But the world would stop dead, wouldn't it, if we all stuck to the rules?'

'I didn't hear a word you said,' said Malone, pious as one of the less tempted saints.

Clements's grin widened, then he listened to whoever was on the other end of the phone. He scribbled down two names and an address. 'Thanks, Stan. You want anyone run in or a ticket fixed, give me a ring.'

'You're a crooked cop,' said Malone as Clements hung up.

'Ain't it a help, though?' said Clements and looked at his piece of paper. 'Their full names are Francisco Paredes Canto and Max Domecq Cruz. In Spanish, as I remember it, you use the middle name as a surname. Nicaraguan-born, but they were travelling on US passports. They gave as their address the White Sails Motel at Rose Bay. That would be less than a mile from old man Hourigan's house.'

'What reason for their visit?'

'Tourists, but that doesn't mean a thing. Remember those two Mafia guys who came in to have a look at the poker machine racket? They were tourists. But Immigration has nothing on file against Paredes and Domecq.'

Malone took his time with his thoughts. 'Can you get anything on them from the FBI?'

'We could try. But since the CIA are supposed to be backing the Contras, you think the FBI are going to help us?'

'From what I've heard from Joe Nagler in Special Branch, the FBI and the CIA aren't exactly buddy-buddy. They go their own way, just the same as we do out here with the Federals. Try your luck.'

Clements ferreted around in his desk, an unlicensed refuse dump; Malone, a reasonably tidy man, was sure that, buried in its drawers, were the remains of old homicides, old lunches, perhaps even a fossilized limb or two. But Clements knew his way around his own garbage. He came up with what he sought, a tattered schedule of world time. 'It's seven o'clock Sunday night in Washington. Do the Yanks work round the clock and at weekends?'

'Let's try them.'

Clements went away to fax a message to the FBI and Malone settled down to getting his notes in order for his preliminary report. He could feel the undercurrent of anger in himself at the political interference in the case; he had half-expected it but not so soon. Nobody, it seemed, cared about the dead nun; she was already garbage. But no, that was unfair: Brigid Hourigan cared. He looked at the paper in his typewriter: without guiding thought, his fingers had tapped out, *Who cares?* and underlined it. Don't get angry, he told himself; angry policemen never see things clearly. This was a case where he could already see the fog creeping in, the political fog that obscured so much political work in this State. Take it easy, he said silently, keep your eyes and your feelings wide open. Keep the courage of your suspicions, let's see whose side The Lord is on, the Archbishop's or the nun's.

Clements came back. 'It's gone off. While we're waiting, I'm going back to Tilly Mosman. I'm still puzzled why the girl was dumped on her doorstep.'

'Who owns the Quality Couch?'

'I've got that –' Clements looked at his notebook. For all his lumbering, seemingly careless style, he was a methodical policeman, one whose mind was always two jumps ahead of his appearance and other people's impression of him. 'Tilly has the lease on the house, but she doesn't own it. It's owned by Ballyduff Properties, they own both sides of the whole street. Guess who owns Ballyduff Properties?'

The coincidences in this case were too tight. 'Fingal Hourigan?' Clements nodded and Malone said, 'I'm glad it's not the Catholic Church. We don't want to take them on.'

'Taking on Fingal Hourigan can't be much better. But I don't think he'd be in the brothel business, not even the up-market stuff. He's way beyond that now.'

'Start digging into his background, see what you can come up with. In the meantime, who's claimed the nun's body?'

'Her mother. They're doing the autopsy today and releasing the body tomorrow for burial.'

'That's quick. No inquest?'

'There's a special one today – guess who pulled strings? I'm due out there in half an hour. It'll be the usual – murder by person or persons unknown.'

'Has Tilly been called?'

'I'm picking her up. Then I'll go back with her and talk to her girls.'

He went away to pick up Tilly Mosman and take her to the inquest; Fingal Hourigan, it seemed, could have court schedules altered.

Malone settled back to clear up his paper-work. He sometimes wondered how much paper-work the modern criminal had to do. White-collar crims probably did much more than the average cop, but they rarely, if ever, committed homicide and so were outside his bailiwick. The law had been invented to protect property and Malone, protecting people, sometimes thought he was working in the slums of the law. But he knew for whom he had the greatest contempt.

The fax to Washington was answered in two hours; someone in the FBI headquarters must be working round the clock, including weekends. But then crime in the US, according to the Sunday newspapers, was a round-the-clock event, a murder a minute . . . All that paperwork!

When Clements came back from the Quality Couch, Malone handed him the message and the two photos. Clements read the message, then said, 'How do the Yanks let guys like that into their country?'

Francisco Paredes Canto and Max Domecq Cruz had been personal aides to the ex-chief of the National Guard. Each of them had been charged with three murders in Nicaragua, but the cases had never come to court. They had been present at the massacre of forty Indians who had been demonstrating against a particular landlord, a crony of then President Anastasio Somoza Debayle, but no charges had been laid against them. They had fled Nicaragua when the Sandinistas had come to power and had been granted US passports two years ago. Their names were linked with a major anti-Sandinista guerrilla movement based in Honduras and their principal source of income was thought to be from a connection with a drug ring in Colombia. The FBI had no proof of any of the charges.

'I think the FBI suffers from politics the same way we do, only more so,' said Malone.

He studied the two photos. Paredes was a handsome grey-haired man; the hair was thick and wavy and glistened like oiled iron. He had a thin moustache of the sort that had long gone out of fashion, and eyes and a mouth that would promise nothing if there was no dividend in return. He was sixty, according to the FBI report, but was lean and looked in fine condition. Domecq was younger, forty-two, dark and saturnine, but running a little to fat. He looked like a successful gambler, the sort who would be at home in any casino anywhere in the world.

'You pick up anything out at Tilly's?'

'The girls heard and say nothing.'

'Did they have any Spanish-speaking clients Saturday night?'

'A couple, but the girls said they were regulars, young guys with plenty of money to flash around. How do these Wogs manage it?'

'Russ, you're getting to be a racist in your old age.'

Clements nodded morosely; then abruptly grinned. 'I'm starting to understand bigotry. You can actually enjoy it if you put your mind to it.'

'Well, don't get too bigoted about these Wogs from Nicaragua. Be objective about them. Do we go and pick them up for questioning?'

'I think I'd like nothing better,' said Clements, trying not to look bigoted and not succeeding.

Malone gratefully put away his unfinished paper-work and he and Clements drove out to the White Sails Motel in Rose Bay. It was on New South Head Road, the main artery from the city out to the south head of the harbour. It had no view of the harbour or the white sails that decorated the waters on most days; but it looked clean and respectable and reasonably expensive. As it should in Rose Bay: the suburb itself was clean, respectable and more than reasonably expensive. It would never have seen itself as a haven for suspected political murderers with links to an international drug ring. It harboured one or two white-collar criminals, but they could not be condemned till they were caught. Rose Bay might have its bigotry, but not against its own kind, the white-collared black sheep.

The manageress of the White Sails came from over the hill, from Bondi and its beach. She was a strawberry blonde, a colour that went incongruously with her deep tan. She had hung on to her figure, her only good feature. She had lain in the sun for years; she had the skin one would love to sandpaper. Malone had met her sort before: the girls always hanging around where men hung out, at surf clubs and rugby clubs and pubs, all their femininity lost in trying to be 'one of the boys'.

'You'd love a beer, wouldn't you?' she said as soon as Malone and Clements had identified themselves.

'No, thanks,' said Malone, to Clements's disappointment, and showed Miss Allsop, as she said she was, the photos of Paredes and Domecq.

'Oh, those South American guys. No, they're not here. They checked out on Sunday.'

'In a hurry? I mean, how long had they booked in for?'

'They'd paid up till tomorrow. They just said they'd decided to go on to Melbourne and I gave 'em a refund. Anything wrong with them? They seemed real nice. I went out to dinner with one of them last Thursday. Mr Domecq.'

Malone was not surprised and was a little sad for her; on her dying day she would be looking for some man to take her out to dinner. 'No, we have nothing serious on them, just routine stuff. Did Mr Domecq tell you anything about himself?'

'Just about life in Miami. He said he was in the import business there.'

'Did he say what?' *Drugs, for instance?*

'No, he was a bit vague. This and that, he said.'

'What was he like?'

'You mean how did he treat me? Oh, he was a gentleman, up to a point –' That was all she expected of men; she gave the impression she would be disappointed if men were gentlemen all the way. 'I like Latin men, they have something about them.'

'We're both Scandinavians,' said Malone. 'No hope for us. What about Mr Paredes?'

'He seemed to be the senior partner, if you know what I mean. He kept very much to himself. He had a sorta, now I come to think about it, a *cruel* look to him. But he was always polite. And they were always beautifully dressed, both of them, real sharp.'

'If they come back here, give us a ring, will you? But don't let them know.'

'Oh, it's like that, is it?' All at once she looked knowing, though she knew nothing.

Malone nodded and winked and she gave him a smile that invited him back. She stood at the doorway of her small office, an autumn girl in an autumn day, and waved to them as they drove away.

'I hope the bastard gave her a good dinner,' said Clements.

'I hope that's all he gave her. Do you ever feel like her, being a bachelor?'

'It's different being a man.' But Clements sounded neither convinced nor convincing.

They stopped at a phone box and Malone made a call to the Hourigan mansion. 'May I make an appointment to see Archbishop Hourigan?'

'No,' said Mrs Kelly, belligerent as ever. 'He's at the cathedral all day today. There's a special Mass at five o'clock and he's preaching the sermon.'

'What's the special Mass for? Some saint's day?' *St Fingal, maybe?*

'It's a Mass against *The Threat of Communism*.' She sounded as if she were reading from some pamphlet, all capitals and italics.

'Will you be there, Mrs Kelly?'

'No, I've got the house to look after.' She knew the priorities and the dangers. Communism was not likely to strike in Vaucluse.

At five o'clock Malone was at St Mary's Cathedral, alone but for about a thousand worshippers. Either the fame of Kerry Hourigan as a speaker had spread wider than Malone had anticipated or there was a greater fear of the threat of Communism than he had imagined. In the last year or two conservatism, never far below the surface of the Land of the Easy Going, had started to rise like methane gas from some marsh hidden beneath the beaches and the sports ovals. The congregation this evening looked ready for a crusade, so long as they weren't taxed for it. Malone could not control his cynicism even in church.

The Mass was a straightforward one, though the hymns were sung with more fervour than Malone remembered and the words sounded martial. Then Archbishop Hourigan

72

climbed into the pulpit like an overweight pilot into a fighter-bomber. Malone had thought of him in the drawing-room of his father's house as urbane, sophisticated, low-key. In the pulpit this evening he was another man, all brimstone and rhetoric. He carved the air with his hands like a man slashing his way through the entire Soviet Presidium; he thumped every Marxist since Karl himself into the pulpit railing with a bunched fist. The chill air in the cathedral began to warm up under his harangue and the response of the congregation; Malone looked up at the huge vaulted ceiling, waiting for battle flags to flutter and fall, but a lone pigeon, disturbed by the unusual fervour, was the only sign of movement there. Communism got a going-over that it had not experienced since the days of Hitler and Franco, and Malone looked up again, waiting this time for the roof to open and the Lord Himself to come floating down. Malone had once attended a Billy Graham revival meeting, looking for pickpockets helping themselves to worldly goods while the born-again Christians were in a state of spiritual ecstasy and ready to give away everything but their children. The American evangelist had been like a bronchial crooner compared to the bellicose wizard up there in the cathedral pulpit.

Then Archbishop Hourigan called for donations to the cause. Baskets were passed round; money and cheques fluttered like manna into them. The Archbishop, a man of the financial as well as the spiritual world, had come prepared; for those with credit cards there were appropriate slips of paper. American Express and Diners Club could now pay your heavenly dues. The baskets were taken up to the altar, Kerry Hourigan gave a blessing of thanks and the celebrant priest came back to finish Mass. It was an anti-climax and Malone, a rebel but still an old-fashioned Catholic in many ways, wondered what The Lord, as the Host, thought of being on the lower half of the vaudeville bill.

When it came time for communion, he went up to the altar. He hadn't been to confession in at least three years, but he took advantage of the new philosophy of conscience: he didn't *feel* a sinner. But then, he guessed, neither had Stalin. He stood in the line waiting to be given the Host by Hourigan and was surprised when he saw Father Marquez up ahead of him. The celebrant priest, two other priests and the Archbishop were all giving communion; Malone had positioned himself to be in the line for Hourigan and so, it seemed, had Marquez. The young priest stood in front of the Archbishop; Malone, only four behind in the line, waited for some reaction from the prelate, but there was none. Marquez took the wafer and walked away; Hourigan's eyes did not follow him, not even for an instant; they could have been complete strangers to each other. Then it was Malone's turn.

He chose the old-fashioned way of lifting his face for the wafer to be put on his tongue rather than having it placed in his hands. He looked straight at the Archbishop and said quietly, 'I'd like to see you after this, Your Grace.'

'The Body of Christ,' said Hourigan and for a moment his hand shook.

'Amen,' said Malone and went back to his seat and prayed, not for himself but for his family, as he always did.

When Mass was over he got up and moved across to where he saw Father Marquez still sitting. He sat down beside him. 'Was that the sort of stuff that upset Sister Mary Magdalene?'

'Not that so much – that was pretty much bulldust tonight. No, she used to argue with his specific accusations about the Sandinistas, about their atrocities against the Church and the *campesinos*. From what my father used to tell me, I don't think they're any worse than the Somoza gang was. Maybe nowhere near as bad.'

'Did he recognize you as a friend of hers?'

'I don't know.'

'Can you hang on a minute? I'd like him to meet you.'

Father Marquez looked uneasy. 'Do I have to?' Then he saw the look of reproach on Malone's face and he nodded. 'Yes, I guess so. I owe Mary that. Okay, I'll wait.'

Malone went round to the vestry. Kerry Hourigan was in there in the middle of an admiring throng; the Cardinal, the head of this archdiocese, stood in the background like an umpteenth Apostle. He was a modest man, part of the wall-paper of the Church, and Hourigan, wearing the aura that Rome alone gives, knew it. Then the Archbishop caught sight of Malone and the light in his eyes, if not the aura, dimmed.

He detached himself from the almost blasphemous ador-ation; Communism, tonight, was responsible for more sin than it knew of. He crossed to Malone, who stood against a wall like a wooden effigy that hadn't been blessed.

'Not here, Inspector. Can't you see I'm holding court?' The arrogance, Malone guessed, would never be dimmed.

'Is that what it is, Your Grace? I thought it was a meeting of NATO.'

Hourigan smiled. 'You love your little joke, Inspector. Meet me at the rear of the cathedral, in one of the back pews. No one will interrupt us. They'll think I'm trying to convert you.'

It was Malone's turn to smile. 'You didn't do that from the pulpit. I don't think you'll do it in a back pew. Ten minutes, or I'll come back and start showing my badge. Your New Right friends here are supposed to be all for law and order.'

Ten minutes later, almost on the dot, the Archbishop came down to the back pew where Malone waited for him. He pulled up sharply when he also saw Father Marquez.

'A friend of your niece's,' said Malone. 'He won't be staying. I just thought you'd like to meet him.'

'I've seen you before, haven't I?' said the Archbishop.

'Possibly, Your Grace,' said Marquez. 'But I was usually in Sister Mary's shadow.'

'She'd have had the world in it if she'd had her way.'

Here we go again with the rhetoric, thought Malone. 'Father Marquez is Nicaraguan. He's had two death threats since your niece died.'

Hourigan was resting a hand on the back of a pew; Malone saw it tighten grimly. 'I'm upset to hear that. One tragedy is enough. I hope you are being very careful, my son.'

'Oh, very much so, Your Grace. Inspector Malone is seeing that I get police protection.'

He may be politically innocent, Malone thought, but he's a shrewd young bugger. Hourigan nodded and said, 'Let's hope we have a quick end to this dreadful business. I'll pray for your safety.'

'Thank you,' said Marquez, but didn't sound reassured. 'I must go now, Inspector. I'll be in touch. Good-night, Your Grace. That was an interesting sermon tonight.'

'You agreed with it?'

'I doubt if it would go down with those I have to work with,' said Marquez and turned on his heel. 'Good-night.'

Hourigan looked after him as he disappeared out the big doors. 'The young are so blind, aren't they?'

'So are some of the middle-aged,' said Malone.

'Meaning me or thee?' said Hourigan with a smile. Then he said, though not aggressively, 'Are you a Communist sympathizer, Inspector?'

'Not that I'm aware of, Your Grace.' It was as if they were using their titles of rank to draw up the battle lines between them; there was a hint of mockery in the voice of each. 'I've probably seen more sin, or anyway the results of it, than you have. I'm not sure any more that everything is cut and dried. Which was what you were preaching tonight.'

'Communism is still the biggest threat to the world, bigger than all the health threats, the economic recessions... Out here in Australia you just don't know what's going on in the rest of the world.'

'Sister Mary Magdalene knew what was going on in Central America. We think that was why she was silenced.'

That silenced Hourigan for the moment. He sat surrounded by the huge silence of the cathedral; it was empty now but for the small figure of a warden putting out the last of the candles on the main altar at the far end of the great church. He was always affected by an empty church, especially a cathedral; he found less peace in it than when it was filled by an overflowing congregation. The bare pews, the vaulted ceiling reaching towards God, the stillness of the air, all of it troubled him. Solitude is no place for a reluctant conscience.

In his heart he believed that religion was a philosophy, something he had never confessed to any confessor. He had been born two centuries too late; since there was no Voltaire these days to debate with, he had chosen to exhibit fervour and faith, as tonight, instead of reasoned argument; the latter never caught the public eye. He had been immodestly ambitious ever since he had first entered the seminary; he had chosen a career, not a vocation. The celibacy had worried him at first, but he had in time become accustomed to it, though sin occasionally lingered in the groin. Yet he loved The Lord and His ways; it was just that he expected The Lord to compromise. He had had no ambition to be a saint, he had just wanted to be a cardinal. It was his father, the make-believe Catholic, the sinner who knew no sin, who had raised his sights. He had chosen as his path his own war against Communism, a philosophy that sometimes masqueraded as a religion.

At last he said, with no hint of arrogance this time, 'Are you accusing me of the murder of my niece, Inspector?'

'I didn't say that. But I think you know more about her and her death than you've told me.'

'You came to communion this evening, but are you a true Catholic?'

'Sort of.'

'What does that mean?'

'I have my doubts about certain things. But I didn't come here to make my confession.'

Hourigan nodded. 'No, I suppose not.' He looked up and about him, then back at Malone. 'Do you know what this edifice represents? It's the Church in stone, the monument to God. I'd stand outside there and defend it with my life if someone tried to burn it down. That's how I feel about the

Church as a whole.' He believed what he said; or tried to. But he sounded convincing, at least to his own ears.

'Let's stick to Mary Magdalene. I don't think she was trying to burn down the Church, neither this cathedral nor the Church as a whole.'

'The people she believed in, the ones she worked for, are trying to do just that. Not only the Church but the whole of democracy, too. You live in a fools' paradise here in Australia. If we don't stop the spread of Communism we are dead, Inspector. Dead!' His voice rose and he thumped the back of the pew in front of him. 'My niece was a menace. So are the religious like her, the ones with their Marxist views and their contempt for the Church's authority!'

'Simmer down,' said Malone quietly. 'The Marist brothers told me never to raise my voice in church, except to sing a hymn. We were taught never to ask questions, too. Your job, and the priests', might have been easier if we had been taught to ask questions. But I didn't come here to debate the threat of Communism with you. All I'm interested in is who killed Mary Magdalene. Did you ever visit Nicaragua while she was there?'

'You asked me that. I told you – no.'

'So you did. What about Honduras? I believe that's next door.' At school geography had been his favourite subject; he knew where the world was, unlike most of his countrymen. 'When were you last there?'

Hourigan hesitated. The lights in the cathedral had been dimmed and it was almost impossible to read his expression. At last he said, 'I was there three months ago.'

'Did you know your niece was in Nicaragua then?'

'Yes.'

'Did you try to see her?'

'I sent for her. She was brought to Tegucigalpa. That's the capital.'

'Brought?'

'Perhaps I used the wrong word there.' He sounded

78

uncomfortable. 'Escorted. She had to travel through danger-ous country getting out of Nicaragua.'

'And what happened?'

'We had a debate – an argument, if you like. She was a stubborn, reckless young girl. Like her mother,' he added, then looked quickly at Malone, as if regretting having said that. 'It's a family trait.'

'It must come from your own mother. I've never heard your father described as reckless.'

The Archbishop looked at him with a shrewder eye. 'You're not a dumb cop, are you, Inspector? You know much more than you show.'

'We're just like priests, Your Grace. It doesn't pay to show you're a know-all till you're at least a bishop. Did you threaten your niece?'

'Threaten her? I'm not a violent man.'

I wouldn't put money on that. 'Threaten her with excom-munication, anything like that?'

'No.'

'Why did she come back to Australia then? I mean if you saw her in Honduras three months ago, then it must have been immediately after that that she left for Australia. Who ordered that?'

'I have no idea.' He turned his head, faced Malone directly. The challenge might just as well have been spelled out. *Prove that I did.* 'Now you must excuse me. If he's on time, and he always is, a most un-Irish thing, my father is waiting for me outside.'

He stood up and Malone followed him. They both genu-flected; Hourigan crossed himself, but Malone didn't. They walked down the side aisle, passed a stone bowl into which the Archbishop dipped his hand and crossed himself again.

'You don't believe in the power of holy water, Inspector?'

'I'm afraid not. I told you I had doubts. But if it upsets you –' He put his hand in the bowl, then crossed himself with the water. His mother would have been pleased to see him do

79

that: she threw holy water around like a religious market gardener.

'It doesn't upset me, Inspector. Symbols have their uses, but true faith can survive without them.'

'You have true faith?'

'Oh, absolutely.' He smiled, turned it into a deep chuckle. 'It's a pity you and I are on opposite sides.'

'I didn't know we were.' Malone chuckled, too, just to show he was joking. But the Archbishop, looking at him sideways, almost fell down the wide steps in front of the cathedral and Malone had to grab his arm. 'Steady there, Your Grace, I'm no Communist.'

As they reached the bottom of the steps a dark Rolls-Royce drew up at the kerb. It was a Phantom V, the biggest model, and Malone knew there were only one or two in the whole of the State. A uniformed chauffeur jumped out of the front seat, came round and opened the rear door. A light came on and Malone saw Fingal Hourigan sitting in the back seat. Beside him was a handsome, olive-skinned, grey-haired man.

'Good evening, Mr Hourigan,' said Malone. 'And it's Mr Paredes, isn't it?'

It was not such a wild guess, and he knew, as a policeman, that shots in the dark sometimes hit home. Even if they didn't, they could cause the target some uneasiness. Paredes's chin came up as if he had been clipped there.

Fingal Hourigan leaned forward. 'Good-night, Inspector. Who our friends are is none of your business.'

The Archbishop stepped by Malone and got into the car, putting his bulk down on the jump-seat. The chauffeur closed the door, went round, got in and the car silently drove off. Malone looked after it, then turned and looked back up at the dark towers of the cathedral.

'Don't fall down,' he told the stones. 'You'll outlast me.'

FIVE

I

Sydney in the 1930s reminded Fingal Hourigan, ex-Jimmy Mulligan, very much of Chicago. Its police and politicians could be bought, though not its judges. There were criminal gangs, but they were amateurs compared to the Chicago mobs; they knew nothing of organization. Australians, it seemed, had a sardonic attitude towards being organized, especially their criminals. There were, of course, sections of the population that *were* organized: political parties, trade unions, returned soldiers, certain crooked trainers and jockeys. By and large, however, the voters preferred to think of themselves as individuals, resentful of being told what they should do, and nowhere was that more apparent than amongst the criminal elements. Though certain crims admired Al Capone from afar and dreamed of imitating him if Prohibition ever came to Australia, none had yet shown his organizational ability. They spent their energies in sly grog selling, prostitution rackets, some uncoordinated bank hold-ups and assorted razor slashings amongst themselves. They were a poor lot, proper descendants of the convict gangs of the past, and Fingal Hourigan decided to have nothing to do with them.

He landed in Sydney on Wednesday, October 30, 1929. In America it was still Tuesday, October 29, and investors and bankers were airborne, like wingless hang-gliders, as they leapt from high windows, the thump of their landings adding to the tumult of the Big Crash. The Sydney newspapers featured the Panic on Wall Street, but the thumps were heard only faintly down in the Antipodes; America's troubles, said the locals, were not ours. Fingal, recognizing fools when they stood in a crowd in the street, got off the ship and instantly started buying property.

His first purchase was a hotel, a pub, in Paddington, a working-class inner suburb. It had taken him only a week to see that Australians, like the Irish, were natural-born drinkers; unlike the Irish, who could blame their drunkenness and misery on the English, the natives had no excuse. In summer they did blame the heat, but in winter they drank twice as much. Fingal saw the market and moved into it. It was noticeable that three out of five hotel owners had Irish names, proving that some smart Irishmen had got out of the Ould Country.

Five months after Fingal's arrival he was startled to read that there was to be a referendum in the neighbouring State of Victoria on the introduction of Prohibition; if the notion spread, his hotels, for he now had two, would soon be out of business. Liquor was not to be sold except for medicinal and sacramental purposes, which presumably meant doctors and priests would constantly have temptation on hand. Fingal at once sent a large donation to the Prohibitionists, assuring them, under an assumed name, of his fervent support. If Prohibition was introduced into Victoria he would move down there and become the bootleg king of Melbourne. Unfortunately for his dreams, the Prohibitionists lost overwhelmingly. The winning margin equalled the number of drunks who voted, though all the pubs were supposedly closed on that Saturday. It was suggested they had had access to the medicinal and sacramental supplies. Fingal did not mind the loss of his donation. He always backed both sides in any contest.

The Depression at last began to settle on Australia; though, since there was a height restriction of 150 feet on local buildings, no one was jumping out of windows. There was no point in attempting suicide if it might mean no more than one's being crippled. Violence broke out between striking workers and scabs; the police, caught in between, flailed in all directions with their truncheons, often knocking out each other. The Labour Government of the day brought in what it proudly claimed was a tough Budget, increasing company tax to 6 per cent; blood boiled in the Union Club and other hotbeds of business conservatism and some saw the end of the world looming up. There was talk of marching on the madhouse that was Canberra, the national capital, but since all the banner-makers were flat out supplying the striking and unemployed workers, that idea was abandoned. Newspapers advised readers how to live on £1 a week, ignoring the fact that on £1 a week no citizen, if he had the strength to crawl to the newsagent's, could afford to buy a newspaper. A cold miserable wind blew through the voters, even in summer, though no one suffered as much as the poorer elements of the northern hemisphere. Starvation, somehow, tastes better in the sunshine: or so the well-fed, volunteer charity workers tried to tell the hungry.

Fingal Hourigan didn't suffer at all. Besides his hotels he now had a widening starting-price betting network; SP bookies had been at work since the first convict had tried to out-run the pursuing soldiers, but Fingal was the first man to organize them into a chain. He also bought up closed-down factories and shops, using his profits from the bookmaking; he bought three more hotels, all of them in good situations. In the course of buying the Windjammer Hotel near the Woolloomooloo docks he met Sheila Regan.

She was behind the bar when he walked into the pub, an ethereal-looking girl who looked as if she should be pulling holy water instead of beer. She was pale-skinned, had blonde hair and dark-blue eyes that said she believed all that the world told her. She was a saint, up to her knees in her father's foaming ale and lager, an unwelcome steadying influence on the hard drinkers from the wharves across the road. Paddy Regan kept her out of the bar as much as possible, but this day he was short-staffed and she had volunteered to be a stand-in barmaid. She stood at the end of the long bar and the drinkers, afraid of conversion, crowded together at the other end.

Fingal walked in, took one look at her and fell in love. He had never been a romantic, never had a girl who walked soft-footed through his dreams. He had had girl-friends, but he had always thought of them as the Drainage Board, there to get the dirty water off his chest. Marriage was a fate that, like cancer or an honest living, never crossed his mind. He had never contemplated the possibility of loneliness: money and possessions would always be the best company. Then he met Sheila.

'I am looking for Mr Regan,' he said and was surprised that he sounded breathless.

'He is my father.' She had a voice that should have been in a choir, singing the softer, more seductive notes. 'What are you selling?'

'I'm not selling, I'm buying.' Somehow he managed to sound unaggressive; he couldn't bring himself to bruise this vision. 'Your father is expecting me. I'm Fingal Hourigan. At your service,' he added, getting his breath back and deciding to be a little flourishing in speech and gesture, something she never got from the dockers.

She smiled: was he wrong or was it a knowing smile? But the eyes were still as innocent as those of a convent novice. 'I'd love to visit Ireland, Mr Hourigan.'

He blinked: had he missed something? 'Pardon?'

'You offered your services, Mr Hourigan. Oh, here's Dad. Be careful of him. He's a hard man for a bargain.'

She gave him another smile and floated away, making way for Paddy Regan. He was a thin, red-faced man with thick wavy hair and sharp bitter eyes, the very opposite of his daughter's. Sheila's looks had come from her mother, a dark-

84

haired beauty who had run away with a sailor from the S.S. *Mariposa* when it had docked across the road. She was now in Long Beach, California, living with yet another sailor, though, to be fair to her, he too was from the Matson Line. She was not promiscuous, she wrote her daughter.

'I've thought about your offer, Mr Hourigan,' said Regan in a voice laced with the best of his hotel's stock. His breath was an advertisement for what he sold, if you were a drinker who bought through your nose. 'It's not enough, not by a long chalk.'

'Mr Regan,' said Fingal, one eye watching Sheila pulling beer for the cautiously suspicious drinkers at the other end of the bar. 'I know your financial position down to every penny owed. I will pay you cash, notes in your hand, no cheques, and we'll alter the bill of sale any way you want to fool your creditors.'

'Cash, eh?' Regan pulled them each a beer, peered into the amber looking for a green light of advice. 'I owe something to the brewery, you know.'

'Indeed I do know. You owe quite a lot. Leave that to me.'

'I'm attached to the place.' Regan looked around him. He was attached to it because, wifeless, he was now afraid of the outside world. Out there were too many sober villains who would take him down. It didn't seem to occur to him that he was standing across the bar from one of them. 'Would you want me to stay on and manage it for you?'

Fingal looked along the bar at Sheila, who now stood watching him. She was silhouetted against a window on which a brewery advertisement was painted: a Walter Jardine rugby league forward looked ready to leap out of the glass and rape her. He said, 'I'd like to consult your daughter on that.'

Regan did not look surprised; he was a weak man who acknowleged that women, or anyway *his* women, always had their own way. 'Be careful, Hourigan. She's a hard girl for a bargain.'

Fingal smiled; how could such an ethereal beauty drive a bargain? 'I once made love to the queen of an African tribe. She sold me the tribe in the morning.'

'Don't waste your mullarkey on me, Hourigan. I'm Irish, too. Are you planning to make love to my daughter?'

'Not yet,' said Fingal. 'Only when it is honourable to do so.'

Sheila advised him to buy the hotel and to engage her father as manager, but not to let him keep the books. He asked her would she go out with him.

'I was wondering when you'd get around to asking me,' she said.

He had been talking to her for less than five minutes. He put her forwardness down to her innocence. 'Where would you like to go?'

'To the fights.'

He blinked again: she was full of surprises. But he took her to the fights that night, sat at the ringside in the old Stadium and watched Jack Carroll chop an American import to pieces and, out of the corner of his eye, watched the angel beside him leaning forward with all the blood-lust of a half-starved lioness. When he took her home he tried a chaste good-night kiss and was instantly devoured by lips, teeth and tongue that burnt him: even her teeth seemed hot.

A month later Fingal proposed to her and she accepted him. 'On condition that you will take me to Ireland for our honeymoon.'

'I'll take you to the moon itself, if you wish,' said Fingal, both feet off the ground as he made love to her, not honourably.

'Ireland will do,' she said. 'Now roll over, it's my turn on top. I've just finished reading *The Perfumed Garden*.'

'Does your father know?'

'No, he thought I was reading the *Annals of Mary*.'

'You look so angelic. How can you be so wanton?'

'It's my mother in me. Don't worry, I go to confession

86

every Saturday – I can see the priest's hair standing on end through the grille. Don't expect me to be wanton on Saturday nights.'

'Sunday to Fridays all right?'

'Every night, three times a night. Oh, I do love you, Fingal!'

Which she did; and he her. They were married on the January day in 1933 when, on the other side of the world, Adolf Hitler became Chancellor of Germany. Both events appeared in the *Sydney Morning Herald*, though the Hourigan announcement was only a paid advertisement in the 'classifieds' column. The general public paid little more attention to Hitler than they did to Hourigan; they were about to declare war on England, whose fast bowlers were hurling cricket balls at the heads of Australian batsmen. The Empire looked ready to fall apart and local weddings and foreign politics were minor events.

Fingal, as promised, took Sheila to Ireland for their honeymoon. She fell in love with the misty, gentle countryside, but said she wouldn't like to live there. He then took her to Italy and in St Peter's she fell on her knees with a force that he thought would crack them and prayed for half an hour without lifting her head; then they went back to the Hotel Hassler and made wanton love for the rest of the day. He took her to Germany and she fell in love with the countryside of that country. But he was not a pastoral lad and the Irish fields and the German forests made no impression on him. But he went to a Nazi rally and watched, fascinated, while Hitler mesmerized his audience. Capone had had power, but never like this. He dreamed for a moment of capturing an audience back home like this, of 50,000 voters standing up at the Sydney Cricket Ground and shouting, '*Heil* Fingal!' But he knew it would never work, that if ever he was to have power in Australia it would not be through rhetoric. The natives back there were too laconic, they would always suspect the orator.

Sheila wanted them to go home through America; she might

87

be a hard woman with a bargain, as her father had said, but she knew how to spend her husband's money. Fingal, however, said they had to hurry home: he had to go back to making money. The truth was that he was afraid to go anywhere near the United States. Al Capone, in and out of jail now, hounded by the US Treasury, was still a force and, as Fingal well knew, he was not a man to forget a treachery. America, and particularly Chicago, was to be avoided like the rock of Scylla, a Greek dame he had read about in the Chicago Public Library.

Eighteen months later, back in Sydney and having watered *The Perfumed Garden* till it was overgrown and had become weedy, as had Fingal, Sheila decided she wanted a child and took out her diaphragm. Nine months later, to the day, she gave birth to Kerry Seamus. She said that was enough children for the time being, as if she had given birth to a litter; she wanted to learn to be a mother, something her own mother had never been. Three years later she decided it was time for another child and she became pregnant with Brigid Maureen. When it came time for delivery it was a difficult birth and Fingal, who still loved her dearly, almost went out of his mind with the fear that he would lose her. She survived and so did the baby, a bawling, brawling infant who entered the world fighting everyone in sight; it was rumoured that when the doctor slapped her to bring her to life, she slapped him back. Her four-year-old brother hated her and she, from some primeval instinct, even before she had her eyes open, hated him.

And then, slowly but steadily, Sheila came to hate Fingal. It began in ways that, at first, he didn't quite catch. There would be a barbed remark about his preoccupation with money; women, he had once told her, knew nothing about the making of money. Then she began to complain about the way he made his money; he turned his back on that argument, because he would never discuss with anyone how he did that. That was how it had been in Chicago with Capone and the other gang-leaders, including the Irish: money matters were no concern of the women.

Then she began to have what she called 'a marital headache'; it always seemed to coincide with an ache in his groin. At last he discovered the reason for her turning away from him, figuratively and in bed. She had given up reading *The Perfumed Garden* and turned to the writings of St Teresa of Avila.

'She's atoning for the sins of her mother,' said Regan.

He was still managing the Windjammer Hotel, living above the premises and staring each morning across the road to the wharf where his errant wife had waved goodbye as she had fled with the American sailor. He never visited the Hourigans in their home in Bellevue Hill and he was slowly drinking himself to death, though at Fingal's expense.

'How are the babies?'

Fingal brought the children down once a month in the big Buick he now owned; but Sheila never came. 'Always on their knees. She's teaching them to pray, even the baby.'

'There's something wrong with us Irish, Fingal. We put too much money on prayer. What does she want to do with the boy? Make him Pope?'

Fingal nodded seriously. 'She actually said that yesterday. I think she's going out of her mind, Paddy.'

'The same thing happened to her ma when she ran away with the Yank.'

In the spring of 1939, two days before Hitler marched into Poland and the world fell into the second war to end all wars, Sheila went completely out of her mind. Fingal was never able to explain to himself or, later, to his children why she did so. She was put away in a home and Fingal engaged a succession of housekeepers and nannies to look after the children; none of them could stand the pious little brats, let alone love them, and none of them lasted longer than six months. The home became no more than a house: love, like world peace, had gone out the window. Fingal turned to making more money, which could be loved without fear of rejection.

The war was kind to Fingal Hourigan. He made money on the black market, in war industries, in property. When the Japanese shelled a harbourside section of Sydney in 1942 he bought up half of Vaucluse from residents fleeing to the Blue Mountains west of the city. He made substantial donations to war comforts funds and in return was rewarded by ladies on the fund committees who couldn't give fleshly comforts to their absent husbands. He made no committed alliances, however. He was still in love with Sheila: not the pathetic deranged woman in the private mental home but the ethereal-looking girl who had smiled at him in a hotel bar long ago.

The war ended and there was no bigger victor than Fingal Hourigan. He had sold out his starting-price business and now he was on his way to being respectable: if being in business where no criminal charges could be made meant being respectable. He indulged in insider trading, though the term was not yet invented; in tax evasion, a legitimate if not honourable pursuit; in mortgage foreclosures, only dis-reputable if pursued against elderly widows; and cheating any Government department, a national sport. He had raised skulduggery (or skulbuggery, as a later acquaintance would call it) to an art.

2

In 1948 Kerry, who was then fourteen, came to him and asked for a man-to-man talk. They had never been close, more like uncle and nephew, and there was a certain constraint between them that had always obstructed any confidences.

'Is it about sex? Don't the Jesuits teach you about that?' Kerry, for the past three years, had been attending St Ignatius' College as a boarder. It was an expensive school and it had been chosen for him by Sheila before she had gone round the bend from sex to religion.

'No, I know all about that. I found one of your old books when I was home for the holidays.'

'What book?'

'*The Perfumed Garden*.'

Fingal didn't disclaim ownership. 'It's a book on acrobatics. Go on.'

'I want to be a priest.'

'*The Perfumed Garden* brought that on?'

Kerry laughed, something he rarely did in the company of his father. Fingal looked at him, liking the sound; Kerry was a big boy for his age, already as tall as his father, and the laugh came up from his belly. Fingal grinned, sat back in his chair and relaxed.

'Actually, I want to be a cardinal.'

'I think fourteen-year-old cardinals went out of fashion when the Popes stopped having bastard sons. Who gave you the idea of being a priest?'

'Mother.'

Once a month Kerry and his ten-year-old sister were taken by the current housekeeper to see their mother. Sheila had occasional lucid stretches – 'some women do,' said her now totally alcoholic father, locked away in his room above the Windjammer bar and no longer managing the hotel – and she spent those moments giving advice to the children on how to avoid the wicked ways of the world she had left. Fingal, carefully guarding the memory of the girl he had once loved, never went near her. He paid the bills and sent her expensive presents and flowers every Friday, but that was the extent of his concern for her.

'She ought to know better,' said Fingal. 'Are you religious, pious, full of faith, all the rest of the bulldust?'

'Yes, I think so. You do good in the world, if you're a priest.'

'And if you're not? You think I'm not doing any good in the world?'

'I don't know. You never tell me or Brigid anything about

what you do. You make a lot of money, and that's all I know.'

There's no need for you to know, thought Fingal; better that you don't. His interests were so wide now that no one who worked for him, not even his accountants, knew the full extent of his holdings or his pursuits. Only this year, after several years of legitimate business, he had slipped back to the criminal side, lured by the money available. He had recently taken over the gold smuggling racket between Hong Kong, Bombay and points west; Sydney was the half-way house, the exchange point, and he now owned the ships that brought in the gold. Taking charge had involved the elimination of certain opposition, though they had never known who *their* opposition was. Crooked cops had taken care of the elimination, though they never knew who paid them. One competitor, a businessman as well-known as Fingal, had held out, but he had been disposed of by being thrown off the back of a ferry one night into the harbour; the two thugs who had done the job had never known who paid for their services. The body had been recovered, half-eaten by a shark, and the coroner had put death down to suicide brought on by worry about the deceased's health. There had been a big funeral attended by politicians and prominent businessmen, including Fingal Hourigan. He had sat in a back pew of the Anglican cathedral, listened to the eulogies, hidden his smile and added up what the gold smuggling would bring him each year. It would be several million pounds at least. More than even the most venal cardinal would ever make.

'That's *my* religion,' he said. 'Making money is what makes the world go round. Not love or prayers.'

'Don't you believe in God?'

'No, But don't tell the Jesuits — they'd be here on my doorstep as soon as you mentioned it. You believe in God, if you like, but I don't need Him.' In his mind he used the pronoun with a lower case *h*.

Kerry looked worried. 'He could strike you dead for that. Aren't you afraid?'

He had been afraid ever since he had left Chicago nineteen years ago, afraid that some day Capone, or someone sent by the Big Fella, would catch up with him. That is, until a year ago, when Capone, racked by syphilis, hatred for the Internal Revenue men and regrets for his lost empire, died in Florida of an apoplectic seizure. Fingal had said a prayer that day, but no one had heard it, probably least of all The Lord.

'No,' he said. 'Fear is for cowards. Are you a coward?'

Kerry thought about it, then said, 'I don't think so. I'm like you, Dad, in lots of ways.'

'Except about religion. Go away and think about wanting to be a priest. I won't say no if you're stuck on it, but don't expect me to give you my blessing.'

Kerry grinned and his father grinned in return: they were growing closer. 'That would be sacrilege, Dad.'

'Sure. Don't tell the Jesuits.'

Kerry left him then and he sat in his living-room in the house in Bellevue Hill and looked down towards the harbour, where he could see one of his ships heading for Hong Kong and another shipment of gold. The house was more than large enough for him and the children and the housekeeper, but it was still too small: the memories of Sheila crowded him. He would build another house, one down on the water at Vaucluse. He began to dream of a castle, something that Al Capone had never owned.

When Brigid came home on a weekend pass from Rose Bay Convent, another expensive school, Fingal took her into the Hotel Australia for lunch. It was the first time he had taken her out alone and she looked at him with a sceptical eye far too experienced for a ten-year-old.

'Why are you doing this, Daddy?'

'I've been a neglectful father. You and I should get to know each other better.'

She played with a chocolate éclair. 'I don't know anything at all about you, Daddy. You've never told us anything about where you came from. Do Kerry and I have a grandfather and grandmother, I mean from your side?'

'No. Some day I'll tell you about myself, when you're older. I was an adventurer.' He changed the subject. 'Did you know Kerry wants to be a priest?'

'No. He's like you, he never tells me anything about himself.'

'Do you want to be a nun?'

'Hell, no!'

'Do they teach you to swear at Rose Bay? Still, I'm glad to hear it. You're too pretty to be wasted in a convent.'

'There are pretty nuns. You don't have to be ugly to be a nun. I just don't want to be one, because I want to grow up and be an artist.'

'Are you any good?' He had never seen any of her work, not even any of her schoolwork. I'm a terrible father, he thought, but would only have given himself a hernia if he had tried to dredge up any guilt.

'The sisters say I'm very good. They don't like what I draw, but that's because they're old-fashioned.'

'What do you draw?'

'Naked men and women,' she said, and suddenly he saw Sheila in her.

She was a remarkably pretty child, with her mother's eyes, but there were already hints that the prettiness would fade and some day there would be a strong-boned handsome woman in her place.

'You can hold back on those. Wait till you leave school and I'll send you to an art school, a good one.'

'I want to go to Paris and live with Pablo Picasso.'

'Paris is no place for a young girl, especially with Picasso. Stay at home and marry a rich young man in Sydney. You can still be an artist.'

'It wouldn't be as much fun. I think I'm like you, Daddy, in lots of ways. An adventurer.'

Perhaps they were right, perhaps there was more of him in them than he saw.

Paddy Regan died in January 1950 from a surfeit of hops and lost hopes. A month later Sheila died; there was a wild happy look in her eyes, as if she had caught sight of The Lord in the moment before He took her. She was buried privately and there was no announcement in the newspapers. Fingal did not look at her when she was laid out in her coffin; she was a stranger, he was not burying his old one true love. The children cried, but with fear more than grief. Two deaths in a month: it was too much for children to be faced with such mortality.

A month later Kerry entered the seminary to study for the priesthood. He still wanted to be a cardinal, an ambition he did not confess to the monsignor in charge. Brigid showed promise at school of being a talented artist; she had given up drawing naked men and women, a retreat greeted with relief by the nuns. She still dreamed of going to Paris and living with Picasso, a dream she did not confess to the mother superior.

Fingal Hourigan went on making money. Then in 1955 he took into his employ Jonathan Tewsday, a crook as devout as himself.

SIX

I

Brothels are like parliaments: no one there ever believes the intentions of the rest of those present. Not even when the police come calling.

'I never expected it of you, Inspector. You've come back for a pay-off.'

'Why would I do that, Tilly? I'm not on the Vice Squad.'

Tilly Mosman looked at him dubiously. 'Why did you have to come back now? It's the girls' rest period.'

'Better now than when they're working. I don't think your clients would be too happy if I'm sitting on the end of the bed asking the girls questions.'

Malone had gone from the cathedral back to Homicide, picked up the fax photos of Paredes and Domecq and come here to the Quality Couch. Tilly Mosman had invited him in, but reluctantly.

'They go back to work at eight. Have you eaten? You can have supper with us. It's only light. The girls don't like to work on a full stomach.'

Malone grinned. 'Theirs or their clients'?'

'No crudity, Inspector, I don't allow that.'

Tilly Mosman prided herself on her taste; it was what distinguished her establishment from similar ones around town. As Malone followed her through the downstairs drawing-room into the small dining-room at the back of the house he noted the expense and good taste. Even the nudes in the paintings on the silk-hung walls had a look of class about them, high-priced whores who posed only for the best painters. The two Vietnamese maids who were emptying the ashtrays and cleaning up after this afternoon's trade did not look like Saigon bar-girls; dressed in demure black uniforms with white lace aprons, they would not have been out of place in a Point Piper mansion. To which Tilly Mosman some day aspired.

Half a dozen girls, dressed in cotton wraps, their make-up removed, sat around the dining-table eating quiche, salad and cake. They looked up as Malone entered and all of them sat very still. 'It's all right, girls,' said Tilly. 'It's not a raid. This is Scobie Malone. He's come to ask questions about that poor nun they found outside yesterday morning.'

The girls relaxed and two of them moved aside to let Malone sit between them. They piled his plate with food, like good wives, then offered him a glass of mineral water. 'Tilly never lets us drink wine when we're at work, says it clouds our minds,' said one of them. 'As if it mattered.'

She was a naturalized redhead, a pretty woman who might have been twenty-two or thirty-two; she had probably looked this age at sixteen. She had a husky voice, cultivated as part of her trade, and a smile with a touch of malice in it. For which Malone couldn't blame her.

'Is this all there are of you? Six?'

'There are eight others. They go home to feed their hubbies or put the kids to bed.'

Malone took the two photos out of the manilla folder and laid them on the table. 'Any of you recognize either of these men?'

The photos were passed around, like severed heads; the girls looked at them dispassionately. No matter what they might think of their own menfolk, if they had any, here in this house men were just livestock, bulls who paid. Malone knew that he could not have chosen sharper eyes or sharper memories.

'Yes,' said a girl sitting opposite him. She was a mixed-blood, part-Chinese, part-European, part-something darker; she was beautiful in a striking way and Malone wondered how long it would be before some well-heeled client took her away from the Quality Couch. He felt the attraction of her and decided he would not tell Lisa where he had been tonight. 'I've entertained him two or three times. Three.'

She pushed one of the photos back across the table and Malone looked down at Max Domecq Cruz. 'What about the other one?'

He looked around the table, but all the girls shook their heads. They all looked interested and ready to help and even a little afraid: if a nun could be killed on their doorstep, why not one of them?

'Sergeant Clements was here and you girls told him you had only two Spanish-speaking clients Saturday night.'

'This man didn't speak Spanish,' said the girl opposite him. 'He said he was an American.'

Malone looked at Tilly Mosman, keeping to protocol: 'Can I take her into another room?'

Tilly nodded. 'Go ahead, Dawn. Don't upset her too much, Scobie. She has to go back to work.'

The girl led him out of the dining-room and into a small, exquisitely furnished side-room. Malone, conscious of all the elegance around him, wondered what the bedrooms upstairs were like. There had been a time when he had been almost totally unaware of his surroundings, when rooms were only furnished by the people in them, but Lisa had educated him to an appreciation of couch and table and drape. She had, he'd told her, also educated him to an appreciation of mortgage.

'Is Dawn your real name?'

'No. Why do you want my name?'

'Righto, we'll forget it for the moment.' He did not want to antagonize her; after all, she was entitled to some privacy if she demanded it. In an hour or so she'd have precious little. 'What was this man's name?'

She arranged herself on a love-seat and gestured for him to sit next to her. The face-to-face seats had been designed for lovers; it was also an ideal arrangement for an intimate interrogation. Malone was surprised that he felt uncomfortable sitting so close to the girl. She was even more beautiful now that he had time to look at her closely; her skin was flawless and he could not find any of her features that was out of proportion to the others. Every gesture, every line of her body hinted at sensuality: he felt the attraction of her again and wished he had not sat down so close to her. The perfume she wore was thick in his nostrils, accentuated by the nervous heat of her body.

'Is this what they call a love-seat?' She nodded, and he grinned and added defensively, 'I should buy one for my wife and me.'

She smiled, showing beautifully even white teeth. 'Nobody's ever said that to me. Nobody ever mentions their wife in this place, it's taboo.'

'What did our friend talk about? What was his name?'

'Sebastian. Raul Sebastian. He never told me much at all about himself. Just that he lived in Miami.' She had put her arm on the division between them; her hand rested on his upper arm. It was an unconscious movement, a trick of the trade that she performed automatically. 'I think he's genuinely keen on me. He asked me if I'd like to go and live in Miami.'

'You could do better than that.'

'Here in Sydney? Don't be silly. There are several guys who come here who say they're in love with me, but none of 'em would marry me. All his friends would know where he picked me up.'

'Why'd you go on the game then?'

'The money, what else? I'm lazy, too lazy to move somewhere else and start again. All I can hope is that some day I'll finish up with my own house, like Tilly.'

He looked at the lovely waste of her. Nature had made her perfect, then left her to her own devices. Or men's vices. 'How did Sebastian come here? Do they come in off the street or are your clients recommended?'

'Oh, recommended!' She looked at him indignantly; she had her standards. 'We're the top of the class.'

'I'm sure you are. Sorry. Who recommended Sebastian?'

'I don't know. Tilly takes care of all that. But I don't think she'll tell you.'

'Let's try her. Will you get her for me?'

'I'm here,' said Tilly Mosman, appearing in the doorway. 'I was eavesdropping. You're a nice man, Scobie, but my policy is, Never trust any man. Dawn is right – I'm not going to tell you who recommended Mr Sebastian.'

Malone stood up, relieved to be away from the side of Dawn. He had always been a faithful husband; was he at last developing the seven-year itch? 'Trust me this time, Tilly.' He told her who Sebastian really was. 'He's connected with the murder of Sister Mary Magdalene in some way, I don't know how. You don't want to be an accessory after the fact.'

Tilly looked suddenly worried and a frown cracked the flawless face beside her. The women looked at each other, then Tilly said, 'Is he dangerous? I mean would he come back and, you know, hurt Dawn or me?'

'I don't think so. If he comes back, get in touch with us – I'll have men here within two minutes.' The Police Centre was only a few blocks away. 'Who recommended him, Tilly?'

She hesitated, jealous of her standards. Then: 'Sir Jonathan Tewsday.'

Malone kept his eyebrows in place. 'Is he a client of yours?'

'Not now.'

So he once was. Malone had met Tewsday only once, years ago when he had been a young detective-constable on the Fraud Squad; he had also then met Fingal Hourigan for the first time. The Squad had been unable to lay any charges against Tewsday or Hourigan; both men had gone on to be ornaments of the Establishment, all tarnish scrubbed away by their wealth. It was said that Tewsday had bought his knighthood, but it would not have been cheap; the dead Premier who had sold it to him had never believed in bargains. It was also said that Fingal Hourigan, the bargain hunter, Tewsday's boss, had refused a knighthood because there was no discount.

'What did Sir Jonathan say about Mr Sebastian?'

'That he was a gentleman who paid his bills in cash. I take credit cards, but I prefer not to.'

Malone grinned. 'What do you put it down to?'

'I call it telex charges. It's a form of communication, isn't it? So's what my girls do.'

Malone looked at Dawn, who smiled lazily. He said, 'Was he a gentleman?

Dawn shrugged, but offered no comment. Then Tilly said, 'He paid his account each night, though he made what I thought was an ungentlemanly remark. He said the devalued Aussie dollar gave him a cheap roll in the hay. None of my girls is a cheap roll in the hay, no matter what the dollar's valued at.'

She had her pride and so did her girls; Dawn gave a slow nod to emphasize what Tilly had said. Malone nodded in reply: he respected any professional, even some crims.

'Righto, let me know if he calls again.'

'You're not going to get in touch with Sir Jonathan?'

'Don't worry, Tilly. If I do, he won't know how I got to him.'

'I'd like to believe that . . .' She knew the power of powerful men, both good and bad. 'Don't call again, Scobie, not unless you have to.'

He smiled, knowing the brush-off wasn't personal. He went through to the front door and Dawn, a good hostess, accompanied him. She put her hand on his arm; he felt the effect of her perfume and her attraction. 'All the girls would like you to find who murdered that nun. Some of us are religious, in a sort of way.'

'Sure, Dawn. Take care of yourself. And don't go to Miami.'

She kissed him on the cheek, looked unafraid but lazily so. Bed, he guessed, was her natural habitat.

'I'll probably never get away from here, not till I'm Tilly's age. When I get my own house, come to the opening.'

'I'll do that. Can I bring my wife? Good-night, Dawn.'

As he went out to his car, a hired stretched limousine drew up at the kerb. Six Japanese men got out, two of them with cameras strung round their necks, stood for a moment as if gathering their courage or their potency, then went into the Quality Couch, like tourists looking for Aussie souvenirs. Malone wondered if they would pay by credit card, if they would think the over-valued yen would give them a cheap roll in the hay.

He went straight home, suddenly feeling worn out. Enough had been done for the day; Sir Jonathan Tewsday could wait till tomorrow, Tuesday. The skies had cleared and he drove home through a beautiful autumn night. He pulled the car into the garage beside the house, got out and, before going inside, stood and looked up at the stars. He had read in the newspapers that a new supernova had just been discovered, the death of a star 170,000 years ago. He looked for it and found it, a tiny bright explosion south-west of the Southern Cross. He had always been interested in the stars, ever since he had been a small boy; not as an amateur astronomer nor as a carnival astrologer but as a dreamer. What a way to die, he thought, 170,000 years ago and only now the word was out. All deaths should be like that, so that those who loved the deceased would themselves be dead before the grief began. He wondered if Brigid Hourigan was sitting beneath the stars tonight and grieving for her daughter.

He went into the house, took off his jacket and dropped it over the back of a couch. Lisa kissed him, then, ever neat, picked up the jacket to put it away on a hanger. She lifted a sleeve and smelled it. 'Arpège?'

'Russ Clements is wearing it.'

'You're holding hands with a detective-sergeant?' She led him out into the kitchen. 'Your dinner's in the oven.'

'I've eaten.' He hadn't eaten much, but he had a sweet tooth that was always hungry. 'What's for dessert?'

'I thought you'd had it,' said Lisa, taking a Dutch apple cake from the oven. 'Maybe mousse Arpège?'

He mock-winced. 'You can do better than that. If you must know, I had dinner with the girls at the Quality Couch. I had a girl on either knee and they fed me with a silver spoon. I think both of them were naked, but I'm not sure. I was too interested in what they were telling me.'

She cut a wide slice of apple cake, put whipped cream on it and pushed it across to him. Then she sat down opposite him and smiled. 'The day I think I can't trust you, I'll walk out. It wouldn't be that I just couldn't stand losing you to some other woman, it would be that I'd be so disappointed. I could never believe in anyone again if I couldn't believe in you. Now eat up.'

'You really know how to give a man an appetite.' There was a lump in his throat; and an oxyacetylene burn of guilt in his breast. He would never be able to tell her about Dawn, the whore of all men's dreams. He clasped her hand, glad that the children were in bed: this was not a family moment. 'I love you. I'll buy you a gallon of Arpège.'

She squeezed his hand, lifted it and kissed it. Then, aware of the worry in him, she said, 'What did the girls tell you that was so interesting?'

Should he burden her with his worries? But who else was there to confide in? Russ Clements, of course; but Russ couldn't hold his hand. So he told her and as always saw the sympathy in her face. How could he have looked at the girl in the brothel, who would be worn beyond sympathy for anyone but herself?

'I think I'm opening a can of worms bigger than tiger snakes.'

Yesterday: a cathedral and a brothel. Today: what?

'How about a visit to a cemetery?' said Clements, as if reading his mind. 'Sister Mary Magdalene is being buried this morning at Northern Suburbs. There's nothing in the papers. I got that from the morgue.'

The forensic report had been on Malone's desk when he came to the office this morning. It said that the killing of the young nun had been a professional job: 'The knife used, I would say, was one designed for killing, possibly the type used by military Special Services or something like it. The knife was driven into the heart at exactly the right angle to a depth of eight centimetres. Death would have occurred within two seconds. Very professional.' One could feel the cold admiration of the writer.

On the way out to the cemetery Malone told Clements about his visit last night to the Quality Couch. 'I think we'll pay a visit to Sir Jonathan.'

Clements looked at him dubiously. 'Scobie, we're opening up –'

'I know. A can of tiger snakes.'

'That wasn't what I was going to say. But –' He nodded, then bit his lip. 'Yeah, you're right. Tiger snakes, taipans, pythons, the bloody lot. Not to mention the Pope.'

'He'd thank you for that, in there in the snake-pit. I don't think we have to worry about him.'

'I dunno. You Tykes have got the influence.'

'Is Tewsday a Catholic?'

Clements shrugged. 'Does it matter, if he's a mate of Old Man Hourigan and the Archbishop? They're all in bed together.'

It was a cool day, the wind coming off the mountains to the west with a whisper of winter. The cemetery struck Malone as being like all others, hectares of loneliness: the dead never kept each other company, no matter what the living intended.

The gravestones, like tablets planted by some minor Moses, stared at each other with messages written by the living for the living: the dead beneath them were beyond any communication. Some of the gravestones were fancier than others, ornamented with marble angels, marble wreaths and a shower of marble snow; but they, too, were messages from the living to the living. Wealth, or the manifestation of it, should never be buried, unless one were an Egyptian king.

There was some evidence of wealth, though not of the Ptolemys, in the parking lot: a silver Rolls-Royce and the latest Jaguar, a bright-red model that stood out like a fountain of blood in the monochrome of the cemetery. Clements pulled the unmarked police Commodore in beside them and got out. Standing apart from the two expensive cars were a small mini-bus and a motor-cycle. Clements made a note of the number-plates and Malone once again nodded in appreciation of the methodical efficiency of the big yobbo.

Further over were half a dozen other cars and three television vans. The reporters and cameramen had already moved over towards the open grave where Sister Mary Magdalene was to be buried; they had the grace to keep apart from the small group of mourners around the grave. The cameramen, however, already had their inquisitive cameras pointed at Brigid Hourigan: no one any longer was entitled to private grief.

Father Marquez was saying the last prayers, his voice sometimes choking. Around the grave there were half a dozen uniformed schoolgirls; Mother Brendan and a younger nun; Brigid Hourigan and her manservant Michele; and a portly, bald man who had the look of an expensive physician. Sir Jonathan Tewsday, however, revived only sick companies, though he was known to have killed off as many as he had cured.

Malone wondered who had invited Father Marquez to say the prayers. When the young priest had finished, his face as sad as Brigid's, the gravediggers moved in as the mourners moved away. Malone felt a touch of unaccountable grief; then he knew he was looking into the future, praying against the burial of his own children. As he turned away he saw the headstone on the neighbouring grave: Sheila Regan Hourigan, 1913–1950. Mary Magdalene was being buried beside her grandmother and Malone wondered why her grandfather and her uncle hadn't attended.

He moved across to Father Marquez. The young priest was still looking down into the grave and he started when Malone touched his arm.

'Oh, Inspector – I didn't see you. I'm glad you came. I was going to phone you later.' He turned away for a moment to give a sad smile to the schoolgirls as they filed past; through their tears they looked back at him soul-stricken. Mother Brendan harrumphed softly and pushed them on, but the young nun paused. 'Yes, Helena?'

Sister Helena, on a better day, would have been plain and cheerful, good company; today she was just plain, her face turned to suet. 'Did you get the letter?'

'Yes. I was just about to tell Inspector Malone about it. This is Sister Helena. She found a letter addressed to me under Mary Magdalene's mattress. It could have caused a scandal . . .'

'I knew it wasn't a love letter – Mary wasn't the sort.' Sister Helena herself might have been, in other circumstances. She was still a schoolgirl, which was a reason she would always be popular with the girls she taught. 'I must be going. There's Mother Brendan cracking the whip.' There was just a faint crumbling of the suet; her energy could never remain far below the surface. 'Nice meeting you, Inspector. Find the devil who killed her!'

Then she was gone and Father Marquez looked after her. 'You see? I told you everyone loved Mary who knew her.'

'Did you?'

Marquez smiled, shook his head. 'Not that way. Here's the

letter. I sort of wish I hadn't read it. There's more in there than I want to know.'

Malone took the letter. He read it, his face showing nothing of his reaction. 'Can I keep it? Why would she have written it d'you think?'

'Sure, keep it, I don't want it. I don't know why she wrote it – unless she thought she was in danger. But she doesn't say anything about being afraid. You don't seem surprised by what's in it?'

'Not surprised, no. But I'm like you – there's more in it than I'd rather know.' Russ Clements had come up to stand beside them. Malone introduced him, then handed the letter to him. 'Read it, Russ, then put it in the murder box.'

He said goodbye to Father Marquez and walked back to the car park. Brigid Hourigan stood beside the red Jaguar, complementing it with the rich blue cape that she wore. Jonathan Tewsday stood beside her, holding her wrist as if taking her temperature.

'I didn't expect you, Inspector,' said Brigid. She had been weeping, but there were no tears now. Her blonde hair was wrapped in a blood-red turban that offset the cloak; she was a ball of style, if a little theatrical. Malone preferred it to the usual mourner's black; at death there should be some challenge that life went on. 'Is this police duty?'

'In a way. Sometimes the murderer turns up, fired by a sort of final curiosity.'

She looked at him with interest. 'You'd know more about the psychology of that than I would.' Then she looked around her; it was difficult to tell if she was mocking him. 'Did you see anyone you suspect?'

'No.' So far he hadn't looked at Tewsday. As casually as he could, he said, 'Your brother the Archbishop didn't come?'

'No. He was afraid there might be some publicity.' Her voice was sour.

He could go all the way to Nicaragua, unafraid of the Sandinistas and their guns: so the letter had said. He could not come to his niece's funeral because he feared reporters and their cameras. 'So far you've kept the Hourigan name out of the papers.'

'Not me, Inspector.' She looked at Tewsday with a smile as sour as her voice. 'Sir Jonathan and my father have done that. Do you know Inspector Malone, Jonathan?'

'I don't think I've had the pleasure,' said Tewsday, exhibiting a convenient memory. 'I take it you're in charge of this awful case. Any clues so far?'

'A few. I think we'll know before the end of the week *why* she was murdered.'

Michele held open the door of the Jaguar and Brigid was about to get into the car. She paused. 'Will you let me know, Inspector? I'm entitled to know.'

'Of course, Miss Hourigan. We'll be in touch again, anyway. There are more questions we want to ask you.' Out of the corner of his eye he saw Tewsday lift one of his chins.

Brigid nodded, then got into the car. Michele closed the door gently after her, got into the front seat and drove the car away. Malone wondered if Brigid always rode in the back seat or whether, today, she too was afraid of publicity.

'A remarkable woman,' said Tewsday. 'Talented and beautiful and headstrong.'

'Her daughter seems to have been something like her. Headstrong, anyway. I'd like to ask you some questions, Sir Jonathan.'

There was the sudden roar of an engine: Father Marquez had kick-started his motorbike. He pulled on his dark-visored helmet, waved a gloved hand to Malone, then wheeled the bike round and sped off as if getting away in some religious grand prix.

'Who is the priest?' said Tewsday.

'A friend of Sister Mary's – her closest friend, possibly.'

'The young – they're so different from my day.'

'You don't have children?'

'Three daughters. When do you want to ask me those questions, whatever they are?'

'Now.'

'Here? This is hardly the place.'

'Are you going back to town? Maybe I could ride back with you?'

'You're intrusive, aren't you, Inspector? Has anyone ever told you that?' He had the sort of voice that had been cultivated as he had gone up in the world; he sounded as if he were juggling his vowels, fearful that he might drop them and squash them.

'It comes with the job. I'm naturally shy.'

'That isn't what I've heard.' Then Tewsday realized his mistake; he lowered the lids on his large pop-eyes. 'Get in.'

Malone signalled to Clements to go back into town without him. The chauffeur, a muscle-bound man who bulged even through his grey uniform, smiled at Malone. 'Mind your head as you get in, sir. A lot of people think these cars are higher than they are.'

'Especially people who travel in Holdens,' said Malone.

He got into the Rolls-Royce. It was a Silver Spur, a later model than Hourigan's Phantom, but it did not have the other's cachet. Tewsday evidently knew his place in the corporate garage.

Tewsday settled back in his seat as the car moved off. He was of medium height but looked shorter because of his bulk. He had a florid complexion and a voice to match: both had come with the indulgences of wealth. He was one of the leading financiers in the country and he knew it and would never be modest about it. He had character, most of it bad, but no one had ever proved it so.

He pressed a window-button and they were cut off from the chauffeur. 'So what are your questions, Inspector?'

Malone nodded at the chauffeur on the other side of the glass panel. 'An American as your chauffeur?'

'Isn't Australia supposed to be a melting-pot, just like America was?'

'I didn't think Americans migrated here to take menial jobs.'

'There's no shame in starting at the bottom, Inspector. I did. I presume you did, too?'

This wasn't going to be easy. He decided to attack at once. 'Are you raising money for Archbishop Hourigan?'

'Raising –? You mean for some Catholic charity? I'm not a Catholic, Inspector.'

'I don't think the Archbishop is really interested in charity. Not from listening to him preach last night at the cathedral. No, are you raising money for his crusade against the Contras in Nicaragua?'

Tewsday laughed, a rich sound, richly cultivated; Malone wondered if he spent half an hour each day in vocal exercises. 'Contras? Good heavens, man, what have they got to do with us? Australia doesn't invest in Central America. We have more bananas here than we can eat.'

'Then what is your association with Mr Paredes and Mr Domecq? What do they have to sell besides bananas?'

Tewsday turned away and looked out the window. The Rolls had pulled up at a traffic light. Standing beside them was the convent mini-bus; the girls who had been at the funeral stared out at them; two of them said something to each other, their mouths opening silently behind the glass like those of pretty goldfish. Sister Helena, who was driving the mini-bus, turned and smiled at Tewsday.

'Nuns,' he said, face still turned away from Malone. 'I'll never understand them.'

'Did that include Sister Mary Magdalene?'

The car moved off again; Tewsday waved some plump fingers at the mini-bus, then looked back at Malone. 'She was a nuisance to her uncle, the Archbishop, but you probably know that.'

'Was she a nuisance to Mr Paredes and Mr Domecq? What's

their connection with you, Sir Jonathan?' Malone kept his tone conversational; it was difficult to be too confrontational sitting beside Tewsday in the latter's luxury. 'Better that you tell me. I'll be taking them in for questioning some time today.'

Tewsday was fiddling with a ring on his left hand; it was a broad gold band with a black opal set in it. On the wrist of the same hand there was a gold watch; a gold cuff glinted on the cuff of the shirt. Over the years he had learned a certain restraint, but he was a man who would always advertise his wealth. All he lacked was power: his boss had that.

'I think you had better ask Mr Hourigan, the Archbishop's father, about that. I run Mr Hourigan's companies, but in the end I am still only his employee.' It hurt him to admit it: his chins seemed to quiver.

'What about Ballyduff? That's the company that owns the freehold on the Quality Couch. Do you think it was just coincidence that Sister Mary Magdalene's body was found there?'

'I have made money on coincidences, Inspector, so I'd never bet against it.'

That was no answer, but Malone let it pass. 'Do you know anything about a company named Austarm? Sister Mary mentioned it in a letter.'

'Who to?'

'To a friend. Do you know anything about it?'

Tewsday looked out the window again, then back at Malone. 'It's a small company in our overall group. I don't think I've ever visited it. It's somewhere in the bush, Moss Vale, I think.'

'What does it make?'

'Small arms, maybe larger stuff. I don't really know. There are over fifty companies in our group, Inspector. There are group managers within the larger organization. They run their own bailiwicks.'

'And all you're concerned with is the profit and loss?'

Tewsday didn't miss the mild sarcasm. 'At the end of the financial year, Inspector, that's all that counts. And I'm responsible for it.'

'Why did you come to the funeral this morning, and not the uncle or the grandfather? Are you responsible for funerals, too?'

It was rude and Malone knew it, but Tewsday had to be shaken out of his set jelly. The plump face flushed and Tewsday sat forward as if he were going to shout to the chauffeur to pull up. His mouth opened, then closed, and he sat leaning forward, breathing heavily; for a moment Malone thought he had had some sort of attack. Then slowly he relaxed and sat back. A hide like his would never burst under apoplexy.

'You're everything I've heard about you, Malone. Intrusive, insulting . . .'

Who have you been listening to? But Malone didn't ask that. He sighed and said, 'If people were more co-operative, I wouldn't need to be like that. Let's cut out the bull, Sir Jonathan. I'm looking for who murdered a young nun, who, as far as I can tell, had more good points than she had bad ones. She had compassion and she cared about people worse off than herself and some bastard killed her for being that way!' He couldn't help the heat that had suddenly appeared in his voice.

Tewsday shook his head, looked more composed now. 'It was not like that, Malone. Not like that at all. But I'm not the one to tell you all about it.'

'What about Paredes or Domecq?'

'You might get somewhere with them.'

'Where do I find them?'

Tewsday hesitated, then said, 'They're staying with Mr Hourigan and the Archbishop.'

Malone had the feeling that Tewsday had said too much and knew it. But he was protecting himself; one could see him hastily building the wall round himself. They rode the rest of the way in silence. At last, when they had crossed the Harbour Bridge and were sliding into the central business district, Tewsday said, 'Where would you like to be dropped?'

'Anywhere will do. It's time I had a think walk.'

Tewsday looked at him curiously. 'Arnold Bennett?' Malone looked at him blankly and Tewsday explained: 'He was an English novelist, before my time, but I read him and other dead writers. Howard Spring, J. B. Priestley, Hugh Walpole, Maugham. I'm an old-fashioned man. Bennett used to go for what he called think walks when he had what they call writer's block.'

'I've never read him. I guess I suffer from policeman's block. I got the expression from my wife.'

'Don't tax yourself. Stay in the car. Gawler can take you where you want to go.'

The car drew up outside Ballyduff House, a seventy-storey glass-and-granite monument to Hourigan enterprise. Tewsday got out, ignoring yet obviously conscious of the curious stares of the passing citizens: princes, especially unroyal ones, like to be acknowledged. That the reaction of the local elements would be more resentment than admiration didn't worry him.

'Good luck with your problems, Inspector. I think you may have quite a few.'

Malone watched him cross the pavement and go into the building, leaning back against the weight of his stomach, his top chin lifted arrogantly. Malone settled uncomfortably back into the luxurious leather of the seat, feeling that the first of the tiger snakes had just got out of the opened can.

He pressed the window-button and the glass slid down between himself and the chauffeur. 'Your name's Gawler?'

'Yes, sir. Gary Gawler.'

'I'd like to go to Homicide. It's up in Liverpool Street. You're American?'

'Yes, sir. I saw the tourist advertisements with that guy

113

Paul Hogan and I decided to give it a try. Give it a burl, as you Aussies say.'

'What did you do in America?'

'Oh, this and that. I'll move on to something else after this, I guess. But Sir Jonathan is a good man to work for.'

'I'm sure he is. Where did you come from in the States?'

'Chicago. Which end of Liverpool Street, sir? I'm afraid I've never had to drive Sir Jonathan to Homicide.'

SEVEN

I

When Fingal Hourigan first met Jonathan Tewsday in 1955 he should have recognized a young man as ruthlessly ambitious as he himself had once been. He was a real estate salesman, a junior one at that, and he would not have been selling the Hourigan home in Bellevue Hill had his boss not been knocked down by a car.

'A woman driver?' said Fingal.

'Yes, sir. His wife.'

'Deliberately?'

'I don't think so. Evidently she got Reverse mixed up with Drive.'

'They're all the same,' said Fingal, who had never allowed Sheila to drive, even before she had become deranged. 'Tuesday? The second day of the week?'

'No, sir.' He handed Fingal his card. 'Some day I hope it will be as well-known as your own. With all due respect.'

Fingal was unimpressed. 'Okay, sell this house and find me another. One with a water frontage.'

Jonathan Tewsday sold the Bellevue Hill house within two days for seven thousand pounds above Fingal's reserve price. The profit was a drop in a bucket to Fingal, but he took note of it; profit was always profit, especially when it was tax free. Within the week Tewsday had come up with a waterfront property at Vaucluse that, he said, was going for a song.

'I don't write songs, I write cheques,' said Fingal. 'How much is it?'

'Thirty-two thousand pounds.'

Fingal went out to Vaucluse to inspect it, bought it, then said, 'Knock down the house. I'll build my own.'

Tewsday all at once caught a glimpse of Fingal's wealth; in the 1950s no one paid a small fortune for a property, only to knock it down. Then and there he decided that, somehow he was going to attach himself to Fingal Hourigan's wagon. He never over-estimated anything (except, of course, prices promised to prospective house sellers), least of all his chances; but, even though young, he was not myopic about the future and could take the long view. He knew that, sooner or later, he could be of use again to Fingal Hourigan.

The opportunity came six months later. There were no commercial developments in the eastern suburbs, where Tewsday operated, that would interest a man of Fingal's investment scope. Tewsday looked across the harbour to North Sydney; he needed a telescope, but he saw all he needed to see. The northern end of the Harbour Bridge promised to lead to a twin city to the main business district on the south side; already the smart developers were moving in. Without his boss's knowledge, Tewsday took a thirty-day option in the firm's name on a row of houses just off the northern approach to the Bridge. Then he went to the offices of Bally-duff Holdings in a building not far back from Circular Quay. It took him three days to get into Fingal's office. While he waited he wondered why such a wealthy company should headquarter itself in such an old unattractive building. He was not to know that it was another manifestation of Fingal's fear, still with his memories of Chicago, of being too conspicuous. The building of the castle at Vaucluse would be an example of conspicuous anonymity, but it would be the first break-out from his long-held fear of the ghost of Capone.

At last Tewsday was shown into Fingal's office. Fingal

looked at this persistent young man for the first time; that is, *really* looked at him. He saw a man in his mid-twenties, hair already thinning, stomach and a second chin already developing, a fastidious dresser who wore expensive English shoes: Fingal always started his scrutiny from the feet up of anyone who interested him. This Jonathan Tewsday had eyes the colour of sultanas, well suited to his puddeny face; his mouth had all the flexibility of a veteran con man's. Fingal decided at once that he couldn't be trusted, so he listened to him, for he believed that trustworthy men never made money as fast as the other kind. Though he did not make the admission to himself, they were vultures of a feather.

Tewsday, for his part, was examining the man he hoped would soon be his employer; or, eventually, his partner. He was a dreamer, though he would give dreams a bad name. Fingal was now fifty years old, but looked at least five or six years younger, despite the streaks of grey now appearing in his thick brown hair. He had virtually lost his American accent and when it did occasionally surface people put it down as Irish. He was soberly but expensively dressed; he had acquired a patina of conservative success. Or successful conservatism, which was of greater value in the Australia of that decade. The new rich did not wear white shoes and tycoons had not yet taken to wearing gold chains; new money tried to look like old money from the feet up. His office complemented his own appearance, all dark panelling, brass lamps and leather chairs; the paintings on the walls were sober Australian landscapes, not a bushranger nor a bared breast in sight. Fingal might have been a Supreme Court judge or the Governor of the Commonwealth Bank. But Tewsday, who had done his homework, knew he was sitting opposite a man as rapacious and unscrupulous as himself. It made him feel good.

'You have ten minutes, young man. Get started.'

Tewsday opened his brief-case, an English leather one bought three mornings ago at Kitchings: he, too, knew the value of looking conservatively successful. 'Mr Hourigan, have you looked at the possibilities for development in North Sydney?'

'Yes,' said Fingal unencouragingly, though he had not.

Tewsday didn't miss a beat. 'Then you know the difficulties of dealing with a suburban-minded council that doesn't know the value of a bribe?'

Fingal smiled; but only to himself. 'What have you got in mind?'

Tewsday told him, producing the sketch plans he had commissioned with an architect friend. 'This row of ten houses overlooks where the new freeway will run. There is room there for a twenty-storey office block, plus half a dozen shops.'

'Are the houses owner-occupied?'

'Only two. The rest are tenanted.'

'Is it zoned for commercial development?'

'Not yet. But if the price is right, it can be. I can guarantee that.'

'What's in this for you, Mr Tewsday?'

'I want to come to work for you, Mr Hourigan. Five thousand pounds a year, plus expenses, to start with.'

'Nobody starts as high as that with me. You have a lot of *chutzpah*.'

It was a word that Tewsday had never heard up till then; the European Jews who would one day be a force in the country's economy had not yet shown the local natives what *chutzpah* was. But Tewsday not only had an eye for opportunity, he had an ear for meaning and he caught it. 'Mr Hourigan, you wouldn't have appreciated me if I'd come in here and under-valued myself.'

'What are you besides a smart-arse who can buy and sell real estate?'

I'm never going to love this man, thought Tewsday; but he had never believed that love made the world go round. 'I'm that rare bird, an accountant with imagination.'

Fingal this time allowed his smile to show. 'Mr Tewsday, I don't employ accountants unless they have imagination. You'll have some competition. I'll give you a six months' trial. Three thousand a year and expenses, supply your own transport, take it or leave it.'

'Those are coolie's wages, Mr Hourigan.' He took a risk with his *chutzpah*.

'Then you'd better get used to dim sims and fried rice.' Fingal pressed a button on his desk and almost immediately the door to the outer office opened and a secretary stood there. 'Miss Stevens will show you out. You can start Monday, report to Mr Borsolino. You'll get on well with him – he's an accountant with imagination.'

Tewsday stood up, closing his briefcase. 'I haven't said I accept your offer, Mr Hourigan.'

Fingal looked up at him. 'You came in here with your mind made up to accept the job no matter what I offered you. It's only because you're so keen that I'm giving you a trial. But you'll have to learn to be less transparent, Mr Tewsday. You'll never get anywhere in business by laying yourself out like an open book. Any imaginative accountant will tell you that an open book is just asking for trouble. Good-day.'

When Tewsday had gone, Fingal got up and walked to the window of his office. He looked out past one or two buildings that partly obscured the view of the harbour, across the water to North Sydney. He should have moved in there sooner; but money had been so easy to make here south of the harbour. Beginning with the wool boom during the Korean War, during which he had bought his first merino sheep stud, money was becoming more manifestly visible than at any time since the 1920s. A new young, aggressive breed of developer was beginning to emerge, some of them refugees from post-war Europe. The old refugee, from Chicago, had to stay ahead of them. The number of upstarts was growing, smart-arses who had no respect for tradition. He had little time for it himself, but one could always call upon it as a last resort.

Jonathan Tewsday reported the following Monday to Robert Borsolino, a slightly older smart-arse who knew a younger one when he presented himself. 'What am I supposed to do with you?' His imagination didn't run to making use of juniors; they might depose one. 'Did Mr Hourigan say?'

'I'm to be left to my own devices.' Fingal had said no such thing, but Tewsday knew that middle-level executives, especially ones not much older than himself, did not go to the chairman and managing director and query his reasons for his directives. 'Or vices, as the case may be.'

'Don't be a smart-arse,' said Borsolino. He was a thin, dark-haired man with a very thin veneer of good temper. 'Three thousand a year, eh? Prove you're worth it.'

Tewsday went over to North Sydney, picked up the deputy-mayor and brought him back to the south side of the harbour to lunch at the Hotel Australia. Bill Oodskirt, the deputy-mayor, was flattered; his usual rendezvous for such dealings was the fish café at Crows' Nest. He was a short, fat little man with plastered-down red hair; he was a butcher by trade and, stripped, would have gone unnoticed in his own shop window. His collar was too tight and he was constantly tugging at it, as if he were choking.

He choked when Tewsday offered him a thousand pounds. 'This is highly unusual, Mr Tewsday.' He meant that he had never before been offered more than a hundred pounds, but Tewsday deliberately misunderstood him.

'Mr Oodskirt, you're worth it, every penny of it. You have the influence in Council, I know your record. You vote and two-thirds of the Council vote with you. All you have to do is have this section of Rogers Street zoned for commercial development.'

'We've been thinking about it,' said Oodskirt, who always liked to find excuses for his venality and corruption. 'Yes, we've definitely been thinking along those lines.'

'Of course you have!' said Tewsday, showing enthusiasm for his victim's imagination. 'Sydney is going to be the New York of the South Pacific and North Sydney will be a major part of it. And you'll be a part of it, too.'

'It's a lot of money,' said Oodskirt, having a sudden attack of guilt, something he couldn't explain, since he'd had no previous symptoms.

It was not a lot of money, if one took the long view. Tewsday knew that within ten years the site would be worth ten times the present price; it took imagination to see that far ahead and calculate such a sum, but Tewsday could feel it in his bones. Oodskirt, on the other hand, though he cut up bones every day in his shop, had no imagination. He never saw further than next week and the next envelope under the table.

'As I said, Mr Oodskirt, you're worth every penny of it. A little more claret?'

'Don't mind if I do.' Oodskirt's collar suddenly seemed to have got looser. He sat back, a big shot whose worth was appreciated. 'Better than the old Porphyry Pearl, isn't it?'

'Indeed it is,' said Tewsday, who wouldn't have drunk the cheaper wine if he had been dying of thirst. He was already a wine snob, for which no breeding is necessary.

The following week the Rogers Street block was zoned commercial. The week after that Tewsday bought the ten houses in Ballyduff's name, withdrew the option money and paid it back into his former employer's agency account. His former employer knew nothing about the withdrawal and the re-deposit till a month later when he received his bank statement. By then he knew there would be no catching Tewsday.

A month later Tewsday was sent for by his new employer. 'You've bought us a parcel of trouble, young man.'

'I don't understand –' For once Tewsday couldn't finish a sentence.

'The two owner-occupiers in those houses in North Sydney

have moved out. The rest, the tenants, are staying put. On top of that, squatters have moved into the two houses the owners have vacated.'

'I don't think we have a problem, Mr Hourigan. The courts will evict them.'

'Borsolino says that could take twelve months or more. Furthermore the Commos in the unions are taking up their cause. That feller Nev Norway has got into the act. You know him?'

'I know of him, Mr Hourigan. I've never met him personally.'

'I met him once, right after the war. He'd turn this country into a Soviet republic, if he had his way. He has no time for capitalists like you and me.'

Tewsday was flattered to have already the same status as his boss. 'Everyone has his price, Mr Hourigan.'

'I doubt it with Norway. Try your luck, but never mention my name. You're on your own. Fall on your face and you're fired.'

Tewsday went down to see Nev Norway, at his union's offices not far from the Darling Harbour wharves. He didn't wear his new Richard Hunt suit or his suede shoes; he went in an open-necked shirt, the collar worn outside his jacket in true working-class style, and a pair of his father's old leather shoes that he dug out of a family trunk. Both his parents were dead, glad to have gone to their graves to escape from a son who had disappointed them by showing an interest in nothing but making money and who, on his father's death bed, had told the old man that he had voted Liberal in the last elections.

'You'd have known my dad,' said Tewsday, flattening his vowels, dropping the accent he had been cultivating. 'He was a tally clerk down there on the wharves. Any Day Tewsday, they used to call him – he'd go out on strike any day you called him.'

Nev Norway was not taken in by his visitor's appearance or his accent; this kid was a toff, or aspired to be one. Norway himself was not built to be a tailor's dummy; he was almost as broad as he was high and had a face to match. He was famous for his red cardigan, worn in all weathers; it was rumoured that Lenin, on a secret visit to Australia in 1904, had been present at Norway's birth and swaddled the new-born babe in his own cardigan. He was shrewd, had a dry sense of humour and was as ruthless as his Russian idols had been. It was said that he had wept for two days when Stalin had died, though no one had actually witnessed that incredible collapse.

'Are you here to join the union?' His humour could be sardonic.

'No, I'm here to talk progress, Mr Norway.'

The union boss suspected anyone who called him Mr Norway; only the enemy, the other bosses, the capitalists, called him that. 'Who do you represent, Mr Tewsday?'

'Ballyduff Properties.'

'Fingal Hourigan's lot? Get out! You're wasting my time.'

Tewsday didn't move. The union boss's office was a cubby-hole, made even smaller by the piles of pamphlets stacked in each corner: Norway was notorious as the most prolific pamphlet-writer since St Paul, a comparison he found odious. The walls were decorated with posters, all of them threatening: non-Communists were made to feel they were being attacked from all sides. Tewsday, no coward, was undaunted. The pursuit of money has created as many heroes as patriotism.

'Mr Hourigan has nothing to do with this. This is my baby.' His vowels had rounded again. 'I want you to withdraw your support for the tenants and squatters over at North Sydney. In return we'll make a substantial donation to your union's funds.'

'We? I thought you said Fingal Hourigan had nothing to do with this? You look as if you couldn't make a donation to the church plate. If you go to church . . .'

Tewsday didn't. 'I'm not a church-goer, Mr Norway. I'm a man of the world, like you. Those people over at North Sydney can't stand in the way of progress. We wouldn't be getting rid of them if we weren't sure they could get accommodation elsewhere.'

'Where, for instance?'

'There'll soon be plenty available out west. Mount Druitt is being developed, lots of cheap housing –'

'Out in the bloody backblocks? Would you move out there, get your arse frozen off in winter and the top of your head burnt off in summer? No bloody fear, you wouldn't! Get out, you young arsehole, and shove your money up it! Your old man must be spinning in his grave, no matter what day it is!'

'You're making a mistake you'll regret, Norway –'

The union boss got up from behind his desk, moving with surprising speed, came round and grabbed Tewsday by the scruff of his neck and the seat of his pants. It was an old-fashioned technique, the headlock had not yet come into style, but it was effective. Tewsday, before he could struggle, was tossed out the office door and landed on his hands and knees in the narrow dusty hallway in front of four hefty wharfies come to pay their dues.

'He was trying to sell me a subscription to the *Catholic Weekly*,' Norway told them.

'Never!' said the wharfies and threw up their hands in horror; they were taking Workers' Education lessons in drama. 'Shall we throw him down the stairs?'

'Not a bad idea,' said Norway, grinning. 'Not head first, but. He might chip the woodwork.'

So Tewsday finished up down in the street, battered, bruised and bewildered as to what to do next. Things, over the next couple of weeks, went from bad to worse. Norway, who had friends amongst the older industrial reporters on the city's newspapers, got the right sort of publicity for his campaign on behalf of the tenants and squatters: the little Aussie battlers arranging a murder. All the young, and old, murderers he had known back in Chicago had been as obvious as if they had worn badges or had been cast in their roles by Hollywood. Since coming to Australia he had had to employ murderers only once and his go-between then had been a lawyer who had looked as murderous as some of the clients he had defended. The lawyer had since conveniently died and Fingal now felt safe from any connection with the murder. He would have to watch any possible connection with the disappearance of Nev Norway.

'Have the police been to question you?'

'Yes, sir. I could tell them nothing.'

'Were they satisfied with that?'

'I think so.' Tewsday was beginning to feel a little easier. If he had been about to be sacked, it would have been over by now. Fingal Hourigan would never slow down the guillotine.

'Have you got rid of the tenants and squatters?'

'Not yet. I think I can arrange that in a week or two.'

'Don't kick 'em out in the street. Buy up some cheap flats somewhere and move them there at our expense.'

'Do we need to go to that expense, sir? It's only a matter of a few days – they've lost the guts to fight since Norway disappeared –'

'You'd better learn something about public relations if you want to keep working for me.' Fingal had never worried before about public relations, particularly in business; all of a sudden he had been bitten by that most debilitating of bugs, an urge for respectability. Or anyway to be outside of any police questioning. 'Buy the flats and move them. Talk to Borsolino about writing 'em off against tax – he'll find a way. No publicity, if you can avoid it. Let this whole thing die down as soon as possible.'

'What about the houses? How soon do you want them knocked down?'

'Leave it as long as you can. The papers won't come back to the story. Let the architects get all the plans for the new

who were being tossed out on to the streets in the name of Progress. Television had not yet arrived in Australia, that would not come till next year, so there were no two-headed demons to record the banners and the parading pickets and the squatters perched on the roofs of their houses like pugnacious pigeons.

Tewsday stayed out of Fingal's way, meanwhile planning his own campaign. He had never gone in for thuggery; real-estate deals, up till now, had never required more than slick words and envelopes under the table. But the situation, or rather his own, was now becoming desperate. He went to certain rugby union clubs where, even though *union* was in their title, he knew there was no love for trade unions. He enlisted a dozen rugby front-row forwards, all of them famous for their thuggery on the field, everyone a capitalist or hoping to be, and sent them over to North Sydney to confront the wharfies who were now picketing the houses. They lost the match twelve-nil: there was no referee and they hadn't expected to be met by pick-handles. The tenants and squatters sat on their front verandas or stood on their rooftops and cheered as the battle went on. Next day the *Daily Telegraph*, contradicting its industrial reporter, ran an editorial on union brutality. All the rugby league, soccer, Australian Rules, tennis and cricket-following readers nodded their heads in agreement, mistaking the union blamed.

Tewsday was now at his wits' end; which, since his wits ran in circles, was not as desperate as it sounds. He went to a night club in King's Cross and spoke to the bouncer on the door. The Cross in those days was not a focus for sleaze and junkies and drug-ridden prostitutes. There were prostitutes, but they were all female, mostly clean and just trying to make an honest living; there were spivs and crooks, but they didn't mug one in the street; and there were the odd one or two professional killers who didn't charge an exorbitant fee. The night-club bouncer, a giant named Jack Paxit, was not a killer but had a friend who was.

'Who you want done? *Him?* Jesus, sport, that's asking for trouble. It'll cost you.'

'How much?'

'It'll take two blokes, I reckon. So me mate'll have to get a helper. Six hundred quid.' A fair price: inflation was not a worry in those days.

'Five hundred.' Tewsday could not forget his real-estate training, it was natural for him to bargain.

'Six hundred, sport, take it or leave it. I gotta get my cut.'

'Can I trust you to forget I ever came to you?'

'Sport, you're the Invisible Man. You ever see that fillum with Claude Rains? I was just a kid . . . I never seen you, sport, never heard your name. When you want it done?'

'As soon as possible.'

Two days later Nev Norway disappeared and to this day nobody knows where he went.

Fingal had conveniently taken himself out of the country during all this. He had gone to Hong Kong, renewed acquaintance with some of his old gold-smuggling contacts who, like himself, were now looking for less dangerous pursuits. In partnership with them he started buying up what little land remained in Hong Kong. From there he had gone to Japan, but the Japanese had defeated him with their bland politeness and smiling masks. He liked to recognize the taste for larceny in the eyes of those he took as partners, but the Japanese had the gaze of neither larcenous nor honest men: blank eyes seemed to look right through him. He came back to Sydney convinced that they would some day rule the world. They had lost only the shortest of wars, the military one.

On his first day back at the office he was driven into the company garage in his three-year-old Jaguar Mark VII. As he got out of the car he saw Jonathan Tewsday drive in in a Jaguar XK 120. He dismissed his chauffeur, then walked the length of the garage to accost Tewsday.

'Is that car yours? How can you afford it?'

'It's second-hand, Mr Hourigan. I'm paying it off.'

'Get rid of it. If my shareholders find out you're something like that, they'll think I'm over-paying you his holding company owned 40 per cent of all his companies, he had no respect for his shareholders, b tradition, they occasionally had their uses. 'See me in m at ten sharp.'

Tewsday, brimming with resentment but keeping on, presented himself to Fingal sharp at ten o'clock. W going to be sacked? Already he was thinking of other panies where he could present himself. He was not general but he had the makings of one: he went into no without making sure of a good line of retreat.

Fingal wasted no time in preliminaries: 'What's happ to Nev Norway?'

'I have no idea, sir,' said Tewsday and succeeded f moment in assuming a cherubic look, albeit that of a fa one.

'You didn't arrange his disappearance?'

'No, sir. He had plenty of enemies, including the Government down in Canberra.'

'You think Menzies had him got rid of?' Fingal laughed sound as dry as a bedouin's cough. 'The Prime Mini doesn't have people bumped off. He's subtler than that. T get postings to Washington or somewhere. He's dead, i he?'

'The Prime Minister?'

'Don't be a smart-arse, son. You'll never hold your with me. Norway.'

Tewsday hesitated, then nodded. He knew he was cliff-edge and for the first time he felt the vertigo c unconfident. 'I've heard that, sir.'

'Where'd you hear it?'

He lied, 'From one or two reporters on the papers, trial roundsmen. And a crime reporter.'

Fingal looked at him shrewdly. He knew this your was crooked, but he would never have suspected

building done and then we'll knock the houses down.'

Tewsday stood up, knowing he was safe. 'I'm sure all this will turn out satisfactorily, Mr Hourigan.' He sounded smug, a tone no employer should ever condone.

Fingal didn't. 'Get rid of your car, get a Holden or something.'

'Of course, sir.' Tewsday swapped smugness for obsequiousness, another mistake. Only kings, presidents and prime ministers can suffer it.

'Don't crawl,' said Fingal. 'And in future, no murders, understand? This is a reputable company.'

'Yes, sir,' said Tewsday, this time neither smug nor obsequious, just afraid. This tough old bastard would always have the edge on him.

Next day Tewsday sold his XK 120, at a profit. A month later Fingal took delivery of his first Rolls-Royce, a black Silver Cloud. It made him more conspicuous than he wanted to be, but, he told himself, he had to have a car worthy of the castle he was having built at Vaucluse. It certainly put all the other cars in the Ballyduff garage in their place.

Two months later the houses in North Sydney were knocked down. The event made none of the newspapers, not even any of the trades unions' news bulletins. Occasionally, when news was dead, references would be made to the disappearance of Nev Norway, but nothing ever came of them. In the atmosphere of that period a dead Commo, even a murdered one, got no more sympathy than a live one. Fragments of what might have been a red cardigan had been picked up in their nets by fishermen off Coogee beach, but they didn't report it to the police; people were always tossing their garbage and old clothes into the sea. The tenants and squatters who, no matter how indirectly, had been the cause of Norway's disappearance, settled down in their new flats, went on being little Aussie battlers, though one or two turned traitor by having a good word to say about Ballyduff Properties.

A year later Jonathan Tewsday was running his own small development division in Ballyduff. He had sold his second-hand Holden and ventured to buy a new Rover; Fingal made no comment. The two met only once a month, when Fingal presided over a management meeting, but Tewsday was now just one of the team. The only contest between the two men was their search for respectability.

Then in September 1956, at the launching of Fingal's new television station, Tewsday met the Hourigan siblings, Kerry and Brigid, for the first time.

2

Television had just been introduced to Australia and Fingal, putting together a consortium of merchant bankers, industrialists, radio executives, plus two writers, two producers and two elderly actors to add a touch of the arts, had applied for a television licence and been granted one. Within two years he would have disposed of all his partners, the artists getting the chop first, and then would have, as a newspaper owned by a failed rival bidder would say, a licence to print his own money.

Television was such a new toy that the launching of the new station enticed Kerry along to one of his father's business functions. He got leave from the seminary and, picked up by Brigid in her new MG, was driven out to Carlingford in the western suburbs to the new complex.

'How's the Jesus business going?'

Brigid was now almost seventeen, looked twenty and had had no trouble getting her driver's licence. She was beautiful, sexy-looking enough to have had Picasso, had he seen her, dropping his brushes and his pants at first sight of her. She had just started art classes with an old local artist who had once been as gamey as Picasso but no longer had any lead in his pencil.

'I hope you don't talk like that about me to your friends.' Kerry was now twenty-one, big, beefy and handsome, ideal clay for the cardinal he still hoped to be.

'I'll never understand you, Kerry. You're no more religious than I am. Oh, you may not go in for sin and all that, but you don't have a true vocation.'

She had inherited her father's shrewd appraisal of men. She had also, unfortunately, inherited her mother's passion for them; or, rather, what they offered her. She had been expelled from the Rose Bay Convent after being found in a garden shed with one of the young gardeners; that suburban Mellors had been the first of half a dozen lovers as the junior Lady Chatterley had moved on up the social scale. She was a sinner, but she would never be repentant, least of all to her brother the trainee priest.

'Are you running away from the world?'

'No.' He would have to be patient with her; she had guessed the truth, or anyway the half-truth, of him. Already he knew that he would never be able to suffer the duties of a parish curate or priest; the hoi-polloi flock would have to look for another shepherd. 'It's useless trying to explain a vocation to someone who doesn't have it. It's not the same as understanding your predilection for sin – I understand that.'

'My predilection for sin! God, you're already talking like an archbishop!'

She couldn't have given him higher praise. 'Keep your eye on the road. I don't want to have to give the two of us Extreme Unction.' At the seminary they taught him to think in Capitals, as if God were a grammarian.

'God,' she said, though He was only a very casual acquaintance nowadays, 'how could I have had you as a brother?'

Fingal, spending the consortium's money, had spared none of it to make the television complex the best in the country. Huge and lavish, it seemed like an affront to the small fibro and timber cottages that surrounded it, the homes of the little Aussie battlers who would look to it for their escape from their drudgery and their debt worries. Fingal knew the venture could not fail; better to spend the money now while the pound still had value. Nowhere in the world were television station owners going broke. BHN Channel 8 was a gold mine standing in landscaped gardens.

As they drew into the parking lot Kerry heard the music coming from a nearby building. 'What on earth is that?'

'They're putting on a separate party for the staff who are going to work here. None of them know anything, but they'll all be experts within a week.' She was repeating her father's opinion.

'No, I mean that awful music.'

'Oh God, what sort of stuff do you hear in the seminary? That's rock and roll, the new music. It sounds like Bill Haley and "Rock Around the Clock".'

Kerry shook his head in wonder. 'Whatever's going to happen to Guy Lombardo?'

The party for the executives was more sedate. The only music was the humming of praise for the opportunities that lay ahead. Jonathan Tewsday, the most junior executive there, stood in a corner and sipped champagne, Australian, of course, since Fingal, seeing further opportunities, had just gone into vineyards. When the sexy-looking pretty girl came in with the young novice priest, Tewsday knew she had to be saved.

When the priest left the girl, Tewsday went up to her, taking two glasses of champagne with him. 'To help you relax.'

'Oh, I'm relaxed, all right. But my father won't let me drink alcohol in public.'

'Who's your father?'

'The chairman, Mr Hourigan.'

Though he had never met or even seen photographs of them, Tewsday now recognized the young girl and the priest. These were the Hourigan heirs, never spoken of by the chairman, never discussed by his executives; but always there in the background, the sometime future bosses. 'I'm Jonathan Tewsday, one of your father's junior executives. Are you at university?'

'No, I'm an art student.'

'What do you paint?' He knew nothing about art and had no interest in it. Endorsement and sponsorship of the arts had not yet become fashionable in the commercial and industrial world; money was still being spent only to make money. Art, and artists, should be self-supporting.

'Naked men, mostly. I'm going to specialize in portraits of penises.' She was learning the youthful pleasure of being outrageous; later she would recognize that outrageousness was the last resort of the untalented. So far she was not certain how much talent she had.

He clenched his scalp, holding on to his already thinning hair. 'Will there be a living in it?' As if, in her circumstances, that mattered.

'Do you think I need to care?' she said, reading his mind. She had already dismissed him as the sort of young man in whom she would never show any interest. Plump and sleek as a young seal, one for whom appearances would be an abiding preoccupation, the urge for riches oozing out of him, he was everything she currently despised. Her father's riches allowed her to be comfortably and snobbishly idealistic, something else she would grow out of. 'Oh, this is my brother Kerry. This is Mr Tewsday, a junior executive.'

She moved off on that insult and Kerry smiled uncomfortably. 'Don't take any notice of her, Mr Tewsday. Underneath, she's really a very nice kid.'

'Are you being charitable because you're her brother or because you're a priest?'

'Oh, I'm not a priest yet, just a trainee. Like you as an executive.' Kerry, too, could toss an insult: he and Brigid were not their father's children for nothing.

Tewsday wanted to ask him why any young man in today's world, so full of opportunity, would want to be a priest; but

133

such a question, he guessed, would be another insult. He knew as much about religion as he did about art.

'Do they let you out much? I mean to parties like this?'

'Oh, they don't make us live a monastic life, if that's what you mean. They like to expose us to temptation occasionally, just so's we'll recognize it.'

'There's plenty here,' said Tewsday, looking around. 'Wine and women.'

'I'm not tempted,' said Kerry, smiling.

'Where will you finish up?'

'When I'm ordained or later on? The Church is just like working for my father. You don't shoot to the top in a rush. I'm patient.'

Tewsday all at once recognized another man with ambition; it surprised him, because he thought all clerics were supposed to be humble. 'You'd like to be a bishop or something?'

'A cardinal, actually,' said Kerry, smiled and walked away.

Tewsday looked after him, then looked across at Brigid, holding court to several of her father's more senior executives. Even so young, she was the best of all flirts, an arrogant one: men like to be trampled on before, as they think, they conquer. The senior executives, Don Juans in their own imagination, middle-aged fools in the eyes of their watching wives, jostled each other to catch her attention. Tewsday turned and saw Fingal Hourigan watching the group. The look in the old man's eyes told him that each of the senior executives had been put on probation. He looked for pride in the old man's face, but there was none, at least not in his daughter. That only showed when he looked across the room at his son. God damn! thought Tewsday: by the time I get to the top in this corporation, I'll have a cardinal as a chairman.

Fingal had taken the monsignor in charge of the seminary to dinner at the Union club. He had joined that conservative establishment last year as part of the consolidation of his respectability; there had been one or two demurs from some of the elderly, stuffier members, but no one had black-balled him. The committee would have preferred a new member whose family could be traced back, preferably on the land or one of the more respected ways of making money; they would not have wanted the tracing to go back too far, for fear that a convict ancestor might have been unearthed; the rattle of chains in a family closet had not yet become a patriotic jingle. At least a man with no family line had no skeletons visible. And he did have money, lots of it, something that was now beginning to have a respectability of its own.

The monsignor was not out of place in the club, even though a Catholic; he came of an old moneyed family and it showed. 'A nice Burgundy, Mr Hourigan. We're producing some fine wines in Australia these days.'

'Do you use them on the altar?'

'Of course.' The monsignor was a cheerful man, only occasionally depressed by the classes he taught. A radical student would have brightened his life, but the seminaries, like the universities of the day, seemed full of conservative youth. He wondered what the coming decades would bring. He had read the new English play, *Look Back in Anger*, and he wondered if, when the play came to Sydney, he should take his classes to see it. 'Why did you want to see me? Are you going to make a gift to the seminary or is it just about Kerry?'

'You're a smart man, Cliff. Okay you'll get your gift. Now what about Kerry? How's he making out?'

'The smartest one I've had in years. We are taught – and teach – not to be fulsome. But I have to say your son is brilliant. He is very sound in theology, history, all that, but he is positively brilliant at administration. He is bishop material, if ever I've seen it.' The Burgundy had made him fulsome.

'Nothing more than a bishop?'

'Ah, that is in God's hands,' said the monsignor and smiled, because he knew it wasn't.

'How do we influence God then?'

'Pray, Fingal, pray. Are you good at that?'

'I'm good at anything I put my mind to.' But he wouldn't know how to start praying.

In the closed room of his mind he had begun to have megalomaniacal dreams. If Kerry had been American-born he would have made him President. Something like that was happening now in the United States; word had reached him of Joseph Kennedy's campaign to have his eldest surviving son nominated as the next Democrat presidential candidate. But, since Kerry was Australian-born and Australia amounted to nothing in the world politically, he had begun to dream of other empires. And so had come, as an extension of Kerry's own ambition, which he recognized now was genuine and strong, to the idea of an Australian-born Pope. So far he had not mentioned the idea to Kerry. He looked across the table and wondered if, half-jokingly, he should mention it to this worldly cleric. But no: the monsignor would treat it as a joke. So would the rest of the Church. The Italians, who ran the Church and thought they had a God-given right to the Papacy, would laugh, then scratch their heads, wondering where Australia was. No Pope had yet found it.

'Can you save him from the backblocks when he's ordained?'

'It'll be out of my hands, Fingal. But I'll do my best to recommend him to some admin. office. I don't think he's cut out for weddings and christenings. I'm not myself, especially christenings. Many's the time I've wanted to hold the squawling brat under the water, instead of splashing him with it.'

Kerry was ordained in 1962. Brigid, rebelling against her father, wheedling money out of her trust account by sleeping with one of the trustees, one of her father's lawyers, had left for Paris in late 1958. She had kissed her father goodbye, the first time she had kissed him in six years.

'Don't be angry, Dad. You have Kerry to fuss over.'

'I don't fuss over anyone.'

'No, that's not true.' Certainly not over her. She had been only fourteen when she had recognized the tribal sign: the son was the one who counted. 'But some day you may be proud of me. I'm a good artist and I'm going to be much better.'

'I'll never understand you,' Fingal had said.

'I don't think you understand *women*. You've never talked about her, but did you ever understand Mother? What made her mental? You?'

'Never!' he said fiercely. He would never have done that to the golden-haired girl who still occasionally slept with him in his dreams. 'It was in her genes. I didn't know when we married, but her grandmother went mad when she was only twenty-five.'

'Then I might go mad, too?'

'I doubt it.' He looked at her, sane, confident and seemingly invulnerable. He loved her, but he couldn't show it. The Irish do share a few characteristics with the English; sometimes he wondered if he were Anglo-Irish instead of pure Irish. He had the piratical inclinations of the English. 'You're a Hourigan through and through.'

'No insanity there?'

None that he knew of; but perhaps his ambition for his son was a form of insanity. Brigid went off to Paris, wrote home twice a year and told her father and her brother nothing. Then she came home for Kerry's ordination.

Fingal threw a reception afterwards in the castle on the waterfront at Vaucluse, where he had been living for the past five years. As if having a new priest for a son were some sort of protection, he invited the half a dozen women he had been sleeping with for the past ten years. They were youngish widows, divorcees and one career woman, a TV chat show hostess. None of them had known of the others, but, with that instinct that is more highly developed in mistresses than in wives, risk always heightening the senses, they recognized the up-till-then unknown competition as soon as they saw it. Fingal greeted each with a peck on the cheek and nothing more, stood safe between his son and daughter, the Church and Art.

'My son, Father Hourigan. And my daughter Brigid, home from Paris and living with Picasso.'

'Unfortunately not,' said Brigid, wondering which one of the women was her father's regular bed-mate.

It was an early summer day and the reception was being held in the garden of the big house. It was an Italian-style garden, all stone balustrades and clipped hedges and pebble paths, a proper setting for a young priest destined eventually for the Vatican; but none of the guests, not even the seminary's monsignor, caught the significance. Only the guest of honour's sister saw it.

'Has Dad booked you into the Vatican yet?' she said when she and Kerry were alone.

'Aren't you pleased I'm a priest?'

She bit her lip and for a moment looked as if she might weep. He was shocked; he had never seen her cry, not even as a child. He knew nothing of the childhood tears in the lonely bedroom.

'Of course I am. It's what you've always wanted, isn't it?'

'Ever since I got the vocation for it.'

She looked at him out of the corner of her eye. 'You really do have a vocation?'

'I really do,' he said, and out on the harbour there was a sudden flash of sunlight, as if God had fired a warning shot.

She looked down at the garden from the terrace where they stood. 'There should be a maze.'

'Do they have mazes in Italian gardens?'

'Didn't Machiavelli invent the maze?' She had no idea if Machiavelli had, indeed, ever been in a garden of any sort; but she had just spent almost four years in Paris and learned the French trick of answering questions with a question. Then below her she saw a face she recognized, though the scalp above it had widened. 'Why, it's – I've forgotten your name. Friday, Saturday? The junior executive.'

Tewsday, thirty now and almost bald, came up on to the terrace as Kerry left his sister and went into the house. 'Not any more – a junior executive, that is. Jonathan Tewsday.'

'Of course! Is there a Mrs Tewsday and lots of little days of the week?'

She hadn't changed in her attitude towards businessmen. An independent income is the best support for an artist's standards; idealism flowers beautifully when watered by a trust fund. She would never need the likes of Jonathan Tewsday.

She was still beautiful, but had become a flamboyant dresser; if her brother ever became a cardinal, it would be a race between them to see who caught the eye. She was dressed in black-and-white chequered knickerbockers, white silk shirt and black-and-white chequered cap, with a red silk scarf tied to the handle of her black handbag. It was her *Jules et Jim* look, but Jules and Jim and Pierre and Yves and Roger and Daniel had all been left back in Paris where, like Fingal's mistresses, they did not know of each other.

Tewsday thought she looked terrific, but wouldn't have walked down the street with her. He knew nothing about women's fashion, he was too intent on his own wardrobe. 'I've learned about Art since we last met. Let's go out to dinner and talk about it.'

'All right,' she said on the whim that was part of her mother's bequest, 'let's go now.'

'Do you want to change?'

'Why? Don't you like this?'

'Love it,' he said and hoped they wouldn't be seen by anyone he knew. 'Do we have to ask your father's permission to go?'

'Never do that,' she said. 'He delights in saying no.'

Fingal, who could see in a dozen directions at once, saw them go. He had come to appreciate the worth of Tewsday, but never gave him any verbal encouragement, just promotion and a salary increase; which was all Tewsday craved, since praise wasn't bankable. He had distinguished himself the previous year when there had been a massive credit squeeze throughout the country. Ballyduff had been awash with liquidity and Tewsday had gained an audience with the chairman. He had brought a list of companies that, unknown to the general market, were on the verge of bankruptcy and ready for takeover. Fingal, though he had said nothing, had been impressed by his junior's inside knowledge. He had also had inside knowledge of the extent of the newly discovered iron ore deposits in north-west Australia, the biggest ever found, and he suggested early investment there. Fingal, after having them checked, had given him the go-ahead on all the suggestions. Tewsday was on his way, a young man to be watched, as business circles said, and no one watched him more closely than his executive chairman. He was not to be encouraged too much, especially by the chairman's daughter.

'Don't worry, Dad,' said Kerry, coming to stand beside his father. 'Brigid can look after herself.'

'It's him I'm worried about,' said Fingal, but that wasn't true. He wanted no one in the corporation admitted to the family. An outsider, once admitted, might want to know the secrets of the family.

Brigid stayed in Sydney a month on that visit. She went out with Jonathan Tewsday three or four times and went to bed with him once; not out of any attraction to him or liking for him but out of her own sexual hunger. She was at a loose end, something she confessed to no one, hardly even to herself. Her development as a painter seemed to be standing still and, almost as bad, her one sustained love affair, with Jules, who was married, was petering out. The future, which for the young is tomorrow, had begun to look like a washed-out fresco.

She went back to Paris, determined not to confess failure to her father, and Kerry, certain of success, taking the long view, went into a desk job with the Catholic Education Office. Tewsday went back to making money for Ballyduff and Fingal sat in his chairman's chair and waited patiently for the future, in which he was certain he would have a controlling interest.

3

Brigid took up again with her married Frenchman, a lawyer who specialized in divorce and large settlements. But he was only a *cinq à sept* lover; he would not leave his wife, who was as rich as Brigid and, when she put her mind to it, a far better cook. In February 1963 Brigid discovered she was pregnant. Trying to force her Frenchman to leave his wife and at least live with her, if not marry her, she refused to have an abortion. Jules the lawyer declined the invitation, all at once honourable towards his wife, an occasional French habit. Brigid went to London and had her baby on the National Health, a choice that was a subconscious thumbing of her nose at the *bourgeoisie*, her lover and her father, neither of whom would ever understand her rebellious nature. Teresa was born on November 22, 1963, a terrible day in history. Brigid wept for her, hoping it was not an omen.

She did not see her father and brother again till Teresa was two years old. Fingal came to London occasionally in that period, but Brigid contrived to be somewhere on the Continent when he was there. She did it out of perversity, another of her mother's bequests; but she also did not want Fingal assuming a proprietary interest in Teresa, though it was difficult to see him as a grandparent, especially a doting one. She had not told him directly of the child's birth, but had mentioned (confessed?) it in a letter to Kerry, who had written back and told her how delighted he was for her sake, if that was what she wanted.

Then the two Hourigan men came to Europe together, Fingal to do business in Germany, Kerry to attend a short course in Rome. They met in Zurich, Brigid coming there from Lerici, in Lyguria, where she now lived.

'You didn't bring the child?' said Fingal.

'I wasn't sure you'd want to see her.'

He wasn't sure himself, but, 'She's my granddaughter.'

'And my niece,' said Kerry, trying to sound avuncular or anyway espiscopal, which is much the same thing.

'What would you have done with her if I'd brought her? Played kitchy-koo with her? Neither of you are child-lovers – you make W. C. Fields look like Santa Claus. You'll meet her eventually, but I wasn't going to bring her here and display her like some toy doll. She's not my toy, she's my child.'

They were having lunch in Fingal's suite in the Baur au Lac, looking out on the lake. She had noticed that Kerry took the luxury for granted; though a priest, he was still his father's son. Luxury, so far, had not concerned her. Her trust allowance allowed her to live very comfortably and she had that reassuring backstop that the children of the rich always have, family money that would pay for any emergency. So far she had not had to call on her father for help and she hoped she would never have to.

'Are you living with anyone?' said Fingal.

'No.' An Italian writer came down from Milan every second weekend to stay with her, but that couldn't be called *living* with anyone. 'Are you?'

Kerry was the one who looked shocked, not Fingal. 'What sort of question is that!'

'It's all right, Kerry,' said Fingal. 'I asked her the same question. She has a right to throw it back at me. No, I'm not, Brigid.'

'Why did you never marry again?'

'Because I'm still in love with your mother.' It was an amazing admission from him: he had never mentioned the word *love* in their hearing. Both of them waited for him to go on; but he had said enough. 'Do you want sweets?'

'No,' said Brigid, 'I want you to talk about Mother, what she was like before ...'

'That's a closed book.'

'You obviously haven't closed it, not entirely.'

Fingal sat silent, suddenly withdrawn, and after a moment Kerry said quietly, 'I think we'd better leave it, Bridie.' It was the name he had called her as a child.

Brigid felt she had almost entered a half-closed door; or rather, the closed book that had been their father's life. She had felt on the verge of *knowing* him at long last, but he had shut her out once again. She decided, then and there, that it would be for the last time.

She went back to Lerici, to the delightful village on the Gulf of La Spezia where she was renting a villa once owned by the Baroness Orczy, where that lady had written *The Scarlet Pimpernel*. Brigid looked down over olive groves, across the village to the old castle high on the point; beyond it was the arm of the gulf that reached round to Portavenere. She had tried painting the landscape and the seascape, experimenting with the interpretation of light, but her brush, she knew, was lifeless. It only came alive when she painted *people*, but even with them as subjects she was finding it difficult to have something to say. Mostly, she sat in the sun on her terrace and took delight in being a mother as Teresa continued to grow.

Three months after her return from Zurich, someone turned up on her doorstep; but he was no pimpernel, even though he carried a bunch of primroses. Tewsday had always been heavy-handed in his courting.

'I was in the neighbourhood, so I thought I'd drop in.'

'The neighbourhood? In Lerici?'

'Well, not Lerici, exactly. Genoa, actually. Your father is buying into a shipping line and he sent me over to look into it.'

'Did he tell you I was living here?' She knew he would not have.

'No. You know your father, he never tells anyone about his family. No, I dropped in on Kerry in Rome.'

'Dropped in again?'

'Well, not dropped in, exactly. Bumped into, actually. I met him at the airport. He was going back to Sydney and I was changing planes to go up to Genoa.'

'Where are you staying?'

'Well, actually —' He was still out on the terrace, had not yet been invited inside. He stood back and looked at the villa. 'I was hoping it was big enough for you to have a spare room for the night. Oh, who's this? One of your servant's children?'

'No, she's mine,' said Brigid flatly and made no attempt to introduce the $2\frac{1}{2}$-year-old Teresa. 'Well, come in.'

It was a Thursday and the Italian writer was not due till tomorrow night. Tewsday took her to dinner that evening in the Albergo Shelley and across the zabaglione and the last of the Tuscan wine he said, 'Kerry told me about your villa and *The Scarlet Pimpernel*. You're like the Pimpernel himself, so damned elusive.'

'You read it?'

'Oh, I used to be a great reader.'

'Shelley lived here in this house, before it became a hotel.' The great reader looked blank. 'Percy Bysshe Shelley. The poet. Byron lived down there, at the Casa Magni. He used to swim across here to visit Shelley.'

'Ah, I never read much poetry. Queers, were they?'

She took him home then, but not to her bed. He tried to get into it, but she kicked him out. 'What about your wife?'

'I'm not married, for God's sake!'

That surprised her. She thought he would be well married by now, smug and snug with a businessman's wife in a businessman's home, the kids, born or unborn, already registered for Cranbrook or Ascham schools, their lives mapped out like business charts.

'Brigid — listen — I want to marry you!' His voice was loud in the bare-walled, marble-tiled bedroom.

She fell back amongst the pillows laughing till she gave herself a stitch. He stood at the end of her bed in his pyjama trousers, Richard Hunt's best silk, the long hair along his temples standing out: his plump face looked like a moon about to fly off in a fury. It is not true that there is no fury like a woman scorned; Congreve, who said that, had never been spurned by a man. Tewsday came close to murder that night. All that saved her was that he did not have the courage to strike the blow himself, there were no thugs to do the deed for him. He had been rejected before, but he could not stand being laughed at. From that moment on he hated her; had he loved her, he might have reacted differently. But he loved only three things: money, success and himself. He stamped out of her room, out of the house, out of Italy, went back to courting success and money. He did not need to court himself: that love was consummated every time he looked in the mirror.

Back in Sydney, meanwhile, Father Kerry Hourigan made his first mistake as a priest. He had been moved from the Catholic Education Office to be an assistant to the Bishop Coadjutor, a man so renowned for his misogynism that he made St Paul look like Don Juan. A newspaper columnist rang the Bishop's office and asked for a comment on Australian women's apparent hunger for the Pill, which they were swallowing at twice the rate of women elsewhere. Kerry answered the phone, said, 'Perhaps they think they're jelly-beans,' and hung up.

It was a harmless, facetious remark; but the columnist that day was short of material. He rang a well-known chain of confectionery shops, asked its opinion of the relationship between the Pill and jelly-beans, then wrote his column. The next day the LOLLY WAR BETWEEN CATHOLIC CHURCH AND DARREL LEA was the joke of Sydney.

Kerry was sent for by the Bishop-Coadjutor and exiled to the bush. 'I have no time for women, but I'm not prepared to be made a fool of because of them and their lust.' He was as purple-faced as his shirt-front.

Fingal got in touch with the monsignor at the seminary, who managed to get him a meeting with the Cardinal, a man known as Cement Crotch because of his habit of sitting on the fence on all controversial matters. The Cardinal was sympathetic, but said he couldn't over-rule the Bishop-Coadjutor.

Kerry was sent to a country town as curate to an old Irish priest who drank beer by the gallon, coached the local rugby team, understood the sins of those who crowded his confessional and gave them lenient penance, and who preached against Communism with all the fire and rhetoric of an old-time evangelist. Kerry hated life in the country town, hated the Saturday evenings in the confessional, but the old Irish priest, unwittingly, put him on to the cause that would lead him to Rome. The Vietnam War was warming up, the Domino Theory was a constant catch-cry in editorials and the Threat of Communism was now more important than the possibility of defeat at cricket by the West Indians or the Englishmen. Kerry had discovered the torch he had to carry into the future.

Brigid wrote to him to commiserate, in a mildly sarcastic way, on his having to go out and wash away the sins of the Great Unwashed. She mentioned, in passing, that Jonathan Tewsday had paid her an unwelcome visit and had reduced her to hysterics by asking her to marry him. *It was not just him*, she wrote, *but the thought of marrying any businessman just breaks me up. I can't imagine anything more boring . . .*

Kerry didn't share his sister's jaundiced opinion of businessmen; they certainly weren't as boring as farmers. He did not, however, like Jonathan Tewsday, whom he had now met several times and he would certainly not want him as a brother-in-law. He wrote his father a weekly letter and in one of them he mentioned Tewsday's visit to Brigid and his proposal of marriage.

A day after receiving the letter Fingal sent for Tewsday. 'Pack your bags. I'm sending you to Wellington.'

'Wellington, *New Zealand*? But that's Antarctica!'

'Then you'd better take a fur coat. You're taking over our office there and I'm bringing Parkinson to Sydney.'

'I'd like to know what I've done to deserve this, Mr Hourigan –'

'You've stepped out of line,' said Fingal.

Tewsday knew at once what he meant. 'I think my private life is my own affair, Mr Hourigan –'

'Not when you try to link it with mine.'

Fingal had thought long and hard last night whether he should get rid of Tewsday altogether. He recognized the social as well as the business ambitions of the younger man; not that he concerned himself too much with his own social status, but he knew that Fingal Hourigan's son-in-law would always be in demand for the big social occasions. He also knew that there was no risk that Brigid would take Tewsday as her husband; she, too, was without social ambition. Tewsday's crime was that he had dared to think of himself as Fingal's son-in-law.

Tewsday pondered a moment, then said, 'I think I'll resign, then.'

Fingal remarked the half-hearted threat. He was tempted for a moment to accept the resignation: he wanted to drive the knife deep into the smug young man. He was, however, a businessman and he could never shut out business, not even to feed his spite. Tewsday was the up-and-coming young man in Sydney's, if not the country's, business world. He would be grabbed by any one of half a dozen other corporations, and Fingal would never give a competitor the time of day let alone his most valued protégé. Yet Tewsday had to be taught a lesson.

'A year in New Zealand will give you time to think about it. There's nothing else there to do.'

Tewsday, for his part, did not want to leave Ballyduff. He knew he could walk into any other corporation in town and virtually write his own ticket. There was, however, no other corporation in town, or indeed the country, which showed the potential to dominate the national scene as Ballyduff undoubtedly would in the next five years. Tewsday had developed the long view into an art; tomorrow was next year, the day after, five years hence. If he stayed with Ballyduff, put up with the year's exile in Wellington, he would be running this company before he was fifty years old. In his late forties, amongst the greybeards then running most of the country's corporations, he would be the Young Turk.

'Just a year?'

'That will depend on what you do with the possibilities there. There must be *something* that can be developed there.'

Fingal never looked in the direction of New Zealand; to him it was just a northern suburb of Antarctica. The national religion was rugby, there were fifteen Apostles called the All Blacks, and New Zealand racehorses always won the Melbourne Cup. He sometimes wondered why, like Tasmania, it was on the map. He was not alone in his myopia in Australia. 'You can leave on Friday.'

So Jonathan Tewsday went to New Zealand to do his penance. He did not beat his breast or order sackcloth from Richard Hunt's. He did, however, take the long view on his growing hatred of the Hourigans. Some day they would all pay.

4

Tewsday returned to Sydney and the headquarters of Ballyduff in September 1967, bringing back with him a pregnant wife. She came from one of the most socially acceptable families in New Zealand, a pioneer clan that had produced some of the finest merino wool in the world, though not from family members; two of the country's leading bankers; a Cabinet minister; and three All Blacks. The family didn't think much of the Australian who had no interest in sheep or rugby, but the daughter of the clan, a good-looking girl named Fiona, had a mind of her own and, like her husband-to-be, a long view. She knew she could never be an All Black, would always be a second-class citizen, always in the shadows in the Land of the Long White Cloud, so she took the opportunity to escape to Australia where, she had heard, women were learning to break free of their chains. She also loved Jonathan, though she sometimes wondered why. She consoled herself that she was probably not the first woman who had had doubts about her one true love. There is no evidence that she was blind in love after she dipped into the fruit.

Tewsday, with that sleek confidence of the unabashable, moved back into Ballyduff as if he had never been away. Fingal gave him no special welcome, did not even bother to mention his stay in New Zealand. He had done his exile term, had brought back a wife and so settled his social course and, most importantly, had trebled the investments and profits of the New Zealand subsidiary. Tewsday had also multiplied his hatred of Fingal Hourigan, but was prepared to bide his time for his revenge.

Kerry also came back from exile. His talents, the arch-diocese soon realized, were too great to be wasted in the bush; the farmers could be relied upon to find their own way to salvation. Word of his understanding of and passion against the threat of Communism had got back to Sydney. He was what was needed in Rome, where there was a new crusade and where, said the Cardinal, separating national pride from religious expediency, there were not enough Australians.

'You're on your way,' said Fingal. 'Now don't bugger it up by making any more facetious remarks. Stick to Communism – you can never be facetious about that. Will you want any more money?'

'I'd like something comfortable in Rome. I don't want to have to share accommodation with some other recruit from overseas – Lord knows whom I might get.' Kerry would always look for creature comforts; he had no wish to be compared with St Francis of Assisi, poverty was for the birds. 'Perhaps you could buy one of the old *palazzi*, say it was your Rome *pied-à-terre*, and I could live in it.'

Fingal smiled, 'You sound just like you did when you were fourteen years old. Show a little modesty for a start. We'll get you a small flat, something that won't make the bishops or even the monsignors envious. We'll get you a car, too.'

'A Lancia,' said Kerry, who, had he been a disciple, would never have followed The Lord on foot.

'A Fiat *cinquecento*,' said Fingal, who had a better sense of the value of modesty.

'I'll never fit into it.'

'Just shrink your ego, that's all you need to do.'

Kerry went to Rome, where Brigid came once to visit him with her new lover, a Communist Party official from Bologna. The two men got on well together, much to the chagrin of both of them and the amusement of Brigid; each recognized in the other a man constrained by the austerities of his beliefs. Brigid took them out to dinner at the Grand Hotel, fed them lobster and pheasant and wild strawberries from Sardinia and had a wonderful time, since she was the only one not troubled by conscience. She did not bring Teresa to Rome and Kerry made only a polite enquiry about his niece.

On her return to Lerici Brigid broke up with her Communist lover, who wanted her to paint pictures of social significance. With Teresa and an Italian nurse she left Italy for London to throw herself into the last years of the Swinging Sixties. She was surprised to find that she now envied Kerry, began to wish she had some vocation of her own. Romance, or lust, call it what one liked, was no vocation.

Fingal, meanwhile, was discovering his own loneliness. He had enough acquaintances to fill in what empty hours he had; but he had no friends and, despite his bouts of loneliness, wished for none. He also had no desire for romance; but lust still troubled him. A young whore named Tilly Mosman satisfied him there.

He had taken a small apartment in the medical specialists' street, Macquarie Street, in a building where all the other suites were occupied by doctors. If he were seen entering the building, which happened every Thursday in the early evening, it would be assumed that he was visiting one of the doctors. He and Tilly were never seen together; she was always waiting for him in the apartment when he arrived and always left after him. She already had a discretion that was advanced for her years.

'Do you have any other clients?' said Fingal, being indiscreet.

'No,' she said, lying.

'Is this what you want to do for the rest of your life?'

'No, I'd like to own my own house, a high-class one, the best in town. I've been reading the business pages in the *Herald*. They say that service industries are going to be the big thing.'

He smiled. 'This is a service industry? Well, yes, I guess it is. If I financed you, would you ever mention my name to anyone?'

'Have I done that so far?'

'I don't know. Have you?'

'No. What would you do to me if I did?'

'I think I'd have you killed.'

'You wouldn't!' She started up in the bed, suddenly afraid of him for the first time.

'No,' he said; but, he thought, he probably would have to have it done. He would have to give up a lot of pleasures when he became the Pope's father. Though by then he would be beyond all *this*. 'When the time comes, I'll see what we can do about setting you up in your own establishment. But not yet – you're too young.'

'That's what I'd like to be – the youngest madam in the country.'

He couldn't blame her; he had been just as ambitious at her age, even younger. 'We'll see, we'll see.'

In 1969 Australia discovered nickel. Holes suddenly appeared all over the Outback; some of the most worthless land on the planet became as valuable as a building site on Wall Street. Companies sprang up like financial weeds; ordinary men, and women, in the street rushed to fertilize the weeds with their savings. Mining shares rose from ten cents to a hundred dollars almost overnight. Entrepreneurs, a word most Australians had never heard of up till then and certainly couldn't pronounce, came out of the scrub, the desert and the woodwork of one-room offices in the cities and became millionaires as fast as one could say, No Capital Gains Tax. It was the gold-rush of the nineteenth century all over again, except that it took place on the stock exchanges of the nation.

Tewsday floated a new mining company for Ballyduff and Fingal let him have his head. But Tewsday made one of his rare business mistakes. In the rush to beat the competition to the bonanza, he only cursorily checked the so-called mining experts who came to him for backing. Bundiwindi Mining turned out to have much less nickel content in its ore than the 'experts' had claimed.

The Fraud Squad called at Ballyduff headquarters and asked to see Mr Tewsday. The two officers were shown into his office: Inspector Zanuch and a young detective-constable whose name was Maloney or something like that. Tewsday, who had always had the potential, had grown into a snob, a man who failed to recognize inferiors, even in his own organization.

'We were duped, Inspector.' He decided to be utterly frank, he laid his case on the table like a saint pleading guilty to over-zealousness. 'We relied upon those we thought were honest experts.'

'They've fled the country, Mr Tewsday.' Zanuch was already the second-best dressed man on the force, a conservative dandy who matched the man opposite him. Alongside them Detective-Constable Malone looked like a vagrant who had wandered into the wrong room. 'We estimate they've made a quarter of a million dollars each, all tax free, which should buy them a nice hideaway somewhere. That, as they say, leaves you holding the baby.'

'You surely don't think a corporation like ours would be a knowing partner in a conspiracy to defraud? Or, indeed, that I would be?' He had been made a Commander of the British Empire in that year's Honours List: the Empire no longer existed and he commanded nothing, but CBE meant something after one's name, even if most of the natives weren't quite sure what it meant.

Zanuch looked at Malone. 'Constable Malone has dug out some interesting facts, Mr Tewsday. Perhaps you'd like to hear them?'

Malone took out a notebook. 'On November the first last you hosted a lunch at the Wentworth Hotel in a private dining-room. You told a group of bankers and stockbrokers that you personally had been to inspect the mining leases in Western Australia, to wit, the Bundiwindi leases, and that you had then gone on to Perth and seen the ore samples tested for the nickel content you claimed, to wit, eight per cent. The true content was a non-commercial one per cent, is that not right?'

'Where did you get that information?'

'From two of the stockbrokers and one of the bankers present. And from one of the geologists on the leases – he said you'd never been near Bundiwindi.'

Tewsday looked at the young detective. He was tall and well-built, a ramshackle dresser, someone Tewsday felt he didn't need to remember; the police force, he guessed, was full of these nondescripts. 'What makes you think I'd risk my reputation by concocting anything like those men have alleged?'

'Greed?' said the nondescript.

Tewsday gave him a hard, second look then. 'That's an indiscreet remark, Constable. You may live to regret it.'

Inspector Zanuch said, 'We have a good deal of evidence, Mr Tewsday. I suggest it might be a good idea if you got in touch with your lawyers.'

Tewsday sat very still, even his plump hand lying like a

dead starfish on his desk. He was barely into his forties now, but he had looked middle-aged for the past five years: this had been the destined portrait of him and he had been growing into it since he was in his mid-twenties. He had a plump pink-marble look to him and, unless he lost weight, one had the impression that the marble wouldn't age any more. There was, however, a crack in the marble at the moment.

'I think I'd better have a few words with someone.' He stood up. 'Will you excuse me for ten minutes? My secretary will get you some coffee.'

'Can we trust you, Mr Tewsday?' said Zanuch. 'Maybe Constable Malone had better go with you.'

'No.' Tewsday's voice was hard. 'I'll be back, Inspector. I don't run out.'

There were two large offices on this floor, his own and that of the other joint managing director. On the floor above, having the space to itself, was the office of the executive chairman. This was accessible without appointment only to Tewsday and the other managing director. Fingal Hourigan had never been a gregarious boss and now he had become almost monastic.

He looked up in irritation as his long-time, long-suffering secretary, Miss Stevens, a durable, patient woman, showed Tewsday in. 'What's the matter?'

'We're in trouble,' said Tewsday and told him about the Fraud Squad's visit.

'Is what they say true?'

'Up to a point.'

'Jesus!' Fingal sat back in his high-backed chair. His hair was iron-grey now, but touches of white were showing through. 'How many times have I told you to cover your tracks? You'll never learn, you youngsters. Did you go over to Western Australia to inspect the leases?'

'No. I took the word of our two experts. You met them, we agreed they looked on the up-and-up. I found out after they'd bolted that there was only one intersection that showed eight per cent, but it would have yielded nothing commercial, it was so narrow and shallow.'

'Well, whatever happened, we've been left holding a crock of shit.' When he was wildly angry some of the old Chicago street argot slipped back on to his tongue. 'You can carry it.'

'You okayed the float, Fingal.'

'Have another look at the prospectus. You won't find my name anywhere on it. But yours is, with that big flash signature of yours.'

The two men stared at each other; the war between them would never end. Fingal had not allowed the enmity between them to blind him to Tewsday's business talent: he had promoted him as he had deserved to be. As a balance and a threat he had created a joint managing directorship: Borsolino, Tewsday's sour rival, occupied that. Tewsday, for his part, had stayed on at Ballyduff, riding out the occasional rude rebuff, because he was on course towards his ambition, some day soon to be chairman and chief executive of what was now one of the five largest corporations in the country. Ballyduff was a battlefield, but no campaign medals would be issued. Both men kept their hatred of each other very private.

'It won't reflect too well on Ballyduff,' said Tewsday.

Fingal reflected on that. 'Okay, I'll see what I can do. Go back downstairs, tell those cops you'll talk to them in a couple of days when you've seen our lawyers. Stall 'em. Handle 'em with kid gloves – you're good at that.' He wanted to say *greasy* kid gloves, but restrained himself. 'I'll get in touch with Joe Redford.'

Tewsday left him, drew on kid gloves and went downstairs to stall Zanuch and Malone. Fingal got up and walked to one of the big windows of his huge office. This new Ballyduff House had been up only a few months; here on the sixty-ninth floor, one floor under the boardroom, where he also ruled, he was king of the city. Here, if he so wished, he could piss on the citizens from a great height. He was already the richest man in the land and in his pockets he had enough politicians to form a party of his own.

Joe Redford was one of them. He was the conservative Premier of the State, a politician who knew he and his party would be tossed out at the next elections. He was in his late sixties and his last hurrah, feathering his nest as fast as he could pick up the necessary. From his window Fingal could look south and almost directly into the window of the Premier's office. He walked back to his desk, picked up the phone and talked to Redford on a private line for ten minutes.

Two days later a senior officer called in Inspector Zanuch and said the case against Bundiwindi Mining would be dropped. Zanuch argued, but only half-heartedly; he could sense corruption, even though he couldn't smell it. Three months later the senior officer was driving a new car, one that seemed expensive for a man on his salary. The Premier's wife had $50,000 deposited in her bank account by Sugarcane Properties, a company registered in Queensland and used by Fingal for such donations. Tewsday emerged unmarked, except for this further debt to his enemy.

EIGHT

I

The letter had said: *My uncle came to Nicaragua last November, a month before I left to come home to Sydney* ...

Mary Magdalene knew exactly where she was, even though the windows were boarded up. She had been to this village several times, though not in the past six months. The Contras had been in control of this mountain area for that long and the Bishop in her own region had forbidden any of the priests, nuns and lay workers to come near any of these villages. No one had expected the Contras to come down out of the mountains on a kidnapping raid.

The village where she worked was on a small lake below a tangle of low mountains. She had set up the school when she had arrived here two years ago; she was assisted by a part-Indian nun, Sister Carmel, and an American lay worker, Audrey Burke. There was a two-room schoolhouse, built of adobe by the villagers, and a two-room hut where the three women lived. A lean-to kitchen had been built on the outside of the hut. It was all very primitive, but then everything, she had learned, was comparative. Audrey, however, brought up in a *House and Gardens* kitchen and who thought a microwave oven was essential to survival, was of the opinion that humility as taught by Christ could sometimes be a drag.

It was Audrey, a thin pretty girl from Kansas City, who had come running in to say there were soldiers in Jeeps at the end of the village's main street. Mary Magdalene had gone out of the schoolhouse into the bright sunlight and the first thing she saw was the mineral-water vendor running down the street, pushing his rattling cart ahead of him. 'They've taken Señor Caracas and his children!'

José Caracas was the village's principal employer. He owned a coffee plantation and also grew corn and wheat for the neighbouring markets. His father had been a Somoza supporter and had fled to the United States when the Somoza regime was toppled. José had stayed on and made his peace with the Sandinistas. Because he treated his employees with respect and good wages and because they had not complained against him, his holdings had not been seized; the Government was a silent partner, in return respecting his ability to run a successful commercial venture. His three older children were at school in Managua, the capital, but his two youngest came here to the parish school, another toleration by the Government.

'Where's Father Roa?' Mary shouted, but the mineral-water man rattled on past her at full speed.

'He's gone into Esteli,' said Audrey.

'Damn! He's never around when we need him.' Father Roa, old and a drunk, had given up the ghost, if not the Holy Ghost, and no longer cared about his flock. They could find their own way to Heaven where, he hoped, he would be waiting for them, young again and sober.

'Why would the soldiers be taking Señor Caracas?' Audrey was not qualified as a teacher or, indeed, for anything. She had turned up out of nowhere one day, fresh-faced and fresh with that American enthusiasm that Mary Magdalene found endearing and exasperating at the same time. They were always so *optimistic*. 'It must be a mistake.'

It was a mistake, all right; they were not Government soldiers. Mary looked up the street and saw now that the few villagers who had been out in the midday heat had disappeared into their homes. Out on the lake two flat-bottomed boats that had been about to come in had turned back and

158

now stood offshore. Four Jeeps, crammed with Contras in camouflaged green battle-dress, were coming down the narrow street; behind them she recognized the battered old Oldsmobile that was José Caracas's only relic of the family's lost affluence. The small convoy came to a halt in front of the school.

'Go back inside.' He was a young lieutenant with a soft wispy beard and hard dark eyes.

'Where are you taking Señor Caracas? Leave the children with us.' She had come out without her hat and she was squinting in the bright reflection flung up from the red dust of the road.

'Go back inside,' he repeated. 'It's none of your business. You outsiders are a pain in the ass.'

'What's the difference between us and the other pains in the ass, the Americans who are working with you?' Mary was glad that it was Audrey, an American, who asked the question.

Sister Carmel stood quietly in the background, as if trying to lose herself in the thin shadow flung by the overhang of the school's roof. Mary could not blame her: Carmel would have to remain here, no matter which side won the civil war. If an old Spanish-blood priest did not want to fight, who could blame a part-Indian nun if she chose to be neutral? God Himself hadn't yet made up his mind whose side he was on in this war-racked country.

'Leave the children with us,' said Mary doggedly. 'Where's their mother?'

Half a dozen parakeets, like small green missiles, suddenly took off from the strawberry tree beside the schoolhouse. The lieutenant turned his head sharply; all at once he looked nervous. Then he looked back at Mary, but said nothing. The three soldiers in the Jeep behind him, mere boys, looked sheepish. Mary stared at them, then wheeled and went up the line to the Oldsmobile. It was a convertible, but the top, ragged and patched, was up against the midday sun. Two soldiers were in the front seat and José Caracas was slumped in the back seat, his arm wrapped protectingly round his two small daughters.

'For your own sake, Sister Mary, don't interfere.' He was a small, jovial man; or had once been. All the joviality had gone and had left just a shell. He wore a white shirt and white trousers, but they were dirty, as if he had been dragged through the dust, and there was a large patch of blood on the shirt. He looked at Mary with glistening frightened eyes and she realized with a shock that he was weeping. 'They have killed my wife.'

The two children shuddered and he wrapped his arms tighter round them.

'It was an accident,' said the young soldier behind the wheel. He, too, looked sheepish, like the soldiers in the Jeep at the front of the column. He believed in his cause, but he hadn't expected to kill women. 'She was trying to protect the children and the gun just went off.'

Mary put her hands on the side of the car and leaned forward, feeling sick and faint. Rose Caracas had been a friend, a quiet plump women who was the right complement to her thin, jovial husband; there had been nothing in her life but him and her children. One heard of deaths every day in this country, but this was the first death of a friend.

She had not come here originally to take sides in the war, political or military. The order had been working here in Central America for over a hundred years, not always in a non-partisan way; in the 1920s it had been known by the locals as the Little Sisters of United Fruit. Over the past two years, however, the younger nuns, more politically aware than their older sisters, had begun to question their own neutrality. Rome might lay down its edicts, but Rome knew little, if anything, of the pain and bewilderment in these red-dust, green-tangled hills. One prayed to God for advice and, if He didn't strike one down with a bolt of lightning, one took it as approval of what one was doing. She was sensible enough, however, to run indoors whenever an electric storm had struck. She had never run away from the Contras.

She straightened up. 'Leave the children with me, Señor Caracas. I'll take care of them till you return.'

'No.' The young lieutenant had come up from the front of the convoy, treading quietly in the dust as if to ambush her. 'Damn you, Sister, get into the car! You're coming with us!'

He swung open the door of the car, grabbed her roughly and thrust her in before she could resist. Audrey came running up, yelling, and attacked the lieutenant, throwing both fists at him at once in the way women do. He took hold of one of her wrists, stepped aside and pulled her head first into the side of the car; some American instructor had taught him unarmed combat. Audrey's head hit the car with a horrible thump and she slid down into the dust and lay there.

'Drive on!'

He ran ahead, jumped into the leading Jeep and the convoy took off at once. Mary Magdalene scrambled up from the floor of the Oldsmobile, looked out over the side and back at the inert figure of Audrey still lying in the middle of the roadway, with Carmel, taking sides at last, running towards her.

Caracas moved over in the back seat and Mary slid on to it beside him. She took one of the children from him and cradled her in her lap. 'There, Teresa, we'll be all right. We'll be all right.' But the little girl looked at her with no faith at all.

Ten minutes later the convoy came to an abrupt halt. The lieutenant came back to the Oldsmobile and Mary and Caracas were both blindfolded with dirty bandanas. Then the convoy moved off again and travelled for another hour, climbing all the time. Once it stopped, not moving for ten minutes or so; Mary heard the clatter of a helicopter and guessed that the convoy must have pulled in under some trees to hide from a Government Mi-24. They must have been well hidden; the helicopter cruised up and down the road, then swung away and was gone out of earshot in a moment. The convoy moved on, then at last stopped; Mary, blind but not deaf, knew they had arrived in some village. She was feeling car-sick from the constant twisting and turning of the road and from the smell of the bandana tied round the upper part of her face: it was like having her face buried in someone's armpit. Teresa was taken from her arms and Mary herself was led, gently, by the young driver, out of the car and into a house. It was a *campesino*'s house: she could feel the dirt floor under the crêpe-soled boots she wore.

The young driver took off the bandana. She rubbed her eyes and blinked at him, standing there in his embarrassment. 'What are they going to do to us?'

'I don't know, Sister, not you, anyway. They're going to take Señor Caracas and the children across the border.' He lowered his voice. 'Don't make the lieutenant angry, Sister. He might kill you.'

She looked at him with horror, not believing him. But he was deadly serious; she could see the horror in his own face. He was part-Indian, but he didn't have the mask that the full-blooded Indians could sometimes wear.

'Why would they want to do that, for God's sake?'

'Not *they*. *Him*. He's a fanatic, Sister.' He couldn't understand fanaticism, that was something that wasn't in the printed-in-the-USA army manuals. His face had started to change; he was putting on the mask. Perhaps, she thought, they never lose it, that the Spanish blood in him can never crumble it. But then, she remembered, there was also a Spanish mask, something that had come out of Africa with the Moors long ago. She began to feel something that had been creeping into her for the past six months, that she might never feel at home in this country. The young driver said, 'What's your name? Are you an American?'

'Sister Mary Magdalene. No, I'm not American, I'm a mixture. Irish-Australian.' She didn't add French: her father, her mother had told her, was dead and best forgotten.

He shook his head, puzzled. 'I just don't know what you're

doing here,' he said and left her wondering the same thing. Doubt is no comfort, no staff: she was suddenly afraid. She took out her beads and began to pray, but she had, too, doubts about the efficacy of prayer.

They kept her in the room for another two days; having abducted her, they didn't seem to know what to do with her. Several times she heard arguments outside the house; she recognized the voice of the lieutenant, angrier than the other voices. It was cold at night and the one blanket they gave her did not keep her warm. They brought her meals twice a day: chicken, beans and rice; at least they were not going to allow her to starve. The young driver brought the meals, still friendly and concerned for her; but when she asked what had happened to Señor Caracas and the children, the mask came down, he was suddenly Indian. The war, she guessed, had become much more complex than he had been led to believe.

On the second day she stood in front of the closed door, barring his way. 'Where am I? I'm in Telgalpa, aren't I? I heard someone say the name.'

She knew the village, a collection of whitewashed houses, rusting tin sheds and a small pottery factory clinging to the side of a mountain; one wondered why it had been built in such a precarious position and outsiders, coming to it, always looked as if they were in a hurry to depart before the whole lot slid off down into the valley below. A dilapidated church, like one of God's hovels, stood at the end of the main street, dominating the one flat space in the village, the Plaza di La Señora. The whole village looked on the verge of ruin, yet somehow it had survived earthquakes and, she guessed, it was now surviving the war.

The driver hesitated, then said, 'We'll be going soon, back over the border.'

Here in the mountains the border was only a line on a map, a figment of the cartographers' imagination. 'Are they going to take me with them?'

'I don't know. Just don't make the lieutenant angry.'

163

But the lieutenant didn't come to see her, not till the third day. Then he opened the door and stood there with a big man in what looked to be army tans and a windbreaker. 'Here she is,' the lieutenant said angrily, as if he resented the newcomer's presence.

'Leave us,' said the big man. He looked around the small room, then said to Mary in English, 'Let's go outside.'

'You can't do that!' The lieutenant's anger grew.

The big man looked at him with contempt; or so it seemed to Mary. 'Don't tell me what I can or cannot do, lieutenant,' he said in poor Spanish. He stood in front of the other man and gestured to Mary. 'Come along, Sister. Let's get some light on all this.'

She followed him out of the house and up a dirt path between narrow terraces of corn. They came out on to a terrace where so far nothing had been planted and he gestured to her to sit down on the low stone wall that held up the terrace above it. A laurel tree threw some shade over both of them and she was able to look at him without squinting. On the way up here, after three days of darkness in the house, she had been almost blinded by the bright sun and had stumbled several times.

The big man sat down on the stones beside her and gazed at her steadily for almost a minute. Then he said, 'I'm Archbishop Kerry Hourigan, your uncle.'

She felt suddenly faint; she swayed and he put out a hand to steady her. In the two years she had been in Nicaragua she had come to expect the unexpected; but this was beyond her imagination. One's uncle, one she had never met, did not drop out of a clear blue sky, no matter how closely he might be connected to God. She recovered and told him what she thought.

He smiled. 'I'm glad to see you have a sense of humour. That's the Hourigan in you.' He had no idea who her father was, Brigid had always kept that secret. If he had known, he would not have remarked on it: his opinion of the French in the Vatican was that they had no sense of humour, only malicious wit. 'But this isn't a humorous situation... Damn it,' he said, suddenly irritable. 'Why are you working in this damned country? They're Marxists.'

'Not the *campesinos*, not all of them. I'm not working for the Government, I'm working for the Church.'

'You know what the Holy Father thinks of priests and nuns who work in a Marxist system.'

'Does that include Poland?'

'Poland is different,' he said, realizing he was up against another Hourigan, no matter who her father had been. The Hourigans always had minds of their own: no one knew that better than he. 'You're helping the system here. I've heard the reports on you.'

'Reports? Who's been taking notice of me? I'm not important enough. All I do is teach in my village school and assist the local priest. Sometimes I help the doctor when he comes to visit the village. What are you doing here, anyway? Does the Cardinal in Managua know you're here? Did he send you to rescue me? Or to tick me off? Is he the one who's got the reports on me?' She was angry that she might have been spied upon, possibly by old Father Roa.

Kerry Hourigan shook his head. 'I'm not supposed to be here. I came in over the border from Honduras – I came here only because of you.' He was lying, but The Lord didn't punish you if you lied in His cause. If He did, Hell would be fuller than it was. 'You're an embarrassment, my child.'

My child: God, how she hated being addressed like that! The Church seniors always put one down: the father figure gave them some protection. 'To you or the Church?'

'Both. Go home, Mary –'

'I don't have a home, Uncle. I've never had one, except the convent.'

'That was your mother's fault. She should have brought you home to Australia. It's criminal that you and I have never met till now, that you've never met your grandfather.'

'I regret it. I've often wondered what you and Grandfather were like – I mean, when I learned who you were. I was sixteen before she told me . . . She only told me after I decided I wanted to be a nun. She never took me back to Australia when she'd go – I'd be left in a boarding school in England or Switzerland.' All at once she was bitter. 'Home is my school down in my village, it's where I've been happiest. That's where I want to go back to.'

'Your mother is back in Australia now.'

'I know. She writes to me every week – I think she's starting to feel guilty . . .'

He was exasperated with her, yet felt sorry for her. She was not his responsibility, that was her mother's; yet he was not without a sense of family duty, he was the one here on the spot. He was just not accustomed to taking care of an individual, he had been trained for bigger responsibilities.

He had come to Honduras with Francisco Paredes Canto and Max Domecq Cruz to talk to the local Contra commanders. With the drying up of American supplies, the guerrillas were looking for a new source of arms. He had the money and the contacts, but he had wanted to assure himself that everything he paid for would reach the Contras. His father did not believe in his money, or any part of it, being hijacked. The venture had to be not only successful but secret: there were certain people in the Vatican who would have his head if they knew what he was up to. He was supposed to be in the United States raising money for the Defence Against Subversive Religions.

Yesterday he had heard about the young nun, Sister Mary Magdalene, and he had known at once who she was. The Contra chiefs in Honduras didn't want her; there had been too much trouble in the past over what had happened to foreign missionaries. They could not leave her fate to the lieutenant in Telgalpa; they knew his reputation. Kerry Hourigan, conscience overcoming his zeal, had volunteered to talk to her, though he had not mentioned his relationship to her.

Now he was regretting his fit of conscience. It was all very well to have a conscience, but, like lust, it should be kept under control.

'If you go back there, what will you do?'

'The same as I've always done. Teach the children.'

'Teach them what? The ways of The Lord or the ways of Karl Marx?'

She laughed: it was a harsh sound coming from such a young throat. 'Oh Uncle! When did you last get down to the level of someone like the *campesinos*? When did you last hear the confession of an ordinary worker? Or the mother of six or seven kids?'

Oh, how simple-minded were the young. Did they really think only the poor could arouse compassion? None knew better than he the agonizing sins of the rich.

'I'm not a Marxist,' she said. 'All I do is listen to their troubles.'

'They have plenty of troubles under the Sandinistas.'

'Are you for the Contras?'

'Yes,' he said almost defiantly. He had no ambition to be a closet martyr; if he was going to sacrifice himself for The Lord, he wouldn't mind headlines. If Judgement Day should prove to be a low-key occasion, he wouldn't attend. But, of course, it was easy to be outspoken here in these mountains; secrecy was still necessary back in Rome. He backed off a little, in case, by some chance, she had a line to the Cardinal in Managua, who, he knew, had a line to Rome: 'Let's say I'm against Marxism. It is the evil of the world.'

'I wouldn't know,' she said simply. 'The world doesn't count for much in my village.'

He looked away from her, out over the valley to the opposite ridge. He saw a flash of brilliant green, as if someone had thrown a huge long emerald down into the valley: it was a *quetzal*, the most beautiful bird in the New World; he had an eye for beauty and it made his heart ache to see it. Then he saw a King vulture drop down out of the sky and alight on the roof beam of the church in the square; he watched it, fascinated by it and repelled. He had seen it in Indian carvings, beautiful yet ugly; somehow it was symbolic of this region. He turned his face away from it, his ear now caught. A big *higuera* tree stood opposite the church; a boy came out from under its shade carrying a transistor radio turned up full blast; an American voice was belting out a rock-'n'-roll song. The vulture took off from the roof of the church as if its ear, like his own, had been offended; it flapped away on black and white wings till it was just a speck on the far side of the valley. No, he thought, I couldn't work here, not at her level. He looked back at her.

'You can't stay here.'

'Here? I don't want to – I want to go back to my village.'

That wasn't what he had meant: he had meant here in Nicaragua. The missionaries always finished up on the wrong side if they stayed long enough; they never saw the whole picture. 'All right, you can go back to your village.'

She looked almost like a *campesino*: scuffed and worn boots, a shapeless skirt, an unpressed shirt, short straggly hair that looked as if she had cut it herself. He was a fastidious dresser, something he had inherited from his father, and he detested anyone, even nuns, who didn't try to keep up appearances.

'Thanks, Uncle. What about you?'

'What about me?'

'Are you coming down to Managua to see the Cardinal?'

'I don't think President Ortega and his Government would welcome me. No, I'm going back to Rome. I think it would be better if you didn't mention that I was the one who arranged your release. The Sandinistas might get the wrong impression.'

'About you or me?'

She had no respect for his rank; he wondered what respect she gave to her superiors in the Order. But then she was not family-related to her superiors: perhaps she saw himself and her only as uncle and niece. 'Both of us. God bless you, Mary.'

'You too, Uncle.' Then suddenly she smiled and put out her hand. 'I'd like to meet you in other circumstances. We could have some ding-dong arguments. Just like you and Mother used to have.'

'God forbid!' But he smiled; in other circumstances he might have come to like her. 'Keep up the good work.'

... But that was a hypocritical remark if ever I've heard one, said the letter to Father Marquez. *A month later I got an instruction from the Order in Ireland that I was being transferred to Australia, that I had done more than my fair share of field mission work. Two years! I've met nuns and priests who have been in the field for thirty or forty years ... It was easy to guess who had applied the pressure. Ireland always does what Rome tells it ...*

2

'Here's the letter.' Clements lifted it out of the murder box. 'What do you want done with it? I mean, do you want to show it to the Archbishop?'

'Not yet. The holy bastard has been stringing me along. He said he'd seen her in Honduras, that she'd been brought out of Nicaragua to Tegal – whatever the capital is. He was *in* Nicaragua – doing what?'

Malone had been dropped outside Homicide by Tewsday's chauffeur. He had stood on the pavement for a while, wishing he had had his 'think walk'. His mind was still muddied. He had more questions to ask, of the Archbishop, of Fingal Hourigan, of Paredes and Domecq, if he could find them. He was not, however, going to go off half-cocked, like a conservationist's gun.

'Why do I expect Archbishops to be the soul of truth?' said Clements, the non-religious.

The phone rang and Malone picked it up. It was Father

Marquez, sounding breathless, as if he had run to the phone at his end. 'Inspector? This is Luis Marquez. Holy God, you know —' He paused to get his breath; for a moment Malone thought he had quit and gone. Then he came back, his voice more under control: 'I've just had another threat. The same guy, Inspector.'

'What did he say?'

'He wanted to know what was in the letter I gave you.'

Malone racked his memory, trying to remember the scene at the cemetery. 'You're sure it was the same man? He spoke to you in Spanish?'

'It was him, all right. He couldn't have been there, Inspector, I mean at the cemetery. I was scared — I'm even more scared now — and I kept looking around to see who was watching the burial. If he saw us, he must have been some distance away, watching us through glasses. Or someone at the funeral saw me give you the letter and told him.'

That thought had already occurred to Malone. 'I'll check up on that angle.'

'Inspector, I'm really scared. I didn't want to get into all this. And now ...'

'Easy, Luis. Where are you — at the University? Do you live alone there?'

'Yes, I have a room here. I eat in the canteen.'

'Can you go and live in some church presbytery, I mean where you'll have company?'

'I guess so. I can go up to Randwick. If I explain to them ... But for how long? And I don't want any of them dragged into this. The parish priest up there is a pretty conservative old stick ...'

'Do you have to stay at the University for the rest of the day? Yes? Righto, I'll send a man out to keep you company, then he can escort you up to the presbytery at Randwick. His name is Detective-Constable Graham.'

Malone hung up, then sent for Andy Graham. The latter arrived, as usual all enthusiasm; Malone felt he should have been a football cheer-leader instead of a cop. He was tall and overweight and had a rather vacant, good-looking face behind which a brain was growing that would one day, perhaps too late, be shrewd enough to temper his enthusiasm. Malone explained what he wanted him to do.

'Right!' said Graham and Malone was relieved when he didn't punch the air. 'Let's hope the bastard shows up, right?'

'Right,' said Malone and hoped the Spanish-speaking bastard would never put in an appearance. 'Just stick close to Father Marquez till you leave him at the presbytery this evening. What are you? Catholic?'

'No, a Methodist. The Uniting Church.'

'Don't get into any argument. Be ecumenical.'

'Right!'

And Andy Graham went off, metaphorically punching the air, the flap of his holster already undone under his jacket. Clements grinned at Malone.

'He should transfer to the mounted section. He'd have jumped on his horse and galloped all the way to Kensington. I felt like shouting Hi-ho, Silver!'

'We're getting old, Russ.' Then he looked down the big room and added softly, 'We're just about to get older. Or anyway *feel* it.'

Chief Superintendent Danforth was lumbering towards them, nodding to the other detectives as he passed them, making a royal progress, though there was nothing regal about him.

'Inspector –' He wheezed down into a chair, both vocally and physically; the chair looked and sounded as if it might collapse beneath him. He might once have been athletic, but that was long ago; he was within a year of retirement and he was wheezing his way towards it, careful not to exert himself. As long as Malone had known him he had been slow-moving and slow-thinking, one of the last of the old school who had risen in the ranks on seniority and not merit. 'You're on this murdered nun case? What's the progress?'

Malone glanced towards the murder box; Clements had slipped the letter back into it and put the lid on the old shoe-box. 'Not much, Chief. You know who's involved.'

'Oh, indeed I do. Definitely.' Danforth ran a beefy hand over his short-back-and-sides. He was a man from the 1950s: he had stopped still in time. He had once been corrupt, but the new regime had put paid to that; he had had sense enough to realize the gravy train had run off the rails and he had been lucky to escape. 'I think you are biting off more than you can chew, Scobie.'

Scobie: that meant this was going to be a man-to-man talk. Malone looked at Clements and the latter took the hint and rose. 'I'll see that Andy Graham has got away.'

Danforth waited till he and Malone were alone, then he moved his chair closer to the latter's desk. They were separated from the other detectives in the big room by several empty desks; none the less, he lowered his voice conspiratorially. 'Scobie, it's not going to be worth all the trouble this will cause. You're going to be up against the Catholic Church.'

'Did they tell you that?'

'Who?'

'The Church.'

'Not directly, no. But you know how much clout they have in this State. Half the MPs are Tykes. So's the Premier. He's never going to give the Church a kick in the bum.'

'I haven't pointed a finger at the Church. I've got a murdered nun and her uncle's an archbishop. That's all.'

'It doesn't stop there, and you know it. There's the nun's grandad.'

'Has he been talking to you, Harry?' Let's keep it man-to-man.

'Not directly, no.'

'Tewsday, then? Sir Jonathan?'

Danforth sat back, ran his hand over his head again, as if putting all his thoughts together under his grey thatch; Malone had the image of a hand of not very good cards being put in order before being played. 'We don't need any names. Walls have ears.'

Malone strangled the laugh that started in his chest; he managed to nod soberly. 'Righto, no names. But we know who we both mean.'

Danforth nodded in return, just as soberly. 'There's too much influence, Scobie. You could never beat it. You could find yourself in charge of the traffic branch out at Tibooburra.'

Tibooburra was in the far west of the State; it had a population you could gather in a single schoolroom. Malone played his own best card: 'The Commissioner is in on this, Harry. I have to report to him.'

Danforth ran his hand over his head again, this time a little worriedly. 'The Commissioner, eh? How did he get into it?'

Malone wasn't going to tell him that. Danforth was obviously the Hourigan, or Tewsday, man in the department. 'I think you'd have to ask him that, Harry. He doesn't take me into his confidence.'

Danforth nodded, still worried. 'Yeah, yeah, I'll do that.'

Then the phone rang and Malone picked it up.

'Inspector Malone? We talked the other night.'

Malone recognized the voice from its faint accent. 'Go ahead.'

'Inspector, the young woman has been buried. Let her rest in peace.'

'Oh, she'll do that, all right. She's the only one who's going to have any peace.' He could feel himself getting angry: first, the threat to Marquez, then Danforth trying to apply pressure and now this.

The voice hardened, though it remained quiet. 'Be sensible, Inspector. We don't want to do anything you'd regret.'

'Are you threatening me –' he took a wild chance. '– Mr Domecq? Or is it Mr Paredes?'

There was silence for just a moment; the man, whoever he was, was used to thinking on his feet. 'You have the wrong names, Inspector. Don't be too smart or –' But he didn't finish the threat.

Malone held on to his temper, aware of Danforth sitting opposite him, both ears strained. 'Whoever you are, let me tell you something. This isn't Latin America. Nobody threatens the police in this country.' At least not since the bushrangers' day; or in a shoot-out. But not over the phone: it was un-Australian. 'Go back and tell your boss, whoever *he* is, that it won't work. If anything happens to me, the whole of Homicide will be down on you and you'll be up shit creek. That's an old Aussie expression. I don't know the Spanish for it, but your boss might translate it.'

He slammed the phone down and looked at Danforth. The Chief Superintendent pursed his lips in a silent whistle. That last message of mine was for you, too, Malone thought; and knew that Danforth had got it. Danforth at last said, 'You'll report that to the Commissioner, I take it?'

'Of course. You know how he feels about his men being threatened.'

'Yes. So he should. Definitely.' Danforth nodded, almost too eager to agree. 'They made a mistake there.' He stood up, wheezing. 'Well, think about what I said, Scobie. It was just between you and me, you understand?'

At least he had the grace not to wink, thought Malone. 'Sure, Harry. I appreciate it. You had my best interests at heart. Definitely.'

'I always had my men's interests at heart. That's how I got to be Chief Superintendent.' He lumbered away, elephantinely smug.

Clements came back as soon as Danforth had disappeared. Malone told him about Danforth's attempt at pressure and of the threat over the phone. 'I'm beginning to wish my leave was due. I'd like to go bush somewhere with Lisa and the kids.'

'Are you going to back off?'

'Would you expect me to? But I'm not sure where the hell

174

to go next. I think it's just as Tewsday told me – Old Man Hourigan is hiding Paredes and Domecq. I've checked with Immigration and they haven't left the country, not unless they went out on different passports to the ones they used when they came in.'

'Let's get a warrant to search the Hourigan place.'

'We'd never get one. He'd pull enough strings to make a shark net.' He looked out the window, at Hyde Park green and peaceful in the autumn sun. 'It's a nice day. D'you feel like staking out the Hourigan mansion? Just sitting in your car and making out your bets for Saturday?'

Clements made a face. 'I can think of things I'd rather be doing. I'd better take someone with me, in case I fall asleep. Are you staying here?'

'I'll be here all day. I've got to finalize the report on the Lloyd case.' The Lloyd case had been a double murder in a family; the murderer, a son who had killed his mother and sister, was in custody and had confessed. It was an open-and-shut case, the sort that made police work easy. If investigating murder ever was easy: Malone hoped he would never become as callous as that. 'When I get that out of the way, my desk is clear.'

'You want to bet?' said Clements.

Malone worked till five o'clock, when his desk was as clear as it would ever be; he would never achieve the barren neatness of the Commissioner. Clements, sounding bored, called in to say there had been no movement in or out of the Hourigan place, not even a delivery man. Malone told him to pack up and go home, then he did the same himself.

As he was leaving his desk a call came in from Andy Graham. 'Inspector, I'm just taking Father Marquez up to Randwick. You want me to stay with him there, too?'

'I don't think so, Andy. Just tell him not to go out tonight. You or someone else can pick him up again in the morning.'

He went down, got into his Commodore and drove out into the peak-hour traffic. He was almost home in Randwick, looking forward to the comfort of Lisa and the children, when he decided to drive on the extra half-mile to the church. Father Marquez might like some comfort, too, though Malone was not sure that he could give any.

He arrived at the church just as Andy Graham, in an ummarked police car, pulled up in the parking lot and deposited the young priest. Graham said good-night and drove off with his usual haste.

Marquez looked after him. 'He drives like one of those Grand Prix drivers. It's the first time I felt I should have been wearing my crash helmet in a car.'

'He's our traffic cops' favourite target.'

'He's a ball of energy, isn't he? He told me he did a year in Arts down at the University, but couldn't stand the slow pace. I gather he used to breeze through a millennium of history while everyone else was plodding through a decade.'

The young priest sounded talkative, as if he were nervous. Malone said, 'Where's your motorbike?'

'I left it down on campus.' He looked at Malone in the dim light of a street-lamp outside the parking lot. 'I appreciate what you're doing, Inspector. But how long is it going to go on?'

The parking lot had once been the extensive grounds of an old house that had belonged to one of the district's best families. Now the house was a community centre, the whole area surrounded by tall, thick ficus trees. The church was on the south side of the parking lot, its steeple piercing the night sky. The lights were on in the church and a few people were arriving for evening Mass, most of them elderly. The young were too busy, who needed to demonstrate his faith seven days a week, for God's sake?

Malone looked around at the shadows. They suggested a menacing silence, despite the noise of the traffic out on the busy street. He abruptly felt uneasy: *we're targets side by side, just waiting to be hit.*

'I'll walk you down to the presbytery.'

At that moment the car swung into the parking lot. It

came in slowly, its headlamps sweeping across the large two-storeyed house as it turned and came towards Malone and Marquez. It was moving slowly, as if the driver was looking for a vacant spot away from the half-a-dozen other parked cars. Malone, blinded by the headlamps, stepped to one side and Marquez followed him.

'It's probably one of the old ladies,' Marquez said. 'They shouldn't be driving at night –'

Then the car was opposite them. Malone caught a glimpse of the driver, but he couldn't tell whether it was a man or a woman; he or she seemed to be wearing a balaclava or a ski helmet. Malone did, however, see the shotgun come up; the driver drove with one hand for a moment. Then he took both hands off the steering wheel and pumped the gun. Malone fell down, rolling away, but Father Marquez caught the full force of the blast. He seemed to jump backwards, hit the parked car behind him and fell in a contorted heap. The assassin's car accelerated, swung right with a squeal of tyres and drove out on to the street. It went straight across the north and south streams of traffic, causing a louder screech of tyres and several nerve-shuddering bangs of crashing metal, and down a narrow street opposite. Malone had scrambled to his feet, but he caught nothing that would identify the car except that it was dark and medium-sized.

He dropped to his knees beside Marquez; but as soon as he touched the young priest he knew he was dead. Then someone was running across from the front of the church: Malone stood up and recognized Father Joannes, the parish priest.

'I heard the shots – Oh, Holy Jesus!' He was a burly man in his sixties, one who had spent all his early years in bush parishes and had helped in the physical labour of building his churches. He was old-fashioned in his theology and moral approach, but he was practical and tough-nerved. 'I'll get an ambulance! Are you all right?'

'I'm okay, Father. You stay here with Father Marquez –

say some prayers. I brought my own car, not a police one – I don't have a radiophone in it.' Other people were now coming across from the church, some of them approaching apprehensively. 'Where can I find a phone?'

'There's one in the community centre. It's open – the cleaners are in there.'

Malone ran across to the old house, feeling weak in the legs, found a phone and called Police Centre. 'Get the local boys up here – I want the parking lot cordoned off. Get in touch with Sergeant Clements – he should be at home – and tell him I want him here on the double. And Constable Graham. Get an ambulance here, but tell 'em the man is already dead.'

'What about the car, Inspector, the one that got away?'

'No description – I missed it.' He hung up and stared at the hand still on the phone. It was shaking like an old man's with palsy. Then he felt his knees beginning to tremble and he leaned against the wall in front of him.

'You all right?' A cleaning woman stood beside him, her hand in the middle of his back, her broad blunt face wrinkled with concern. 'Here, sit down.'

He straightened up, shook his head at the chair she pushed towards him. He clenched his fists, trying to force the nervousness out of them. He had felt shock before, but never like this. He looked at the phone, wondering if he should call Lisa, wanting to hear the reassuring sound of her voice; then he decided against it. He wanted to be fully in control of himself before he spoke to her. What was happening to him must not be allowed to touch her or the children.

The police from the local station arrived within two minutes; the ambulance was only three minutes behind them. The parking lot was filling up with spectators, most of them from the church: this was more interesting than Mass. Some of them bent their heads in prayer and crossed themselves as Father Marquez's body was lifted into the ambulance. Father Joannes, ashen-faced in the glare of the cars' headlamps, which had been switched on to shed more light, came across to Malone.

'Why? He rang this morning and said there was some trouble he wanted to avoid –'

'It had to do with the murder of Sister Magdalene, from the convent. Father Marquez was an innocent victim – they should never have touched him –'

'Who's *they*?'

This was no place to tell him; if ever he was to be told. The early evening was busy: the glare of the headlamps, the flashing roof-lights of the police cars and the ambulance, the dark figures moving restlessly in silhouette, the shriek of tyres as the traffic out in the street pulled up to see what was going on. Three cars had crashed into each other when the killer's car had cut across the traffic streams; they had been pulled into the kerb and two tow-wagons had already arrived like four-wheeled vultures. The Moreton Bay fig trees loomed against the night sky like dark clouds underlit with green and there was a touch of damp in the air, as if rain was building up to drown out the whole scene. It would be a good thing if it did, Malone thought.

'I'll explain some other time, Father,' he said, wanting to get away before the media reporters arrived. 'But you don't have to worry. They won't be back.'

'I hope not,' said Father Joannes and blessed himself. 'I can't keep up with what goes on today.'

'Neither can I,' said Malone, but he knew they were speaking in different contexts.

Russ Clements and Andy Graham arrived within ten seconds of each other. The media vans and cars were right on their tail. Malone gave Graham instructions: 'The local sergeant seems to have got everything under control – let him handle the reporters.'

'What about Father Marquez's family?'

'There's only his mother, I gather. Let the local police handle that, too.'

'I'm glad you're not asking me to do it,' said Graham, all enthusiasm suddenly unconscious. 'That's a bastard of a job. Do we try and trace the killer's car?'

'Scout around locally, see if it's been abandoned – it might have been a stolen job. He used a shotgun – he got off five or six shots, I didn't count.

Graham went off, still showing no enthusiasm; he knew as well as Malone that he had virtually nothing to work on. Malone turned to Clements, who was studying him carefully.

'He meant to get you too, didn't he?'

'I think so.'

'It knocked the shit out of you, didn't it?'

Malone looked at his hands; they had stopped trembling. 'How did you guess?'

'I know how I'd feel if it was that close – shotguns aren't like hand-pieces. Half-a-dozen times I've seen the damage it can do. The older we get, the sight doesn't get any better. You want to go home? I'll take over here.'

Once again Malone felt the warm, if unstated affection that Clements felt for him; the big man was as upset as himself at how close he had come to being blasted. He had shut his mind at how Father Marquez had looked. He had seen him only dimly in the shadow of the car where he had fallen; when he had come out of the community centre and the cars' head-lamps had been switched on, he had not gone near the body. But in his mind's eye he knew the terrible damage that had been done to the handsome young priest and, unless he could keep that eye shut, he knew the lasting unnerving effect it would have on him. And Clements, too, knew it.

'No,' he said, 'I'm going out to Vaucluse to talk to Arch-bishop Hourigan.'

3

On the way they stopped at a public phone-box and Malone rang Lisa. 'You'll hear it on the radio – they may even have it on the seven o'clock TV news. Father Marquez has been shot. He's dead.'

There was a gasp; then Lisa said, 'Are you all right?'

'Why shouldn't I be?'

'I don't know. I – Were you with him?'

It would be in the papers tomorrow morning. 'Yes. But I'm okay. I'll be home in an hour or so. What's for dinner?'

She knew him too well. 'Don't start acting casual. You've got no appetite. Take care, darling.'

She hung up and in his mind's eye again, that weakness that always makes us vulnerable, he saw her close her eyes and lean against the table on which their phone stood. In the background would be the noise of the children, but she would be deaf to them. But then, he knew, she would recover and take up again whatever she had been doing when he had called. Married to him, she had become a woman for all emergencies.

It started to rain as he and Clements drew up outside the Hourigan mansion. Parking was always easy here; the Vaucluse elements had their own off-street parking. Malone got out and crossed to the intercom on the big gates. Mrs Kelly, the warden, answered. 'What would you be wanting this time? Mr Hourigan isn't receiving visitors.'

'The police are never visitors, Mrs Kelly. We're just gate-crashers.'

He waited patiently; she was gone almost five minutes. Two dogs came down the driveway and barked savagely at him on the other side of the tall gates. Then the intercom crackled again; her voice sounded like broken glass being rattled in a tin cup. 'You're lucky he's such a gentleman. Come in when I've put the dogs away.'

There was a further delay, then the gates swung open. The

first thing Malone saw as he and Clements walked up to the house was the red Jaguar parked in the driveway. Michele sat behind the wheel, his head laid back as if he were asleep.

Mrs Kelly was waiting for them at the front door. 'Don't keep Mr Hourigan too long. He's going to a dinner, a business dinner.'

No mourning period here, not whilst there was more money to be made. Fingal Hourigan was in black tie and dinner suit, looking like a crafty penguin, an emperor who, given the chance, would have made money out of Antarctica. His daughter Brigid, still in the crimson turban she had worn to the funeral and a blue woollen dress, was seated at the grand piano, the keyboard open in front of her.

'I hope this isn't going to become a regular habit, Inspector.' Hourigan was a frank host; in one's eighties, politeness only wastes valuable time. 'What's it about now?'

Malone told him bluntly, watching both him and Brigid. The old man showed no expression; Brigid dropped her hand, made a discordant thump on the keyboard. 'Both Father Marquez and I had threats over the phone today. I'd like to interview Mr Paredes or Mr Domecq. Are they staying here?'

'What makes you think they have anything to do with what you've just told me?' He was still standing, leaning on the silver walking-stick; he made no gesture for them to be seated. Behind him Brigid had quietly closed the keyboard lid and stood up.

'I'll tell you that, Mr Hourigan, when I've talked to them. Are they here?'

'No.'

'Yes,' said Brigid. 'They're in the study. I'll get them.'

She had to pass her father to go out of the drawing-room. He put up the walking-stick, blocking her way. 'You've just made me out a liar.'

'That's what you are, Dad. I didn't make you one.'

She pushed the walking-stick aside and went on out of the room. She moved with dignity and grace, Malone remarked,

182

almost queenly. The Hourigans, no matter where they had come from, had learned the touch of class that arrogance gives.

Fingal looked at Malone. 'Do you have daughters, Inspector? They're much harder to handle than sons.'

'Even when the son is an archbishop?'

Fingal ignored that, looked at Clements. 'What do you do, sergeant? Just stand in the background?'

'Most of the time, yes,' said Clements. 'Sometimes you learn more that way.'

Then Fingal looked at them both, his bright-blue eyes glinting in the light of the expensive lamps surrounding him; he was afraid of shadows, there were all those gathered in his past like a black storm. 'You're a couple of smart-arses.'

'We try,' said Malone.

Then Brigid came back into the room with Paredes and Domecq. They were better- and more prosperous-looking then their photos had shown. Both of them were immaculately dressed in navy-blue mohair, their white shirts with the starched collars reminding Malone of a fashion he had seen in old magazines. They had the air of men prepared for any situation.

'This wasn't my idea that you should meet Inspector Malone,' Fingal told them.

Paredes smiled politely, looking unperturbed. 'There is nothing to be concerned about, Mr Hourigan. Back in the States we are always being interviewed. The FBI, Congressional committees . . . It is the lot of political refugees.'

Malone had met this ploy before: be frank, lay everything out in the open. Well, *almost* everything. 'Mr Paredes, did you ever meet Sister Mary Magdalene?'

Paredes glanced at Brigid, who had gone back to sit at the piano. 'Miss Hourigan's daughter? Never. A dreadful tragedy . . . We came here today to pay our respects to Miss Hourigan.'

'What about you, Mr Domecq? Did you ever meet her?'

'I never had the pleasure. If she was as charming as her mother ...' He gave Brigid a gambler's smile, all charm and challenge under the dark moustache. She gave him no smile in return. She had opened the keyboard and now she struck a note, one that sounded curiously flat.

Domecq's voice was the one Malone had heard over the phone. 'Where were you this evening, Mr Domecq? Say three-quarters of an hour ago?'

'Why, I was here.' Domecq looked surprised; or feigned it. 'I was upstairs, having a bath.'

'I can vouch for that,' said Fingal. 'You're barking up the wrong tree, Inspector. You're also being bloody insulting. I think I'll have a word with your superiors.'

'I think you already have, Mr Hourigan. He passed on the word this morning. But maybe you'd like to have a word with the Commissioner? I'm working directly under him.'

Fingal said nothing for a moment, then he nodded his head in appreciation. 'You are a smart-arse.'

'I'm glad to hear that,' said Brigid from her place at the piano. She looked as if she might at any moment start playing, perhaps some martial music. 'I'm relying on you, Inspector, and you too, Sergeant, to find out who murdered my daughter. Nobody else seems to care.'

Most other mothers, Malone thought, would have broken down at that. But Brigid Hourigan was in control of herself; whatever turmoil of grief and anger was going on inside her, none of it showed on the surface. Malone recognized an ally, though he wondered how much she, being a Hourigan, would demand of him and Clements.

'I might have cared more if you had brought her home sooner,' said Fingal. 'I hardly knew the girl.'

Malone felt suddenly uncomfortable; behind him he sensed that Clements felt the same way. Even Paredes and Domecq looked as if they wanted to be gone from the room. Family tensions were the smallest of wars, understood by everyone and the wounds felt accordingly.

Brigid seemed to sense the others' embarrassment; she changed the subject. 'Did Father Marquez have any family?'

'Just his mother, as far as I know.'

'I must call on her – I feel we owe it to her. If it had not been for Teresa... I think I need a drink. Where is the liquor kept, Dad?' Evidently she didn't know her way round her father's house.

He hesitated, then nodded towards a flamboyantly inlaid bureau. 'In there.'

She went to the bureau, pulled at a handle and the whole top opened up to expose two shelves of cut-glass decanters and expensive glasses. 'How cute! Where's the ice – in the bottom drawer?'

It was: the bottom drawer was a shallow refrigerator. Fingal realized that none of his visitors, least of all his daughter, was impressed; or if they were, not in the way he had intended. The bureau would be thrown out tomorrow. He had begun to weaken: he could be made to look small. And all because of his daughter.

Brigid took her whisky straight, except for one ice cube. She held the glass up to the men enquiringly, but they all shook their heads. Then, still moving with dignified grace, she went back to the piano stool. She looked at Paredes and Domecq with calm hostility.

'Both of those young people died because of what you two gentlemen are trying to do.'

'You are mistaken, Miss Brigid,' said Paredes, as calm as she. 'Our visit to Australia has nothing to do with Nicaragua.'

'Bullshit,' said Brigid without raising her voice; somehow she even made the word sound dignified. 'They are here, Inspector, with my brother the Archbishop to raise money for their precious Contras. Teresa told me all about it.'

'You are treading on dangerous ground here,' said her father. 'You're committing slander.'

'Dad –' She smiled, took a sip of her whisky. 'When I was growing up, our house stank with slander. You never had a good word to say for anyone, even the nuns who taught me. If Señor Paredes and Señor Domecq think I'm slandering them, let them sue me. They have two good witnesses, *police* witnesses. Would you speak for the plaintiffs, Inspector?'

The interrogation had been taken away from Malone, but he didn't mind. 'I don't think so, Miss Hourigan. But as your father says, you're treading on dangerous ground.'

She caught the warning; but she seemed careless of the risk she was running. She looked into her glass and, with her face turned downwards, Malone saw the tears glistening on the long eyelashes. The grief in her was about to burst out.

'Mr Paredes, Mr Domecq,' said Malone, 'I'd like you to come with us. We have some questions – I think it would be better if I didn't ask them here.'

'Do you have a warrant?' said Fingal.

'It's only for questioning, Mr Hourigan. But if you want to make an issue of it, I'll see the Commissioner . . .'

Fingal stared at him, then he turned to the two Nicaraguans. 'Go with him, Francisco. I'll have my lawyer there as soon as possible.'

'I'd like your son to come with us, too,' said Malone. 'Where is the Archbishop?'

There was no smirk; but there was a flash of triumphant satisfaction on the shrewd old face.

'You've missed him. He left for Rome an hour ago.'

NINE

I

'You can go in my car, Señor Paredes,' said Fingal Hou
then abruptly changed his mind: 'No, I'll need it. Tr
police cars – they're comfortable enough.'

The change of mind was abruptly rude; but Ma
amused, saw the reason for it. Fingal, at this stage, wa
no public connection with the Contra agents; the Hou
Rolls-Royce would be too obvious an advertisement. Let
Paredes and Domecq travel in a slum for tonight.

On the ride in to Homicide Domecq looked bewildere
if, in what had seemed like Heaven, God had turned o
have no influence. 'Don't you know who Señor Houriga

'No,' said Clements dead-pan into the driving mirror,
is he?'

Malone, half-turned in the front seat, saw Paredes
thinly. This isn't the first time he's ridden in the bac
police car, Malone thought; the older man was a vete
many and varied situations. Interrogating him was no
to be easy.

He said something in Spanish and Malone said,
English, Mr Paredes. It will make it easier for you.'

'In what way, Inspector? You're not threatening us
I just told my friend we are in the hands of honest c
only a matter of adjustment.'

That's the way we seem to be going on both side
case; but he was not going to tell Paredes that. M

Nicaraguan had already guessed it. He looked as confident in the back of the police car as any Police Commissioner.

Clements pulled the car up in front of the Remington Rand building. 'I thought you might like to take 'em in the front entrance, Inspector. I'll put the car in the garage.'

Malone got out and waited for Paredes and Domecq to follow him. He was not sure that he wanted to see any reporter idling his time up on the sixth floor, but if one should be there and ask embarrassing questions, could he be blamed if the reporter made the wrong inference from the evasive answers?

There were, however, no reporters visible. As they had come in across the pavement to the front door of the building, four young men had passed them. One of them made a *moue* of his lips and blew a sour kiss to Domecq, who glanced in puzzlement at Malone.

'He thinks you're a cop,' said Malone. 'The gay district starts just up the street.'

'You have a gay community here?' Paredes sounded as if he found the thought distasteful; behind the sleek conservative look was an old-time Latin macho man. 'A district?'

'Oh, we're up with everything here. We're not as behind the times as you seem to think.'

When they got out of the lift on the sixth floor both Nicaraguans looked around them, as if not believing where they had been brought. '*This* is Police Headquarters? A private office block?'

'No, this is just Homicide.'

Paredes smiled, still looking around him. 'And you say you're not behind the times?'

'Remington Rand sponsor us,' said Malone. 'Next year IBM are taking us over. Or is it the CIA? You'd know about them, wouldn't you?'

'The CIA? Never heard of them.' Paredes smiled again, but Malone could see that, for the first time, the Nicaraguan looked unsure of himself. Malone decided to push him a little more off-balance.

'Who made the decision to threaten me and Father Marquez?' he said bluntly. 'You or Mr Domecq?'

'I have no idea what you are talking about.' Paredes had recovered; the acting was perfect.

Malone looked at Domecq. 'We have a tape of your last call, Mr Domecq. You probably know that voice-prints are as good as finger-prints, they're just as incriminating.'

Malone's own acting was perfect. So was Clements's, who had just arrived: he didn't even blink at Malone's bald lie. Both men, however, knew they would be marooned like shags on a rock if, or rather when, Domecq asked for a copy of the tape.

They were saved by the belle. She came walking down the aisle between the desks; the other detectives in the big room stopped work and turned to stare after her. She wore a revealing cocktail dress, with a matching shawl thrown over her shoulder; she was blonde and glamorous, but she also looked business-like; she gave the impression that she would be business-like even if she were naked. But she would never be any man's whore.

'Inspector Malone?' She had a pleasant voice, made only slightly artificial by the fluting vowels taught her at one of the more expensive eastern suburbs schools. Malone privately thought of it as the Ascham accent, easily acquired by the poor but socially ambitious just by standing outside the school gates and listening to the mums waiting for their daughters. 'I'm Zara Kersey.'

He recognized her now, if only from her photos which were a constant feature in the Sunday newspapers. She was known to the society columnists as the Queen of the Freeloaders; no charity ball, no gallery opening, no fashion launching was complete without Zara Kersey. A widow, she had once been married to a lawyer who, suiciding, had finished up at the bottom of the harbour with the load of tax evasion schemes he had devised and for which he was to have been prosecuted. She had been left three children and no money; that was when she had taken up freeloading. She had also taken up her husband's shattered practice; she had a law degree that she had never used up till then. Now, seven years later, she was one of the most successful commercial lawyers in Sydney. Malone wondered why Fingal had sent her and not a criminal eagle.

'Mr Hourigan sent me to represent and advise you,' she told the two Nicaraguans.

Domecq almost fell over himself to show his appreciation; he would have followed a skirt into Hades. Paredes, however, was not impressed. 'I am accustomed to lawyers looking less – seductive?'

She flicked a finger at the low-cut silver dress she wore. 'Take no notice of this. I've just come from a party to launch a new perfume.' She held out a wrist to Domecq, the ladies' man, and he sniffed at it like a bloodhound doused with a bucketful of clues. 'Like it?'

'Let Sergeant Clements have a sniff,' said Malone. 'He's been seduced by half the girls on the perfume counter at DJ's.'

Mrs Kersey withdrew her arm and was suddenly brisk. 'Is there any charge against my clients, Inspector?'

'None so far. We're just having a little get-together.'

'I've heard of you. You're supposed to be a hard nut to crack.'

'Just non-seduceable, that's all,' said Malone.

It seemed to him that she would be above using what had once been called womanly wiles; but he was in no mood for a skirmish between the sexes. She was a lawyer and he was a cop and he wanted no gender differences. He had a natural sympathy for women, but he was uncomfortable with them as opponents. He had always been glad that women had never played his class of cricket.

'Your clients don't have to talk, but it might pay them to listen to some of the questions we have to put to them.'

'Questions such as what?'

Malone looked at Paredes. 'Are you doing any business

with a company called Austarm?'

Paredes looked at Zara Kersey and she said, 'Austarm is a perfectly legitimate business, Inspector. I myself drew up its articles of association. It makes small arms. It supplies the Australian Army, if you are looking for credentials. What's the relevance of that question?'

'Relevant to what, Mrs Kersey?'

She had made a mistake; but she had got out of worse traps. 'You're not interested in legitimate business deals.'

'If they're legitimate, Mr Paredes won't have anything to hide. What are you buying?'

Paredes hesitated; then, on a nod from Zara Kersey, he said, 'Rifles and machine-guns.'

'Austarm is one of Mr Hourigan's companies, a subsidiary of Ballyduff Holdings?'

'Correct,' said Mrs Kersey.

'Is there an export licence for these arms?' said Clements, and Malone looked at him gratefully. Clements always had a good practical question buried away amongst his notes.

'Yes. Mr Hourigan has arranged that.'

'I'm sure he has,' said Malone, wondering which conduit Fingal had used to make the connection in Canberra. 'But why him and not Sir Jonathan Tewsday? He runs Mr Hourigan's companies, doesn't he? Is Archbishop Hourigan involved in all this? Is he the one who's arranging the finance?'

'Where did you get such an outrageous idea?' Zara Kersey, too, could act.

'From a letter his niece wrote to a young priest, Father Marquez. He was murdered tonight.'

She had apparently been briefed before she got here; she showed no surprise. 'Neither my clients nor Mr Hourigan and the Archbishop had anything to do with murder.'

'The murderer tried to kill the Inspector too,' said Clements quietly.

That shocked Mrs Kersey. 'I wasn't told that! I'm sorry, Inspector ... Well, now I can understand your prejudice ...'

'I'm not prejudiced,' said Malone, though he knew he was. Clements's quiet remark had brought back the event of an hour ago with shattering clarity. He could feel himself trembling inside, as if his very foundations were about to give way. He was silent for a moment, gathering some control, then he said, 'I'm just curious. You're not a criminal lawyer, but you must be used to entanglements in your own field. This one is chock-a-block with entanglements. And –' his voice hardened, though it got no louder – 'I'm going to get to the bottom of it! If that's being prejudiced, then that's what I am!'

'There may be cross-connections, Inspector – life is full of them, as you well know. But there is no evidence of any connection on the part of my clients with the murder of the priest and the attempt on your life.'

'The Inspector says he was threatened by Señor Domecq,' said Paredes. 'He says he has a tape of the telephone call.'

'Is that so, Inspector?' Zara Kersey gave Malone a hard stare. 'You'll let us hear it, of course.'

'No.'

'Why not?'

'You'll hear it when we lay charges against Mr Domecq.'

'You're bluffing, aren't you, Inspector?'

'No more than you, Mrs Kersey.' He looked at Domecq, changed tack: 'When you came out of the Quality Couch last Saturday night, did you bump into Sister Mary Magdalene? Had she followed you there?'

'The Quality Couch?' Domecq tried to look as if he were being questioned about a bedding store.

'The brothel in Surry Hills.'

Paredes and Zara Kersey looked sharply at Domecq; he just sat very still, a gambler who had been dealt a very bad hand. It was obvious that Paredes did not know his colleague had been to the brothel; anger darkened the older man's face, but he said nothing. At last Zara Kersey said, 'You don't have to answer that question, Mr Domecq. It may incriminate you.'

'He was at the Quality Couch last Saturday night,' Malone told her. 'He's already been identified.'

'You'll produce the witness or witnesses?'

'When the time comes. Well, Mr Domecq, what about Sister Mary Magdalene? Was she outside the brothel when you came out Saturday night?'

Domecq's head was bent, as if he was ashamed of having been in a brothel. Or maybe, Malone thought, he's afraid of Paredes. The latter's silence was more threatening than an outburst of anger.

At last Domecq lifted his head. 'She wasn't there – at least, I didn't see her. I told you – I never met her.'

'Not even at Mr Hourigan's house? She'd been there.'

'We never met the young lady,' said Paredes, his voice gravelly.

'Did you ever meet Father Marquez?'

'No.'

'Were you with Archbishop Hourigan when he was in Nicaragua last year? Oh, we know he was there, all right. It was in the letter I told you about.'

Paredes hesitated, then nodded. 'Yes, we were with him. We flew down with him from Miami.'

'But you didn't meet Sister Mary, his niece?'

Again the hesitation, then: 'We saw her only from a distance. I tell you, Inspector, we had nothing to do with the death of this young woman! Why should we kill an innocent girl like that?'

'I don't know. Why should Mr Domecq threaten me and Father Marquez?'

'You're making unfounded charges, Inspector,' said Zara Kersey flatly. She stood up, wrapping the silver shawl round her shoulders with an extravagant fling. 'I think you have taken up enough of my clients' time. Unless you care to produce a warrant or make some sort of definite charges, we'll be leaving.'

Malone said nothing for a long moment; then he stood up.

He looked at Zara Kersey, not the two Nicaraguans. 'It looks, then, as if we'll have to bring Archbishop Hourigan back from Rome. He seems to be the key to this whole mess.'

'I'll tell Mr Hourigan.'

'If you don't, I'm sure someone else will. Good-night, Mrs Kersey. I don't think that perfume you're wearing has much future. It's already wearing off.'

She wasn't offended; she had become that much of a lawyer. She just smiled and shook her head. 'You're just not a ladies' man, Inspector.' Unlike Domecq who, bouncy again, as if he had found good cards at the bottom of the deck, had offered her his arm. 'You'll be hearing from me again.'

'I'm sure I will.' Then he looked at Paredes. 'And from you, too, Mr Paredes? Or Mr Domecq?'

The older Nicaraguan just stared at him, then turned on his heel and followed Domecq and Zara Kersey down between the desks and out of the big room. The other detectives looked after them, then turned towards Malone.

'She has a lovely arse, Scobie. How come you get all the cases with good-looking birds!'

'Anyone can have this one,' said Malone, but under his breath.

'What do we do now?' Clements looked lugubrious, ready to throw in the towel.

'I shove my neck out.' Even in his own ears it sounded like suicidal bravado.

2

'Daddy, why do people kill each other? Especially a nun?'

'If I knew that, Claire, I'd be the smartest cop in the world.'

'Well, I gotta admit,' said Maureen, the TV addict, 'Sonny Crockett in *Miami Vice* is puzzled, too, sometimes.'

'I'm glad to hear it. I'm tired of being compared to those two over-dressed smart alecks.'

'Smart-arse is the word,' said Maureen, who occasionally sneaked a look at ABC telemovies, where language was freer.

'Not in this house it ain't,' said Malone.

He was in the girls' bedroom saying good-night to them. When he had arrived home they had just finished their homework, had their baths and got into bed. Tom was already asleep in his room, dead to the world and its cares. Malone, very much alive to its cares and worn out by them, had hoped for a quick good-night kiss, but as soon as he had walked into the room he had seen that Claire was troubled. It turned out that the murder of Sister Mary Magdalene had been the talk of the school yesterday and today and then this evening, on the TV news, there had been the story of the killing of Father Marquez.

'She didn't teach our class,' said Claire. 'She taught Year Eleven and Twelve. But she was always fun to be around when we were playing netball. Sometimes she'd play – she was pretty rough, a real tomboy, you know?'

'Why did they call her Red Ned?' asked Maureen.

But he wasn't going to get into politics, not tonight; the day had been political enough and tomorrow would be worse. 'It's time you went to sleep.'

They lay on their pillows looking at him. Claire, blonde and promising to be beautiful, with a composure that was old for her years; Maureen, dark and vivacious, with his mother's long Irish lip and plenty of the cheeky lip he himself had had as a boy. All his and Lisa's and to be protected. But he knew, better than most fathers, how difficult it would be to shelter them, even against the possibility of murder.

Lisa came to the doorway. 'It's late, girls, and Dad's tired.'

'Is it any use saying prayers for Sister Mary and Father Marquez?' said Claire.

'It's always worth saying a prayer for anyone. I say them all the time.'

'Who for?' said Maureen, who had confessed to asking questions of the priest in the confessional.

'You. Claire and Tom. Dad. Everyone.'

'God, I didn't know you were so *holy*!'

Lisa switched out the light and led Malone out of the room and down to the kitchen, where his supper was on the table. 'Steak and kidney pie.'

'You always know just what a man needs. How do you do it?' He sat down and she poured him a glass of red wine from a cardboard cask. He raised the glass to her. 'I'm glad I'm home tonight.'

'So am I.' She poured herself a glass and sat down opposite him. 'Were you close to Father Marquez when he was shot?'

He hesitated, then nodded. The wine in her glass shook; then she put it to her mouth and gulped, as if it were medicine she was loath to take. He watched her carefully, waiting for some tears; but he should have known better. She lowered the glass, looked at him steadily. 'How close to him were you?'

'Let's talk about something else –'

'No!' She spilled some wine, but ignored it: she who was so careful of any crumb dropped or food splashed by the children. 'Let's talk about what happened tonight! Did they try to kill you, too?'

'I don't know,' he lied. The meat in the pie was already in small chunks, but he applied himself to cutting the chunks even smaller. He picked up a piece of kidney, chewed on it, hardly tasted it. 'The point is, I'm here, safe at home.'

'For how long, though? Safe, I mean.'

She looked around the kitchen, as if she were trying to imagine it as a bunker. It was her pride, all quality timber and copper and brass; a combination fridge and freezer, a double-oven stove, a Swedish dish-washer: it had been their biggest extravagance in their renovation of the house, but he had never begrudged her a penny of it. He had realized after he had married her that, despite her education, her wide travels and her successful career as a government private secretary and then in public relations, she was a *hausfrau* at heart. She was an almost perfect mother to the children, a wonderful lover to him in bed, but it was from this kitchen that she ran her life, the children's and, as far as the Police Department would allow, his.

She had put down the wine, no longer able to taste it. Almost automatically she now reached for the salt cellar and sprinkled salt on the red stain on the tablecloth.

The refrigerator suddenly started up: the sudden humming seemed to bring all his nerves together in an electric shock. 'Darl, for Christ's sake – I'm all *right*! If they meant to get me tonight, they won't try again –'

'Why not?' She lifted the tablecloth, put a paper napkin under the stain.

'Because it won't help their cause –'

'Who's they?'

He sighed, pushed his plate away. 'I wish I knew. I'm going round in bloody circles on this one. The only constant is Archbishop bloody Hourigan stuck there in the centre of it all ...'

'What if they come *here*?' She looked around her again, as if she meant *here*, this kitchen, not the rest of the house. 'I don't want any threats against Claire and Maureen and Tom ...'

'Do you want me to get you police protection?' He hated the thought, but it had to be faced.

'No. Well – I don't know ...' She stared at the red stain on the tablecloth. 'It looks like blood, doesn't it?'

'Stop it!' He had never seen her like this before. 'No, it doesn't. Blood goes darker ... Christ Almighty, why am I talking like this? Look, I'll get on to Jack Browning, the sergeant down at Randwick. We'll work something out. The thing is, I don't want a police car parked outside the house twenty-four hours a day.'

'Neither do I.' She had slumped forward, but now she straightened up. 'Finish your dinner, there are poached pears for dessert. An empty stomach's not going to do you any good. Are you going to arrest Archbishop Hourigan?'

'He's gone back to Rome.'

'What are you going to do then?'

'I'm going after him, if they'll let me.'

3

'No!' said Assistant Commissioner Zanuch emphatically. 'The idea is ridiculous!'

'I agree,' said Chief Superintendent Danforth, who never disagreed with his superiors, not now, so close to retirement and his superannuation.

'Let's hear your reasons, Inspector,' said Commissioner Leeds.

The four of them were in the Commissioner's office at headquarters. Malone had put in his report, a copy to each of his superiors rising in rank; it was unusual for a daily report to go direct to the Commissioner, but neither Zanuch nor Danforth had remarked on it. They knew their places in this particular case. Malone had been sent for a half-hour after he had filed his report and, five minutes into this room, he had asked for an extradition warrant against Archbishop Kerry Hourigan.

'Because I don't think we're going to get anywhere in this case without him. He's the key, sir.'

'It's too hot,' said Zanuch. 'We'll get our arses burned off.'

'That only happens if you sit on something,' said Leeds. 'I don't think we can sit on this one. Apart from the two murders, I'm bloody angry at the attempt on Inspector Malone's life!' He was too cool to show obvious anger, but the tension in him was apparent. He clenched a fist, the knuckles showing pale, but refrained from thumping his desk with it. 'For that reason alone, I'd like the Archbishop back here in Sydney so that we can question him.'

'It's not going to be easy,' said Zanuch, backing down. 'I

don't think it's possible to extradite anyone from the Vatican. Even the Italians can't get anyone out of there.'

'I'm afraid the Assistant Commissioner is right,' said Malone when Leeds looked questioningly at him. Clements, the non-Catholic, had done some homework. 'They treasure their own – I read that somewhere. The Pope makes his own judgement about his sinners – I read that, too.'

'What sort of books do you read? said Danforth, who read none. Then he saw the Commissioner's cold look and he ran a hand over his head, searching for another thought: 'What's the point of going to Rome, then?'

'I think we can scare him into coming home. He and his old man don't want a fuss. And neither do those Contra blokes, Paredes and Domecq.'

'Do you think those are the two who ordered those murders?' said the Commissioner. 'You don't come out and say that in your report.'

'I don't have any evidence, sir. None that would stand up in court. For all I know, it could have been Old Man Hourigan.'

He glanced at Danforth out of the corner of his eye as he said that. The big beefy hand went to the top of the short-back-and-sides, but there was no thought there at the moment. But Malone knew there would be before the morning was out, even if Fingal Hourigan had to put it there.

'You sure as hell have some wild ideas,' said Zanuch; then he looked at Leeds. 'What's the Premier going to say about this? He'll have to have a say in it, won't he?'

'Oh, I never thought he wouldn't,' said Leeds, unperturbed. 'I'll just let Inspector Malone argue his case before him.'

He looked at Malone and smiled his cool smile. Bugger it, thought Malone, why don't I transfer to something easy like Traffic or Public Relations?

In the Commissioner's car going down to the State Office Block, Leeds said, 'This is a messy one, Scobie.'

'I'm thinking of applying for a transfer out to Tibooburra.'

'You think there aren't any politics out there? Scobie, if ever you finish up in my job —'

'God forbid, sir.'

Leeds grinned. 'I think the chances are very slim. But if ever you do, you'll find out that police work is about fifty per cent politics.'

'I know that, sir, even at my level.'

They got out of the car outside of the tall black building at the corner of Macquarie and Bent. Malone wondered if any of the Premiers who had occupied the offices in this government building had ever been embarrassed by their address. He knew that the incumbent Premier wouldn't be: he had been bent all his life.

He was in a bent, bad mood this morning. 'Holy Jesus, John, bursting in on me like this! I'm Police Minister, but do I have to be worried by every little thing that goes wrong? Hullo, you're Malone, aren't you?' He never forgot a name: voter, friend, enemy. 'Oh Christ, it's not the Hourigan affair, is it? My secretary just said you wanted to see me, it was urgent ... What's up now?'

'I want Inspector Malone to go to Rome and bring back Archbishop Hourigan.' Malone was grateful for the way the Commissioner phrased the suggestion; he wasn't going to put one of his junior officers out on a limb on his own. Not in this room, where the toughest axeman in the country reigned. 'An extradition order won't work, so it'll have to be by persuasion.'

'Stand-over stuff, you mean?' Hans Vanderberg might mince a phrase, but he never minced a meaning. 'You think the Vatican will put up with that?'

Leeds looked at Malone, the Catholic, assuming he knew

more about Vatican history. But Malone had never been interested in the Vatican till now; he was the sort of Catholic for whom it and its ruling were too remote. There were other ways to Heaven; or so he occasionally hoped. He had read bits and pieces about the intrigues and influence of the popes and cardinals; he knew that in the past some of them had used the gun and pike as much as the cross. He didn't fancy his chances, but he would ask Lisa to pray for him. She seemed to be praying for everyone else.

'I'd like to try my luck, sir,' he said.

'It'll cost money,' said the Premier, who had spent millions on memorials to himself; he was known not only as The Dutchman but also as the Human Foundation Stone. 'How do you cops travel? Economy?'

'Overseas, I think he should go business class,' said Leeds.

'Jesus!' said Vanderberg. 'Haven't you heard a penny saved doesn't make a pound look foolish?'

'No,' said Leeds and wondered if anyone else had.

The Dutchman grinned. 'If you were one of my Ministers, John, you'd be on the back-benches in no time. Well, all right, Inspector, you can go to Rome, but for Christ's sake, keep it discreet. Are you discreet?'

Malone didn't look at his Commissioner. 'I try to be, sir.'

'Well, try your hardest in Rome. No publicity, you hear? You run into any of them *papapizza*, whatever they call 'em, them Italian photographers, you turn and run, okay?' Then he looked at Leeds. 'What are you going to do with the Archbishop when you get him back here?'

'That depends on how far Inspector Malone gets with his interrogation of him. We have to get to the bottom of this, Premier. This could get much bigger. If a firm in this State becomes a major supplier of arms to the Contras in Nicaragua —'

Vanderberg sat up. 'You didn't say anything about that!'

'I was saving that for the final argument,' said Leeds and told him about Austarm.

'Holy Christ!' God the Son was being called upon so frequently, Malone wondered whose side He was on. Maybe all the odds were not with the Archbishop. 'Can you smell the stink? We'll have every lily-livered group in the country, the anti-war mob, the Mothers for Peace, the Greenies, they'll all be out there in Macquarie Street demonstrating!'

'Not the Greenies, surely.'

'They'll join any bloody demo!' The Dutchman had never found a vote amongst the conservationists, so he couldn't be expected to be fair-minded about them.

'Are you in favour of the Contras?' said Leeds mildly.

'Christ, I'm in favour of no one!' Which was true; excluding himself, of course. 'Foreign policy's no concern of mine. Nothing that happens outside Sydney Heads has ever won or lost a vote for me. Who's this crowd – Austarm?'

Leeds looked at Malone and the latter said, 'They are one of Fingal Hourigan's companies.'

The Premier's head shrank into his shoulders, he sank down in his big leather chair. He looked like an ancient turtle that had just found major cracks in its shell. 'Jesus, what other bad news have you got?'

Leeds couldn't resist a small smile. 'I think the sooner we get the Archbishop back here, the better, don't you?'

On the way back to headquarters Leeds smiled. 'You can have a week in Rome, no more. I'll have Mr Zanuch arrange your ticket and expenses – it'll come out of the Special Fund. If anyone wants to know where you are, you've gone on compassionate leave. Do you have a sick grandmother who lives somewhere out of Sydney? Tibooburra, maybe?'

'I'll have to tell my sidekick, Sergeant Clements. He can keep his mouth shut. What about Superintendent Danforth?'

'I'll attend to him.' One knew that he would: the Commissioner had no time for the veteran detective.

Malone wondered if he should tell the Commissioner about Danforth's connection with either Hourigan or Tewsday; but what proof did he have? He decided to remain quiet. Fingal

Hourigan or Tewsday would learn no more from Danforth than they would know from the Archbishop in Rome as soon as Malone landed there.

'Is your passport in order? Good. Leave tomorrow, on Qantas. The sooner we get this over and done with . . .' Leeds looked at his junior officer. 'How do you and I get ourselves into these situations, Scobie?'

'I don't think it's our fault. If human nature were different, it wouldn't happen.'

Which, of course, is the explanation for History.

5

Next morning Lisa drove Malone to the airport. He had said goodbye to the children, all of whom wanted to know why they couldn't go with him – 'It's business.'

'Who with?' said Maureen. 'Mussolini or the Pope?'

'Mussolini's dead and the Pope is travelling somewhere – he's never home these days.'

'Neither are you,' said Claire.

'I'll bet he takes his wife and kids with him,' said Tom.

'The Pope doesn't have a wife and kids. He doesn't know how lucky he is.' But he pressed Lisa's hand as he said it.

'That's enough,' said Lisa. 'Kiss Dad goodbye. Maybe he'll bring you back an Italian T-shirt or something.'

'Yuk,' said Claire, already rolling herself into a ball of style. 'Italian is *last* year.'

'What's this year?'

'Japanese.'

'I'll come home via Tokyo. Hooroo. Take care of Mum.'

'I don't think I'll be a policeman,' said Tom. 'Always leaving your wife and kids.'

'Who's been coaching you? Get off to school before I arrest the lot of you.'

When the children had gone to school, Malone and Lisa

went to bed. 'I hate goodbyes at airports,' she said.

'They wouldn't let you do this at Mascot. Not even in the VIP lounge.'

'Ah, that's nice. I love you. Be careful.'

'You haven't stopped the Pill, have you?'

'I don't mean *that*. In Rome, stupid. Oh yes!'

Then they both forgot Rome and danger and politics. Here in each other's arms was the safest place in the world. Love isn't blind, but it can provide a merciful fog.

At the airport Clements was waiting for them. 'Thought I'd come out and see you off. Wish I were going with you.'

'Why don't you go instead of him?' said Lisa.

Clements looked at the two of them, then bit his lip. 'Like that, eh? Have I turned up in the middle of a domestic situation? When I was in uniform, I always hated those sort of calls, a domestic situation.'

Lisa kissed him, which did something towards making his day. 'I wish you *were* going with him. I'd feel happier.'

'Keep an eye on her and the kids, will you, Russ?' said Malone. 'The boys at Randwick are going to be dropping by, but Lisa doesn't want a car parked outside the house all day and night.'

'Changing the subject,' said Clements, 'look who's just checked in.'

Zara Kersey, looking like an advertisement for travel out-fitters, the Vuitton luggage brand-new and discreetly obvious, was standing at the first-class counter. She turned, saw Malone and smiled at him.

'Isn't that Zara Kersey?' said Lisa, who, disdainfully, never missed the social pages of the Sunday newspapers. 'How do you know her?'

'She's Fingal Hourigan's lawyer.'

'Is she going to Rome?'

'Probably,' he said gloomily. The word had already been got to Fingal Hourigan and the battalions were being drawn up. 'The Swiss Guards will probably be out to meet her.'

'She'll probably to able to accommodate them. I think I'd better come with you.'

'What about the kids?'

'Let Russ look after them. I wonder what perfume she wears – Arpège?'

'I think I'll leave you two,' said Clements, grinning. 'Look after yourself, Scobie. My old Congregational mum says you can never trust the Pope.'

'It's not him I'm afraid of. Look after Lisa and the kids, Russ.'

They shook hands, then Clements lumbered away. Lisa said, 'I wish I had a sister to marry him. He'd make a wonderful uncle for the kids.'

'Two cops in the family? You'd worry yourself stiff.'

They went up to the Qantas private lounge, poured themselves some coffee and sat down. Then Zara Kersey came in, looked around and saw that the only vacant seat was next to them. She looked at Malone enquiringly and after a moment's hesitation he shrugged and nodded. She came across, sat down and arranged her body and legs like a model and smiled at Lisa.

'I'm sorry to intrude. Husbands and wives should have a special section set apart for them. You *are* Mrs Malone? I'm Zara Kersey.'

Malone got up and went to get her some coffee and Lisa said, 'How did you know I was Mrs Malone?'

'Oh, he has that look. A happily married man.'

Lisa looked across at Malone at the coffee bench, then back at Zara Kersey. 'How do you know? I don't think I've ever noticed.'

Mrs Kersey smiled. 'Come on, Mrs Malone. Wives notice *everything* about their husbands. Especially anything they themselves are responsible for.'

Malone came back with the coffee. He had noticed that most of the men in the lounge had turned to look at Zara Kersey, but she had the knack of seeming unaware of their stares. Now Malone realized that the men were also looking at Lisa and suddenly he felt that simple-minded pride that all men feel when in the company of beautiful women amidst a group of envious men. He sat down, all at once relaxed. He knew who was the more beautiful of the two women, and she was his. He should have been disgusted with his smug possessiveness, but love is a form of possession.

'Seems we're going to Rome for the same reason, Inspector.'

'I guess so, except that we're on opposite sides. You're lucky to get away, aren't you? I thought you were the busiest lawyer in Sydney.'

'There are degrees of busy-ness, Inspector – you know that. When the Commissioner calls, do you tell him some Superintendent has first call on you? What are his priorities at home, Mrs Malone?'

'Oh, the children and I are a long last,' said Lisa, but she held his hand to show she was still in the race. 'What's it like working for a man as powerful as Mr Hourigan?'

'Exhilarating. Demanding. He thinks all women should be slaves.'

'You'll feel at home, then, in the Vatican.'

'I doubt it. I think your husband and I are going to be the odd ones out in Rome, even though we're on opposite sides.' Then their flight was announced and she said, 'Are you travelling first, Inspector? Perhaps we can sit together, if Mrs Malone doesn't mind?'

'He's in business class,' said Lisa. 'That's what he's on – business. Have a nice trip, Mrs Kersey.'

They smiled at each other like ice queens: Mary of Scotland and Elizabeth of England might have shown the same warmth towards each other. Zara Kersey got up and left and Malone sniffed the air.

'She's not wearing Arpège. You think I'm safe?'

Lisa held his hand all the way down to the passport control gates. There she kissed him and clung to him. 'If it gets dangerous, come home at once. Nothing is worth losing you.'

'Are we talking about Mrs Kersey?'

'You know we're not!' she said angrily; then softened and kissed him again. 'Ring me every day. Reverse the charges if you can't put it on expenses.'

'Make it short and sweet. It's a dollar-eighty a minute – I looked it up.'

'Tightwad.'

He left her with an aching regret, as if he were leaving her for ever. He was sometimes amazed at the depth of his love for her; but he knew from experience that the human heart had never been fully plumbed. In its depth could be found all the slime of human nature; but that was not all. Love went as deep as anything else, or everybody was a lost soul. He had only vaguely thought it out, but he believed it.

At Singapore Zara Kersey sought him out as he walked up and down the splendid transit lounge. When he had come through some years ago, the new Changi terminal had not been built; now it was one of the palaces of travel, the wayside station, the coach-stop raised to the luxury level. But outside it, he had read, in the city itself the hotels were empty, the stores uncrowded, the economy shaky.

'I thought you'd be in the duty-free shops,' she said.

'I'm not a shopper, never have been, even back home.'

'I love shopping, but not for bargains.' She said it without snobbery. 'Scobie – do you mind if we drop the Inspector and Mrs Kersey bit? – what do you want with the Archbishop?'

'Some answers, that's all.'

'That's all? You're not planning an arrest?'

'Is his old man expecting one? Zara –' he wondered what Lisa would think of this sudden intimacy, '– I don't think you realize what a mess you've landed in. I'm not sure of the proportions, but this is a bloody sight more than the murder of a nun and a priest.'

'But they're *your* interest, aren't they? You're just Homicide.'

'Sure, but this looks to me like a case of murder just being the stone in a pool.'

She looked at him with friendly amusement. 'You can be quite literary, can't you?'

'It's my wife's influence. What's that perfume you're wearing?'

'Poison, by Dior. Two drops and men have been known to fall dead at my feet.'

He grinned. 'My wife inoculated me just before she kissed me goodbye.'

'You're a nice man, Scobie. It's a pity we're on opposite sides.'

TEN

I

When the plane landed at Fiumicino airport there were no Swiss Guards to meet Zara Kersey. There was, however, Captain Aldo Goffi to meet Malone.

'Your Commissioner, Mr Leeds, met my chief, General della Porta, at an international conference of police. They are friends, by letter. Commissioner Leeds called the General and explained the situation. We understand your visit is *sub rosa*. Do you speak Italian?'

'*Ciao* and *arrivederci*.'

Goffi was an amiable man in his middle forties, thin and hollow-cheeked, his uniform sagging on him. He looked sad and experienced; on the drive into Rome Malone recognized the scars of police work. 'Are there politics in this, Inspector?'

'Sort of.'

'Ah, wouldn't it be splendid if all police work were just a shoot-out between the goods and the bads? Like in the old John Wayne films. I think I should have been a cowboy sheriff, a spaghetti Wyatt Earp. Where are you staying?'

'There wasn't time to book me in anywhere. What can you recommend that's cheap?'

'Is your police force as tidy with money as ours? Yes? Then I know a good *pensione*, run by a cousin of mine.' He smiled, showing big crooked teeth. 'Everyone has cousins in Italy.'

Malone had never been in Rome before. He had been abroad twice, once on a direct police trip to and from London, the other on a cheap excursion world trip with Lisa on their honeymoon; he had won $12,000 in a lottery and blown half of it on the trip. Rome had not been on their itinerary and now he looked out at the Eternal City with that scepticism that those of Celtic descent, bruised into cynicism by invaders, have about places other than their homeland. He would have been surprised to find that most Italians felt the same way, though for different reasons. After all, the Renaissance had been only yesterday.

The *pensione* was in a side street near the Forum. The cousin and his wife, Signor and Signora Pirelli, were of a size and disposition: they were built for laughter and Malone, a man of dry mirth, could see floods of it ahead. 'You like Italian food?' The signora rolled about with laughter, as if she had cracked a joke.

He always thought Italian food was for gummy gourmets; he liked food one could *chew*, a good steak or lamb chops. But: 'Love it, signora. That's why I've come to Rome.'

The Pirellis went off laughing and Goffi, a lugubrious man compared to them, said, 'You'll need a little sleep, eh? You must have jet lag. But General della Porta would like to see you this afternoon at four o'clock. He thinks you should see him before you approach anyone at the Vatican. He has his contacts there.'

'Cousins?'

Goffi smiled, shook hands with him; Malone, a modest man, was relieved when the captain didn't kiss him on both cheeks as he had his cousin. 'You and I are compatible, Inspector. I shall pick you up just before four.'

Malone slept till three, got up, showered, ate the fruit, cheese and bread that Signora Pirelli brought him and was waiting downstairs in the narrow entrance lobby when Goffi arrived at ten to four. 'The General is most un-Italian – he likes everyone to be punctual.'

'A man after my own heart.'

Goffi had a driver this afternoon, a ghost from the long-dead Mille Miglia; he drove through the Rome traffic as if the cars were no more than phantoms. Malone, a poor passenger even at dead slow, held his breath and kept his feet buried in the floor of the car. Goffi sat beside him relaxed and eager for compliments for his native city.

'You like Rome?'

'What I've seen of it,' said Malone, eyes glued on the impenetrable traffic ahead at which the driver was hurtling the car. 'Do you fellers ever have any accidents?'

'Not many,' said Goffi. 'And it's always the other driver's fault. Is that not right, Indello?'

'Yes, Captain,' said the driver, turning round and taking both hands off the wheel. 'All the time.'

Somehow they reached the Via del Quirinale and *carabinieri* headquarters. As they got out of the car Malone, legs shaking, looked back at the huge building that dominated this hill. 'What's that?'

'The Quirinale Palace. The President of the Republic lives there.'

'So close to police headquarters?'

Goffi caught the inference. 'Politics and the police go together, Inspector. Hasn't it always been the way.'

Malone grinned. 'I think you are going to be a great help to me, Captain.'

'It will be a pleasure.' Goffi's big ugly smile softened his gaunt face.

He led Malone into the big bleached ochre building that was *carabinieri* headquarters and up some wide stairs to the first floor. General della Porta's office made Commissioner Leeds's back home look like a closet; it was fit for the President of the Republic, if he wished to move from next door. The tall walls, separated from each other by what seemed to Malone a small ballroom, held aloft an elaborately carved ceiling. Tall narrow doors, two pairs of them, opened out on to a small balcony that overlooked the square below and the city beyond. Seated with his back to the doors, behind a huge desk, was a man who fitted the room. General Enrico della Porta had the look of a man who thought he should be commanding armies instead of a police force. He had a strong handsome face, if a little plump around the jowls, a grey military moustache which he kept brushing up with the knuckle of his right forefinger, and shrewd belligerent eyes. He would take not only the long view and the short view but the medium, too: he would be ready for any emergency.

But he was friendly: he got up and came round his desk, a small journey, to shake hands with Malone. 'Ah, Commissioner Leeds telephoned me and explained the situation. We have a problem, haven't we?' His English, like that of Goffi, was good. Since crime, and terrorism, had become international, police chiefs had had to improve their linguistic ability. Malone doubted that Leeds could speak anything but English, but that was his British heritage. It was the foreigners who had to broaden their languages. 'I have had dealings with the Vatican on many occasions. God's bureaucracy is far worse than any we have in the rest of Italy.'

'Did the Commissioner give you all the facts as we know them, General?'

'No, sit down and give them to me, Inspector.' He made the return trip to his chair behind the desk, sat down and stroked his moustache. He was wearing uniform, a sartorial splendour that added to his handsomeness; and he knew it. A braided cap lay on the desk, one that suggested, even at rest, that it would be worn at a jaunty angle. The General's vanity was often difficult for those who worked for him; what they didn't know was that it was difficult for him. He was that odd dichotomy, a vain man who wished he could be modest. 'Take notes, Captain Goffi.'

Malone gave them the history of the case, leaving out nothing; no Sydney newspapers or even Fingal Hourigan had a line into *carabinieri* headquarters. General della Porta listened without interrupting, something that Malone, with his small prejudices, had not expected from an Italian.

At last della Porta said, 'It is not going to be easy, Inspector. If the Vatican agreed to your taking the Archbishop back to Australia – indeed, if he agreed to go with you – it would be creating a precedent. And the Vatican hates to create a precedent, unless it holds a Vatican Council on it. It's the way with all religions. Are you a Catholic?'

'Sort of,' said Malone. 'I don't think they'd call me a *good* one.'

'We seem to be in the same mould, Inspector. But Captain Goffi here is a good Catholic, one of the best.' Malone would have had his doubts, but piety wasn't all pursed lips and steepled fingers. 'He's our conduit to the Vatican. He knows our contacts there and he'll lead you straight to them. I think you should talk to Monsignor Lindwall, he's English, before you approach Archbishop Hourigan. He works for the Archbishop in the Department for the Defence Against Subversive Religions.' He shook his head. 'What medieval titles they go in for! Sometimes I wonder that they don't drive around in chariots instead of their Mercedes-Benz.'

Malone, an iconoclast though a slightly reformed one, hadn't expected such disrespect for the Vatican so close to home. But then the Romans had had to live longer and closer with the Church than anyone else.

'Monsignor Lindwall was a missionary in Africa for thirty years. He has no time for bureaucracies, even though he works in one. He will tell you the best way to get over all the hurdles you are going to find over there.' He got up and motioned to Malone to follow him to the tall doors. They were open to the spring sunshine and he stood in the doorway and pointed across the city to the west. 'That's it, Inspector. The citadel, one of the smallest yet easily the most powerful city-state in the world. We Italians invented the city-state – well, perhaps the Greeks were ahead of us, but we developed it much further. That's the last survivor. Don't try storming it, that won't get you anywhere. The only way in is by trickery and subterfuge and burrowing. Monsignor Lindwall will tell you that – he's a Jesuit.'

Oh Christ, thought Malone in half a prayer, what have I got myself into? He looked out across Rome, across the old, pale-coloured buildings to the huge dome of St Peter's dominating the city as towering commercial buildings dominated the other cities he had known. Like most Australians he had little sense of ancient history, but a sediment of his Celtic heritage stirred in him, ghosts whispered to him out of long-ago mists that all men were connected by events. People had lived in this city for God knew how long, there had been voters and polling-booths here when Australia Felix was just a wilderness, there were buildings here far older than Australia as a nation or even a colony. And the Vatican, though its power was now limited by treaty, had ruled longer than any of those who had tried to challenge it. Now he, in a way, was challenging it again.

'We'll help you all we can, Inspector, but not in an obvious way. We have to live with them over there, but you can go back to Australia. So all our help will be unofficial and, as they say, under the lap. We Italians,' he smiled, showing what looked like more than the usual complement of teeth, 'are very good at under the lap. Good luck, Inspector. Please come back and see me before you return home, with or without the Archbishop.'

Malone thanked him and left, saying to Goffi as they went down the stairs and out of the building, 'I think he's on our side.'

'Up to a point, Inspector. Nobody at the top in Italy is ever fully committed to one side or the other. Except, of course, the Pope.'

'And Archbishop Hourigan.'

'Ah, but he's not Italian.'

There was another hair-raising drive down the Via Maggio XXIV, along the Corso Vittorio Emmanuel, over the Tiber and up the Via delle Conciliazone to St Peter's Square. Malone saw only sidelong flashes of what they passed and he vowed he would walk back to the *pensione*, wherever it might be. Better to be lost in the city than laid out in the morgue.

The Department for the Defence Against Subversive Religions was in a building across a small garden from the tower that housed Vatican Radio. It was a small department; evidently subversive religions were not as big a problem as Archbishop Hourigan made out. Or perhaps the Vatican, like the rest of the world, was cost-cutting.

Monsignor Guy Lindwall was a small-man; indeed, he was tiny. All his life he had been plagued by his lack of inches. Amongst the extraordinarily tall Denka tribesmen in the southern Sudan, he had been only head-high to their navels. It had seemed to him that he had spent years preaching St Paul's Epistles to the Genitalia. A midget of the cloth, he just hoped to God that when he reached Heaven that God was not tall. But he had a sense of humour, was voluble as a fishwife in a gale, talked a blue streak but with only the occasional blue word. He would, however, never preach cant.

He listened attentively, if impatient to say something, while Malone told him something, but not all, of the case. When Malone had finished the little man ran his fingers through his unruly white hair and shook his head.

'I don't believe Kerry would have anything to do with a murder, not a nun and particularly his niece. He's a decent man at heart, a moral man. He just has this obsession with Communism. We call him Archbishop Rambo and around here we're all scared of what he's going to do next. Every time he opens his mouth, the Sacred Heart fibrillates.' He pointed to a religious print hung on the wall of his tiny office. 'You can see the glass is already cracked. Does anyone in the Curia know you're here?'

'I don't know. The Archbishop's father has friends and spies everywhere. I wouldn't be surprised if someone isn't whispering in the Pope's ear right now.'

'The Holy Father only got back from China last night – he has more on his mind than the Archbishop. No, it's the cardinals in the Curia we have to be careful of. If Kerry goes to them and complains about you harassing him, nothing short of a miracle will get him out of here. You can take out all the warrants you can think of, he won't be moved from here.'

'Maybe he won't broadcast too much. He's got plenty of reasons for keeping all this quiet.'

'True, true. None of us here in the Department knew he'd been in Nicaragua. His Holiness wouldn't like that.'

'Does anyone in the Curia back him on the Contras?'

'One or two. They're divided over there, just like Washington is. There are some of us here in the Department who think that some day, perhaps soon, Islam will be as big a threat to Christianity as Communism – it may even threaten both of them. But all Rambo can see is the Red menace.'

'How did he feel about the Pope going to China?'

'Oh, he was dead against it.' Lindwall smiled, showing badly fitting false teeth. He had lost his own years ago while surviving on a poor diet in Africa. He still suffered from malaria and there were traces of bilharzia in his bloodstream that had to be checked regularly. He had suffered for Christ, but none of it had left him bitter; he had a true vocation. In the next day or two, as he got to know him better, Malone would come to have the highest regard for the tiny priest: he was the best sort of advertisement for the Church, a priest who understood and did not just condemn sinners. 'He preaches that one should never get into bed with a Red, especially in his own country. His Holiness, I think, prefers not to know too much about what we get up to. Or what our Archbishop gets up to.'

'So all we have to watch out for are the cardinals in the Curia?' Malone had had some opponents in the past, but never a battalion of cardinals.

'They are enough. Captain Goffi will tell you how powerful

they are. Even the Holy Father has trouble with some of them.'

'Where's Archbishop Hourigan now? Does he live in the Vatican?'

'No, he lives across the river, in a riverside apartment.' He gave Malone the address. 'Do you want to telephone him?'

'No.' That would only be a warning. Kerry Hourigan would have Zara Kersey there waiting for him. 'He might call out the Swiss Guards.'

'I shouldn't be surprised. He's a loose cannon, as the Americans here in the Department say.' Lindwall escorted Malone and Goffi to the door. 'Have you seen the Basilica, Inspector? Come back this evening at six, you'll see it at its best. His Holiness is saying Mass to celebrate his trip to China.'

'What'll we have at communion – rice wine?'

'Tell that to Archbishop Hourigan. He'll probably agree with you.'

Out in St Peter's Square Malone gently but politely declined Goffi's offer to drive him to the Archbishop's apartment. 'I need the exercise, Captain. And I think it's better that I see him on my own. He may just shut up shop altogether if he knows you're involved, unofficially or not.'

Goffi looked disappointed, but nodded. 'I understand, Inspector. But take care. Rome isn't as safe as it used to be.'

Malone walked down the Via delle Conciliazone, passed under the shadow of the Castle of St Angelo, crossed the bridge and walked along the eastern bank of the Tiber. He could feel the city brushing against his consciousness; he began to wonder at the history of Rome, though he knew none of it. What secrets had been dreamed up behind these sun-drenched walls he was now passing? The sun beat off them as if the stone were alive. He touched one of the walls, felt the warmth of it; when he took his hand away, there were flakes of paint on his fingertips. I've left my prints on Rome, he smiled, being literary. Maybe the city did that to you, though he didn't know the name of a single Roman poet.

Archbishop Hourigan's apartment was on the third floor of a *palazzo* that had once been the home of one of Rome's richest and most powerful families. The grandeur was shabby now: paint peeled, dust floated, the busts on the wide marble staircase were chipped, like experiments in cosmetic surgery that had gone wrong. Malone passed several big doors, glanced at the names: Contessa This, Principessa That. The *palazzo* was a crypt for the past and Malone wondered what the Archbishop was doing here.

When he came to the Hourigan door he saw at once that it was new; or refurbished. The thick oak was polished, the brass door-knobs were bright. There was no title on the brass name-plate beside the door, just the name *Hourigan*. Perhaps clerical rank had no rating on this side of the river.

A butler in black uniform with white gloves answered Malone's ring. He was an elderly man with a rugged face that reminded Malone of that of a Mafia boss he had once arrested back in Australia who, true to the form of the period, had been acquitted. The butler showed no surprise when Malone introduced himself, but stepped back and gestured for him to enter.

Then Kerry Hourigan, dressed in street clothes (Why did I expect him to be in full regalia? Malone wondered. Did Rome do that to you?), came into the entrance hall, his heels clack-clacking on the black-and-white marble.

He put out his hand. 'I've been expecting you, Inspector. I was told you were in Rome. Come on in.'

He led the way into a high-ceilinged room too big to be called a living-room; Malone guessed this was what was called a *salon*. There was no seedy grandeur here; though nothing looked new, everything was stylish and expensive. The paintings on the walls were Old Masters, for all Malone knew: to his inexpert eye, they looked it. He noticed there were no religious paintings, no agonized saints sitting on red-hot pokers or Madonnas airborne by the Renaissance equivalent of Alitalia; perhaps the Archbishop got enough of that sort of art on the other side of the river. Hourigan waved Malone to a silk-covered chair.

'I never thought you'd have the persistence to follow me all the way here to Rome.' He appeared friendly enough; or anyway relaxed. He's at home, Malone thought: Rome is home. 'I understand there's been another murder.'

'Yes. Father Marquez – you met him that evening in St Mary's.' It seemed a year ago. Did jet lag and 10,000 miles do that to you? Or was it because he was in another world altogether? 'They tried to kill me, too.'

That upset the Archbishop's composure. 'They? Who are *they*?'

Malone decided to be blunt. 'I was hoping you might give me a clue, Your Grace. I tried my luck with Mr Paredes and Mr Domecq – they suggested I try you.'

Hourigan shook his head. 'You're bluffing, Inspector.'

'That's what your father's lawyer said – Mrs Kersey. Why does everyone think I'm bluffing? You're connected to these murders, Your Grace, whether you know it or admit it or whatever. All of you are bluffing much more than I am. Or lying.'

The Archbishop flushed at that. 'That's insulting! Dammit, man, who do you think you are? I've told you – I know nothing about the murders! Good God, don't you think I've felt *something* about my niece's death, some grief, horror? I feel for that young priest, too, though I never knew him. I have no connection with the murders – they are as much a mystery to me as they are to you!'

'They may be a mystery to you, but I'm still convinced you're connected to them. We want all of you brought together for questioning – you, your father, Paredes and Domecq. We can't bring Paredes and Domecq here to Rome, but we can stop them leaving Australia –'

'How?' The Archbishop was almost too quick with his query.

Malone grinned. 'You're in a bureaucracy – you know there

are ways and means. Come back with me, Your Grace. It'll cause less of a stink.'

'You mean you'll cause a – a stink if I don't?'

'It's on the cards.'

The Archbishop sat silent, his chin on his chest. His hands were folded, but he was not praying. The Lord, for Whom he was working, had let him down; the murders were accidents which should never have been allowed to happen. The Lord had made a mistake in allowing man his free will.

At last he looked up. 'If I come back, if all your investigations prove I had absolutely nothing to do with this, can you keep it quiet? Out of the newspapers? I have work to do, Inspector – it's God's will –' There was a glint of passion in his eyes, almost of fanaticism. 'I don't want it ruined!'

'I can't promise anything, but I'll do my best. Can you leave tomorrow night?'

'No,' said Fingal Hourigan from the doorway. 'He won't be leaving Rome at all.'

He did not look out of place in this *salon*. With his white hair, thin aquiline face, dark suit and silver walking-stick, he could have been a Roman aristocrat; only the bright Irish eyes gave him away. There were still rumours of power and intrigue in the corners of the big room; he looked as if he intended to revive them. It suddenly struck Malone that this was *his* apartment, which explained the name without rank on the door-plate; the Archbishop was living here as a rich man's son, not through some indulgence by the Church. Once again he wondered what had happened to vows of poverty. But he would get nowhere asking such a question of the Hourigans. The Archbishop probably looked upon luxury as one of God's casual gifts; Fingal would look upon it as a deal with the Almighty. He sounded at the moment as if Rome itself was part of the deal.

'My son belongs here, Inspector.' He came into the room, moving a little cautiously on the marble tiles; the silver

220

walking-stick tapped bone-like on them. 'He's outside your domain altogether.'

'Not entirely, Mr Hourigan.' Malone had stood up, not wanting to be dominated by the old man. 'I can ask the *carabinieri* to arrest him and hold him. He's outside Vatican City.'

The Hourigans looked at each other quickly, as if this possibility had not crossed their minds. Then Fingal coughed a small dry laugh. 'You don't know Italy, son. When did the *carabinieri* last arrest an archbishop? One from the Vatican? I'm not without influence here, Inspector.'

'The Mafia?' It was a stupid remark and Malone knew it as soon as he uttered it; but he was becoming frustrated. 'Forget that. You'd be further up the scale than them.'

'I'm glad you think so. You're not that dumb – I don't do business with hoodlums. I don't do business with murderers, either.' He had once, long ago, but it never troubled his conscience. 'Neither does my son.'

'Paredes and Domecq have both been charged with murder in Nicaragua.'

'Charged and acquitted.'

'No, not acquitted. Never brought to trial. There's a difference.' He looked at Kerry Hourigan, who had remained in his chair, silent and with his hands still clasped together. 'You must have known their record?'

'They were fighting Communists,' said the Archbishop. 'There was a war ...' But he sounded as if he were trying to forgive sins that were beyond his comprehension. 'They are the leaders of an honourable army.'

'Bullshit, Your Grace,' said Malone. 'With all due respect. The FBI have them also tagged as being the leaders of a drug ring, tied up with some mob in Colombia. You're dealing with crims and you're a bloody fool if you don't face up to it!'

The Archbishop stood up, drawing some dignity into himself. 'I think you'd better leave, Inspector. I'll take my chances on my own judgement.'

Malone knew when to retreat. He was too experienced a policeman to go plunging on; there were other ways of going forward than by a direct line. At the moment, however, he wasn't quite sure where he was going. He felt the loss of back-up that could be relied upon. He had been like this twice before, in London and in New York; and he felt a recurrence of the same lack of confidence. But he didn't let it show.

'Then you'd better move back into the Vatican. A *cara-binieri* captain told me less than an hour ago, Rome isn't safe any more. You'd better believe it.'

As he went out into the entrance hall he heard a sound that gave him some small comfort. It was the nervous tap-tap of Fingal Hourigan's stick on the marble tiles.

2

Malone was both weary and tired; which can be two different conditions. Jet lag was catching up with him: he felt like falling into bed and sleeping for a week. But the weariness was greater: the weight of this case was exhausting him. Sitting here in a side pew in St Peter's he wanted both to fall asleep and throw in the case. Then, like the apparitions that sometimes appear in the moment before one falls asleep, the faces of Sister Mary Magdalene and Father Marquez, the one dead and serene, the other alive and afraid, would jerk him awake. Perhaps it was the setting. Both of them, the religious, would have been thrilled to be sitting where he was, to be so close to what was going on.

Once inside the great basilica he had been amazed at the size and splendour of it. He was not to know it, but a philosopher, Giovanni Papini, had once written, 'It is like the hall of an imperial palace designed for splendid gathering, rather than the mausoleum of a martyr intended for the public appearance of the Vicar of Christ.' Russ Clements's old

Congregationalist mum would have sneered at it and retreated to her tin-roofed chapel, but Malone, against the grain of his nature, found himself impressed.

The Pope had made a modest entrance; if popes, surrounded by a regiment of cardinals, archbishops, bishops, liveried laity and Swiss Guards, could ever move modestly in the huge basilica. He had not been carried in on the *sedia gestatoria*, the chair usually used during his public appearances; perhaps he, too, was suffering from jet lag and did not want a reminder of his long flight from Beijing. Newspapers had reported that, crossing the Muslim countries, the Alitalia flight had been subjected to intense air buffeting. The *sedia gestatoria* was rarely on an even keel: carried by Italians, it always tended to list to the right or left, depending on the current government in power outside the Vatican. Popes never looked more uneasy than when in the shoulder-borne chair.

'I'm glad you came,' Monsignor Lindwall had said when Malone had presented himself back at the Department for the Defence Against Subversive Religions. 'A lot of people may sneer at all the panoply of a papal Mass, but honest human nature needs panoply occasionally. The Communists go in for it on May Day. The Presbyterians are dour in church, but they get carried away by their pipe bands at the Edinburgh Tattoo – so do I, I must confess. I missed all the panoply during those years in Africa. I made up for it by going to watch the tribal dances, dreadfully pagan occasions, and enjoying them. A papal Mass is extravagant and I sometimes wonder what Christ would have thought of it, but the soul needs the occasional circus, even if it's a solemn one. It doesn't make one a better Christian to attend one, but it beats the hell out of self-flagellation.'

Malone had grinned at the little man. 'Who hears your confession?'

'Oh, I have a friend, another retired missionary. We try to out-do each other in imaginary sins. How did you fare with our Archbishop?'

'I think he's winning on points at the moment. But it's a long way from over. I think he may retreat into the Vatican, but he can't hide here for ever.'

'How much time have you got? There are over ten thousand rooms in the Vatican. There are nine hundred and ninety-seven staircases you may have to run up and down. Thirty of the staircases are secret – the Vatican has had more experience at hiding people than any other organization on earth. I sometimes think the CIA and the KGB and MI5 come here for instruction in safe houses, or whatever they call them. If Kerry goes to His Holiness or the Tardella –'

'What's that?'

'The Pope's inner cabinet. If he goes to one of the senior cardinals in the Tardella, you've had it, my son. You may just as well go back to the Colonies.'

'The Colonies? You're eighty-seven years out of date as far as Australia is concerned. I didn't think you'd be an imperialist Pom.'

'A figure of speech, Scobie. I was thinking in Roman terms. Everywhere outside of Rome is the Colonies.'

'How does a cynic like you last in a place like this?'

Monsignor Lindwall smiled. 'Better to have me inside, shooting my mouth off, than outside. Shall we go to Mass?'

Despite his lack of liking for panoply, Malone was impressed by the papal Mass. He could see that this could be part of the Church's seduction of converts; they expected Heaven to be even better. The basilica was packed; it seemed to him that people were even squeezed into niches in the walls, like flesh-coloured effigies. There was constant movement, even during the Consecration; Italian congregations evidently didn't consider it rude to wander around in The Lord's presence. One item did thrill Malone: the singing. This was *real* music: if The Lord could listen to guitars and banal hymns after this feast, He was straining His charity or had a tin ear. Then he found himself dozing off again.

Guy Lindwall woke him with a digging elbow. 'It's over.

Do you see who is on the other side of the altar?'

Malone shook his head, opened his eyes wide to get them working again. During Mass there had been so many people between him and the opposite pews that he had been able to see no one. Now, amongst the chromatopsia of cardinals, he saw the two Hourigans, Zara Kersey and General della Porta standing together in a group. With them were two elderly cardinals, one white-headed, the other bald, both of them looking like the princes they knew they were.

'You see?' said Lindwall. 'He's already with the Tardella.'

'And the *carabinieri*, too, it seems,' said Malone and all at once wanted to give up, to fall into bed and wake up in Randwick with Lisa beside him and the case wiped from his memory.

But it wasn't to be. As they began to move out of the basilica, Zara Kersey looked across and saw Malone. She smiled at him, then turned and said something to Fingal Hourigan. The old man shook his head, then he turned and stared across at Malone. He said something to his son, then the two of them pushed through the crowd to Malone and Monsignor Lindwall. Only when they had come through the throng did Archbishop Hourigan look down and see the little man.

'Hello, Guy, do you two know each other?'

'He's my spiritual adviser,' said Malone.

'I've been explaining the difficult ways to Heaven,' said the Monsignor. 'He's a stubborn man.'

'Don't we know it!' said the Archbishop.

'Inspector –' Fingal Hourigan had barely glanced at Lindwall. 'Mrs Kersey has suggested we get together for one last conference. She thinks we may be able to work something out. I doubt it, but I don't pay her to give me advice I ignore. Can you have dinner with us?'

'I'm bushed, Mr Hourigan – I have jet lag –'

'So have I,' said the old man. 'How do you think I got here? By transubstantiation, changing one body for another?'

'I wouldn't be surprised,' said Malone, dredging up some reserves that he thought he had lost; this old bastard acted like a battery charger on him. 'Where will we have dinner?'

'The Hassler. Nine-thirty. Is that too late for you? These Eyeties evidently can't cook anything before nine o'clock.'

That would give him time for at least an hour's nap. 'I'll be there. Will General della Porta be there? He didn't tell me he knew you.'

'He's an old friend,' said Archbishop Hourigan.

'I might have guessed it. What about the Pope?'

He left them on that, clearing a way through the crowd, with Monsignor Lindwall following in his wake. He walked quickly, almost hurling people out of his way and Lindwall had to run to keep up with him. Once outside, however, in the cool air of the spring evening, he slowed down, took a deep breath.

'I'll pray for you,' said the Monsignor as he said goodnight.

'Will it help?'

'I don't know. I prayed every night in Africa, asking for something better of The Lord. Look where He landed me. But if we don't keep hoping and praying, what's the point of anything? Good luck.'

'Luck isn't a Christian symbol, is it?'

Lindwall smiled. 'I told you – I used to go to those pagan celebrations and enjoy them. Not all pagan things are bad.'

Malone went back to the *pensione*, asked Signor Pirelli to call him at nine o'clock, went up to his room and was asleep as soon as his head hit the pillow. It seemed only a moment later that Pirelli was shaking him awake. He got up, had a quick shower, dressed and, after getting directions from Pirelli, walked up to the Hotel Hassler at the top of the Spanish Steps. He was ten minutes late, but, usually a most punctual man, it didn't worry him. The Hourigan party had not arrived and he was shown to their reserved table. It was a window table with a view over the city. This was one of the perks of the rich, he guessed, and felt the natural envy of a poorer man.

The Hourigans and Zara Kersey arrived fifteen minutes later. Fingal made no apology and his son and Zara Kersey said nothing about their tardiness. Perhaps they felt that in Italy one did not need to.

'I thought you might not have waited,' said Fingal.

Malone had had two cups of the strong Italian coffee, felt more awake. 'General della Porta didn't come with you? I only stayed because I wanted to talk to him.'

'We'll keep the Eyetalians out of this,' said Fingal. 'What do you want to eat?'

Malone had already glanced at the menu and was glad that he was not paying; eating out in Rome was expensive. He ordered fish; judging by its price it had been landed in a Bulgari gold-mesh net. While he was eating it he could taste money; but he enjoyed it. It was Fingal Hourigan's money and it might be the only thing he would get out of the family. The Archbishop ate extravagantly; Malone tipped he might have asked for seconds at the Last Supper had he been there. Both Fingal and Zara Kersey ate sparingly. Nothing much was said during the meal, though Zara did try to keep some conversation going.

'You should have brought your wife to Rome with you, Inspector. Rome is a city for women.'

'Better than Paris?'

'Any city where they can spend money is a city for women,' said Fingal. 'Do you want dessert?'

'Yes,' said Malone. 'If you don't mind spending the money.'

Fingal grinned. 'It's a pity you're a cop, Malone. I could have found a place for you. I still could,' he added without the grin.

'Are you trying to bribe me? In front of your lawyer, an honest lady?'

'Let's not get into that,' said Zara. 'The bribery, I mean, not my honesty. If Mr Hourigan meant it, it was meant only

227

as a joke.' She gave Fingal a hard stare. 'Right?'

He stared back at her, then retreated behind his menu. Kerry Hourigan said from behind his menu, 'I'll have the stuffed peaches. I think it's time Mrs Kersey put our case to you, Inspector.'

Zara put a cigarette in a holder and lit it. Fingal put down his menu and said, 'I don't like smoking at the table.' Zara put out the cigarette, made no apology and looked at Malone. This is like family, he thought. Fingal treats her as he does his daughter and he gets about as far with her as he does with Brigid.

'Inspector, the Archbishop tells me you have threatened to create a stink back in Sydney if he doesn't return with you.'

'That's about it,' said Malone. 'It's time I started playing dirty.'

'Where will you create the stink, exactly? Mr Hourigan is a major shareholder in two of our biggest newspapers, through one of his subsidiary companies.'

'There's the ABC – something like *Four Corners* or *The 7.30 Report*. You seem to forget, Mrs Kersey. Most of the journos in Sydney are left-wing or that way inclined. And I don't think any of them are particularly religious, probably the opposite. I don't think we'd have any trouble creating a stink.'

'We?'

He almost said *Me and the Commissioner*; but he knew just how far he could go in taking the Commissioner's name in vain. 'The Police Department. We're all pretty tired of people saying we're corrupt – we're looking for chances to show we're not. What was it you wanted to put to me?'

'I don't think this is the place.' She looked at Fingal. 'Can we go back to your apartment, Mr Hourigan?'

'I don't like entertaining cops in my home.' But then he nodded. 'Okay. We'll have dessert and coffee first. We don't want to disappoint my son.'

Kerry laughed. 'Gluttony is my only constant sin.'

Malone forbore to ask him what his occasional sins were.

They rode back to the Hourigan apartment in a Mercedes limousine driven by the elderly butler, who evidently doubled as chauffeur. Once inside the apartment he did a quick change, appeared again in his black livery and white gloves and served them liqueurs and more coffee.

'This is a forty-year-old Grande Fine Champagne,' said Kerry, sniffing his brandy glass. 'One of the best cognacs, another of my sinful indulgences. A religious war, or rather the end of one, was responsible for the creation of cognac. Did you know that, Inspector? Henri the Fourth of France stopped the war between the Huguenots and the Catholics in whenever-it-was, Fifteen – something. The Huguenots had learned about "burned wine" from the Dutch . . .'

He trailed off when he saw his father looking stonily at him. He had drunk too much wine at dinner; but something else had undermined him. Is he afraid? Malone wondered.

When the butler had retired, Malone said, 'Well, what do we have to talk about?'

Zara Kersey looked at Kerry Hourigan. 'I think you'd better speak for yourself now, Your Grace.'

'Be careful,' warned Fingal.

The Archbishop, replete and seemingly at ease now, as if a full stomach were some sort of assurance, sat back in his chair, re-gathering himself. It was a high-backed chair covered in rich red velvet; he looked cardinalate in it, almost papal.

'I have the strongest possible alibi for myself and Señor Paredes for last Saturday night. We were in Moss Vale, some hundred and forty or hundred and fifty kilometres from Sydney. We didn't leave there to return to Sydney by car till three-thirty in the morning.'

'Where were you? At Austarm?'

'You know about Austarm?' He seemed surprised.

'We've done some homework.'

'H'm.' Kerry Hourigan looked at his father. 'Do I tell him everything?'

'I wouldn't tell him anything. But now you've started . . .'

'Only as much as you have to,' Zara Kersey advised.

Fingal suddenly changed his mind. 'Tell him everything. Otherwise we'll never get rid of him.'

Malone, tiredness all at once hitting him like a bilious attack, grinned. 'Thanks.'

'Well –' Kerry Hourigan seemed a little less assured now, as if he had expected to get away with telling much less. 'Señor Paredes and I were there to buy arms. You must understand, this is in the strictest confidence. If this got out, it would be a bigger scandal than the Irangate affair in the United States. Do I have your word on that?'

'No,' said Malone. 'This isn't the confessional. You know I have to put in a report. I can see that it goes to the Commissioner and nobody else, but I can't guarantee what he'll do with it.'

The two Hourigans looked at each other again and Fingal said, 'Leave that with me.'

I know the Commissioner isn't in your pocket, thought Malone; but maybe the Premier was and the Premier was the Minister for Police. All at once he felt unutterably weary. The world was full of conspiracy, of connections, of payments made and favours done. Why did he think he could beat it all?

'The Vatican doesn't know I'm involved in our programme in Nicaragua – the Contras' programme, that is.'

'Some people in the Vatican know you're involved. You mean the Pope doesn't know.'

'Well, yes . . .'

Out of the corner of his eye Malone saw that Zara was disturbed by the Archbishop's frankness, reluctant though it might be. Or perhaps she had been shocked by what she had been told beforehand, whatever it might have been.

'When it comes off, when it is successful – as it will be –' Again there was that glint of passion (of fanaticism?) in the eyes. 'When it happens, I'll be a hero. Not a public one, but here in the Vatican – yes. A success against the Communists – one that will wipe out that canker in Latin America – is what we want here in Rome. But there are ways it has to be done – well, ways Rome would rather not know about. The Lord understands, but Man sometimes doesn't –'

'Don't get too pious,' said the Archbishop's father, who would never be that.

Kerry smiled, not offended: the zealot can never be insulted. Malone understood that. Archbishop Hourigan was no foam-mouthed raver, but he was a zealot or a fanatic, all right.

'Señor Paredes and I went to Moss Vale to buy arms –'

'On a Saturday night? In the middle of the night?'

'We didn't want any of Austarm's staff to know about us. We dealt only with their two top executives.'

'What was the order?'

'Ten thousand rifles –'

'What sort? Old ones or new?'

'Austarm's newest – it's based on the Belgian 7.62 rifle. Do you know it?'

'I've seen it.' He was surprised that the Archbishop should know one rifle from another; he was a Rambo, all right. 'We confiscated half a dozen from a gang of bikies. They're pretty lethal.'

'Rifles are supposed to be – you know that.' He could see himself at the head of an army, another Julius II, that most war-like of popes. 'We also ordered a thousand machine guns and I've forgotten how many gross of grenades and land-mines.'

Just something to fill up the shopping basket. Malone looked at Zara, seemingly the only sane one besides himself in the room. Fingal seemed unperturbed by his son's bizarre militarism.

'Do you believe all this?'

'Yes.' But he recognized the reluctance in her voice; or was there a hint of outrage, of disgust? 'It's all true, Inspector.

That's why I didn't want this conversation held in the restaurant.'

Malone looked back at the Archbishop. 'An order like that – how are the Austarm executives going to explain that to the factory production manager? What would it be worth?'

'Including the ammunition, shipping, everything – just on ten million dollars.'

'And you expected nobody to ask questions about an order like that?'

'It was being arranged.'

'That's not good enough. I want to know everything or I'm on my way back to Sydney, with or without you, and I'll start work again on Paredes and Domecq.' He looked at Fingal. 'You'd better tell him, Mr Hourigan – I'm a bastard for persistence.' He just wished he were not so exhausted.

'The end justifies the means, Inspector.'

'Hitler said that.' Had he? It seemed something that all the fanatics of history would have said. But, as he was honest enough to admit to himself, probably a host of honest men had also said it. 'Go on, Your Grace.'

Kerry Hourigan hesitated, then went on. 'The bill of sale says they are for Saudi Arabia. The export order will say the same.'

'Does anyone in Canberra know about that?'

Again the hesitation; then: 'Yes.'

'Do the Saudi Arabians know?'

'Yes.'

'Who's paying for it? Them?'

'No.'

'Who, then?'

'I am,' said Fingal Hourigan.

Malone kept his surprise to himself; then after the initial reaction, there was no surprise. Ten million was nothing to a man of Fingal's wealth; some profligate playboys spent that much on a yacht or a plane. But Fingal had never had a public profile as a rabid anti-Communist. Was he being just an indulgent father? It was hard to believe such a proposition. Fingal, he would have thought, was the sort of father because of whom charity would have left home.

'Do the Saudis know that?'

'No,' said Fingal. 'They don't need to know. They're willing to put their name to the order in support of a good cause.'

'That's a great combination – the Saudis and the Catholic Church. How ecumenical can you get? All that, just to get rid of the Sandinistas in Nicaragua? Okay, you've told me all that and that explains where the Archbishop and Mr Paredes were Saturday night. It doesn't explain where Domecq was after he left the brothel. It would take only one man to kill your niece, Your Grace.'

He said it brutally and it had its effect on the Archbishop. The big man seemed to slump in his chair: he had been hit by conscience, against which even a full stomach is no defence.

'When was my – my granddaughter murdered?' said Fingal.

'The medical examiner put it between ten p.m. and two a.m., give or take an hour or so.'

'Then it couldn't have been Señor Domecq. He was with Mrs Mosman, Tilly Mosman, till seven in the morning.'

'How do you know?'

'I checked with him and then with Mrs Mosman. He didn't leave the brothel, as I gather she told you. He was upstairs in her private suite.'

Who isn't in your pay? But Malone didn't ask that question. That would mean laying his cards on the table and Fingal would see that it was a dead hand.

'How do you know Tilly Mosman?'

'I don't.' He knew she could be trusted. 'I had someone visit her. I'm investing money in these two men. I investigate everybody I back. It's just plain business sense.'

Malone suddenly felt light-headed. He wanted to adjourn the interrogation. But that would mean losing his grip on the whip-handle; it was tenuous enough already. He sat up, held out his cup and Zara, the closest he had to an ally in this room, poured him more coffee from the silver pot. He gulped it down, forced himself at least to sound alert, if not to feel so. How did statesmen, shuttling across the world, keep wide awake when bargaining for peace? Would historians in the future take into account the effects of jet lag as now, writing of the past, they took into account those of syphilis and porphyria and a dozen other maladies of the past? He finished the coffee and put down the cup.

'Righto, that's Saturday night accounted for. Now we have Tuesday night, when Father Marquez was murdered and someone tried to do me in, too.'

'I was at the airport, waiting to board the plane for here,' said Kerry Hourigan.

'And Señor Paredes and Domecq were at my home,' said Fingal Hourigan. 'You have my word for that, Inspector.'

What's that worth? Ten million? But insults would never get him anywhere, not even if he were wide awake and on top of the situation. They might arouse the unintelligent, who might lose their tempers; but Fingal would never lose his, any rage would be instantly under control. He stood up, knowing he had lost this round.

'I'll sleep on what you've told me. I'll be back again tomorrow.'

'I'll have Paolo drive you home,' said Fingal, not bothering to rise. He had the smug look of a manager who, with his boxer, had just scored a knock-out. In his own eyes, though, he would never have given himself such a lowly image. He was a king-maker; or anyway a pope-maker. He was looking for a throne, not a champion's title belt.

'No, thanks, I'll walk,' said Malone curtly and left.

Outside in the night air he breathed deeply, trying to clear his lungs and his head, trying to stay awake. He knew that if he had accepted the lift back to the *pensione* he would have been asleep in the car before they reached there and Paolo, and probably Pirelli, would have had to carry him up to bed.

It was still early by what he guessed were Rome's standards;

the streets had none of the deserted look of midnight Sydney. He felt less light-headed, but he knew that if he had to break into a run for any reason he would just stumble and fall headlong. He walked carefully; how did modern cricketers turn out for net practice only a day after a twenty-four hour flight? He'd better have a check-up when he got back to Sydney; maybe there was something wrong with his blood pressure. Maybe the Hourigans were a health hazard.

He passed the ruins of the Forum, where the ghosts of ancient assassins lurked, and turned into the street where the Pensione Pirelli was, glad that he had only a few yards to go to his bed. Then he heard the footsteps behind him, heard them quicken into a run and he turned. The quick turn-round, with his light-headedness dizzied him and at the same time saved him; he fell against the man as the latter came at him with the knife. The fall saved him: he hit the man in the midriff with his shoulder, a thumping tackle. The man staggered back, hacked at him with the knife; Malone felt the blade hit the bone in his shoulder and he gasped. He fell away, kicking at the man as he came at him again, rolled over and came up on his feet and saw the attacker coming at him with the knife thrusting up for the kill. Then a gun went off right beside his ear.

The attacker stopped in his tracks, a gaping wound in his throat. He stood upright for a moment, his mouth open as if in surprise, then he toppled backwards. Malone turned and saw Captain Goffi, his gun still held for a second shot. Then the last thirty-six hours caught up with him in a black wave and he fell in a limp heap beside the man who had tried to kill him.

3

'He was a Mafia hit-man named Morello, brought in from Milan,' said General della Porta. 'Captain Goffi has identified him.'

'I don't believe the Mafia are involved in this,' said Malone.

'Of course not.' The General sounded as if he wanted no Italians involved, not even the Mafia. 'Morello was a contract man, he did outside work if the pay was good enough.'

They were in della Porta's office. After Goffi's shot had rung out in the quiet side street it had been only a moment or two before an excited crowd had gathered. Goffi had been kneeling beside Malone when the latter had regained consciousness. He had leaned down and whispered in Malone's ear, 'Don't say a word, just keep quiet.'

Then Signor Pirelli, in pyjamas, dressing-gown and a state of high concern, had appeared. 'Signor Malone! What have they done?'

Goffi had taken over at once, giving Malone no chance to reply. 'Get back to your phone, Dino, and call the ambulance.'

'And the police?'

'I am the police!' Goffi snapped, not wanting the city police to poke their noses into this affair. 'Start running!'

The ambulance had arrived within five minutes. Malone, his shoulder numb, had remained dumb. He had got shakily to his feet and leaned against the wall behind him. He had looked down at the dead thug, but someone had thrown a sheet or curtain over him and he was now just an anonymous lump. When the ambulance arrived the body had been lifted in and then Goffi, who had disappeared for a few moments to talk to his cousin, had come back and helped Malone into the ambulance.

'I've told them to take us to *carabinieri* headquarters first. We'll have a police surgeon look at your shoulder. If it's bad, we'll have to take you to a hospital. If it's not, then we can keep this to ourselves. I've told my cousin not to speak to the newspapers.'

'I don't care who knows,' said Malone. 'I was bloody near killed tonight! If it hadn't been for you . . .'

'You'll think differently in the morning.'

'I wouldn't bet on it.'

But this morning, after ten hours' sleep, he had felt differently. The police surgeon had said last night that the wound would heal without any serious consequences; the knife had skidded off his shoulder-blade and plunged down without much damage to the muscles. The shoulder was still sore and hurt when he moved his arm; but it was his left arm and he was right-handed. When he had woken he had had a bath instead of a shower, keeping the wound dry; the long sleep and the bath had made him feel much better. When Goffi had picked him up and brought him here to *carabinieri* headquarters he had been prepared to listen to what General della Porta had to say.

On the way across town he had said to Goffi, 'Were you tailing me?'

'Yes,' said Goffi. 'The General told me I wasn't to let you out of my sight.'

'Was that bloke tailing me, too?'

'No, he was waiting for you in a doorway. He knew where you were staying –'

'Nobody else did but you and the General.'

Goffi smiled, unoffended. 'Are you suspecting me or the General?'

'No. Sorry. Yes, there was someone else – Monsignor Lindwall.'

'Don't be too suspicious, Inspector. I think you may have been tailed from the moment you landed at Fiumicino. You were fortunate I was right behind you. Otherwise I think you would have been dead.'

'He used a knife, the same way they killed the nun back in Sydney.'

'There may be a connection, but I don't think so. Knives are just quieter than guns.'

'You can say that again.' Malone could still feel, rather than hear, the roar of Goffi's gun beside his ear.

Now, in della Porta's office, he said, 'Had Morello been in Australia?'

'No,' said the General. 'We checked with Milan – he was seen twice there last week. He didn't commit your Sydney murders, Inspector.'

'Have you interviewed Archbishop Hourigan or his father?'

'No.'

Malone wanted to ask why not, but managed to bite on the question. His concern, however, must have been apparent, because the General said, 'Is something worrying you, Inspector?'

Well, here I go for the high dive, Malone thought, and not for the first time: 'General, how well do you know Mr Hourigan and his son?'

Della Porta stared at him coldly, all the friendliness suddenly gone from his plump handsome face, bone seeming to show through the jowls. 'You dare to ask me a question like that in front of one of my junior officers? You may go, Captain.'

Goffi rose. 'Yes, General.' As he turned away, with his back to della Porta, he shot a warning glance at Malone.

When they were alone the General said, 'I have been trying to help you, Inspector. I don't like to be rewarded by that sort of insult, especially in front of a junior officer.'

Malone had had to eat crow before, but it had never been his favourite dish and it had never tasted worse than now. 'I apologize, General. Twice in the past week someone has tried to murder me. I think I'm becoming desperate . . .'

Della Porta's face didn't soften. 'You're an experienced man, Inspector. Commissioner Leeds said he had the highest regard for you. You should know that someone in my position can't always choose his bedfellows. I have to be a politician as much as a policeman – and sometimes a priest, too, since I have to deal with the Vatican. I was very good friends with Signor Berlingeur when he was chief of the Italian Communist Party, but that didn't make me a Communist. I sat beside

Licio Gelli, the head of P2, at dinners, but that never made me a Fascist. I'm sure it happens back in your own country, Inspector. Archbishop Hourigan, whom I've known for several years, telephoned me and asked me to join him and his father at the papal Mass. Perhaps they were using me as window-dressing – I don't know. I may have been in the window, Inspector, but I assure you – I am not a store dummy!'

Malone could see the genuine anger in the man, even though he was holding it in control. He felt a sudden shame at his suspicions; and a quick stab of apprehension. If Commissioner Leeds got to hear of this, he would be reduced in rank and bound for Tibooburra.

'I'll try biting my tongue, General, when I get out of here – *if* I get out –'

Della Porta's stern face abruptly broke into a smile. 'I accept your apology, Inspector. You just needed to be taught a lesson. I'm not sitting in this chair because I scratched people's backs and genuflected in the right direction. I occasionally have to do that, but it's not the reason I hold the job. Corruption is endemic in public life in Italy, but nobody has ever offered me money – they know they would be in prison before they could put their hand back in their pocket. I hope you are the same way. Now what are we going to do about Archbishop Hourigan?'

'I want to take him back to Sydney. I think if I leaked something of the story to the media –'

'No.' The *carabinieri* chief stroked his moustache with his knuckle. He had once cultivated the media: he had thought of himself as unique, an honest civil servant, but the media, made cynical by local history, hadn't believed him. 'Let's keep it between ourselves and the Vatican. Perhaps if Monsignor Lindwall could be persuaded to drop a few hints to those who run the Curia ...'

Malone was driven across the Tiber with the General; the driver this time was a man who had had no Mille Miglia ambitions. 'I like a stately progress,' said della Porta and in a moment of frank immodesty added, 'I think I was a king in a previous existence. What were you, Inspector?'

'I've never considered the possibility, General. Whatever I was, I don't think I was on the side of the angels. If I was, the buggers have let me down in this life.'

General della Porta smiled. He had never thought of himself as on the side of the angels, even in a fanciful existence as a king. They, he thought as they crossed the river, were with those on this side of the Tiber.

Monsignor Lindwall's white eyebrows rose when he saw Malone's arm in its sling. 'What happened? Has the General been twisting your arm?'

'No, Monsignor,' said della Porta, smiling at the little man; these two had a great deal of respect for each other, they were real friends, not political ones. He told Lindwall what had happened, then said, 'We need your help, Guy.'

'What happened to the man who tried to kill Inspector Malone?'

'He committed suicide,' said della Porta blandly, ignoring Malone's quick glance.

'Voluntarily or involuntarily?'

'Don't ask too many questions, Guy. It's not your mission to straighten out the truth, not on our side of the river. Now what can you do for Inspector Malone to get the Archbishop on a plane for Australia?'

'Can you leave the Inspector with me? Let's see what can be done with the truth on this side of the river.'

General della Porta stroked his moustache, left them with a wink and a nod and went back across the Tiber, into the country of poets, plotters and lions that, before they turned to stone, had once had a fundamental way of dealing with those in the Church. Perhaps, he thought, I was an emperor and more than a king . . .

Guy Lindwall took Malone for a walk in the Vatican gardens. The spring sunshine was warming up; the statuary looked as if sap might begin to flow in it. Staff were coming and going, all carrying folders, like good civil servants, all looking preoccupied if not busy: bureaucrats are the same the world over, Malone thought. Two cardinals passed, neither carrying a folder: Permanent Secretaries who had to do nothing to justify their employment.

'Cardinals Fellari and Lupi,' said Lindwall. 'Two men we might talk to if it's necessary ... They, too, dream of being Pope some day.'

'Too? Who else?'

'Why, our own Archbishop, of course. He'll be a cardinal before long and then it's just another step ... He thinks we don't know about it, but we do, at least those of us in our Department. But we never discuss it. Who knows – he might make it. And who wouldn't want to be on the Pope's personal staff? On the periphery of the centre of attention, the trips abroad ... And, of course, guaranteed entry into Heaven.'

'Not you, I'll bet.'

The little man grinned, looked like a white-headed mischievous boy. 'Think of the chaos I could cause!' Then he sobered. 'I think we should go and see His Grace now.'

Malone put his free hand on his arm. 'Guy, wait a minute ... I don't want you shoving your neck out on this. You have to live with this man. If I don't nail him on some charge back home, he'll be back here. And where will that leave you?'

'My dear boy –' Guy Lindwall suddenly sounded very English, more so than at any time since Malone had met him. The public school, the manor house in the Cumbrian dales, Oxford: all of it was a long way behind him. He was, if anything, more colonial than Cumbrian; but three centuries of influential family can't be wiped out in a lifetime spent in foreign climes. Malone knew the feeling: sometimes he felt he pissed Irish bog-water. 'My dear boy, at my age there are no risks, only whims. Detective stories are my favourite reading. Conan Doyle, Freeman Wills Croft, the American, Raymond Chandler – they were my salvation out in Africa, not my breviary. If I can help you solve who murdered your young nun and the priest, The Lord will take care of me. He always has up till now.'

Malone grinned. 'If ever I go to Confession again, I think I'll wait till you're in the confessional.'

'Glad to be of service. Now let's see how much service I can be in this other matter.'

Archbishop Hourigan was in his office, a room small enough to have compacted his conceits. He started up in surprise when he saw Malone. 'Inspector! What happened? An accident?'

'No, Your Grace, it was no accident. Someone tried to kill me again. With a knife this time.'

Hourigan looked at Lindwall as if he expected the latter to explain. The little man just shrugged and Hourigan turned back to Malone. 'So you've come to say goodbye.'

It was a statement, not a question. Malone said, 'Not quite. I've been putting pressure on the Monsignor here ...'

The Archbishop looked at the Monsignor again. 'How did you get into this, Guy?'

'Kerry, I don't have any conflict with the police. Inspector Malone asked me some questions and I answered them.'

'Questions such as what?'

'Did the Curia know what you are doing in Nicaragua, do they know you've been there –'

'Who told you that?'

'I did, of course,' said Malone.

'Go on, Guy. What did you tell him about the Curia?'

'Kerry –'

Lindwall had sat down; he didn't like being overshadowed by two tall men. He had adopted the same tactic in the Sudan; the six-feet-six Denka tribesmen had spent more time on their haunches, listening to him, than at any other time in tribal history. Malone and Hourigan remained standing for a moment, then the Archbishop sat down and gestured for Malone to do the same.

'Kerry –' The Monsignor might have been talking to a novice seminarian. 'If certain cardinals got to hear what you've been up to ... You have your rivals, you know that as well as I do. His Holiness listens to them more than he does to you –'

'He knows my dedication to what we're trying to do.'

'We all know it, Kerry, none of us better than I. But buying rifles and machine-guns?'

Hourigan looked angrily at Malone. 'You told him everything?'

'Everything,' said Malone. 'Just like in the confessional.'

The Archbishop's lip curled. 'Go on, Guy.'

'What he told me won't go outside this room. Except –'

'Except what?'

'Kerry, if what you have done ever got out, if *L'Unita* ever got hold of it and spread it across their front page, all our good work would be undone.'

'You're wrong!' The Archbishop hit his desk with his fist. 'With the Holy Father behind me –'

'How do you know he would be? He's trying to build bridges.'

'He's as anti-Communist as I am!'

'I haven't heard of him using Peter's Pence to buy rifles and machine-guns. Be sensible, Kerry – just take a cool look at the bomb you're putting together. Being over-zealous has helped the Church in the past –'

'I'm not some wild fanatic!' But he looked it at the moment, sitting tensed in his chair, his eyes hard and bright.

'No,' said Lindwall, half-conciliatorily, half-sarcastically. 'It's always the other chaps who are the fanatics.'

Malone sat watching the small battle between the two clerics. There was long-standing antagonism between the two. There was the resentment of the old man, who had paid his dues in the field, towards the younger man who had come to Rome on a much easier, more comfortable road. Equally, there was the impatience of the crusader with a tired old man who wanted to show tolerance towards the enemy. There was no real hatred, just a clash of temperament. Which, as he knew, could produce just as long and fierce a battle. He didn't, however, want this one to go on: Guy Lindwall deserved better than that.

'Don't blame the Monsignor for any of this,' he said. 'I bailed him up against a wall. I said if he wouldn't talk to you, try and persuade you to come home with me, I'd go straight to the Curia cardinals myself.'

'They'd never let you in the door,' said Hourigan scornfully.

'They would if General della Porta pushed me in.'

'Is he on your side, too?'

'Everyone's on my side.' There were no titles of rank between them now: they were man to man. 'I'm not bluffing any more. I'll go to the cardinals and lay the whole lot on the table for them. They may tell me to go to hell, but none of it will do you much good. I think you'd be out of this Department before you could say Hail Mary ... They'd find some backwater for you ...'

'I can recommend the southern Sudan,' said Lindwall with an impish grin and some malice. 'Or Ethiopia. No comfort there, but it's full of Communists. Your map shows that.'

He nodded at the map of the world on the wall behind the Archbishop. Great patches of it were coloured red. It reminded Malone of old school maps he had seen, before all the colour ran out of the British Empire. Now there was a new empire, one that had to be conquered by any means: rifles, machine-guns, possibly even prayer.

Hourigan sat silent and stiff-faced for a long moment; then abruptly he smiled. It was a weak, slightly puzzled smile, but it was genuine. 'Why can't you and I get on together, Guy?'

'God knows, I've tried, Kerry. But I'm too old for your sort of – enthusiasm.' There was just a faint pause before the last word.

Hourigan hadn't missed it. 'My fanaticism, you mean? I *believe* in what I'm doing, Guy. If I sometimes get carried away ... The end justifies the means.' For the moment he believed what he was saying. The end, of course, was something different from what they thought. When he was Pope there would be so much he could do ... But you never confessed your ambition to be Pope, certainly not to someone who, if he had the vote at all, would never vote for you. He looked at Malone. 'I'd like to talk to my father before I make a decision. And I'll want some sort of guarantee that if I come back to Sydney, there won't be any publicity.'

'I'll do my best, but I can't guarantee anything. Paredes and Domecq may shoot their mouths off.'

'I don't think so,' said Archbishop Hourigan, and his voice had a threat to it that didn't go with his smile.

4

Captain Goffi drove Malone to the airport, Monsignor Lindwall going with them. There had been a quick farewell of General della Porta in his office. 'It is a pity you did not have an opportunity to see our city, Inspector. The externals of it are very attractive.'

'I'll try and come back, General. And stay on this side of the river.'

'We can't promise you Heaven on this side, but they don't make it any easier for you over there ...' He waved towards the tall doors and the distant dominating dome. 'There was an English writer, a convert, who once wrote that anyone who could spend a year in the shadow of the Vatican walls and still retain his faith, need have no fear that the gates of Heaven would be closed against him. I hope he was right.' Then he blessed himself, smiled when he saw Malone's blink of surprise. 'I told you, I have to play both sides. Good luck, Inspector.'

On the way out to the airport Guy Lindwall said, 'I hope you can keep all this out of the newspapers.'

'Don't tell me you're now on the Archbishop's side?'

'Not at all, old chap. I just don't enjoy seeing the Church taking the bumps for what its zealots do. You must feel the same way about your police force. Even democracy gets a bad name when certain Americans think they are the only defenders of it.'

Malone nodded. 'How will you feel if he comes back here lily-white and takes up where he's left off?'

'Ah, then I think I shall play dirty,' said the one-time missionary. 'I didn't waste my time out there amongst the pagan, unsporting Denka.'

When he got out of the car Malone shook hands with two old friends; or so it seemed they were. One had saved his life and the other had saved his morale. He felt a gratitude that he could only express with the firmness of his grip. The other men understood and their handshakes were as sincere as his.

'Take care, Scobie,' said Goffi. 'The third time you may not be so lucky.'

Malone left them and walked across to the three-engined Dassault Falcon 900. He had hesitated when Fingal Hourigain had insisted that they return to Australia in his private aircraft – 'It's the only way to ensure we land there without publicity. I came over in my own plane and I'm going back that way. What's the matter, Inspector? Are you afraid I'll have you tossed out from thirty thousand feet?'

'I'd take someone with me if you did.'

Fingal had smiled. 'I think you would, too. But not me, Inspector – I'd be standing well back.'

So now Malone climbed the steps to the aircraft, stood at the top and waved to Lindwall and Goffi, then went into the forward cabin. It was the first time he had been aboard a private jet and he was impressed by the luxury and comfort of it. In the forward cabin deep lie-back chairs faced each other across console tables. In the middle section there was a similar set-up for dining. In the rear cabin there was a work-station and a lounge that could be converted into a bed. The furnishings were luxurious: Fingal Hourigan's caravan was designed to make him feel at home even above the clouds. But then, Malone mused, he probably has options on air space all over the world.

The two Hourigans were already aboard and so was Zara Kersey. A uniformed steward took Malone's bag and went aft with it. Then he came back with coffee and biscuits.

'I employ only male stewards,' said Fingal. 'Women are a distraction.'

'Thank you,' said Zara Kersey.

'You too,' said Fingal. 'But you're smart and that makes up for it.'

'I don't think I'll last this journey,' said Zara to Malone. 'I think I'll be getting off somewhere about half-way.'

Archbishop Hourigan had remained silent, greeting Malone only with a nod. Malone sat down opposite him, the console table separating them. Fingal and Zara were on the other side of the aisle and Malone was aware that both of them were watching him.

'I think we'd better declare a truce till we get home,' he said.

Kerry Hourigan looked stonily at him. 'You're interrupting my work.'

'You interrupted mine, when I had to chase you here to Rome. I'm only doing my job. I'm not going to get any promotion out of this. I stand a good chance of things going the other way for me.'

'I can promise that,' said Fingal from the other side of the aisle.

Malone buckled his seat-belt, sat back as the plane taxied out on to the runway. He looked at Zara and smiled wearily. 'It's going to be a long twenty-four hours.'

'I hope the movie is a good one,' she said. 'What's on?'

'*The Untouchables*,' said Fingal. 'I didn't choose it. It's about a cop who's a pain in the arse.'

'My autobiography,' said Malone and felt a glimmer of

relief when he saw the glimmer of a smile on the Archbishop's lips.

They flew by way of Dubai and Singapore, stopping at each landing for only two hours while the aircraft was refuelled. At Dubai and Singapore men came to the airport to confer with Fingal. He made no mention to Zara and Malone of who the men were, but Kerry, who by now appeared to be his old confident self, explained: 'My father never loses an opportunity to do business. He would consider it a waste of time to pass through these places and not make money.'

'I might have guessed he wasn't just picking up duty-free grog,' said Malone.

He was no longer amazed by human behaviour; but he had not become impervious to it. Hate and anger, jealousy and revenge, all those he could understand, though at times it was difficult to forgive the results of those emotions. Greed was the hardest instinct to swallow: it was not his meal at all. He wondered what the Archbishop thought of his father's greed, but did not ask. The truce was fragile, but he wanted it to last till they reached Sydney. Truces are often no more than a blind for the worst of intentions, but they are the best currency for buying time.

At Singapore he went to one of the duty-free stores and bought perfume. As he walked back to board the plane Zara joined him.

'I thought you didn't like shopping?'

'It's perfume for the wife. Arpège.'

'Is that her favourite?'

'I don't think so. But she wouldn't have liked it if I'd brought back that one of yours. I saw it in the store – Poison.' He pronounced it English style. 'I didn't get anything for the kids. I didn't know what to buy them. I'm a dead loss as a father.'

'I doubt that, Scobie.'

When they got back on board the plane he was moving up and down it, inspecting it again, when he saw Kerry Hourigan looking at him with amusement. He said, 'If it's not a rude question, how much does a plane like this cost?'

'It is a rude question, but I suppose you're used to asking them.'

'We're taught to ask them. Just like lawyers,' he said, smiling at Zara, certain now that she was as much his ally as an adviser to the Hourigans.

'Eighteen million dollars,' said the Archbishop. 'US dollars, that is. Are you shocked?'

'Stunned, I think would be closer. It's a lot of cash for convenience.' It was – what? Thirty times more than he would have earned by the time he retired? He would sit down on the way home and work it out. Whatever *he* earned, no one could say it had bought him convenience.

'It's also for security, Inspector. My father is worth enough to be the target of kidnappers. How would you feel as an ordinary passenger on Qantas if some terrorist, or even ordinary gangsters, took over the plane and held my father to ransom? This isn't just an indulgence, though I suppose that's how it looks. In any event, it's his own money, not his shareholders'. That's more than can be said for a lot of other barons.'

And what happens to all the money, and to this aircraft, when your old man dies and it all comes to you and your sister? But that, of course, would have been a really rude question.

Then Fingal came back on board showing, as much as he ever could, some pleasure. 'I've just given some Chinese a lesson in patience. We've been two years on that deal, trying to out-sit each other. I lasted longer than they did. How much patience do you have, Inspector.'

'Not much.'

Fingal sat down opposite this time as the plane took off. 'You will never out-last me.'

'I didn't know the competition was between you and me.'

'Oh, it is, Malone, it is. I'm not going to let you ruin my

son's career. You're a Communist.'

Malone laughed at the other man's prejudice. 'Your son accused me óf that a week ago. I don't have any politics. If it turned out Gorbachev murdered your granddaughter, I'd be down on him like a ton of bricks. The same goes for our Prime Minister. Or the President of the United States.'

'That's fantasy. Top men never pull the trigger.' He knew: Capone hadn't pulled any trigger in the St Valentine's Day Massacre. Of course the Big Fella had killed people himself, but those murders had been personal. Which was different and understandable.

He sat back and stared at Malone across the cabin, the pale-blue eyes suddenly almost opaque. Malone stared back at him and all at once, with a tight feeling in his stomach, was certain he knew who had paid for the murders of Sister Mary Magdalene and Father Marquez. And for the attempted murder of himself in Rome.

Fingal at last turned his head away and looked out of the window. He had just had another moment of self-questioning, a disturbing weakness that had begun to occur too frequently. Why so many enemies? Brigid had asked him that back – when?

ELEVEN

I

'Why do you have so many enemies, Dad?'

Brigid had asked him the question on one of her few visits home to Sydney, back in the Sixties. She had also wanted to ask him why he had no friends, but one cruel question was enough.

He had smiled and shaken his head, 'Nobody loves a rich man, not in this country.'

'You're talking about the poor, the workers. Other rich men might love you.'

The smile remained. 'You don't know the rich. You see, I'm the *richest*. It's the same with a group of beautiful women. One of them's got to be the most beautiful and she's the one who'll always be the most envied.'

It was a cynical answer, but Brigid knew she should never have expected any more from her father.

She went back to England, where she saw the Swinging Sixties go out without any regret on her part. They would remain vivid only in the memories of those who would not go on to much better; there had been a spuriousness about those years that had never convinced Brigid they were something special. She had believed in free love and free thought long before those pursuits became wildly fashionable; miniskirts, which didn't suit her legs, and rock music, which, like her brother, she had now grown to hate, were minor manifestations to which she turned a blind eye and a deaf ear.

She slipped into the next decade with relief, found at last her true *métier* as a painter.

Her natural irreverence, her sceptical opinion of her brother's vocation, led her to look at religious paintings with a suddenly discovered new eye. She began to paint religious subjects as they might have been viewed by a tabloid news photographer, a biblical *paparazza*. They stopped short of being sacrilegious, but they raised comment. One or two of the more progressive Anglican bishops, those who didn't believe in God, praised them; more conservative clerics, including her own brother, condemned them, though Kerry only did so privately. Museums and private collectors bought them and all at once she was no longer a part-time painter, a talented dilettante, but a working professional artist.

Teresa was now nine years old, a replica of her mother at that age. Brigid, caught up in her painting, sent her to boarding school and the nuns took over the raising of the bright, opinionated child. Brigid, without realizing it, was creating the same situation that had separated her from her father.

In Rome Kerry had already come to the notice of certain influential members of the Curia. He knew now that he was safe from pastoral work in Australia; his administrative brain was not going to be wasted totting up parish funds and throwing holy water on the heads of indifferent infants. He not only had an excellent administrative brain, he was financially clever, an inheritance from his father; he also had something his father did not have, a gift for public rhetoric, an ability to fire an audience or congregation. He was now attached to the Congregation of the Council, a body which administered, among other affairs, ecclesiastical properties and revenues. It had been founded by Pius IV, a sixteenth-century Medici pope who knew the value of ecclesiastical favours: he sold cardinals' hats as if they were summer straw bonnets. He raised taxes in the Papal State by 40 per cent and let rich defendants, who should have been imprisoned, buy their freedom with exorbitant fines. Kerry, not without some irreverence of his own, thought of Pius as his father's patron saint.

In 1976 he was made a monsignor and in 1980 became a bishop. It was then that Fingal, coming to Rome to celebrate the occasion, for the first time raised the subject of Kerry's becoming Pope.

'Now don't say it's a crazy dream –'

'I wasn't going to, Dad. Don't you think I've dreamed of it myself?'

'Is it possible?'

'It's a lottery. All you can do is buy as many tickets as you can.'

'You mean the cardinals can be bought, just like the pollies back home?' Even Fingal was surprised at the thought.

'No, not like that. You just make opportunities to be noticed. But I have a long way to go yet, two more steps. I have to make cardinal first.'

'How long will that take?' He was impatient now, he was seventy-five years old and occasionally he caught a whiff of the grave on the wind.

Kerry shrugged. 'Who knows? There are eighty-year-old cardinals over there in the Curia still hoping they'll get the vote.'

'Then we'll have to see you get noticed. Do they vote for saints as Pope these days?'

'I wouldn't fit the image, Dad.' He knew his limitations. 'No, I know my road. Communism is the enemy – if I can beat that wherever it's making inroads, then I'll be noticed. We'll just have to be patient.'

In 1983, by which time he had engineered his own small congregation, the Department for the Defence Against Subversive Religions, he was made an archbishop, one of the youngest in the Church. Fingal once more came to Rome to celebrate the elevation and to buy the apartment in the *palazzo* on the Tiber.

'It won't be out of character for an archbishop, you living

there. You can get a better car, too. What's the going model for an archbishop?'

'A Mercedes.'

Fingal shook his now white head. 'You haven't changed.'

'Have you?' said Kerry.

'What does that mean?'

'Isn't it time, Dad, you told me who you really are? You're – what? – seventy-eight this year. I think it's time you told me – and Brigid – who you were before we were born. The newspapers have already been on to me, they're already writing your obituary.'

'Who cares about the newspapers?'

'All right, forget the newspapers. What about Brigid and me? We have a right to know who you were. What have you got to hide?'

'Are you wanting to hear my confession?'

'In a way, yes.'

Fingal sat in a chair which had once seated a pope. This room, the main salon of the *palazzo*, held more secrets than he could ever divulge. He had at last begun to feel *old*: every road from here on was downhill, even though he sometimes felt he was *climbing* them. Winter (memories of Chicago) had begun to assail him once more. He spent his year now in perpetual summer, coming to Europe for it, going home for it. Like most old men he was beyond surprise but not beyond feeling. It both pleased and hurt him to learn that Kerry (and Brigid: it was always an effort to think of her these days) wanted to know who he really was. He had forgotten, if he had ever known, that a father owed more to his children than just their well-being.

Chicago and its ghosts were safely behind him now, though he had never been back there. O'Banion, Drucci and Moran were almost forgotten names; minor ghosts are kept alive only by discussing them and there had been no one with whom to discuss them. He still remembered Capone. He could close his eyes and see the Big Fella as clearly as on those days when he had faced him in the suite of the Metropolitan Hotel or in the back room of 2145 South Michigan, in Dr Alphonse Brown's surgery. But Capone was long dead and so was everyone who might have sought revenge for him; no dynasties die out so quickly as gangland ones. It was safe to kneel in the confessional:

'This is just between you and me. Brigid isn't to be told – I don't know she can be trusted to keep her mouth shut. You know what artists can be like.'

Kerry nodded, wondering what sort of sins he was about to hear. 'I shan't tell her, at least not till you're dead.'

Fingal hesitated, then accepted that. It might be a joke, if there were any jokes in the grave, to know how shocked some people would be to learn that Australia's richest man had begun life as a con man. Or maybe they would not be: Ned Kelly, the bushranger, was still a national hero.

'I was born in Ireland, in a village called Ballyseanduff, but I was taken to Chicago when I was six months old and I grew up there. I worked for Dion O'Banion and Al Capone –'

'You were a *gangster*?' It was Kerry who was shocked. He knew all about venality and skulduggery, but he was an innocent, though an archbishop, to real sin.

'No, I was not.' Fingal had his pride. 'I dealt in bootleg liquor, but I never belonged to any gang.'

'You said you worked for Al Capone –' His father had worked for one of history's worst villains, a latterday, low-class Borgia. He could see his whole career going up in smoke, but not the white smoke that signalled the election of a new Pope.

'Only as a consultant.' Fingal smiled: it was a joke that had lasted almost sixty years. 'I never carried a gun. Nor ordered anyone killed.' *Not till I came to Australia*. And that, now, was forty years behind him. 'I lived by my wits, the same as I've done in Australia. Only in Chicago I had to deal with gangsters.'

'Why?'

'Because in Chicago in those days a poor boy from a poor family got nowhere unless he worked for those with influence. And the gangsters had the influence. They ran the city. You've never seen corruption like it, not even here in Italy. If I wanted to get uptown, I had to forget everything my mother tried to tell me – she was a good Catholic woman, always praying for me, even took her rosary beads into the bath with her in case she had a seizure and drowned. I had to stop listening to her and listen to my father, who knew what the score was.' He sounded sincerely regretful, an honest moral boy who had had to bend his standards to survive. Old men have a tendency to colour not only their youth but their intentions. 'It wasn't easy.'

'Why did you leave Chicago?' Kerry was not taken in by his father's penitent tone.

Honesty, even towards one's son, could be taken too far: 'I could see myself getting too involved with Capone and the others.'

'Why did you choose Sydney, of all places?'

'I read it was warm.' That, at least, was the truth. He sat waiting for absolution; but none seemed forthcoming. At last he said, 'Well?'

'I don't know what to say,' said Kerry, never lost for a word. 'I always suspected you must have had something to hide. I thought you might have had another wife before Mother, that you'd run away from her . . . But Chicago in the Nineteen-Twenties! With Al Capone! God, if it should ever get out . . . !'

'It won't. That's why I don't think you should say anything to Brigid – you know what women are like.' Women and artists, the blabbermouths of the world. 'Well, maybe you don't know . . .' He sometimes forgot that his son was celibate. 'You've come this far. Nothing must spoil it now.'

Kerry nodded, still absorbed in what his father had told him; and what he had not told him. For he knew that only half the truth had been told. He had lived too long with his father not to recognize that he was a consummate liar. He didn't feel disappointed that he had been lied to: perhaps it was better not to know the whole truth.

Later, over dinner in the apartment's big dining-room, with the newly acquired staff hovering over them in black-and-white livery, like trained magpies, Kerry said, 'Are you thinking of retiring?'

'What would I do? I'll retire when you become Pope. I'll come here and live, maybe I'll become a born-again Catholic. Just for appearance's sake.' He knew The Lord would never accept him.

'You may be ninety years old before that happens.'

'I'll live that long, if it's necessary.' He would do his best, would get up-wind from the grave.

'You're not going to keep on with the day-to-day running of Ballyduff?'

'Why not? I'm still two streets ahead of anyone who works for me.'

'Give it away, Dad. Ease up. Let Jonathan take over.'

'Not a chance.'

He chewed carefully on *scaloppina al marsala*. He still had most of his own teeth, preserved at great expense by Sydney's best dentist, but he had a small bridge that occasionally caused him trouble. He usually solved the problem by taking out the bridge and wrapping it in his handkerchief, no matter what company he was in; the very rich and the very old have their own rules of etiquette. He took out the bridge now and a manservant, accustomed to either the habits of the rich or just ordinary sensible Italians, appeared at his elbow with a fresh napkin. Fingal, impressed, took it and wrapped his bridge in it and put it on the table beside his plate. He had always thought the Italians had plenty of imagination but no common sense; maybe he had been wrong. Al Capone had had both, but then he had gone to America.

'You don't mean it.' Kerry was surprised. He had never interfered in the affairs of Ballyduff, never ventured an opinion. He had, however, never missed a line of the annual reports, never failed to check the stock prices of the holding company and its myriad subsidiaries. 'I thought it was taken for granted that he'd . . .'

'No. It's never been in my mind that he would.'

'Who, then?'

'Bob Borsolino.'

'Does Jonathan know that?'

'No. Neither does Borsolino. They work better together if they're kept guessing.'

'Jonathan is the better of the two of them, I think that's generally recognized. When he got his knighthood, I thought you'd arranged that.'

Fingal shook his head. 'Not me. He arranged it himself.'

'I've often wondered why you didn't get one yourself.'

'What would Sir Fingal be beside Pope Kerry? People would always say you'd upstaged me.'

'But what about Jonathan? Why are you so against him? The board and the shareholders won't agree with you.'

'I have my reasons for not wanting him to take over.' It was difficult to explain enmity born out of plain hatred, so he didn't bother. Wars have been started for simpler reasons. 'That's where you and Brigid will come in. She has no time for him, no more than I have. When I go, you two and your trusts will have 51 per cent of the holding company – and the holding company has the preferential voting shares in the subsidiaries. I've seen to all that in my will. All you have to do is vote against him.' He looked up and across the table at the son to whom he had given so much. 'That's all you owe me.'

2

Four years passed before Jonathan Tewsday learned that he was never going to have the top job at Ballyduff.

258

He was within touching distance of his target in the business and social firmament. He was equal No. 2 in what was now the nation's largest and richest corporation, above even BHP and the other, more recently arrived high-flyers. He had a wife who was one of Sydney's leading hostesses, a charity Queen Bee, and three bright daughters who, he suspected, didn't think as much of him as he did himself. He had a sixty-foot cruiser, the Rolls-Royce and a BMW for Fiona, his knighthood, a country property outside Bowral and a mansion at Pymble on the North Shore. Pymble reeked of respectability, like the smell of old mouldering money; he had arrived in the land he had promised himself. It was not Israel; for some reason, there were few Jews in Pymble. He and Fiona were both anti-Semitic, though they would never admit it. Some of their best friends were Jews, but they didn't want to live amongst them. To do him justice, Tewsday didn't dislike Jews as much as he did the Irish. Or anyway the Hourigans.

In the Pymble house he now had a library: Fiona had introduced him to books. He was now known as a collector of antique books, though he had to rely on an antiquarian bookseller to guide him; it did, however, give him a certain cachet, it set him apart from other newly rich men who collected paintings. He did not read the antique books; they were for show. His reading consisted of what he called 'solid' books: biographies, English sagas by long-dead authors and books about business chicanery, which he enjoyed the most. He never read 'modern' authors, certainly not women authors, and still had never ventured into poetry.

When they moved into the big home in Pymble, Fiona decided she wanted live-in staff. Up till then she had got by with a cleaning woman coming in every day and a cook coming in late on the afternoons when they were having dinner parties. Tewsday had had a company chauffeur for several years, but he had been available only during business hours; Fingal had insisted that he and Bob Borsolino had to drive themselves in their own time. Now, Fiona said, it was time they engaged other people to look after them.

They advertised for a couple. They chose Gary Gawler and his wife Sally, the only couple to apply whose native tongue was English. No Australians applied: to be 'in service' was against the native grain. Gawler, however, was an American and his wife English, each from a country where helots could still be found if the price was right.

They were a couple obviously in love, a pair who looked as if they might have arrived at true love rather late and for the first time. He was in his early forties and she in her late thirties, he quiet and controlled, she jovial and outgoing. Each was good at his or her job and the Tewsdays were glad to have them.

Yet Tewsday never felt entirely at ease with Gawler. It was not because he lacked the confidence, so endemic amongst the newly rich, to handle personal staff. It was just that Gawler was always slightly distant, a superior slave; it was as if he carried with him an invisible screen to match the one that had been specially fitted between the driver's seat and that of the passengers in the Rolls-Royce. He never ventured any information about himself other than what had been in his references: that he was Chicago-born, had served in the US Army in Vietnam, had worked as chauffeur for retired widows in Missouri and Kansas. He was polite, a hard worker, never complained; but as enigmatic as one of the Chinese jade statuettes that Fiona was always buying. Nothing, it seemed, could disturb his cold equanimity except the sight of the cheerful Sally waiting for him when he drove Tewsday home each evening.

On one occasion the Rolls-Royce ran over a dog. The fox terrier sprinted out into the middle of the road; Tewsday, later, thought there would have been time for Gawler to brake. He didn't: he just went straight over the dog. He did draw in then to the side of the road and went back to see if the dog was dead.

When he came back Tewsday said, 'You could have avoided that, Garry.'

'Yes, sir.' Gawler was unperturbed; he might just have run over a road marker. 'But the car behind me would have run into us. I think humans are worth more than a dog, sir.'

There was no answer to that, unless you were an animal welfare enthusiast; which Tewsday was not. 'Is the dog dead?'

'Yes, sir. There doesn't seem to be anyone coming to claim it. Shall we drive on?'

Tewsday, feeling a little sick, nodded. He was upset more by Gawler's apparent callousness than by the death of the dog. The screen between them had thickened.

He tried to sound out Sally Gawler on her husband, but Sally, though loquacious, told him nothing. 'That's just him, Sir Jonathan. He's kindness itself to me, the best thing that's ever happened to me. He doesn't say much, unlike me, but that's the way some people are. It'd be a pretty noisy world, wouldn't it, if everyone was like me.'

Then, one night, Tewsday worked back in his office. His secretary had gone home and when he finally left the office there was no one in the building but the cleaners, the security men and the two caretakers. He went down in the lift on his own, from the sixty-eighth floor to the basement garage.

He stepped out of the lift into the half-lit garage. Most of the cars had gone; there were no more than half a dozen parked in the vast cave. His mind was still occupied by the desk work he had just left; Ballyduff had made a raid on one of its smaller competitors. His wits were not about him as he got out of the lift and turned towards where the Rolls-Royce was always parked. The youth, long-haired, unshaven and grubby, wielding a long-bladed knife, seemed to materialize out of nowhere.

'Okay, shit-head, gimme everything you got on you!'

Tewsday was pushed hard against the wall; the long-bladed knife was pricking the skin between his first and second chin. He was paralysed by fear; physical courage had never been

261

one of his attributes. He was on the verge of fainting; he knew his legs were going to fold under him at any moment. He could do nothing with his hands to give the mugger what he wanted; he just stood with his mouth and eyes wide open, an animal whimpering coming from him. The youth, with his free hand, began to rip at Tewsday's pockets.

Then Tewsday saw Gawler come out from behind the Rolls-Royce. He moved so silently, on the balls of his feet, that he was on the mugger before the latter saw him. Tewsday, closer to a killing, his own or anyone else's, than he would ever again be in his life, saw everything in frightening close-up. He saw Gawler take the youth from behind, wrapping a muscular arm round the scrawny neck. The knife flicked away from Tewsday's chins, cutting the top one; it went backwards to swipe at Gawler, but the American grabbed the wrist of the hand that held the knife, twisted, and the wrist was broken. The youth tried to scream with the pain, but the arm round his neck was pressing too tightly. Only a foot from him, watching the agony and the fear in the wide, drug-crazed eyes, Tewsday saw the youth die. Gawler gave a last savage jerk that broke the youth's neck, then let him drop to the floor.

'Come on, sir, let's get out of here!' Gawler was breathing heavily, but there was no sign of any emotion. He picked up the mugger's knife and put it in his pocket. 'I'll get rid of him. Pull yourself together!'

He grabbed the corpse's shoulders and dragged it across into a corner at the side of the lift. Tewsday was still leaning against the wall beside the lift door. His bladder had abruptly given way on him; he could feel the piss running down his legs. He gestured weakly as Gawler came back.

'What about the police?'

'We don't want any involvement, sir. Come on, sir!' Now Gawler sounded angry. He grabbed Tewsday by the arm and began to drag him towards the Rolls-Royce. 'Come on, for Christ's sake!'

Tewsday was a limp wreck, sodden from the crotch down. He was both terrified and embarrassed; he was certain the mugger had intended to kill him. He could not think straight; his mind, too, might have been full of piss. He made no effort to argue with Gawler. He let himself be dragged into the car, heard the door slammed behind him. Then Gawler was in the front seat, starting up the car without fuss or panic and a moment later the Rolls-Royce moved sedately up the ramp and out into the street. Tewsday twisted round and looked back. The garage was still deserted.

He said nothing all the way home to Pymble, just sat uncomfortably in his sodden trousers. Ever careful of his possessions, he had, however, picked up the floor mat, turned it over to its rubber side and put it between his wet behind and the leather of the car's seat. He knew that the acid in the urine could stain the leather and he did not want to have to explain it.

When they drew up in front of the house he got out at once, standing with his legs apart. The cut on his chin had stopped bleeding, but his handkerchief was blood-stained. He had regained some of his composure, but not much. 'I think we should have reported it, Gary.'

'No, sir. You would have been upset by the publicity, once it started.'

The shocking incident hadn't entirely dulled Tewsday's perceptions. 'I don't think you wanted publicity, either. Am I right?'

'If you say so, sir. This is just between you and me, okay?' He looked down at Tewsday standing with his legs apart, then back up at the big strained face. This was man to man, not servant to master. 'Nobody else is to know, not even Lady Tewsday or my wife, okay?'

Tewsday hesitated, then nodded. 'All right. Where did you learn to kill a man like that?'

'In Vietnam. Good-night sir. I'd get out of those trousers before you see Lady Tewsday.'

'What will you do with the knife?'

Gawler took the knife out of his pocket, looked at it as if he had forgotten it. 'I think I'll keep it as a souvenir. Goodnight, sir.'

Usually, when a servant saves a master's life, a bond is established; or so some classical tales would have us believe. It usually is a sense of debt on the master's part. Tewsday, however, was not allowed to feel any such thing; for which he was glad. Gawler made no mention of the incident again, not even the next morning. Tewsday, still embarrassed by his own abject behaviour, still shocked by the cold-blooded way Gawler had disposed of the mugger, could find no way of broaching the subject. He had not even thanked Gawler for saving his life, yet he felt it was already too late to do that. The killing of the junkie seemed as inconsequential as the running down of the dog. Gawler was colder and more distant than ever.

Tewsday managed to hide his stained trousers from Fiona, but she was intrigued by the cut on his chin. 'Been duelling with Fingal?'

'That's not funny,' he said and gave her no explanation.

The youth's body had been discovered later that night by one of the security men. A Sergeant Clements from Homicide came to interview Tewsday, but he could tell the detective nothing – 'Yes, I worked late last night, but I saw nothing when I went down into the garage. I gather my driver saw nothing.'

'I've already talked to him,' said Clements. 'Nobody seems to have seen anything.'

Was the big lumbering oaf being sarcastic? 'You sound as if you don't believe us, Sergeant.'

'Why would I do that?' said Clements and went away. Nothing more was heard from the police. The case, it appeared, was closed. The mugger, a known junkie with a record, was expendable.

Gawler continued to trouble Tewsday. He had always

prided himself on knowing what made people tick; he told himself that even Fingal Hourigan was no secret to him. Knowing who Gawler really was, what was behind that cool façade, became an obsession with him. He finally phoned a man he had not spoken to in thirty years, someone he had hoped never to see again.

Jack Paxit came to the offices of Ballyduff. He had long ago given up bouncing at night-clubs and now ran the best-known private detective agency in the city. He was in his early sixties now, as beefy as ever but smoother, someone who would talk a man out of a situation rather than throw him out. He had once had a cauliflower ear, but had had cosmetic surgery done on it and it now looked like a white eggplant. He wore an expensive navy-blue suit, but he somehow looked out of place in it, as if he had only borrowed it for the occasion.

'Sir Jonathan, long time no see. You're still the Invisible Man, remember? But I hope it's not that old case, is it? I'm respectable now.'

'Who isn't?' said Tewsday, regretting now that he had sent for Paxit; but it was done and so must be gone through with. 'I want you to trace the background of someone who works for me. Do you have access to computer systems?'

'If the price is right, you can have access to anything you care to name. It's the Freedom of Information Act.' He was the sort of man who had to grin to tell you he was joking.

If the price is right: how many times had he heard that? 'Overseas systems? The US Army, the FBI, systems like that?'

'Computer systems don't know any boundaries.' Paxit screwed up his blunt face. 'This guy must be special?'

'I don't know,' Tewsday confessed. 'My suspicions may add up to nothing. He's my chauffeur – he and his wife live in at our place. I want to know more about him than he's prepared to tell me.'

'If he's just your driver, why not get rid of him if he worries you?'

'There's more to it than that.' Though he would never be

able to explain it. 'This is strictly between you and me – it's not a company matter. I'd like the information as soon as possible, but be thorough. Name your own price.'

'My price is reasonable, Sir Jonathan – you must remember that from the old days. It's what the others will charge that will cost.'

'The others? Will others need to know?' He was technically, or anyway technologically, ignorant. He appreciated the worth of computers, but he could not work one. He had grown up in an age when sums were done on scraps of paper; he was a brilliant mental mathematician, faster than the whiz kids with their calculators, but was an idiot in front of a computer. 'Can't you do it?'

'Sir Jonathan, in computer exercises there's always someone who has to know. The systems don't work on their own. It's the human beings who make it dangerous, not the machines. You still want me to go ahead?'

'Can it be traced back to me? I mean the line of enquiry?'

'It'll be traced back to me. I'm a private enquiry agent, that's what my licence says. They won't want to waste their time going past me. Not if the price is right. There's a certain honesty about computer hackers.'

'Really?' said Tewsday, who always doubted anyone who claimed to be honest. They were like those who claimed to have a sense of humour, jokers who found it hard to take a joke against themselves.

Paxit came back with the information on Gawler in two weeks: the price must have been right. He put down the envelope on Tewsday's desk. 'It's all in there, Sir Jonathan. Everything you need to know. I'd be careful of him.'

'Is that your comment or the computer's?'

'Computers don't have opinions, only facts. Would you care to pay me in cash?'

'I thought you were respectable now?'

Paxit smiled. 'Taxation makes it difficult. There are limits a man can go to. If only cash changes hands between us, who's to know we've done any business? You can be the Invisible Man again. Or was it me?'

'Twenty-five thousand – I don't have that much on hand. I'll send it by courier tomorrow.'

'No receipt, no pack drill – okay? Good luck, Sir Jonathan.' He looked around the big elegant office. 'You've come a long way.'

There's an even bigger, more elegant office one floor above: I haven't finished climbing.

Paxit went back to his agency, to his flexible respectability, and Tewsday looked at the record of Gawler's life. He had indeed been born in Chicago, as he had said, but his name had not been Gary Gawler. It was Alphonse Brown and he was the son of a petty crook with a long list of convictions. He had served in Vietnam, but with a counter-terrorist unit run by the CIA; he had been credited (credited? Tewsday wondered) with no fewer than seventeen killings and probably more. After the end of the Vietnam war he had stayed on in South-east Asia, moving to Bangkok, where he had worked freelance for the CIA; the report had nothing specific on what he had done for the agency. His contract had been abruptly terminated, no reason given, and he had moved on to Hong Kong. He had worked there for a year; again there were no details. He had gone back to the United States, had various jobs, no specific details, and had served three years in Joliet Prison, Illinois, for manslaughter: he had killed a man in a bar-room brawl. When he had been released he had changed his name to Ray Karr and had disappeared, at least from the computer records, for three years. When he surfaced again he was back in Bangkok, working for an American drug smuggler (here, a reference code was given). He was suspected of three more killings, but they were expendable victims, other drug smugglers, and the Thai police had not bothered following up the murders. It was in Bangkok in early 1986 that Ray Karr had met Sally Heston, spinster, on holiday on an organized tour. He had followed her to Hong Kong and they had been married there; he had signed the register as Gary Gawler, business consultant. The information ended there, except for the Australian immigration records that the Gawlers, man and wife, had arrived back in Australia in June 1986. If there was any further information in the Australian system it had not been accessible or the price had not been right. No matter: Tewsday knew all he wanted to know. Possibly more: he felt a deepening sense of fear.

He said nothing to Gawler of what he had learned. As he was driven to the office each morning he studied the chauffeur from the back: I'm employing a professional killer, he told himself with horror and wonder. Yet he made no attempt to dismiss Gawler; it was a week or two before he admitted to himself that he was afraid to. Gawler, for his part, seemed unaware of the deeper scrutiny to which he was being subjected. He was as coolly self-contained as ever; the killing of the junkie might never have taken place. He drove Tewsday home each evening and only then did his composure show the slightest crack. His face would light up at the sight of Sally waiting for him. Tewsday, angry with himself, would envy him; there was none of that feeling left between him and Fiona. He wondered how much Sally knew about her husband's past life, but he knew he would never again attempt to question her. He was afraid of what Gawler might do to him.

So the odd situation continued and after a while Tewsday grew to live with it. The Rolls-Royce became a merry-go-round, though he felt no merriment: he rode behind Gawler on a carousel from which he couldn't alight.

3

Brigid Hourigan came back to Australia in the spring of 1986, bringing with her a young handsome Italian who, quite obviously, was her houseman in more ways than one. Though not an alcoholic, she had become a regular drinker, another characteristic which set her apart from her father, the tee-totaller. She bought a waterfront house on Pittwater, twenty-five miles north of Sydney, set up a studio but painted only spasmodically. With her salaried lover, her daughter the nun now in Nicaragua, her father and brother more estranged from her than ever, she had become bitterly aware of the gaping holes in her life. She blamed no one, but that didn't help: she might have done better to have had a focus for her bitterness.

Fingal was glad to have his daughter at least within driving distance; but he could not bring himself to tell her so. He had never feared loneliness before; he had always found a certain safety in it. Now, however, safe at last beyond all danger and worry, he had begun to hanker for company and (yes, though he found it hard to believe) love. Kerry loved him, or so he made himself believe; but Kerry now spent all his time in Rome. Fingal went there every northern summer, but as soon as the cold winds came down the spine of the Apennines he would leave and return to Sydney. There the loneliness would creep in on him again, another kind of winter.

Sometimes he even thought of calling up Tilly Mosman and asking her to visit him. He had not seen her in twelve years, not since he had had the property division buy up the whole street in Surry Hills and then told Tilly to take up a long lease on the two big terrace houses. He had given her the money to pay the first three years of the lease, then bade her goodbye. To his chagrin and embarrassment, the lead had started to slip out of his pencil; too often Tilly, for all her tricks, failed to arouse his erection. To his further embar-rassment, because he had always prided himself on his appear-ance, his body, if not his face, had become an old man's, stringy and wrinkled. He had never been one for making love in the dark: Sheila had liked it best in broad daylight. Now he had turned out the light for ever on love-making and Tilly had become only a memory, occasionally revived.

Jonathan Tewsday revived the memory on one occasion when they were alone after a board meeting. 'Did you know we own the lease on the Quality Couch?' Fingal looked at him feigning puzzlement and Tewsday explained. 'The top brothel in town.'

'Are you visiting brothels now?'

'Don't be sanctimonious, Fingal. Yes, I've been there a couple of times. Fiona and I are not the best of friends, well, not *that* way.'

Fingal was embarrassed; he did not like people to confess their bedroom problems. 'You're taking a risk, aren't you? You'd be recognized.'

'I went twice, that was all. Some of our Japanese clients had heard of it and when –' he named a top Japanese industrialist '– came out here, our PR man put on a party there. I went along.'

'That was once. Why twice?'

'I enjoyed myself, if you want the truth. I don't think being recognized would cause any harm – you'd be surprised who I saw there, girls as well as clients. Even two of our best-known girls-about-town work there.'

He waited as if he expected Fingal to show interest; but the latter had never been interested in gossip, not even when Tilly had been coming to his bed in the flat in Macquarie Street. 'Is it a good house?'

'The best. Five star.'

'They ever troubled by the police?'

'Not as far as I know.'

Good: it seemed that Tilly had taken care of herself. He felt pleased for her: she had made him happy at one time. 'So long as they pay the lease, leave 'em alone. We'd only get bad publicity if we closed them down.'

'Are you thinking of your son the Archbishop?' said Tewsday shrewdly.

'No. He's never been a customer there,' said Fingal. 'I was thinking of you.'

Tewsday left him then, angry that he had raised the subject of the Quality Couch. The old bastard could never resist scoring points.

He went downstairs and into Bob Borsolino's office. The other managing director looked up in annoyance; he was a workaholic, a man who hated wasting a minute of office time. Tewsday sat down uninvited and Borsolino sighed and leaned back in his chair.

'Bob, you ran the properties division ten or twelve years ago, right? Who recommended we buy up the whole of Sandhill Street, Surry Hills?'

Borsolino frowned. He had a narrow bony face that seemed to be continually frowning, as if he were deep in some financial problem, an accountant squeezed thin by heavy ledgers. 'Hell, I don't know, Jonathan – no, wait a minute. Is that the street where they have that brothel, what's it called?' He was a highly moral man, except when it came to creative accounting.

'The Quality Couch.'

'What a name!' He shook his head, his lank hair falling down over his brow. He had none of Tewsday's smoothness, tailored or otherwise, but then he had never aspired to appearances. He had other aspirations, though he had never confessed them to anyone, not even his wife. 'It was the boss who told me to buy up that street. I can't remember if he said anyone had recommended it to him. We looked it up and thought it was a good buy for the future, in case it was re-zoned. It's still residential and I guess we've just hung on to it.'

'Did Fingal recommend the lease to the brothel owner, Tilly Mosman?'

Borsolino frowned again, then laughed. 'Jonathan, d'you think the old man's been making money on the side out of a brothel? I don't know who recommended the owner, or if anyone did. When she took out the lease, she certainly wouldn't have said she wanted it for a brothel. All I can remember is that she wanted a long lease, renewable every five years, and the old man okayed it. Those were the days, you remember them, when he poked his finger in every pie.'

'An unfortunate phrase, but thanks, Bob.' And Tewsday went back to his own office satisfied that, even if not now, there had once been a connection between Fingal and Tilly Mosman.

Then he heard that Fingal's granddaughter, the nun Sister Mary Magdalene, had come to Sydney from Nicaragua. He discovered the fact by accident when he rang Fingal at home one Sunday and Mrs Kelly, the housekeeper, said she didn't want to interrupt Himself because he was entertaining his granddaughter – 'A lovely young nun, she's just come home from one of them South American places, Mick or Nick something-or-other.'

Tewsday hung up, then called Brigid. 'Your daughter's home, I hear. Congratulations.'

Brigid was cool. 'Thank you, Jonathan. But we're keeping it as quiet as possible, if you don't mind. She's a nun, she doesn't want to be bothered by the Hourigan name.'

'Of course not. It must be nice to have her so close to you again.'

He told Fiona and she, being a society hostess, which meant not missing the opportunity to examine any newcomer with the proper connections, even if she was a nun, suggested a dinner party for the Hourigans.

'You must be out of your head!' said Tewsday, though the idea intrigued him. 'Nuns don't go to dinner parties, do they? And Fingal would never come. Neither would Brigid, for that matter.'

'Leave it to me,' said Fiona. 'It's time I met Brigid. I'm told you once had a yen for her.'

'Who told you that?'

'I heard it at the bottom of a football scrum.' She had never forgotten her All Black heritage. Her approach to her society hostess competitors was said to be as rugged as that of her rugby compatriots.

Tewsday never learned how she did it, but she brought the three Hourigans to dinner at the house in Pymble. Twelve sat down at the table, all well mixed: the Tewsdays, the Hourigans, a politician, a businessman, a lawyer and their respective wives and a young gallery owner looking for buyers. The two older Hourigans, father and daughter, were quiet, as if uncomfortable with each other's company as with that of the other guests. Only the granddaughter, the nun whom everyone expected to be mum, was voluble and gay.

'I was teaching some girls in Year Twelve the other day and I mentioned adultery. What's adultery? said one of them. Some sort of kinky sex, said another one of them. I'm not even sure they were pulling my leg. The kids of today are way out, I can't keep up with them.'

'I suppose it's much different in Nicaragua?' said Fiona.

'Where is it?' said the businessman's wife, brain as feathery as her teased-out hair. 'I keep seeing it in the headlines, but I've never tried to find it on the map.'

Mary Magdalene stopped being gay, gave her a withering look. 'Oh, it's on the map, all right. I'd like to come and talk to you some time about it, Grandpa.'

Grandpa Fingal took a moment to recover from being so addressed. 'You should talk to your uncle, the Archbishop. He knows more about that part of the world than I do.'

'Oh, I have talked to him,' said Mary Magdalene, and Brigid, sitting beside her, looked at her sharply. 'I want to talk to lots of people about Nicaragua, now I'm here in Sydney.'

'We have our own problems, my dear,' said the politician, whose party was not in power and didn't look like winning it.

'I'd love to go there,' said the gallery owner. 'I just adore Aztec art. It's so *knowing*.' Whatever that meant.

'I tried to talk Mother into coming there to paint.'

'We'll go there together!' exclaimed the gallery owner.

'I'd love that,' said Brigid without enthusiasm.

Fingal contributed little to the dinner conversation, but at least he succeeded in not being ungracious. He was fascinated by his granddaughter, still finding it hard to believe that his blood ran in her veins. His mother, whom he had not thought of in a long time, would have been in a fit of religious ecstasy: a grandson an archbishop and a great-granddaughter a nun. He was covertly gazing at the young nun, looking for signs of himself in her, a hopeless search, when Fiona touched his arm. 'Fingal?'

He blinked, then looked at her. 'Eh?'

'You seemed miles away.'

'I was.' He had always tolerated Fiona, neither liking nor disliking her. Sometimes he wondered what she had ever seen in her husband. 'I'm just getting used to the idea of having a grandchild. It's a shock to a man of my age.'

'I'm looking forward to having mine, when my daughters get around to it. I like the idea of the continuum of the family – I've traced my own family back three hundred and fifty years in Scotland. The present and the past, the now and the then, they are always connected, don't you think?'

'The now and the then,' he repeated. 'Yes, I guess you're right. Which do you prefer?'

'Oh, the now,' she said. 'The present. At least we know that, don't we?'

'I guess so.' But he had an old man's memory and the past was clearer for him than it was for her.

At the other end of the table Tewsday had been studying Sister Mary Magdalene. He could see something of Brigid in her; they were both iconoclasts; the young nun had already made some joking remarks about Big Business, though she had been polite enough to make out she was referring to the Americans. There was something in her, however, that suggested something more passionate in her beliefs than Brigid had ever shown. He had the feeling that Sister Mary Magdalene, for all of her mother's statement that she wanted to be divorced from the Hourigan name, would some day look for publicity for whatever causes she adopted.

When dinner was over and the guests were leaving, Fingal offered his granddaughter a lift back to her convent in Randwick, but Brigid intervened. 'She's coming home with me, Dad. She has the weekend off.'

He was disappointed, but didn't show it. 'Well, come and see me some time, Teresa.'

'Oh, I'll do that, Grandpa. I want you on my side.'

He looked at Brigid, who had never been on his side; then back at his granddaughter. 'What side is that?'

'I'll tell you when I come to visit you.'

But she did not come to the castle in Vaucluse till Kerry arrived home unexpectedly with the two Nicaraguans, Paredes and Domecq. Fingal had already had hints of what was expected of him in the way of financial support; he had looked at his fortune and knew the money wouldn't be missed. He was just unprepared for the sudden arrival of Kerry and the two Nicaraguans and the speed with which they wanted the arms deal done.

It was the day after Kerry's return that Teresa (Fingal could not bring himself to call her Mary Magdalene or even Mary) came to Vaucluse. For the first time Fingal saw the passion in her when she confronted her uncle; she was even more of a zealot than he because she had no control over her temper. There was a stand-up fight in the big drawing-room, a substitute set for the Nicaraguan mountains; she hurled threats and insults at Kerry and he responded with heated rage. Fingal suddenly turned against his granddaughter; she was his daughter's daughter and more. The threats, he saw, were a real danger: she could throw Kerry's progress right off the rails. She knew too much and she would use that knowledge in her cause. It didn't matter whether she was a Marxist or not, he had no time for labels; she was a threat to Kerry and that was enough. So Fingal turned against her and, as always when opposed, became implacable.

He was sitting in his office next day, a Friday, his mind still stewing with yesterday's fight, when Tewsday, unannounced, walked in. 'I think we'd better have a talk, Fingal.'

Fingal stared at him a moment, then he pressed the button on his intercom. 'We're not to be interrupted. No calls, nothing.' Then he settled back in his high-backed chair. 'Shoot.'

'An appropriate word,' said Tewsday, who had never been noted for his humour, 'in the circumstances. Austarm, where we make things that shoot.'

'Don't be a comic, Jonathan. What's biting you?'

'This deal that Kerry is trying to put through with his Nicaraguan mates. You're out of your head, Fingal, if you think the board will let you get away with that. Not to mention what Canberra will say.'

'Who told you about the deal?'

'It doesn't matter who told me.' It had been the managing director of Austarm, a man stunned by the size of the foreign orders. So many Australians, Tewsday knew from experience, were frightened by bigness. 'I *know*.'

'It's none of your business. Ballyduff won't be paying for the arms. It's a deal between Austarm and the Saudis.'

'Oh, come off it! The Saudis have nothing to do with it. Jesus, Fingal, what's the matter with you? Has Kerry got you wrapped round his little finger with all that anti-Communism stuff he's been peddling? Is he running for Pope or something?' It was a random remark, but Tewsday saw at once that there was a target he had never suspected. The discovery stopped him in his tracks for a moment; he was not religious, but he had just been confronted with a vision. 'Good Christ! He's really thinking about that, isn't he?'

'You're the one who's out of his head,' said Fingal, wondering how much had shown in his face; nothing showed now but cold hatred of this man across the desk from him. 'Go on.'

Tewsday sat a moment, heady with his discovery. He had no idea how the Catholic Church worked; he was a money

276

man and he assumed that money, as in every other field, could buy position in the Church. *If the price was right* ... And Kerry, more than any other cleric in the world, would have the cash behind him. He could see now why Fingal was taking risks that he would never have otherwise contemplated.

'Your secret's safe with me, Fingal.' He all at once felt confident, in control here in this office that, some day soon, would be his. 'It doesn't concern me. But Ballyduff's name does. If this gets out, have you thought about what will go down the drain? We are up for renewal of our mining leases in Western Australia – the State Government there would be glad to kick us out and give the leases to their local boys. We're just about to sign that Federal ship-building contract for our yards in South Australia – 280 million dollars' worth. Canberra would cancel that without a moment's notice. For Christ's sake, Fingal, you're going to walk all over the people we have to cultivate – and for what? So your son can give arms to a bunch of right-wing nuts in some Central American jungle!'

'I always thought you were a right-wing nut. You bent your knee every time you mentioned that nut up in Queensland.'

'That's in my own country. And I wasn't supplying him with arms, busting up Ballyduff's contracts to do it! It's not on, Fingal. I'm seeing Bob Borsolino when he gets back from Melbourne and we'll call a board meeting for Monday afternoon. You're not going to take Ballyduff down the gurgler because your son has some crazy idea about being Pope!'

'Sit down, Jonathan.' Tewsday had risen, but he sat down again as Fingal waved a stiff hand at him. 'First, you're wrong about the Pope bit – you just don't know how the system works. If Kerry wants to be Pope, that's his ambition, not mine.'

'You're a liar, Fingal – I saw it in your face when I first mentioned it.'

'You're wearing out your welcome,' said Fingal softly. Tewsday found himself leaning across the desk to hear him.

'Second, *I* run this corporation, not you, not Borsolino and not the board. Third, you're finished!'

'*Finished?*'

Fingal nodded. He could not have imagined that he would enjoy this moment so much; but there was no outward sign of his enjoyment. His voice was still soft, but every word had a hard edge to it. 'You can go back downstairs and write out your resignation. Say anything you like, so long as you say it in two lines.' He sat back, raised his voice a little. 'I've already worked out your golden handshake. I'll have Miss Stevens type it out and it'll be on your desk in ten minutes.'

Tewsday was still leaning across the desk, but now he needed its support under his stiff arms. 'You really are out of your head! You think I'm going to *resign*? Just because you've told me to? I'm not the office boy, Hourigan – I'm the joint managing director! I'm lined up to be executive chairman when we finally push you out of here!'

'You couldn't be more wrong, Jonathan. It was never on the cards that you'd sit in this chair ...' He had had power for years, but he had never felt as powerful as at this moment. He wondered if Capone had felt like this when he had ordered Moran and the others eliminated. Holding a man's fate in your hands was the ultimate power, he told himself. But, as Tewsday had said, he was out of his head, though he would never have admitted to any madness.

'You'll have to fire me! You'll have to get the board to back you – and that'll never happen! You'll be the one to go!'

Fingal shook his head. 'You're being stupid, Jonathan. You know who has the voting stock. *I've* got it – and it doesn't matter a bugger what the board says or does. Goodbye, Jonathan. Try and say it all in two lines.'

He swung his chair round and faced the window. When he turned back a minute later Tewsday had gone. Then the reaction set in. What if Tewsday went downstairs and called a press conference, brought everything out into the open? A vindictive man knows what another vindictive man can do.

All at once he felt the vertigo that can affect old men. Here on the sixty-ninth floor, at the top of this most tangible monument to himself, he suddenly felt Ballyduff House begin to tremble beneath him.

4

Tewsday did not call a press conference. His rage almost blinded him; but not quite. Ballyduff had to be saved, not destroyed; which was what Fingal was going to do. He didn't write out his resignation; how can one resign in two lines after thirty-three years? Kings could, perhaps; but not he. He would spend the weekend marshalling his forces.

He went to bed that Friday night with his mind in turmoil. He and Fiona now slept in separate rooms; occasionally they met for love-making, like a senior citizens' wing-ding. He could not have slept beside her that night; he was an open book to her and she would have read every page of him. He tossed and turned all night, his rage increasing. All the years of enmity turned him mad, though, like the other madman, he did not recognize the madness.

In the morning Fiona, their daughters and Sally Gawler left for the Bowral property for the weekend. 'Will you be down this evening?' Fiona said.

'No. I've got too much to do.'

'Are you all right? You look as if you've spent the whole night at the bottom of a ruck.'

Christ, why did she have to drag up these bloody rugby similes? 'I'm all right. Get on your way or you'll be caught up in the traffic.'

She and the girls and Sally Gawler drove off in the BMW. He stood for a moment, abruptly lost; Fiona, for all their disagreements and the growing distance between them, was his only support. Maybe he should have confided in her ...

'I don't think I'll wash the car, sir.' He became aware of Gawler standing in the driveway between the house and the garages. 'It's going to rain. Will you be needing me today?'

'I'm not sure, Gary. Stay around.'

He went back inside, tried to phone Bob Borsolino at his hotel in Melbourne and missed him. He did not want to contact the other board members until he had talked to Borsolino. He spent the rest of the day planning his attack at Monday's board meeting. By Monday evening Fingal would be cut out and he would be executive chairman. Tomorrow he would go down to Pittwater and woo Brigid. Hers would be the deciding voting stock.

He did not believe in fate; yet it was fate, he appreciated, that brought the phone call from Fingal's granddaughter that Saturday afternoon. 'Sir Jonathan, may I come to see you? It's important.'

'What's it about?' His voice was sharp. Had her grandfather arranged this, was this some cunning ploy on Fingal's part?

'It's about a company called Austarm, one of my grandfather's subsidiaries.'

'Does he know you're calling me?'

'Heavens, no! Don't mention it to him – he'd kill me! Please, Sir Jonathan, let me see you – it's important! I can come to your house this afternoon –'

'No!' He had never felt like this before, his nerves worn ragged. Well, yes, he had: the night the junkie had threatened to kill him. But this was worse: his whole life was threatening to crash down around him, yet he would still be alive. 'I'll – wait a minute. You've caught me by surprise. Come – can you come at eight o'clock this evening?'

'That's later than I'd like –'

'Eight o'clock,' he said firmly. 'Do you know how to get here?'

'Sir Jonathan, I found my way around the mountains of

Nicaragua for two years. I don't think I'm likely to get lost in Pymble.'

She arrived on time. She was wearing a grey raincoat against the rain that had started to fall in mid-afternoon; only a sharp-eyed observer would have noticed her as a nun. Tewsday, always a man with an eye for what other people wore, thought she looked smart and not too obvious. Nuns were not regular visitors to this house.

'Does anyone know you've come to see me?'

She gave him a quizzical look, one of her grandfather's. 'Does it matter? No, Sir Jonathan, nobody knows. At the convent they think I've gone to stay with – with a friend.'

'Have you had dinner?' He was ambivalent towards her: he wanted to be rid of her as soon as possible, yet he wanted to know more about her. She was the only Hourigan towards whom he had no antagonism.

'Yes, I had supper before I left.'

'I hope they feed you well at the convent?'

'Bread and water.' She smiled, but he could see that she was nervous and highly strung.

He took her into his library. Gawler, playing houseman for the evening, brought them drinks: a Scotch for Tewsday, vodka on the rocks for Mary Magdalene. 'I need a little strength,' she said when she ordered it. 'I'm trying to be Joan of Arc or something and it's a little scary.'

He had only a smattering of knowledge of European history, but he had seen the movie. 'Didn't she take on the archbishops?'

'Oh, she took on everyone. I'm not going to do that. Though I'm taking on *one* archbishop.'

'I shouldn't imagine you'd be scared of anything,' said Tewsday. 'Not if you've been in Nicaragua amongst all that's going on there. Pymble is considered pretty safe. Even for socialists,' he added tentatively and she smiled, humouring him.

She sipped her vodka: a Russian drink, Tewsday noted. But then it was also the favourite drink of Fiona, a Presbyterian and female All Black. 'I think you should know about Austarm and what my Uncle Kerry and those two Contra men are trying to do ...'

Then she proceeded to tell him what he already knew; but more. He said nothing, listening to her without expression. At last he said, 'What do you want me to do?'

'You're the managing director of Austarm – you should be able to stop it!'

'It isn't that easy –' He couldn't tell her how powerless he was, that her grandfather held all the cards and all the voting stock.

'Nothing's easy! God, don't you think I know that?' She was beginning to boil beneath the surface, but she was still in control of herself. 'You have to do *something*! That's why I've come to you – you're my last hope. Well, almost ...'

'What do you mean by that? Almost ...?'

She took a deep breath; all at once there was a look of despair on her pretty face. 'I'm going to tell it all to the newspapers and to television, to *Four Corners* or some programme like that. I was hoping I wouldn't have to do that – that you would help me – you're one of the managing directors. I tried to get in touch with Mr Borsolino – I've never met him – but he's away somewhere –'

'He's down in Melbourne, he'll be back tomorrow night ... I don't think you need to see him. I don't think you need to talk to the newspapers, either.'

'Oh, I'm going to talk to them!' She took a long gulp at her drink; it took a moment for her to recover. 'Grandpa threw me out of his house – even my uncle threatened me. They're mad, you know. They've got to be stopped. The only way to do it is to give the story to the newspapers.'

'That will have more effect than you realize. It could bring down a whole corporation, the biggest in the country, drop its prices on the stock exchange –'

'Does it matter?'

Oh Christ, he thought, she's mad, too, the whole bloody

Hourigan lot are mad. 'I think your vows of poverty have warped your vision, my dear ...'

He sounded patronizing, episcopalic. She saw her uncle in him and began to bridle.

'There are hundreds of thousands of people who depend on Ballyduff for their jobs and income ...' He really didn't care about Ballyduff shareholders and employees. The *hoi polloi* always survived: there was always the dole.

'There are hundreds of thousands of people in Nicaragua who could be killed if a full scale war breaks out there. Do the Ballyduff people want their jobs and income to come from that?'

'You're exaggerating everything. You're cockeyed with your Marxism –'

She laughed, a harsh sound in such a young throat. 'God, you sound just like my uncle! I'm not a Marxist – I've never read a political pamphlet in my life – all I'm concerned about is the people I lived amongst ... Are you in favour of selling the arms to my uncle and his friends?'

'No, I'm not. I'm trying to prevent it. But it shouldn't be done by going to the newspapers. There are left-wing journalists here in Sydney who'd make hay out of that –'

'They're the ones I'm looking for, someone who'll make a big splash ... I'm going to them, Sir Jonathan. I don't trust anyone any more. I thought you might back me up – from what I understand, you run the corporation from day to day ... But you've known about this all along, haven't you? I'm telling you nothing new.'

'No, I found out about it only yesterday. And I'm telling you – I'll do my best to stop it. But I'll do it my way!'

'No, you won't – not if you won't go to the newspapers. You'll hide it all there in the boardroom – my grandfather will find some other way of getting those arms to the Contras. You won't stand up to him – nobody does. I've only known him for a few months and I can see he rules everyone – he's a despot! I should have known – all you people care about is making money! You may not have any time for the Contras, but if it'll make you money, you don't care!'

He didn't know if it was the drink; not just one glass of vodka on the rocks, surely. She was drunk on something else: zeal, fervour, whatever it was that drove these religious cranks beyond reason.

'Sister, sit down – listen to me –'

She had risen, was heading for the door. He plunged after her, got between her and the door. 'Get out of my way!'

He put out a hand, grabbed the lapel of her raincoat. 'Listen to me! You can't go to the newspapers – that will ruin everything! I can stop the arms sale – I can beat your grand-father! Listen to me –'

All at once she was beyond listening, there was something in her (a madness? fanaticism?) that had turned her deaf. She saw her friend Rose Caracas, dead and buried now, the frightened José Caracas and his children, the unconscious figure of Audrey Burke lying in the dusty village street, Sister Carmel torn between neutrality and beliefs ... She hit at Tewsday with her fist: he was a dozen men: her grandfather, her uncle, the Contra lieutenant, everyone who had to be fought. Her fist struck him on his plump cheek. Without thinking, he hit back. The heel of his hand caught her beneath the jaw. Her eyes abruptly rolled back in their sockets, she moaned, then fell in a heap at his feet. Just as the junkie had done ...

The door was pushed against his back. He fell forward, just managing to avoid stepping on the unconscious girl, grabbed the back of a chair and spun round to see Gawler standing in the doorway. 'You all right, Sir Jonathan?'

All he could do was nod. He was trembling, his legs shaking under him. Was he going to piss himself again?

'I heard most of that, sir. You want me to get rid of her?'

Tewsday looked at him, uncomprehending.

'It'll be easy, sir, no trouble. She's a Commie, isn't she? I saw her kind in 'Nam ...'

'*Kill* her?'

Good Christ, was murder this easy? He had no memory of how he had felt thirty years before when he had purchased that other murder. That had been a hands-off affair, the victim had not been lying at his feet. He looked at Gawler – was he another fanatic, a Commie killer? No: he was just a plain killer. *It'll be easy, sir, no trouble . . .*

'How?' he croaked.

'Leave it to me. I'll dump her somewhere –'

'No, not anywhere. Dump – put her –' He was still trembling, even his voice; the plummy tone had gone, it was the flat voice of his youth, the barren country he had escaped from. 'Do you know the Quality Couch?'

'The brothel, the one in Surry Hills? Sure, sir.'

'Yes, yes. Put her there – on the doorstep –'

Gawler smiled as he picked up the still unconscious Mary Magdalene. 'A nun on a brothel's doorstep. You got a nice sense of humour, Sir Jonathan.'

Tewsday's mind had always been a calculator; it had stopped working for a while, but now it was in gear again. It was only his nerves that were not under control. He began to giggle, but it was from hysteria, not humour. He was going to avenge himself on the Hourigans with one deed.

Gawler took Teresa Hourigan across to the garage. There he put the junkie's long-bladed knife into her heart. He laid the body out on the garage floor on sheets of newspaper till the wound had stopped bleeding. Then he buttoned up the raincoat and put the body in the boot of the second-hand Toyota that was his and Sally's own car. He then got into the front seat of the car and slept till three a.m. when his wrist-alarm woke him. Ten minutes later he drove out of the grounds and headed for the south side of the city and Surry Hills. He felt a certain excitement being back on the job he did best. He was glad, however, that Sally had not been home.

Fingal Hourigan was deeply shocked by the murder of his granddaughter. He did not show it when Inspector Malone and Sergeant Clements came to the Vaucluse mansion on the Sunday morning; he acted the opposite to what he felt, because it was natural for him to resent any invasion of his privacy. When the two detectives had gone, he said 'I'll stay home. You go, Kerry, and say Mass.'

Kerry, equally shocked, said, 'I'll say it for her.'

'Keep it to yourself. Don't announce it publicly.'

'You're not going to be able to keep this out of the papers. They'll be here as soon as they know who Teresa was.' When she had called him and asked could she see him again yesterday, he had unhesitatingly agreed. The urge to convert is an appetite; but it worked both ways. She had arrived with all her arguments still intact and after a while he had replied with the same anger. But she had not deserved to die, not in such a way.

'They'll never get past the gates.'

'You'd better call Brigid.'

'Not yet.' The old man had sat down. 'I – I've got to get myself together. I'll call her soon.'

Kerry had never seen his father like this before; not since Sheila, his mother, had died. 'I'll be back as soon as Mass is finished.'

He left and Fingal sat alone in the big drawing-room. Mrs Kelly came in to ask if he wanted anything, a drink or coffee, but he just shook his head and sent her away. He sat on there for another half-hour, the silver stick occasionally tapping the carpet like an extension of a nervous tic. He had never been repelled by violence, though he had never physically indulged in it himself: it was a fact of life and he accepted it. He had, however, never been able to accept or understand violence against women. His granddaughter had been a major aggravation, provoking temper in him and Kerry; but he had recognized something of himself, and even of Sheila, in her. She had the courage of her convictions, wrong as they were, and she had been admirably, if irritatingly, persistent. She should not have been murdered and all at once he was angry.

He rang the White Sails Motel in Rose Bay and spoke to Paredes. 'You'd better check out of there at once. Bring your stuff over here to the house.'

'Is something wrong, Señor Hourigan?'

'A bloody lot's wrong! Get over here!'

Paredes and Domecq arrived at the same time as Kerry returned from saying Mass. The two Nicaraguans came in rather tentatively; it had occurred to them that Fingal Hourigan saw them as no more than minions. That offended their pride, especially Paredes', but this was the man with the money and certain concessions had to be made. He was obviously angry and their first thought was that he was going to cut off their funds, that the Austarm deal would be stopped before it had begun.

'My granddaughter has been murdered,' said Fingal bluntly and looked at them accusingly.

Paredes was the first to recover. Though he spoke English well, his mind could be slow in it. He was genuinely shocked, at the murder and at what seemed to be the accusation that he and Domecq might be responsible. 'What can I say? She was an enemy –' That was the wrong word, he saw at once. 'No, not an enemy. An opponent? But to be murdered for what she believed ...?' It was a good performance. He had murdered others, including a woman, for what they believed. 'We know nothing about it, Señor Hourigan, believe me.'

'Nothing,' said Domecq, shaking his head.

Fingal stared at them for a moment, then said, 'Then who did it?'

Domecq spread his hands and Paredes said, 'Where did it happen?'

'They found her outside a brothel in the inner city, in Surry Hills.'

Domecq's face closed up, but he said nothing. Paredes said, 'Outside a brothel? Then perhaps it could have been anyone who killed her? The brothel area in Miami, no one goes there alone, certainly not a woman.'

'Maybe.' But Fingal was certain Teresa had not been murdered by some casual stranger. These men, he was sure, had something to do with her murder, no matter how remotely. 'Anyhow, we have to keep you away from the police. They're getting nosey.'

'Would your granddaughter have told the police anything before she was − she was killed?' said Domecq, face still closed up.

'Why would she?'

Domecq shrugged. 'She never made any secret about how she felt about us. Isn't that right, Your Grace?'

Kerry had been silent up till now, sitting stiffly in a chair as if still in a state of shock. He looked up now, took a moment to catch the drift of Domecq's question. 'What? Oh, yes. Yes, she's been talking to groups around the universities.'

'There's a young priest,' said Paredes, 'a Nicaraguan. He's been encouraging her. Perhaps he will talk to the police.'

'How much does he know?' said Fingal.

'Who knows?'

'Have you spoken to him?'

'No.'

'Maybe someone should.'

'Dad −' Kerry looked anxiously at his father. 'This could get out of hand. Don't let's get any more involved . . . It's bad enough Teresa being murdered. I never . . .' He looked as if he might break down if he went on.

'Go upstairs and lie down.' Fingal spoke as he might have to a six-year-old; but his voice was tender. 'I'll call Brigid.'

Without another word Kerry got up and left the room. All at once it seemed that God had turned His back; Teresa's murder was a warning. But was it a warning of disapproval or just one that the road ahead would always have such tragedies, that the victory would not be easy? He would pray for an answer, but he didn't really believe in the efficacy of prayer. That required another sort of faith.

When his son had left the room Fingal said, 'You'd better have a look at that priest. What's his name?'

'Father Marquez.'

'Get someone to have a word with him.'

'I can do it over the telephone,' said Domecq. 'A few words ... It has worked in Miami when we have found people causing trouble.'

'That's all it needs sometimes,' said Paredes, the voice of experience.

Fingal looked at them, understanding them; it had been like that in Chicago all those years ago. 'Okay, do it then. But go to a public phone box, don't do it from here. Then have someone keep an eye on him, see if he takes the warning. You have someone here in Sydney can do that?'

'Oh yes, we have our supporters. It can be done.'

Then Fingal left them, went into his study and called his daughter. In the best of circumstances it would not have been an easy call for him to make; this was the worst of circumstances. He was surprised how sorry he felt for her.

'I have some bad news –'

'The police have already been here.' Her voice was calm and cool, almost cold.

'I – I'm sorry, Brigid.' Father and daughter, he thought, and we're strangers talking to each other. *And whose fault is that?* That sounded like Sheila, her voice coming out of the grave.

'If this happened, Dad, because of you and Kerry –'

'No,' he said sharply. 'No, Brigid. Kerry is shattered ... Would you care to come here? I think we need to be together.' It was the closest he could come to expressing love.

There was silence at the other end of the line; he thought she had just walked away from the phone. Then she said, 'I'll be there in an hour,' and hung up.

She arrived an hour later, as promised. Grief, however, did not reunite them. Kerry tried, but Brigid had retired behind an invisible wall. 'I only came to find out how much you were responsible for her death.'

'Bridie –' He tried to take her hand, but she moved it away from him. 'Do you really think I'd have my own niece *killed*? I saw her in Nicaragua –'

'She told me.'

'A Contra lieutenant there wanted to kill her. I prevented it.'

'No, I don't think either of you would be capable of killing her. I should hope not,' she said, looking at her father as if she had doubts about *him*. 'But those men you're dealing with – Paredes and Domecq. She told me about them. Are they here?'

'They're staying with us,' said Fingal. 'They had nothing to do with the murder. I swear that.'

She smiled cynically, 'Dad, your oath has never been worth a spit in the wind. But I'll believe you ... I *want* to,' she said and her voice was full of despair, as if she had suffered enough and she wanted it all behind her.

Oh Sheila, cried Fingal silently, *where did it all go wrong?* But he knew the answer. Long ago in Chicago, when what few scruples he had inherited from his own mother had been smothered, like fragile flowers, beneath his father's corrupt advice and his own ambition. It was too late now.

6

The war with Jonathan Tewsday had been put aside for the moment. Tewsday's resignation did not arrive on his desk Monday morning and he did not send downstairs for it. The newspapers now had the full story on Sister Mary Magdalene, Teresa Hourigan; Ballyduff House and the castle at Vaucluse had been besieged by the media jackals. Brigid had not gone back to Stokes Point, but had remained at the house, occupying the room she had slept in as a child. The reporters and cameramen had looked as if they were about to camp outside the high gates, but Fingal called Chief Superintendent Danforth. The police arrived and within ten minutes the street had been cleared. The media men and women went away, complaining loudly about the violation of the freedom of the press, and the police agreed with them and gave them another kick up the bum. Both sides knew that democracy could sometimes be a comedy.

'Kerry and I won't go to the funeral,' Fingal said on Monday evening. 'The press would just turn it into a stampede. You don't want that.'

'No,' said Brigid, but it was impossible to tell whether she was grateful or hurt. In truth, she did not want either of them at the burial. If it could have been arranged, she would have wanted no one there but herself. She had to ask the dead Teresa, her one and only child, for forgiveness.

Late Tuesday afternoon Paredes knocked on the door of Fingal's study and came in. 'Did you watch the funeral on TV this morning, señor? The eleven-thirty news.'

'Yes.' He had watched it only till the coffin was lowered into the grave and then it had been too much for him and Kerry. They had switched off the set. 'What happened? You've got something to tell me.'

'The camera remained on Señorita Brigid. In the background were Father Marquez and the detective who came here Sunday morning, Inspector Malone. The priest gave Malone a letter. Father Marquez looked very worried.'

'Has Domecq spoken to him, given him a warning?'

'Twice. He also spoke to Inspector Malone.'

'Jesus!' Fingal raised his silver stick and for a moment Paredes thought the old man was going to hurl it at him. 'Why, for Christ's sake, did he do that? Of all the fucking stupid –' It was the first time he had heard the old man swear. 'This isn't fucking Nicaragua – you don't threaten our police!

You talk to them – you bribe them –'

Paredes spread a hand, as respectful as ever. The cause must not be lost, the money must still be promised. 'I'm sorry, señor, we all make mistakes –'

It took Fingal a moment or two to come off the boil. 'You'd better keep him under control. Christ knows what he's likely to do next. Where is he now?'

Paredes hesitated, 'He – he's gone out.'

'Where?'

Again the hesitation; then, 'He's gone to dispose of Father Hourigan.'

'*Who?*'

It had been a slip of the tongue; this old man was fast turning into another enemy in his mind. 'Sorry. Father Marquez.'

Fingal opened his mouth, but nothing came out but a coughing gasp; it was as if he were beyond words. He stood up abruptly, grabbed his walking stick and came round the desk. Paredes stepped aside, throwing up an arm to ward off the expected blow; but Fingal went right by him and out of the study, hurrying with surprising agility for such an old man. He went up the curving staircase in the big entrance hall, suddenly pausing half-way up as if he were about to collapse. He drew a deep breath, looked down at Paredes with a terrible expression of rage on his face, then went on up to the landing and disappeared.

Brigid, an empty glass in her hand, came to the doorway of the drawing-room. 'Do you know where the liquor's kept, Mr Paredes?'

'No.' He was still staring up at the empty landing.

She followed the direction of his gaze. 'Something wrong with my father?'

'I don't know, señorita. He'll tell you, I suppose.'

'I doubt it,' said Brigid and went back into the drawing-room.

Upstairs in Kerry's bedroom Fingal was explaining what

Domecq had gone to do. 'Get packed! We've got to get you out of here! *Now!* Do you hear me, for Christ's sake – *now!* Get back to Rome tonight –'

'I can't leave just like *that*! How can I get on a plane at such short notice? Planes don't leave for Rome every hour –'

'Just get out to the airport – I'll have the Falcon ready for you. If you can't get Qantas or Alitalia or one of the others for Rome, I'll have our crew fly you to Perth. You can pick up something there and change at Singapore. But you've got to get out *now*! You hear me?'

'I can't believe it –' Kerry, in this bedroom where he had harboured all the doubts and fears of boyhood, was nothing like the confident, arrogant man he presented to the world. He was still suffering from the shock of Teresa's death; and now this. The Lord was deserting him; he felt both hollow and angry. His devotion had always been narrow, a thin rod of sustenance; now it threatened to break. 'God, it's not worth it –'

'What's not worth it? Of course it's worth it! It's just bloody stupid, that's all, the way they've gone about it. Get packed! I'll have the car round the front in ten minutes. You're going back to Rome!'

It was an order. Or a coronation: Fingal was not going to be denied his ambition.

TWELVE

I

When the Falcon 900 landed at Kingsford Smith airport Malone said a brisk goodbye to Fingal and Kerry Hourigan and walked quickly across the tarmac to the main building. He had had enough of the Hourigans for the moment; he breathed in the crisp autumn air as if it were smelling salts. He would not even think about them for at least twenty-four hours. He knew, however, that thoughts could be as slippery as criminals.

He stopped at the duty-free store on his way out to Immigration. Zara Kersey, looking as fresh as if she were about to begin a journey instead of just finishing one, came in after him. 'I'm buying something for my children.'

'So am I,' he said, conscience-stricken that he hadn't bought something in Rome or Singapore. 'But what? Kids today are so choosey. My thirteen-year-old actually reads *Choice* magazine. A thirteen-year-old consumer!'

She helped him choose: Italian boat shoes for the girls, a model airplane for Tom. 'Boat shoes? I don't own a boat.'

'It doesn't matter. Believe me, Scobie, those shoes are going to be the *in* thing for kids next summer. If I know anything about something, it's fashion.'

He grinned. 'You know more than that, Zara.'

She nodded. 'I've learned a few things on this trip. Good luck, Scobie. This case is a long way from over. Don't get in the way of any more knives.'

Lisa was waiting for him outside Customs. He had discarded his sling, hoping that they would be home before she discovered another attempt had been made on his life. But she rushed at him, embraced him; he let out a gasp of pain as she flung an arm round his wounded shoulder. She drew back in alarm.

'What's the matter? Have you been hurt?'

'Not here – I'll tell you about it in the car –'

She seethed with concern all the way to the car-park. Six overseas airliners had arrived within twenty minutes of each other; the path from the terminal to the car-park was a United Nations reunion. A party of Greeks blocked the Malones' way; Lisa pushed through them with discriminatory prejudice. A large family of white natives, back from a holiday in the tropics, shivering in their thongs and shorts, got the same treatment. She had only one nationality this morning, that of her family and him in particular.

Once in the car she demanded, 'What's the matter? Have you been hurt?'

'Not here – wait till we get home –'

'*Tell me!*'

He did, flatly and in as few words as possible. 'I'm okay. They got the cove who tried it –'

'They arrested him? You've got to go back to Rome?'

'No-o. They – they shot him.'

'Oh Jesus!' She rarely, if ever, swore. She slumped back in the seat of the car, stared at him as if she didn't believe what he was telling her. '*Twice!* Twice they've tried to kill you!'

'It won't happen again –'

'How do you know?' He couldn't remember when he had last seen her so angry.

'I don't. Darl – Please . . .'

He looked and sounded unutterably weary and abruptly she relented. 'I'm sorry. I'm selfish – all I think about is myself and the kids.'

'No. No, you're not selfish.' He put his arm round her and

kissed her again. 'I'm just in the wrong job for a family man.'

They drove home and he was reunited with the children when they came home from school. Zara Kersey had been right: the girls were delighted with their boat shoes ('Daddy, how did you *know*?') and Tom wanted to take off at once in his airplane for the moon ('Planes don't go to the moon.' ... 'Mine does.'). As numerous times before, he rediscovered God and was grateful to Him: his family was his harbour. Sunday he would go to Mass with them, suffer the boring sermon and the banal hymns and the monotonous guitar music, and say a heartfelt prayer of thanks. It suddenly occurred to him that he could not remember saying a single prayer while at Mass in St Peter's.

Clements came to the house at six o'clock. 'I guess you're ready for bed, eh? The Commissioner told me to ask how you were. Rome rang to tell him about the guy knifing you. You okay? Who paid for the job? Domecq and Paredes?'

'I don't think so.'

Clements bit his lip. 'Not the Archbishop?'

'No. It might have been his old man. I just don't know.'

Clements sat chewing on his lip. Then he said, 'Well, that's another tiger snake out of the can. If we bust this case, I hate to think where you and I are going to finish up. Still, that's all to come. I'd better brief you before you come in tomorrow. I've got them all together tomorrow morning at ten – the Archbishop and Paredes and Domecq. Mrs Kersey will be there, too, I guess. You want me to bring in old man Hourigan?'

'No. You made any progress with Domecq?'

'A little. I've found out how he could have known about you and Father Marquez and the letter. I went around all the TV stations checking if they had any Nicaraguans working in their crews.' He shook his big head. 'None. But a guy at Channel 8, Hourigan's own station, said they'd run a piece on the funeral on their eleven-thirty news last Tuesday morning. He got out the tape and ran it for me. You and

Father Marquez are there plain as day – he's giving you the letter and you're reading it. There's a second shot and you're saying something to him and he's looking pretty worried. If Domecq saw that clip, he could put two and two together.'

'We've got no proof that he did.'

Clements grinned. 'Don't be obstructive, mate. We have to hit him over the head with anything we can. How'd you go with the Archbishop?'

Malone shrugged. 'I don't know. How much resilience have martyrs got?'

'He's a martyr? You could have fooled me. Go to bed, Scobie, get a good night's sleep. I'll see you in the morning.'

On his way out he said to Lisa, 'Take care of him. He looks beat.'

'So am I,' she said, but good-humouredly. 'Who's taking care of me?'

'Uncle Russ,' he said and put his arms round her, the first time he had ever done that.

Next morning when Malone went into Homicide, Kerry Hourigan, Paredes and Domecq were waiting for him. Clements had procured a separate room for the interrogation; it was small and the five big men made it smaller. When Zara Kersey arrived, looking much fresher than Malone felt, she looked around and smiled. 'Whose lap do I sit on?'

Clements squeezed in a chair for her between the Archbishop and Domecq. The two detectives sat on the opposite side of the narrow table with Paredes beside them. It looked more like a conspiracy than an interrogation.

'We're taking Mr Domecq into custody on suspicion of murder and attempted murder,' Malone said without preliminary. 'Specifically, the murder of Father Luis Marquez and the attempted murder of myself at Randwick.' He turned his head and looked at Paredes. 'Someone also tried to kill me in Rome. Did you know that?'

Paredes showed no surprise or concern. 'How would I know it, Inspector?'

'I thought His Grace might have told you.'

Kerry Hourigan flushed, but said nothing.

'Have you any evidence against Mr Domecq?' said Zara Kersey. 'Any witnesses?'

'We'll be calling Archbishop Hourigan as a witness for the prosecution.'

It seemed for a moment as if the room were going to burst; the walls, Malone was sure, were pushed back. The Archbishop grew bigger with shock and indignation; beside him Malone felt Paredes swell. Domecq pushed his chair back, half-rose as if he were about to bolt through the door. Only Zara remained calm.

'You can't do that, Inspector.'

'Oh, yes, I can.' It was a gamble, but he had been mulling it over in his mind since four o'clock this morning when, his body still out of rhythm with Sydney time, he had woken. 'If he doesn't tell the truth, we're going to leak all we know about his work for the Contras. Rome will be interested in that.' He looked at Kerry Hourigan. 'There's another thing, Your Grace. You've told enough lies – but so far they've only been to me and Sergeant Clements and we're used to them. If I get you into the witness box, you can act as a hostile witness, but you're going to be no advertisement for the Church. People, even the non-believers, expect archbishops to tell the truth. Your father once told me that truth is a dangerous weapon. You'll have your chance to prove it.'

Paredes and Domecq looked at the Archbishop. He avoided their gaze, unable to suffer their anger and contempt if he showed that he might go against them. How could he explain to them his ambition? They would laugh, even though they had ambitions of their own. They were Catholics, but in name only: it was a good cover in Latin America. They would never understand the ambition of a man to be head of all the Catholics in the world, or the ambition of the father of that man to make him so. He had discovered in the months he had known them that they were men of little imagination, especially Domecq. Paredes *might* understand, but he was not the one who would be sacrificed.

'We didn't come here to be betrayed,' said Paredes and there was no mistaking the threat in his voice. He showed no surprise, it would not be the first time he and his fellow Contras had been betrayed. 'Especially if you have to lie.'

Kerry Hourigan's own voice was just a rumble in his throat. 'I didn't come home to see my niece murdered. Nor that young priest . . .'

'We had nothing to do with your niece's murder – you know that!'

'We're not charging Mr Domecq with that murder,' said Malone quietly.

Paredes saw his mistake, looked quickly across the table at Zara Kersey. 'Do something, señora. They are trying to rail-road Señor Domecq!'

She stood up. 'May I see you outside, Inspector? You too, Your Grace.'

Outside in the corridor people were coming and going busily; homicide, it seemed, was on the rise today. Oh, for a nice simple homicide, Malone thought, an open-and-shut case with the murderer still standing over the victim yelling that he had done it. But those were usually domestic murders and sometimes they could be worse, far worse, especially when the children had to be told what daddy had done to mummy or vice versa. At least there were no kids in this one.

'Will you be a witness against Mr Domecq?' Zara Kersey said.

Archbishop Hourigan was going through agony. 'If I do, I'm going to crucify him –'

'Don't let's get too religious,' said Malone. 'I know who threatened me and Father Marquez over the phone. I know who shot at us – I can *feel* it every time I'm near him –'

'That would never be accepted in court, Scobie,' said Zara, but she sounded sympathetic. She was out of her depth in a murder case, especially this one; her pool was white-collar crime where only money and not blood was spilt. Fingal Hourigan had made a mistake in calling her in on this and when she left here she would call him and tell him she was withdrawing from the case.

Malone said, 'Was Domecq still at your father's house at Vaucluse before you left for the airport that evening?'

Kerry hesitated, then shook his head. 'No.'

'Where had he gone?'

'I don't know.' Then he thought better of the answer: 'My father said he had gone looking for Father Marquez.'

'Did he have a gun?'

'He – yes, I suppose so.'

'What do you mean, you suppose so?'

Kerry hesitated again. 'When we were down at Austarm, at Moss Vale, he told the men we were talking to that he often went hunting in the States. He said he wanted to go pig-shooting while he was here – he'd seen it in some travel movie, he said. They presented him with the gun. It was a heavy, pump-action shotgun.'

'The sort they use for security?'

'I wouldn't know, Inspector. We don't go in for that sort of security in the Church.'

'You were going in for 7.62 rifles, ten thousand of them.' The Archbishop made no answer to the jibe and Malone went on, 'So he had the shotgun with him at your father's house?'

'I saw him showing it to Paredes. He'd confessed to me on the way back from Moss Vale that he really wasn't interested in pig-shooting, he just collected guns. He's the sort of man who likes people to give him things.'

'Will you testify in court that Domecq had the shotgun at your father's house?'

'God, do I have to?' There was real anguish in his voice. Pope Judas – would it be worth it? 'Do I have to, Mrs Kersey? Isn't there some way out?'

'You can refuse to answer any questions.' She showed him no sympathy.

'If I testify against him, he'll bring everything out into the open. I can't risk that!'

'You should have thought of that before you got yourself involved with them,' said Malone, equally unsympathetic. 'I don't know about the other Contras, they may be honest patriots, but these two are gangsters. You should have looked into their credentials, Your Grace. Well?'

The Archbishop looked at Zara Kersey again, but now he could see he would receive no help from her. He felt no bitterness towards her, though life itself had never tasted more bitter. He sighed, gave himself up to God, Who also might offer no help. 'I'll testify.'

2

Fingal Hourigan fell headlong into a terrible rage when Kerry went home and told him what he intended doing. 'Holy shit, do you know what you're doing?'

'Of course I do,' said Kerry gloomily, offended by his father's language as much as his rage.

'You're throwing everything out of the window! Years of effort, God knows how much goddam money –'

'Do you want me to pay you back?' A spark of rebellion showed. 'With interest?'

Fingal ignored that. He stomped up and down his study, swearing and yelling till Brigid opened the door and came in. 'I think every window in Vaucluse is open and listening to you. What's the hullabaloo?'

'Tell her!' Fingal stormed; the silver stick threshed the air like streaks of lightning. 'Tell her!'

Kerry told her, leaving out only that he was throwing away his ambition to be Pope. It was bad enough to be raged at; he could not bear to be laughed at. And he knew Brigid would laugh. 'I'll probably be asked to leave Rome.'

'Not necessarily,' said Brigid. She was the only calm one of the three of them. She had lived in Italy and she knew the Italian talent for accommodation. And the Vatican, after all, was still Italian, or almost. 'Doesn't The Lord look after His own? They'll probably make you a papal knight or whatever they do to cover up your mistakes.'

'They only do that in the civil service.' Fingal was simmering down. His eye was not so filled with fury that he missed his daughter's reaction to the crisis. But, of course, she did not know of the real prize that had been sacrificed. He looked at Kerry. 'What are the police going to do with Domecq?'

'They're holding him,' said Kerry. 'They're going to oppose bail. Paredes has stayed with him for the time being. He says he'll move out of here.'

'He won't be missed,' said Fingal. 'I never liked either of them.'

'Did Domecq kill Father Marquez?' Brigid asked, still calm.

'Yes.'

'Did he kill Teresa?' Icily calm now. 'If he did, I'll have him killed.'

She's like me, Fingal thought with wonder. She *would* have Domecq killed; just as I tried to have Malone killed in Rome. He had no conscience about that; it had been a mistake to have commissioned the contract. Brigid would have a conscience: he recognized enough of Sheila in her to see that.

'No. No, he didn't kill her. It wasn't Domecq. Nor Paredes, either.'

'Who was it then?'

All at once, unaccountably, he wanted to save her from herself. If she tried to have anyone killed, she would never cover her tracks as he could.

'We don't know. Unless . . .'

'Unless what?'

She was staring at him, and so was Kerry. The latter said, 'Be careful, Dad, If you have no proof . . .'

302

'You're thinking the same as I am.' He had not even thought of the possibility up till now.

'*Who?*' demanded Brigid.

'I'll tell you when I've done a little more checking.'

'No, tell me now!' She had lost her calm, was standing opposite him, pounding his desk. 'Dad, I have to know!'

'You will know,' he promised her and meant it. But she mustn't be allowed to endanger herself with her own revenge. 'But let the police do it. Let Inspector Malone do it – he owes it to us.'

She stared at him, not trusting him; yet suddenly wanting to. Blood bound the three of them here in this room; she was caught in it, as in a whirlpool. She looked into the once-bright blue eyes, now dimmed by age and pain and loss, and saw something she had never seen before: an effort at love.

She could find no words for him. She turned abruptly and went out of the room. She was running by the time she reached the stairs, stumbling as the tears blinded her.

Fingal reached for the phone book, then dialled Police Centre. They put him through to Inspector Malone at Homicide. 'This is Fingal Hourigan. You're holding Mr Domecq.'

'That's right, Mr Hourigan. We're going to oppose bail, if that's what you're calling about.'

'No, I'm not. I'm calling about something else. How far have you got on the murder of my granddaughter?'

'We're still working on it.'

'Which means you haven't got anywhere. Ask Sir Jonathan Tewsday what he knows about it.'

'Are you accusing him of it, Mr Hourigan?'

'You know better than that,' said Fingal and hung up. He looked across his desk at Kerry. 'There, it's done.'

'It's malicious,' said his son. 'You have no proof whatsoever.'

'None at all. But who else is there left to suspect? Tilly Mosman? She wouldn't dump the body on her own doorstep.'

'How do you know anything about the brothel-owner?'

'I set her up in business. We were – friends, once upon a time. Don't look shocked. Fornication is an everyday – or everynight occasion.' He was feeling better. In his inflamed imagination he could see the police cars screaming towards Tewsday. 'Jonathan knew about it. He hates me, Kerry, always has. I sacked him – he'd do anything to get back at me. We've hated each other for years. I've enjoyed it. He never did.'

Kerry had always suspected this uglier side of his father; it shocked him now to see it so openly displayed. 'But why poor Teresa? An innocent –'

'I don't know. He wouldn't have killed her himself – he's pure yellow all through. But he would have paid someone. Once, long ago, he did that ...' But then he stopped. Too much confession was not good for the soul; or the neck. 'If he did have Teresa murdered, Malone will nail him.'

At Homicide Malone had looked at the dead phone, then also hung up. He believed in the law of coincidence, though it was rarely recognized in a court of law. In the hours he had been awake in bed at home the murder of Teresa Hourigan had been as much on his mind as that of Father Marquez; one could not be thought of without thinking of the other. He had run down a list of everyone remotely connected with the dead nun; Tewsday's name had been there only because he had been at the funeral and there was no explanation for that. He was also connected with Ballyduff and Austarm; on top of that he had been less than forthcoming on the ride back from the funeral. Perhaps Tewsday *should* be asked a few more questions. But why had Fingal Hourigan suggested it?

'What do we know about Sir Jonathan Tewsday?' he asked Clements.

'I don't think there's a file on him, is there?'

'There's probably one over in Fraud. When I was on the squad over there, oh, I dunno, fifteen or twenty years ago, we thought we had a case against him. Bill Zanuch was in charge of it.'

'What happened?'

'I don't know. They just suddenly shut up shop on it.'

'I interviewed him a couple of years ago, him and a few others at Ballyduff. That Pommy junkie they found with his neck broken in the garage at Ballyduff House.'

'What happened on that one?'

'Nothing. We couldn't trace any of the junkie's relatives. He was better off dead, anyway.' Clements was not callous; he just had his own ideas of justice. But he never voiced them to anyone but Malone. 'We just put the file in a drawer and turned the key on it.'

'Whom else did you interview?'

'*Whom?* I'd have to look up the file. The only one I remember was Tewsday's driver, a Yank, I can't remember his name.'

'Gawler. Why did you remember him?'

'Yeah, Gary or Larry Gawler. I dunno, he just wasn't – forthcoming?'

'That's a good word. Put an enquiry on the telex to the FBI in Washington, see if they have anything on him. Do the same with Immigration here. In the meantime, let's go and have a word with him. And Tewsday, too.'

'Mind if I ask – who put this bee in your bonnet?'

'Fingal Hourigan.'

Clements bit his lip. 'This mob, they really love each other, don't they?'

Clements sent off the telex to the FBI, then he and Malone went to see Gary Gawler, Tewsday's unforthcoming chauffeur. 'Where do drivers hang out when their bosses are in their offices?'

Their first call hit the jackpot: Gawler was in the Ballyduff House garage. He had the bonnet of the Rolls-Royce up and was tinkering with the engine when Malone said, 'I didn't think anything ever went wrong with Rolls-Royces.'

Gawler put down the bonnet, wiped his hands on a clean rag. 'Hello, Inspector. Just a battery connection, that's all. Nothing is perfect.'

'So they tell me. Mr Gawler, can you remember where Sir Jonathan was last Saturday week, the night of the fifteenth?'

'I'd have to look up my book. Sir Jonathan has me write down every trip. He's very meticulous like that, with the fringe benefits tax.'

'I didn't think you'd have to look this up. It was the night Sister Mary Magdalene was murdered.'

Gawler was still wiping his hands, but now suddenly they were still, the rag held tightly between his fingers. A car went out of the garage, its tyres screeching a little as it went up the ramp into the street. At the far end of the garage a radio was playing: a talkback guru was listening to the woes of housewives whose husbands wouldn't listen to them. It was cold here in this concrete cavern and Gawler seemed to be feeling it. He abruptly dropped the rag and reached for his uniform jacket hanging on the car door.

'Yes, I remember. Sir Jonathan was home all day that day. The night, too. His family had gone down to their place at Bowral. He had a lot of paperwork to do. I cooked the evening meal for him.'

'He never went out? He doesn't drive himself?'

'I sleep over the garages, my wife and I have our flat there. I'd have heard him if he'd taken the car out.'

'You didn't go out yourself?'

'No. I was on my own. My wife had gone down to Bowral with Lady Tewsday and the girls.'

'And I suppose you watched television?'

'Maybe an hour or so, I can't remember. I don't watch much TV.'

'You read?'

'No, I watch videos.'

'What sort?'

'Anything with action in it. Sylvester Stallone, Arnold Schwarzenegger. It relaxes me.'

'It bores me,' said Malone. 'Is Sir Jonathan up in his office now?'

'Yes.' Gawler looked at his watch. He seemed warmer now that he had his jacket on, more at ease. But he hadn't liked Malone's remark about the action videos. 'I have to take him out in twenty-five minutes. He's always punctual.'

'We'd better get a move on, then. Thanks, Mr Gawler. We may be talking to you. What floor is Sir Jonathan on?'

'The sixty-eighth.'

As they walked across to the lift Malone said, 'What did you think?'

'He's used to being questioned,' said Clements.

'Yeah, not a stutter or a stammer. I wonder where he got the practice?' Malone pressed the floor button in the lift. 'Sixty-eight. I've never been this high before.'

'Getting into a lift is the only way I'm going to go up in the world.'

'Don't put yourself down. If we solve this case, they may make you inspector.'

Clements grinned. 'I got the feeling, we solve this case we're both going to end up out at Tibooburra.'

Sir Jonathan's secretary said he was *terribly* busy. 'So are we,' said Malone. 'We've got homicides piling up like those letters in your *In* basket.'

She gave him a look that said she didn't think either he or his remark was funny. But she spoke to Tewsday on her intercom, then stood up and ushered them into his office. 'You have your Reserve Bank appointment in twenty minutes, Sir Jonathan,' she said pointedly.

Malone smiled at her. 'We'll see he's not late.'

She nodded coldly and closed the door. Tewsday remained seated at his desk, but waved a hand to the two chairs opposite him. Malone, aware as ever of his surroundings, remarked the quiet elegance of the office; he guessed that more money had been spent on this one room than on all the rooms in the Malone house at Randwick. He was not to know that the man sitting behind the big antique desk was spending his last day in the office.

'I won't waste time, Sir Jonathan, since your secretary made a point of telling us how busy you are. Where were you last Saturday week, the fifteenth, from say eight o'clock in the evening till two o'clock Sunday morning?'

'Last Saturday week?'

'The night Sister Mary Magdalene was murdered.'

A flush darkened the pink marbled face. 'Are you saying – are you saying I'm some sort of suspect?'

'I haven't said you're anything. I'm just asking a question.'

'You're *implying*.'

'Only if you want to take it that way, Sir Jonathan. Sergeant Clements has been doing a lot of leg-work on the case. Nobody has been able to tell us where Sister Mary Magdalene went between leaving the convent at Randwick at six-thirty that evening and when she was found next morning outside the Quality Couch. She rang her mother at seven o'clock – what did she say, Russ?'

Clements had his notebook open, saving Tewsday's precious time. 'She didn't say where she was ringing from or where she was going. They had a date to go to the opera, but she said she'd have to put it off. Her mother was at the Regent Hotel – they were booked in there for the night.' He glanced at Malone. 'Under the Hourigan name. We didn't think to ask when we were looking for her that Sunday morning. We were looking for Miss O'Keefe, remember?'

'I remember,' said Malone, but he had forgotten.

Clements looked back at Tewsday. 'She said she'd see her mother out at Stokes Point on the Sunday. She didn't turn up, as you know.'

Tewsday was solid jelly; but at any moment he would begin to quake. He had been expecting just such a call as this; yet he was unprepared for it. In a desk drawer, hastily put away when Malone and Clements had been announced, was a note from Fingal sent down half an hour before. It told him what his golden handshake was to be and it demanded his delayed resignation by 5 p.m. today. Fingal was back in business, no longer put off by mourning. Tewsday's mind had been full of further threats against Fingal, but he knew now they were as empty and lethal as party balloons. *He* was the one under threat and he had no proper answer.

'I think I was home. Yes, I was. I had work to do.'

'Your wife or your family can corroborate that?'

'Yes. No. No, they were down at Bowral. I have a property down there.'

'Your driver, Gawler – what about him?'

'He was at home with me.'

'So he'd be your only witness if –' Malone let the sentence dangle in the air like a looped rope.

'If what?' Tewsday was moving his opal ring round and round as if trying to unscrew his finger.

Malone stood up. 'You'll be relieved to know, Sir Jonathan, you and your driver have told the same story.'

'You've already seen him? You have a lot of gall!'

'It's one of my few talents,' said Malone. 'That and persistence. Goodbye, Sir Jonathan. I don't think we've kept the Reserve Bank waiting.'

'Give them my regards,' said Clements, who had great respect for banks, even though so many of them were being held up these days. He wondered what sort of crim it would take to hold up the Reserve Bank. Someone like Sir Jonathan Tewsday? No.

Going down in the lift he said, 'He was as nervous as an old-fashioned virgin.'

'I didn't know there were any left. You're right, though. I thought he had piles, he was moving around in his chair so much. But why would he kill Sister Mary? Unless he's tied up in this Austarm deal more than we know. How'd you like to drive out to Pymble and talk to the Tewsdays' neighbours?

They might give you morning tea – they're very keen on morning tea up that way. Check if any of them heard him drive out during the night. Or if he had any visitors.'

'Now? Okay. You want me to drive you back to the office?'

'No, thanks. I'll have a think walk.'

'What's that?'

'Ask Arnold Bennett.'

He left Clements bemused and walked back to Liverpool Street; but the think walk produced no solutions. The telex to the FBI did. When Clements returned from Pymble, Malone, smiling with satisfaction, laid the telex in front of him. 'Get a load of that. We're getting somewhere.'

Clements read the report, sucking on his bottom lip as he did so. Then he looked up. 'That tells us he has a police record. But what do they mean – check with CIA? Don't they know the CIA never tells foreign police anything? We're not in the spy business, we're low life.'

'I'll get on to Joe Nagler over at Special Branch. He's got contacts at ASIO.' ASIO was the Australian Security Intelligence Organization. 'They work with the CIA. In the meantime, what did you get?'

'Morning tea.' Clements brushed imaginary crumbs from his lapel. 'They're just like the rest of us up in Pymble – stickybeaks. Or anyway the Tewsdays' neighbour is, Mrs Prunello. I think she must spend all her weekend at the front window. Someone did go out on the Saturday night – or rather, Sunday morning early. She was awake. She doesn't know what time it was, but she heard a car go out of the Tewsdays' drive. Not the Rolls, she thought it was a smaller car. I had a peek in the Tewsdays' garages – the doors were open. They have a BMW and what looked like a Toyota.'

'Will Mrs Whatever-her-name-is keep her mouth shut?'

'I doubt it, though I don't think she'll talk to the Tewsdays. She didn't seem to have much time for them, thought they were uppity.'

'What's she doing living in Pymble then? I thought everyone

up there was uppity.' He sounded like his father, the worker from the south side of the harbour. 'You learn anything else?'

'This is the bit I've been saving. Tewsday had a visitor Saturday night, a young woman. Mrs Prunello saw the taxi arrive there about eight o'clock. It dropped whoever it was out in the street, then drove off. I've got the cab companies checking with their drivers. They're going to ring me when they find out who had the fare.'

There is always something where they slip up, Malone thought. He had known so many criminals who had overlooked the small, inconsequential links that bound the world together: a forgotten phone call, a taxi ride, an inquisitive neighbour. There was no proof yet that Tewsday had done anything criminal; but yes, now he was a suspect. There was a gleam of hope in Malone's eye. We all like to have our suspicions confirmed, no matter what prejudices they arise from. The truth of the matter was, he didn't like Sir Jonathan. Cops, after all, are human.

He reached for his phone, called Detective Inspector Joe Nagler at Special Branch, told him what he wanted, then hung up. 'Joe'll see what he can do.'

'What do we do now?'

'Wait. And put a stake-out on the Tewsday house.'

'What about Domecq?'

'He's been refused bail.'

'Paredes?'

'I've got Andy Graham tailing him. He's safe.'

'The Archbishop?'

'I guess he's out at Vaucluse praying hard. He's more a politician than a priest. And now he's going to find out that politicians can't fall back on the privilege of the confessional.'

'You Tykes,' said Clements. 'You make life so bloody complicated for yourselves. It's never like that with the Congregationalists.'

The meeting between Tewsday and Fingal was short and bitter.

'You've got your handshake – six times your salary. You own six hundred thousand shares – if you sell those at today's prices you'll have another twelve million. If you want to go on working, there'll be head-hunters rushing to offer you another job. You won't starve.'

Tewsday hadn't sat down when he entered Fingal's office. He stood on trembling legs, wanting to leap at the smug old man behind the desk but knowing he could never bring himself to that peak of violence. Cowardice is a good self-defence. 'I'll get you, Hourigan! I'll break this corporation –'

'If I owned a bakery, you couldn't break a piece of stale cake. You've only got as far as you have because I've let you. You're a number two man, Jonathan, you always will be . . . Goodbye!'

He swung his chair round, disappearing from Tewsday's view behind the high back of his chair. Tewsday stood a moment longer, fury making him ugly; but there was no one to see it, not even the man at whom it was directed. He was full of words, but they were incoherent, even in his head; it takes a cool mind to be properly abusive. He spun round, almost toppling over on his unsteady legs, and galloped out of the office. This was the highest office in the land, the peak where he had always dreamed of sitting, and he had just been kicked out for ever. He felt he was falling from a great height.

Going home to Pymble he sat in sullen silence in the back of the Rolls-Royce. Gawler said nothing till they were held up in stalled traffic on the Pacific Highway. Then, without looking round, he said, 'Have the police been back to see you, Sir Jonathan?'

'Eh?' Tewsday came back to the back seat. He had been miles away in the past, a region he hadn't visited in years. 'You mean this afternoon? No. Why?'

'I didn't like the sound of their questions this morning.' There had been time for only a brief discussion on the short ride up to the Reserve Bank that morning. 'That Inspector Malone, I don't think he'd ever take maybe for an answer.'

'No,' Tewsday agreed. 'But we have to sit tight.'

'Yeah,' said Gawler, but for once he sounded less than cool and distant.

Tewsday had not mentioned to Fiona the ultimatum Fingal had given him; till five o'clock this afternoon he had refused to admit, even to himself, that his career with Ballyduff was finished. Injustice had been done; which is more soul-destroying than justice being done. Though no one had ever accused Tewsday of having a soul, not even Fiona.

'What are you going to do?' she said when he told her he had resigned. She didn't believe his resignation had been voluntary, but she did not want to humble him. He looked sick and she felt a certain pity for him; love had finished up as pity, but the latter was still a genuine feeling. 'Why don't you retire? Don't look for another position.'

'No, I'm too young –' Though he felt older than he had ever dreamed he would be. 'I have to see Fingal go first –'

'Don't get too worked up.' She recognized the signs. He had never told her of his hatred for Fingal Hourigan, but he had never been able to hide it from her. She was still a good wife in that respect, keeping a husband's secrets, even though he had not revealed them to her. 'We'll go away on a holiday. Somewhere on the Barrier Reef, Lizard Island, perhaps –'

'No, I can't go now.' An earthquake was about to happen and he wanted to be there when the victims were counted. Including, he hoped, Fingal Hourigan. Then he said, 'Can I sleep with you tonight?'

'It's still a double bed.' She said it kindly, almost with some of the old love.

4

In the morning he was half-dressed for the office when he remembered he would not be going to Ballyduff any more. After breakfast, which he only nibbled at, he wandered about the house, getting in the way of Sally Gawler, till finally he was told by her would he mind going into his library and staying there. There is no one so demanding of the territorial imperative as a woman doing housework. Fiona went off in the BMW to one of her charity meetings; his daughters, as usual, were at their weekly boarding school. At last he went out into the garden where Gawler was cutting back a big camellia bush.

Gawler said at once, 'I'm worried, Sir Jonathan. There's a car parked up the street with two guys in it. It was there early this morning when I went down to the gate to pick up the papers. It's still there.'

'Police or someone else?' But who else? Fingal no longer had any interest in him.

'I'd lay money it's police.' He snipped at the bush with the big sharp secateurs. 'I think I'd like to take a vacation.'

'You had your holidays only – oh, I see.' He shivered with the cold; or so he thought. A south-west wind was blowing, bringing hints of an early winter; a brown snow of leaves blew across the lawns. 'It'd be foolish to start running away, Gary. That would only raise suspicion.'

'It's already raised.' Gawler knew an ill-wind when it blew, warm or cold; he had been chased in all climes. 'Those guys aren't sitting out there just because they like the neighbourhood.'

'Have you said anything to Sally?'

'No. She's right outside this, okay?' There was a threat in his voice.

'Of course, of course. We mustn't panic. Let things take their course.' But he really didn't know how the police worked. They were in a different business altogether.

He watched Gawler cutting the camellia bush; the secateurs sounded as if they were slicing through bone. He said, poised ready to run if necessary, 'I know all about you, Gary.'

Gawler paused, the blades open round a branch. 'You know what?'

'About what you did in Vietnam, in Bangkok, back in the United States. Everything. Alphonse Brown, Ray Karr. Everything.'

Gawler lowered the secateurs, held them like a dagger for an upward thrust. 'How long have you known?'

'Since about a month after you killed that junkie who attacked me.'

'Who told you?'

'It doesn't matter. Your secret's safe with me.'

'Is it safe with the guy who told you?'

'Yes. Alphonse Brown. *Alphonse*? Did you have a French mother or something?'

Gawler smiled; the secateurs were hanging loosely in his hand now. 'No. My daddy worked for Al Capone, *Alphonse* Capone, when he first come up to Chicago from the Kentucky hills. He was only small-time, the old man, but he thought Capone was the greatest. Capone used to call himself Al Brown one time, I dunno why. My daddy thought he was doing me an honour, y'know? What kid would want to be called Alphonse?' Then he raised the secateurs again. 'So what are we gonna do?'

The wind had dropped; the cold seemed more deadening now. In the garden next door Tewsday could hear Mrs Prunello calling to her cat: like to like, as Fiona would say. He wondered if she had heard any of their conversation. Fiona had warned him that she had ears like satellite dishes; gossip was her energy current. He lowered his voice, which in his own ears sounded as if it had a shiver in it.

'We just trust each other, Gary.'

Gawler looked at him, cool and distant again. 'We better, Sir Jonathan. We better.'

Malone and Clements arrived at lunchtime. Tewsday was not surprised to see them; just depressed and afraid. He had had home-made pea soup and hamhocks for lunch; they curdled in his stomach when he opened the door to the two detectives. 'Why, Inspector Malone!'

'Sir Jonathan,' said Malone, too tired for preliminaries; jet lag had started to catch up with him again, 'we'd like to talk to you about your driver Gary Gawler.'

Tewsday hesitated, then stood aside. 'Come in.' He led them into the library, closing the door so that Sally Gawler would not hear what he knew was about to be said. 'What's all this about, Inspector?'

'We went to Ballyduff House, but they told us there that you resigned yesterday afternoon. A bit sudden, wasn't it?'

'It's going to be announced today, after a board meeting. My health has not been good. Blood-pressure, heart – I've been advised to take a long break.' He felt ready for intensive care. 'What about Gawler?'

'We've got two reports on him, one from the FBI in Washington, the other from the CIA.' Joe Nagler's contact in ASIO had used his contact in the CIA; even in the world of spooks, Malone had remarked to Clements, it was not what you knew but whom you knew that counted. 'Maybe you'd like to see them?'

Tewsday glanced at them, making a pretence of his surprise. 'I never knew ... His references were excellent!'

Malone took back the telexes. 'I think these are more reliable. Where is he?'

'Over – over in his flat.' He was trapped; Gawler would not take the rap on his own. 'Is – do you think he'll be dangerous?'

'I hope not.' But Malone looked at Clements. 'You'd better get the two fellers from out in the street, Russ. Just in case.' Clements hurried out and Malone turned back to Tewsday. 'Why did Sister Mary Magdalene, *Teresa Hourigan*, come to see you the night she was murdered?'

'Eh?' He put out a hand to steady himself, it fell on the big antique globe beside his desk; the world spun round, giving him no support at all. 'The Archbishop's niece? She wasn't here! Where did you get that –?'

'We've traced the cab driver who brought her here from Pymble station. We have another witness who saw her arrive.' But he did not name Mrs Prunello; he didn't want to start a neighbourhood war. 'Why did she come?'

The earthquake had started and he was to be the first victim. He had never been philosophical; there wasn't a philosopher on the surrounding library shelves who could help him. The 'good solid reads' were full of men like himself, successes who were flawed. But he had learned nothing from them.

'She – she called me, said she wanted to talk to me about her uncle and a deal he was trying to put through with one of our companies ...'

'Austarm.'

'Yes, yes! I agreed to see her because I wanted to stop the deal – it was bad for the corporation, bad for Australia –' He was babbling, wrapping the flag, anything, round him. 'We were on the same side, she and I –'

Then Clements came bursting back into the room. 'He's gone, Scobie – bolted! Raudonikis and Harris have been out in the drive, in front of the flat, ever since we came in here. But he's not there – he must have scooted over the back fence.' He looked at Tewsday. 'What's at the back of your garden?'

'A small reserve – a park. He can't have – bolted!' He felt a prick of hope: with Gawler gone there would be no one to testify against him.

'Get a call out!' Malone snapped. 'Stay here, Sir Jonathan – don't *you* try to bolt!'

Malone and Clements left the room on the run; but Malone was back within a minute. Tewsday had slumped down in his chair and Sally Gawler, who had come in from the back of the big house, was standing beside him. She looked in bewilderment at Malone as he came back in.

'What's going on? I can't get a word out of Sir Jonathan – who are you?'

'Police. Who are you – Mrs Gawler? Where's your husband?'

'Gary? He's, I dunno, over in the flat. I was just going to call him for his lunch – why do you want him?' Suddenly she looked even more worried.

Malone took the telexes out of his pocket. 'Did you know any of this, Mrs Gawler?'

She read the dispatches, then shook her head dazedly. 'The FBI? The CIA? My Gary?'

'I think you'd both better come with me. I'll take you into Homicide.'

Tewsday at last regained his voice. 'I'll have to call my wife.'

'Of course. I think you'd better call your lawyer, too.'

'Does Mrs Gawler need to come?' He was not totally taken up with himself: he saw how shattered she was.

'Just for her own protection.'

Sally Gawler was shocked at the suggestion. 'Gary would never hurt *me*!'

'I'm afraid he's already done that,' said Malone and wondered again at the number of women who fell in love with the bastards of the world.

5

Malone managed, on one pretext or another, to keep Tewsday at Homicide and then at Police Centre for almost five hours. He wanted to hold him till Gawler had been picked up, but he spent the afternoon battling Fiona Tewsday, two lawyers, a State Member of Parliament and finally Commissioner Leeds himself.

'You'll have to let him go, Inspector,' Leeds said on the phone. 'The Premier himself has been on the line.' *And on my back*: Malone heard the unspoken words. 'If you can't lay charges, let him go.'

'Yes, sir,' Malone agreed reluctantly. 'I was just hoping we'd pick up this other feller Gawler, put them up against each other.'

'You can do that when you do pick him up. Tewsday's not going to skip the country. I think you'd better come and see me when all this is over.'

'When do you think that will be, sir?'

'That's enough, Inspector.' But the Commissioner's voice sounded more sympathetic than sharp.

Tewsday was released at six o'clock. He and Sally Gawler were driven back to Pymble by Fiona in the BMW. Fiona, a true All Black, drove straight at the assembled reporters and cameramen gathered outside the Police Centre, and the media crowd had to scatter for their lives. Accusations of mayhem, it seemed, bred thoughts of mayhem. Or maybe all the latent Kiwi antagonism towards Australians had come to her blue-rinsed surface.

On their way back to Homicide Malone said to Clements, 'I want a tail kept on Tewsday around the clock.'

'Is the Commissioner still on our side?'

Malone shook his head. 'I think he's had enough of me. It's better that we go on our own on this one.'

Clements gave him a quizzical look. 'Tibooburra's getting closer and closer. I can already hear the flies buzzing and the kangaroos bouncing up and down.'

The phone was ringing in the house at Pymble when the Tewsdays arrived home at 6.50. Tewsday was first into the house and picked up the receiver. It was Gawler ringing from a public call-box.

'Just a minute,' said Tewsday as Fiona and Sally Gawler came in the front door. 'I'll take it in the library. It's one of the newspapers about my resignation.'

'Tell them to get stuffed,' said Fiona, though her vowels were still rounded.

He switched the connection, hung up and went through into the library and closed the door. 'Where are you?'

'I'm not telling. Listen – what did the cops want?'

'You. They've been questioning me in the city for the last five hours. It's bloody embarrassing.'

Gawler laughed. 'Embarrassing? You dunno what embarrassing is. Listen, I need money.'

He had guessed that the demand would come some time. 'How much?'

'I want enough to get out of the country, get me set up again. I'll go somewhere where there's no extradition treaty. I'll get my wife to meet me there. Fifty thousand, how does that sound?'

'Are you trying to blackmail me?' He had expected a demand of pehaps ten thousand; he had lost track of the price of murder. 'You don't want to forget, she was still alive when you took her out of this house.'

'Don't bullshit me, Tewsday!' It was the first time he had ever heard Gawler raise his voice. 'You knew what was gonna happen to her! The same will happen to you –'

'Calm down,' said Tewsday, anything but calm. 'I just can't produce that sort of money out of the blue –'

'You're still bullshitting. I've seen the evening papers, they got it all about you resigning from Ballyduff. You got a big golden handshake, they said. What was it? A million, a coupla million? You owe me one, Tewsday, a golden handshake.'

Tewsday had seen the papers; Sally Gawler had gone out at one point in the afternoon and brought them back. It had been the lead story on the financial pages: BOARD-ROOM WAR? one headline had asked. Suddenly he heard himself say, 'Would you like a handshake of a hundred thousand?'

There was a moment of silence, then: 'Doing what?'

'Getting rid of someone else.' In for a penny, in for a hundred thousand. 'Fingal Hourigan.'

'You're outa your fucking head, you know that?'

'No.' But maybe he was; madness, after all, was just another state of mind. 'Do you want to earn the money or not?'

There was another silence; then: 'It's not enough. Two hundred and fifty thousand.'

'Don't be ridiculous!'

'You're the one being ridiculous. More than that, you're crazy. You want me to be crazy, too, that's the price.'

He sighed; he hated parting with his own money, even to win back a hundred times as much. Which he could do so, if Fingal was gone. 'You're a hard man, Gawler.'

'You got to be in my trade. Is Sally there?'

'I don't think you should speak to her now. She's pretty upset. I'll tell her you called and you'll talk to her tomorrow. Get the job done first.'

'Payment first. Give Sally ten thousand in cash, just for starters. Tell her it's my redundancy pay. The rest of it cable to my account in Switzerland. Take it down.' He gave an account number and a bank in Zurich. Tewsday was not surprised that Gawler should have such an account; there was still so much he didn't know, and would never know, about the American. 'If it's not there within forty-eight hours, I'll be back to take it out of your hide. You know what I mean?' He was cool and distant again, the professional killer. Tewsday felt weak, wondering that he should be dealing with such a man. 'Where do I find Hourigan? At home or in the office?'

Tewsday thought a moment. 'At Ballyduff House. I'll have him there at eight o'clock, in his office on the sixty-ninth floor. You be waiting for him.'

He hung up, sat staring at his desk. He *was* mad, he knew that; but it was not much to live with if it brought him vengeance. He had lived for thirty-two years with ambition: perhaps that had been a madness, too, but he had weathered it, indeed thrived on it. Fingal Hourigan could not be allowed to win. He had to go.

He picked up the phone, dialled the number at Vaucluse.

6

'You'd better come with me, Kerry,' Fingal said as he hung up the phone.' That was Jonathan. He says he's got something that concerns you. He wants to see me in my office.'

'Why there?'

'At eight o'clock at night he thinks that's the last place we'll see any reporters hanging about. Are they still camped outside our gates?'

'No.' The Archbishop, for whom publicity had once been like another state of grace, was tired, even afraid, of it now. 'They've given up. They'll be back as soon as something else starts up. What's Jonathan got on me this time?'

'He didn't say.' Fingal went out to the entrance hall, put on his topcoat and hat, picked up the silver walking-stick. He looked over his shoulder as Brigid came down the stairs. 'Kerry and I are going out for a while. Jonathan wants to see us at the office.'

'You businessmen – why can't you keep business hours?'

'This is different sort of business.' He paused as he opened the front door. 'All of a sudden I feel tired.'

'Stay home,' said Brigid gently.

'No, not that sort of tired. Just as if . . .' But he couldn't explain the weariness that had abruptly overtaken him. 'Come on, Kerry. Wait dinner for us, Bridie. We'll have it together.'

Bridie. Oh Dad, why did you leave it so late?

In the car going into the city Kerry said, 'Why didn't you tell Jonathan to go to hell? You're bone-tired . . .'

Fingal looked out at the drizzling rain. The roadway was a black mirror patterned with moving white, amber and red lights; he was dazzled by it and had to shut his eyes. Small things were beginning to defeat him; this was the way healthy old men died, bit by bit. Was there any point to anything any more? Maybe he should have told Jonathan Tewsday to go to hell. But he had not been able to resist the opportunity to give the screw one last turn. He had no fear that Tewsday could do any more damage to himself or Kerry; the man was beaten. Still ...

'I'm trying to protect you,' he said 'We don't know what the sonofabitch might do.'

'It doesn't matter any more. I'm finished with Paredes and Domecq.'

'There are others. You can't give up now!' He had to whip up the protest, though with a tired hand.

'I'll wait and see. I'm still young – they don't elect young popes any more. I still have to make cardinal.' But he had begun to lose hope; or ambition. Someone (Galen?) had once said that the temperaments of the body led the faculties of the soul. If so, his body was winning out, leading him to resignation. He had been running towards Rome for years and now he was suddenly as tired as his father. He had been caught up in the greatest sin of all, murder, and he could not give himself absolution. Especially since one of the victims had been his own sister's child.

'Don't give up,' Fingal insisted, but he knew in his heart that it really didn't matter any more. He would not live long enough to see the dream.

The Phantom V pulled into the basement garage of Bally-duff House, gliding in like a royal barge. There were half a dozen other cars in the garage, plus two vans; the contract cleaners were at work. As the chauffeur opened the door for Fingal to get out, the old man paused and looked around the garage.

'I can't see Jonathan's car.'

'It would be like him to keep us waiting.' The Archbishop decided this was no time for Christian charity. He began to look forward to being a sonofabitch, though he was not sure how one went about it. Then he reasoned that all he had to do was mimic Jonathan Tewsday. Up till now he had not realized how much he disliked the man. He might even come to hate him, as his father did.

They rode up in the lift to the sixty-ninth floor. As they got out, a thin balding man in white overalls was waiting to go down. He was carrying a heavy vacuum cleaner, the long cord rolled in loops over his shoulder.

'You finished on this floor?' said Fingal.

'Not quite. You're Mr Hourigan, right?' There was no touching the forelock, even if he'd had one; he didn't work for this big shot, he worked for his own boss. 'There's a guy waiting in your office. He told me to come back later. I like to keep me routine, you know what I mean? Start at the top and work down.'

'You'll never get anywhere that way,' said Fingal.

He walked on down the wide corridor, unbuttoning his topcoat but not taking it off; the meeting with Tewsday would be short. Kerry followed him, wondering what lay ahead. He was tired of scenes, he who had dreamed of a coronation.

Fingal opened the door into his secretary's office, crossed the room unhurriedly and opened the door into his own office.

'Tewsday?'

The man at the big window turned, Sydney brightly lit at his back. 'Sir Jonathan couldn't make it, Mr Hourigan.' Then he saw Kerry standing in the doorway behind his father. 'Ah shit!'

Fingal stepped into the room and, after a moment's hesitation, Kerry followed him. 'Gawler? What the hell are you doing in my office?'

Gawler moved quickly and lightly away from the window; before the Hourigans could move, he was between them and the door. He closed the door, took out a long-bladed knife.

'Two for the price of one. It wasn't in the contract, but I guess you're out of luck, Your Grace.' It was a black joke, but he didn't smile.

'Why?' Kerry was shocked, but, to his own surprise, he was not frightened.

'I don't even know,' said Gawler. 'With me, I got problems and I need the money. It's an old story – for me, anyway. Ever since I was a kid in Chicago.' He wasn't about to reminisce. He had come prepared for one killing, now he had to adjust himself to two.

'You're from Chicago?' Fingal was the coolest of the three of them. Or maybe just the most tired. After all these years he recognized fate when it was in the same room with him.

'Yeah, Chicago originally. What's that got to do with it?'

Fingal nodded. 'I might have guessed. Now and then.'

'What?' But puzzlement wasn't going to stop Gawler. He stepped towards Fingal, the knife blade sweeping upwards.

7

'Where's Paredes now?' said Malone.

'He's in the Crest Hotel up at the Cross,' said Clements. 'Andy Graham's in the lobby and he's got someone watching out the back. It looks as if Paredes isn't going to do a bunk, not yet.'

'He's a cool bastard. I thought he'd be on the first plane out of Sydney as soon as we charged Domecq. I was hoping he'd try it. Then we could have picked him up on suspicion.'

'We still could.'

Malone shook his head. 'We had no luck with Tewsday. He's free till we pick up Gawler.'

'Are the two murders connected?'

'I still don't know. The bloke in the middle of it all is the Archbishop and it seems he's the only innocent one, excepting for getting all these buggers together.'

'Him or his old man,' said Clements. 'There's someone else we never really questioned. Brigid Hourigan.'

Malone pondered the suggestion; then he looked in his

notebook for a number. He rang the house at Stokes Point and the phone was picked up almost immediately. *'Pronto? Is that you, signorina?'*

'No, it's Inspector Malone. Where is Signorina Hourigan?'

'She is at her father's house –'

Malone hung up in Michele's ear, quickly dialled the Vaucluse house before the houseman could call his mistress and warn her that the police wanted to speak to her again. Mrs Kelly, another keeper of the flame, answered this time. 'Miss Brigid? Yes, she's here. Who's calling? Oh, it's *you*.' Malone felt like the Devil himself. 'You don't give a soul any peace, do you? I'll get her.'

Brigid Hourigan came to the phone. 'No, Inspector, I really don't have anything further to say. Perhaps when you've caught whoever murdered my daughter –'

'We're still trying to do that, Miss Hourigan. That's why I want to ask you some questions. About Sir Jonathan Tewsday, for a start –'

'You should ask my father about him, not me.'

'We'll do that, too. Is your father at home now?'

'No.'

'Where is he?'

'Do I have to answer that? He's not under house arrest or anything –'

'*Where is he?*'

'He – he's gone into his office with my brother. Sir Jonathan called him, asked him to meet him there.'

'How long ago did they leave?'

'Not more than ten minutes –'

Malone hung up, was on his feet, dragging on his jacket. 'Ballyduff House, as fast as we can make it!'

'What's going on?' Clements was running after him down the aisle between the desks.

'I don't know! But I bet we're going to find the answer to everything in the next ten minutes!'

Fingal died instantly as the knife went in under his ribs and upwards. It was not an easy stab for Gawler; he had to drive in through the thickness of the topcoat. Fingal said something that sounded like *Now and Then, Amen*, but it was indistinct in what also sounded like a laugh, though there was no mirth in his face or the wide blue eyes. He stepped away from Gawler and, the fugitive from Chicago winters of long ago, fell into the coldest, darkest winter of all.

Gawler withdrew the knife and spun round as Kerry, a huge black figure of terrible rage, came at him with a roar. He swung with the knife, but Kerry took it on his left arm. He fell on Gawler, crashing him to the floor. The killer went down, but he had no hope under the bulk on top of him. The Archbishop was astride him, smashing at his face with a bloodied fist, when the door burst open and Malone and Clements came in. It took their combined strength to drag him off the unconscious Gawler.

'That's enough, Your Grace,' said Malone. 'That's the last of it.'

THIRTEEN

I

'We'll give him a State funeral,' Premier Hans Vanderberg told his Cabinet colleagues.

'Y-y-you c-c-can't do th-that!' The Minister for Culture had a shaky voice and an even shakier department.

'All the unions will go out on strike,' said the Minister for Industrial Relations, an ex-union man. 'A State funeral for a boss! You must be joking.'

'He gave the Party over a million dollars at one time or another,' said the Treasurer.

'H-he g-g-gave the other side tw-twice as m-much,' said the Minister for Culture.

'You'd like a State funeral when you go, wouldn't you?' said the Premier.

'I-I wasn't th-thinking of g-g-going,' said the Minister for Culture, but felt the knife already in his back.

So Fingal Hourigan had a State funeral. The country's richest man could not be buried without a salute in a country where wealth, till something better was recognized, was the main yardstick. Fingal, a clear-eyed cynic, would have understood. The obituaries put his fortune at between two and four billion dollars, but they were only guessing. Obituaries are never meant to be truly accurate: the laws of libel are too strict, something for which the heirs are always watching. Nobody would ever know the full truth about Fingal Hourigan. Which was the one thing he had in common with the rest of us.

Domecq, Gawler and Jonathan Tewsday were all sentenced to life imprisonment; the judges marked them all eligible for parole at the turn of the century, an appropriate time to start all over again. Paredes, against whom no charges were laid in New South Wales, went back to Miami, where the FBI picked him up at once; the law, with that talent it has for eventually finding the right charge, sent him to Federal prison for ten years for tax evasion, a crime that, as a Latin American, he had always thought was a joke. Fiona Tewsday sold up the house in Pymble, the property at Bowral, the sixty-foot cruiser and took her three daughters, Sally Gawler and the Rolls-Royce back to New Zealand, where the All Blacks turned out and did a *haka* for her on Eden Park. She was forgiven eventually for marrying an Australian.

Archbishop Hourigan went back to Rome, where he is still head of the Department for the Defence Against Subversive Religions. On his return he had a private audience of the Pope and came out looking like an elderly choirboy, as Monsignor Lindwall wrote to Malone. 'We forgive our sinners, Scobie. If they didn't, what church, of any persuasion, would last even a decade, let alone two thousand years?'

Brigid Hourigan sent her Italian houseman back to Italy. Then, unexpectedly revealing to the world that she was more her father's daughter than it had suspected, she became non-executive chairwoman of Ballyduff Holdings. Kerry, at last succumbing, after a great deal of soul-searching, to vows of poverty (well, almost; he still lived in the *palazzo* apartment), turned over the bulk of his inherited trust to Brigid. She thus became Australia's richest person and the land was loud with feminist hallelujahs. She was, however, still poor in spirit, though she hid it well. Part of her had died with Teresa, the young nun who might have taught them all true love.

One night at the end of winter Malone was sitting in the living-room in the house in Randwick. It had been a dull day at Homicide, just as he liked it; nobody dead, no attempts at murder. The front door was open, letting in the cold night air, but he hadn't the heart to yell at the children to come in and close it. He could hear them:

'Look at the stars!' said Tom. 'Tens of 'em!'

'Millions!' said Maureen. 'There are *millions* of 'em!'

'I can't count that much,' said Tom. 'Tens is good enough for me.'

On television an old, old man was being interviewed on *The 7.30 Report*. It was his hundredth birthday, but he looked much older, his face blotched and pinched and wrinkled by centuries. Malone turned up the sound:

'And what do you think is the secret of your great age?'

'No sex.'

'You mean you have been celibate all your life?'

'No, I mean I aint (*beeped*) a woman since I was ninety!'

The wrinkled old face broke into a wicked grin, then disintegrated as the toothless old mouth opened up and a happy, happy cackle came up out of a hundred years' of memories. Malone switched off the sound and fell back laughing.

Lisa came in from the kitchen. 'What's the matter?'

'Nothing! Nothing.' He reached for her, pulled her down on to the couch beside him as the children came in from the front veranda, slamming the door behind them. 'Everything's normal!'

'What's normal?' said Tom.

'We are,' said Claire, and her father looked at her gratefully. That was something she had worked out for herself, *Choice* hadn't had to tell her.

Then the phone rang. Lisa got up, went out to the hallway and answered it. Then she put her head in the doorway, sighed. 'It's Russ Clements. Normal?'

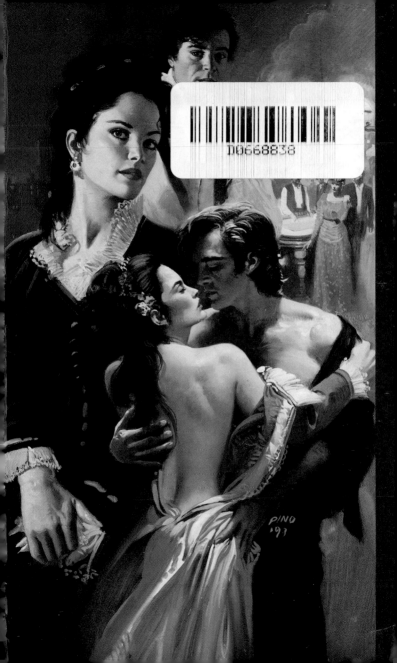

"Don't call me Cat. My name is Catalina."

"Is it?"

"Is yours really Taylor Canton?"

The last two questions were spoken softly, dangerously, both trying to probe weaknesses, and both recognizing the tactic of the other.

"I would swear to it on a Bible," Marsh said, his mouth quirking.

"I'm surprised you have one, or know what one is."

"I had a very good upbringing, Miss Cat." He emphasized the last word.

"And then what happened?" She asked caustically.

The sardonic amusement in his eyes faded. "A great deal. And what is your story?"

Dear God, his voice was mesmerizing. An intimate song that said nothing but wanted everything. Low and deep and provocative. Compelling. And irresistible. Almost.

"I had a very poor upbringing," she said. "And then a great deal happened."

For the first time since she'd met him, she saw real humor in his eyes. Not just that cynical amusement as if he were some higher being looking down on a world inhabited by silly children. "You're the first woman I've met with fewer scruples than my own," he said, admiration again in his voice.

Bantam Books by Patricia Potter
Ask your bookseller for titles you may have
missed

NOTORIOUS
RENEGADE
LIGHTNING
LAWLESS
RAINBOW

NOTORIOUS

PATRICIA POTTER

BANTAM BOOKS
NEW YORK • TORONTO • LONDON • SYDNEY • AUCKLAND

NOTORIOUS

A Bantam Book / December 1993

ISBN 0-533-56225-8

Published simultaneously in the United States and Canada

---

*Bantam Books are published by Bantam Books, a division of Bantam Doubleday
Dell Publishing Group, Inc. Its trademark, consisting of the words "Bantam
Books" and the portrayal of a rooster, is Registered in U.S. Patent and Trademark
Office and in other countries. Marca Registrada. Bantam Books, 1540 Broadway,
New York, New York 10036.*

PRINTED IN THE UNITED STATES OF AMERICA

OPM 0 9 8 7 6 5 4 3 2 1

PROLOGUE

Just before daybreak...

DENVER, COLORADO
WINTER 1879

Marsh Canton kept his face expressionless. Across the table a man who called himself Darcy wiped nervous sweat from his brow.

"About—about that marker . . ." Darcy stammered.

Marsh said nothing. He merely waited.

"I . . . I can't pay it."

"You will," Marsh said coldly, "one way or another."

Sweat beaded like tears at the corners of Darcy's eyes; it dripped down his cheeks. His face was red, mottled from heavy drinking, and his hands trembled. "I do ... do have something," he managed to say. His expression was a study in fear as he reached inside the breast pocket of his coat.

Instantly a gun was in Marsh's hand. The movement was so fast, it seemed to onlookers as though Marsh hadn't moved at all. The three other men at the table pushed back their chairs, and silence fell over the crowd in the Purple Sage Saloon.

"No!" Darcy shouted. "I wasn't reaching for a gun. I swear it!"

The gun didn't waver. Marsh's eyes were very dark, framed by hooked black brows that gave him a perpetually lazy look. But no one took Marsh Canton for lazy. He had the reputation of being one of the most ruthless, and deadly, men in Colorado, perhaps in the entire West.

"You were saying?" Marsh prompted. His words echoed in the cavernous hall, and men inched away even as they tried to position themselves to better hear what transpired.

Slowly, Darcy slid the paper from his coat. "A ... a saloon. In San Francisco. This is the deed."

"And what would you be doing with a saloon in San Francisco?"

"A debt. I took it, like ... like now ... in a poker game."

"You must have been a better poker player a while back than you are now," Marsh said in a low, contemptuous voice. He hated welshers. But then, he didn't like anyone much.

He took the deed. There was a legal-looking seal, and the deed appeared legitimate enough. But why in the hell would he want a saloon? He was a gunfighter. One of the best. He brought the highest dollar.

Darcy was sweating even more profusely. Marsh cursed to himself. He wouldn't get anything else from the man. It was very plain there was nothing more to get. Marsh could kill him. But damn, he was tired of killing—so damned tired.

His last job had made him realize exactly how tired. He had been hired by a rancher who feared a range war was in the making. One of Marsh's competitors, a man called Lobo, had been hired by an opposing rancher. In the end Lobo and he hadn't been forced to confront each other, but Lobo had been drawn into a show-down with another hired gun and been shot, his gun hand shattered. In that moment Marsh had imagined himself in Lobo's place.

Nearly forty now, Marsh knew he was old for a gunfighter. He was losing his edge, those split-second responses. More and more often he awoke from a dream in which he saw himself dying on a dirt street in a worn-out, no-name cow town while people stared as if he were a freak.

And he *was* a freak. No heart. No soul. A shell of a man. But he didn't want to die that way, not with an ambitious young gunfighter bending over him as a crowd cheered him on.

He looked at the crinkled piece of paper in his hand. His deliverance, perhaps? A sign? Hell, he didn't believe in such tomfoolery. Yet . . .

He smoothed the paper and saw Darcy release a long breath. "This had better be real," he said in a voice that rumbled threateningly. "Or I'll find you."

The man's red face went white, something Marsh would have thought impossible.

"It's real," Darcy mumbled.

"Sign the deed," Marsh commanded, pushing it back. The man did as ordered, the signature barely legible because his hand shook so badly.

Marsh Canton took the deed back, folded it carefully, and placed it in his pocket. He stood, casually sliding his gun into its well-used holster. No one moved. He took one careful look around the saloon. Only the usual fear registered on the faces of the men.

He was used to the fear. He expected it. He discovered he was also weary of it.

Marsh turned his back, satisfied that no one would try to stop him.

No one did. They simply watched the lean blackclad figure stalk out of the saloon. And they were damned glad the gunfighter had gone.

No one heard Marsh's mirthless chuckle as he left the silent crowd behind. The gunfighter was about to become a saloon owner. Maybe the odor of fear and death, which had been his companion for more than twenty years, would no longer shadow him. . . .

Maybe.

PART ONE

Bright Midnight

CHAPTER 1

Cat bolted upright, her hand sliding under her pillow to seize the derringer she always kept there. She heard a loud bang, then muted thumping. Fear engulfed her, and she struggled to calm herself.

So much had changed. So very much. But not the fear. Loud noises at night brought it back . . . along with images of another time when men tramped the hallways and banged on doors. Years later, banged on *her* door. And forced their way inside.

It wasn't night, she realized. It was nearly dawn, and the noises that had awakened her were coming from outside, not from within the safe home she'd made for herself above the Silver Slipper Saloon, where she, Catalina Hilliard, reigned. She slipped the derringer back to its hiding place and got out of bed, walking slowly to the window, throwing aside the blowing pale-green curtains as she searched outside for the source of the sound. San Francisco was a raucous town, haven to the newly rich and the recklessly adventurous—a town of mavericks, like her, and the city was never still. But the banging noise was different, oddly compelling and demanding of attention.

The window was open as always. She loved the cold wind that blew off the bay, fresh and tingly, so unlike the humid, almost suffocating, heat of Natchez Under the Hill and so many other towns up and down the Mississippi.

The sharp bang came again, and through the silver glow of an oncoming dawn, her gaze found the culprit: a wooden sign on the building across the street. One end had fallen from its hinge and was banging against the wooden side of the building. She could barely make out the words from the awkward position: "Glory ole." It should have been the "Glory Hole," but one of the letters had faded, and now the rest of the sign was joining it in ignominy.

The sight almost revived her spirits. She'd had no small part in its present abysmal condition. She'd run four owners out of business, and she would continue to do the same to anyone who tried to revive the saloon.

She'd seen her competition try everything from cheap watered whiskey to prostitutes, two practices she abhorred, and she'd defeated them so completely that no one had tried to reopen the saloon in the past two years. The empty building had sunk into disrepair, most of its furnishings taken to pay the bills of its last owner, and the interior was used now by a variety of human and animal flotsam.

Little remained within its fairly strong walls other than a long scarred bar and a damaged piano too big to cart off. She didn't even know who owned it, though she had heard that one of the creditors of the last owner had taken the deed.

If anyone did try to reopen it, she would ruin them as she'd ruined the others.

The sign banged again as if to accentuate that vow. No one in his right mind would try a fifth time. Everyone in San Francisco knew the Glory Hole's history of failure.

With that happy thought, Cat turned away from the window, her hand pushing back the thick mane of dark hair that had fallen partially over her face. She'd been too tired last night to braid it as she usually did, so she would have to fight the tangles. She lit an oil lamp and glanced in the mirror, looking at herself critically. Her face was still smooth, her eyes still a vivid green. No lines yet, thank God, despite late nights and long hours. She was thirty-seven, maybe thirty-eight years old; she didn't know when she had been born, not the day or even the year.

She knew she was beautiful, but in the past her face and figure had been a curse. They had, however, become assets in making the Silver Slipper successful. Beauty at a distance. Out of reach. No one laid a finger on Catalina Hilliard. People called her the Ice Queen, a name she relished. It was part of the image she had assiduously cultivated. In a few years she wouldn't have to worry about her looks or her image because she would have enough money to fulfill her heart's desire. She longed to pull up stakes and move into the countryside, somewhere near the sea, to a place where she could enjoy anonymity and the security that meant to her. A few more years. A few more years without competition.

The Glory Hole sign banged again. Now the noise comforted her, proclaiming her success, her competitors' failures.

Cat decided that she liked that noise very much indeed.

The lawyer looked at Marsh Canton as if he had suddenly contracted leprosy. Or insanity.

Marsh didn't much care for the expression on the lawyer's face or the peculiar feeling he was getting. Something was wrong, very wrong. He fixed the lawyer with a stare that quelled most men.

It had an impact, though not as great a one as Marsh was used to; but then, lawyer David Schuyler Scott was not a man who was easily impressed or intimidated.

The lawyer had been recommended to Marsh by the owner of the hotel where he was staying, a man named Quinn Devereux. Scott was a rarity, Devereux had said, an honest lawyer in San Francisco. Now that Marsh thought about it, Devereux had also looked at him a bit strangely when he'd mentioned the Glory Hole.

"You plan to do what?" Scott asked.

"Take possession of the Glory Hole," Marsh repeated as patiently as he could. His eyes narrowed. "This is a legal deed, isn't it?"

"Oh, yes. It certainly seems to be. But why don't you try to sell the property? It would be suitable for . . ." His voice trailed off. What would the property be suited for with the Silver Slipper across the street? Not a home, or a school, or even a respectable store. Respectable women didn't patronize that area.

"A saloon," Marsh finished for him.

David Scott leaned toward his new client. The man disturbed him in more ways than one. He called himself Marshall Canton, and the name had an odd familiarity to it, though David couldn't place it at the moment. But he did perceive a certain aura of trouble exuding from the man. Trouble and danger. His first impulse had been to turn away Marsh Canton, but Quinn Devereux, an old and valued client, had sent the man to him, and David owed Quinn and his wife, Meredith, a favor or two.

"I think I should warn you, Mr. Canton, that the last four owners lost everything they had with the Glory Hole."

Marsh Canton shrugged. "Why?"

"The lady across the street doesn't like competition," David said.

"The lady?"

"Catalina Hilliard. They call her the Ice

Queen of San Francisco. She owns and operates the Silver Slipper."

"A woman saloon owner?"

"Yep," David said, a bit pleased that he finally startled the stoic man across from him. "A very pretty one. And a very determined one."

"And how does she get rid of her competitors?"

"Various ways, I hear. An unexpected visit from the police. A small riot. Accusations of watered whiskey and card cheating."

"Were they true?"

"I expect some of them were."

"I don't intend to allow either."

David cleared his throat. He suspected if Catalina couldn't defeat him by legal means, she'd find extralegal ways to drive him out.

"It's in very bad shape," David said quickly.

"I'll fix it," Marsh countered.

"It will take a lot of money."

"I have a lot of money."

Frustrated at the way his new client so casually pushed aside objections, David sighed. Canton's clothes weren't fashionable, but they were made from expensive fabric. And striking. All black. Shirt, trousers, coat, even his gunbelt. The gunbelt was disquieting in itself; guns were becoming a rarity now in San Francisco, where once they had been as common as boots. His client's dark gray eyes and ebony hair matched the darkness of his clothes, and the gaze, though steady, was most unusual. David had never seen eyes that betrayed so little; they were like glass, reflecting pools that caught images of others while safeguarding the person behind.

"Why, Mr. Canton?"

Marsh's eyebrows arched. "Why what?"

"Why are you so insistent on the Glory Hole?"

"I won it."

"You won trouble."

"I'm used to trouble, Mr. Scott."

David didn't doubt that for a moment. But this was, he suspected, a different kind of trouble. He was acquainted with Catalina Hilliard.

"There are other properties," the lawyer said.

Marsh didn't know why the Glory Hole had become so important to him, but it had. All the way from Colorado he had thought about it, thought that maybe this was his one chance to get away from the gun. It had become an obsession with him, even if he didn't understand all the reasons why. He did know, however, that when he set his mind on something, nothing changed it. And he had his mind set on the Glory Hole. So he simply said, "No."

"What do you plan to do with it?"

Marsh shrugged. "Gambling. Whiskey. What else do you do with a saloon?"

"And you're prepared to run it?"

Marsh nodded.

"You don't exactly inspire frivolity," David said with the slightest of smiles as he thought Marshall Canton's eyes alone would daunt most customers. Not to speak of the grace with which he wore the gun, a grace that came only from familiarity and long use.

Marsh's lips twisted in an approximation of a smile. There was so little warmth in it, David thought, that Canton might as well have frowned.

"That's why I know I need someone else. A front man. I hoped you could help me."

The last was said with obvious reluctance. It was easy for David to see that Marshall did not like asking for help. And for the first time, he warmed up to this client. There was something to say for honesty, for a man who realized his limitations. "Perhaps," he said. "But why don't you take a look at it before you make a decision?"

"It's not necessary."

David shook his head. "I won't have anything to do with it unless you do."

Marsh stood, studied David with such a measured gaze that he had the sudden feeling he was being sized for a coffin, then nodded. "I'll be back."

David watched him turn and leave the office and felt relieved. Canton wouldn't be back, not after seeing the condition of the Glory Hole.

Still, he thought, Marshall Canton would make an interesting client. A *very* interesting client—and an interesting challenger to Catalina Hilliard. David grinned suddenly. His client wasn't like the others who had tried to make a success of the Glory Hole. Now that he thought about it, there were certain similarities between Canton and Miss Hilliard. Both seemed to have a streak of stubbornness that would make a mule proud, and their eyes . . .

He was suddenly struck with the thought

that both Canton and Catalina had the same look in their eyes: wariness and detachment, a warning not to venture too close. It was part of Catalina's appeal, that touch-me-not aura that alternately challenged and bewitched.

David Schuyler Scott leaned forward on his chair and rested his elbows on the desk, a thoughtful look on his face.

Marsh took one look at the Glory Hole and understood the attorney's reluctance to proceed.

A wooden sign dangled on one chain, hitting the side of the building with an occasional thud. He stood transfixed, remembering a similar scene fifteen years before. A thud, just like this one, reflecting the same bleakness . . .

Someone shouted, and he realized he was standing in the middle of a street, in the path of an oncoming carriage. He moved deliberately to the wood sidewalk, making the cursing driver slow his horses. Danger was a word that had little meaning. He had no fear of death, only a reluctance for a certain kind of dying.

He could touch the sign from where he stood now, and he did, his fingers running over the faded *H*. Appropriate, he thought, for something essential was missing, too, from his life.

He turned to the front entrance. Only one of the pair of four-feet tall swinging doors remained in front of a substantial door. He tried the solid door and found the lock gone. The door opened easily, and he stepped inside.

He heard a growl. A dog—if you could call it a dog—was rising from where it evidently had been sleeping. It was the ugliest animal he had even seen—as ugly, he thought with dry humor, as the wrong end of a Winchester rifle.

He looked over at a broken window, guessing that was how the animal had entered. The dog was fairly large, his sides bony and scarred, his head not distinctive of any breed and his salt-and-pepper coat layered with dirt. Only the dog's teeth seemed to be in decent condition, and they were bared threateningly. It crouched, growling, and Marsh spoke evenly. "I won't hurt you," he said as if conversing with a human, "if you'll grant me the same courtesy." His tone of voice pacified the animal, which relaxed slightly and lowered his growling to a warning rather than threatening sound.

Marsh took several more steps inside. There was only a bar and a piano in the huge room. He thought of another piano, one from years back, and looked down at his hands, hands that had once been so facile on piano keys before they had become even more talented at delivering death. He walked over to the forlorn-looking instrument, detouring around the wary dog. He stroked an ivory key and heard a dull thud. The sound sent anguish through him; it seemed to echo his own dead soul.

He shook his head at the morbid thought. He'd given up on his soul and heart long ago. There was nothing left of either in him, nothing of grace or worth. Only survival drove him now, a survival that was becoming more and more difficult.

Like this place. Perhaps he did fit here in this rotting, desolate building. He grinned at the dog, feeling at one with it. The dog cringed, and Marsh chuckled mirthlessly. "Don't like the comparison?" he asked in the same conversational tone he had used before, and the dog growled more forcefully.

The dog had a great deal of sense, Marsh thought, as he took a more searching inventory of his property.

Windows were broken, the paint on the walls peeling, and there was the inescapable odor of unwanted visitors. He leaned against the wall and took from his pocket a long, thin cigar, lit it, and studied the interior by the light that filtered in through the broken windows.

He had lied to the lawyer. Well, not exactly lied, but certainly he'd left a misconception. He had said he had money. He did. But not a great deal. He had been well paid for his jobs, but he had expensive tastes, and there had never been any particular reason to save. God knew there wasn't anyone to leave it to. So he always stayed in the best hotels, ate the best food, and bought the most expensive wines. And he gambled, often not really caring if he won or lost but finding it a way to wile away time. Or to ferret out information.

His gaze went to what remained of a mirror over the bar. Not much. A couple of pieces of glass, just enough to catch a glimpse of his black coat. Jagged pieces of glass . . . like those he'd found in the charred ruins of his home.

The room started spinning, and he placed his hand against the wall for support. . . .

He was leading his horse up the once-broad drive that led to the main house, to Rosewood. Both he and the horse were weary and half-starved. The animal had served him well, and despite his need to get home Marsh was damned if he was going to kill the horse to do it.

He fought his anticipation. Anticipation and a terrible gnawing fear. He had passed too many burned and abandoned plantations in this part of Georgia not to worry about what he would find. While fighting in Virginia, he had heard about Sherman's brutal march to the sea and the subsequent occupation, but the reality of what he had found surpassed any horrors he had imagined.

He'd thought he had few illusions after four years of bitter fighting, but he'd somehow managed to keep his image of home, of the green grass, rich fields, and fine Greek Revival house. But most of all he remembered the gentleness of his mother and sister. His brother and father were both gone, killed in the early days of the war, but a distant cousin had taken on responsibility for the plantation, and though he hadn't heard from his mother and sister in a year, he'd forced himself to believe it was only because a Union army lay between them.

He took the bend of the road, looked up eagerly, and stopped in his tracks. Where the house had stood, only the skeletons of two of the six chimneys of its fireplaces remained.

There was an eerie silence, perhaps because there was little left to harbor birds or block the slight hot breeze. Even the oaks that had once led to the house were gone . . . cut for firewood, perhaps, or burned by sparks from other fires.

Of all the outbuildings—the two barns, stables, and slave cabins that had once sat in neat rows behind the great house—only half of one cabin remained, its door listing from a single hinge. It swayed on that hinge, occasionally hitting the partial wall that remained. The sound from that collision emphasized the overall silence, the sense of abandonment and bleakness. The garden his mother had loved was overgrown with weeds, although a few red roses had valiantly fought their way through them. The once-fertile fields were also covered with weeds. Slowly he walked to the small family cemetery shaded by one of the few surviving trees. Looking oddly out of place among the great stone monuments were two simple wooden crosses. Sally Canton and Melissa Canton. Beneath their names was the same month of death. June 1864.

Marsh Canton, a colonel in Mosby's guerrillas and veteran of four years of some of the most bitter fighting of the war, stood still and felt heat gather behind his eyes. He wasn't aware he was crying until he felt moisture hit his hand, which still held the reins of the horse. It was then, at that moment, when what was left of his soul died.

He was twenty-five that day.

And he had turned from his heritage and walked away, never to return, not after he dis-

covered exactly what had happened in that month of June. . . .

He shook his head. He had walked away once. He should walk away again. Once more his gaze moved around what remained of the saloon. Why did it hold an attraction? Why was he so determined to have what he'd sworn didn't matter to him—a place of his own?

The goddamn deed had seemed a sign of some kind, a start.

A start? More like a finish, he thought wryly as he mentally totalled the cost of renovation. It would take everything he had. He *could* just ride on.

And do what? Another job? More killing? Christ, it was already too easy. It had been so natural on his last job that it scared him. He had killed two men there, one who had challenged him and the other who had shot a child. Both needed killing, but when he'd left that town and all that had occurred there, he'd known a confusion and gnawing ache he'd never experienced before. Now in a blinding moment of self-examination, he realized he was seizing this opportunity for personal salvation.

The Ice Queen. A woman saloon owner. Apparently she was responsible for the dismal shape of this place. A challenge. Perhaps that's what he needed to feel alive again.

Hell. He whisked aside the thought. The whole thing was nonsense anyway. He didn't need this place—especially if it was going to revive memories best left alone.

He dropped the cigar on the floor and crushed it with his booted foot.

Right now he needed a drink. Badly.

And why not across the street? The mirror fragment above the bar reflected his wolfish grin. He unbuttoned his broadcloth coat, sauntered through the door, across the street, and into the Silver Slipper.

CHAPTER 2

The Silver Slipper was everything the Glory Hole wasn't.

In fact, Marsh thought, it was probably the finest saloon he'd patronized since before the war, when he'd visited the most fashionable ones in Richmond and Washington. It certainly was one of the biggest.

Yards of hardwood floor, polished to a fine sheen, stretched to a rich mahogany bar that spanned the width of the room in the rear. To one side was gambling paraphernalia: two roulette wheels, several poker tables, a blackjack table with an elegantly dressed dealer presiding. To the left was an elevated stage with a piano. Stairs at the back led up to a landing that disappeared into a hallway. Dazzling chandeliers lit the room, light dancing off the mirrors and gleaming floors. Pale-blue velvet curtains framed windows as well as the stage.

The saloon was welcoming, friendly even, and Marsh never before had had that impression in a public drinking place. A table laden with food was near the front door; tables with chairs were placed around the room. Small groups of men, several enjoying the company of pretty hostesses, sipped from frosted mugs, another rarity in western saloons, and Marsh thought the cost of ice must be astronomical.

He went to the bar and hooked his right boot on the brass footrest. The bartender was there immediately with a smile. "Your pleasure, sir?"

"Whiskey," Marsh said, and the man nodded and poured a generous dollop in a clean glass. Marsh was impressed, despite himself. Cleanliness was rare in western establishments. He sipped the whiskey, savoring its fine rich taste. No rotgut here.

"You're new in town?" the bartender asked.

Marsh nodded.

The bartender, obviously trained as to when and when not to pursue conversation, looked down at the glass. "Another?"

Marsh nodded again. He needed it after comparing the Silver Slipper with the Glory Hole. He only wished he had that welsher in his gunsight.

A woman with light-brown hair approached him with an oddly hesitant expression. "Like some company?"

Marsh eyed her speculatively. She, like the whiskey, was premium. She looked about eighteen or so, a bit young for his taste, but she was very pretty in a soft way, and she had an appealing vulnerability about her. Her eyes were an expressive coffee color, and her smile was appealingly tentative rather than practiced.

If he'd been of a mind for company, he might have sought information from her, but he wasn't. He was in a foul mood. The unwanted memories sparked by the wreck across the street, and the knowledge he'd been gulled by a tinhorn, fed a simmering anger.

He watched the woman's face as her gaze met his, and he saw the familiar withdrawal in them. Philosophers said the eyes were the mirror of the soul, and he knew his had become about as black as sin. Not many people looked at him without flinching and inching away. The lawyer had been one of the few, and even he had been wary.

The young woman was moving slightly backward, even as a question remained in her eyes.

Why not? Marsh thought suddenly, changing his mind. The girl was unusual. She couldn't be as vulnerable as she appeared, not if she worked in a saloon. Perhaps he could learn more about the Ice Queen, who, apparently, was not in the saloon this afternoon.

He nodded and gestured to the bartender while keeping his eyes on her face. "Your pleasure?"

"Champagne," she said, her voice a little shaky.

More like tea, Marsh knew, at champagne prices, but he gave the order to the bartender along with one for another whiskey. That would be his limit. It always was. He held his liquor well, but it was pure stupidity for a gunfighter to drink more. A fraction of a second was often the difference between life and death.

When the drinks came, he took them and followed her to a table where she sat down, her hands nervously taking the glass of champagne.

"My name's Molly," she said, obviously waiting for him to reveal his.

"Canton," he said curtly, hoping there would be no recognition. He doubted there would be, for he had not worked in California, but there had been one of those god-awful dime novels about him. Mostly fiction, of course, but with a grain of truth.

"First or last?"

He shrugged. "Just Canton."

The girl looked even more nervous. "First time here?"

He gave her a slight smile and nodded.

Her gaze wavered, apparently unnerved by what she saw in his smile, in his face. She bit her lip and took a nervous sip of the drink, and he watched with interest. She was nothing like the saloon girls he had met in the past. There was something rather . . . uncertain about her. He wondered whether there were upstairs rooms, whether the Ice Queen dealt in prostitution as well as liquor, gambling, and bribery. It was a matter of interest, rather than desire. He was becoming intrigued. Shy, frightened bar girls were unusual.

He waited for her next question, not making it easy for her with his hard, steady stare; but then, he never made things easy for anyone.

She was tongue-tied now, whether because of lack of wit or his intimidation, he didn't know. One hand tapped the table while the other clutched the empty champagne glass.

He gave her as close to a real smile as he could manage. It was meant to disarm, but it apparently had the opposite effect, for the glass shattered, cutting her hand. She gave a sudden cry, and the bartender moved quickly to her side, glaring at Marsh as he wrapped a towel around the wounded hand.

"Aw, Molly," he said with real concern. "I'll get Catalina."

Marsh sat back, watching with a bemused air. A skittish saloon girl. A protective bartender. Strange. He looked around, and even the customers were glaring at him.

Was he that frightening these days?

He heard movement above him and looked toward the stairs, his gaze riveted on the woman descending them. Marsh Canton had never been awed by a woman. Christ knew he had seen enough of them and bedded a good many, but the woman who was approaching was unique, and he couldn't immediately give a reason why.

But he understood why she was called the Ice Queen, and it certainly wasn't because of her coloring. He had expected her to be blond and blue-eyed for some reason, but her hair was as black as his own and her eyes the most spectacular emerald green he had ever seen. It wasn't her vivid beauty, though, that caused her to be called Ice Queen. It was an aura that cloaked her, one that proclaimed her separateness from the rest of the world.

The thought was so quick, so certain, that it astounded Marsh. Intrigued him. Fascinated him. Very little did that these days, and the sudden surge of interest surprised him. He rose as she approached.

Her gaze was only for Molly and went directly to the bloody towel. "Are you all right?"

Molly nodded, a shamed, half-frightened expression on her face. "It's just a little cut. I'm . . . sorry."

Cat gently unwrapped the towel and examined the cuts; then she looked over at Marsh, as if seeing him for the first time. Anger sparkled like green fire in her eyes. "Are you responsible for this?"

Of everything Marsh had been accused of in his ill-directed life, hurting a woman had never been one of them, and he stiffened.

But Molly shook her head. "No . . . Miss Catalina, he didn't do anything. . . . I was nervous and broke the glass." Marsh recognized the courage the girl had to muster to speak up, and wondered why.

"He didn't say anything to you?"

Molly shook her head.

The woman turned to the bartender. "Take her upstairs and send Wilhelmina for the doctor." She turned her attention to Marsh, studying him as if he were a specimen under glass.

He was used to perusing other people that way. He wasn't sure he liked the turnaround.

"Mr. . . . ?"

"Canton," he replied easily. "You must be Catalina Hilliard."

This time she stiffened. It was obvious that she liked control and equally obvious that somehow that control was drifting between them.

"I don't allow manhandling of the girls who work here," she said in a frigid tone.

He raised an eyebrow. "Unusual policy for a saloon," he remarked. "However, I think anyone in here would tell you that I wasn't close to her." His voice grew harsh. "And I don't care for the implication."

Their gazes met, held. Something flashed between them, a recognition of sorts. Two strong wills probing, testing. Marsh almost lost himself in her eyes; the depths were limitless, yet they revealed little.

Now he saw every feature, every perfectly molded feature. He tried to judge her age but discovered that he couldn't. She was one of those few women who were ageless, whose fine bone structure would mask years. Her wary eyes were experienced, and a few fine lines, which she didn't try to conceal, spread from their corners. He didn't think they were laugh lines.

He knew she was weighing him in the same cold, methodical manner, and he knew she was experienced enough to see, and sense, the killer in him. Strangely enough, it didn't seem to frighten her, even as he saw the awareness enter her eyes. He suspected it was that recognition again, a recognition that would make them wary of each other, but not afraid.

Instead, she relaxed slightly. "A visitor to San Francisco, Mr. Canton?"

He shrugged. "I'm thinking about opening a business here."

"The same kind of business you have been in?"

He smiled. "Not exactly."

Heat suddenly radiated in waves between them. A peculiar kind of heat. A dangerous kind of heat. The kind he had felt in the Midwest just before a tornado hit.

She felt it too. He could tell from her startled expression.

"I have to go look after Molly." She started to turn and then looked back at him. "She's new here," she added in an explanatory but not apologetic tone. "The drink is on the house."

He bowed low, as he used to in Georgia so many years ago. A lifetime ago. He had been the scion of a plantation family, a student at the Virginia School of Law. He'd had exquisite manners and had been gifted with a number of talents, from riding and shooting to playing Mozart and reading law.

He'd been all that, before the war had sifted out all the gentler pursuits and left only the deadly ones.

He hadn't lost his touch, however. He saw a certain appreciation, then amusement in those brilliant eyes that were as cold as the gems they resembled.

She walked away, her dark-green silk dress floating around an exceedingly fine female form.

He had been so absorbed with the face, he hadn't noticed the rest of her. The neck of her dress was fairly high, and the sleeves covered the upper part of her arms. It was modest for a saloon owner, but as he felt a sudden hardening in the groin area, he realized the modesty was even more enticing and challenging than a revealing gown would be.

He sat back down, spreading his long legs out under the table as he considered the last few moments. She fascinated him, as, he'd surmised from the attorney, she fascinated much of San Francisco. Otherwise she wouldn't have the power she did.

She was an odd combination, showing such concern for the girl and real outrage at him before deciding he was innocent—in that matter, at least. But there was also a coldness in those eyes that he had rarely, if ever, seen in a woman.

Catalina Hilliard was interesting. Extremely interesting, and would make a worthy adversary. He felt a flicker of excitement, the first in a very long time. He thought he had been deadened to human emotions. Did he really want them? Could he afford them?

Maybe not, but anything was better than the emptiness of the past few years, the absolute black void that had become his life. It had been growing, almost swallowing him whole as he realized he no longer felt anything when he killed another human being, nothing at all. Not regret or pain, or even relief that it was someone else lying dead in the street, or some hot desert, or lonely mountain valley. That indifference would kill him someday, someday soon.

And God knew he could spend what money he had. If the Glory Hole didn't pan out, he could command almost any price in Colorado for his particular specialty.

A certain unfamiliar exuberance took hold of him. And he wondered only for the briefest of seconds whether he was really looking for a new life, or if he just wanted to see whether he could melt the Ice Queen.

Cat waited with Molly for the doctor, but her thoughts remained in the saloon . . . with the stranger.

She would never forget that face, that too-handsome face that had no soul in it. She wouldn't forget his hard, lean grace, his all-black attire, his worn gunbelt—or his air of danger. She had damn little use for most men, or this kind in particular.

What kind of business could he have in San Francisco? Nothing respectable. She was sure of that. Well, she wasn't very respectable herself, and she certainly had no right to judge others. But why couldn't she erase him from her mind? Something baffling had transpired with him. She had felt what must be desire, and that had never happened to her before, not in a lifetime of altogether too many—

It couldn't be desire, she told herself. Couldn't be.

Using all her willpower, she banished him, temporarily at least, from her thoughts. And she sighed. What to do with Molly?

The girl sat stiffly in the chair, clutching the

bloody towel wrapped around her hand, her soft brown eyes pleading like some wounded doe. Cat had had reservations about trying Molly as a hostess. It was unfortunate that one of Molly's first attempts was a man who would probably scare most women silly, or else seduce them right in the middle of a crowd.

Dear Lucifer, why had she even thought of that?

She turned her attention back to Molly. Cat considered herself hard-hearted, her emotions almost untouchable, but Molly had somehow cut a swath through her usual defenses. Perhaps because she reminded Cat of another girl so long ago. Scared. With no place to turn.

Cat didn't know Molly's history, but she recognized fear when she saw it, the kind of fear that came from abuse of some kind, and she felt a peculiar protectiveness. She knew Molly was desperate for a job and shelter, and that had been enough.

Molly wasn't like the other girls who worked at the Silver Slipper. Cat had chosen each of them carefully. They were all attractive, all vivacious, and all experienced. Cat paid them well, well enough that they wouldn't have to sell their bodies, and many of them eventually married customers.

"I'm sorry," Molly said. "He tried to be pleasant, I think, but . . ."

Cat knew. She had looked into his eyes too. But she had not felt the fear Molly had. She'd felt challenged to a duel of sorts, almost as if he'd thrown a gauntlet. She had lowered her eyes first, simply because her body was doing unexpected things as their gazes had met, searched, weighed.

She wondered if he would be back.

She hoped not. She didn't like the reckless emotions he stirred in her.

Canton. He'd said his name was Canton. It had a familiar ring to it.

Where had she heard that name?

Marsh returned to the law office. He had to wait, but he used the time productively, envisioning improvements to the Glory Hole.

The attorney finally ushered a client from his office, and by the nod of his head invited Marsh in.

"Record the deed," Marsh instructed.

"You've decided to keep it?"

Marsh nodded. "You've done your duty in warning me, and I agree it's in abysmal shape. But it does have promise."

"Promise?" David Scott's voice was full of doubt.

"Of a sort," Marsh said with a smile tight enough to cool hell. It certainly didn't invite more questions.

Still, David hazarded one. "Did you visit the Silver Slipper?"

His new client's obsidian eyes flickered as he inclined his head.

"And you still want to proceed?"

"I think there's room for a different kind of drinking establishment in that part of town," Marsh said.

David shrugged. He'd warned his client.

"I'll get the deed recorded in your name today. How do you want it?"

"Just Canton."

The attorney started to protest.

Marsh hesitated. Perhaps he would discover how honest this lawyer was. "I have a certain . . . reputation that I would rather not advertise."

"Do you have a middle name?"

"Taylor."

"We'll use that, then."

"Good. Now, do you know some good carpenters?"

Another kind of banging woke Cat up. She had become used to the slamming of the sign against the building across the street, but this was something else. Not so random. Steady. As if controlled by a human hand rather than nature's.

She had a very bad feeling about it.

With a slight groan she rolled out of bed. Early. Much too early, especially when she'd had a restless, unsettled night. She went over to the window.

A small army was working on the Glory Hole. The sign had been repainted, the gold-colored letters bright and gaudy, and it had been neatly nailed in place.

Cat swore.

And prepared to do battle once more.

CHAPTER 3

Marsh watched the activity around the Glory Hole with satisfaction.

David Scott had been something less than enthusiastic about this venture, but he'd obviously known the right people to speed it along. Marsh had met with a foreman last evening, directly after Scott filed the ownership deed, and work had started at daybreak.

Marsh had discarded his black clothing, just as he hoped to discard his past. He stretched out comfortably in denim trousers and cotton shirt, although he still wore a gunbelt under a leather jacket. The gun was too much a part of him to set aside. He had enemies, probably more than he knew, and he'd lived too long on the razor's edge of danger to go unprotected.

The sky was pale blue, the sun still low and drowsy looking through a lingering light fog. A fresh breeze swept across the street, as he was discovering it often did in this city. After the heat of the Colorado plains, Texas, and Arizona, he relished this constant rush of cool, sometimes cold, air from the ocean. He liked the excitement of San Francisco, the color, the tolerance he found in the city.

The dog he'd discovered in the saloon was still about, slinking under some wooden boards, eyeing him malevolently. The dog had as much right to the saloon as he did, Marsh felt, perhaps more.

He looked back up at the sign nailed neatly above the door, each letter boldly outlined in the gold that had had so much to do with this city. He'd halfway thought about leaving the *H* off the Hole, but then reconsidered. His irreverent sense of humor might not be shared by others.

Marsh sauntered inside. Workmen were replacing the broken windowpanes; carpenters were working on the door and shutters. He felt an odd sense of proprietorship. He'd owned nothing but a horse, a saddle, and a gun since the war.

He took measure of what else needed to be done. The walls could remain as they were. He needed furniture: tables and chairs. A new piano. And then liquor, of course, and glasses. He'd obtained a list of dealers from David.

And employees.

He'd told David he wanted to open within two weeks.

Christ! Hiring employees.

He'd been a loner for more than fifteen years. A gunfighter didn't have friends. You might have to kill one of them someday.

Like Lobo. They'd come damn close to facing each other several times. In the end, however, Lobo had hired Marsh to aid in his retirement from gunfighting and from being hunted. After his hand was crippled, Lobo, with the help of folks in a Colorado town, had faked his own death. He named Marsh heir to his estate, predated the will, and assumed the name of Jess Martin. Marsh took a share of the proceeds and transferred the remainder back to his old adversary under the new name.

Marsh grinned as he recalled the startling transition of Lobo into Jess Martin, renegade into respectable citizen.

He doubted his own transmutation would be anywhere as complete. He was, after all, older than Lobo, a hell of a lot more experienced. He'd often wondered which of them was faster, and now he would never know. He wasn't sorry. He'd respected the man for his professionalism, his cool competence. They had been among the last of their breed, and when Lobo retired, something inside Marsh had known his own time had come.

Through a newly installed window, he looked over at the Silver Slipper, and his gaze traveled upward. He saw Catalina Hilliard standing at her window, hair down, her loose garment blowing against her tall, slender fig-

ure. She looked almost ethereal standing there.
The very thought made him smile wryly. No
ghost she.

Who dared to start up the Glory Hole, Cat wondered.

She stretched, thinking she would have to
send Teddy to find out. Teddy was the only man
she trusted, had ever trusted, other than Ben
Abbott, who had died years ago.

Which reminded her of Molly again. Teddy
tried to hide it, but he obviously was taken with
the girl. Big, gruff Teddy, who maintained order,
was really as gentle as a kitten. The fierceness
was all on the outside.

After taking one last glance at the invaders
across the way, she dressed quickly in a stiff
white blouse and green skirt and went downstairs.

The saloon had already been cleaned from
the night before, but the chairs still sat awkwardly on the tables. The floors were wet from
mopping, and the smell of soap had replaced the
sharp odor of alcohol.

Teddy stepped out of the back room, where
barrels of beer and bottles of whiskey were
stored. He was surprised at seeing her this early.

"The noise," she explained.

Teddy's expression was cautious. He, too,
had seen the activity across the street, and he
knew it boded trouble. And change. He didn't
much care for change. "Want me to find out?"
he asked. He didn't even have to ask. He had
been with Cat Hilliard since the beginning of the

Silver Slipper, probably knew her as well as anyone could, and he was positive she would want
to know every detail about the Glory Hole.

She nodded.

Theodore Brown located his jacket, set a
cap on the curly top of his head, and made for
the door. He was a large man, solidly built, and
his steps appeared lumbering, but he could be
surprisingly quick, as troublemakers were wont
to discover.

Cat went into the kitchen. Teddy—all his
friends called him Teddy, which was far more
apt than Theodore—had already fired the stove
and started a pot of coffee. It would be as black
as the stranger's eyes, she thought, wondering
why she still couldn't banish that damnably attractive, though chillingly cold, face from her
thoughts. She had seen handsome men before—
her late husband had been disarmingly attractive—and they mostly repelled her. A handsome
exterior often hid rot underneath, she'd learned.
She shivered, reliving the night when she'd
learned her husband, the man she thought would
finally be her protector, had bartered her body to
a gambler to whom he'd lost. The betrayal had
numbed her that first time, but not the succeeding ones. Since then she had trusted only two
men—and only after years of wary vigilance.

He probably wouldn't even return, the
stranger. He had been new to the city; she was
sure of that, since he'd openly worn a gun with
such assuredness. His was the kind of presence
people noted, and word about him would have
reached her.

Which raised another question. Why had

she heard nothing about the revival of the Glory Hole? In the past her suppliers, or city officials, or the men who controlled the liquor distribution had told her about each competitor long before he opened.

There simply was not enough business for two saloons, at least not enough to satisfy her goal. She didn't want to compete with a saloon that watered drinks and offered more than simple female companionship, as did her former competitors. It brought a rougher crowd to this area, sullied her own hard-won reputation, and, of course, reduced her profits.

She poured herself a cup of coffee, and it was, as she expected, strong enough to walk. The cook would be here soon to prepare the midday buffet. The Silver Slipper would officially open in two hours. Another day, another deposit. Another evening of being polite and charming to customers. She winced as she thought of the incessant ordeal of being nice to men whose lust was plain in their faces. But it was far better than doing other things with them.

She went to the door and looked over at the Glory Hole, and her body suddenly stiffened. Two men were talking, one in workman's clothes, the other in a pair of tight trousers and a shirt that stretched across broad shoulders. A gun was in the black leather holster tethered to his thigh with a leather strap. He seemed totally oblivious to the fact that it was out of place in a sophisticated city like San Francisco.

The wind ruffled his dark hair; his profile was unforgettable. Even from this distance, she noticed that lean, sleek grace that had been so apparent last night. The impression was lethal, hard and implacable.

The stranger!

He'd exuded the sensation of power yesterday, even of menace easily stirred. Could he be the new owner?

Cat couldn't think of a more unlikely saloon owner.

To blazes with waiting for Teddy.

She was drawn across the street, as much by attraction to the stranger as curiosity. The fact was difficult to admit, although undeniable if she was honest with herself. And she always was these days. She had spent half her life avoiding truths, running from them, and learning to face them had been another diffi cult lesson.

She didn't like her odd interest in the stranger, but there it was, and it was better to satisfy herself and explore the reasons than to allow it to fester.

Cat knew he was aware of her approach, though he was turned away from her. It was a change in his stance—not a stiffening exactly, but an awareness. She wondered if he had eyes in the back of his head, but perhaps he did if he was what she sensed. She'd spent more time than she'd intended last night thinking of him, wondering at the sense of recognition, of awareness that had flared between them. She tried to categorize him, to put him into one of the slots she usually reserved for her men customers, but he didn't seem to fit in any of them. And then she'd remembered the gunmen she'd seen in the innumerable mining towns she'd worked her way through. There was a particular aura about them, and he had it: the alertness in his eyes, the danger that radiated from him.

But what was he doing in San Francisco? More important, what was he doing at the Glory Hole?

He turned then, a slight smile on his face as his eyes measured her in more than one way and glinted suddenly with appreciation. The smile, however, was as chilling as she remembered.

He bowed, not low exactly, but with an amused gallantry that she remembered from the past evening. It might have been laughable with anyone else, but nothing about this man was laughable. It was almost as if he were testing her in some way, teasing her with a mocking gesture.

"Miss Hilliard, isn't it?" he drawled, and she tried to place the accent. She thought she heard the South in it, but she wasn't quite sure. It could just as well be Texas or a border state.

"Mr. . . . ?" She remembered his name very well, but she wasn't going to let him know it.

"Canton," he said, the grin on his lips spreading as if he'd read her mind.

She gave him her most insincere smile. "You're up early this morning."

"I might say the same about you."

"Ah," she said softly as she surveyed the work that had already been completed this morning, "but I suspect you've been up since . . . very early."

"I hope I—that is, we didn't disturb your rest," he said. "That would be most unforgivable." But there was no true concern in his voice, only a challenge, and she knew suddenly that he *was* the new owner of the Glory Hole—and that he was very much aware of her reaction to previous owners.

"Of course not," she said. "I'm most interested, Mr. . . . Stanton."

"I hope the construction won't take too long. We are using double crews to keep from disturbing our neighbors for too long a time."

"Very thoughtful," Cat said, trying to keep the hiss from her voice. She didn't like being baited.

"I try to be a good neighbor," her adversary said with a grin that wasn't quite as cold as it had been. Neither, however, did it have any sincerity, only a personal amusement that made her simmering anger flare into full antipathy.

"I suppose you know the Glory Hole has been . . . well, unlucky. I would hate to see you waste money on it."

"It's very kind of you to concern yourself," he said solemnly. "But I don't believe in luck, good or bad, and I can afford to lose what might be required."

Cat bit her tongue to keep from saying that she planned on making him lose every bit of what he could afford—and more. Instead, she gifted him with a smile every bit as insincere as his. "If you need anything . . ."

"I'll know who to call upon," he finished smoothly, his eyes glowing with a dark flame of mischief. "I'm sure you will be an inspiration. Your Silver Slipper sets a standard to emulate. There's nothing that improves quality as much as worthy competition."

Cat counted to ten, keeping her face absolutely still, her gaze cool and distant. Competition, indeed! The Glory Hole had never been competition, never would be. Certainly not under the direction of this . . . arrogant donkey. "Are you going to be running it yourself, Mr. Stanton?" she asked sweetly.

"Canton, Miss Hilliard," he corrected. "It *is* Miss, isn't it?"

"It is," she said in her best dulcet tone.

"Since we're going to be neighbors, why don't you just call me Taylor? It's probably easier to remember than Canton." Now he made no pretense at hiding his amusement, as if she had been caught in some particularly childish prank.

Cat felt checkmated, and she didn't like the sensation at all. She was used to winning. And she would win, no matter what it took! She started thinking again of ways to thwart him, starting with distributors and moving more dishonorably to some of Teddy's disreputable friends. Just thinking about this arrogant man's downfall put a genuine smile on her face.

"So it is," she agreed readily and made one last attempt to discover useful information. "I suppose you have experience?"

"I have a great deal of experience, Miss Hilliard," he replied. The words were obviously open to interpretation, and the sudden glint in his eyes said his experience wasn't limited to business.

"I have little doubt about that," she said, "and it will be most interesting to see how that . . . experience works in San Francisco." Her gaze went down to his gunbelt, and when she looked back up at him, she saw that she had scored a point of her own. The amusement was gone from his face, replaced by a momentary bleakness that took her by surprise, but then vanished in an instant.

"You will have to come to our opening," he said.

"And when will that be?"

"Two weeks, three at the most."

She showed her surprise then. She would have wagered a goodly sum that it would take at least a month.

"Do you also plan to live there?"

He shrugged. "The living quarters come last," he said. "I'm currently living at the Pacific Palace."

"Quinn Devereux's hotel?" There was surprise in her voice as if she couldn't believe he was staying in such a respectable—or expensive—hotel.

"You know him?"

Cat hesitated. She knew of Quinn and Meredith Devereux, but she had never met them. They simply didn't move in the same circles, and Quinn Devereux was one of the few civic and political leaders who hadn't patronized the Silver Slipper. There were legends about the couple, about how they had worked in the Underground Railroad and barely escaped capture. Meredith Devereux was a painter of renown, and her husband was well known for his many civic contributions, and particularly for charity for the poor. Part of her envied this "golden couple" as they were sometimes called by the newspapers. They seemed to have everything, especially respectability and security. She'd given up on respectability years ago, but security . . .

"I only know of them," she answered honestly.

"It's a fine hotel," he said. "One of the best I've stayed in."

"And how many have you stayed in?"

"More than I want to remember," he said, and for the first time Cat heard something other than complete assurance in his voice. There was weariness in it for a fleeting second that made him appear vulnerable, that took some of that icy hardness from his face and softened something in her. She, too, knew that kind of weariness. He suddenly was more the man and less the untouchable, fallen archangel. Their gazes caught, and that charged magnetism that rushed between them took on the force of a runaway train headed down a mountain.

Cat felt a longing pull deep inside, a craving she'd never experienced before and had thought she never would. She'd hated even the touch of a man, and now, inconceivably, she felt her body betray her with needs she had never even known it harbored. Even worse, she was responding to him in an odd empathic way.

She didn't want to be touched in that way, any more than she did physically. People betrayed. Men betrayed, and it would be well for her to remember that. James Cahoon, the man she had trusted and married, had male beauty, too, and charm. She bit down on her lip and tasted blood. A good warning.

Her gaze flicked away from his, and when it returned, his eyes were hard again, hard and cold, and she wondered whether she had imagined the attraction. Her glance studied him anew, the dark taut skin that stretched over high cheekbones, the dark thick eyebrows. There was the slightest dent in his chin, which on another face would be charming but on him was incongruous, almost mocking features hewn by years of violence. The mouth was sensual, too sensual.

Hot blazes. She had made a certain peace with herself, and now it was disintegrating. Cat felt anger building inside that he could do that. He had no right. He had no right to be here, to open the Glory Hole, and by his mere presence to break barriers no one else had been able to breach.

The sooner she destroyed his business, the sooner she would have her peace returned. She would talk to the liquor distributors today, talk to the police captain to whom she paid a rather large tribute. Maybe she could keep Canton from obtaining a license.

She sensed it wasn't going to be as easy as in the past. Canton wasn't like any of the former owners. He wasn't even like any other man she'd ever met.

His lips curved slowly, and she wondered what a real, honest-to-God smile would do to that face.

She didn't want to know. Destroying him was no longer a business necessity but a personal one. Her legs were trembling slightly. She never trembled. Her lips wanted to do the same, and the only thing preventing them was the iron will she'd forged. One of these days she might not be able to control it, and, she sensed, a moment's weakness with Canton would doom her.

"Another example . . . of quality to emulate," he said into the silence between them.

She tried desperately to figure out what he referred to. Ah, the Devereux hotel. They were talking about the hotel. One of the finest he had stayed in, he'd said, before that moment of weariness had crept into his voice.

"Do you never do anything of your own, Mr. Canton?"

"You remembered the name," he said triumphantly. "And the answer is yes, at times, but don't forget, Miss Catalina, that imitation is the sincerest form of flattery."

"Really?" Cat said. "I would call it a lack of imagination, even theft."

"Oh, I intend a few twists of my own," he said easily.

Cat gnashed her teeth. Not if she could help it. But she smiled at him. "I had better let you get back to work. I know how much you have to do."

"That's very thoughtful," he said dryly. "It's so pleasant to have friendly neighbors. And I hear your food is exccllent. I'll have to try it."

Cat thought about poisoning the buffet, but then she might kill off too many of her other customers. "I'd be glad to accept your money," she said. "And remember, if you need anything . . ."

Like a bullet between the eyes, she thought wistfully, as she turned around without waiting for a reply. She was gratified to discover her legs still worked properly.

• • •

Marsh leaned against the bar of the Glory Hole and surveyed the interior. The swinging doors had been fixed and a lock added to the solid door. Glass was back in the windows. Some of the layers of dust and dirt were gone from the floor, but now there was sawdust. He liked the aroma. There was something clean about the smell. He looked down at the blisters on his hands. Sometime during the afternoon he had taken a hammer and gone to work with the carpenters. There was only so much standing and watching he could do, and after a few awkward strokes he had caught the rhythm. Hell, he'd even enjoyed it.

Christ, how long had it been since he had built instead of destroyed?

The workmen, hampered by the encroaching darkness, had left minutes ago. Tomorrow he would purchase some lamps. The soft dusky glow of a setting sun hid the many imperfections of the room. It looked quite attractive and gave him a sense of satisfaction. He was tired, but it was more a relaxed exhaustion than that to which he was accustomed.

For years he had slept lightly, very lightly, certain senses awake even when his body cried for rest. He had hunted, and he had been hunted, and he'd seldom known an easy night's rest.

Tonight, he thought, would be different.

If, that is, he wasn't haunted again by a pair of watchful green eyes.

They were, unquestionably, the most striking eyes he'd ever seen.

God knew he'd seen green eyes before. And beautiful women. Gunmen were exceedingly attractive to some women. He'd never understood it, but he realized that what made him good with a gun also made him good with women. Practice. Deliberation. Control. He always knew instinctively when to climax, when to bring both of them to the ultimate pleasure. It wasn't so much out of thoughtfulness as the recognition that his own physical satisfaction was greater when it matched the woman's. But he never bedded the same woman twice.

And he never changed his rule. Just as he never changed any of his other self-imposed rules: never stay long in one place, never permit a friendship, never get personally involved in a job, never take on a partner. It was a lonely way to live, but the devastating grief he had felt during and after the war was worse. He'd vowed never to love again, to care again.

And he hadn't.

The dog, hostility still bright in his eyes, had come inside and regarded him warily. Marsh put down some food he'd taken from the Silver Slipper, where he'd indulged in the bountiful buffet earlier in the afternoon; he'd justified the action as being for a worthy cause.

The buffet was free, and he understood that a number of other San Francisco bars and saloons offered free food. He'd watched carefully and speculated about the cost, amused with himself as he did so. Marsh Canton. Concerning himself with the price of oysters. It was ludicrous, or would be to any number of people who had seen him behind a gun.

The dog looked at the food and backed off, as if it were a Greek gift. Marsh grinned, understanding the distrust only too well. He moved away, opened one of the windows so the dog could come in and out. He doubted if any human would try to crawl through that window with the dog inside. And, after all, the dog had been here first.

Someone was playing a piano at the Silver Slipper. Catalina Hilliard had not been evident earlier when he went over for a beer and something to eat. She would be there now, he thought, weighing the idea of a return visit.

And then he thought again about those green eyes, and the odd effect they'd had on him today. He'd best leave well enough alone at the moment . . . if he wanted any sleep.

CHAPTER 4

———❖———

The sound of hammers at daybreak became more and more an irritant to Cat.

Canton's presence in the Silver Slipper in the afternoon was even more of one.

She didn't like feeling hesitant about going downstairs in her own establishment. Even less did she like the feelings stirred by the sight of the man. He always took a chair and table by himself, making sure he faced the door. There was a natural wariness about him that spoke of aloneness, and Cat hated the way something inside her responded to it.

Cat didn't think of herself as lonely. She was independent. She was successful. She didn't need anyone. Those three factors alone had given her a sense of satisfaction, a sense of accomplishment that precluded anything like loneliness. She worked hard, often falling into bed exhausted but pleased because she was getting closer and closer to her goal of security.

She dreamed of that security, of owning a house that overlooked the ocean, of wandering the shores and watching sunsets. That was all she asked of life.

But now she was experiencing one frustration after another. She had talked to the distributor who supplied liquor to the Silver Slipper, asking him not to service the upstart at the Glory Hole. He had hemmed and hawed and finally admitted that Canton had been introduced to him by Quinn Devereux of the Pacific Palace Hotel, and he couldn't antagonize one of his biggest customers.

Cat had forced a smile and said, "Of course not." She also started thinking about finding another distributor.

Her next move met with more success. She met with the local police captain, Mike Delaney. She had been making payments to him for the last three years "for extra protection."

"He doesn't look very respectable," she'd started carefully. "Downright dangerous, in fact. No telling how much trouble he'll bring. Remember the last time?"

Indeed the captain did. There had been a riot at the Glory Hole when someone discovered the house was cheating. He'd secretly wondered whether the whole fracas had been plotted when he saw some very familiar faces among the crowd hustled off to jail, faces he usually saw in the Silver Slipper. Catalina had never been stingy, whereas the former owner of the Glory Hole had been.

Delaney smiled. Although Catalina had never shown amorous interest in him, he still had his hopes . . . and dreams.

"I'll try to stop the license," he said, looking at the soft skin just above the neckline of her dress.

Cat gave him a heart-stopping smile of gratitude, and he felt ten feet tall. Some day . . .

Forty-eight hours later he, too, admitted failure. Mr. Canton's lawyer had already obtained the license.

"There has to be something," she wondered aloud to Delaney.

The captain looked thoughtful. He wanted Catalina's gratitude. "Perhaps there is," he said finally.

One more week! Marsh eyed the interior of the Glory Hole with something close to proprietary pride, which surprised even him.

A perpetual student of human behavior, as one had to be to live long as a gunfighter, he was amused and intrigued by his own obsession with this venture. For one who had avoided commitments for so long, he had grasped this one with the stubbornness of a one-eyed mule set on a clover patch.

When he wasn't supervising the reconstruction of the Glory Hole, he was exploring San Francisco. He'd discovered there were really two cities: the sophisticated city with fine hotels and residential area, especially Nob Hill; then there was the other San Francisco, as rough and corrupt as any place on earth.

The Barbary Coast, an area along the waterfront, attracted him, as did Chinatown. He'd been in nearly every mining and cow town in the West, from Mexico to Canada, but he'd never seen such open debauchery as he witnessed in those sections. Opium dens and cheap prostitution cribs flourished openly. And he'd learned quickly that San Francisco operated on corruption. He'd experienced it firsthand when he discovered the expense of obtaining a license to operate the Glory Hole. An ordinary business expense, his lawyer told him, as he paid nearly two thousand dollars for a license.

Both Devereux and David Scott had warned him against taking a drink in the Barbary Coast saloons, lest he end up drugged and robbed, or at worst, a sailor on his way to China. "Shanghaied" was a new term, he was told, and one unique to San Francisco.

But one late evening, after the workmen went home, he hesitated before returning to the hotel. He was strangely restless, harried by a gnawing need he couldn't identify, perhaps attributable to the new piano that had been delivered that day. He'd sat down on the bench to try it, and after a few tentative notes it all rushed back, the emotion, the joy he'd once taken in discovering his talent, a talent inherited from his mother. . . .

And then his fingers had crashed down on the keys, creating a cacophony of sound. That world was gone, had been gone for years. The damned piano. But he had to have it in his saloon. He planned on offering entertainment to compete with the Silver Slipper. Food. Honest gambling. Everything that the Silver Slipper did. And more.

But a chill swept through him. And daring fate, he decided to visit the Barbary Coast's most notorious establishments: the Moro, the Thunderbolt, the Dew-Drop-In, where, it was said, many visitors who did indeed decide to drop in never dropped out, at least not through the front door.

He left a plate of food for the dog and opened the window just enough for it to come and go. The dog never ate while Marsh was there. The food disappeared in his absence, and the dog didn't appear quite as starved as it had in the beginning, though his disposition hadn't improved. Well, Marsh thought, neither had his own over the years.

His gun was strapped to his hip, partially hidden by the black broadcloth coat he wore. Marsh locked the outside door and moved swiftly along the street. He decided against riding the cable cars, which he liked very much, in favor of walking. He needed the exercise to drain his excess energy, to calm his restlessness.

His natural wariness was dulled, he knew, by this new environment. He had no declared enemies here—though God knew he had left enough vengeful brothers, cousins, and other assorted relatives in his wake—so he decided to ignore a man who seemed to be following him. He was a small man, and Marsh's sharp eyes had already determined he didn't appear to have a gun. And then the man disappeared, and Marsh told himself he had been overly suspicious in even noticing the fellow in the first place.

When Marsh entered the Thunderbolt, he quickly noted that his gun was not out of place here as it was in many sections of the city. The tavern was frequented almost entirely by villainous-looking characters, armed with knives and clubs.

He barely rated a moment's notice in the loud, noisy room, a fact that amused him. Marsh almost felt like Little Lord Fauntleroy among the sailors and ruffians. His entrance usually brought a saloon to silence. He remembered Devereux's advice about drugged drinks and asked for an unopened bottle. It was grudgingly given by the bartender and carefully inspected by Marsh before he opened it and poured a generous dollop into a glass. He carried the bottle and glass to an empty table and seated himself with his back to the wall.

Marsh leaned back in the chair and surveyed the action. Lots of prostitutes. One, her hair uncombed and her dress only half-buttoned, spied Marsh and, ignoring the calls of other men, came directly over to him. She leaned against his table, drawing up her dress to reveal plump legs, and one of her hands played with his hair. "What's a gent like you doing here?"

He didn't have an answer. Even he didn't know why, except it suited his dark mood.

His lips twisted into a cynical smile, and her hand moved away as if she suddenly encountered something she didn't expect. His eyes, he

suspected. He'd been told they could freeze an
Arizona rattler. And tonight he expected they
might be even colder than usual.

"Buy a lady a drink?" she asked, trying
again.

He remembered the girl a few days earlier
in the Silver Slipper, that odd fear in her, even the
innocence that was so surprising in a saloon girl.
There was no innocence in this woman, who obviously had just returned from a short business
engagement.

A sudden abhorrence rose up in him, a distaste that was as strong for himself as for her,
and he knew then why he had come. To be
among his own kind. He was reminding himself
where he belonged. Not with the likes of Quinn
Devereux and David Scott but with the scum of
the earth. What was the use of trying to be anything else?

He shrugged. "Why not? I have a bottle
here."

Her eyes looked at him warily. "I would
prefer champagne," she said with a smile every
bit as practiced and meaningless as his own.
Again he remembered Molly and her request for
champagne.

"As you wish," he said, not sure why he
was doing this. Her painted face, too-blond hair,
and overblown figure repelled him. He kept seeing, instead, Catalina's almost patrician features
and angry green eyes. His fingers tightened
around the glass as he downed its contents in
one gulp and poured another.

The woman was watching him carefully, as
if he were a snake she first thought harmless,

and about which she was having second thoughts. His smile widened, and he knew it did nothing to comfort her. Well, he damn well didn't feel like comforting or reassuring anyone. Let her run like hell. Like Molly.

But this woman was made of stronger stuff. "Just thirty dollars," she said, "if you want some private fun, sugar. Anything your heart desires."

"No," he said, and pushed his chair away from the table. He threw down some bills.

"Too good for me?" the woman asked angrily.

He gave her a crooked smile. "Just the other way around, darlin'. Just the other way around."

Marsh strode toward the swinging doors, and he saw the small man again, huddled now against the bar, a drink in his hand.

Coincidence, Marsh told himself as he moved outside into the fresh air and took a deep breath. Christ, that place smelled. He shook his head to clear it of the smoke and odors of cheap perfume, unwashed bodies, and rotgut whiskey. He thought of the Silver Slipper, of its quiet, discreet elegance, and that led his thoughts once more to Catalina Hilliard.

His normal alertness was dulled by whiskey consumed too fast and by thoughts of Catalina. He paused for a moment. The back of his neck was crawling, and he knew he'd been careless. He leaned against a wall, taking stock, trying his damnedest to look unconcerned. All his instincts were working now, but it was too late. Three, no four, men were approaching him. Three had clubs. The fourth needed no weapon other than his huge six and a half feet of height, and hands that looked like grizzly paws. Their faces and their aggressive movements made no secret that he was the quarry. He remembered Devereux's warning about the dangers of being shanghaied. And then he remembered the little man who seemed to follow him from the Glory Hole.

Marsh realized suddenly this was no random attack, but an ambush. He also knew what had to be behind it.

His hand went to his gun in a lightning-fast movement, and he heard the explosion as well as the cry of the man to the right of him. He then heard exclamations, a curse, and felt a bat ram into his chest.

He fell, desperately clutching his gun in his hand. He rolled over to avoid another blow and aimed at one of the approaching men, firing again. The man fell on him, blood spurting from his body. Marsh was pinned down long enough for one of the toughs to kick the gun from his hand. He pushed the injured man off him and reached for his gun, but a foot impacted with his stomach and he doubled over, and then there was a stunning pain at the back of his head.

Teddy was closing up, and Catalina had wearily climbed the steps to her rooms. It was past three in the morning, and she'd had precious little sleep during the past few nights. She went over to the window and looked out. There were no lights shining in the Glory Hole windows, not as there had been on previous nights.

She unpinned her hair, letting it fall down

her back, and she started brushing it with long strokes. She remembered those few haunting notes of music she'd heard earlier from across the way as she had dressed for the evening; she had wondered at the beauty of them until they'd suddenly ended in a clash of sound.

Cat didn't know who had played them. She could only speculate that Canton had hired a musician. But it hadn't been saloon music. The notes had been quiet and lovely and poignantly lonely. She didn't know much about "good" music, but she suspected that was what she had heard. Perhaps someday she would visit the concert hall. . . . No. She was an outcast.

Still, that melody remained in her mind, playing over and over again. She'd even found herself humming it this evening.

She wondered if the piano meant that the Glory Hole would be providing entertainment. She had, for a while, but found it interfered with conversation and also the amount of liquor imbibed. Her customers drank more if they weren't distracted. But perhaps . . .

Damn him, anyway.

She'd just started to braid her hair when she heard a knock at the door and opened it to Teddy. His usually stoic face showed concern.

"Molly?" she asked, knowing that Teddy worried about her.

"No," he said. "She's in her room."

He hesitated, and she tipped her head in question.

"Captain Delaney sent word that your troubles are over," he said.

"Troubles?"

"The Glory Hole."

"How?"

"He's arranged to have ... the owner shanghaied. He wanted you to know you won't have any more problems."

"When?" she said.

He shrugged. "Tonight maybe."

"Do you know what ships are leaving in the morning?"

He shook his head.

Cat bit her lip. Most shanghaied sailors didn't come back. The captains and owners couldn't afford to let them tell their stories. Accidents were often arranged near the end of a voyage. She thought of the tall stranger, his arrogant smile and pantherlike walk. He wouldn't last long under the harsh discipline of a ship. Damn Delaney. She'd never wanted him to go this far. A problem with a license, with the building, perhaps. If that hadn't worked, she would have seen whether Canton tolerated cheating at cards, and if so, she would have set him up. None of those tactics bothered her conscience a whit.

But being shanghaied was equivalent to murder. She'd killed once. She still felt the blood on her hands from that time, the shock that had numbed her brain. She still had nightmares about that night. She didn't want more.

"No," she said suddenly to Teddy. "Tell Captain Delaney no. Go yourself if you must. But I'll not have this done in my name."

Teddy gave her a rare smile that lit his prizefighter's face. He really was a gentle soul under that brigand exterior, Cat thought. She closed the door, sat back on the chair in front of her dressing table, and started once more to braid her hair. She should have felt satisfaction, but she didn't. She felt empty. Intolerably empty.

Marsh woke painfully. His head felt like mush, and there was a strangely familiar odor that hung like poison in the air. He tried to think what it was. It seemed like a good thing to do, to focus his mind on that problem rather than the pain that assaulted him every time he moved.

Such a familiar smell. Then he knew. Unholy groans and cries. The sound of a medical saw gnawing through bone. Field hospitals. Chloroform. His mind ran through all the steps and reached the final logical conclusion. Besides being nearly beaten to death, he'd been drugged.

He opened his eyes slowly. The light was dim, very dim, and at first he was grateful. He didn't think his aching head could tolerate any kind of brightness. Then he started to assimilate his surroundings, and he noticed the light was shadowed, cut by lines of some kind against a filthy stone wall. He moved his head carefully, but even then it seemed someone was pounding on its interior like a hammer on an anvil.

Bars! Iron bars decorated a window so filthy, it was amazing any light filtered through. He turned his head again, looking to the other side of the small room, and saw more bars; beyond those, another set of bars. A jail of some kind.

He looked down at his wrists. Rope marks still burned them, although they were free. He had been tied recently.

Marsh tried to move again, but he knew a rib had been either cracked or broken, and every part of his body hurt. It took all his will not to groan, but he never gave in to weakness. Never.

He ran his hands over his body gingerly, wincing as they touched bruised parts. He remembered the bats, the kick. The battering must have continued after he lost consciousness.

Where was he? And why?

The small man. The one who looked like a rat. Christ, he had been ambushed like a tenderfoot. And there could be only one person responsible. Any other enemy would have simply killed him.

He swore, using words that would have brought a look of horror to the face of his gentle mother.

At least he wasn't in the hold of some ship. Some part of him reasoned that could have been the intention. Why else the rope burns and the chloroform? He looked down at his waist. The gunbelt was gone, his shirt bloodied. His jacket and his boots were gone also.

He ran his hand through his hair and found it crusted with blood.

Marsh looked around the small bare cell. It was little more than a cage with barely room for the iron cot on which he now half lay. There was a bucket in the corner, and that and the cot constituted the only furniture, if one could charitably call it such.

In twenty years of the most violent kind of life, this was the first jail he'd ever been held in. It was really quite remarkable, he thought, in the objective, distant way he often viewed himself.

But he'd studied law, and he had observed it, walking warily on the sharp edge between legality and murder.

Except once, and then he'd made quite sure there were no witnesses.

He tried to stand, but his body rebelled. Goddammit. Was there no place on him left untouched? He needed medical help. He knew that. His ribs needed binding, for one. A cut on his forearm needed stitching.

And why in the hell was he here? But suddenly he understood. The corruption of the police force. Catalina. He'd been prepared for a battle of wits. Had even relished it, but his neighbor had declared war, and he could be every bit as underhanded and vicious as she.

Catalina Hilliard didn't realize it, but she'd roused a wounded tiger. Marshall Taylor Canton didn't forget. Much less forgive. A number of men could attest to that.

From hell.

CHAPTER 5

Work had ceased at the Glory Hole. A scarred old dog stood like a sentry in front, as if waiting for something. Or someone.

Cat had learned from Teddy that Canton had not been put aboard a ship, but instead jailed and charged with assault and disorderly conduct, a ludicrous charge at best. There was no such thing as disorderly conduct on the Barbary Coast.

She felt twinges of guilt, but they weren't too severe. At least she had saved him from an unwilling trip to China. That she had set things in motion in the first place was something she decided not to dwell on; she'd never told

Delaney to go to such lengths, though she prob-ably should have expected it.

But there was nothing she could do about it now. And he *was* stopped. Perhaps he'd learned a lesson and would fold his hand and go back to wherever it was he came from . . . if he ever got out of jail. He'd made an enemy of Captain Delaney when he hadn't allowed himself to be taken without a fight. Delaney didn't like com-plications, nor having to pay more money to two of the more seriously injured thugs. It wounded his pride.

She hadn't been surprised, however, when she'd learned the details. Canton had almost killed four of the city's most vicious toughs. If one hadn't landed a lucky blow . . .

Damnation. Why couldn't she go two min-utes without thinking of him? It had been ten days since his disappearance, and she still found herself looking for a tall, lethally graceful man who, by only his presence, dominated a room.

Ten days. Ten goddamned hellish days in a damned cage before he finally convinced a guard he could obtain bribe money if only the man would contact his lawyer.

He still hurt. His ribs remained sore, and his skin retained a yellowish spotting where some of the worst bruises were finally fading. The cut on his arm was healing slowly, leaving a great jagged scar because it had not been stitched.

Only the injury to his pride hadn't im-proved.

And his anger.

And both had festered each of the past days, each humiliating moment stored in his mind for retaliation.

The first few days were still somewhat a blur of pain. He hadn't really cared where he was, and he reasoned that the hard bed was as comfortable as a feathered one, considering the extent of his injuries. Softness would have made movement more of a probability. Movement was pain.

But on the third day imprisonment became a reality, along with inedible food, filth, lack of privacy, and most important, the impotence of being caged. There was barely space to walk five steps before bumping into walls or bars, and his natural restlessness screamed for relief.

He asked repeatedly and to no avail to see David Scott. His rage grew with the sense of hopelessness. He thought of dozens of ways to even the score with Catalina Hilliard, the most rewarding of which was taking her to bed. He knew how to torment, not by crude pain, but by exquisite temptation. He knew how to bring a woman to the edge . . . and then leave her in expectant agony.

Or perhaps financial ruin. He was willing to risk everything now to win.

Catalina Hilliard had raised the stakes. He didn't plan on losing the game.

David Schuyler Scott eyed his bearded, blood-stained client with no little trepidation. Canton had seemed fierce before, but that was nothing to the way he looked now.

"Don't say it," Marsh said. "You warned me. Now, how do I get the hell out of here?"

"You want to tell me what happened?"

Marsh met his gaze directly. "I went to the Barbary Coast."

"Should I ask why?"

Marsh shrugged. "A whim."

"An expensive one, you'll find, in more ways than one," Scott said. "I talked to a Captain Delaney, who lodged the charges and got nowhere, so I went a step above him." He paused. "Fortunately, the two men you shot have long police records. They also have long connections with Delaney." He paused again. "And Delaney is frequently seen in the Silver Slipper."

"I rather thought that," Marsh said without a change in expression.

"I didn't think Catalina Hilliard would go this far," David said slowly.

"I think her purpose was even more ominous," Marsh said. "Like having me shanghaied. You see, I was chloroformed. Why do that merely to cart me to jail?"

David looked puzzled. "But you *are* here!"

Marsh smiled humorlessly as he looked around. "That's very observant of you. Now what do we do about it?"

"It's already been done," David said. "You performed a public service for the city, disabling those thugs. It was simply pointed out that no one, particularly Captain Delaney, would want the newspapers to look too closely into the circumstances, which, if your case went to trial, might happen."

"I didn't know I'd hired such a clever and influential attorney."

"You didn't," David said. "As much as I would like to take credit, I can't."

"Then who . . . ?"

"The only man I know who has that kind of power: Quinn Devereux."

For one of the few times in his life, Marsh was stunned. "But why?"

"Damned if I know," the attorney said. "He seems to take on odd causes."

Marsh didn't like the idea of being a cause. Or of owing anyone. He wondered what Devereux wanted.

It was as if David read his mind. "You can always stay here."

Marsh gave him a cold smile. "My boots?"

David looked down at his client's stockinged feet, remembering the first time he had seen Marsh Canton, and his eyes moved upward over a filthy shirt and torn trousers. While not elegant, his client had always been well dressed and groomed. These last ten days must have been hell. He did not miss the determination in Canton's eyes. They were even colder than before, and he knew he wouldn't care to be in certain shoes. He also wondered whether Quinn Devereux knew what he was unleashing. "I'll see what I can do." He started to leave.

Marsh didn't hesitate. "To hell with the boots."

David nodded and watched as Marsh

moved slowly, painfully, toward the barred door. "I think you might want to visit a doctor."

Marsh shook his head. "I have other business first."

David looked at him warily. "You may not be so lucky next time you . . . visit here, or the Barbary Coast."

"I have no intention of doing either," Marsh said harshly. He didn't like explaining himself to anyone, but he owed this man something for his freedom. And Devereux. He supposed he would discover soon enough what the hotel owner wanted.

"Then—"

Marsh cut off David's warning. "I know the legalities, Scott," Marsh said. "I'll stay within them." Except, he added to himself, for a few minor circumventions. Like a little bribery of his own. He'd had ten days to think about retribution, and how to go about it.

"I have a carriage outside. The hotel?"

Marsh looked down at himself. His odor was rank, as were his clothes. And that was a charitable way of describing both.

David understood. He should have thought to bring some clothes. He knew San Francisco jails, though not well. He usually represented businessmen, not criminals. Canton was proving an interesting diversion in more ways than one. "I'll take you to my home," he said. "You can take a bath there and borrow some of my clothes."

"I'll pay for them," Marsh said abruptly.

"Not necessary."

"It is," Marsh said in a tone that finished

any argument. It was one thing to pay a man for services, another to accept favors. He hadn't accepted one in fifteen years, and now in one day he was forced to take two. Well, he could minimize at least one of them.

"If that's what you want."

"It is," Marsh said curtly, and followed the attorney out of the filthy cell, down a filthy corridor, and through another pair of doors to sunlight.

David Scott's wife regarded Marsh with interest, not horror, and he wondered whether her tolerance came from simple good manners, experience with her husband's clients, or the fact that there were probably few surprises in a city said to be full of odd characters.

Whatever it was, he liked her, her easy smile and affability. He had also been surprised at the force with which Scott had urged a very good suit upon him. He was not used to being taken in and treated kindly, and he didn't care for the way the gesture initially pleased him. He didn't need any cracks in an interior he'd worked hard to fossilize.

Quinn Devereux had been the next stop. Marsh had already decided to leave the Pacific Palace's comfort for the far less lavish rooms of the Glory Hole. With the costs involved in rebuilding the place, he could scarcely afford expensive lodgings.

Devereux had been in his office, which was remarkably designed. One wall was all windows; the other three walls were graced with some of the finest paintings Marsh had ever seen, one of which he considered particularly outstanding. It was a rainbow that seemed so real, Marsh imagined he could reach out and touch it.

"My wife painted that," Devereux said, his voice laced with pride.

"She's very good."

"Yes," Devereux agreed simply. "Some night you'll have to come to dinner and meet her."

The same kind of pang that had struck Marsh earlier at the lawyer's home invaded him again, and he tried to shove it away. Christ, was he really that desperate for the companionship of someone other than the usual gamblers or gunfighters he met? For just the briefest or moments, flashes of another life returned, of sociable evenings and gay balls, of hunts, of evenings spent in companionable discussion over fine bourbon and excellent cigars. And then he stiffened. He had chosen a certain kind of life that precluded the niceties of civilized society, and it was too late now for regret.

He gave Devereux a noncommittal nod that bespoke reluctance, and Devereux smiled as if he had some kind of secret knowledge.

It made Marsh downright uncomfortable. "I just wanted to thank you," he said in a raspy voice that revealed inexperience in thanking someone. "Scott told me you were the one who arranged my release. I don't know why. . . ."

Devereux raised dark eyebrows, which seemed incongruous in a face framed by gray hair. His age was impossible to determine, Marsh thought, because of the strength of the face and eyes. There was an energy around the man that defied time. His eyes were blue, almost brilliant, and his body was exceptionally fit. There was something about Devereux that told Marsh he was no ordinary businessman, and not a man to cross. And yet there was humor and even compassion in his expression.

"I don't like injustice," Devereux said easily. "I don't like four men attacking one, who was jailed for it."

"How did you know?"

"I hear a great deal."

"It wasn't a random attack."

Devereux hesitated a moment. "I've heard rumors."

Marsh decided to dig for information. "About the glorious Miss Hilliard?"

"I don't know the lady, but I do know of her. This doesn't sound like her. Perhaps I'm wrong, but at least now you know what you face. Are you sure you want to continue?"

"More than ever," Marsh said with a faint smile.

"I suspected as much. If there's anything I can do—"

"Why?" The question was sharp and suspicious. "Why should you care? Why should you concern yourself?"

Devereux didn't answer that question immediately. Instead he went over to a cabinet, opened it, and took out a decanter.

"Drink?"

Marsh refused with a curt gesture of his hand. "Why?" he repeated.

"I suppose you remind me a little of myself years ago."

Marsh looked at him with disbelief. Quinn Devereux was one of the most respected men in San Francisco, a philanthropist, it was said. "There's nothing you want?"

"Absolutely nothing."

"I don't like owing people."

"Neither do I, nor having people owe me. So forget it. Consider it a whim of mine. I don't like Captain Delaney. It amuses me to annoy him."

"Delaney?"

"The man behind your arrest. Watch out for him."

Another favor. Marsh winced. "I'll do that." He started for the door, then turned back. "I still owe you." Before Devereux could reply, Marsh had opened the door and left.

That odd tune she'd heard days ago from the Glory Hole kept nagging at Cat.

She grimaced in the mirror as she twisted her hair into a French knot for the evening. Would that melody never go away? Perhaps if she knew its name, but she didn't know how to discover it, although the melody stayed firm in her mind. She knew songs like "Skip to My Lou," and "The Yellow Rose of Texas" and some pretty bawdy chants and maudlin ballads; her knowledge ended there.

She frowned as she considered her lack of education. She'd acquired what she had as an adult, mostly from Ben, and that had been pretty much limited to the basics: reading, writing, and ciphering. Ben had introduced her to some good books, but they were hard to come by in the mining camps, and she'd had little time here in San Francisco. Someday, though . . .

But she'd had a really wide education in human nature.

"Go away," she whispered to the melody that was haunting her. And when it wouldn't, she suddenly realized it wasn't in her mind. She *heard* the piano, the notes drifting up through the evening air.

He must be back. Canton. Somehow he had gotten out of jail. Canton was playing?

It couldn't be. Not with that hard face and those soul-dead eyes. Not something this soft and lovely and enticing.

He was back. Released. A chill swept through her. He must have guessed what had happened. And why.

How did he get out of jail?

And how would he take revenge?

The music changed from the plaintive melody to an almost violent piece. She shivered as she imagined a threat in it.

And then she pushed that odd feeling away. She had learned to fight. And she didn't mind fighting dirty for what she wanted.

Marsh sat at a table in the rear of the Silver Slipper. Cat was surprised by the rush of guilt she felt when she saw his fading yellow bruises and the stiff way he held himself as if he were still in pain.

Cat knew how to bluff. She also knew one should never avoid an encounter with an enemy set on one. Especially when she was on her own ground.

She walked up to him. "Mr. . . ."

"Canton," Marsh said with a small smile. "Taylor Canton."

Cat met his gaze directly. "It's been quiet the past few days."

His eyes betrayed nothing. Neither did his face, nor the small, enigmatic smile. "Some business to take care of," he said easily. "But I'm afraid your respite was a short one. We begin again in the morning."

Her gaze never left his. "You're going to stay?"

"Oh, yes," he said. "Once I start something, I stay to the bitter end."

For the first time there was a hint of emotion in his cool voice, a trace of menace, a warning so subtle, Cat almost missed it. "We have something in common, then," she said with a patently insincere smile of her own.

"I think we may have a great deal in common, Miss Catalina."

"Very little I would say." She shrugged with contemptuous dismissal.

His smile broadened. "Now let me see. We both own saloons." His gaze left hers and lazily, but very thoroughly, examined her body. Cat suddenly flushed, something she hadn't done in years. Without words but very definitely with his eyes, he confirmed something else they had in common: the almost painful physical attraction that was impossible to hide. It was so strong, the air vibrated with it.

He allowed that knowledge to simmer, daring her to deny it, as his eyes undressed her in a way no man ever had—with lazy sensuousness, with the knowledge that her body was involuntarily responding . . . aching suddenly with exquisite yearning that was plain torment.

She hated him then. She hated him for making her feel like a woman. She hated the weakness it spawned in her. She hated the sudden doubts that made her question who and what she was.

And he sat there, unreadable, watching with eyes that were like mirrors, not of himself, but of her, mirrors that bored into her.

That was the most menacing of all. Much more than open threats or visible fury.

She thought about explaining that she'd meant him no physical harm, but any explanation would involve the police captain. And in the end it would mean nothing. She'd set events into motion, and she doubted whether he would believe anything she said, especially the fact that she'd prevented his voyage to exotic places. After all, the possibility wouldn't even have existed if not for her, so she doubted his appreciation.

And she couldn't apologize. Cat was not a hypocrite. And she knew she would probably do the same thing over again. And next time, she thought a tad viciously, she wouldn't be so quick to interfere. The thought of him swabbing a deck was suddenly very sweet. In any event, she thought self-righteously, he'd deserved it. Anyone who visited the Barbary Coast was a fool.

That's it, she told herself. Think of him that way. As a fool. Not as a man whose masculinity sent hot shivers down her back.

"And then," Marsh added softly, "we seem to have something else in common. . . ." He seemed to be searching for words, but Cat knew it was only for effect. She instinctively knew a great deal about him.

"A lack of charity," he said with sudden inspiration accompanied by a wolfish smile. "You would agree, perhaps?"

"Perhaps. Or perhaps 'ruthlessness' is the word you seek," she said slowly, meeting the challenge frontally.

"As good as any," he agreed amiably.

Her gaze ran over his face again, over the discoloration from the bruises. It did nothing to detract from the masculine appeal of the features, of the hard lines and angles that so oddly attracted her.

And she knew that the tactic she'd tried, to consider him a fool, was as useless as the others. She didn't know why he had ventured down to the Barbary Coast, but it wasn't because he was a fool.

She sat on the table, her hand rubbing across the smooth wood, taking confidence in it. This was hers. She had built and nurtured the Silver Slipper, and she was the Ice Queen of San Francisco, held in awe, if not respect, by many. She wanted to wipe that lazy look off his face, even though she suspected how dangerous that action might be . . . how touching him in any way would be fatal.

Danger mixed with the hot sensuality that

had settled like a cloud around them. It was in-
toxicating. Exhilarating. And terrifying.

Mindful of the danger, yet unable to stop,
she asked, "Did you have an accident?"

"A minor mishap," he said carelessly. "A
miscalculation." He waited a moment before
adding, "By others."

"Oh?"

"There are two in the hospital, I think.
Maybe three. I'm not sure."

"Ah, San Francisco can be a very dangerous
place. You have to be careful where you go."

"It's kind of you to warn me," Canton said,
a gleam in his eye.

"Of course, you look well armed," she said
innocently, her gaze moving from the wounded
face to the gun he was wearing.

Canton nodded. "Now that I'm fully aware
of the city's pitfalls, I'll be more on guard."

Cat switched to another subject. "I heard a
piano earlier . . . coming from the Glory Hole."

His expression didn't change. He ignored
her question as if it weren't worth answering and
sipped his whiskey.

She had been roundly rebuffed, but she had
to know. *Because one should know one's enemy.*
"Were you playing?"

Canton looked through her, still not answering. He was the kind of man who didn't
have to answer. She suspected that he did this
frequently. Merely fixed that dark gray gaze on
someone until they were so intimidated, the
question just fell away as if into an abyss. Had
he tired of their game? A warning had been

given, acknowledgment made, war subtly declared.

He rose suddenly, lean and lethal, the gun so very evident at his hip. "It's been . . . enlightening," he said as he reached out and took her hand, bringing it almost to his mouth in a cavalier manner.

Cat was struck motionless by his gesture, even more so by the heat that scorched her hand when he touched it, scorched and traveled on, like a brushfire, along her bloodstream. For a moment she thought he was going to draw the palm to his mouth, but then his lips twisted into a mocking smile.

"For now, darlin'." He allowed her hand to drop, threw a couple of coins on the table, and strode out, Cat staring after him.

The dog growled at Marsh when he entered the Glory Hole. He lit an oil lamp and considered his companion. "We'll just have to tolerate each other," he told the animal.

Marsh decided to stay in the main room this evening. He placed his bedroll and gear next to the bar. The dog stayed a fair distance, growling whenever he deemed Marsh encroached on his territory.

The dog had been sitting in front of the saloon when he'd arrived earlier. Marsh had had the odd feeling of being greeted. He'd not been greeted by a living thing in more than a decade. At least it was some kind of homecoming after ten days in jail.

Marsh stretched out on the blanket. He

heard loud noises from across the way. The Silver Slipper was alive with activity. He saw Catalina in his mind again, those sparking green eyes as he'd taunted her. She played the game well. Very well.

He would take the greatest of pleasure in besting her. And he would. One way or another.

CHAPTER 6

The Glory Hole was beginning to look respectable again.

Cat couldn't ignore the obvious, no matter how hard she tried.

In fact, she conceded grudgingly, it looked far better than she'd thought possible.

Canton's workmen had painted the exterior a bronze color that, when the sun hit the building in the afternoon, looked like pure gold. For a saloon called the Glory Hole, it was perfect. Part of her admired the imagination; the other less generous part scorned it.

The Glory Hole was gaudy, she told herself, where the Silver Slipper was a model of elegance.

Still, the Glory Hole represented trouble, and its owner, with all his male arrogance and amused eyes, even more so. She felt it deep in her bones.

And in other places she didn't wish to consider.

Her resentment smoldered, just waiting to break into white-hot flame. This was *her* corner. She had built it through damned hard work. He had no right to take advantage of her success. Why, for all that was unholy, had she not allowed him to be shanghaied?

It gave her the smallest crumb of pleasure to imagine she had, to conjure the picture of Canton climbing masts—or worse. At least she had a powerful secret weapon: a spy planted in the enemy camp. Word had gone out that the Glory Hole was looking for a bartender/manager, and Teddy had encouraged his cousin to seek the job. It had not taken much convincing, since Hugh O'Connell was out of work and had five children and a wife to support.

Cat glanced through her bedroom window toward the Glory Hole, even as she hated herself for it. It was almost as though she'd sensed he would be there. And he was! He was leaning against the railing in front as newly painted shutters were being hung. He started to turn, and Cat stepped back, out of sight.

Cursing herself as much as him, she put just the slightest amount of color on her cheeks and prepared to go downstairs. She looked around the room: the rolltop desk where she did the books, four-poster bed, the small sitting area with its fine chairs. She had to admit that the room looked far warmer than usual with some whimsical pillows and a colorful covering for her table. She'd finally discovered something Molly could do well—sewing—and secretly she was preparing a future for the girl, unless, of course, Teddy overcame his timidity and Molly her fear of most men. There was an obvious attraction between the two. Molly seemed to relax around him, and Teddy . . . well, his face showed adoration.

As for her other girls, three of whom lived in two rooms above the Silver Slipper and four others who lived elsewhere, she felt a certain amount of satisfaction. One had announced she would marry in a month and would be leaving. Two others, including Wilhelmina, who had been with her three years, were being courted by customers.

San Francisco was still a town with a shortage of available women, and her hostesses, as she called them, were uniformly pretty and personable. She didn't employ those whom she thought might want to do business on the side. Much of the attraction of the Silver Slipper was its respectability, at least as much as possible for a saloon. It attracted the politicians and businessmen who needed a private place to do business as well as take a drink and play a game of poker. While a pretty face was welcome, nothing more was required.

She wondered what her neighbor planned. Those hard gray eyes were pitiless, and yet Molly, when questioned at length, had absolved him of any aggressive behavior. It had been the gun, she'd said, the gun and that steely-eyed hardness that had so frightened her.

It also frightened Cat, but not in the same way. For the first time in her life, she felt like a woman. A woman with desires. She had thought that any such prospect had been wrenched away a long time ago, in the house where her mother had sold her and later in countless hotel rooms when her husband had done the same.

What frightened her even more was the fact that she had actually enjoyed her exchange with Canton the other day, had been stimulated by the challenge in his eyes, had felt so completely alive as her every nerve reacted to him. She wasn't afraid of him in a physical sense, but by the way she was so drawn to him.

Like attracts like. Heaven help her if that was true.

Even if she didn't believe in heaven. Only hell.

And fallen angels.

Hugh O'Connell was the fifth man David Scott interviewed.

Marsh had spent the entire afternoon listening to prospects in David's office, only occasionally throwing in a question of his own. He hadn't liked any of the candidates until O'Connell. The others had eyed him warily, had wriggled in their seats after understanding Marsh would be their boss, then fairly bolted for the door, despite Scott's quiet questioning.

Hugh O'Connell did none of that. He was not a big man, but he carried himself with confidence. He did not appear rattled when told the hard man with the icy eyes would be his boss.

"I need this job," he said.

"Why?" Scott asked.

"I have a wife who's expecting and five younguns already here," he said. "I was the head bartender at the Cairo in the Barbary Coast area before it burned down a month ago and haven't found anything steady since."

"It'll be long hours," Marsh said.

The man nodded. "I'm used to them."

David looked at Marsh a moment and then at the applicant. "There could be trouble. Mr. Canton has already been attacked, and we believe it's because he's reopening the Glory Hole."

O'Connell stared straight ahead. "I'm used to trouble. I worked on the Barbary Coast."

Marsh stepped in again. "I want to run an honest place. No crooked gambling. No prostitution."

O'Connell looked relieved. "Good, I hated the Cairo," he said. "I would like the chance to work at a clean place."

"You would be working for me."

O'Connell didn't blink.

"Can you handle the hiring of a staff?"

O'Connell grinned. "I know some bloody good men."

"Can you start tomorrow?"

"This afternoon," O'Connell said.

Marsh looked over at Scott, who shrugged helplessly. He knew Marsh had made a decision. "Of course I'll have to check your references," the attorney said.

O'Connell nodded.

"In the meantime, you can start," Marsh

said. He didn't like dickering, especially when he'd made a decision.

"When do you plan to open?"

"Three weeks from now," Marsh said with a smile. "I had hoped to make it earlier, but I had a slight complication." He rose lazily. "You know where the Glory Hole is?"

"Everyone knows where the Glory Hole is. It has an . . . interesting history." O'Connell didn't add "unfortunate," but the implication echoed in the room.

"It's going to be even more interesting," Marsh said dryly. "Oh, and there's a dog there. Just ignore him and he'll ignore you."

"I like animals. He got a name?"

Marsh remembered his first thought when he'd seen the animal: as ugly as the wrong end of a Winchester.

"Winchester," he said. "Win, for short," he added with a slight smile that seemed to hint at a joke only he understood.

Miss Lotta Crabtree, one of San Francisco's most popular entertainers, will reopen the Glory Hole, San Francisco's newest palace of entertainment, Saturday night.

Miss Crabtree has been appearing in New York, Philadelphia, and Boston and has returned home for a month's engagement at Maguire's Opera House. Prior to that engagement, however, she will perform as the first entertainer at the newly renovated Glory Hole.

Many of our readers may remember that the Glory Hole closed two years ago. The new

*owner, Taylor Canton, a distinguished business-
man from Texas, has promised that the refurbished establishment will take its place among
the most sparkling entertainment centers in the
city.*

*The announcement that Lotta Crabtree will
perform there lends substance to that claim. We
welcome Mr. Canton to San Francisco.*

Catalina crushed the newspaper. She'd read
similar articles in the other city papers. Damn
him. How in the name of Lucifer had he engaged
Lotta Crabtree?

And "distinguished businessman" indeed.
More like a . . . a brigand. A plague. She wondered how much he had paid for those little an-
nouncements.

She muttered to herself. Lotta Crabtree was
a legend in San Francisco. The daughter of a
ne'er-do-well miner, she had started performing
as a child in the mining camps and had been the
rage of San Francisco's music halls until she went
east, where, rumor had it, she was the highest-
paid actress in America.

But she still occasionally returned home to
San Francisco, although she rarely performed in
the city now, certainly not in saloons. Which renewed Cat's original question. How had Canton
enticed Lotta Crabtree to perform in a mere saloon? Especially the notorious Glory Hole?

And why hadn't Cat heard the news from
Teddy via his cousin instead of from the newspaper?

She threw the newspaper across the room.
The opening would attract a tremendous crowd
to the Glory Hole, the disreputable Glory Hole

with the sullied reputation. This one event would erase every bad thing that had ever been said about it.

How did he do it?

He didn't appear to be the type of man who had friends. He was always alone, and she suspected that when he was with people, he was still alone.

She always was, and she recognized that same isolation in him.

She knew about David Scott, because Teddy had described his cousin's interview. She had asked a few of her customers about the attorney and had received precious little information other than he appeared to be honest, a virtue many of her customers avoided in an attorney. The source of the coup could be Quinn Devereux, whom Canton had mentioned, but why would he help a man who appeared to be totally ruthless?

It didn't make sense, and Cat didn't like things that didn't make sense.

She liked even less being checkmated.

Did the announcement mean that Canton would continue featuring entertainment after the opening? If so, Cat would have to do the same. Now, how on God's green earth could she surpass Lotta Crabtree? But she must—unless she was to lose face . . . and business. Everyone in San Francisco knew, or suspected, she was at least partially responsible for the previous problems of the Glory Hole. Her power and reputation as hostess to the powerful in San Francisco had been heightened by an aura of invincibility. It was an aura that protected her personally as well. She had promoted a rumor of a great love killed during the war, an everlasting love that she would always honor. She had even found and purchased an oil painting of a handsome uniformed man, which hung in a conspicuous spot.

But she knew the first sign of weakness would crack that wall she so carefully kept between herself and her customers.

Damn Canton.

She picked up the paper again and smoothed it out, ignoring the item that had so offended her. She was looking for something else now, something that would strike a chord.

On the sixth page she found it.

Teddy was taking her for a walk. Molly looked from under her wide-brimmed bonnet. Only the steady presence of him beside her kept her legs moving in any kind of stable manner. It was the first time she'd ventured more than a stone's throw from the Silver Slipper in the six weeks she had been there.

Her gloved hand trembled. Apparently Teddy noticed, for he took it, tucking her arm in his protectively.

What if she saw *him*?

The thought made her shiver, although the midmorning was warm. She had already taken risks, the greatest one working, however briefly, as a hostess for the Silver Slipper. *He* wouldn't find her there, she knew. *He* decried the use of alcoholic beverages as the work of the devil. The hypocrisy of those pronouncements would have made her laugh, if she'd had any laughter in her.

Instead, there was only a crunching terror that never left.

She had been so very desperate when she'd arrived in San Francisco, desperate enough to swallow her fear of being with a man, even in a crowded place.

She had run away, wearing a modest wool dress. She'd had no money, only a chance to hide herself in a wagon of hay bound for San Francisco, and when she'd arrived, she had been at a complete loss as to what to do next. Hungry and frightened, she had found a dark corner to pass the night and the next day had sought a job. But the owners of the shops she approached glanced over her disheveled appearance, listened to her stuttering, hesitant voice, and sent her away quickly.

When asked about skills, she hadn't known how to answer. She hadn't thought of the samplers she'd been required to sew since she could pick up a needle, perhaps because she had hated them so much, had hated everything they represented. So she hadn't mentioned she could sew.

The next few days were full of hunger and terror. Terror that she would be found, terror of the streets, of the dark nights that had, for so long, held their own devils. And then she overheard someone say a cook at the Silver Slipper had left. Swallowing the knowledge that she knew nothing about cooking, but desperate for something to eat and a safe place to sleep, she decided to try. Cooking couldn't be that difficult. She had watched Inez cook, until Inez had disappeared and was replaced by a woman who never allowed anyone in the kitchen.

Molly had tried to hold her head up when she entered the back of the Silver Slipper and found Teddy, who had looked at her with curious pity. And then Miss Catalina had appeared. At first Molly had been tongue-tied and frightened at the elegant perfection of the woman, at the cold green eyes that seemed to peer deep inside her.

The questions had been sharp. Where had she worked? How much cooking had she done? Molly had lied, had made up several places, and she had seen the doubt in the woman's eyes. But the cold green had seemed to soften for the slightest of seconds, and she was hired on trial. Miss Catalina had offered her a room and, after another searching look, said she needed several days of rest before starting—and different clothing. Molly had been grateful beyond words.

But then, unfortunately, she burned the first bread she baked and almost set the saloon on fire.

Molly had gone to her room, taken off the dress Miss Catalina had given her and put on her woolen one. She'd left the dress on the bed, looking at it with regret. It had been a pretty blue calico, brighter than any she had ever owned, though not nearly as expensive, but now the sleeve had a burned patch. Even then she would have kept it, but it wasn't hers, and she couldn't steal from someone who had been kind to her.

Miss Catalina's voice had stopped her just as she started to close the door behind her. "Molly?"

Her hand had frozen on the doorknob. She

couldn't conceal the shiver that ran down her body; she was used to punishment, both verbal and physical.

Miss Catalina's facial expression was as indecipherable as always, but the eyes had a sort of sad understanding in them that stopped the quaking within Molly. Her employer was so beautiful, Molly sometimes thought she wasn't real, that she was someone who had stepped out of a painting. But now there was a question on her face.

"Are you going someplace?"

"I thought . . . I'm so sorry."

"Because you lied about being able to cook, or because you almost destroyed the Silver Slipper?"

Molly felt an inch high, but the fear was fading. "Both," she said.

"Where do you plan to go?"

Molly could only shrug hopelessly.

Miss Catalina sighed. "And that dress . . ." She shook her head.

"I didn't really think I was lying," Molly stuttered. "I really thought I could."

"But you hadn't before?"

"No, ma'am."

Miss Catalina had smiled at that. "Well, what *can* you do?"

Molly wasn't up to any more lies. She hung her head. "Nothing, I'm afraid."

Catalina studied her carefully. "You speak well. You could be very pretty if you wore your hair down. Would you like to try as a hostess?"

Molly went very still. A chance. Another chance. A chance to hide and perhaps make enough money to go east, far enough that he could never find her. But what would she say to the men? Could she even talk to them? She knew from the bartender that no one was allowed to mishandle or mistreat the hostesses, that nothing more was expected of them than to look pretty and drink tea. She'd had that confirmed when one unruly customer, who'd made another kind of demand, was forcibly ejected from the establishment the previous night. She had heard about it from the two girls with whom she shared a room.

But still . . .

She remembered hands, those reaching hands that wouldn't be stopped, and she wasn't sure she could talk easily to men, not like the others.

But she had no place to go. Nowhere to hide. Here, at least, was some protection. She would try. And she had tried.

She shivered in the warm San Francisco air, moved closer to Teddy, and increased the tempo of her steps. She looked up, and her eyes met Teddy's. It had been a long time since she'd had a friend, much less a protector. It felt good having both.

If only she felt safe.

CHAPTER 7

———◆◆◆———

The streets outside the Glory Hole were overflowing with people. Ladies who would never have thought about entering a San Francisco saloon had come to hear Lotta Crabtree.

Catalina hadn't even tried to compete this night. Any entertainment she might offer would pale in comparison. But her time would come shortly. Very shortly.

She couldn't prevent a flash of admiration for Canton's ingenuity as she dressed to attend the opening of the Glory Hole. It was not going to be a happy experience. Yet he had extended an invitation, and she wasn't going to let him think her a coward, nor that he had gotten the best of her. She would wear her very finest gown—a black velvet creation that dramatically punctuated the ebony of her hair—and smile brilliantly.

Cat took her time dressing. She brushed her hair until it glowed, then twisted it into a French knot held by pearl pins. She used the barest amount of paint on her cheeks and lips, just enough to give them a rosy sheen.

She stepped back and regarded herself in the mirror. She looked her best. She drew on a cloak and took the first steps toward the serpent's lair.

Catalina Hilliard would come. Marsh knew it as well as he knew life ended in death. She would come because she couldn't bear to give him the satisfaction of not coming.

He had saved the best table for her. For them. The second-best table was reserved for Christopher Buckley, "Blind Chris" as he was called. Buckley owned the Snug Cafe near the city offices and was, according to all sources, the power behind the politicians in San Francisco. He was a man, Canton was told, to cultivate if he wanted to stay in business. Buckley had sent word that he wished to attend, and Marsh had been warned to give him the best table in the Glory Hole. Instead, he gave him the second-best.

Marsh tried his damnedest to look pleasant. Christ, but it was difficult after perfecting a stare of pure menace for so many years. Hugh O'Connell had made several suggestions and finally gave up with a disgusted grunt. "It'll have to do," he muttered as he'd stamped off.

This was the first time since the end of the war that Marsh had worn formal clothes, and they took him back to times and places he didn't want to revisit. He was also tired of black. He had worn it for years as part of a legend he had established. The greater the reputation, the more business came to you; the bigger the reputation, the more shaky opposition became. The black brought back the gunfights. The range wars. That displacement of feelings.

When he'd looked into the mirror this night, he had wondered for a moment who was standing there. He'd been to a barber who'd cut his hair, and now the tiniest bit of gray showed through the ebony strands. The fine clothes did nothing to ease the lines on his face, but they distinguished them in some subtle way.

It wasn't a killer facing him, not the killer he'd seen so many times reflected in the glass.

Could clothes really make that much difference? Or was it something else?

Or was he only imagining it? Wanting it to be so?

He'd turned away in disgust, wishing the night were over, wishing he hadn't started to question so many things, wishing he was alone, with the dog. The dog had been there this morning, but as the number of bartenders and waiters had increased during the day, he'd slunk off someplace. Marsh wished he could do the same.

With one last disgusted look, he'd turned around and made for the stairs, and, perhaps, a new life. Or the discovery that it was no longer possible.

Catalina Hilliard made an entrance. Perhaps it was on purpose, or perhaps her mere presence always created a stir.

Marsh had long ago become jaded about women, but even he took a deep breath when Catalina swept into the Glory Hole.

He always had admired her beauty, but tonight she was breathtaking. She wore a black velvet dress that hugged a very desirable body, then fell gracefully to the floor. It was not fashionable; there was no bustle, no elaborate decoration or bows, but the very simplicity emphasized her dark beauty. Her hands and arms were clothed in black silk gloves; her only other adornments were a gold necklace with a small emerald that matched her eyes and pearl pins in her dark hair. The simple elegance made every other woman in the room look overdressed and fussy. He was impressed, even as he reminded himself that this was the woman who'd probably had him beaten, jailed, and very nearly shanghaied.

Every head turned away from him, away from the stage where musicians were warming up for Lotta Crabtree's appearance, away from seeing who else had been able to gain entrance to one of the most popular events in recent San Francisco history. And every set of eyes remained on the elegant woman who moved toward Marsh with an assurance and challenge that was undeniable.

Marsh met her halfway as the room hushed. Rumors had already been flying about a feud between the two. In fact, he had encouraged them, knowing, as he had learned over the past years, that such speculation spurred interest.

And interest spurred business.

He also realized immediately that he and Catalina, with their black hair and formal wear, were striking together.

Marsh bowed with great courtliness. "Welcome to the Glory Hole," he said. "You are most gracious to come."

"Ah," she replied sweetly, "I don't think 'gracious' is quite the word. Let's say 'curious' instead. I like openings—almost as much as I like closings."

"Do I detect petulance, Miss Catalina?"

"Of course not, Mr. Canton. You are to be congratulated on obtaining Lotta Crabtree. And I would like to return the invitation. I hope you will find . . . the time to attend my . . . little gift to San Francisco."

He raised his eyebrows. "When is this?"

She gave him a beatific smile. "You can read about it in the paper tomorrow."

Marsh's smile widened, and this time he didn't have to work at it. The exhilaration he had felt with her before surged through him. It was wild and heady and unpredictable. And completely new.

He saw the sparkle of combat in her eyes, deepening them to an almost unbelievable shade of green, and he bowed again. The scent of fresh flowers hovered around her, not sweet, but with the tangy, enticing aroma of fields of wildflowers. "I look forward to it, Miss Catalina," he said, tucking her hand in his arm. "I hope you will share my table."

She nodded, unable to detach her hand without making a scene. She wouldn't give him that satisfaction. She was surprised, however, by the jolt that ran through her as his white-gloved hand touched her black-gloved one. Cloth should have protected her, but it didn't. His body warmth flowed through and burned right to the core.

He felt her reluctance, the slight recoil, and yet she showed no distaste, only awareness. Their eyes met, dueled, and she dropped her gaze first, only, he realized, because she didn't want to make a point of it, not because he'd won. He silently applauded her again. She stole the show with aplomb.

But then the music ended with a crescendo, and all eyes went to the stage and to Lotta Crabtree.

Marsh guided his reluctant partner to the table and seated her with a flourish. But no one was paying attention now, and he immediately understood why David Scott had so insisted on spending such a large portion of Marsh's money on the redoubtable Miss Crabtree.

From the second she took the stage, Lotta captivated every person in the audience. As a girl she had been befriended by Lola Montez, another California legend, who had tutored her. Lotta had a contagious laugh. Her hair was red, and her eyes a bright black, and she danced and frolicked, inviting everyone to join in the fun.

The Glory Hole rang with laughter, and Marsh felt an unusual burst of pride at the transformation that had taken the place from the derelict it was only weeks ago to the pleasure palace it was tonight. An accomplishment that had nothing to do with his gun hand, it was deeply affecting.

And so was the woman beside him, who couldn't quite hide an occasional smile during the performance, a contagious smile that he instinctively knew was as rare as his own. Once, she'd leaned over to share a joke but then obviously caught herself and turned away quickly. He felt a sudden, unaccountable loss.

When the first performance was over, she asked, "And what are you going to do with the Glory Hole after this?"

"I'll think of something," he said complacently. "But now the Glory Hole's respectable again."

"For how long?" The question was sweetly asked.

"Oh, I plan to run an exemplary establishment," he said with dry humor. "I have great respect for the law."

"I never would have expected it, Mr. Canton."

"Taylor," he insisted, almost saying "Marsh" instead, before reminding himself that he was distancing himself from Marsh Canton, the gunfighter. Somehow, suddenly, that life seemed aeons away. But still, he knew only too well, the shadows would always be there.

She cocked her head. "You don't look like a Taylor."

Marsh wondered whether the name had sounded new on his tongue. He had to be careful. If she had been behind the attack on him, as he so strongly suspected, she would dearly love to know who he really was. Then the newfound respectability of the Glory Hole would be shot to hell. He shrugged. "You don't look like a Catalina."

"And what would you suggest?"

"Perhaps a shortening . . . to Cat."

"Cats have claws."

"That's why it suits you so well." He smiled, his eyes telling her that he was only too aware now of her attempt to rid herself of him. "And I've always been fascinated by them, their . . . cleverness. I've always wondered if one could be tamed—by the right master, of course."

"There is no such thing as a right master, Mr. Canton."

"No exceptions?"

"No."

"Such certainty," he said, amused. "There are always exceptions."

"I didn't expect such . . . flexibility from a man like you."

"And what kind of man am I?"

"Uncompromising. Dangerous."

"Coming from you, that's a compliment," he said. "What do they say, it takes one to know one?"

"Exactly, Mr. Canton."

The challenge was there again, and he reveled in it. He had never dueled like this with a woman before, and it was exhilarating. His gaze didn't leave hers as his hand reached for a glass of champagne that had been placed in front of him. The green eyes *were* like a cat's, lazy and superior and sensuous—and unblinkingly fixed on him.

Marsh's groin tightened. He ached to touch the ivory skin above the inky blackness of the velvet dress, to run his tongue over the hollow of her throat, to lay his head against that dark hair that looked as if it were soft as silk.

Christ, he was panting like a dog.

For a woman who was his declared enemy.

But that was what made it so exciting. At least, he thought that was part of it. He didn't want to think it might be something else.

He barely heard the enthusiastic roar of approval as Lotta Crabtree appeared again onstage. He felt only the heat that was radiating between Catalina Hilliard and himself, heat that he knew she also felt, because her cheeks had turned rosy.

She blinked.

So the Ice Queen did feel!

His hand brushed hers. The flush deepened on her cheeks, and she moved her hand as if it were burned.

"Champagne?" Even he knew his voice was huskier than usual.

"I wouldn't want to bankrupt you too quickly," she retorted, but her voice too had a new sensuality to it. What was obviously intended to be a waspish tone was almost a purr of invitation.

Bankruptcy sounded good in that warm, seductive voice.

They were still then, listening to Lotta Crabtree, but his eyes rarely left Cat's. Despite their silence, they were communicating in another way altogether, a soundless conversation filled with expectancy and challenge, which grew with each passing moment.

He didn't want to let go of those moments. Christ, but they were oddly pleasurable, a sharing of feelings so personal, so private. He was barely aware of another round of applause as Lotta Crabtree finished her last song of this particular series, and Hugh O'Connell mounted the stage to announce that the finest in entertainment would be offered nightly at the Glory Hole.

The room then exploded into conversation. People crowded over to Marsh's table to congratulate him, curiosity evident.

The brief, unique pride he'd felt dissolved as he realized that the only thing he wanted at the moment, needed at the moment, was the woman who sat across from him. But as he accepted the congratulations, he saw her ease from the chair, then toward the door, and he could do nothing about it. Not now. Not without appearing to run after her.

But the pure need of his body didn't go away as he moved among the crowd, trying to look pleasant and not quite knowing whether he was succeeding. Christ, but he was out of practice with the simplest of civilities, he who had once been master of them, one of the most sought-after young gallants in Georgia. At last he gave a nod to Hugh and made his way to the back door and out into the alley, into the fresh air, away from the lingering scent of wild-flowers.

The Silver Slipper was busy with the overflow from the Glory Hole. Cat offered the customers drinks on the house, and the somewhat sullen mood turned good-natured. Catalina never offered drinks on the house.

And she mingled, as she rarely did, making each customer feel uniquely privileged and not at all displeased that he had missed Lotta Crabtree.

She talked of politics and asked of their families, always keeping a certain emotional distance while making the recipient of her attention feel honored. When one hand of a newcomer reached out to touch her, she fought a familiar revulsion, but then recovered quickly, giving him a polite smile but quickly moving away.

Why didn't Canton's touch do that to her, incite that wave of distaste, of memories, that had protected her all these years? Why, instead, had he awakened something in her that was so intense in its yearning, that ached so painfully, she could scarcely bear it? She didn't even know where the ache had been birthed; it simply flooded the whole of her with such strength that it occupied every part of her body and soul.

The feelings terrified her even more than those dreaded visits years ago. She had given her heart and hope once and had been so bitterly betrayed that she knew she couldn't face such a thing again.

She had to get rid of Canton. She refused to think of him in any other way. Certainly not as Taylor. He was too . . . too earthy for such a civilized name. Nothing fit other than "Canton." A harsh name. A harsh man.

Somehow she got through the evening, fixing her attention on each of the customers in a way she'd never done before. But her real attention was on a tall, black-haired man in formal clothes who was too handsome by far, with eyes too magnetic, even as they chilled. Chilled some. Not her. If only they did, instead of filling her with such dangerous heat.

She wondered whether he was watching Lotta Crabtree, perhaps even sharing a private dinner later. And she was seized with a jealousy she hadn't known she possessed.

Lotta Crabtree eyed her host with speculation as she puffed on a big black cigar.

He had sent her a huge bouquet of flowers, along with a box of cigars it was rumored she liked. She liked him for doing that. Most men wouldn't have thought of the last.

She sat across from him in her dressing room, drinking a glass of champagne, wondering whether she dared pursue anything more with Taylor Canton.

She dared anything.

But he was different. She had accepted this offer because David Scott had requested it, and David had once done her a very great favor. She was opening in a play tomorrow night in San Francisco, and this seemed a small enough favor, though her manager had screamed about it. Performances in a saloon diminished her, he'd argued, but Lotta did exactly what she wanted, and she felt intense loyalty toward those who had helped her in the beginning . . . when she was a child performing in mining camps and later as her fame increased.

From the first moment she'd met Taylor Canton, she'd been intrigued. He was as unlikely a saloon owner as any man she'd ever met, and she wondered briefly at David Scott's connection with him. She'd seen men like Canton before in the mining camps, the wolves among sheep.

And yet he had the manners of a gentleman even while his eyes said otherwise. No tame suitor, he.

"Is that a southern accent?" She asked.

He smiled. "I thought it long gone," he said. "But yes, Georgia." She noticed the smile didn't reach his eyes.

"Just a trace, but I have an ear for accents," she said, pleased with herself as she studied him. "A wealthy family?"

"Once upon a time."

"Before the war?"

"Before the war," he confirmed.

"And how did you become a saloon owner?" She puffed on the cigar and discovered the conversation had so involved her that the cigar had gone out. She looked at it in disgust. Marsh leaned over to light it again, amusement dancing in his eyes. Amusement but not warmth.

"I won it."

"A gambler?"

"In part."

"And the other part?"

Now he leaned back and lit a cigar for himself, letting the silence answer for him.

"You think I ask too many questions," she said. "I do. That's how you become a good actress . . . knowing people. Understanding them."

"And do you understand me?"

"I doubt if anyone understands you, even yourself."

He did smile then, a smile that even touched his eyes. He leaned over and his lips met hers, and he felt her respond. But the stirring he'd felt earlier, the raw hunger, wasn't there, and he knew it immediately. He tried to will even a fraction of that emotion, that need, but it wouldn't come.

He cursed silently. Lotta Crabtree was a beautiful, fascinating woman, desired throughout the country, and he didn't feel a damn thing, except perhaps a slight, pleasant sensation.

Lotta Crabtree allowed herself to explore for a moment; then she disengaged herself. "That was a beautiful woman you were sitting with," she observed with a slight smile.

He nodded warily.

"She left," she noted.

"She owns the saloon across the street."

"Friendly competitors?"

He shook his head. "She tried to have me shanghaied."

Lotta Crabtree sat back and chuckled. "I could almost feel the heat from where I was standing. I didn't think it was dislike."

He grinned. "Something . . . does seem to happen when we're together. Fireworks."

"Too bad," she said with real regret as she eyed him with a certain amount of desire. "It would have been interesting. . . ."

She didn't have to explain what she meant. Marsh wished for a fraction of a second he'd never set eyes on Catalina Hilliard. "It still could," he said.

Lotta shook her head. "I never settle for being second."

"No," he agreed. "You wouldn't."

"And now would you like to take me to my hotel?"

"My pleasure, Miss Crabtree."

Cat was braiding her hair when she heard the sound of a carriage outside. It was near dawn, and silence had long since fallen over both saloons.

She went over to the window. Canton was handing Lotta Crabtree into a carriage. She waited until he nimbly joined her on the seat and the driver flicked his whip. Canton had moved close to the actress, and in the first gray light of dawn Cat saw Lotta turn toward Canton and break into laughter.

Cat felt a tightness in her chest, almost as though she were being smothered.

With an oath that would make a sailor

proud, she flung her brush across the room, watching as it headed toward a glass of port awaiting her. The glass broke, flinging the dark-red liquid across the silk sheets of the bed.

Stains. Dear God, the stains.

CHAPTER 8

Stains.

Lizzie Jones had stared at the filthy sheet, at the red stain that stared back. The blood. Her blood.

She had thrown up. Her stomach hurt like the rest of her. She'd felt torn apart inside.

She had closed her eyes during most of it, had willed herself someplace else. But the pain had been awful, like a sword jammed inside her, and it kept bringing her back to her terrible reality.

She was supposed to have turned thirteen that day, her ma's guess at her birthday. She'd never had a birthday before. And now this had been the first and only birthday gift she'd ever received.

She had known it was coming. She had seen the men looking at her, felt their hands taking squeezes on different parts of her body as she served drinks. And she'd heard about the bidding. She'd tried to run away then, but the sheriff, who was paid off by the madam, brought her back. She'd been locked in her room, the one window boarded over.

She had survived every attempt to prevent her live birth, and then almost total neglect as a child. Except that there had always been some softhearted whore who gave her some small care before disappearing. It had never been her ma.

Lizzie had been little more than a slave most of her young life. She'd never gone to school, had never realized there was another life beyond the one of noisy coupling and drunken fights and screaming arguments between the women. She had survived simply because she was basically too tough to die, but survive was all she did.

And then she started turning pretty, and her ma noticed her.

After that first time with a man, she had a room of her own, but she never got any of the money. Her ma took it, and Lizzie learned to shut off her mind when the men came. She thought about running away again, but then she remembered being dragged back by the sheriff and locked up. What would she do, anyway? Her ma kept telling her she was worthless, no good for anything except whoring.

So she pretended she was someplace else,

that her body belonged to someone else. She'd seen a picture once of the sea, and she would picture that, because it looked so clean and pure. She thought of it all the time the men were at her.

And then James Cahoon started visiting on a regular basis. He seemed to have money, enough to visit her several times a week, anyway, and he made some attempt to be gentle. She was about fifteen when he asked her to run away with him, to become his wife. He said he would take care of her.

He loved her.

Hope found a place in her life. It was short-lived. . . .

Cat shook herself. No more past! She refused to remember that she had started life as Lizzie Jones, a miserable little river rat, then a whore.

The dog woke Marsh, and instinctively he reached for his gun, which was in a holster hung on the bedpost. He felt like a damned fool as light from the window shone only on the four-legged intruder.

He also felt a flash of apprehension. He must be getting older than he'd thought. He used to wake up at the slightest sound: the breaking of a twig, horses' hooves against pine needles, the creaking of a floorboard.

Marsh glared at the dog, which glared right back. It was obvious the mutt was disgruntled, apparently by being crowded out last night. "Something you'll have to get used to," Marsh muttered, even as he wondered about his own sanity in talking to a damn dog.

A gnawing uncertainty ate at him. His hand took the pistol, cocked it, felt it, almost soothed it, seeking the familiarity that had made it one with himself. He couldn't afford this kind of carelessness. No matter how far away he might travel, there were likely those with a grudge out there. Or even those seeking a reputation. They might find him.

Where had his edge gone, that split-second awareness of everything around him? Where were the skills he'd accumulated during three years with General Mosby scouting behind enemy lines, then perfected as a gun for hire?

He stretched, testing the muscles that were as taut as ever, and he sprang to his feet in one movement. He was naked, and he enjoyed the freedom of that nakedness. He hadn't slept that way since he was a university student, not until he'd come to San Francisco. He'd never known when he might need to move quickly, and he'd often slept fully clothed. Now he reveled in this tiny bit of liberation. But he had to be careful and not be lulled into a false sense of security. There was no such thing for him. Never would be, which was why the unaccustomed heavy sleep worried him.

After closing up, except for leaving the window open for Winchester, he had gone to his room and fallen with exhaustion on the hard mattress.

But now sunlight dappled the floor of the room, meaning the sun was well above the horizon. Hugh should be here soon, preparing for another day. He heard a low growl and looked over at the dog.

Marsh had still not touched the animal, but he had talked to it. Winchester kept his distance, although he no longer waited more than a moment to gulp down whatever food Marsh provided. "Getting greedy, aren't you?" Marsh said now, knowing that it wasn't his company the animal craved. The thought amused him. How long had it been since anyone had wanted his company?

A long time.

Fifteen years ago he had stood over an unarmed man and killed him. Slowly. Bullet after bullet in painful places. He had even taken unholy pleasure in it. He'd had his reasons, but he'd also known in those minutes that he had surrendered his soul. It was the final act that placed him outside of humanity.

Marsh had never allowed an attachment after that. Not to a person, a place, or even an animal. He'd never named a horse and often traded them to avoid any attachment. His few pleasures were superficial, a momentary indulgence in a fine meal or superior wine or an hour with an enthusiastically uninhibited woman.

When had it become not enough?

The dog growled again. Christ, Marsh thought, he had to stop this . . . this questioning. He went to the window, still naked, and looked across to the Silver Slipper, to the window he knew belonged to Catalina. And smiled. Damn, but she was beautiful last night. Beautiful and dangerous. His body recalled, with vivid warmth, the sizzling heat that had run along every nerve when they'd touched. No woman had ever done that to him.

Too bad she wanted to ruin him. It would be interesting to explore just how hot the fire could get. Perhaps it would even burn itself out, like a backfire.

And then he could lay it aside, once and for all.

He dressed slowly in his work clothes, hesitated a moment, and then reached for the gunbelt and buckled it on. He needed it today. He needed it so he'd know who he was.

He went to the doorway. Winchester followed him at a distance.

A pot of coffee and some food. Perhaps a long ride this afternoon.

And maybe a seduction tonight. He'd always been very good at that.

Teddy entered Hugh O'Connell's home without a knock, as he was used to doing. He and Hugh had grown up together, Hugh's parents dying at a young age and Teddy's mother taking him in.

Hugh had been Teddy's manager when he had been in the boxing ring, but Teddy had never really been that good. He didn't have the killer instinct, and he knew, after several years, that while he might win a bout now and then, he would never be among the best. Hugh had fallen in love by then and needed a steady income, and Teddy reluctantly dropped out of fighting, because Hugh wouldn't leave him until he did.

When Hugh had married, Teddy was best man, and he was godfather to the oldest boy. He adored Elizabeth, who had always made him feel part of the family and was constantly trying to pair him with one good Catholic girl after another. But Teddy had always been shy with them, realizing that his bulk and battered face were not the stuff of which a woman's dreams were made.

Catalina Hilliard, who had originally hired him as a bouncer, was one of the few people who had looked beyond his brawn and given him a job with responsibility that made him feel more than a has-been fighter. He'd gained confidence in himself, even though he knew his surface roughness still repelled young women, and, in most cases, it didn't really matter. Most were young and silly and shallow and only shadows of the strength he saw and admired in his employer. His loyalty to her was absolute, even fanatical, because, without her faith, he knew he'd probably be lying in an alley someplace, remembering in a drunken stupor those very few hours of glory in a ring. Now he had respect, a life he enjoyed, a feeling of worth.

And he was falling in love with someone who didn't seem to care about his smashed face and large size. He was filled with expectation . . . and gratitude, even as he realized that his courtship might be very slow. Molly was afraid of something, and he knew he had to go slow. But she trusted him, and that alone made him feel . . . well, like a king.

The noise inside the O'Connell house was comforting, even the crying of the youngest one. There was always noise here with five little ones between the ages of one and ten. Two were in school, but the two middle ones, Betsy and

Terrence, hurled themselves into his arms as Elizabeth came into the front room with the youngest in her arms.

She beamed at him. "Thank you for telling Hugh about the job," she said. "It's been a godsend."

Then Hugh emerged from the bedroom, apparently dressed for work in a new suit. Teddy was obviously curious.

"Mr. Canton," Hugh explained awkwardly. "He paid for some new clothes."

Teddy felt indignant for his cousin. He knew how much Hugh and his wife needed money; he had, in fact, tried to lend them money, but they always refused to take it. "He made you buy new clothes?"

Hugh shook his head. "No, he's paying for them himself. Said they gave the place"—he struggled for a word—"style."

"Let's talk alone," Teddy said.

Hugh looked distinctly uncomfortable, but nodded as Elizabeth disappeared into the kitchen to let the men talk. She called the other two children to come with her.

Teddy took a chair, overflowing on it. He towered over his cousin. "What is Canton up to?"

Hugh hesitated. When he'd first met Mr. Canton, he hadn't suspected he might have a problem with loyalty. The man had been as cold as Alaska ice, but something in the past few days had nibbled at Hugh's conscience. He supposed it was his innate loyalty to the person who paid him, along with Canton's unexpected offer of an advance when he'd learned that Hugh's wife was expecting. Or perhaps because Canton treated him with dignity after years of none in the Barbary Coast. But Teddy, who was closer than a true brother, sat there looking at him expectantly.

What could it hurt?

"He has a new singer, a regular. Mr. Devereux from the Pacific Palace recommended her." Hugh hesitated. Dear Lord, he felt like a Judas, but Teddy continued to look at him expectantly. Years of kinship, blood ties, overtook his scruples, but he didn't feel good about it, and he let Teddy see it. "He's bringing in more gambling equipment," he said finally. "Almost double that at the Silver Slipper, and he's hiring very pretty girls to deal."

"Women?" Teddy asked, startled.

Hugh nodded reluctantly. He hadn't agreed with his new employer. Girls were usually employed to serve drinks, to dance with customers, not as dealers. But Canton had made it very clear that he wanted something the Silver Slipper didn't offer and had said he would train the girls himself.

Teddy remained silent for a moment. Catalina had made the Silver Slipper into a place for conversation and business more so than a place for gambling, although gambling was available during certain hours. But that was changing now, what with her new plans to fight the Glory Hole with everything she had. He didn't think it was necessary; the Silver Slipper was well established and well respected. Time would take care of the problem. But his employer was obsessed with eliminating the newcomer, and he knew her

obsessions. They didn't go away. It was one reason, he figured, that she had come as far as she
had. She followed her instincts all the way.

"Will they be crooked?" he asked his
cousin now.

Hugh shook his head. "Mr. Canton's very
definite on that. Anyone caught cheating will be
fired."

Teddy was decidedly unhappy at the news.
He had hoped they might rid themselves of the
Glory Hole in the usual way . . . and without
guilt. And he didn't like Hugh's reluctance to
speak. Not at all.

"There has to be something wrong. . . ."

Hugh shook his head. "Not that I can tell.
Perhaps," he offered tentatively, "perhaps both
saloons can do well."

"You don't know Miss Catalina."

"I don't think he's like the others. He won't
give up easily."

Troubled, they stared at each other. Hugh
had sought the job because he needed the money
and he wanted to help his cousin. He had
thought it only temporary, knowing the history
of the Glory Hole, but now he felt as if he had
a new chance in a fine job with a man he was
beginning to respect, if not particularly like.

Teddy felt a tightening in his belly, the sure
sign of big trouble. He saw the first rip in a life-
long relationship. He rose and shifted uncomfortably from foot to foot. "I'll be saying
good-bye then to Elizabeth and the little ones."

CHAPTER 9

Catalina Hilliard, owner of the Silver Slipper, has announced she will bring the cancan to San Francisco for a two-week engagement.

The dance, which originated in France and has created a stir throughout the world, will be performed by a company of French dancers now touring the United States. It will be the first performance of the cancan on the West Coast.

The event is seen as a response to the appearance last night of Lotta Crabtree at the revival of the Glory Hole across the street from the Silver Slipper.

The feud between the owners of the two es-

tablishments is certainly benefiting San Francisco's night life.

This reporter looks forward to even more excitement in the coming weeks.

Marsh read the item in the *San Francisco Chronicle* several times. A similar announcement had appeared in the city's other newspapers. He'd bought the papers after hearing a newsboy chanting "Cancan coming to San Fran." The singsong words had caught his attention.

He was sweaty but exhilarated from a long ride along the coast. Christ, but he was beginning to enjoy California, especially the fresh bite of the sea wind.

It was almost as if he were awakening from a long sleep, parts of his body and mind coming alive again, appreciating small pleasures he had denied himself for so long. His mind was fully functioning again, not just his senses and his gun hand.

And now the next move had been made in what he was coming to think of as a chess game between him and the fascinating Miss Hilliard. A game he didn't intend to lose. He wanted her to concede. And make amends for his attempted kidnapping and stay in jail—and he knew exactly the form in which he desired those amends from her.

He closed his hand around the newspaper and entered the Glory Hole. It was satisfactorily filled for a late afternoon; Marsh supposed that people were curious after all the publicity. He was glad. He had to keep them coming, especially during the two weeks the cancan was being performed.

His women dealers should help. He was interviewing the next day and would start their training immediately. The novelty of women dealers and croupiers would bring in customers and encourage them to play more. He also had a new singer, highly recommended by Quinn Devereux.

Hugh was behind the bar, working with another bartender he had hired. He looked harried, and Marsh stopped to speak with him before going to his room to change clothes. "Everything all right?"

"The new singer's accompanist is sick. She says she can't sing without him.

Marsh swore softly. They had distributed handbills throughout the city. Jenny Davis, a popular young singer, had gained a strong following. A nonappearance after Lotta Crabtree's success would do incalculable damage. For a fleeting moment he wondered whether Cat had anything to do with it. "Where is she?"

"In the dressing room. Waiting for you. She wanted to tell you herself. Uh, have you seen the newspapers?"

Marsh nodded. "The cancan?"

Hugh fumbled with the glass he was holding. "I just thought you should know."

"I know," Marsh replied dryly. "But if I can get in my dealers, along with Jenny, we may minimize the effect—unless Miss Catalina brings in women to run her gambling."

The glass fell and broke, and Hugh knelt swiftly to retrieve the pieces, keeping his face averted. "I'm sorry, Mr. Canton."

Marsh suddenly felt kicked in the gut. He

wasn't used to loyalty and had no reason to expect it. Hugh had worked for him only three weeks now. Marsh had no reason to expect anything. But he did, and he knew in that instant that Hugh was not his.

The quiet pleasure of the morning faded as his cynicism returned. His first impulse was to fire the man; the second was to use him.

His jaw tightened. "It's all right. We have plenty of glasses. Just see about getting those young ladies in here for me to interview."

Hugh nodded, his eyes fixed on the broken glass.

"I don't think we can depend on Hugh any longer," Teddy told Cat.

She looked up from the ledger. Bringing the cancan to San Francisco was costing her a fortune. An investment, she told herself, both an emotional and business investment. She had to get rid of the troublesome neighbor across the street.

It takes money to make money.

Money is power and protection.

How well she remembered Ben Abbott's words. They had been among the first lessons he'd taught her.

She tried to concentrate on what Teddy had told her. "What did you say, Teddy?"

"I don't think I can get any more information from Hugh. He doesn't want to be disloyal."

"How about his loyalty to you?" she asked indignantly.

"That's just it, Miss Cat. He doesn't feel right about either."

"He *likes* that . . . that man?"

"I don't know how he feels about Canton, but he's taking his money."

Cat muttered under her breath about damn principles.

"He did tell me that Canton's hiring women as dealers.

Cat felt the now-familiar tightening in her chest as she thought about it. It was a good idea. A very good idea. Why hadn't she come up with it?

She could counter by doing the same, but then that would be conceding defeat in some way. She didn't need to imitate him. She could do better, just as she had by bringing the cancan to San Francisco. She just hadn't dreamed he would be so . . . imaginative.

"Hugh also said Canton won't allow any cheating."

"Sweet Lucifer," Cat said. "He's not a saint. I know he's not a saint."

"It's obvious the usual means won't work."

"We can try Captain Delaney again," Cat said hopefully.

Teddy shook his head. "Not now. He's still angry about your stopping the shanghaiing."

Another grudge against Canton. Because of him she'd used up a valuable marker with Delaney.

"The cancan will bring in new customers," Teddy said. "All San Francisco's talking about it."

"We'll get the girls new dresses, dresses that

will be similar to those worn by the dancers. Perhaps they can learn the dance, and we can keep it going."

Teddy grinned. "Bare legs are better than lady dealers any day."

Cat didn't smile. "I liked the Silver Slipper the way it was."

"We can always go back . . . we'll still get our usual customers."

"Will we?" she asked. "People always go after something new, something different."

"We were doing just fine."

Maybe. Cat didn't know anymore. She just knew everything had changed. And Taylor Canton was the reason.

What would she do without Teddy? He was her only real friend, the only person she could talk to, the only one who knew the photo of her supposed husband was a fraud, the only one who knew how much she needed to succeed. He'd heard her one night when she'd had a nightmare, and though he had never questioned her, she'd known from his expression that he'd learned a great deal—but she also realized he would never repeat a word of it. He looked worried now, and she wondered whether it was because of her or Molly. "Has Molly said any more to you?" Cat asked.

Teddy shook his head. "But I know she's scared about something."

Cat nodded. "I wish she would talk about it," but she knew the girl wouldn't, just as Lizzie Jones hadn't. For the longest time Cat hadn't been able to distinguish friend from foe; betrayal had been too frequent and too hurtful.

"I'll keep close to her," Teddy promised.

Of that Cat had no doubt. "Don't get too involved," she warned, knowing it was probably too late.

Teddy only looked sheepish, a ridiculous look on a face that could be as fierce as any in San Francisco, and Cat felt a deep surge of affection for the man who had become like a brother. She didn't want him hurt, and despite his rough exterior she'd learned he had a big heart that he protected as she protected her past. But now, at this moment, she suspected he was as vulnerable as she.

He was peering at her with a concern on his face that probably equaled her own for him. "Why don't you go out for a while?" he asked, looking around the room. "Get some fresh air." There was a lull right now in the saloon, the time between the midday rush and late-afternoon crowds.

The idea struck her as a fine one. Fresh air, that's what she needed and some time away from the Silver Slipper, away from the Glory Hole across the street.

She smiled and nodded, suddenly pleased with the idea. "I'll take a walk." Cat picked up a shawl. She wished she had time to take the rig and go to the shore, but she knew her presence was important to her customers, and now, more than ever, she needed their loyalty.

Still, she found herself crossing the street when she didn't have to. Passing the Glory Hole when it wasn't necessary. Drawn there by some invisible cord. To see what he was up to now, she told herself.

Cat slowed and gazed into the saloon—to judge how many customers were inside, she told herself. Then she heard the sound of a piano, and she moved closer. She recognized the tune as "The Girl I Left Behind Me." The keys were being caressed, rather than merely touched. She'd heard enough piano players to know this was a particularly good one, and she remembered the haunting melody from nights earlier.

And then she saw the player's back, the head of thick dark hair turned toward a pretty girl standing beside the piano. Her breath stopped momentarily and she couldn't move.

Canton was sitting at the piano, his fingers ranging easily over the keys. He seemed oblivious to the customers, to the waiters.

His sleeves were rolled up, and she saw mostly his back, which seemed even broader than ever. The usual grace was in his movements, but it was as if an angel played rather than the man who was anything but angelic.

Cat couldn't stop herself from entering, pulled by the same force that had drawn her to walk by the Glory Hole when she could have easily avoided it. Canton—she couldn't think of him in any other way—stopped and looked up at the girl next to the piano, who hummed a few notes. His fingers went back to the keys, and the music floated out with such elegance that Cat was stunned.

She saw the muscles move in his arms, in his back. She sensed a barely harnessed energy and, remembering the earlier passion of the night music she'd heard, wondered whether it was difficult for him to mold his playing to what was required now for accompanying the girl.

He looked up. "Will I do?"

The singer grinned. "I wish I could take you every place I go. You wouldn't like a permanent job, would you?"

Cat saw a slow smile transform his face, and she felt the strangest ache inside.

"I'm afraid I have one, for the time being. I'll keep it in mind, though."

The girl laughed. "Will you play something else?"

He rose slowly, lazily. "I only know what I hear," he said as he started to turn, his eyes showing only the briefest surprise at seeing Cat. They studied her for a moment with the wary amusement she now expected, even as his words hovered in the air. She knew them as a lie, and wondered why he so disparaged what even she knew was extraordinary talent. He knew a great deal more than what he merely "heard." No one could play as well as he had the other night without training. She just didn't know why he lied about it.

"Miss Cat," he said as his gaze ran over her dress and shawl. "What a very pleasant surprise to have you visit again. Can't stay away?" His voice was low and teasing.

She thought fast. "I'm just returning your courtesy," she improvised sweetly. "A special invitation to sit at my table for the opening night of the cancan." And then, because she realized that there was something about his musical ability he wished to hide, she continued, "How interesting to discover you have . . . a talent. Are there any more I should know about?"

Something flickered in his eyes. Anger, perhaps. Or something even stronger.

"Are you sure you want to know, Miss Cat?" Now his voice purred, but not like any house pet she'd ever known. There was a sensual invitation in it that sent prickly shivers up and down her spine. She felt herself being expertly unclothed, piece by piece by those damnable eyes of his. The shivers turned to raw, ragged heat that seemed to claw at her insides.

The girl standing next to him looked decidedly confused. The air was alive with challenge . . . and the heat that crawled inside Cat was making her existence plain hell. It reached outside her. It wrapped around him. She saw it plainly in the smile that was disappearing, in the sudden tightness of his trousers.

A muscle twitched in his cheek, and she took satisfaction in it. He wasn't nearly as indifferent as he wanted to appear. But then, as if through sheer force of will, the muscle quieted and a grim smile came to his lips. "I've forgotten my manners," he said in that natural way that told of breeding in his past. "Catalina, this is Miss Jenny Davis, who will be entertaining here, and Jenny, this is Catalina Hilliard, our worthy competitor from the Silver Slipper."

Jenny flushed and Cat wondered why. She'd seen the quick looks the girl had sent toward Canton, and that bubble of jealousy she'd felt about Lotta Crabtree bobbed back to the surface of her awareness. Damn the man. Did he have every woman in the city panting after him?

He didn't seem to notice as he nodded to the girl. "I'll see you this evening, Jenny. I have some business to discuss with Miss Catalina." It was an abrupt dismissal, but a slight, practiced smile softened the impact, and the girl nodded, though it was clear from her expression that she was curious.

His eyes were intent on Cat, and there was something very dangerous in them now. She wasn't surprised when he took her arm and guided her toward the door. His fingers pressed into her arm in a possessive way, with a fierceness that indicated he wasn't going to let go. "Will you accompany me for a ride?" The question was not a question at all, but an order, and Cat bristled. She thought of pulling away, damn the consequences of a scene, but then he leaned down, his warm breath tickling her ear in a way that dulled her intent but excited less reasoning and more combustible parts of her anatomy.

She tried to say no, but his hand on her was as confining as a shackle. "Of course, you will," he whispered as though he heard her declining his invitation. "We have some very important matters to discuss ... a certain police captain, for instance."

"I don't know what you mean," Cat said with the composure she'd practiced for so many years.

Canton smiled. "You're very good, you know. You would have made one hell of a gunfighter.

She leapt on the words. "Is that what you are, Mr. Canton?"

His smile widened, and Cat knew it was no

slip of his tongue. As part of his invitation—or order—he was offering a slice of temptation, a hint that he might reveal what she desperately wanted to know.

"I didn't say that. I merely said that you would have made a good one."

"And why is that?"

"You give very little away, Miss Cat. And then there's a certain ruthlessness about you."

"You're describing yourself, Mr. Canton."

"I thought we'd gone beyond *Mr.* Canton." That infernal chuckle was in his voice, that deep sensuousness that was half invitation, half challenge, and all deadly. Her wayward body felt the craving she heard in his voice, the pure lust that astounded and horrified her.

She summoned every bit of willpower and tried to pull away, but his hand was like a steel band on her arm. "I have to get back."

"Then I'll have to carry you off," he said in a low voice no one else could hear. "I'll try to make your abduction far more pleasant than the one you arranged for me."

"I have no idea what you're talking about."

"Of course, we could discuss it here." They had reached the door, away from Jenny Davis and customers, but all eyes in the establishment were fixed on them.

She lifted her chin. She didn't like the way he called her Cat. No one called her Cat, although a few had tried, before she'd fixed them with what Teddy called the look that turned men into bumbling, apologetic fools. She had mastered that look to perfection, but it didn't work on this man. He seemed only amused by it, as if he understood all the insecurity and pain that lay behind it, that he knew it for the fraud it often was.

"We have nothing to discuss," she said coldly, even as she struggled to keep from trembling. All her thoughts were in disarray. He was so adept at personal invasion. That look in his eyes of pure radiance, of physical need, almost burned through her.

Fifteen years. Nearly fifteen years since a man had touched her so intimately. And he was doing it only with his eyes!

And, dear Lucifer, she was responding.

She'd thought herself immune from desire. If she'd ever had any, she believed it had been killed long ago by brutality and shame and utter abhorrence of an act that gave men power and left her little more than a thing to be used and hurt. She'd never felt this bubbling, boiling warmth inside, this craving that was more than physical hunger.

That's what frightened her most of all.

But she wouldn't show it. She would never show it! She didn't even like Canton, devil take him. She didn't like anything about him. And she would send him back to wherever he came from. Tail between his legs. No matter what it took. And she would never feel desire again.

But now she had little choice, unless she wished to stand here all afternoon, his hand burning a brand into her. He wasn't going to let her go, and perhaps it was time to lay her cards on the table. She preferred open warfare to guerrilla fighting. She hadn't felt right about the kidnapping and beating—even if she did frequently regret her moment of mercy on his behalf.

She shrugged and his hand relaxed slightly. They left, and he flagged down a carriage for hire. Using those strangely elegant manners that still puzzled her, he helped her inside with a grace that would put royalty to shame.

He left her then for a moment and spoke to the driver, passing a few bills up to him, then returned and vaulted to the seat next to her. Hard-muscled thigh pushed against her leg; his tanned arm, made visible by the rolled-up sleeve, touched her much smaller one, the wiry male hair brushing against her skin, sparking a thousand tiny charges. His scent, a spicy mixture of bay and soap, teased her senses. Everything about him— the strength and power and raw masculinity that he made no attempt to conceal—made her feel fragile, delicate.

But not vulnerable, she told herself. Never vulnerable again. She would fight back by seizing control and keeping it.

She straightened her back and smiled. A seductive smile. A smile that had entranced men for the last ten years. A practiced smile that knew exactly how far to go. A kind of promise that left doors opened, while permitting retreat. It was a smile that kept men coming to the Silver Slipper even as they understood they had no real chance of realizing the dream.

Canton raised an eyebrow. "You *are* very good," he said admiringly.

She shrugged. "It usually works."

"I imagine it does," he said. "Although I

doubt if most of the men you use it on have seen the thornier part of you."

"Most don't irritate me as you do."

"Irritate, Miss Cat?"

"Don't call me Cat. My name is Catalina."

"Is it?"

"Is yours really Taylor Canton?"

The last two questions were spoken softly, dangerously, both trying to probe weaknesses, and both recognizing the tactic of the other.

"I would swear to it on a Bible," Marsh said, his mouth quirking.

"I'm surprised you have one, or know what one is."

"I had a very good upbringing, Miss Cat." He emphasized the last word.

"And then what happened?" she asked caustically.

The sardonic amusement in his eyes faded. "A great deal. And what is your story?"

Dear God, his voice was mesmerizing. An intimate song that said nothing but wanted everything. Low and deep and provocative. Compelling. And irresistible. Almost.

"I had a very poor upbringing," she said. "And then a great deal happened."

For the first time since she'd met him, she saw real humor in his eyes. Not just that cynical amusement as if he were some higher being looking down on a world inhabited by silly children. "You're the first woman I've met with fewer scruples than my own," he said, admiration again in his voice.

She opened her eyes wide. "You have some?"

"As I told you that first night, I don't usually mistreat women."

"Usually?"

"Unless provoked."

"A threat, Mr. Canton?"

"I never threaten, Miss Cat. Neither do I turn down challenges."

"And you usually win?"

"Not usually, Miss Cat. Always." The word was flat. Almost ugly in its surety.

"So do I," she said complacently.

Their voices, Cat knew, had lowered into little more than husky whispers. The air in the closed carriage was sparking, hissing, crackling. Threatening to ignite. His hand moved to her arm, his fingers running up and down it in slow, caressingly sensuous trails.

And then the heat surrounding them was as intense as that in the heart of a volcano. Intense and violent. She wondered very briefly if this was a version of hell. She had just decided it was when he bent toward her, his lips brushing over hers.

And heaven and hell collided.

CHAPTER 10

The kiss had been as inevitable as day following night.

Marsh had known it from the moment he saw her in the Glory Hole.

The only way in hell to get her out of his system was this, and he was deadly determined to accomplish it. He'd hoped that the fireworks which constantly surrounded them would prove to be nothing more than a brief flurry of sound and fury, signifying nothing.

He hoped Shakespeare would forgive him for his literary liberties, but the diversion helped in reestablishing some kind of equilibrium.

Until his lips touched hers.

He hadn't really known what to expect. Ice that would cool the damned heat burning him inside out? Emptiness that would swallow his unexpected and disturbing need?

But there was no ice. No emptiness.

He knew she was as unwilling a participant as he in the damnable attraction, the veritable hurricane of desire that engulfed them. It was explosive, filled with the hot expectancy of a pending lethal storm. Her lips, at first reluctant, wary, suddenly yielded, yet he knew she wasn't surrendering. Instead, he suspected, their mutual astonishment stunned her into a certain acceptance. He wanted to explore, to taste, to test. Even savor the currents of hot pleasure that surged through him.

He felt her arms go around him, just as his had wrapped her tightly against him. Gingerly at first. Even reluctantly, but inevitably, as if some force propelled her against her will. He felt every movement in her body, every quiver, every stiffening awareness as his own arousal pressed into her. How long had it been since he'd felt this alive? Had he ever felt like this before . . . even before war, and hate and revenge had robbed him of feeling?

A low moan rumbled through his body as, unaccountably, his mouth gentled in a way it hadn't since long, long ago. It was new, so new, so enticing, this very odd tenderness. He didn't understand where it came from, where it had been lurking to emerge at this damnably inconvenient time. Still, it was . . . pleasant. More than pleasant as their lips explored this strange new sensation. Some instinct told him it was as new and strange to her as it was to him.

Her mouth opened hesitantly under his lips, greeting him with an unexpected longing that he felt straight through to his core, and his tongue ran knowingly over the sensitive crevices of her mouth. He lifted his head slightly, his gaze moving to her eyes, and he was almost lost in the smoldering green of them, even as he sensed the hostility that was still there.

He closed his eyes against them, against the confused yet heated emotion in them, and his lips hardened against hers. He forced anger. He forced it because he didn't know how to deal with the tenderness. He forced it because he *was* angry, angry that she was stirring things best left alone, angry because he knew he couldn't trust her. She was the woman who had had him beaten, almost shanghaied, who caused his imprisonment in a filthy cage. His kiss became harsh and bitter. Punishing.

He opened his eyes and saw hers flare in apprehension, and he deepened the kiss, demanding in a physical way. Yet he still felt her response, unwilling now, and he took a sudden cruel pleasure in the fact that she was as helpless against this goddamn attraction as he was.

The swaying of the carriage turning a corner threw them hard against each other, and he was aware again of that faint scent of flowers he'd noticed the night before. She was one of the few women who didn't overdo, but allowed the elusiveness of the scent she applied to tantalize rather than overpower.

God, but she was beautiful. And soft. So damned soft.

His lust reached monumental proportions as he felt the surge of heat reach his loins. Christ, he hadn't meant this to happen. He'd wanted to punish in some way for those ten days, indignity and pain in jail. He'd recognized her physical reaction to him, and he'd wanted to tease and tempt and make her beg for more. But he was the one who would soon be begging, damn her. His lips tightened almost brutally against her as he tried to regain control. But the intended punishment, the hard demanding lips against hers, seemed no punishment at all, because it only stoked the fires in him and, he sensed, in her.

As if they needed any stoking. They were like match and kindling together. No, more like fire and dynamite.

His fingers went to her face, wanting to touch the smooth perfection, to go beyond the mask, and he felt her tremble.

Anguish coursed through him. A kind of anguish he hadn't felt in years. There was something about this contact, something more than physical lust that made him ache with yearning.

Christ, what was happening?

You don't even like her, he told himself.

But his hands wanted to do gentle as well as violent things, and he had to hold himself back. He could not betray this weakness to her. She would take that weakness and use it . . . as he would do to her.

After the one time in his life he'd lost his self-control, he had spent the rest of his life honing it. He always had been able to distance himself from events; even his participation as a principal in them was somehow apart, as if he were standing aside and watching himself.

But he was not standing away now, not any part of him. Every sense was engaged, every nerve that had been numb for so long was tingling.

His hand moved to her breast, fondling it through the cloth and stays. His fingers moved up to where the skin was unprotected except for the starched cotton of her blouse. Heat radiated through the material, and he started to caress her shoulders, his fingers making their way under the material as his lips moved from her mouth to nibble at the soft, vulnerable part of her neck. He felt shivers run through her body. He felt similar spasms rock his body, and his hands became even more invasive, one starting to unbutton the blouse in back.

His other hand slipped down farther underneath the cloth, under the stay until his fingers found the soft flesh of her breast. It was firm, so firm, the nipple erect with excitement.

She suddenly wrenched away with a little cry, staring at him with a kind of horror that stunned him into stillness. For the first time since he'd met her, he saw fear and vulnerability in her that struck him like a blacksmith's hammer.

He was used to seeing fear in people's eyes, in men's eyes and even women's. Christ, he'd lived practically his entire life stoking that fear. But not a woman he'd been kissing. And the last person he'd expected to reflect the kind of terror he was witnessing now was San Francisco's Ice

Queen. He'd wanted to incite need in her; he'd wanted to shatter the cool, remote perfection she affected.

He hadn't wanted this.

He watched her fight for control. He should feel satisfaction, but he didn't, only an even greater emptiness that he inspired this kind of terror. He knew, dammit, that she'd responded to him, that she'd been as aware as he of the physical attraction between them.

So he watched her with narrowed eyes, wondering if this was some kind of game, even as his intuition told him it was not. No one could manage that look of humiliation she wore or struggle so gallantly to hide it. He half expected an explosion of abuse, of blame, but it didn't come. But then she seldom did the expected; it was part of his fascination with her.

She put on her usual controlled expression. He silently applauded, sensing it had not been easy, especially when he saw the glint of chagrin in her eyes. She had shown a weakness, and he knew he was probably the last person in the world to whom she wished to do that.

"That was a mistake," she said.

"Yours or mine?" His question was cool, as unemotional as the expression on her face, although his body was still caught in the storm of physical need, aching unmercifully.

"Mine. I should never have come with you."

"I didn't give you any choice."

"I always have a choice, Mr. Canton."

He leaned back against the seat of the carriage, surveying her ruthlessly. "I would suspect that once you didn't."

"You know nothing, Mr. Canton."

"I know you responded to me. I didn't imagine that passion. I'm just not sure why you suddenly—"

"Ah, you're not sure of something. What a surprise."

She was trying to divert him. He knew that, and he had no intention of letting it happen, not when spasms of want still raked his body.

"The icy Miss Catalina," he said in a silky voice. "Fire and ice. Exactly what are you?"

"Nothing for you."

"That's not what you were telling me minutes ago. You wanted me every bit as much as I wanted you."

"Male arrogance," she said superciliously. "You're not nearly as . . . interesting as you seem to think you are."

He raised an eyebrow. "No? Let's try it again."

Marsh didn't give her a chance to protest. He pulled her over to him, ignoring her struggle as his lips feathered softly over her face before reaching her lips, tempting them to open.

She resisted longer than she had before, but in only a few moments she stopped fighting him. Instead she tried to keep herself cold, but then his mouth gentled, and the smoldering fire flamed again, and she couldn't prevent her own surrender.

He waited just long enough to make his point, and then, summoning all his self-control, he pulled back, ignoring the throbbing of his body.

"Damn you," she said.

"Didn't anyone ever tell you what happens to little girls who lie?"

"Or tell you what happens to big boys who are arrogant bullies?"

He chuckled mirthlessly. "They get shanghaied?"

She didn't blink. "That's a thought."

"I wouldn't try it," he warned softly, "again."

"If I had intended for you to be shanghaied, you would be on your way to China."

"Just beaten and jailed, then?"

"Do you always talk in riddles, Mr. Canton?"

He wished she didn't look so damn beautiful when she was angry. "We could call a truce, Miss Cat." He hadn't meant to make the offer. She had started this war; he had lost only one in his life—and he hadn't really lost that one, others had. He certainly had not surrendered.

"No," she said flatly. "I've worked too hard to build the Silver Slipper."

"So the war continues."

She shrugged. "Call it what you will."

"No more ambushes, Miss Cat."

"Who was it that said war is hell?"

He raised her chin with a gentle touch of his fingers. "A northern general, I think. But you know nothing of hell, Miss Cat."

"And you do?" The sparks were there again, darting back and forth like heat lightning in a Texas August. Energy pulsed between them. Dare and counterdare. Thrust and counterthrust. Each searching out weaknesses. He moved his fingers along her jaw, watching as her cheeks turned from ivory to rose.

"Don't touch me," she said, jerking away.

"Why, Miss Cat? Does it disturb you? Burn you?"

It did, but Cat wasn't going to admit it. She felt like a rabbit hypnotized by the unblinking stare of a snake. If only her body didn't react in such unfamiliar ways. If only she didn't want to reach out and touch him. If only she didn't remember the moment of sweetness when his lips first touched hers. That moment was so rare and gentle. And she'd responded in a way unfathomable to her.

"I don't like you, Mr. Canton."

"I don't think I asked if you liked me."

"Take me back to town."

"Not quite yet."

"Exactly what do you want?"

He leaned back and took a cheroot from his shirt pocket, then some matches from his trousers. Without asking her permission, he lit the cheroot and inhaled deeply, sending out lazy smoke rings to bounce against the ceiling of the carriage. "Do you have any idea what a jail cell is like?"

His eyes were no longer smoldering, but like mirrors again, reflecting rather than revealing. The mouth was grim, and Cat had a sudden urge to put her finger alongside it.

"No," she said, "but I suspect you have more than once."

"*Only* once, Miss Catalina. And it wasn't much larger than this carriage, and not nearly as comfortable. I always give back in good measure what I get. I'm making this one exception."

"Another warning?"

"A promise."

She bristled. Catalina hadn't apologized to anyone in a number of years. "You don't belong here, Mr. Canton."

He raised an eyebrow. "Where do I belong?" He really wanted to know.

Cat swallowed. There was just a hint of wistfulness in his question. Not enough to invoke sympathy. Enough to be intriguing. She remembered again that very brief illusion of gentleness. Her imagination? It had to be.

"Where did you come from?" She didn't expect an answer.

He shrugged carelessly. "A place that no longer exists."

She knew she shouldn't have asked the question. She didn't want to know. The conversation was too personal. She didn't want to like him, or feel the slightest interest. She just wanted him to disappear. She wanted the Silver Slipper back the way it had been. She wanted her life back too. No complications. She wanted to be respected. She wanted to be rich. She wanted to . . . be safe. Which meant to be alone.

Alone. The word had never hurt before. It had always represented paradise. Why not now?

You can't trust him. You can't trust any man, her inner voice whispered. Except maybe Teddy.

"I want to go back," she said again, and she despised the catch in her voice.

"Coward."

"I just don't like the company."

"But I do, and right now I'm in control."

"I'll have you arrested for kidnapping."

He moved his fingers across the skin of her arms. "Then I might as well make it worthwhile."

The warmth of his touch made her skin prickle, made those internal woman parts ache again with longing. And in pure reflex, she slapped him. She gasped. Dear God, she had done what she had vowed never to do again: attack another human being. As the stunned look on his face registered, she remembered another face. Scenes came tumbling back, like pieces of paper caught in a windstorm. . . .

And she was back in a cold, dirty little room.

The gloating sneer on her husband's face turned to stunned surprise as the object in her hand ripped into him. "Lizzie . . . ," he said as he stumbled back, his hand grasping the table in their room.

"No more," she heard herself whisper. "I'll never do it again. Never."

He reached out for her as he fell to his knees. "You can't get away from me, Lizzie. Never . . . you little whore."

She backed away from him, from the blood splattering the floor of the cheap rented room. He moved toward her on his knees, his hand still reaching for her like the obscene talon of a vulture. She took a step back, and then she was against the wall, and there was no place to go.

The stunned look on his face was replaced by pure hate, even a certain glee.

*A few inches. That was all she had. She
looked frantically for escape. His hand caught
the bottom of her dress and then her ankle. In
desperation she reached out, her nails ripping
trails in his face. He cursed as his hand went to
his face, and then he seemed to lose his balance.
He fell, his chest hitting the floor, driving the
knife in deeper. . . .*

Marsh's first response to the slap was to
grab her wrist. He wanted to shake her. If she
wasn't a woman, he would. Then saw her face.
It had gone white as paper. Her eyes, those magnificent eyes, were stark with terror. He doubted
if she even knew he was beside her. She was
someplace else, someplace that was vividly alive
in her mind.

His anger bled away. "Catalina," he said
softly. But she didn't seem to hear.

"Catalina," he repeated a little louder, and
her eyes moved as if she was trying to focus.

"Cat!" His voice was still low, but now it
was insistent, demanding, and he watched her
shake her head as if to shake away demons.

He wanted to reassure her in some way,
though he didn't know how. Christ, it had been
twenty years since he had comforted anyone.
Even longer ago than that. When his sister had
been bitten by a hurt raccoon she was trying to
rescue from a trap. He'd had to kill it because it
had been too injured to save. She had looked at
him as if he were a monster. The pain then had
been raw, for she had always adored him and
thought he could do no wrong. It was weeks before their father had convinced her that killing
the raccoon had been the merciful thing to do.

He felt like that monster again. Christ, he *had* meant what he had told her during that first meeting. He would never intentionally hurt a woman. This had been a contest, one in which she'd seemed a willing participant. His throat tightened as he tried once more to call her back.

"Catalina." This time his voice was soft, coaxing, and he saw her blink. Her lips trembled slightly as he watched her visibly gather her wits. She had inched into the corner of the carriage. Now, gradually, she relaxed. Life came back into her face; so did awareness of everything he'd probably seen.

The carriage came to a stop, providing both of them with a reason, or excuse, to say nothing. The silence, however, was heavy with unspoken emotions.

Marsh tore his gaze from her and opened the door. He stepped out, taking a deep breath. And then he reached out a hand to her. She stared at the red splotch on his face where her hand had connected.

He grinned suddenly, and it was a very real smile, unlike any she'd seen, and she almost melted with its impact. "You have a very good right."

She wondered whether her face had revealed anything to him. It must have been only an instant, that memory. He was the kind of man who would take advantage of any weakness he found, picking at it like a vulture. He wasn't doing so. Obviously he hadn't found out a thing about her.

She ignored his hand and stepped down. She recognized the place. It was a cliff overlooking the ocean, one she had visited often. Rocks broke the sea below, turning it into many colors of blue highlighted by white foam. The sky was ribbed with the soft pastel colors of a sunset just beginning. In minutes it would darken, turn vivid with violent reds and golds so effulgent, they could make a heart ache as they reflected in the sea below.

It was beauty too strong not to hurt. And she knew she didn't want to share it with Canton. She could share it with no one.

There had been too many intimacies with this man, making too many cracks in the world she had built. She could afford no more. She would never depend on a man again, would never really trust one, or herself. She could trust on an impersonal level, as she did Teddy and even her second husband, Ben Abbott. But never again in an intense, emotional way. Her judgment was too faulty.

And Canton, of all men, was more dangerous than most. His ruthlessness equaled hers; his mesmerizing attraction for her was threatening. He gazed no longer on her but on the sea.

She wished she knew what he was thinking, but he was as unreadable as always.

"I have to get back," she said again.

He turned then and studied her, the golden glow of the sunset forming a halo around his head. Her legs trembled as she remembered her first impression of him . . . a fallen archangel, God's favorite who had fallen from grace. Lucifer the rebel. She'd heard enough hellfire sermons from itinerant preachers who had frequented the mining towns to pick up biblical references, and she had chosen "sweet Lucifer" as her favorite oath, in lieu of less acceptable ones she'd learned as a child. She had certainly never expected to *meet* her "curse."

"I'm not sure *I'm* ready to return," he said at last.

"I'll walk, then," she said.

"But I wouldn't be a gentleman if I allowed you to walk."

She turned back. "I would call you many things, but a gentleman isn't one of them."

His white teeth shone bright in his sun-browned face. "Considering the circumstances, I have been the epitome of restraint and gracious manners."

She disputed the statement with one rather pointed glare.

He ignored it, offered his arm. "Shall we go?"

Fuming, but sensing this was one battle she wouldn't win, she shrugged, ignored his arm, and climbed back into the carriage.

Canton smiled. "Something to remember, Miss Cat. I always finish what I start."

"So do I," she said softly. "So do I."

CHAPTER 11

Marsh hadn't dreamed in a long time. He sometimes wondered whether he'd simply willed dreams away, or whether he'd just become too empty to have them.

But when he woke at dawn the day after the ride with Catalina, he had traveled through several dreams, and he remembered every one in vivid detail.

He was back at Rosewood, the Canton plantation in Georgia, before the war. He even remembered the occasion, a Christmas ball, one of many social events given by his parents in hopes of creating opportunities for making desirable matches for their two sons and one daughter, all of whom were of, or nearing, marriageable age. Marsh had returned from law school at the University of Georgia, and his older brother had already taken up permanent residence at home, assuming more and more of the day-to-day duties of running Rosewood, which one day would be his.

Lanterns hung in the trees lining the road up to the main house, and the house itself was fragrant with the smell of pine and spices. Overnight guests had filled the rooms with talk and laughter despite the war clouds on the horizon. Marsh had taken shameless pleasure in a way of life he treasured. Love was as much a part of his life as air to breathe.

He and his mother played the piano on request, once joining in a duet while his sister, Melissa, sang in a sweet, pure voice. And then he and his mother dueled on the piano, much to the delight of the onlookers. She would play a melody, and he would elaborate on it, then they would reverse roles, each taking the other's melody and embellishing it. The ability to hear music and then play from ear was a talent only he of the children had inherited from her. She had also taught him to read sheet music, and he knew many of the classics from memory.

He had often thought that his mother could have been a concert pianist. She'd once encouraged him in that direction, but his own interests were too varied to devote himself entirely to music. But he enjoyed it, enjoyed the rare talent he knew he had.

The ball that year had been even more gay than usual. The specter of war made it so. His mother had banished talk of a possible conflict, but it was on everyone's mind. A current of fear and excitement ran through every conversation, every flirtation.

Even he was caught in the frenzy of expectation. He was twenty-one, and he would live forever. In the meantime, the prospect of war gave him reason to snatch forbidden kisses and fondle more than was permissible. He met any rebuke with a tragic look. . . .

Margaret. Annie Laurie. How many others? How many names forgotten?

And his sister Melissa had looked so pretty at sixteen. So eager and so full of life. He'd always protected her, had always relished his role as big brother.

Then the figures seemed to fade during the dream, to become little more than wisps of fog. He reached out to keep them with him, but there was only cold air where they had once laughed and danced.

Life had held promise then. Gracious and comfortable and so damn good. He had buried thoughts of it. And with them that talent his mother had nurtured. He had not touched a piano since the war, not until he'd entered the Glory Hole.

He knew exactly why. Who and what he was today had nothing to do with that former life. He didn't even recognize that boy who'd played so well. And his mother with all her laughing kindness would have been horrified at the son she'd raised to honor the best things in life: music and books and kindness. Well, kindness had been banished from his soul long ago, replaced by cold, hard vengeance that had systematically destroyed every good thing in him.

Marsh closed his eyes and swore. He felt warm breath on his hand and opened his eyes again. Winchester sat next to his bed, apparently wakened by his companion's fitfulness. Solemn brown eyes stared at him as a scarred ear cocked. Marsh stretched out a hand, and the dog backed away.

"Suspicious bastard, aren't you? And rightfully so."

Still, he was uncommonly grateful to the animal. For a moment, anyway, the dog had banished the ghosts. "Hungry, huh? I think there might be some beef."

Gratitude was obviously not one of Winchester's attributes. He kept on staring.

"Don't," Marsh warned. "This is a temporary arrangement. Two renegades hooked up temporarily. Nothing more."

The dog seemed satisfied enough with the arrangement. He rose from his haunches, padded toward the closed door, then waited.

Marsh glared for a moment, trying to remember letting the dog in. But he didn't. And then he remembered the almost silent ride back to the city with Cat, his accompanying Jenny on the piano last night, and finally getting drunk. He *never* got drunk.

His gaze went to the table, where a bottle stood nearly empty. At least he'd had enough sense to drink by himself, out of sight of anyone who might see it as a weakness. Which it was, he admitted to himself. One he had no intention of repeating.

Hell. A damn dog. Getting drunk. Dreams. He didn't like any of it.

Damn. *She* was responsible.

His seduction had failed yesterday. But perhaps not entirely. She had kissed him back. She *did* feel something, however much she resisted that feeling. He'd just taken things too fast.

Slow and easy, he told himself. Very slow and easy. And then rip her from your mind. He was convinced that once he bedded her, he could do exactly that. A woman had never held his interest longer than a night in bed. Never.

Teddy looked down at the circular in his hands. The woman pictured there was Molly.

A thousand-dollar reward was offered for information about Mary Beth Adams, the daughter of Edwin Adams of Oakland. According to the circular, the girl had disappeared under mysterious circumstances, perhaps kidnapped.

He'd picked it up in the general store. The proprietor had said a man who claimed he was a private detective had left it there. He could be reached at the Jefferson Hotel.

The drawing was not good. He crushed the paper in his hands, wishing he knew what she was running from. A thousand dollars. That was a lot of money. Her family must care about her. But then why was she hiding?

Several explanations darted through his mind. A baby, perhaps. Even a lover who had abandoned her. Neither explained the stark fear he sometimes saw in her eyes. And if she had been with child, it would be obvious by now.

Should he show her the circular? Warn her? Or would it make her run? He felt gutshot at the thought.

Teddy decided to show the circular to Cat. Cat would know what to do. She always did. And then he paused in midstride. Or did she? She had not been herself lately. He didn't want to bother her with something else, not now that she was fighting so hard to keep the Silver Slipper competitive.

His gaze went back down to the circular. Molly. He'd never thought that name fit her. But Mary Beth did. It had a sweet sound on his tongue. Soft. Vulnerable. Too vulnerable.

He wouldn't bother Catalina with the circular. Perhaps he would go to Oakland himself. Make inquiries of his own about this Edwin Adams.

"Oakland?" Catalina stared at Teddy. He'd never before asked for time off, had never seemed to have any personal life other than the Silver Slipper. She'd never really thought about it before. She'd learned to take his dependability and loyalty for granted.

Now she felt a stab of guilt at doing so. Had she really closed herself off so much that she was oblivious of the feelings of those around her? She'd tried to be a good employer, to pay decent wages, but she had been reluctant to go beyond that.

She focused on Teddy. "Of course," she said. "Is there anything I can do?"

He shook his head. "Just personal business."

His answer hurt her, although she knew it shouldn't. She really hadn't invited confidences, much less given any. She nodded. "Take as long as you need."

"I should be back before those Frenchies arrive," he said with a twinkle in his eye.

"Do you need any money?"

He shook his head and then looked toward the steps. "But keep an eye on Molly, if you will. Don't let her out alone."

"Is there something I should know?"

"Just that she's afraid of something. Or someone."

"I'll make sure someone's always with her," she said. "Wilhelmina really likes her. I'll ask her to stay with Molly. She'll be safe here."

He nodded. "I'll be back as soon as I can." He hesitated. "I saw you return yesterday with the owner of the Glory Hole." He had said nothing yesterday, not after seeing the sparks in her eyes and her flushed cheeks. "He didn't—"

"Of course not," Cat said. "He just wanted to . . . to talk. I told him there was nothing to talk about."

"You know our business has improved since he opened. . . ."

Her green eyes flashed fire again. "It won't forever," she said shortly. "You know what happened that first time someone opened the Glory Hole."

He did. The owner had cut his prices down

to nothing. Cat had almost lost the Silver Slipper, trying to bring back customers lured by low prices and gambling. It had been Teddy who'd discovered the gambling was crooked and hired several thugs to make a scene. The Glory Hole soon closed, but Cat had never forgotten that lesson. She'd installed her own gambling equipment, making sure, the games were honest. And she vowed then that she wouldn't risk her future again, no matter what she had to do. No one else had had a chance. She made sure everyone remembered the old stories. Each time the Glory Hole reopened, she'd paid the police to raid the place, to refuse permits.

And now it wasn't only business at stake, but her peace of mind. No one had ever shattered it like Taylor Canton.

Teddy's expression was inscrutable, and yet she had the peculiar feeling that he thought she was wrong.

"Just let me know if you need anything," she said in a voice that closed the discussion.

He left, knowing her well enough that any argument would probably only further strengthen her resolve.

San Francisco loved the cancan. So did Marsh.

He hated to admit it but booking the dance into the Silver Slipper was a brilliant stroke on the part of Miss Catalina Hilliard. He was attracted by the exuberance and the color of the dance. He admired the flashes of leg shown so frequently by the dancers.

But he couldn't help but wonder whether

Catalina's legs would put them all to shame. He still couldn't guess her age but, with the information he'd gathered in the last several days, knew she had to be in her late thirties. According to Quinn Devereux, she arrived in San Francisco nearly seventeen years before, not long after the Devereuxs themselves had come to the city.

He could glean few other details from either Quinn or his attorney. San Francisco apparently took great pride in ignoring pasts; too many residents had backgrounds they didn't particularly wish examined. It was an attitude for which he was grateful, with the exception of Miss Catalina Hilliard. The mystery of Cat.

Marsh had never been in a city like this one. Whereas most towns took great pride in talking about scandals or ostracizing those who violated their mores, San Francisco honored its citizens' privacy and treasured its characters. The more bizarre they were, the greater the collective fondness. Emperor Norton was a prime example; at every theatrical performance three front-row seats were reserved for the "emperor" and his two mongrel dogs. The self-declared emperor, whose privately printed "royal currency" was accepted throughout the city, was a bit of a madman who had once sent a telegram to President Lincoln, ordering him to marry the widowed Queen Victoria in an effort to bring peace to a nation on the brink of war. But his every undertaking in his empire of fantasy was meant for the good of mankind in general. San Franciscans therefore not only tolerated him but became his royal subjects.

On the evening of the opening of the cancan, Marsh accepted Cat's invitation and attended in evening clothes made just for the occasion. Knowing that reporters from every newspaper in town would be present, he intended to make every bit the appearance she had. Their public feud and one-upmanship had spurred business at both saloons. And now that he felt relatively safe with the name Taylor Canton and the very long distance from his "Duel at Sunset" notoriety, he found himself taking pride in building a thriving business—and irritating Miss Hilliard.

Greeting her, he bowed elegantly, taking her hand and bringing it to his mouth. "You are very lovely tonight," he said, meaning it.

She looked at him with suspicion, but he merely smiled complacently, though it was difficult. He had kept away from her for the past week, ever since he had handed her down in front of the Silver Slipper after their carriage ride, and she had sniffed disdainfully as she turned on her heel and disappeared inside.

He'd played the piano each night after the last customer and employee had left, when he thought no one was listening. Only Winchester was there to hear; the misbegotten mongrel would sit next to the piano with his head tipped, and his half ear cocked. Marsh was never sure whether it was his playing or the prospect of food that kept him there. But the company had been unexpectedly welcome.

Marsh had warned himself to keep away from Cat, to allow her anger to fade before he renewed his campaign. Also, if he was entirely honest, to give himself some time to rebuild his defenses. She had affected him in extraordinary ways that day on the cliff. And he had no intention of allowing that again.

She led him to a table, aware of the sensation they both made. He seated her with a flourish as the music began. The troupe included its own small group of musicians, and its enthusiasm more than substituted for size. Marsh found his foot tapping as six very pretty women, dressed in red flounced dresses, ran on stage. The Silver Slipper itself was full of motion: clapping hands and feet and whoops of approval. The gambling apparatus had been moved out; the hostesses were dressed in costumes similar to the dancers. The audience was all male—the cancan apparently considered to risqué for the proper ladies of San Francisco.

Marsh tried to concentrate on the dancers, but Cat kept drawing his attention. Her face was flushed with triumph, and he wanted her as he'd never wanted before. Her success was suddenly his success, her excitement his.

What idiocy!

She was out for his blood.

He moved suddenly, his knee touching hers. She jerked away just as the applause died down after the dancers had run off the stage, and her hand hit her champagne glass. Champagne splashed Marsh's shirt and dinner jacket.

Cat flushed and fumbled with her napkin.

"You should keep your knees to yourself," she whispered.

"An accident," Marsh said with a shrug. "And I think you owe me a new suit."

"Nonsense," she said. "A few drops of water should be sufficient to repair—"

"I thought you treated your customers with more consideration."

She glared at him. "I'll . . . see to it."

"Now!" he demanded with a twisted grin. "I'm a little damp."

"You can always leave."

"Such hospitality," he chided her. "Surely you wouldn't allow a guest to leave in this condition. Not in front of everyone, not without making amends of some kind."

"All right," she said. "As soon as the music starts." They had already made a spectacle of themselves. She tried to put on a concerned but pleasant smile.

"Upstairs?" His eyes were more than a little suggestive.

She bit the side of her lip, one of the few uncertain reactions he'd seen her make. He savored it.

A waiter returned with some towels, and she stiffly gave several to Marsh to soak up the champagne in his lap.

He grinned again. "I think *you* should do it."

She glared at him again. "Don't overplay it, Mr. Canton," she warned in a low voice. "Or you might find a whole bottle in your lap."

The music started again, and the dancers came back, drawing the attention of the audience to the stage and away from them.

Cat smiled graciously and rose. "Come with me," she said. She swore to herself. This was to have been a night highlighting her new entertainment, not herself and the upstart from across the street.

Despite Teddy's assurances days ago, he had not yet returned, though she had received a telegram saying he should be back tomorrow. She led her nemesis to Teddy's room across from the kitchen, and used a match to light the oil lamp there.

She watched as Canton took stock of the room. It was plain and masculine. A bed, table, and trunk. A small bureau and mirror.

"Your watchdog's," Canton said pleasantly.

Catalina bristled. "Teddy is much more than that."

Canton raised his eyebrow with a certain insinuation, and Catalina felt an unusual defensiveness. "He manages the Silver Slipper," she said tartly. "Silver Slipper Hugh manages . . ." She immediately realized her slip and hoped it went unnoticed as she went back to the door. "I'll get some water."

But Canton caught her wrist. "'Just as Hugh manages . . . '? Do finish the sentence, Miss Catalina. I didn't realize you knew Hugh O'Connell."

"I know a lot of people in San Francisco," she said icily. "They come to the Silver Slipper."

"Somehow Hugh doesn't seem like your usual customer."

"I don't have a *usual* customer. The Silver Slipper appeals to everyone."

"Really?" he drawled, angry that his suspicions about Hugh had been confirmed. He wasn't angry at Cat, though; he was angry at himself. He had started to like Hugh and had been hoping he had been wrong.

She tried to shake her wrist free as she

looked up at him directly, challenging him to say something more, to make an accusation. He felt the delicacy of her wrist, so slender yet strong. He didn't want to let go.

Cat tried to break free again. "If you want me to do something about those stains before they set, you'd better let me go."

He released her, eyeing her lazily. "Hurry back, Miss Cat."

The door slammed behind her. The champagne had stained both his dinner jacket and his linen shirt as well as his cravat. It would be difficult, he mused for her to clean them while on his body. As for his trousers . . .

With a wicked grin on his face, he started to undress.

CHAPTER 12

◆━━◦⬦◦━━◆

Cat balanced the bowl of water carefully and nudged open the door. She nearly dropped the bowl. She was no child to blanch at the sight of a man without a shirt. Yet her heart seemed to stop, and her gaze unwillingly went directly to his bare chest and remained there. It was magnificent . . . and battered.

She saw at least three scars, one long and jagged down his side, the other two small and puckered, obviously bullet wounds.

Canton followed her gaze. "A saber," he said. "During the war."

"The others?"

He shrugged. "Bullet wounds."

"Also during the war?"

"No," he said flatly, his dark eyes obviously watching for her reaction.

"Should I ask which side you fought for?"

He grinned unexpectedly. "Why the correct side, or course."

"Was that the winning side or the losing side?"

"I suppose it's all in the way you look at it."

"You enjoy talking in riddles, don't you? A way of protecting yourself?" she asked shrewdly.

The grin disappeared. "Perhaps. As you use the Ice Queen pose, shall we say?" He moved toward her, all lean, lethal, masculine perfection. "We both know you're not cold."

True. No one knew that better than she as the temperature in the room spiraled upward at least ten degrees with each step he took. She couldn't control herself, much less the man who was approaching.

She tried. "Where's your shirt?" The question was full of a bravado she didn't feel. She congratulated herself for keeping the quiver from her voice.

"On the bed," he said. She didn't realize three words could convey so much invitation. He grinned. "I was considering taking off my trousers."

She knew she was being baited and ignored the comment, even if she couldn't ignore him.

She started to ease herself around him, and to her surprise he allowed it, moving just a little to the side, but not enough that she didn't have to brush by him, her chin almost touching his chest.

She noticed that oddly enough, his chest hair was sandy-colored, not the near black of the hair on his head. Enticing little tendrils curled against a chest that looked as hard as a washboard—but ever so much more inviting. His dark formal trousers were tailored to a snug fit around his lean waist and muscled thighs. Her gaze moved upward, stopping at the jagged scar, and she found herself yearning to touch it, to absorb some of the pain that once had been there.

It was insane! She clasped the bowl tighter before setting it down on the table, along with a towel she carried on her arm. Ignoring him, she dampened the towel and picked up his shirt. It smelled of him, of musk and soap and danger. Trying to ignore him, she sat down at the table and scrubbed furiously on the linen cloth, but the faint gold stains resisted.

She bit her lip. She wanted him gone. From this room, from the Silver Slipper, from San Francisco. From her consciousness.

But he was too real to disappear. Too vibrant.

She scrubbed harder.

"An exercise in futility? Would you like to try the trousers?" He accommodatingly started to unbutton the fly.

Cat thrust the shirt at him. "No need. The Silver Slipper will pay for a new suit."

"Not necessary," he said, suddenly deciding he had gone far enough. He didn't want to chase her away again. His hands relaxed at his sides. "Just watching you scrub is recompense enough. I'm glad I'm not that shirt."

A roar of approval came from the other

room, and then loud applause that almost shook the walls.

He smiled. "Your cancan is a great success."

The smile seemed to make him even more attractive, more . . . human. She wasn't sure she wanted him to be human. "It was expensive," she admitted suddenly, surprising herself. But, then, he would most certainly know that already.

He held out his hand to her, and she placed the shirt in it. The shirt wasn't what he wanted, she knew, but she wasn't prepared to give him any more. A dimple suddenly showed in one of his cheeks as he accepted it. "It's wet," he observed. "I don't think I want to put it back on."

Now she raised an eyebrow. "Are you going out there like that?"

"Not if you have a better suggestion."

"There's a back door," she said helpfully.

"That's not a better suggestion," he retorted, his smile broadening into a grin.

Cat knew she shouldn't spar with him. He was much too dangerous for that. She knew exactly how dangerous, as his hand allowed the shirt to fall to the floor and reached for hers, pulling her to him. Insistently.

And then her body was pressed to his chest, her cheek against his bare skin, her velvet dress suddenly crackling with electricity from his body. He felt so good. Smelled so good.

She had seen so many bodies, but she had never been attracted to one before. And his body was like a furnace, his heart beating like a big bass drum she'd seen in parades. Strong and steady and hypnotic.

Cat felt dazed. "I'll get you one of Teddy's shirts," she finally managed to say. But she couldn't force herself to pull away as she knew she should.

There was a mob of people right outside. And she didn't care. All the fear, all the distaste, all the horror inspired by men who came too close, suddenly disappeared. There was nothing at this moment but his head bending down to meet hers, those sensuous lips playing with hers with such violent delicacy—two incompatible words, she would have thought before meeting this man.

But even as he obviously reined back the violence from a kiss that he tried to make tender, she felt it radiate in the shiver that ran the length of his body. The kiss deepened as their lips melded in eager contest. Not surrender. She knew instinctively that she could never surrender to this man, or he would overwhelm her. And crush her. As he would anyone who stood in his way.

But dear Lucifer, what he did to her!

Cat found herself responding in ways she never thought she could, her hands going eagerly around his neck, her body swaying against his, her mouth seeking to take him deeper. She felt his swelling manhood against her, and that strange yearning that had been plaguing her intensified.

She felt weak and strong. Happy and immeasurably sad. So this was what being alive meant! But it was too late. It had come far too late and most certainly with absolutely the wrong person.

But she didn't want to give it up. Not now. Was it so wrong . . . these few moments?

His lips slipped away, and her head somehow relaxed against his chest. She felt his own head rest on her hair, heard his soft sigh, felt his arms circling her with a gentleness she hadn't expected.

It was insidious. He was a master seducer.

But so pleasant. So incredibly warm and pleasant. She swallowed deep against a need that had nothing to do with the physical craving that was so strong. For the first time in her life, she felt protected.

She knew it was deceptive. That he represented exactly the opposite of safety. But she still couldn't tear herself away, ruin a magic moment.

Her gaze met his, and the darkness, the mirror that usually blanked his eyes, was pierced. A kind of hopelessness was in the cracks, a pain so strong, she felt as though she had been ripped apart.

She felt his chest quiver as he held her tightly, and watched his eyes dart away as if trying to hide what was lurking there. But it was too late.

He kissed her again, and the tenderness erupted once more into the explosiveness that inevitably haunted every physical exchange between them. Cat was stunned again by the way everything within her reacted. She shouldn't be . . . not now, not after those other encounters with this man had turned her ordered world inside out. She found herself doing the unthinkable, tracing her fingers along his back as if she couldn't get enough of him, even as his hands were digging themselves now in her hair, pulling it down from the sophisticated knot that had taken her nearly an hour to arrange. She felt her hair falling over her arms, falling in silken waves against his bare skin.

His eyes closed, and so did hers, and there was nothing between them now except a frantic need to finish what had been started.

Suddenly he stiffened, and slowly she emerged from the sweet haze of feeling, and she heard it too.

An insistent pounding on the door.

"Miss Catalina. Miss Catalina. Are you all right?" It was Harry's voice, her second bartender, who had apparently taken over Teddy's vigil.

Cat swallowed. She wasn't all right. She wondered whether she would ever be all right again. Like Pandora's box, Canton had released something she knew would be better locked away forever.

An ironic smile replaced the blatant sensuality on Canton's face. "You'd better answer, or we might have everyone from the saloon in here."

Cat suddenly realized how she must look. Hair tumbling down, dress mussed. The pounding came at the door again.

"It's all right," she said through the door. "I'll be out in a few moments."

"The mayor's here," Harry called.

"Sweet Lucifer!"

"I'll help you," Marsh said unexpectedly. "After all, it is *my* fault."

"Just dress," she said acidly.

"I don't have a dry shirt," he observed. "Or dry trousers," he added.

She went to the bureau and opened one of the drawers, feeling as if his eyes were burning a hole in her back. She found a white shirt Teddy used for special occasions and pulled it out. It wasn't the same quality as the one Canton had been wearing, and she knew it was much too large. Although he was a large man, he didn't have Teddy's bulk.

She thrust it into his hands, and before he could refuse, she turned and looked in the mirror. Her worst fears were realized. She looked like a schoolgirl caught out in the hay. Frustrated, she searched for a comb, but there was none. Teddy must have taken his with him.

"Are you quite sure you don't want me to repair your hair?" Canton's voice was silky. "*I* have a comb, and the mayor *is* waiting."

"You can give me the comb."

"Oh, no," he said. "But I suppose you could go through that crowd to get upstairs."

Cat gritted her teeth. If only he didn't sound so damnably smug. "All right," she finally said, noting that this was the second time he'd taken advantage, the first being that infernal carriage ride. But she couldn't stay here forever, and she couldn't leave with her hair in this state.

She'd think of a suitable reprisal. A riot at the Glory Hole would be nice.

In the meantime she glared at him while he pulled on Teddy's shirt, leaving it unbuttoned and looking even more tantalizing than before as he rolled up the sleeves.

He grinned at his victory. "Sit down," he ordered.

She obeyed. Anything to keep from looking at him. She felt the comb run through her hair, and then his fingers—every sweep slow and sensually indulgent.

Knowing.

Sweet Lucifer!

He stopped, and a moment went by. She felt her hair being lifted, twisted, and then it fell back down. There was another moment of silence.

She turned, and he looked a bit abashed, an expression unexpectedly endearing.

He shrugged. "I know how to comb," he said. "The other looked rather easy, but . . ."

Cat barely held back a smile. She felt unexpectedly good. He *couldn't* do everything. And also, she admitted to herself, she was rather pleased he didn't know more about dressing a woman's hair. She held out her hand, and he placed the comb in it.

Cat rose from the chair and went to the mirror. She watched him watching her as she started twisting up her hair. The pins were missing! And then she saw him kneeling, and he handed them to her with that slight smile that she was halfway coming to like.

It wasn't going to be as smooth as before, but then, she didn't have an hour to spend. But at least she didn't look like . . . well, like . . .

She turned slowly toward him. He was buttoning the shirt. It *was* too big, but he would look elegant in a sack.

Cat had expected him to try to accompany

her back to the table, and she had already formed several arguments. He surprised her.

"I'll go out the back way," he said. Without fixing his cravat, he pulled on his coat, his shirt still open at the neck. He looked pleasingly untidy. Black bristles darkened his chin slightly, and a thatch of hair fell over his forehead. He took her hand, lifting it to his lips. "I thank you for a very fascinating evening."

He went to the door and slipped out without another word, leaving her to stare at the opening, torn between relief and desolation.

You can't trust Canton.

Catalina knew that. The one time she had trusted had turned into disaster. And murder.

It hadn't taken Catalina long to discover that her supposed savior so many years ago had been her worst betrayer. And if she needed a reminder of his treachery, she only had to look in the mirror at the scars on her back made by James Cahoon's belt buckle when she had balked at servicing the men who had bested him in poker.

Would Teddy be back tomorrow? Or was it today? She missed him. Needed him. Perhaps he could bring some sanity back into her life.

Cat stood in the main room of the Silver Slipper. The last customer had left, the last glass had been washed. The girls had gone upstairs to bed. So had Molly, who had come down to help. Molly, too, missed Teddy.

She looked around the empty room, seeking the comfort she often found in knowing it belonged to her. Chairs were placed on tables so the floor could be mopped. In the glow of the one oil lamp still lit, they looked like skeletons in some macabre dance. Her hand went to one of the tables and clutched the edge of it.

Don't think about it. Don't think about those months of terror after James fell down on the knife. Murder. Murderess. She had run for her life ... changing her name frequently ... moving from one saloon to another because she didn't know anything else. She couldn't even read or write. But trouble followed her wherever she went. A drunken miner or cowhand wouldn't take no for an answer, and a fight would ensue. She would be asked to leave town, or the local law would put her on a stagecoach.

Until she reached a silver mine in Utah ... and Ben Abbott. Ben had come west years earlier because of his sick lungs, and also to chase gold. He'd soon learned his stamina prevented him from being a miner. He simply didn't have the strength to pan gold, to stand for hours in the biting cold. So he opened a saloon, following the miners from one location to another, and made more money than those who panned.

When Cat appeared at the Silver Slipper in Alta, Utah, a stop along the stagecoach line on which she had unceremoniously been ordered, he had offered her a job, though she made it very clear she would not prostitute. Her name was Selina then. Ben was only forty, but he looked a decade older, his eyes sad, his cough racking. He had taken her under his protection, asking nothing in return, and she hadn't understood why until a year later when he'd told her how much she resembled the girl he left in Boston, the girl who had died waiting for him to send for her.

He had taught her to read and write and, when she showed an ability for numbers, how to keep the books. He himself was an educated man, the possessor of a degree from Harvard University, and she realized he'd quite enjoyed transforming her from, he used to say, a raw piece of coal into a diamond.

But his health steadily declined, even in the cool, dry mountains, and Cat, grateful for everything she had learned from him, nursed him and finally, at his request, married him. He wanted no problems, he'd said, in leaving his property to her.

Ben knew something of her past and her aversion to the physical side of marriage, and the marriage had never been consummated. He was too ill, in any event. He had wanted only companionship in his last days and the assurance she would be cared for. He had left her the saloon and some money, but she no longer had protection in a mining town that was infamous for killings and violence. She decided to sell the Silver Slipper and move on to a place where no one knew her.

The stage line ended at San Francisco, and she found an old building suitable for a saloon, the only business she knew. She changed her name again, this time to Catalina because she liked the sound of it, the same name as an island off California. But she named the saloon the Silver Slipper in memory of Ben. . . .

She knew what she wanted even then: to build it into the most successful gathering place in San Francisco, then sell it and retire to some remote, beautiful place. A safe place where she could earn the respectability she'd sought since she was a child. It had been difficult, but she'd succeeded.

Cat stared through the window at the darkened windows of the Glory Hole. Why didn't safety and respectability seem as important now as a month ago?

Why?

A man leaned against a building within sight of the Silver Slipper. He watched the last window darken.

He had learned patience a long time ago. His business as a private detective demanded it.

His hand curled around one of the circulars he'd been passing around. Someone had told him the girl, Mary Beth Adams, had been seen going into the saloon. It didn't make sense to him, not a girl with her background, but he had to check it out.

So he'd gone into the Silver Slipper tonight, one of many men lining the walls, and he'd searched the face of every girl there, including the dancers. None fit the description he had.

Still, it was the first lead he'd received. He would hang around for a few more days. He was being paid well enough, and if he found the girl . . . well, the fee would be substantial—very substantial.

CHAPTER 13

The rumored battle between the owners of two San Francisco saloons became public during a performance of the much-publicized cancan at the Silver Slipper.

Taylor Canton and Catalina Hilliard engaged in an argument during which a glass of wine was thrown. The two then disappeared, Mr. Canton apparently leaving the premises.

The altercation took place during the performance of the cancan. The risqué dance, banned in Paris, drew a standing-room crowd and was enthusiastically received. Miss Hilliard has employed the French dancing troupe of

*Barnard Duvier for a two-week engagement.
Performances are nightly at the Silver Slipper.*

*Mr. Canton recently reopened the Glory
Hole, located across the street from the famed
Silver Slipper. The establishment has been
plagued with bad luck since its founding in
1865, changing hands four times and being
abandoned two years ago. Mr. Canton has
vowed to restore it to its popularity of the
mid-1860s and lured Lotta Crabtree as his opening act. Miss Hilliard has pledged to match, or
better, any entertainment offered by her competition.*

*It is a duel that fascinates this reporter, and,
we believe, San Francisco.*

As he read the San Francisco *Globe*, Marsh
leaned back in his chair, balancing precariously
on its hind legs. He wanted the Glory Hole to receive attention, not himself.

Christ, he hoped no one associated Marsh
Canton, Colorado gunfighter, with Taylor Canton, saloon owner. But who would? Who could?
Unless that damned dime novel showed up. It
had a sketch of him, though not a very good
one.

He tried to relax. The novel had been published a year ago. *Duel at Sunset*, it had been
called, purporting to be a "true account" of a
gun battle between Lobo, the Apache-raised gunfighter, and Marsh. Nothing about the story was
correct. There had been a gun battle all right,
but not between him and Lobo. And Lobo
hadn't died. But the tale had become legend all
the same.

Marsh wondered if his former competitor

had really been able to set aside his gun for good. But then, Lobo hadn't had a choice; his gun hand had been all but destroyed.

He looked at his own right hand—the long fingers whose speed nothing had diminished. He flexed them. A musician's hands, his mother had said. A killer's hands, so many others had charged.

Marsh relaxed, letting the chair fall forward as he folded the paper. He heard the lock on the door click. Hugh. It must be just before eleven. The cook would be there soon—along with the other help—to prepare a dinner buffet. He remembered Cat's slip last night about Hugh. Hell, he remembered too much from last night, particularly the way she felt in his arms.

But now it was Hugh he had to worry about. He felt his lips tighten as disappointment in the man sliced through him once more. How to use Hugh O'Connell?

As Hugh entered, Marsh nodded and slowly rose.

"Hugh," he said. "Right on time." His voice was cordial. He made sure of that.

"Mr. Canton. We had a good night last night despite—"

"I know," Marsh said. "I went through the receipts. We might even make a profit this month."

A smile lit Hugh's face. "Miss Jenny's real good, but she said she missed you."

"I would think she would be glad to have her usual accompanist with her."

"She said no one's as good as you, sir."

Hugh took off his bowler hat. "I don't think so, either, Mr. Canton."

Marsh shrugged and tossed him the paper. "We're news again."

Hugh read the item slowly, the smile fading from his lips. He looked upset.

Marsh watched him carefully. "It didn't exactly happen that way," he said. "Miss Hilliard accidentally spilled the wine and graciously agreed to have the clothes cleaned."

Hugh didn't say anything.

"Interesting woman," Marsh said. "Have you ever met her?"

Hugh's expression set. At least, he wasn't a very good liar, Marsh thought.

"I've been in the Silver Slipper," Hugh finally said.

"Lovely, isn't she? A little treacherous, though."

Hugh shifted slightly. "I don't know much about her."

"No one seems to," Marsh replied laconically. "A situation I plan to change."

Teddy went to the Oakland Farmers and Merchants Bank. It was time to meet the man who was seeking the woman called Mary Beth. He had spent five days in this city, and he'd learned very little of value.

He knew that Edwin Adams was a widower for seven years now, and that he was president of one of Oakland's most substantial banks. From everything he'd heard, Adams was a prudish, upstanding family man, a pillar of the church.

Whenever he asked about Adams, he was told of the tragedies that had befallen him: a wife with a lingering illness, a daughter who had disappeared, but no one knew much about her.

It didn't make sense to Teddy. Why would Molly—Mary Beth—leave a fine home? Why was she so frightened? Why couldn't she go home?

Teddy was a good judge of character. You got that way in a saloon. A good barkeep quickly sized up the troublemakers, the customers who got mean when they drank, the ones who wouldn't pay their bills. He knew his appearance was deceiving, that people didn't pay much attention to him; that gave him a chance to pay attention to others. He had thought about the best way to approach Edwin Adams, to try to form his own opinion about the man.

He squared his shoulders and went inside.

The man at the desk closest to the door peered at him through heavy spectacles. "Can I help you, sir?"

Teddy moved over to him. "I'm thinking about buying a farm around here," he said. "I saw your bank said 'farmers' and wondered whether you make farm loans."

The man looked over his visitor's face, his large frame and ill-fitting suit. "Do you have collateral?" He looked superciliously at Teddy, as if he doubted he knew what the word meant.

"Collateral?" Teddy said, although he knew exactly what collateral was. He had learned a great deal from Miss Catalina. "I got a stash, if that's what you mean. Made it in mining. The lode ran out, though, and I plan to go back to farming. Got enough to buy the place but don't know about seed and animals."

The man's posture changed, straightened slightly. "Where is this farm?"

"Ten miles to the north. The Alvin Becker place," Teddy said. He'd read the notices of sale in the local newspaper.

The man still looked doubtful. The Becker farm was prosperous. Teddy could almost see his mind work, reevaluating his first impression.

"I would like to see the top man," Teddy said, setting his jaw obstinately.

"I'm his assistant, Frank Redd. I can help you, sir," the man said, suddenly more polite.

Now it was Teddy's turn to look arrogant. "I'll only talk to the top man," he said.

The clerk looked doubtful. "I'll see if he has time," he said, and rose from the desk, making his way to a back glass-enclosed office. He knocked and spoke for several seconds to the man inside, and then returned, looking anxiously at his pocket watch. "Mr. Adams will see you for a few moments. He has an appointment at noon."

Teddy lumbered into the back office, surprised when the man rose courteously, a smile on his face. "I understand you're considering buying the Becker place. Good farm, Mr. . . . ."

"Stanton," Teddy said. "Theodore Stanton."

"Have a seat, Mr. Stanton," the man said. "I'm afraid I have an appointment shortly, but I can spare you a few minutes now."

Surprised, Teddy sat. The man was wrapped in cordiality, a broad smile above a neat beard, but his pale blue-gray eyes caused a chill to run through Teddy.

In the way that he imagined a miner or farmer might in the presence of a bank officer, Teddy squirmed in the seat. "I was wondering . . . if I do buy the Becker place . . . can I git loans?" he started. "And would my money be safe here? I've seen banks go bust."

"How much money are we talking about, Mr. Stanton?" Adams's eyes were gleaming now.

Teddy shrugged with a man's reluctance to discuss personal business with someone he didn't know well. "Enough," he said uncomfortably.

"Of course it will be safe. We're the soundest bank in Oakland." There was smugness in the claim, not pride, and Teddy recognized the difference. "We're very stable. Ask anyone."

"I like to know who I deal with."

The man's smile faded slightly, but held. "What would you like to know, Mr. Stanton?"

"I place a big stock in family. Got a big one of my own," Teddy lied.

"Well, then," the banker said, "I have a daughter myself, though my wife died seven years ago. Haven't had the heart to marry again."

"A daughter? I got one. Eighteen, she is. Joy of my life."

The banker tried to smile, but now Teddy definitely felt the chill in him deepen. Something odd flickered in the man's eyes, an almost burning light that had a hint of madness. Teddy would have sworn it had nothing to do with grief over losing a daughter, and everything to do with obsession. He *had* seen obsession before.

The banker fidgeted with a gold watch on a chain stretching across his vest. "You'll have to excuse me, Mr. Stanton. An appointment, you understand."

Teddy stood and reached out to grasp the man's outstretched hand. It was curiously limp. "I'll be back, Mr. Adams."

Marsh spent four days hiring and training his women dealers. He employed eight so that six would always be on duty daily, from early afternoon to closing. He was very careful in his selection, not as concerned with beauty as he was with intelligence and character. He did not want cheating. But the dealers were all attractive, and he made it clear very quickly that any infraction of his rules meant instant dismissal. He had been assisted by Hugh, who convinced some of his Irish friends that their daughters would be safe at the Glory Hole, and it was he who suggested that the young ladies' dresses not be too revealing.

Marsh paid well. His receipts had been far better than he expected. He'd nearly reached the end of his bankroll when the Glory Hole opened; now, despite the costs, he was replenishing it. And finally something other than death was occupying his mind.

Teaching eight females roulette and blackjack and poker was not easy. He found himself learning an entirely different kind of patience from that of waiting on the street to face another gunman.

If Marsh's gaze occasionally wandered to

the doors, and to the Silver Slipper across the street, he yanked it back. Nothing about the attraction between him and his neighbor was any good. After the evening of the cancan, he questioned his original assumption that bedding Catalina would end his growing obsession with her.

It would be best, he'd decided, to remain at a wary distance, at least until he had the Glory Hole, his second obsession, well established.

So he'd thrown his complete energies into that, hiring and instructing and keeping books. He'd always been good at figures, and he found he enjoyed the mental exercise they demanded. It had been a very long time since he'd exercised any of his abilities other than instinct, and now he felt that strange sense of loss that was recurring with disturbing regularity. He was remembering law school, the mental games required and how he had relished them. In the years since, so much of himself had been walled off; now chunks were peeling away, leaving exposed raw pieces of himself.

As if to continue to deny any change, however, he took several hours each morning to himself, riding off to the hills and practicing with his Colt, reminding himself that the gun was still who he was, the life source of what he had become. To forget it was to deny the last twenty years, and he couldn't do that. And he could never forget the danger that would always follow him because of those twenty years.

One of the girls, who was practicing shuffling cards, caught his glance, and the cards went into fifty-two different directions. Her face colored, and he gave her a soothing smile. "It'll come," he assured her. Did he really frighten young ladies that much?

He stood, needing air, needing to get away from the looks of his students. He had tried to make it clear he had no interest in anything but their employment as dealers. But he wasn't used to self-denial. And his manhood had certainly been stirred by the lady across the street.

He reached the door. A man was lounging against the side of the building. He had been hanging around for several days, and Marsh had taken notice. The man's gaze continually seemed to go to the Silver Slipper, and he had taken several drinks at the Glory Hole, each time choosing a chair and table next to the window.

There was something about the man that gave Marsh pause. A furtive quality. He measured the man more closely. Dark-brown hair slicked back. Sideburns that needed trimming. Tan-and-yellow-checked suit that had the ill fit of store-bought frugality.

Marsh told himself it was none of his business. The man was obviously staking out the Silver Slipper, not the Glory Hole. Anything bad that happened to his neighbor was only good for him. It was what he wanted, wasn't it? Catalina Hilliard deserved every misfortune after the beating he'd taken, the humiliation of jail.

Yet . . . he couldn't prevent the onslaught of a certain amount of protectiveness. Besides, it was *his* battle. His revenge. No one else's, goddammit.

He didn't want anyone else to destroy what belonged to him.

He walked over to the Silver Slipper.

• • •

The big man was still absent from his customary place behind the bar. But Catalina was there.

Marsh went up to the bar, hooked his foot on the long brass footrest, and regarded her carefully. She looked just as pretty in the daylight as she had in the glow of oil lamps. He'd never seen such clear eyes. And if he hadn't known better, he would have sworn he saw a moment of greeting in them.

"Whiskey," he said peremptorily.

"Our whiskey is better than yours?" Her smile was taunting.

"Perhaps there's a certain . . . pungency to your hospitality."

"Pungency?"

"Sharp . . . painful," he explained with a slight smile.

"Then why inflict it on yourself?"

"So I keep asking myself."

"Bad example. You preferring the Silver Slipper."

"Are you suggesting I leave?"

"Oh, no, I'm glad to take your money."

Marsh threw a coin on the counter. "I'm just trying to be a good neighbor."

"You?" she asked with disbelief.

"Just thought you might like to know there's someone taking an uncommon interest in the Silver Slipper."

Catalina's glance quickly went to the door and then back to Marsh. "Why should *you* care?"

"I have my own plans for the Silver Slipper," he said. "I don't like interference."

"How thoughtful of you," she said, but she left the bar and moved to the window, quickly studying the man leaning against the wall of the Glory Hole. "One of your thugs?"

"*I* don't hire thugs."

But Cat didn't retort as she usually did. She studied the man more carefully. Now that Canton mentioned it, she *had* seen him earlier. She should have noticed him still lurking around. She usually would have, if she hadn't had other matters on her mind. She turned back to Canton. "How long?"

"How long what?" he asked innocently.

"How long has he been there?"

"I noticed him last night when I closed and again this morning. He was in my place earlier."

She chewed her lip. It was an endearing habit, Marsh thought. And out of character. He knew she hated to show any kind of uncertainty—to the world or to him.

She walked back behind the bar and shoved his coin, still lying there, back at him. "The drink's on the house," she said easily, as if she'd made some kind of decision. It was, Marsh thought, as much of a thank-you as he was likely to receive. He nodded.

"And send me a bill for the suit," she said, as if it were an afterthought.

He shrugged this time. "Not necessary. Your cancan brought me customers too."

Cat hesitated, not sure she really wanted to prolong his stay, but not particularly eager for him to leave either. He had something up his sleeve. She knew it. Otherwise, why would he warn her about the stranger?

"I hear you have some women dealers."

"Word sure does travel in this city."

"It does, doesn't it?"

Their gazes met and dueled. She recognized the initial onslaught of that disquiet that always flooded her in his presence, and she resented it.

His gaze swept around the room. "I haven't seen your bartender . . . the big man."

Did he notice everything? She suspected so. "He's been out of town . . . on business . . . for a few days." Marsh straightened his shoulders. "Nothing to do with you," she added hastily.

"How nice of you to reassure me," he said, the slightest bite in his voice.

"It is, isn't it?" she purred. "Now if you will excuse me, I have work. We expect a very big crowd again tonight."

"Ah, so does the Glory Hole. A bit of gambling before the cancan. Remind me to thank you appropriately some day."

"Anything for a neighbor," she said sweetly.

"And just for that, I'll keep an eye on our curious friend outside."

She shrugged, wanting to appear indifferent to him, although she was worried far more than she'd ever want him to know. She still had a past. Which included murder, in fact. And part of her always lived in fear of being discovered.

"As you will," she said and turned away. It was an abrupt and effective dismissal.

He chuckled. She made entrances and departures better than anyone he knew. But then the chuckle died as he noticed her hand clenched in a fist at her side.

Miss Catalina Hilliard was not nearly as indifferent as she seemed.

He wondered whether it was the man outside. Or himself.

Either way, it was intriguing. He gave her back a brief salute and took his leave. He might do a little investigating on his own.

CHAPTER 14

Cat saw the man in the checkered suit later that day. He came into the Silver Slipper, took a table near the door, and ordered a beer. His gaze scoured the room as if seeking someone.

She set the beer down in front of the man and paused. "You're new here," she observed in as friendly a tone as she could manage.

He shrugged and took the beer but only sipped at it.

"From around here?" Cat persisted. She forced a certain sultriness into her voice, a low husky quality that usually got her anything she wanted from the man she used it on.

"Oakland."

"Business?"

"Look, miss, if it's the same to you, I'd just like to drink my beer."

Cat shrugged. "Your pleasure, mister. If you need anything, I'm Catalina Hilliard, owner of the Silver Slipper."

"Owner?" he said. His eyes went down, and Cat saw a folded piece of paper protruding from his pocket. He seemed indecisive for a moment, then shook his head. "Just the beer," he said.

Cat went to the bar. "Keep an eye on him," she told the bartender. "Let me know when he leaves."

She decided to go upstairs and work on the books. She felt a bit spooked and needed to concentrate on something orderly and neat that ended up giving her definite answers. On impulse she stopped by Molly's room and knocked.

"It's Catalina," she said.

The door opened, and the girl stood there, her long light-brown hair flowing free, looking impossibly young. She gave Catalina such a tentative smile that it hurt. Cat suddenly felt very old.

She looked around the room that Molly rarely left and wondered whether it mustn't be rather like a prison.

"Is Teddy back?" the girl asked shyly.

Cat shook her head. She was beginning to worry.

She watched the shy anticipation on the girl's face fade, and she felt a loss herself. She wished Molly would confide in her, but she seemed to trust only Teddy. Perhaps Molly saw the same innate gentleness that Cat had noticed years ago.

"I was going to work on the books," she said, "but it's such a fine day, perhaps I might take a carriage to the cliffs and watch the seals. Would you like to go?"

Molly smiled and nodded her head.

"I'll order a carriage," Cat said, pleased at Molly's rare pleasure. Cat needed to get away herself, to feel the sea breeze and watch the sea. It always renewed her in some mysterious way. She needed renewal at the moment. She needed to forget Canton, to get away from the knowledge that he was only steps away.

Part of her wanted to run away. Again.

But she'd stopped running.

The last thought settled inside, and she felt suddenly free. Free and young. She nearly skipped when she went down the stairs and told Harry to have someone call a carriage. She saw the man in the checkered suit finish his beer and head for the door, and she felt a moment's relief.

After finding a shawl for herself and a cape for Molly she collected the girl, went out the front door, and got into a waiting carriage.

Once inside and settled down opposite Molly, Cat remembered another carriage ride just days ago. The thought drained some of the excitement she felt. She wished for Canton's overwhelming masculine presence and then banished the thought and smiled at Molly.

At last the carriage rolled to a stop, and the driver hopped down to help them out. Catalina led the way to the edge of the cliff. The rocks below were home to a colony of seals. It wasn't the same place where Canton had taken her; she didn't want to relive that experience and the sensations its memory invoked.

Molly relaxed as she watched the seals play, sliding off the rocks in chase of a fish or flapping their flippers in the warmth of the sun. They were so free. So oblivious to the dangers around them. She shivered in the sun.

"Cold?" Cat asked.

Molly shook her head.

Cat sighed. She'd hoped that Molly would talk to her, tell her what she feared. But she also knew how difficult it was to do that, and that no one could force it. Cat had confided a small piece of her past to only one person, and that only after years. "I've been thinking," she started carefully, "that you sew so well, you might think about your own shop."

Molly's eyes widened. "But I can't . . . I don't have any money."

"My dressmaker has said she needs some help. Perhaps you can work with her, learn the business. The Silver Slipper is no place for you."

Molly's lips trembled. "I . . . I don't want to leave."

"Then you don't have to. But do think about it." In one of the few spontaneous gestures in her life, she put her arm around the girl and led her back to the carriage. And to the Silver Slipper.

Marsh muttered to himself. It was none of his business.

He'd gone to the door when Cat and the

young girl he'd seen at the Silver Slipper slipped out and left in the coach. The man in the checkered suit was lurking in the shadows as usual.

The mutter turned into an oath. Marsh was no longer a hired gun, for Christ's sake. He didn't need to protect anyone. And he had warned Catalina Hilliard, though he suspected she didn't take the warning seriously. The hell with it. She'd obviously looked after herself for a long time. And well too.

At least the man didn't follow the carriage.

Marsh went behind the bar, poured a glass of whiskey, and gulped it down. It tasted like poison, goddammit.

The Glory Hole was crowded, particularly around the gambling tables. He should feel good about this place, but all he felt was a nagging worry he didn't understand.

A low growl came from his left, and he saw Win bare his teeth at a customer who stepped too close. He should ban the damned dog during the day, but he couldn't force himself to do it. Winchester had become something like his shadow, though the dog still wouldn't tolerate even the suggestion of a touch.

Like Catalina.

Well, not exactly. Catalina tolerated it up to a point.

Tolerate. Well, perhaps more than tolerate, but then . . .

His mind went back to the stranger. Should he mention the man's continued interest to Cat?

He decided against it. She hadn't believed him the first time. Why now?

But still, he thought, it wouldn't hurt to

keep an eye on the man. Perhaps he even had some information about Cat. . . .

The prospect didn't excite him as it should.

What in God's name was happening to him?

He would ride out again, he thought, and do some more shooting. The one absolute in his life. The one thing he did better than anyone else.

He strode out of the saloon to the livery stable, saddled his horse, and rode out. He'd ridden for about fifteen minutes when he realized he wasn't going to the spot in the hills he'd selected for target practice; he was heading to the place he had taken Catalina—the one place where he might escape this increasing loneliness, the isolation that had never bothered him before but was beginning to eat at him now.

Don't go there, he told himself.

But he continued on, drawn by something he couldn't explain.

Calvin Tucker fingered the bills. He'd just told Adams where his daughter was.

"Did you talk to her?"

Calvin shook his head. "I didn't know if that was what you wanted. You just said information."

"You've done well, Tucker. Now there's something else I want you to do."

Calvin didn't like the look in Edwin Adams's eyes. But he liked the man's money. He liked it very much indeed.

"I'm at your service, Mr. Adams," he said,

trying not to sound like the ex-policeman he was. He had been fired when his graft offended even his superiors, because he hadn't shared sufficient amounts of it.

"I want you to bring her back here."

Calvin rocked on his feet. "She's obviously not being held against her will," he said. "What if she doesn't want to come?" He had privately wondered why the girl would run from wealth to a saloon, no matter how fashionable the latter.

"She's my daughter," Adams said icily. "It doesn't matter what she wants." He paused for effect. "There's five thousand dollars in it for you, when you bring her home."

Calvin hesitated. "I might need to hire some men to help me."

The banker turned around in his swivel chair and bent down to a safe. His fingers worked the combination, then reached inside, withdrawing a stack of bills. He counted out several before putting the others back in the safe and closing the door.

He straightened up in the chair and reached out with the bills. "There's two hundred for additional men. And I expect results."

"Yes, sir," Calvin said, thinking he had just hit the jackpot. He could hire a few thugs for less than fifty dollars. He started to add the sums: one thousand for the information, five thousand for the girl, and now an extra hundred and fifty.

"And I expect discretion," the banker added. "No one is to know of this."

Calvin nodded. He would use his hired men

to grab the girl, and then he would return her himself.

"Well, get on with it," Adams said with curt dismissal. "I expect to have her back this week."

Calvin touched the tip of his hat. "I'll have her back," he said confidently, before strutting from the room.

Teddy returned the day after the carriage ride. He walked into the kitchen where Cat, Molly, Wilhelmina, and two of the other girls were finishing the noon meal.

A look of relief spread over his broad face when he saw them, and then his gaze settled on Molly. A smile replaced relief—a sweet, protective smile, Cat thought.

Cat looked at him quizzically. "Glad to have you back."

Teddy's gaze didn't leave Molly. "Any problems?"

A big one across the street, Cat wanted to say, but she resisted. Canton was *her* problem.

She shook her head.

"The cancan?"

"An unqualified success. Customers are packing in."

"The Glory Hole?"

She shrugged. "It's still there."

"I noticed that," Teddy said with the faintest twinkle in his eyes. "Doing a good business, from what I can see."

"Temporarily," Cat muttered.

"No other problems?"

"There are always problems." She wondered whether she should mention the man in the checkered suit but decided against it. She still couldn't dismiss the possibility it was only one of Canton's tricks to worry her. In fact, she had grown more certain of that as she had reviewed her own conversation with the man in the checkered suit. There had been no flicker of recognition in his eyes at seeing her, or hearing her name—no undue interest.

Molly's gaze had darted between the two of them. She clutched the shawl around her shoulders, sensing that they needed to talk. "I'll go upstairs," she said, starting to turn away, then looked back and smiled hesitantly at Teddy. "I'm glad you're back."

Cat rose and went over to Teddy, drawing him away from the others even as he stared at the girl disappearing out the door, an oddly vulnerable look on his face.

"Was your trip successful?"

Teddy flushed. His hand dug down in his pocket, and he pulled out the folded flyer. He watched as Cat took it, unfolded the paper, and quickly perused it. "Let's go up to my room," she said then. Without giving him a chance to answer, she led the way up to her room, which also served as her office.

The door firmly shut, Cat asked, "How long have you had this?"

"Since just before I left."

"Have you told Molly?"

He looked miserable. "No. I thought I would see what I could find out about this man."

"And?"

"He's a banker in Oakland. Respected. I . . . met him, and . . ."

Cat waited patiently.

"I didn't like him," Teddy said flatly. "I don't know why."

Cat paced around the room. She was remembering how Molly looked when she first came to the Silver Slipper. Hungry. Tired. Desperate. Why would she run from her own father?

Unless . . . he was like Cat's first husband. Or she was pregnant, but if so, Cat would have noticed by now. Molly had been here nearly two months.

"Wealthy?"

Teddy nodded.

That explained her ineptitude at so many things. And why she could sew. Most young girls, even wealthy ones, learned how to sew. Cat thought for a moment. "Canton's noticed a man hanging around for the past several days."

"Canton?" Teddy started. "He told you?"

"I thought he might have been making it up," Cat said. "A tale to worry me." Cat shrugged. "The man Canton described came in earlier. I tried to talk to him, but he didn't seem interested. He left after drinking a beer."

"Could he have seen Molly?"

"I don't think so," Cat replied. "She's been staying upstairs except for when we went for a carriage ride. And the man had already left by then."

Teddy's brows furrowed. "Should we tell Molly . . . Mary Beth?"

"She has to be warned," Cat said, taking

the poster and smoothing it out. A thousand dollars. How many people had seen it? Sweet Lucifer. Even Canton. Canton would take advantage of this. But then she thought of his warning and wondered whether she was being fair. But that didn't matter now. Only Molly mattered now.

Cat nodded. "I'll tell her."

"She can still stay here?"

"Of course."

Teddy started to turn toward the door and then glanced back as an afterthought. "The can-can really did well?"

"Customers are standing against the walls," Cat said. "And the dancers are teaching some of our girls how to do it. We can continue after they leave."

"I'm sorry I've been gone so long."

Cat's green eyes softened. "I missed you, Teddy, but you're family. Whatever, whenever, you need anything . . . ?"

Teddy looked embarrassed. "I'd better go downstairs. Check the inventory."

She nodded as he disappeared out the door, and she wondered how she was going to talk to Molly. She had no experience at protecting and mothering. Crisp authority? Gentle sympathy? But she knew nothing about gentle sympathy. Crisp authority—that was the best.

Molly overheard parts of Teddy's and Cat's talk, and knew she had to leave. Immediately. She would run until she couldn't run anymore.

She moved silently back to her room and gathered her few belongings, and the dollars

Miss Cat had paid for her sewing. At least she had something this time, thanks to the owner of the Silver Slipper.

Now to leave without anyone seeing her.

The thought was excruciating. Teddy and Miss Cat were the first true friends she'd ever had. And Teddy, with his kind eyes and inherent sweetness, had given her so much hope. But she had to protect them as well as herself. They had no idea what her father was capable of, to what lengths he would go in destroying people who befriended her.

Molly moved swiftly to the hall door that opened onto the steps leading down to the alley.

The alley was empty. She walked quickly to the street that fronted the Silver Slipper, then hesitated. Where to go? There were carriages for hire in front of a hotel a few blocks to the north.

Molly glanced around. Two men were loitering in front of the Silver Slipper. Neither looked familiar. They approached her. Something told her to run. She turned back toward the Silver Slipper, but a hand caught her; another went across her mouth.

A scream died in her throat as she felt a piece of cloth stuffed against her mouth and nose. She struggled as a sickening sweetness filled her nostrils.

CHAPTER 15

———◆◆◆———

Marsh looked out at the street almost empty now. He'd been keeping an eye on the Silver Slipper and just noticed a closed carriage. Two men walking toward the carriage seemed to be struggling with a large bag. He stepped farther out into the street and saw the "bag" was a woman. Limp. And then the man in the checkered suit got out of the carriage and went over to the two men carrying the woman.

All Marsh's instincts started working. There was a furtiveness about their movements that signaled no good. And the man had raised Marsh's hackles from the first moment Marsh had seen him watching the Silver Slipper. And the woman. Catalina? He couldn't tell since a shawl covered the hair and face.

His hand went automatically to the gun at his side. Catalina was his, by God, *his* to torment. His to ruin if he chose. No one else on earth had a right to lay a finger on her.

His hand on the butt of the gun, he quickly crossed the street as the men were trying to load the woman into the carriage.

"I don't think she wants to go," he said in a quietly lethal voice.

The men swung around, all three of them. The one in the checkered suit reached inside his jacket, but Marsh was faster. His gun was out before any of them could blink.

"This ain't your business, mister. It's my . . . sister, and I'm taking her home."

"Let me see her face."

"I told you, this ain't your business."

Suddenly one of the men let go of the woman, and the other shoved her at Marsh. She fell toward him, and he had two choices, to drop his gun and grab her or step back and allow her to fall. The choices flickered through his mind instantaneously, and he stepped back. Better for her to fall than for both of them to be taken.

But as he did, one of the men darted toward him, and the other came around to attack him from the rear. He swung the gun around, hitting one man with the barrel and jabbing his knee in the other's crotch.

The woman fell, the shawl falling from her head, and he saw the light-brown, almost blond, hair. It wasn't Cat, but it *was* the girl he had seen that first night, the shy one. Just then he caught a movement by the man in the checkered suit, who had pulled a derringer from his pocket and was aiming it at Marsh.

Instinct took over. Marsh didn't even think; he just squeezed the trigger. The sound echoed in the street as the man doubled over, blood spraying from a wound in his chest. There was a noise behind Marsh, and he whirled around to see people pouring out of the Silver Slipper. The big bartender. Cat. Customers.

The two men who had grabbed the girl were doubled up on the street; the man in the checkered suit lay motionless in the growing pool of his own blood.

Catalina rushed over to the girl while the bartender, holding a club, glared at Marsh. "What happened?"

"These three . . . gentlemen were trying to put the lady in the carriage," Marsh said.

"You stopped them?" the bartender's voice was incredulous.

Just then a policeman ran up, blowing a whistle as more and more people congregated, the gamblers from the Glory Hole joining the drinkers from the Silver Slipper.

The policeman bullied his way to the front, knelt in front of the man in the checkered suit. "He's dead." Marsh had already holstered his gun.

Cat took over. "I think he drugged one of my girls. Trying to kidnap her." She looked to Marsh for confirmation. "This man prevented it."

The policeman looked at the two thugs still on the ground. "What do you have to say?"

One of them groaned, his hands still protecting his crotch. "We wuz jest taking this girl back to her family ... where she belongs ... that's what he told us."

"By drugging her?" Clearly the policeman didn't believe the man. His glance went around the crowd and settled on Marsh, who by far dominated the crowd. His eyes moved downward to the gun holster. "You do the shooting?"

Marsh nodded. "Self-defense. He drew that derringer on me." He gestured toward a small gun lying in the gutter.

The policeman held out his hand for the gun, and Marsh gave it to him, watching his eyes as the man studied the handmade butt. The barrel was still warm.

"You three," he said, including Marsh in his glance, "will go to the station house with me until we sort this out."

Two other policemen joined the first, apparently summoned by the whistle. One of them stared down at the dead man. "That's Calvin Tucker. Used to be one of us," he said. "Detective now, I hear."

"Sergeant," Cat pleaded again, promoting the man. The officer obviously knew her, Marsh noted. It seemed everyone did. "Can we take her inside?"

The officer flushed with pleasure, and Marsh knew exactly how he felt. Cat was using those incredible green eyes to advantage. He also recognized a familiar sinking feeling. Jail again. And it appeared as if Miss Catalina Hilliard couldn't care less.

He and the officer watched as the burly

bartender picked up the still-unconscious girl and carried her inside. Cat waited until they were gone, gazed at Marsh for the first time, then at the officer. "I don't see why you have to take Mr. Canton in. My bartender and I saw everything. That man"—she gestured to the ground—"has been lurking around for the past several days. He obviously took a fancy to one of my girls. Mr. Canton was defending her, and himself. I saw the man go for his gun, and so did my bartender."

The officer looked at her dubiously, then at Marsh, apparently seeing something he didn't like. "Your full name?"

"Taylor Canton," he said easily enough, though inside he was in turmoil. He'd thought he was through with killing, goddammit, but it still came easily. He suddenly realized his right fist was clenched, and he tried to relax it but couldn't. He struggled for the detachment that served him so well. "I own the Glory Hole across the street."

The officer's face cleared slightly as if ownership of the Glory Hole made Marsh acceptable. He took out a notebook and wrote the name down. "You aren't planning to go anyplace?"

Marsh shook his head.

The officer turned to Cat. "You willing to testify to what you saw?"

"Yes," she murmured.

"I need to talk to the girl."

"Tomorrow?" Cat asked.

The policeman sighed, helpless in the onslaught of that bright green gaze. "All right, Miss Catalina, but I expect to see her then."

Cat nodded.

"I'll be back to talk to you," the police officer said to Marsh. "You," the officer then said, turning to one of the newly arrived policemen. "Wait here for the wagon to pick the dead one up. I'll take these two men in." He handcuffed them as they looked at Marsh with stunned hostility.

Cat went to Marsh. "Would you have a drink, Mr. Canton? It's on the house."

He raised an eyebrow. "Again?"

"Payment of a debt," she said curtly.

His mouth quirked. "You don't place a very high value on the young lady."

"I place a very high value on her," Cat replied. "What do you want?" The question was very low, audible, he knew, only to himself.

"I'll let you know," he said in a voice just as low. "After due consideration."

He felt her anger, her chagrin at being indebted to him. He took advantage of the moment, putting his arm around her waist and steering her toward the Silver Slipper, knowing she must hate the possessiveness of that gesture. He certainly hadn't intended this, but he wasn't above taking advantage of it, either.

They went through the door, aware that a crowd was following them. Marsh understood himself well enough to know that his outward indifference to the episode was misleading. He had told himself he had interfered because he thought the lady might be Cat. But he would have interfered in any case because . . .

Because . . .

The images came back, the ones conjured in his mind when he'd heard the truth, or rather part of the truth, about his sister and mother. A band of Yankees foraging for Sherman. Rape. Fire. Murder. He hadn't been able to do anything about that, though he had spent years avenging his family's deaths. But he had no intention of standing by and allowing anything like it to happen again.

Marsh knew his fist had tightened again into that ball as they reached the bar, and he tried to relax. He kept trying to reassure himself that it had been the woman's danger that caused it. It hadn't been the killing, the pulling of a trigger again—or had it? But no matter how hard he tried to bring his attention back to Catalina, he still saw the man's eyes, the man he'd just shot. Somehow the old detachment was no longer there, the shell that had protected him from his own actions.

Cat's voice interrupted his thoughts. "What would you like?"

"Whiskey."

A small glass was filled, and he took it in one swallow, feeling the burning straight down to his gut.

Cat watched him carefully. Something tortured him.

She poured him another drink, and though his fingers wrapped around the glass, he didn't pick it up. His gaze bored into hers. "Why did you lie for me?"

"I didn't lie," she said simply. "Teddy and I were alerted by a customer and had just reached the window when that man took aim." She hesitated, then added, "Sweet Lucifer, but you were fast. And," she added after a pause, "accurate."

She saw him tense, then shrug. "A talent I picked up in Texas."

"You have a number of talents, Mr. Canton. Playing the piano. Handling a gun. I hear you're very good at gambling too. How many more are there?"

He wanted to change the subject, and he knew just how to do it. "I can show you one, anytime you say," he added.

"Men overestimate themselves," Cat retorted quickly.

"Do they now, darlin'?" he drawled, his insinuation only too clear: how much experience did she have?

She flushed down to her toes. She'd never done that before she met him.

Cat did something she rarely did: poured herself a drink and downed it just as efficiently as he had.

It was enough to reestablish her composure. She set the glass down. "I have to go up and see how Molly is."

His expression changed from taunting into a smoothness she couldn't read. "Do you know what all this was about?"

"No," she said, and then hesitated. "But I thank you on her behalf."

"Does that mean our little war will . . . cease?"

She shook her head. "No," she said flatly. "I've been here a long time. I've built this place from nothing through sheer hard work."

"And you don't want competition?"

"There's not enough business for both of us."

"Ah, but you're wrong, darlin'," he said. "I expect you've never done better."

"It won't last."

"So you'll do anything to rid yourself of it?"

"Yes," she said defiantly. She knew her voice was too strident, and she wondered whether she was trying to convince him or herself.

His eyes locked with hers, and they were so dark, she felt as if she were being drawn into a black night sky. Limitless. Uncharted. She knew she should break away from them, but she couldn't. And, she discovered with shock, he couldn't draw away either. But there was something unsure, despite his bold words, ever since the shooting. In that minute his hand had moved so fast, she couldn't follow it. Sweet Lucifer. The pure reflex of the movement spoke so eloquently of experience.

The dark, mysterious Taylor Canton. Canton. And then she remembered what she had been trying to remember since she'd met him.

She'd seen gunfighters in Colorado, in Utah. Now she knew what she'd recognized in Canton. That stalking grace. The way he always positioned himself where he could see the entire room. The familiarity with which he wore a gun. The cold eyes. The lethal danger she'd sensed since she'd first met him. Canton. She searched her memory for names, but she'd been in San Francisco so long now. Yet she'd read the name somewhere. Heard it. She hadn't found the connection earlier because he was out of place as a saloon owner.

But then, she was out of place too. A fugitive from a past that was also dangerous. Canton. Why did the name haunt her? But she *would* remember. And then what?

She turned to Harry, the second bartender. "See that he has anything he wants."

The man nodded.

Canton's mouth quirked as if to ask whether she was really going to see about Molly, or if she was running from him. "You'll let me know how she is?"

Cat hesitated. "Would you like to go up and see for yourself?" She was surprised at her own question, but his concern threw her off guard, just as that look of pain had earlier.

"No. I have to get back."

"Are you still accompanying the singer?"

Something flickered again in his eyes. "No," he said shortly.

He turned abruptly and, in that effortlessly graceful way of his, walked to the door.

Molly continued to sleep through the afternoon. A doctor had been called and he'd sniffed the air. "Chloroform," he pronounced. He checked her breathing, her heart. "I could try to wake her," he said, "but there's really no reason. I'd just let her wake naturally. It will be an hour or so, no more." He gave Cat, who'd appeared in Molly's room at almost the same time the doctor did, a bottle of pills. "If she has a headache, give her one of these."

Cat took them. "Send me the bill."

He nodded. He took care of everyone at the Silver Slipper.

Teddy paced anxiously, and Cat looked at him sympathetically as the doctor left. "Why don't you go help Harry? I'll call you when she wakes."

"What if they try again?"

Cat smiled. "I think it'll take some time for whoever sent them to realize what's happened. I'll try to make sure those two men are held for quite a while."

Teddy hesitated at the door. "Why do you think he helped?"

"I don't believe he thought about it. He just reacted."

"He was real fast."

"Too fast," Cat grumbled.

"If it wasn't for him . . ."

"He'll find a way to exact payment," Cat said dryly.

"Maybe we misjudged him."

"No," Cat said flatly.

"But—"

"No," she said again. The man really was Lucifer. He was even turning Teddy around now.

Teddy said nothing else, but closed the door behind him with a softness that, like Canton's capability with a gun, was eloquence in itself.

Cat closed the curtains in the room, blocking out the early-evening light. She sat in the semi-darkness, beside Molly. Her thoughts jumped between Molly and the man who had saved her— saved her from what? She had to know or they couldn't protect her.

She wondered exactly how old Molly was. At least eighteen.

By that age Cat had been a prostitute, had lost a child, and had killed a man. But she had never looked innocent. She'd been as tough as bark on an oak tree. She'd had to be to survive.

But Molly? Mary Beth. Cat suddenly felt very, very old.

She reached over with her hand, touching the girl ever so gently, wondering what it would have been like to have a daughter. She would have protected her own with her life. She'd tried. When she'd been Lizzie, when she'd been fourteen, she'd discovered—or the other women had—that she was with child. She hadn't known enough to realize what was happening to her body, yet once she did know, she'd wanted the child. Desperately. Someone to love. To love her. But her mother had called in a woman to rid her of it. Lizzie had refused, but in her ignorance, played into the old woman's hand. She took tea with her. Then she'd felt woozy and everything had started whirling around her. When she woke hours later, she knew the baby was gone. In its place was agonizing pain.

She'd never gotten with child again, despite two more years at the Natchez Under the Hill brothel and then the god-awful time with James. Whatever had happened during those black hours of unconsciousness had apparently made her unable to conceive again.

She'd told herself in the succeeding years that it didn't matter. But she was so alone. Perhaps it had taken Canton to show her just how alone she was. The impression of aloneness hovered around him like a dense San Francisco fog, but it never dissipated as the fog did. He hid in fog. And so, she reluctantly admitted to herself, did she.

CHAPTER 16

Marsh looked at the invitation again. Tea with Meredith and Quinn Devereux tomorrow at four P.M. The Pacific Palace.

The man who'd delivered the invitation had worn the livery of the Pacific Palace and had patiently waited for an answer.

Hell, Marsh might as well find out now what the city was saying about yesterday's shooting. There had been nothing in the papers that morning, but he didn't know how long the silence might last.

He turned to the messenger. "Tell Mr. Devereux I accept."

"Thank you, sir," he said, and turned away, heading for the door.

Marsh watched him leave, then turned back to the invitation. He wondered whether it had been written by Devereux's wife. An artist, he remembered. He wondered whether she had any idea whom she was inviting. She would probably rescind it if she did.

He looked down at his pocket watch. Almost eleven. The cook was already here. Hugh would arrive shortly.

Winchester growled in the corner, and Marsh went into the kitchen to retrieve some scraps for him. He tried to keep the dog inside now. Because there were so many mongrels in the streets, a law had been passed decreeing that stray dogs were to be shot on sight. Unfortunately, Winchester didn't understand and managed to disappear for hours at a time. And, dammit, he worried about the beast.

Everything was getting too damn civilized. Tea, huh?

Hell, he wasn't ready to be civilized. Not yet.

Still, he found himself looking forward to visiting the Devereuxs tomorrow afternoon. He wondered whether tea really meant tea. Such niceties had escaped him these past two decades. Teas and balls and conversation. That odd wistfulness was snaking into his awareness again. Laughter. Affection. Warmth.

One of the afternoon newspapers ran a front-page story about the shoot-out. It revived all the rumors about the feud between the owners of the Glory Hole and the Silver Slipper, and called Taylor Canton, the Texas businessman turned San Francisco saloon keeper, a hero. There was a sketch of Cat. Thank God there was none of him, but the article did hint at some mystery about him.

Marsh threw the paper down. All he needed was for someone to link Taylor Canton with the Marsh Canton of the dime novel *Duel at Sunset*. He hadn't been that concerned with the earlier stories: they had mentioned only Canton the saloon owner. But now, because of the shooting, the link was there for anyone to see.

He knew from past experience he could expect more reporters this afternoon. Best thing to do was disappear for a few days until the story died. It would mean added hours for Hugh, since notoriety always seemed to spur business.

Marsh cursed long and fluently. He still wasn't sure how far he could trust his manager, and that bothered him more than he wanted to admit.

Why in the hell did he ever think this would work?

But he was enjoying it. For the first time since the war, he had started to forget the stench of death. He had started to live in ways he had forgotten were possible.

Christ, but he enjoyed seeing the Glory Hole fill with customers. Hearing Jenny sing. And most of all seeing Cat's eyes spark with anger—and passion. For the first time he envisioned a future that had nothing to do with death.

He was still staring at the crumpled newspaper when he became aware of a stir of interest in the place. He turned and watched as Catalina walked straight to the bar he was leaning against.

Elegant and striking, she was wearing green taffeta that made her eyes seem incredibly green—and so lovely, they made him ache inside.

"Miss Cat," he said graciously, just a hint of mockery coloring his voice.

"Mr. Canton," she said, also in a slightly mocking way, but with a twinkle in her eyes. He'd always thought her beautiful, but now she was enchanting.

"I thought you might be interested in how Molly is doing," she said.

He raised an eyebrow, which could be interpreted in any number of ways: he was; he wasn't; why should he be?

The gesture put her at a disadvantage. Just as he meant it to.

But this time she didn't appear a bit perturbed. As if she knew exactly what he was trying to do and was amused, rather than annoyed. It was disconcerting.

"She's going to be fine. For the moment."

He said nothing, remaining as still and quiet and watchful as a man could be. Waiting. Always waiting. The now-familiar warm shiver crawled up Cat's backbone and down her legs, and then back up through the most private part of her. How did he cause that to happen? By his intense masculinity? Or by the danger that hovered around him? Or the competence. The cool aloofness that she now knew hid a passion that

ran deep. And his music. The night music that
revealed a love of beauty that was surprising in
a man who lived by the gun.

For she was sure now that he had lived by
the gun, that he had been a gunfighter. Perhaps
still was.

Sweet Lucifer, but she wanted to touch him.

And she was going to ask him for a favor.
Dear God, what would he ask in return?

To keep from looking at him, her gaze went
down to the newspaper and was held by the
sketch. She felt the color drain from her cheeks.
Who had done it?

His gaze followed hers and then returned to
her face, studying it with interest. A weapon. She
was giving him a weapon, and she knew it.

Cat forced herself to relax. A sketch. Would
someone from the old days see it? And remember? But it had been so many years. No one
would even care, not about a gambler lying dead
in a Mississippi rooming house.

She forced her attention back to Canton.
"Molly's afraid for you. I said I would warn
you."

For the first time since Cat had met him,
Canton looked startled. Astounded, in fact. She
felt the warm shiver turn to warm honey running
up and down her veins. She didn't know whether
he was astonished because someone thought they
should be afraid for him, or because someone actually worried about him. But whatever it was, it
rocked that usual unruffled composure and
made him suddenly seem less like that fallen
archangel she always imagined him to be.

"Me?"

Cat had to smile at the absolute disbelief in his voice. "You," she repeated.

"Why?"

Cat looked around. Eyes were on them. Many eyes. Fascinated eyes. "Can we speak alone?"

He shrugged. "Why not?" His eyes were speculative now, the surprise gone. "My room is the only place."

Apprehension stabbed Cat. She needed to be in a room with him alone like she needed a knife in the heart. *For Molly's sake, she told herself. Only for Molly.* Or was she lying to herself?

He took her arm gently, with that same old-world courtesy she had seen in him before, and before she realized what was happening, she had accompanied him to his room and he was opening a door. The mongrel dog she had seen several times before followed at a cautious distance.

"Winchester," he said conversationally to the beast. "You'll have to wait outside."

"Winchester?"

He shrugged and looked just a little abashed. "He's ugly as hell," Canton explained, helpfully. He stood back and allowed her to enter, closing the door behind him.

And then there was just the two of them. Without even the dog for distraction.

Nervous, Cat looked around. The room was even more Spartan than Teddy's. A bed. A worn, scratched bureau. A mirror. There were no chairs.

Canton bowed and gestured to the bed. "Would you care for a seat?"

No! But she held the exclamation and shook her head instead.

He merely grinned, the kind of grin, she thought, that the spider wore as it invited the fly into its parlor. She knew exactly how that fly felt.

Leave.

But no part of her body worked properly. Not her mouth, nor her mind, nor her legs. Catalina Hilliard, the Ice Queen, stunned into silence. *Fight. Fight for your survival. You've done it before.*

He moved closer. She felt his warm breath on her, the heat of his body radiating the same kind of excitement she knew hers was.

She stepped back. A small step. But it was a giant step of will. "About Molly . . ."

"About Molly . . . ?" he mocked in that low drawl that seeped through her body, turning the warm honey into hot bubbling desire.

"She . . . she . . ."

But he stepped toward her. His face was so very close to hers, his mouth moving toward her mouth, his hand touching her arm like a fiery brand.

"Darlin', you talk too much," he whispered, and before she could protest that she hadn't talked at all, his mouth closed on hers.

And the explosion, the explosion that had been on the verge of erupting so long, came. The world seemed to rock with it as his lips met hers, plundered hers, made love to hers.

Cat thought she would drown in sensations, in the natural responses of her body to his.

She probably could have resisted if his lips

hadn't turned as tender as they had in the carriage that day. And his eyes were closed. He was a man who always kept his eyes open—so he trusted her in some way. An odd satisfaction flooded her.

She opened her lips under his prodding, and his tongue entered her mouth, teasing and searching but still with a tenderness that shattered her usual defenses. His arm went around her, drawing her hard against him as their tongues played love games of their own.

Her hand went up around his neck, touching the thick dark hair that curled ever so slightly around her fingers. Amazingly, her other hand moved down, to his neck, massaging it in increasingly fast circles as her body writhed.

His eyes flew open in surprise, and for a fleeting second they were unguarded. There was a raw, aching longing in them, a yearning that was only part passion. She felt it in his hands, in his lips, in his possessive arms. Then his eyes closed again, as if he realized he'd revealed something very private, and she closed hers, too, drinking up the almost magical closeness of a moment shared between two people who didn't know how to share.

Cat had never known a man and woman could feel this way. A bittersweet ache grew inside, a poignancy for herself, for what she had missed, and sensed that Canton had missed. It grew into a loneliness so vast, she felt tears gather behind her eyes, the kind of tears too deep to shed.

Her mouth tightened against his, demanding oblivion from her too-unbearable thoughts.

She felt his body shudder, and then his lips move away from her, moving along the contours of her cheek, hesitating at the corner of her eye as if sensing the tears she held back. They hesitated there, and then she felt his tongue feathering her cheek, his lips caressing skin now burning with his touch.

Desire ripped through her, blocking out all the old fear and distaste, as his lips moved again so carefully, so gently back down her cheek and to her ear, nuzzling until she knew nothing but this consuming need for him. His hands became tentative, devoid of the usual sureness with which he moved, as if waiting for her to break away, as she had before.

But she couldn't break away now if her life depended on it. The past was obliterated by the sensations, the incredibly exquisite sweetness of the moment.

"Darlin'," he said in a ragged whisper that was devoid of the usual mockery. "Darlin' Cat." She heard her own raw need in the sound, her own wonderment at what was happening. Her own yearning. And she felt herself shiver with a mixture of apprehension and expectation. Her hands moved with a fierce tenderness along the side of his neck, tracing small patterns of possession.

She drew a shaky breath, trying to restore some calm in a body possessed by a storm, but it only drew his attention back to her mouth, and his lips clamped down, kissing her slowly, deeply. Her hands ceased their wandering, clasping together behind his neck, pulling him closer until her body strained against his. She felt his arousal and heard his soft moan.

When his lips left hers, she knew a second of terrible loss, but then they pressed against her cheek for the barest of moments, and she sensed he was remembering the other times, the times she had torn herself away from him.

She looked up, and she knew her eyes were bright and clear, that they answered the question his hesitancy was asking. If she'd had any doubts, that question had answered them. He was giving her a choice, even though she felt the straining need in him.

"I won't hurt you," he whispered, and she wondered how he knew she feared pain—but then, both of them knew a great deal about each other in unspoken ways. They always had. From the moment they met.

She was still afraid, not physically, but of the magnitude of the feelings betraying her, betraying her body, betraying everything she knew and had believed. The tenderness she felt was worst. The urge to touch him, to run her fingers along the crevices of his face.

He picked her up, carrying her over to the bed, his mouth touching hers as he did. She stopped thinking, lost in the immediate beauty and mystery of his kiss.

Marsh tried to tame the fire licking at his groin, dampen the fierce tenderness that somehow had emerged after a very long sleep. It wasn't because he cared, he told himself. He couldn't care. He wouldn't allow himself to care. It was merely part of the seduction, the only way to cure himself of an obsession that could ruin him.

Why didn't he believe that? He looked down at her, at the face that had tormented him and now regarded him with a steady gaze that asked so many more questions than he could ever answer. She had always made him feel alive, had made him so acutely aware of forgotten emotions. The sun was brighter, the cut of the wind more invigorating, the stars more dazzling.

Elation tugged at him; little darts of pleasure struck his skin as he saw her questioning smile and the brilliance of her eyes that sparked at him, whether from desire or anger. Joy—how else to explain the sudden exuberance, the smile that had started someplace inside at the sudden trust that shone in her face?

He sat down, Cat still in his arms, nestling there as if she belonged. He moved one of his hands slightly so his fingers could get to the buttons at the back of her dress. He half expected her to object any moment, but she didn't. His hand slid inside the dress, meeting the resistance of her corset. His experienced fingers suddenly turned into those of an eager boy and fumbled.

It simply wouldn't work with her sitting on his lap, looking up at him with such unabashed interest, as if she had discovered something totally unexpected. There was a softness there he'd never seen before.

Marsh felt uncertainty again. What if things didn't go to plan? What if she only dug herself deeper into his life? He couldn't afford that. She couldn't.

He closed his eyes for a moment, remembering the last time he'd cared for someone. The aftermath. People he loved died. It was as simple as that. So he'd simply stopped loving.

But that had nothing to do with Catalina Hilliard. He didn't love her. He couldn't.

Yet something slammed into his ribs as he looked at her, and his heart seemed to stop beating for a moment. She was breathtaking. He wanted her desperately, so desperately, he was afraid to take her, afraid the addiction would become even stronger.

Her hands suddenly reached up, touching his face gently. It had been forever since he'd been touched with anything even remotely like gentleness. It was potent. Overwhelming.

To hell with the consequences.

This time he moved her slightly, giving his hands more freedom as he pulled her dress from her and then attacked the ribbons of her corset. She stiffened for a moment, then relaxed slowly as his hands ran up and down her arms. As he had in her room, he sensed that something had happened to her to make her wary. Rape, perhaps.

The thought gentled his hands, although a fierce anger assaulted him at the possibility. He wanted to kill whoever had hurt her, whoever had made her afraid.

He swallowed the budding rage, though a simmering anger lingered deep inside, fueling the hot, hungry blaze that was spreading like wildfire in his body. He leaned down and kissed her again with barely restrained passion.

Her response was unflinching now, though her lips trembled slightly under his. He undid her hair, watching it tumble in black waves around her face and down her back. One of his hands ran through the strands to relish their silkiness.

Marsh wished he knew what she was thinking. He took his lips away, and she rested against his chest as one of his hands unbuttoned his shirt and then his trousers. Marsh felt her tension, and yet there was no fear in her eyes. Only expectancy. And hope? He wanted to give her pleasure. More than pleasure . . . though he didn't know exactly what.

And then he did. He wanted to hear her laugh. He wanted to see her smile. With him. For him.

He felt her gaze stay on him as he finished undressing. She was so still. So solemn.

But as his hands stroked her possessively, caressing her shoulders, then her back, and finally her breasts, he felt her body tremble. Her hand went tentatively to the jagged scar and touched it with a tenderness that made him ache.

"Catalina," he said in a harsh whisper. "Oh, Catalina."

She smiled then, a kind of wondering smile that made him hurt even more inside, that made his arousal even more painful. He turned her around so she lay on the bed, and then he stretched out next to her, leaning over to kiss her breasts. Her body was lovely, slender and firm. She didn't need that corset, he thought, as he ran his hands along her waist, then her hips. He had never been so patient, so carefully tender, yet her stillness was almost unnatural to him, like that of a deer frozen in the light of a lantern. He felt the instinctive reaction of her body to his touch, yet she seemed to give in to it. He knew she wanted him; he knew it in ways men knew, but he also knew there was something holding her back.

Christ, he wanted to kill whoever had caused this.

His sudden fury transferred itself to his hands. He wanted to wipe away memories, to wash away the touch of anyone else.

Cat held herself very still, feeling trapped by her own weakness. She couldn't ignore the desire he created in her, but she was terrified that it would be followed by revulsion.

But still she wanted this. There was a magic she'd never known before, a wonderment that her body had these feelings, that she wanted to touch him, wanted to kiss him, wanted even more from him. *Wanted to give to him*. And now tremors ran through her as his hands moved up and down her body, trailing fire wherever they went. The pressure behind her eyes grew as did the pressure in the core of her.

His mouth touched her breast. His tongue teased and flicked and circled. The nerves in her body came alive, raw and burning. Her body moved toward him. His hand slid down to the triangle of hair, his fingers soothing, creating shock waves of sensation just as his mouth moved up to her lips. She strained against him, her fears lost, her reservations tumbling away like grains of sand caught by a wave.

He moved slightly, positioning that hard body above hers, his swollen manhood probing but not invading. He was waiting for her; she felt the hard tension in him, the rigid control it took for him to hold back. Giving her choices again. Not taking.

No one had offered her choices before. The pressure in her head and body exploded. She felt tears seep onto her cheeks, the first tears in many years. Her arms went around him, urging him down, cherishing the warmth of his body while seeking something more. She didn't know if he could give it to her; she didn't even know what it was, but she felt a need as big as the California sky.

His gaze fastened on the tears, and his smoldering gray eyes grew startled, then filled with an aching understanding that sent quivers through her body. He started to move away, but her hands held him and she shook her head, her words blocked by emotion.

His eyes closed and his tongue licked the tears from her face as she felt the throbbing of him farther down, and she sensed what this was costing him, what agony he must be in.

And now she was in agony too. Her arms tightened around him, and he lifted his head and looked steadily into her eyes. "Are you sure?"

She was. At long, long last she was. She nodded, her eyes feasting on his beautiful arch-angel face.

He moved slightly, and she felt his penetration, his slow entry—and then, astonishingly, she felt ripples of pleasure. Triumph, coupled with billows of delicious sensation, surged through her.

Marsh forced himself to be deliberate, slow, although he was burning like all the fires in hell. He ached. But years of selfishness and indifference to others had fallen away, and he wanted to heal and give pleasure. He wanted to make everything right. He wanted to wipe away that unbearable sadness in a face meant to laugh. He wanted his feisty Cat back.

His. At this moment. He planned to make the moment as fine as possible. He stroked her hair, then her face, before he continued, his body joining hers with loving patience, holding back until he felt her respond, felt her body move to his, welcome his, dance with his, with hesitant yet growing movements.

And then he could wait no longer and plunged inside, feeling the tightness of her, knowing it had been a very long time since she had been with a man.

Her arms wrapped tighter around him, and he suddenly felt worthy. Wonderful. He heard her small gasp of pleasure, his own small moan as the initial streaks of exquisite pleasure rushed through him. He felt her body quiver in response to his quickening rhythm, clasping tightly around him and reaching.

He had never made love like this before, his mind and emotions as involved as his body, and now he knew what he had missed. There was a startling brilliance in the pleasure, a satisfaction that had always been absent. "Oh, God," he whispered with a kind of reverence as he felt her internal explosion, the tremors, just before his own came.

Cat couldn't believe what had happened. In the mellow afterglow of their lovemaking, she felt transformed, reborn in some mysterious way. No longer soiled. No longer half a woman.

She nibbled at her lower lip as he put an arm under her head, pulling her close to him. He didn't just use her and roll off with a curse. He wanted to stay. And she wanted him to stay.

There was such comfort in cradling, and in being cradled.

She turned, and her lips nuzzled the scars on his chest, as if she could take today the pain that had been his yesterday.

"Taylor," she murmured, and she looked up at him as she did so, seeing the surprise on his face. Taylor was not a familiar name to him.

Who was he?

She didn't care at the moment. She only knew he had given her a gift, a gift of feeling.

It wasn't one that could last. She knew that. Yet it would have a lasting impact. No longer would she think of lovemaking as ugly, as a violation. She knew what it was to soar, to dance with the brightest stars, to feel the force of a racing comet.

He was still, so very still, and she wondered whether he regretted this. She looked at his face. So guarded. Even now. She saw questions there. But she wanted to ask them, not answer them. She couldn't answer them. She could never describe her past, the crime that had made her a fugitive. In that, she had to be alone.

She had given him part of her soul, and she wasn't sure how he would treat it. She put a finger to his mouth and traced its outlines, placing into memory every small line.

He caught her finger in his mouth and nibbled on it. "You taste good, Miss Cat," he murmured.

Cat stared up at him, wanting him in ways she'd never wanted a man before. She wanted tender nothings. She wanted touches. She wanted—sweet Lucifer, she didn't know what she wanted. Not when she was this close to him. She closed her eyes, wondering whether it was all a dream, a sweet nightmare meant to torment her. A hell of particularly exquisite torment.

She tried to be as light as he. "You taste good, too, Canton."

"What happened to Taylor?"

"It doesn't seem to fit you."

"What *does* fit me?"

"Canton," she said. "Just plain Canton." *Or Lucifer. The tempter. The thief of souls.*

His hand ran along her backbone, and she felt heat building again. A soul-deep heat. She was already beginning to respond, her nerve ends tingling, her skin burning to his touch, the core of her anticipating, growing taut and needy.

Her gaze met his dark one. His hands moved along her body, exciting her until she trembled with need.

He covered her again, this time with none of the caution he'd used before, none of the sweetness.

And this time she wanted neither.

She was as fierce in her demands as he was. Appetite spurred appetite into ever more ravenous hunger. Cat knew now what to do, what to expect, and this time she participated fully, meeting thrust for thrust. She wanted to crawl into his mind as well as take his body into hers.

"Oh, Cat," he said in a voice that was almost a moan.

She heard a similar moan coming from herself, or was it a whimper? He moved within her, hard and demanding.

Her legs went around his, an instinctive act that startled her as much, she realized from the sudden jerking of his body, as it did him. His movements became fiercer with the welcome she was now offering so freely.

Marsh rejoiced in the change, in the open declaration of need he'd only sensed before. She was giving herself to him without question, without reservation, and he felt as if she had presented him with the greatest possible gift. There was so much he didn't know about her. He was surprised at his hunger to know her, know everything about her. Dammit. Damn. The silent curses followed the same rhythm as his body, as need drove him deeper and deeper. Her body moved with his, meeting and challenging and demanding. And then he felt her shudder, and in one last thrust he felt his world explode in satisfaction. And from her cry he knew her world, too, had exploded.

He held her, rolling her over so she lay on top of him and he could watch her face. But she rested it on his shoulder in a gesture of trust that turned the pang he'd felt into something like agony. He was the last person anyone should trust with any part of her self.

They lay there, once more so close and yet . . . separate in silence. The secrets again, he thought.

The secrets. Cat felt them weighing upon

her like lead. Her hand traveled over the scars on his chest. There was so much she wanted to know. But if she asked, he might ask questions of his own. Questions she could never answer. She now trusted him with her body, but not her life.

So she merely snuggled into the curves of his body, soaking up the heat still permeating from it. She felt young, alive. She wouldn't allow the past to intrude. Not now.

The shadows of the late afternoon shifted and began to close in around the bed. She heard his heart beat, felt his warm breath, his hands around her now in soothing ways. And she knew she would never get enough of him. She suddenly felt panicky. She had to put some distance between them. Cat rolled off and moved next to him in the bed, but his hand kept her with him when she would have left.

"Don't go," he whispered huskily.

She didn't want to go. But she had to. Before he took everything that she was.

"I . . . I must go. I had really just come to warn you. Molly asked . . ."

His finger stopped her words. "*You* were worried about *me*." It was an amused statement, and she wondered if he doubted that she would worry about him.

"Molly was worried about you."

"You may tell her I have one great skill above all others," he said lazily, "and that is self-preservation."

Her eyes went to the scars on his body and then up to his eyes, a dubious expression on her face.

He chuckled. "Appearances to the contrary," he admitted. His hand tangled in her hair. "You're quite beautiful, you know."

Cat tried to ignore the new onslaught of desire. Of heat. "You're changing the subject."

"There's nothing I can do *now*," he observed, secretly pleased by her concern.

"Canton . . ."

He liked the way she said his name. He would have liked to hear his given name on her lips. Marsh. But that would be dangerous. In too many ways. He took her fingers and brushed them with his lips. "Hummmm?"

"You haven't asked who was after Molly."

He shrugged. "Some smitten suitor?"

"I wish that were so," she said, trying not to let him divert her again. Still, the heat moved from her fingers up her arm. She had to force herself to remain sitting, to retain some dignity. It wasn't easy when she was naked. And he was naked next to her.

"Then who?" he asked, as though pacifying a child. He suddenly had a bad feeling about this conversation.

"Her father," she said, recalling the strained conversation she'd had with Molly just hours ago. "A banker in Oakland."

Marsh stiffened.

"I think she's terrified of him. She says he's killed at least one person who's tried to help her and badly hurt others."

His gaze fastened on her. "What are you going to do?"

"I don't know. Teddy thought maybe you . . ."

Marsh went cold all over. So that was why she'd come to him. What a fool he was to think otherwise, to think that she might actually care.

He released her fingers and sat up, stretching with feigned nonchalance. "Me, what?"

Cat heard a subtle warning in his voice, saw the way his eyes shuttered. She shivered at the sudden chill in the room. "Nothing," she said, but she knew it was too late. Whatever had been between them minutes ago was gone.

"Don't stop now," he said silkily. "I always pay for services, darlin'."

The words slammed through her with a pain deeper than any she'd ever known. That warmth, that wonderful warmth, drained from her. Pay? Services? She looked at him with hatred and reached for her clothes with as much dignity as she could muster. She wanted to slap him, to wipe away that suddenly hateful smirk on his face. But then she remembered that other moment of violence years ago.

No!

She dressed quickly, keeping her face averted from his. She couldn't bear looking at him. Bile rose in her throat. She had fooled herself once more, had taken a hint of caring and made so much more of it than it was. A seduction pure and simple. She'd supposed he was very good at it. She hadn't known how good. And then he'd looked at her as if she were dirt. A whore.

You're nothing but a whore. Everything she'd accomplished crashed down around her. *Nothing but a whore. Nothing . . . nothing.* She heard her husband's voice saying the words over and over again. And now Canton. Tears burned inside her as nausea threatened to humiliate her even more. She wouldn't let him see how his barb had wounded her.

She hated him. Dear God, how she hated him at this moment.

She finished her last button and found her shoes. After slipping her feet into them, she started for the door.

Cat was almost there, almost safe, when his hand caught her arm and swung her around. Goddamn him. She clenched her teeth together as she forced herself to look up at him. She wouldn't give him the satisfaction of avoiding his gaze.

"Let me go," she said frigidly.

"I told you I pay my debts," he said, just as coldly. "What do you want?"

"For you to drop dead," she said.

"That's not what you wanted minutes ago." The old mockery was in his voice, and she wondered whether she had imagined those hoarse whispers, the gentle lips, the way he had kissed her tears away.

"But it's what I want now," she said.

He smiled through clenched teeth. It was much like the snarl she'd seen his dog make. "You can join a long line then, darlin'."

If she had not forsworn violence, she probably could have slain him then and there. Her eyes wandered to the gunbelt thrown carelessly over a chair.

His eyes followed her glance. His hands started moving up her arms again in the seductive way they had moved before. She felt the same heat, but this time she ignored it.

"If you touch me again, I will kill you."

"You will *try*," he said in a harsh voice. But he took his hands away and stood, feet apart, his naked body suddenly tense. She couldn't prevent her gaze from lingering for the slightest of seconds, hating the perfection of the man, perfection marred only by the visible trail of violence. Dear Lucifer, but she wanted to mar it even more at the moment.

She lifted her chin and turned again. This time her steps were quick, and she knew he wasn't following. She opened the door and gracefully moved away, trying to curb her instinct to run. She made it through the saloon and out the door. She rested for the briefest of seconds against the wall of the Glory Hole. Cat looked at the Silver Slipper. Her Silver Slipper. Her life.

She felt sick, sick and even more alone than she had ever been. How could she have given herself like that? To a man like Canton.

The enemy she'd thought she had in him was magnified many times now. She would force him out of San Francisco. Even if she ruined herself in the process.

Marsh watched Cat walk across the street, her shoulders squared like a soldier going into battle. Determined. Defiant. Proud.

He watched as she went inside, and then he stalked, still naked, to the bed where the sheets were in a tangle. He closed his eyes for a moment. He had felt free. And so damned good. He'd thought then that she'd wanted *him*.

He remembered how her eyes had widened after he had shot the man who'd grabbed her young charge. He'd know then that she realized he was a hired killer.

Then this afternoon she'd used that knowledge. And he'd died a little inside. She'd wanted a killer after all, not the man he was struggling to become.

His hand went up to his neck and rubbed it. He thought of the stricken look on her face when he'd mentioned payment. Maybe . . . maybe he had leapt to conclusions.

He groaned like an animal in pain. He hadn't jumped to conclusions. He knew that. What else would she want from him? He had to remember she was the woman who'd had him ambushed, beaten, jailed.

Christ, there was no way of changing the past. No way of changing what he was—even she recognized that.

He'd been a goddamn fool to think otherwise.

A stupid goddamn fool.

PART TWO

Shadowed Dawn

CHAPTER 17

Cat used the stairs on the outside of the building. It was usually unlocked during daylight hours for the girls to go in and out.

She knew how she must look. Her hair down and tangled, her face probably still flushed with anger. She wanted the safety of her room, to hide there. Forever. But she knew that after a few furious moments she wouldn't continue to shut herself away.

She was through with that. But white-hot anger stayed with her. If Canton had tried, he couldn't have landed a more lethal blow. And she hated him for striking at her greatest weakness: her past.

The fact that she had plunged from such an exquisite happiness to a hell she had spent a lifetime trying to forget only exacerbated her fury. It strengthened her determination to even the score. She would hurt him as he had hurt her.

Cat knew she couldn't bear to see him every day, to remember the sweetness and yet another betrayal. And his pocketbook was the best way to rid herself of him.

The French troupe would be here only a few more days. But Wilhelmina and several of the other girls had learned the cancan, and she would employ musicians—then slash the price of drinks to next to nothing.

And gambling. By Lucifer, if it took women dealers, she would do that too.

Lucifer. She would have to find a new oath. That one reminded her too much of Canton. She closed her eyes against a new onslaught of pain.

In the meantime, there was Molly. While sitting with her, Cat had gotten lots of important—and frightening—information. What to do about the danger to the girl?

Canton was certainly no longer a possible source of help. Cat wouldn't ask him for a drink of water if she was thirsting to death.

She combed her hair into a bun at the nape of her neck and looked in the mirror. Her face was still flushed, her lips swollen. Her body felt . . . odd. It would have been a pleasant feeling under any other circumstances, but now she hated every reminder of Canton. She hated her body for still feeling tremors. She hated it for wanting him.

Cat splashed water on her face. What she

really wanted was a bath. A bath to wash away this afternoon. But she knew she could never wash it away. Not the memory of how she'd responded to him, how much she gave to him, nor the bitter aftermath, that cold, contemptuous archangel's face.

She shivered with the memory. With the humiliation. Then she tried to block that part of her away, as she had blocked other parts. She could do it. She'd done it before. He no longer existed for her in any way but a rival to be eliminated.

With a last quick look in the mirror, she turned and went to find Teddy.

He was behind the bar, his eyes fixed on the steps leading up to her room, and she knew he must have caught sight of her through the window as she crossed the street.

Ice Queen. She could do that. She fixed a smile on her face and moved deliberately to the bar, going to a section that was empty.

Teddy moved quickly over to her. "Are you all right?"

She nodded. "But Canton can't help us."

"He refused?"

Cat looked away as if surveying the half-filled room. She didn't like lying to Teddy. "His price was too high."

"Price?"

Cat didn't elaborate, and she didn't have to. Teddy's face darkened, and he looked ready to kill. "I'll . . ."

"You won't do anything," Cat said. "I'll do it. In the meantime we have to find a safe place for Molly."

"I'll ask Hugh," Teddy said. "Perhaps she could stay with them for a while. His Elizabeth could use some help."

Cat nodded. It was the best they could do at the moment. But they would have to think of a better long-range plan.

He nodded. "Oh, and this came for you."

Cat looked curiously at the elegant envelope and slowly opened it. She read it quickly, and then again, more slowly, surprise replacing some of her cold fury. "An invitation to tea from Mr. and Mrs. Quinn Devereux."

Teddy's face showed the same surprise. Many of the city's most important politicians and business leaders patronized the Silver Slipper, but never had Cat been invited to a private home. The invitation was something she had coveted for a number of years as an indication of respectability. Ordinarily, she would have been delighted, but now she wondered whether anything could delight her again.

The Devereuxs. The golden couple of San Francisco. Why?

Canton had stayed at the Pacific Palace, but that really didn't mean anything. A lot of people stayed there. And the Devereuxs certainly wouldn't have anything to do with a man like Canton.

Curiosity fought with caution. Curiosity won. She would go.

Tea at the Pacific Palace!

She turned her attention to Teddy. "You'll talk to Hugh."

He nodded. "In the meantime one of us will always be with Molly. Wilhelmina is there now."

Cat hesitated. "Legally her father is her guardian, and he can make his claim on her. We must act as soon as possible in case he goes to the authorities."

Teddy's gaze avoided her as he fumbled with a glass. "Why do you think she's so afraid?"

Cat thought she had learned enough from Molly to guess what the girl would not, could not talk about. God only knew she'd seen and experienced the worst of men, and the fear in Molly's eyes, the humiliation she saw there, didn't come from discipline. Cat's own mother had sold her. She shuddered to think of what Molly's father had done.

Damn Canton. She hadn't realized how much hope she'd rested in him. With absolutely no reason, just instinct. And her instinct had failed her. That cold shiver rippled through her again.

Teddy's eyes had a strange look. "I wonder why Molly's father didn't go to the authorities in the beginning. Why would he have thugs try to kidnap her?"

"Makes you wonder, doesn't it?" Cat replied. "Perhaps exposure is the answer. We must get Molly to talk more about that man."

"Elizabeth might be able to help. Everyone talks to Elizabeth," Teddy said about Hugh's wife.

Cat doubted it. She knew she had never been able to talk about her past, no matter how kind someone had been—even Ben, who'd married her. She had warned him when he'd asked her to marry him. She had wanted to be honest with him, to tell him that she had killed someone. She hadn't been able to tell all of it, even to him. Shame and guilt always went too deep. She hadn't known how deep until this afternoon when Canton— To hell with Canton.

"Why don't you go talk to Hugh now?" she said, hating the thought of Teddy's presence at the Glory Hole. But the sooner Molly was moved, the better. Cat knew that in her bones, knew it from running herself. The cardinal rule was never to stay anywhere long.

"And Teddy," she added as he started to move away. "See if you can't find some women dealers for us."

"What *are* you thinking?"

"I'm thinking Canton's taking customers away because of his lady dealers."

"But we've never done much with gambling."

"It's time to change."

He obviously didn't agree, and she watched his expression as he struggled with himself. He never openly disagreed with her. She knew his loyalty was as deep as the ocean, and sometimes it bothered her that he never argued. He apparently took dissent as a sign of disloyalty. She didn't.

"Say it, Teddy," she commanded.

"The Silver Slipper is successful because of the kind of people it attracts," he said finally, almost stuttering in his earnestness. "They come here to transact business, to relax with a drink."

"But," Cat argued back, "our revenues are up since the cancan, and the Glory Hole is certainly profiting from the women dealers."

"But your *profit* is down," he said. "And after the excitement of something different dies, our new customers will find someplace else that's exciting, and our regular customers might be gone."

"I'm not going to let him win," Cat said stubbornly.

"So you both lose?" His steady gaze met hers.

"It's too late," she whispered. "It's gone too far."

"How far?"

"You'd better hurry. I'll need you later."

"Catalina?"

She stopped but didn't turn around.

There was a silence, then, "If he hurt you ..." There was a rough threat in his voice, and also a little reluctance. Canton *had* saved Molly yesterday.

Cat shook her head. No one had hurt her. She'd done it all herself. "He's just ... damned arrogant," she said stiffly. "And he's trouble."

The gambler absently picked up the San Francisco paper lying next to him on the table of the Sacramento hotel. He wanted to look relaxed, prosperous. His bill was overdue, and he had been receiving anxious looks from the management. He would sneak out tonight.

His luck had been bad. But then, it had never been very good. Of late he had won only when he cheated, and a month ago he had been caught and beaten; he had been afraid to cheat since. He was down to his last ten dollars. He needed a new stake. Then his luck would change. He was sure it would.

His eyes glanced over the headlines without a great deal of interest. Then he saw the picture of the woman and felt a jolt of recognition.

He quickly read the story as a hand went up to a faint scar on his face, rubbing it absently. Could it be? Lizzie?

He had spent years looking for her, scouring the Mississippi River towns and then the mining camps. He had lost the scent years ago and figured she had died.

He looked again. Twenty years had passed, but he would never forget that face.

Catalina Hilliard. A fancy name. Owner of a saloon. Famous enough to get her picture in the paper. She must have a lot of money.

Maybe even enough to make him forget his vow to kill her.

Maybe.

He wondered whether ten dollars would get him to San Francisco. If not, he'd find a way.

He tucked the paper under his arm. His luck was changing just as he had known it would.

Meredith Devereux had gone over the menu with her housekeeper. Tea, of course. Brandy for the men. They usually preferred that. Certainly her husband did, and from what she'd heard of the mysterious Mr. Canton, he would too.

She wasn't sure about Miss Hilliard. She wasn't even sure why her husband had suggested this afternoon event, though he'd had a familiar gleam in his eyes. It was one that usually made her wary—wary and often delighted.

He enjoyed mischief. She did, too, up to a point. But she also liked to know what to expect. She'd told herself she'd had enough of adventuring in the Underground Railroad, though sometimes she might long a little for those days, particularly those wonderful, tormenting moments when she and Quinn had met, and fought, each thinking the other was the enemy. She loved him more today than she ever had, but those days had been incredibly exciting.

So what was he up to now? He was certainly up to something.

When she'd asked, he'd merely said that Mr. Canton was interested in becoming a substantial citizen and might be interested in supporting some of their charities.

And Miss Hilliard? she'd asked.

He'd just grinned.

She did read newspapers—she knew about the rumored feud between the two saloon owners—and she'd looked at him suspiciously.

But he'd flatly refused to say any more.

She could have strangled him, not a new urge. She'd had it the first day she'd set eyes on him, when his startling blue eyes had appeared to see right through her disguise as a simpering husband-hunting belle. He was still as handsome, though the premature white that had once sprinkled his hair now dominated it. At fifty-five he looked a good ten years younger. He was as lean and graceful as ever, vibrant and successful, with so many interests, he made her head spin. Life was never dull with Quinn Devereux. The eight hellish years he'd spent as an English prisoner in Australia had stolen so much from him, he still tried to compensate for it—just as he tried to right every wrong he encountered. Her Quinn was the most compassionate man she'd ever met if, at times, quite roguish. As she feared he was being now.

She was fascinated with the legend of the Ice Queen and was looking forward to meeting her. Meredith had, after all, been a fugitive from justice, had spent nights in the house of an infamous madam and had escaped slave hunters. Her half sister was an escaped slave, and her husband's best friend was a former slave, who now had his own thriving business. She'd learned long ago to judge the nature of a person rather than his appearance or occupation.

Still, there was that rumored feud. She poured a larger amount of brandy into the decanter. She might need some herself.

Meredith looked around the penthouse of the Pacific Palace. It had a wonderful view of the ocean, which was why she and Quinn moved here after their two sons left home, first for college and then one with the railroad and the other with the Pinkerton Detective Agency. Adventure, she feared, ran in the family. Both boys had wanted to make their own way, rather than take the easy route in the family business.

A knock came, and May Ling, the housekeeper, hurried to open the door, Meredith following. Where in tarnation was Quinn?

A lovely woman in a stylish green dress stood at the entrance, curiosity bright in her very brilliant green eyes. There was also the slightest uncertainty, and Meredith instinctively held out her hands.

"Miss Hilliard. I'm Meredith Devereux and I'm so delighted you came. Come in. My husband is tardy, but he should be here any minute."

Cat hesitated, then surrendered to Meredith's charm. She smiled and followed Meredith into the room, taking a seat as her hostess indicated. There was an openness about Meredith Devereux that prompted her to say what she was thinking. "I don't know why I was invited."

Meredith laughed, a clear, happy sound that made Cat smile. "I'll tell you the truth, Miss Hilliard. This was my husband's idea, but I heartily approved. I warn you, though, he might well be up to some mischief. He can be . . . unpredictable. But I imagine it has something to do with our charities."

Cat relaxed. It wasn't some hoax. And she instinctively liked her hostess. There was no reservation in her, no condemnation. She seemed, in fact, genuinely happy to meet Cat.

There was the sound of a key turning in the front door. "My husband," Meredith said. "Watch out for him. He is charming and unscrupulous in trying to get money for his causes."

Cat couldn't help but hear the affection in the other woman's voice despite the admonition. It was clear Meredith Devereux was still very much in love with her husband.

That sharp, agonizing sense of loss, that loneliness she hadn't acknowledged until Canton appeared weeks ago, assaulted Cat again. It was a trembling weakness inside, an overwhelming sense of emptiness. She tried not to let it show on her face. She wasn't lonely for Canton. She despised him. As he obviously despised her.

But the feeling lingered as a tall, handsome man confidently entered the room. She had seen him, of course. But she'd never been introduced to him, nor had he ever been in the Silver Slipper.

He bowed to her. "Miss Hilliard. It's really quite kind of you to come on such short notice." And Cat understood exactly what Meredith had tried to tell her. He was indeed charming, warmth exuding from him like heat from a fireplace.

Why did he remind her of Canton? There was much more natural warmth to this man. A twinkle in the eye. Yet there was a residue of that quality that so set Canton apart from ordinary men. As if they had gone through a crucible and emerged changed forever. Like steel. Except with Canton, it was flawed.

Stop thinking about Canton, she warned herself. These two men were nothing alike. Canton would never have that gentle smile.

But he had. For just a few short minutes, he'd had one. But it was fraud.

A knock came at the door, and in a few strides her host was there, opening it, and it was as if she herself had conjured up Canton by thinking of him. Dear Lucifer, that was the last thing she wanted. He was the last person she ever wished to see. Her hand clenched tightly, and it was all she could do to control her face, to try to keep a pleasant smile in place.

For a brief second she thought he might

have planned this, but she saw the surprise, and displeasure, that flickered very briefly before his face became ice, even when the mouth twisted into a practiced smile.

A sudden tension permeated the room. It was so strong that Cat knew the other two people must sense it. Hostility flashed between them, hostility and the familiar thunder. Why did he have to look so superb? He wore tight but very well-tailored fawn-colored britches, a lawn shirt, and a beautifully fitted afternoon coat. Her gaze went to his hip; he wasn't wearing his gun.

He saw her gaze, and his features became even harder, if possible. His eyes narrowed and a muscle twitched in his jaw. He turned to Quinn.

Although the host seemed perfectly relaxed, Cat again caught the impression of two men very much attuned to each other, recognizing each other, although Quinn's expression was sincerely amused, and Canton's was—not angry, but tense.

"You know Miss Hilliard?" Devereux asked smoothly.

Cat wanted to commit murder. Everyone in San Francisco knew they had met.

"I've had that . . . most interesting experience," Canton said with a slight mocking smile.

Cat saw Meredith wince and glare at her husband, but he seemed not to notice.

It was a good thing Cat didn't have something in her hands, or Meredith Devereux's china would be hurtling at Canton's head.

"Yes, indeed," she said silkily instead. "I've tried to make him . . . welcome. Compensate for his first few unfortunate weeks. Someone should have warned him about the Barbary Coast. Terrible thing to happen in our city." She turned to him. "Tell me, Mr. Canton, is the jail really as . . . dismal as I hear?"

"You should try everything once, ma'am," he said. "I know of a certain police captain who can probably assist you in a guided tour."

She shrugged, unable to hold her tongue. "Some experiences are greatly overrated, and I don't think I would care much for the company incarcerated there." She made it clear what company she meant.

"Tea?" chirped Meredith.

"Brandy?" offered Quinn with an easy smile that included both of them. He seemed not to notice the tension. But that was quite impossible. Cat wanted to throw something at him too. He was enjoying this, by God.

"Brandy," Marsh said curtly.

"Brandy," echoed Cat, hating to agree with anything Canton said or wanted, but needing it just the same.

"Brandy," Meredith said to her husband's surprise. He ignored her suspicious look.

Quinn grinned as he started to pour. Everyone ignored the sandwiches strategically located on nearby tables. Cat's defiant gaze was locked on Marsh's carefully blank one. Meredith was watching her husband, wondering what he was up to with these two people who obviously loathed each other. There were undercurrents so strong, the room was practically vibrating with them.

Quinn graciously presented the glasses. He sat down lazily with his own drink, folding his long legs as if he were in the most amiable company. He turned to Marsh.

"Understand you had a bit of trouble day before yesterday."

Marsh eyed him with hostility. He had been neatly manipulated into this, and he didn't like it. He wondered whether Cat had been involved and then decided not. She looked too damn angry, but then, she was a good actress.

"No trouble," he said in the same curt tone he'd used asking for brandy.

Quinn's grin broadened. "A modest hero. I understand you saved a young lady from kidnapping."

Marsh winced, his eyes growing even icier.

Cat gulped her brandy, feeling it burn her throat. She coughed. Canton didn't have one decent bone in his body!

Quinn turned his attention to her. "And I hear fine things about you, Miss Hilliard, and the way you take care of the girls who work for you."

Cat took another sip of brandy.

"Which is why Merry and I invited you here today," he said, avoiding Meredith's questioning look. "She and I are supporting a house for young ladies who need help. We thought you might be interested."

Marsh looked stunned. Cat gulped her brandy.

"White slavery is not unknown in the Barbary Coast," Quinn said. "Both for Chinese and white girls. Our housekeeper, May Ling, told me a few days ago of an example. We want a safe place where they can go, learn an occupation, get an education if they need it. We're raising money now, hope to open it in a few months."

Silence followed his announcement. Cat felt excitement rise in her. If she had known of a place like that years ago . . . and if Molly had known of one . . .

Cat had done little in the past years but build the Silver Slipper; now she was being handed an opportunity to help girls who had no place to turn. But she did have a reservation.

"Would . . . the other contributors . . . approve of my participation?" she asked hesitantly.

Meredith smiled. "Of course they would," she said softly. She knew all about being an outsider. "We would love to have you." She hesitated, then added quickly, "And Mr. Canton, too, of course."

Cat grimaced. "You can count on me."

"Taylor?" Quinn asked.

Marsh almost missed the name. Christ, he had to become more accustomed to it. But, then, he was looking at Cat, and at this moment she could divert any man's thoughts. Her green eyes had softened. They looked almost wistful. And vulnerable. Very, very vulnerable. Uncertainty knifed through him. He remembered the tears on her face, then the sudden joy before he'd leveled his blows.

He was so damned unused to trust, to belief in anyone. In the last two decades, he'd always assumed the worst; he'd had to in order to stay alive.

Now he wondered whether he had been mistaken. But still . . . he couldn't let go of his mistrust. He was suddenly aware of Quinn

Devereux's eyes on him, a request for an answer to his question indicated by his raised brows.

Marsh thought rapidly. He thought of his own sister and mother. Both raped before being killed. He thought of Molly's unconscious form. He shrugged. "If Miss Hilliard believes it a good cause, how can I possibly disagree?" he said, a bite in his tone. "This has been most interesting," he continued, "but I fear that business calls, especially now that I have an added expense." He downed the rest of his brandy, rose with that lazy grace of his, bowing to Meredith and Cat. "Ladies."

"I'll show you out," Quinn said.

Marsh fell into step with him.

"A lovely lady, Miss Hilliard," Quinn said as he opened the door.

"Is she?" Marsh said caustically. "You must like claws."

"They make life interesting," Quinn said. "I know from experience."

Marsh gave him a cold look, turned around, and disappeared down the hall.

Cat left minutes later after asking a few questions about the proposed home.

As the door closed behind her, Meredith turned to Quinn. "Why?"

He leaned down and kissed her. "Mr. Canton paid me a visit several weeks ago, asking about Miss Hilliard. His interest was"—he winked—"interesting."

"But they dislike each other."

"Do they?" He moved his mouth to her neck, thinking she was just as lovely as she had been years ago. Lovelier in fact. "Remember when we first met. . . ."

Her face flushed. It had been a battle royal, and now that she thought of it . . . the sparks between their two guests had sizzled in a most familiar way.

CHAPTER 18

Reluctantly, Molly moved into Hugh and Elizabeth's home that evening. She feared her presence endangered them and the children, but Cat and Teddy assured her there was no way anyone could trace her movements. What had really eased Molly's mind was Cat's argument that she would be a great help to Elizabeth, who was expecting. Teddy had pointed out that Molly would be needed to care for the children.

Molly's eyes had lit at that. She loved children.

And eventually, Cat said, perhaps Molly could help at the home that the Devereuxs planned to support. Until they found a more permanent way of protecting her.

Teddy had suggested hiring a private detective of their own to investigate Molly's father. If he had been responsible for some of the acts Molly thought he was—the disappearance of a maid for instance—there might be a trail.

Molly had demurred. A detective was expensive, and Catalina and Teddy had already done too much, had even put themselves in danger for her.

Teddy had taken her hand. It had been so small in his big one, and Cat had smiled at the expression of absolute trust Molly had given him. There was something else, too, a flickering of light in her usually shy eyes.

She might lose Teddy soon, Cat thought. Not entirely, of course, but a part of him. Meredith and Quinn Devereux came to mind and the way they had smiled at each other—after two decades or more of marriage. She'd never thought love lasted that long. She'd never really believed in love at all.

An inexplicable longing swept through her, leaving a residue of bitter loneliness. It was bitter because of the last few days. She had discovered a moment of joy, of what joy could be, only to have it snatched away in the most brutal manner. Never to know was one thing. To know and not to have was almost beyond bearing.

If only . . .

She sighed. "Hugh won't tell his employer?" she asked Teddy.

He shook his head. "No one but the four of us knows: you, me, Hugh, and Elizabeth. Elizabeth will tell the children Molly's a cousin from the East."

The move was made during the busiest time at the Silver Slipper, when crowds of men were leaving the last performance of the cancan. Molly was dressed as a boy and spirited to a carriage; no one had been spotted taking a special interest in the comings and goings at the Silver Slipper, but it was wise, Cat and Teddy decided, to be very cautious . . . and secretive.

Cat would hire a private detective tomorrow, possibly ask Quinn Devereux for a recommendation; he seemed as if he might be knowledgeable about such matters. So did Canton, but it would be a freezing day in hell before she asked him anything.

After the last customer left and the girls who lived in the Silver Slipper retired, Cat locked up and went upstairs. She undressed and put on a gown and wrapper and, watching her image in the mirror, brushed her hair. It was just as lustrous and dark as ever, but she saw the tiny lines around her eyes. Nearly forty . . . she thought. Whatever her precise age, she was much too old for the kind of giddy feelings that had so disrupted her life of late.

Cat went over to the open window, her eyes inevitably drawn to the Glory Hole. A lone light still flickered in the main room. She heard the piano again, and the melody that had lingered in her mind despite her attempts to oust it. She leaned against the wall next to the window, listening as an eavesdropper might, knowing she was intruding on something private and intimate. She had missed the music lately. The com-

bination of power and sadness struck her in
peculiar ways, stretching the loneliness in a poignantly sweet way. She hurt, but she knew with
sudden insight, that was better than not feeling
at all. She ached now for life, not for the living
death she'd known so many years. If for no
other reason, she should be grateful to Canton
for that, at least.

The music grew in power and strength. And
anger. She could hear the anger in it. The passion. The passion she'd felt with him.

Why? She wondered why he had changed
so suddenly yesterday afternoon. Why his eyes
had gone from warm to frozen. She had thought
she had been used, but now she wondered. The
music made her wonder. There wasn't coldness
in it. Or indifference. Or cruelty. But there was
anger.

She stood by the open window for a very
long time. He finished what he'd been playing
and started something else: a wistful, haunting
melody that seemed full of loss. She wanted to
cry with the sound, but she didn't. Her tears had
been locked away for years, released only briefly
the other afternoon, and she thought never
again. Not after what had happened.

The music died away and didn't start again.
Instead there was the lonely sound of a single
carriage in the street. Someone going home. She
saw Canton walk into the street. He was alone
except for that dog she had seen on several occasions.

But then there was always a sense of aloneness about the man.

He was wearing a leather coat, and she noticed the familiar bulge under it. The gun. The gun he'd used so effectively. She thought again of the music and wondered how beauty and death could be so compatible in the man.

He turned suddenly, casting his gaze up at her window, and she thought about ducking back, then decided against it. She wasn't going to hide from him, or herself. She wasn't going to run.

The gaslight showed his lean form well, but the night hooded his face. He obviously saw her and he watched for several moments, his body stiff. She felt that he called to her. But then she remembered his taunt. Deliberately she shook her head, turned away, and went to the lamp to turn down the wick. She took off her wrapper and sat down on the bed. She wouldn't sleep tonight.

Marsh looked away from the window. Emotions were tumbling through him now, fired by the music . . . and Cat. He had thought he'd subdued that anger of his, the soul-deep fury that had spurred him to do the unforgivable, the fury that had forever scarred him and turned him into a killer. But it was still there, boiling inside, released by the other emotions now screaming for an outlet. No woman had ever affected him as she had. He wondered whether it was the beauty or the challenge or the strength he saw in her. The other afternoon she had awakened so many things in him, emotions that made him feel like a young man again . . . still idealistic and loving, as if there really was a world beyond the cold, distrustful one he had inhabited half his life. Until she'd suggested . . .

Suggested what?

Christ, he couldn't bear to think of the way her face had changed that afternoon. He clenched his fists. He hadn't been wrong. He couldn't have been wrong. Just look at the way she'd turned away from him today. And tonight.

He turned a corner, walking toward the ocean, Winchester trotting behind him. The dog often accompanied him now, although still not venturing too close.

Christ, before long the world he was building might fall down. He was keeping in his employ a man he thought disloyal to him; he couldn't get Cat out of his mind; and even that little Molly haunted him. What had Cat intended to say when he'd cut her off?

Marsh smelled the water now, that tangy combination of sea and wind that was unlike any other smell. The sharp wind cut across the bay. Wrapping his jacket tight against his body, he felt the gun that was so much a part of him. To his left, across the bay, was the island of Alcatraz, which looked intolerably barren and lonely across the foam-flecked waves.

Fog crept in, slowly obliterating the island from view. If only other scenes could be obliterated. Erased.

Michael Callahan. Marsh knew he would always see Michael Callahan in his mind. A Georgia farmer, whose small plot of land had bordered a section of Rosewood, Callahan had been bitter that his family had never prospered as did the Cantons. He had lost piece after piece of land through ineptitude and laziness. There had been no reason, no reason at all, for Marsh to question the accusation that Callahan had participated in the murder of Marsh's mother and sister. In selling them out to save his own small farm. In leading a small band of Union deserters from Sherman's army to the Canton plantation in exchange for part of the gold rumored to be there.

The accuser had been Canton's overseer, who, Marsh discovered later, had coveted Marsh's sister and hated her when rebuffed.

Marsh had jumped to judgment then. After learning that his mother and sister had been raped and left to burn to death in their own home, he went into a blind rage. Already hardened by years of death and nearly senseless with grief and exhaustion, he had sought out Michael Callahan and killed him in cold blood. But Michael Callahan had been innocent. Marsh had tracked down the deserters, one by one, learning along the way that the overseer had lied, that he had been the one to suggest the attack, that he himself had raped Marsh's sister.

When he'd discovered his mistake, killing had already become a way of life. The only life he knew anymore. The knowledge that he had killed an innocent human being might have deterred another man from further killing, but not him. He'd felt he'd surrendered his soul when he'd killed Callahan; the need for revenge had grown ever stronger, darker, deeper.

Marsh had returned then and found the overseer. He had not been merciful, but had coldly shot him in the groin and listened to him scream before finishing him.

The overseer didn't haunt him. Michael Callahan did.

A void grew where his heart had once been, a heart deadened when his family died so brutally, buried when revenge became a nightmare he couldn't stop.

It had taken two years to track down every man involved. And when he'd finished, there was no satisfaction. No finish. The emptiness made him court death with the one skill he'd honed to perfection. And because he didn't care about his own life, he became invincible. He had no fear, and that was conveyed in his eyes, and that always gave him the edge with other men who did care about living. *His* hand didn't shake.

In all those years of earning his way with a gun, he had been hit twice, both times in ambush. Both times he'd survived and hunted down the ambushers.

God's own joke, he'd told himself often enough. He didn't die because he didn't care. Those who did care died. They made mistakes.

Now, all of the sudden, he wanted to live too. He wanted to feel the wind and taste the sea and love a woman. He wanted everything he'd once dreamed about as a privileged young man before the war. He had opened a door, only a crack, but now there was irresistible pressure to push it all the way open.

Which probably meant his life expectancy was plummeting.

Winchester growled as if he understood.

"We're fools, both of us," he told the dog. "It's too late to change."

The dog whined. Marsh had never heard that particular noise from him before. He stooped and reached out for the dog. This time it didn't inch away. Its dark-brown eyes looked at Marsh steadily.

"You don't think so?" Marsh asked. The dog whined again. "And Miss Cat? What do you think about her?"

The dog regarded him solemnly. "I don't know either, Winchester," Marsh answered his own question. "Christ, I don't know anything anymore."

He stood. "Let's go home, Win," he said, realizing as he said the words that it was the first time in two decades he'd had any kind of home.

Quinn Devereux was surprised when a clerk announced the arrival of a Miss Hilliard.

"She said she didn't have an appointment," the young man said, "and not to bother you if you were too busy."

Quinn was not too busy. He'd liked Catalina Hilliard, and so had Meredith. There was a strength about the woman, as well as a peculiar vulnerability that didn't quite fit his perception of a saloon owner. She had obviously felt out of place in their penthouse, and he sensed it had taken no small amount of courage on her part to accept the invitation. He'd also been touchingly amused at the charged anger between his two guests, and yes, they had reminded him of himself and Meredith when they'd first met.

His mouth twisted as he thought about those days. Sometimes he even longed for them. He had once longed for peace, but now he missed some of the old challenges. Or thought he did. A sign of growing old, he supposed, to think kindly of unkindly days.

"Show her in," he told the clerk as he stood up, awaiting her entrance.

Cat swept in with the grace he'd observed earlier. She *was* a beauty, made more so by maturity. She had to be close to Meredith's age, as Catalina had been in San Francisco since the early 1860s. She, like Merry, was one of those rare women who grew more attractive with years.

"Miss Hilliard," he said, showing her to a seat. "How can I help you?"

"Catalina," she said. "Please call me Catalina."

He nodded.

"I . . . I need a private detective," she said. "I hoped you might recommend one. An honest one."

"Now that's more of a problem," he said. "Can you tell me why?"

She hesitated. It was Molly's secret to keep. But she trusted this man. And she needed his help. "The girl you heard about," she said slowly. "It wasn't just a kidnapping."

The interest in his sharp blue eyes grew.

"It has something to do with her father. She's terrified of him. She believes he's capable of killing anyone who helps her."

"You can't tell me who he is?"

She shook her head. That required too much faith.

"Is she safe now?"

"For the time being."

He leaned forward and wrote down a name. "This man is with the Pinkertons. Completely trustworthy. And discreet." He handed the paper to Cat. "Does Taylor Canton know about this?"

Cat stiffened, as she always did at the name. "I told him," she said curtly.

"He won't help?"

"There's no need for him to be involved."

"I think he already is involved . . . if there is danger."

She shrugged. "He can take care of himself."

A lazy smile crossed his lips. "Most likely. But still . . ."

"Mr. Devereux, I appreciate your help, but I don't like Mr. Canton, and he doesn't like me."

He frowned as if he didn't believe her. Then he shrugged. "If you need any more help, please call on me."

Cat rose, feeling the dismissal. "Thank you," she said, "and thank you for tea."

"Even if you didn't approve of the company?" There was an impish amusement in his eyes, and she had to smile back.

"It was . . . interesting."

"But uncomfortable?"

"A little," she said.

He chuckled as he rose when she did. "I think that's an understatement. I haven't seen sparks like that since my wife and I met."

She stared at him. She'd never seen so much harmony between a man and a woman as between the Devereuxs.

"In the beginning," he added, "and for months after. Someday you might enjoy hearing the story."

She would. Unquestionably she would. Any story with a happy ending. And she liked Quinn Devereux and his wife. It would be nice to have them as friends, but that, she knew, was quite impossible. She was not in the same class, by any means. She wouldn't build herself up for disappointment as she had with Canton. Quinn Devereux was merely being polite.

T. J. Simmons stared at the letter as he sat in the nearly bare rented room in Denver.

Another rejection. However, the editor had said he would be interested in another story about Marsh Canton, a sequel to Simmons's one big success, *Duel at Sunset*.

But Marsh Canton had disappeared. T. J. Simmons had his sources: lawmen who liked to see their names in his novels; newspaper people he cultivated in his search for western stories. All he needed was a kernel of an idea, and then he could spin a tale. He didn't really care whether it was true or not. The only requirement was that it concerned a real western figure.

He'd had some success, but none like *Duel at Sunset*. And its success had practically ruined him. Everyone wanted a story of similar magnitude. But how often do you find two such famous gunfighters as Canton and Lobo going against each other?

He disregarded the fact that they had not really gone against each other. They could have. One had lived. One had died. That was enough upon which to build a story. And it had been a great story. He'd even found someone who'd known Canton to help provide an artist with enough information for a sketch.

Simmons had later been hunted down by a man with a grudge against Canton, a Tom Bailey, who fancied himself a gunman and whose brother had been killed by Marsh in some long-ago dispute. Bailey had sworn to kill his brother's murderer, and Simmons had agreed, for a price, to contact the gunman if he discovered Canton's location.

Simmons had additional plans. He would go with Bailey to confront Canton and have a front-row seat at his first real gunfight. He relished the thought. So did Tom Bailey, who was seeking a reputation as well as vengeance.

The letter in his hand made the mission even more urgent. He needed another success—a big one—and Canton would assure him a very big one indeed.

He would check at the *Denver Post* again. Sometimes they received papers from other states. Perhaps one of them would have word of Canton. The man couldn't have just disappeared. He was bigger than life, and his reputation followed him everywhere.

Perhaps some investigation into his past might also help. Simmons had been a newspaperman prior to coming west and taking up writing pulp novels. He knew how to dig into a person's past.

He would start with the War Department. Canton was at an age where he might have served in the Civil War. And then he would go on from there.

Perhaps he could write an even bigger book: *The Life and Times of a Gunman.*

Excitement stirred in him.

With an eagerness he hadn't known in years, he dressed in his best western garb and started out for the telegraph office.

Three days after the tea at the Devereuxs, business at the Glory Hole dropped abruptly.

Marsh had to do no more than look out his window to find out why. Signs declared that drinks were half-price for the 17th anniversary of the Silver Slipper. They did not say how long the anniversary offer would last.

Hugh reported that now that the French troupe was leaving the Silver Slipper, Cat also planned to employ women dealers. The cancan, a big draw for the Silver Slipper, would continue to be performed on weekends by local dancers. Marsh didn't ask where Hugh had obtained his information. He didn't want to know; his manager's loyalty was still very much in question.

Marsh shook his head in reluctant admiration for Cat's continued assaults on the Glory Hole. He suspected he'd caused this war. The growing notion that he might have wronged Catalina Hilliard had nagged him for the past few days. No one could fake the simple—or not so simple—wonder they'd shared that afternoon.

I had really just come to warn you. He remembered his amusement at her words, and the surprise that someone gave a damn. He remembered how good it felt. If only for a few moments.

Before his mistrust spoiled everything.

He hadn't seen Molly in a few days, but then he hadn't had reason to. He'd more or less holed up in his saloon, nursing his anger until it had dissipated with time and reason. He directed all his energies into the Glory Hole, trying to convince himself that his business was all that was important. He went over the books, hired several new dealers and waiters, even interviewed a new cook, wondering all the time what his new employees would think if they knew they would be working for a notorious gunslinger.

But now that all that was done, he knew the Glory Hole wasn't enough. He found himself increasingly restless, dissatisfied, and he lay much of the blame at the feet of Catalina Hilliard.

He'd purposely stayed away from the piano. It brought back too many memories. He also consciously stayed away from the windows, particularly in the early-morning hours. He didn't want to see that light, know that she was up there, remember the way she'd felt that afternoon.

He thought about going over to the Silver Slipper to try to make amends of some kind, but then he remembered the calculated cruelty of his comments and knew it was futile.

Molly. Perhaps he could offer to help

Molly—without the nastiness with which he'd first presented the offer.

Cat would probably shove the offer back in his face. She might think it was because of her latest move, the so-called anniversary. She might even think she'd won this battle, and he wasn't sure he wanted that.

Dammit. He had checkmated himself. So he searched for other diversions. He sent a sizable sum to Quinn Devereux for his project, probably more than he could afford, partly because the man had helped him get out of jail, partly because he didn't want Cat to outdo him, partly because of his own sister. Both noble and ignoble reasons, he admitted to himself.

But nothing helped. Nothing erased Cat's face from his mind, nor all those emotions he remembered from that afternoon in his room.

And finally, defeated by his own obsession, he found himself walking out the door, across the street, and into the crowded Silver Slipper.

Cat was losing money. She knew she was losing money. But it would be worth it if she could rid herself of Canton.

He had taken her mind and heart and twisted them into things she no longer recognized. She'd learned to control them, but now there was no control. She wanted him, nearly every moment of every day.

Why did he have such a hold on her?

She shook her head, as if to shake away thoughts of the man. She tied on her bonnet, a very pretty, elegant bonnet, which depended on the quality of the fine green velvet and the simplicity of the lines rather than on the flowery decorations so many women used. She was off to see the Pinkerton detective, and she wished to make a good impression. Molly's father probably had a great deal of influence, too much for some people to tackle.

Cat looked at her reflection. The lines around her eyes seemed to have deepened in the past weeks. From lack of sleep? Or was she simply more critical these days? But her hair looked as lustrous as ever, and she gave herself a quick, practiced smile.

She went down the stairs. The Silver Slipper was full for an afternoon, men lined up at the bar. She glanced around, looking again for someone out of place who might be after Molly.

Her gaze moved around the tables, the men at the bar, and then hesitated at a table where five men were playing poker. Something familiar stopped her. She looked again and her very life breath caught in her throat.

It couldn't be!

He was dead! She knew he was dead. She saw that embedded knife nearly every night of her life.

He was looking at his cards. Don't let it be him, she prayed fervently.

She found herself hugging the wall. She closed her eyes, then opened them again, willing him to be a mirage or specter.

But he sat there, his thinning blond hair almost white in the glare of the chandelier. The face she once thought handsome was lined now from dissipation.

How, for God's sake?

A look-alike?

But she would never forget that face, nor that particular habit he had in dealing cards, licking his second finger after dispensing a card. She would never forget that gesture. It meant he was nervous. Losing. It had usually meant that he would send someone to their room that night.

She moved quietly back upstairs, into the safety of the hall. Her room. Safety. But for how long?

How had he found her? Or did he even know she owned the Silver Slipper?

She didn't believe in coincidences.

She took several gulps of air.

What did he want?

She closed her eyes, thinking of the implications. She wasn't a murderess.

On the other hand, Cat knew she was a match for him now. She wasn't a girl. She wasn't afraid of him. He couldn't scare her. It had taken years for her to understand he was a coward. Only a coward used women as he did. Only a coward hit women. Only scum lived off them.

And she was married to just *that*! The knowledge sank in slowly, with terrible certainty.

The sketch in the newspaper! She expelled a long breath. That had to be it. Canton and their feud. If it hadn't been for Canton . . . Even she knew that wasn't fair. If it weren't for Canton, Molly would be gone to God knew what. And she, Cat, was in a far better position to take care of herself than Molly. But the irony didn't escape her.

Husband. She'd read enough to know

about husbands' rights. A husband's right to property owned by his wife. Could he take the Silver Slipper?

Dear Lucifer. Everything she had built. Everything she had earned. Years of working day and night. Her safety. Her security. Her pride.

She felt herself trembling. And she knew that at least part of it was hate. Pure, undiluted hate that he could do this to her again.

Why hadn't he died? How had he survived?

But that didn't matter now. What did matter was protecting what she had. She wouldn't let him take it.

He couldn't take what she didn't have. Cat hadn't survived this long in a very difficult business without using—sometimes misusing—the laws to her own advantage, just as she had in ridding herself of competition. A bribe here. A bribe there. But she needed time.

And she didn't have time. She knew James Cahoon. She knew his sickness for gambling. And she knew he was very bad at it. He would lose the Silver Slipper within weeks, if not sooner.

Unless she deeded it to someone.

Her head was spinning. She tried to think exactly what the newspaper had said. Had it said she owned the Silver Slipper?

She had to deed over the Silver Slipper before James Cahoon could take any action.

Cat took off the bonnet and reached for a shawl, wrapping it around her head, hiding her dark hair. Her mind was working feverishly, going over possibilities and rejecting them.

Every possibility led to Canton. He probably would be delighted to buy the Silver Slipper. If it was done fast enough, she could take the money, give Teddy a share, and then run again before James knew what had happened. She would lose the Silver Slipper, but she would have something. And God knew Canton could take care of himself—and James.

But how could she ask Canton for a favor? It wasn't a favor, she argued with herself. A business transaction. Only that. But even with that justification, the very idea was excruciatingly painful.

Yet the idea of James taking everything she had worked for hurt even more. At least this way she would have something.

Maybe . . . she thought of Quinn Devereux, but then she would have to explain everything. She couldn't bear to do it.

Cat felt sick, so sick that she doubled over. The Pinkerton detective. He was probably waiting for her now. But he couldn't do anything about this problem.

Only Canton could. But she couldn't trust him. Not any more than she could trust her husband. But then she didn't need to trust him. She just needed his money. An exchange. Something he wanted for something she wanted. She prepared herself for a hard bargain. He would know there was trouble because of her urgency. And she more than suspected he would take full advantage of it. She had to look normal. She had to look as if it were a sudden impulse and make him believe that he must take advantage of it.

Dear Lucifer, but her thoughts were in fragments. *Don't panic. Don't let him know you're desperate.* So little time.

She wanted to look down again into the main room. Her creation. Her accomplishment. Her life. Fury overwhelmed her. She forced it away. She couldn't indulge in anger or self-pity. She was a survivor. She would salvage what she could. She would never allow Canton to know she was desperate, at least not too desperate. She needed a story. A sick relative, perhaps. He could never know about her husband, about James Cahoon.

The mere thought of her husband made her sick again.

She went back to the mirror, pinched some color into her white cheeks. She used a little lip color. She didn't want Canton to think . . .

How was she going to do it? Especially after her insults?

But he was her only hope. Her enemy was the only man who could help her. She went to the small safe in her room, opened it, and took out the deed to the Silver Slipper. She then gathered the shawl about her head, slipped out the door and down the hall to the side door. She went quickly down the stairs, kept to the side of the building, then hurriedly crossed the street, only too aware that her path was in full view from the windows of the Silver Slipper.

The Glory Hole was nearly empty and she swallowed hard, wondering whether the fact that she had stolen most of his customers would hurt or help her cause.

Dear heaven, how she hated running again. But she had no choice. She looked around, trying to keep her anxiety hidden. She felt her fist ball around the deed she had tucked in a pocket.

She approached Hugh, who was standing behind the bar, saw his eyes widen.

"Mr. Canton?" she asked.

Hugh stared at her, and Cat wondered whether her nervousness showed, despite all her attempts to hide it.

"Is something wrong? Is someone looking for Molly?"

She shook her head. "I just . . . have a business proposition to discuss with him."

Hugh studied her for a moment. "I saw him go over to the Silver Slipper."

Cat's heart plummeted. There was no way she could go back. And what if he heard something? What if James loudly proclaimed their relationship? She wouldn't put it past him. He was a noisy drunk as well as a poor poker player.

"Would you send someone for him?" she finally said, feeling another chink of broken pride fall away. She couldn't even go into her own place of business.

Run. It was all she could do to stand and pretend that nothing was wrong when everything in her urged her to run away.

Hugh stood there for a moment, studying her curiously, then waved for one of the waiters. "Ask Mr. Canton to come back," he said. "I think he's at the Silver Slipper."

Cat felt her legs tremble. "Thank you. Is there someplace private I could wait?"

Hugh considered the request, then thought of everything she had done for Molly, whom he liked very much. And for Teddy. Yet it might mean the loss of his much-needed job. He simply didn't know how Mr. Canton felt about Catalina Hilliard. He only knew his employer had been short-tempered since that afternoon the two of them had retreated to his room. He had been even more short-tempered when he saw the new signs outside the Silver Slipper.

Still, there was a kind of desperation in Catalina's eyes that made Hugh feel protective. He nodded. "Why don't you wait in Mr. Canton's room?"

Cat nodded.

"The dog's back there," Hugh warned.

Cat gave him a smile. The dog was nothing much to worry about . . . compared to her other problems.

She walked to the back, through the hall, and to Marsh's all-too-familiar room, opening the door gingerly. The dog growled and she hesitated, but then opened it all the way. She remembered Canton calling the dog Win.

"It's all right, Win," she said. "I'm not going to hurt you."

The dog rose from where he apparently had been sleeping, stretched, and growled, but he made no other move. She went inside.

The room was still plain, ridiculously so. Everything was neat, too neat. There was no individuality here, except for the dog, and even that was hostile. Her gaze was drawn to the bed. It was the only thing that wasn't neat. The covers were thrown back, and it looked as if a battle had gone on there. She couldn't help but think of the other afternoon, when they had . . . But she also couldn't forget his bitter, parting words. She wanted to flee again.

She avoided the bed and stood against the wall where she could glance out the back window. There was no view here, only an alley, and her gaze kept going to the bed, her mind's eye seeing something that had happened days ago as her body kept feeling things better forgotten.

To try to rid her mind of both, she turned her attention to the dog. It was the ugliest dog she had ever seen. Its paws were too big, its body too long, its tail too short. Nothing went together. And it was glaring at her with the welcome a sinner gave Satan.

She leaned a hand over to see what would happen, and the dog shied away as if expecting a blow. It reminded Cat of herself years ago. It reminded her of now. All of a sudden her strength drained away, and she buried her head in her hands.

Cat suddenly felt the dog's head against her knee, and she looked down. The dog's eyes were still wary, yet it seemed to be offering some kind of understanding.

She reached out her hand again, and this time the dog didn't move but tolerated her touch, as if he felt and understood her misery. He comforted her.

But just at that moment she heard the sound of boots against the floor, and the door flew open.

Canton looked at her, down at the dog, back to her.

"What an unexpected pleasure," he drawled. "Welcome to my parlor."

CHAPTER 19

Few things in life surprised Marsh Canton. He seldom underestimated an opponent or was surprised by one. He understood human behavior even when he didn't much like it—including his own.

But he had been startled when he was summoned back from the Silver Slipper with a whispered message that someone was waiting for him. He was stunned to learn that it was Cat Hilliard waiting in his room.

Nothing, however, prepared him for the impression he suddenly had as she lifted those great green eyes to look at him after his carelessly suggestive words, uttered out of pure astonishment. He deeply regretted them.

Her face was composed, as he had come to expect. And admire. Her eyes didn't flare this time at his words but were shrouded instead. He had never seen a woman before who could hide her feelings as she did. As he also did. He knew the discipline and control it required.

Yet he was only too aware of tension in her body. That was unusual—not only unusual but, in some way, poignant. If she needed something badly enough to come to him, she needed it very badly indeed.

"Is it Molly?" The sarcasm, the tease, was gone from his voice as his gaze met hers.

Cat found herself surprised that he knew something was wrong when she had tried diligently to hide it. She was usually so good at it. But Canton and she had always been able to see through each other. It was one of those odd things that had always attracted, and repelled, her.

She shook her head. "There's nothing wrong," she said.

"I would like to think you're here because of my charm, but somehow I can't quite accept that," he said, watching her face closely.

"You're right," she replied in a cold voice. "I have a business proposition."

Marsh didn't let his surprise show. Instead he walked over to where she stood and peered down at her. "Business proposition?"

"I find I have to go out of town. I've decided to sell the Silver Slipper," Cat said steadily. "I thought you might be interested."

Marsh didn't move. The announcement was too stunning. He tried to think. Why? She had owned the Silver Slipper, from all accounts, nearly two decades. Was it because of him? He didn't believe that for one moment. He'd sensed she relished the battle as much as he, until that afternoon in his room. That, he knew, wouldn't result in her surrender. If anything, it would have spurred her on, as he'd thought it had when she'd cut the prices of her drinks.

"Well?" she said abruptly, interrupting his thoughts.

"Are you in such a hurry?"

"I have to leave tomorrow," she said. "I want it settled before then."

"Why?"

"That's none of your business."

"I think it is," he said. He looked at her shrewdly. "Is there something wrong with the title?"

Cat glared at him and reached into her pocket. "Here's the deed," she said, waiting for him to take it. "If you don't want to make an offer, say so. I'll go to someone else."

"Why come to me first?" He couldn't keep the suspicion from his voice.

"I thought I could get the best price. No more competition."

"That sounds like the Catalina Hilliard I know," Marsh said, partially satisfied. "But the Silver Slipper is worthless without the Ice Queen."

Cat felt her heart thump. Be calm. "It's one of the best locations in the city."

Marsh detected a certain desperation despite her cold demeanor. He wondered why. He wondered even more why he cared. But he did.

"What is it, Catalina?" he asked softly.

Cat was mesmerized by his voice, by his eyes. She'd thought he would jump at the opportunity, but instead she saw concern in his eyes. Curiosity, yes. She had expected that. But concern? It unsettled her.

"I told you," she said. "I have to leave town. A . . . a sick relative."

"A dear old mother?" he asked sarcastically, angry at his own concern. It was none of his business.

"If you have to know, yes," she said.

"Why don't I believe that?"

Cat stood. "I don't care what you believe. Make an offer, or don't. I've had others express an interest. I just thought I would give you first refusal."

"Out of the goodness of your heart?"

"Yes!"

"You're a liar."

"And you're a scoundrel."

"It takes one to know one," he snapped back. "That's why there are always fireworks between us."

"There's nothing between us."

"Don't lie to yourself, Miss Cat," he said as he leaned down, his lips touching hers. She shied away, her anger sparking.

But his hand was on her arm now, and she could go only so far. His lips met hers again, this time insistently. He could feel her tension, the tautness of her body, the determined refusal to respond to him. Yet he felt her tremble slightly, and he wished he knew why. Desire. Dislike. Or the fear he sensed was inside her.

His hand played about her face. "What is it, Catalina?" He repeated the question he'd posed earlier. His voice was soothing, compelling, almost mesmerizing.

I can't. Despite everything that had happened between them, Cat wanted so much, suddenly, to tell him. Caution stopped her. He *would* take advantage. Men did that. Except for Ben Abbott, who had not really been her husband, after all. She whimpered involuntarily.

Canton backed off suddenly, the concern in his eyes turning to something hard, then bleak.

He was a stranger again. Hard. Cold. Distant. And Cat knew a depth of despair she hadn't felt in years. Why had she come here?

She tried to move, but her legs were unsteady, so she stood still, trying to find some balance. "I'm sorry I bothered you," she said, hating the catch she heard in her own voice.

He watched her for a moment. "What are you going to do now?"

"Find a buyer."

"You really mean it?"

"No," she said rudely. "I just came here to be insulted."

"Cat . . ."

"Miss Hilliard to you."

"Miss Hilliard," he said obediently and in a soothing voice, "what in the hell is going on?"

She gave him a cool look. "I told you."

"You told me nothing."

"I told you everything you need to know."

He sighed. "How much do you want for the Silver Slipper?"

"Ten thousand." There was a note of hope in her voice that worried him. It was an amazingly low price. In fact, it would be thievery on his part, and now he *knew* something was wrong.

"I don't have that kind of money," he said frankly. "I've put everything I have into the Glory Hole."

The glimmer of hope left her eyes. She shrugged. It was a gallant gesture, but he didn't believe the implied indifference.

"I might be able to get it," he said, surprised at himself.

"When?" The sharpness of the question belied her pose.

"I'll let you know this afternoon."

Cat hesitated, then said quietly, "I'll come back."

"How is Molly?" He'd wanted to take her by surprise, to learn whether this had anything to do with the girl. Had Cat been threatened? He would tear whoever was responsible to pieces. He didn't even wonder at his rather unexpected protectiveness.

"She's fine," Cat said as she tried to move her legs once more. She hesitated for a moment, then thought he should know, just in case anything happened to her. "She's staying with your Hugh."

He felt his jaw tightening. "So he is working for you?"

She shook her head. "That was the idea in the beginning, but . . . he changed his mind." She tipped her head. "He has a strong sense of loyalty to you." She hesitated. "Please don't fire him."

Ordinarily, he would have left her hanging, although he had no intention of firing Hugh. Hugh was much too valuable, even if his loyalty had been in question. Marsh had grown to like him, too, and to trust him. Up to a point. But now he looked into Cat's pleading face. "I won't," he said.

Strangely, she trusted him in this. Perhaps even in other ways. Perhaps that was why she'd come here. She didn't like him, she told herself. She didn't like him at all, but neither did she think he lied. He didn't have to. He was infuriating enough without lying. She closed her eyes, trying for a fraction of a second to will away that attraction that still lingered between them, that overpowering sexual pull that never went away, no matter what he did or said.

Cat felt his hand on her face again, and she remembered that brief gentleness days ago. She wanted to lean her face into his palm, to forget the panic that was bubbling inside her, threatening to boil up and spread stark desperation through every cell.

And then his lips touched hers with a lightness, a tenderness, that sapped all her resentment. Her lips responded with reckless abandon, a need so strong, she couldn't harness it. She was losing everything, and she needed this inexplicable drawing of strength from a man who had so much of it. That flicker of concern in his eyes, that calm assurance, was irresistible.

His kiss deepened, and the heat between

them became blue hot, like the deepest part of a flame. She felt shudders run through her body, and she hated the way she succumbed so easily to him, the way she craved his nearness.

She wanted to whisper his name, but she wouldn't give him that weapon. She wouldn't let him know how very much she needed him.

He took the shawl from her hair, letting it drop on the floor, and his fingers freed the knot she'd so carefully constructed. His lips moved to her ear, and the shudders turned into hot spasms. She struggled against them, finally moving slightly until his lips left the ear he had been nuzzling and he cocked his head, looking at her. "Don't leave San Francisco," he commanded softly.

She couldn't look at him. If she did, she would melt again. And she couldn't do that. But she let her head fall against his chest, resting there, feeling a sense of belonging that had been missing all her life.

He allowed her to remain like that, his breath light against her hair. Marsh was afraid to move, afraid to break this fragile moment. He held her tightly, but not too tightly. He knew instinctively that she was near a breaking point of some kind, and he felt wanted, trusted—though not trusted enough.

And why *should* he be trusted? He winced and tightened his arms around her possessively, leaning his head against her dark hair. "Ah, Cat," he said. "I won't let anyone hurt you."

Except me. His thoughts went back once more to that afternoon. He'd done a damn good job of hurting her, and now she didn't, wouldn't, trust him, and he couldn't blame her. He suddenly knew he *would* find the money to buy the Silver Slipper.

It was Marsh who finally separated them, withdrawing ever so slightly so he could look into her eyes. "I'll find the money," he said. "Will you stay on if I do? Manage the Silver Slipper? Buy it back when you can?"

Astonishment stilled her completely. "Why would you do that?"

He chuckled. "I like the challenge of your competition."

Cat hesitated, and then she liked the idea very much. She liked the idea of not running again, of outsmarting James Cahoon. If he thought she owned the saloon, she would love to see his face when she told him it wasn't so. She didn't own the Silver Slipper. She only managed it. She could hide the money due her on the sale, say she gambled it away. But could she trust Canton?

She looked up into his face, trying to find an answer. She had trusted so few times, after Cahoon. Ben, but only after years. And Teddy, again only after a long time. Teddy, dear God. If she left the Silver Slipper, what would happen to Teddy?

Canton's face was unsmiling as he waited for a decision. Perhaps it was that silence, the lack of questions, a kind of trust he was giving her, despite all their confrontations.

And she was a gambler. She had gambled when she had come to San Francisco. He was offering her a chance to keep what she had. If he was lying to her, if he didn't return the Silver

Slipper, she wouldn't be any worse off than now. But she did believe him. In this one thing, she did. She still didn't know why she had faith in him, but she sensed he was a man who kept his word, regardless of the other things he did. And this way she could take care of Teddy.

"All right," she said.

"A deal?"

She smiled. A small smile, but a smile nonetheless. "A deal."

He thought he had never seen anything quite as lovely as her smile. It had been a very long time since anyone had smiled at him like that.

Marsh leaned down and kissed her lightly. "Do you want to stay here while I see what I can do about finding ten thousand dollars?"

She shook her head. She still had Molly to think of. The Pinkerton detective. Sweet Lucifer, but she was late. Very, very late. And then the bank. She had to take out everything she had in the bank and put her cash under another name.

"I have a few errands," she said. "I'll come back."

"Will you be all right?"

She was surprised again. He obviously sensed something was wrong, and yet he still asked no questions. She lifted her chin. "Of course."

He went to one of his drawers and took out a small gun. "This is a derringer. Do you know how to use one?"

She nodded. "I have one at the Silver Slipper."

"I'll remember that," he said, a crooked grin on his face.

"Is that what you were trying to find out?"

He shrugged, leaving the question unanswered. But she knew he wasn't afraid of anything.

"Thank you, anyway," she said.

Marsh hesitated. He wanted to ask more, but questions would probably only make her bolt. Christ, what was wrong? He could always sense fear. Like death. "Would you like an escort?"

Cat hesitated, then shook her head. She needed to get away from Canton. He was too close. He made her braver than she should be at this moment.

She turned away from him and went to the mirror, rearranging her hair and putting the shawl back over her head. He watched, then said quietly, "Then let's share a carriage. I have to go out too."

Cat wondered how he sensed her reluctance to go back into the street. But then he'd surprised her completely today, as he usually did.

Both were silent as they went outside, and he found a carriage for hire. He helped her in, asked her destination, and made no comment when she mentioned her bank. His presence in the carriage was both comforting and disconcerting. Something had changed between them. A small element of trust. Tentative. Fragile. Not yet the kind to be tested by assurances or questions.

Cat leaned back against the cushion of the carriage, feeling his knee touch her, knowing the same poignant wanting she always did with him, only now there was something else, something that made her inexplicably shy and uncertain. He had offered help, asking for nothing in return. She refused to offer anything, for fear it would be misunderstood as it had before.

"A business proposition," he said suddenly, as if reading her mind. "Nothing else, Miss Cat."

She felt a now-familiar tremor, tremors that often preceded earthquakes. Disasters. Would anything between them just be a business proposition?

"I still don't understand why—"

"I expect to make a profit on it." He grinned. "Don't worry yourself, Miss Hilliard."

"Are you sure you can get the money?"

"I'm not sure about anything, Miss Cat," he said, making his reply light and slightly mocking. "Especially when I'm around you, but I would think so." He wished he was as confident as he sounded. He had damned little money left. All he had was the Glory Hole. Collateral.

Hell, he was getting bored, anyway. He was never meant for the peaceful life of a business owner.

Cat withdrew all but one hundred dollars from her account. She had already considered her next move. A different bank where she wasn't known, a different name. She didn't dare keep the cash.

But that infernal sketch in the paper.

Perhaps the detective could help . . . if he would even see her now.

She was just a few blocks from his office,

and she walked swiftly, only too aware of the money in her reticule, which, despite the large-denomination bills, still felt stuffed.

Cat found the office tucked on the second floor of a building on a side street. Unpretentious for such a famous agency, she thought, and remembered Quinn Devereux's words. *Completely trustworthy. Discreet.*

She tried the door, found it open, and walked in. There were several desks, a young man sitting behind one of them. He looked up as she entered. "Can I help you?"

"Mr. Templeton," she said. "I had an appointment. . . . I know I'm very late but . . ."

He nodded. "Mr. Templeton is still here." He rose and knocked at a door, entering at a muffled sound, then returned. "Miss Hilliard?"

Cat nodded.

"He'll see you."

Cat moved toward the door and entered.

A man behind a desk rose and came to meet her. "I'm Booth Templeton. I've heard a lot about you, Miss Hilliard," he said, and grinned as Cat winced slightly. "From Mr. Devereux," he added with a wink. "All very interesting and complimentary. Now, how can I help you?"

Cat hesitated. "I'm sorry I'm late . . . something came up."

"That's all right," the detective said as he went around to his chair behind the desk. "Please sit down."

Cat didn't feel like sitting. She was too restless, but she found a straight chair and forced herself to sit. "Mr. Devereux said you were very . . . reliable," she said, wanting to get some kind of impression of her own. Her initial one was confidence. The Pinkerton man had a solid kind of face, the kind one tended to trust. Intelligent brown eyes that probed while giving little away. They weren't shuttered like Canton's, as if protecting secrets, but more like reserving judgment. Eyes that weighed without judging.

"I've . . . we've done some work for Mr. Devereux," Templeton said.

Cat hesitated. "Did you see the story in the paper a few days ago? The shooting in front of the Silver Slipper."

He nodded.

"The young lady involved . . . believes her father was behind it. She's terrified of him, and although she won't say why, I think I can guess at least some of it." She hesitated, wondering whether he would understand.

"How old is she?"

"Nineteen."

"He's still her rightful guardian, then?"

Cat nodded.

"What can we do?"

"She . . . Molly . . . thinks he's been responsible for her friends being hurt, perhaps even killed. A maid named Glynneth, who tried to help her. She just disappeared."

"Why does she think something happened to her?"

"The girl, Glynneth, was betrothed and very much in love. She never said anything to her fiancé before disappearing. Others . . . were beaten."

"And you want me to find this maid? Or try to find out what happened to her?"

Cat nodded. "And see what else you can find out about . . . my friend's father."

"Who is this man?"

Cat hesitated. "Will you take the case?"

He studied her for a moment. "A prominent man?"

Cat nodded again. "A banker in Oakland."

"Do you want to tell me what you suspect?"

"I think he's . . . abused her in ways a father shouldn't."

"That's damn hard to prove. Begging your pardon, Miss Hilliard."

"I know," Cat said. "That's why you need to start with Glynneth. And perhaps follow him. If I know his kind, Molly's not the only young girl he's used."

The detective's eyes grew harder. "Unfortunately, I think you're right." He hesitated, watching her carefully. "I'll have to talk to the girl."

Cat expected that. "I'll arrange it, but I doubt she'll tell you much. She . . . well, it's very difficult."

Templeton's face softened. "I understand."

Cat liked the emotion on his face. He would be careful, and yet he would have a measure of compassion. He was the man she wanted. "Now how much . . ."

"One hundred to start," he said.

"Done," Cat said. "There's something else."

He merely waited for her to continue.

"Mr. Devereux said I could trust you. Completely."

He waited for her to continue.

"I want to put a sizable amount of money in an account under another name. I'm . . . too well known. Can you act as my agent?"

"Is it against the law?"

She shrugged. "I don't think so. It's my money. But a . . . relative I thought dead has just shown up."

"Husband?" he guessed.

Cat winced. She didn't want to think of Cahoon as her husband. The thought alone was sickening. "He's a gambler. He'll take everything and lose it."

"You'll trust me?"

"I trust Mr. Devereux."

"Smart lady." He hesitated, then seemed to make a decision. "I'll deposit if for you. Name of . . . Kelly Edwards. That could be a man or woman. I'll write you a receipt for it. I'll get back to you on the other matter as soon as possible."

Cat spent nearly an hour with him, giving him the details about Molly, telling him to contact Teddy if he couldn't reach her. And finally, turning over to him the money she'd just taken from the bank.

She felt better as she left his office, even as she realized that she was doing an awful lot of trusting all of a sudden. For someone who had done precious little of that in the past years, it was astounding to her.

And not just a little frightening.

"You want to do what?"

David Schuyler Scott seemed to remember

he'd had a similar conversation before with this particular client. But then Marsh Taylor Canton never ceased to amaze him.

"I'm buying the Silver Slipper," Marsh explained again. "But I want it in writing that I'll sell it back."

"For the same price?"

Marsh shrugged.

"What happened to the feud?"

"I don't think that's changed any," Marsh said with a slight grin.

"You wouldn't care to tell me what's going on?"

"No."

David surrendered. It wasn't his business. All he could do was advise and assist. He'd discovered this particular client wanted none of the first.

"I'll have it ready in an hour."

Marsh's next stop was his bank. He used Quinn Devereux's name as a reference, and that got him into the vice president's office. He pledged the Glory Hole as collateral for a ten-thousand-dollar loan. The banker was obviously curious, but Devereux had initially steered Marsh to him, and Devereux was one of the bank's wealthiest clients. And the banker had been impressed with what Mr. Canton had done with the Glory Hole. He promised to have the money the next day.

As Marsh walked back to Scott's office, he realized it was the first time since the war that he had done anything for anyone—without getting paid for it.

• • •

Molly was happier than she had ever been. She loved children. She loved caring for them. She particularly liked Hugh and Elizabeth's rambunctious imps.

Molly had been shy at first when she'd arrived at Hugh O'Connell's home a week earlier, but she couldn't be shy long as children crawled into her lap and smeared wet kisses on her. They were five in number, soon to be six, and totally uninhibited, obviously used to being loved by their parents and "Uncle Teddy." They were like little steps when they stood beside each other, which wasn't often, because they had too much energy to stay still long enough even to line up.

They had accepted her unconditionally. She was "Uncle Teddy's friend, Aunt Molly."

Not only had she warmed to the love in the house, but she had felt needed. Elizabeth O'Connell was nearing the time of birth, and though she denied it, Molly could tell she tired easily. Molly had taken over as though born to it. She could watch over the children, dress them, play with them, put them to bed, say prayers with them. She was even learning a little bit about cooking.

At the morning meal Hugh would linger, talking about the night before at the Glory Hole. He would discuss politics and gossip and who had gone bust, a frequent occurrence in San Francisco, where fortunes were being made and lost at dizzying speeds. Hugh was uncommonly thoughtful of his wife. Molly had never seen two people who really cared about each other before;

she hadn't, in fact, believed that people really loved each other.

Teddy had joined them several times. There was some strain at first between the two men, but then it had seemed to disappear. Molly enjoyed watching Teddy eat, then light his pipe. She warmed to the way he winked at her when one of the children climbed all over him and the cozy, safe way she felt when he was around.

Then several nights ago, on Sunday when both Hugh and Teddy were off, Teddy had taken her for a walk. . . .

She'd enjoyed his respectful touch on her arm, the way it made her tingle inside. She had never thought she would like a man touching her, but there was something warm and affectionate and safe about Teddy's touch that made her heart thump in a happy way. She found herself looking forward to his visits, not just as a friend, but as someone she cherished being with.

The fear was still with her, but she had been able to push it aside during the day, during the times she was busy. At night, however, it always came back. Night was always when *it* had happened, when he came to her bedroom. She wondered whether she would ever welcome night, instead of fearing it so.

Teddy tried to reassure her. Miss Catalina was taking steps, he said, so her father couldn't come after her. He didn't say what those steps were, but she had a great deal of faith in Miss Catalina. She was so strong. *She* wasn't afraid of anything. Molly remembered Miss Catalina talking to her, telling her, "I was born in a brothel. . . . My mother sold me when I was thirteen."

Those words had helped. If Miss Cat had overcome something like that, then Molly could too. She didn't even feel like Mary Beth anymore. She was Molly, who'd had the strength to run away, who'd defied her father, who'd made friends. And now who felt needed. And capable. And wanted.

And she did so look forward to Teddy's visits, to those walks with him. She looked up at him now, feeling his eyes on her. Brown and warm. He treated her so gingerly, as if she were a piece of crystal easily broken.

"Molly," he said tenderly, "Catalina's going to talk to a Pinkerton detective about your father. You'll probably have to talk to him."

Molly felt the usual sickness rise in her at the thought of her father. Teddy's eyes were steady, expectant, and she would die before she disappointed him. If he and Catalina cared enough to take chances for her, to defy her father, then she could do no less, even if she had to talk about what had happened.

She nodded and was rewarded with a smile. She suddenly discovered she wanted more from him than a smile. She saw him swallow hard, a muscle moving in that face that was becoming so dear to her, his face moving down toward her until . . .

He stopped just as his lips were about to reach hers. Stopped. Hesitated. Retreated. Shaking his head as if in disbelief at his own action.

"Teddy . . ."

He closed his eyes for a fraction of a second

as if pleading with a higher being, then opened them again. "Don't look at me that way," he said, a catch in his voice.

"Why?"

"Dammit," he said angrily. "I'm too old for you."

Molly saw his jaw work. "Sometimes," she said, "I feel a hundred years old."

One of his big hands went up to her chin, his hard fingers caressing it. "You have your whole life ahead of you."

"Only because of you and Miss Catalina."

"Gratitude," he muttered. "That's what you feel. All you feel."

She shook her head. "I don't think so."

"I'm old enough to be your father," he said roughly, and saw her face blanch. He could have kicked himself. Worse. He wished he could bang his thick head against a brick wall.

His expression must have shown his self-disgust because one of her small hands wound its way into the fist that had fallen from her face. "You're nothing like him," she said fiercely.

He felt that small trusting hand, its fingers clinging to his, and the self-disgust faded. He felt as if someone had given him the greatest gift in the world, and yet it wasn't a gift he could accept. She deserved much more than a broken down ex-fighter.

He had watched as she laughed with the children, that sad, wistful look disappearing for those brief moments as the peal of her laughter decorated the room. He had watched as she so carefully assisted Elizabeth with the meal, her face furrowed in concentration. He had watched her bandage a cut on small Betsy's hand with unabashed sympathy as if she felt the hurt herself. She was a gentle creature, too gentle for a great oaf like himself. Too gentle and fragile and wounded.

But he couldn't help but think what it would be like, living with her. Sharing things. Looking across a table at her. He felt a hurtful ache inside at the thought. He knew he dare go no further with such ideas. He would drive himself crazy.

"I'd better take you home," he said roughly.

Home, Molly thought. Hugh and Elizabeth's was as close to one as she'd ever had. She'd never really known what the word meant until she'd come to live with them. A place of warmth and love. A place to laugh and care. And have people care about her.

Someone like Teddy. She admired him so much. His gruff gentleness with Hugh's children. His competence at the Silver Slipper. His protectiveness of everyone there. His sharp and decisive mind, though she knew few realized exactly how sharp under that rough exterior. He seemed to want it that way, though Molly had seen the number of times Miss Catalina had sought his advice.

But she didn't know how to break that reserve of his, how to let him know how much she liked and admired him. And cared in other ways too.

Canton was back at the Glory Hole when Cat arrived. He was leaning against the bar, looking relaxed. Yet the gun was strapped to his waist, and as always, Cat sensed that outlaw spirit lurking beneath the lazy pose. He turned to the man tending bar, said something, then strode over to her, that slight, indecipherable smile on his lips. "I think we've some business to discuss."

Hope sprang up in her. Hope and yet a kind of despair. She felt his hand on her arm. Strong. Firm. She allowed him to lead the way to his room. The dog was inside, and he growled at being disturbed. Marsh shrugged. "The ordinance about shooting strays . . . I've been trying to keep him inside."

Glad for a brief reprieve, a subject away from her current troubles, Cat went over to Win, stooped, and regarded the dog as steadily as he regarded her. All of a sudden Win turned over on his side, exposing his stomach to her, and she rubbed it gently. Win growled. But it wasn't exactly a threatening growl. The dog simply didn't know any other sound to make, Cat surmised.

"I'll be damned," Marsh said, and Cat turned her head. "The cursed animal has barely allowed me to touch it." The chagrined look on his face made her smile, although she knew it was probably a very stiff smile. She felt so brittle at the moment, so tense. If anyone touched her, she feared she would shatter into hundreds of pieces. She had been doing one thing after another, automatically, as if it were someone else doing them. Each had kept her from returning to the Glory Hole and then to the Silver Slipper, from confronting what eventually had to be confronted: her past.

Now she had to face something else. Canton and his proposal. Canton, who made her blood run hot and her anger rush cold.

She stood, facing him. "Are you going to accept my offer?"

"Yes," he said simply.

"Do you have the money?"

"I will tomorrow."

Cat struggled to keep the disappointment from showing. Her hand touched the deed in her pocket. She couldn't take it back to the Silver Slipper with her. She wanted it in Canton's possession tonight, so there could be no proof that she'd known her husband was still alive when she sold it. But could she trust Canton?

His dark eyes flickered in the light of the late-afternoon sun seeping into the room. "You want it now?" His words were curiously soft, that southern accent she'd detected at their first meeting more pronounced than she'd ever heard it.

She nodded.

"You believed I had that kind of money at hand?"

She inclined her head.

"Sorry to disappoint you, darlin'. But I had to borrow it." He didn't know why he explained. Now she would probably guess he'd used the Glory Hole as collateral. But he had seen that stricken look, that sudden panic in her eyes.

Cat was jolted. "The Glory Hole?"

He nodded, and she didn't doubt him for a moment. He was risking the Glory Hole for her.

She just stood there. "Why?" The question came out flatly.

He turned away from her and walked to the window, staring out.

"Why?" she repeated.

"It's a good investment," he said.

"You don't even know why I want to sell."

He turned abruptly. His face was grim in a way she'd never seen it before. He'd always worn that slight smile which disguised his thoughts. "If you want to tell me, you will. I'll have the money tomorrow. You have to trust me on that. In the meantime I had my lawyer prepare an agreement." He walked over to the bureau and picked up a paper, then handed it to her.

Cat scanned it quickly, then again more slowly, her eyes widening as she looked up at him. "You . . . didn't have to do this."

"I thought it would make you feel better."

"Why do you care how I feel?" The grim set of his mouth didn't change as he regarded her without answering. "Canton . . . ?"

"What?"

"Why . . . why do you care how I feel?"

"You've made life interesting, darlin'," he said, trying to insert mockery into the words.

It didn't quite work. There was an element of concern he couldn't hide, and Cat sensed it surprised him as much as it did her. She tried to remember the other afternoon, the one during which he so effectively stripped the hide from her.

"Who can I best if you're gone?"

"You haven't done that yet," she retorted, but there was little sting in her voice.

"You see," he said, "that's why."

Cat looked down at the paper again. It was simple enough. She recognized the attorney's name and remembered her earlier reaction when she discovered David Scott was Canton's attorney. One of the few honest lawyers in the city. The agreement, already signed by M. Taylor Canton, stated that Canton was purchasing the Silver Slipper for ten thousand dollars. It said further that Canton, or any subsequent owner, agreed to sell back the Silver Slipper at no more than ten thousand dollars upon demand by Catalina Hilliard within a three-year period.

It further stipulated that Catalina Hilliard would operate the Silver Slipper and keep ninety percent of the profits.

The agreement, signed and witnessed, was generous in the extreme. It meant that Canton couldn't sell the Silver Slipper from under her without the subsequent purchaser agreeing to the same terms for three years. No one, she knew, would buy a property under those conditions.

"You didn't have to do this," she said. "I would have sold you the Silver Slipper without it."

Now *his* body was tense. He didn't like the questions. He most definitely didn't want gratitude. He had only wanted to alleviate some of that desperation he'd felt in her earlier. And he would lose nothing. The ten percent in profits would more than cover his interest.

But he knew his action went deeper. Much deeper. He didn't want her to leave. Not San Francisco. Not the Silver Slipper. Not this room.

The walls closed in on them. His hand touched her hair, gently urging her head toward him, and those startling green eyes were intent on him, watching, still obviously wondering whether to trust.

Christ, it had been so long since he had even wanted trust. Now he did. And he was afraid to show it, afraid she would throw it in his face as he had thrown her trust away days ago in this very room.

That knowledge was a raw sore in his gut. He wanted her. And that want had grown into obsession. A splendid obsession until something ugly inside him had refused to accept it, had taken and twisted it to better meet his bitter expectations of life.

Her fear earlier, mixed with that fierce, determined pride to do what had to be done, had touched him in ways no one had since before the war. Made him feel protective, for God's sake. Made him risk the one thing that had given him a little self-respect again. But what good was the Glory Hole without Cat Hilliard across the street?

He wanted to kiss her, to enclose her body in his arms, and then to make love to her. But how could he? How could he not expect her to misunderstand this time, to think he was demanding payment? He had been neatly caught in his own trap, and every part of his body and mind was paying for it now.

Marsh leaned over and kissed her lightly. He placed his hand on her shoulder and felt his own fingers shake. Shake with efforts to keep from drawing her toward the bed, from clasping her close to him.

He'd never wanted anything in his life as much as to do that.

His hand went up, his fingers tracing a line down the fine contours of her face. She was absolutely still, and he didn't know what she was thinking. She was as damn good at hiding her feelings as he had trained himself to be. He wondered again why. Why did she guard herself so? Why all the contradictions in her?

"Cat," he said in a low voice. "I'm sorry . . . the other afternoon." And he was. If he could take those words back, even at the price of one knife wound for each sick word, he would. But he'd never apologized before, not since the war, and the words were rusty. Thick. Almost choking.

He recognized the awkwardness of the words, and it cut a painful swath through him. For what he had been. For what he had become. For what he wanted to be now, not knowing whether it was possible. Need, that had nothing to do with lust, filled him with a completeness that was agonizing. How do you grab a moment and keep it? How do you take back unforgivable words? How can you change a soul that has ceased to exist in any meaningful way because it couldn't tolerate the things you had done?

Filled with a kind of pain he didn't know how to alleviate, he turned abruptly away from her.

He wanted to do so much for her. He wanted to run out and slay whatever dragon was haunting her. Now, that really was a new path.

An uncharted one. Yet he knew her well enough to know she wouldn't share this dragon with him. He waited. He waited for her to accept the agreement. He waited for her to respond to his rough apology, but she seemed as frozen as he.

"It doesn't matter what you said the other day," she finally replied, apparently in answer to the latter.

He turned to face her again. "It does. It does to me."

"There was some truth in your . . . observation," she said with a dismissive shrug, but something terribly sad lurked in her eyes, a glimpse, for once, of the complicated lady inside. Marsh felt worse, knowing that somehow that day he had dealt a blow much stronger than intended.

He reached out, his hand touching her arm lightly. "Ah, Cat, I don't know whether we're the worst thing that happened to each other, or the best. Or whether it's too late for either of us. I just know no one has ever affected me as you do. It tends to bring out the demon in me. I don't quite know what to do with it."

"Canton unsure of himself?"

Her words made him wince. He hated the image of uncertainty. He hated the fact of uncertainty. He hated it being applied to himself. Nonetheless, he decided on honesty. Nothing else would work with her. And even that might not. "Perhaps. A little."

Cat smiled a tremulous, breathtaking smile he hadn't seen before. Perhaps, he thought, honesty had a lot going for it.

Marsh swallowed. She had never been more

desirable. And she had been very desirable indeed. He leaned down, his lips skimming along hers, waiting for an invitation.

It didn't come. He couldn't stem a tide of disappointment. And frustration. Yet he couldn't blame her . . . not after his last performance in this room. But he knew she wasn't unaffected. She was tense, and she couldn't hide the very slight trembling of her hand, the sudden fire in her eyes.

He admired her control, even though it tormented him. But then he admired a great deal about her. More each day, in fact, and never more so than now.

Marsh stepped back, not wanting her to think her response, or lack of it, had anything to do with his offer. It was one of the most difficult things he had ever done in his life, but he'd earned this particular punishment. "Take it," he said of the agreement.

Cat stared at it a moment as if trying to remember what it was, and then she carefully folded it and put it in her reticule.

It had been difficult, so damned difficult, not to respond seconds earlier, when his lips feathered her cheek, the sensitive area around her eyes. He had been waiting for a response, she knew, and she also knew she couldn't give it. She would never again put herself in the position she had days ago. She wouldn't thank him with her body, wouldn't let him think again that it was so easily sold these days.

But, sweet Lucifer, how she wanted to.

Cat had already decided she would face James Cahoon tonight. She wouldn't, couldn't, put it off. She would do it, though, in her own time under her own precautions.

Suddenly decided, she pulled out the deed to the Silver Slipper. She looked up into dark-gray eyes that now looked puzzled. "You will have the money tomorrow?"

He nodded.

Cat took a deep breath. She would rather Canton have the Silver Slipper than James Cahoon. "If anything happens to me, you'll see that Teddy gets the money," she said. "Your word on it?"

His hand went to her arm again. "What might happen, Cat?"

She shrugged. "Probably nothing. Do you have pen and ink?"

He nodded and fetched both from a drawer, then watched quizzically as she took out a paper from a pocket in her dress, unfolded it, and quickly scribbled her name on the deed. "Hugh can witness this," she said.

Marsh took it from her, staring in astonishment at the deed to the Silver Slipper. She had signed it over to M. Taylor Canton. "Are you . . . sure?"

"No," she said honestly. "But it's the only thing I can do now."

"Cat?"

She stiffened against the concern in his voice. "I expect the money tomorrow."

"What's wrong, Cat?" His question was raw now.

"The past," she said simply. "I can handle it."

Marsh felt sick. If he hadn't been such an

ass, perhaps . . . But looking at her face, he knew he wouldn't learn any more. "If you need anything . . ."

"I won't," she said abruptly, "except your word about Teddy."

"You have it."

Cat forced herself to move toward the door when, more than anything, she wanted to go into his arms. She wanted to drink in his strength. She wanted the gentleness she'd tasted for such a short time. She wanted so much, but not enough to destroy herself for it.

First James. And then she would deal with Canton.

She turned toward the door and moved, hearing a low growl behind her. She glanced down. The dog had risen and was baring his teeth. "Fierce thing, aren't you?" she whispered. "Maybe I can learn to do that."

"You already do," Canton said. His voice was low and intimate . . . and even admiring. She looked at him suspiciously, but then the expression changed to something more hesitant. "Thank you," she said stiffly.

It was as awkwardly said as his apology. Another rarity?

"Be careful, darlin'," he said, wanting to say more but knowing this was not the right time.

"I'm always careful." *Except with you.*

He nodded. It hurt to watch her leave, but he had little choice. She had made her wishes known, and he respected them.

All the same, he planned to keep an eye on the Silver Slipper tonight. A very close eye.

CHAPTER 20

A knock came on her door, and she went to answer slowly. It was late, and she'd been alone, thinking, in her room for hours. She suspected Teddy was at her door, and opened it without asking.

"Dear Jesus," he said, "I'm glad you're here. I've been worried."

"Anyone left?"

"A few hangers-on. I'm ready to close."

"A blond man? Gambling?"

Teddy looked at her closely. "Yes. He's been asking about you."

Cat's hand went into her pocket, feeling the

derringer. "I'll be down in a few moments. You can tell him that."

Teddy's expression said she was acting oddly, that he was concerned. "It's all right," she said. "He may be someone I used to know. But except for him, let's close."

He nodded.

"And Teddy." He stopped at her words. "Tell the girls to finish up and go to bed. We'll clean up in the morning."

"Catalina, is there trouble?"

"There might be. I don't know."

"I'll be nearby."

"Teddy . . ." Cat hesitated. "I saw that detective today. Booth Templeton. He has your name. He agreed to check out Molly's father. He's been paid in advance." She stopped, then shrugged as if nothing were out of the ordinary. "I just thought you would like to know."

He nodded.

"If you need anything," she added, "go to Canton."

"Canton?" He didn't even try to hide the surprise in his voice.

She nodded, and before he could say anything else, she turned back into the room, effectively dismissing him. He closed the door slowly.

Cat took the two precious pieces of paper, the receipt for the deposit and Canton's pledge to sell back the Silver Slipper, and held them tightly for a moment. She then found a needle and thread, ripped one of the seams in an older dress, and sewed the papers inside, hanging the dress back up. She gave herself one more look before slipping out the door and down the steps.

Cat's gaze went straight to the man still sitting at the poker table, a half-filled glass of whiskey in his hand. His gaze lifted from the glass to her as she came down the steps. She saw it widen with recognition, then a leering appreciation.

He started to stand, nearly fell over a chair, and sat back down as his eyes followed her progress toward him. When she reached his table, he leaned over, using his elbows for support.

"You've improved with age, Lizzie."

"I can't say the same for you," she said contemptuously.

His hand went to the faint scar on his cheek, the one made years ago by her fingernails. "Your fault, Lizzie girl, but I'm prepared to forgive. For a price."

His hand reached out and tried to grab hers, but she was too quick and took a seat at the other side of the table. She glanced around. Teddy was ushering the last customer out. She looked at Wilhelmina and two other girls who were lingering behind.

"I'll take care of this," she said. "You go to bed."

Wilhelmina hesitated. "You sure, Miss Catalina?"

Cat nodded.

"Miss Catalina," the man across from Cat said with a sneer. "Pretty fancy name. What would everyone think if they knew it was really Lizzie? Lizzie Cahoon?"

"They would probably be as sick in their gut as I am," she said, her speech roughening. She felt it was the only language he would understand, and she wanted to make herself very clear.

He tried to stand but fell back down. Too much whiskey. Just as there had always been too much whiskey. "You ain't no better than a whore, Mrs. Cahoon." The last was stretched out, his voice insinuating and nasty.

"I'd rather be a whore than your wife," Cat said coldly.

"Too bad you can't do anything 'bout that," he said with a menacing smile. "Though you tried mighty hard. I wonder what your customers would think if they knew you stabbed your husband."

Cat forced herself to remain relaxed.

"You could go to prison," he continued. "Of course, I could be a forgiving man." He looked around the Silver Slipper slowly, and Cat followed his gaze. Teddy was across the room, still behind the bar, too far away to hear her low voice. Yet she knew he was aware of something odd going on. A bat wouldn't be far from his hands.

"Looks like a gold mine," James said, greed written all over his face. "I hear you own the place. The Ice Queen. Now that's a real joke. Wonder if the good people of San Francisco would still think that if they knew just how hot you were."

Cat felt rage. Red-hot rage squeezing her head. And revulsion. Waves and waves of revulsion. She wouldn't show it. Damn, she wouldn't show it.

She just smiled. A Canton smile. A smile that mocked without revealing anything.

"This must bring a lot of dollars," he said.

"It does," she agreed. "Too bad it doesn't belong to me."

"The paper said . . . ," he started, the sneer turning to what he probably thought was menace. But he couldn't compare to Canton in that regard. The thought made her smile, which obviously infuriated James.

She shrugged. "I can't help what the paper said. I just run this place."

"I don't believe you."

"I don't care what you believe."

James's eyes were a washed-out blue. Cat hadn't remembered how weak they were, how darting. Now they narrowed. "You lying bitch."

Cat started to rise, but his hand grabbed her. "Don't you walk away, wife."

Despite the fact he'd been drinking, or perhaps because of it, his grip was strong, and unlike Canton's, it was abhorrent. Teddy had started to move from behind the bar. She shook her head slightly, not wanting him to interfere. She could manage this. She knew she could.

"Take your hand off me," she said, her voice authoritative and cold, the same voice she used to quell unruly customers but even harder. To her surprise, he did.

"You're my wife," he said eyeing her expensive dress. "Even if I did believe you about not owning this place, you make plenty. I want it."

She shrugged. "Small habit I picked up from you. I gamble. It just so happens I have very little."

"Then you'll steal some," he said. "Or I'll tell all of San Francisco about their Ice Queen."

"Go ahead," she said. "More notoriety will only help the place. The owner will be pleased. San Franciscans admire their notorious people."

"I'll make you so notorious, you'll land in jail," he said in a voice that was all fury. "Don't forget you tried to kill me."

"Prove it," she said.

His face went a mottled red. She knew he had expected something else altogether, perhaps even the cowering illiterate girl she'd once been.

"For that matter," she added, "prove that we're married."

Panic flickered in his eyes, and suddenly she wondered whether they'd really been married at all. She tried to remember that ceremony so many years ago. It had been in the dead of night in some river town. The preacher had been so drunk, he could hardly say the words, but Cat—Lizzie—had been so frantic to get away from her mother's place that she'd accepted everything.

"Prove it," she said again.

"I don't have to prove it. You know it. We lived as man and wife. I could find people who remember."

"I don't know anything. And go ahead, find someone. We'll see what they remember, like your bringing men to my room. Husbands don't usually do that," she retorted in a low, bitter voice.

"By God, I'll prove it," he said.

She started to rise. "I have friends in San Francisco. Lawyers. Police officials. The mayor." Her gaze went over him contemptuously. "Who do you think they will believe?"

He jerked back, the legs of the chair scraping against the floor. "Think you're too good for me now, Lizzie? Well, you're still my wife, and what's yours is mine. I think I'll take a little look in that cash drawer.

"You'll do nothing but get out of here."

He stood. "I've been looking for you for years, Lizzie. You're going to pay for what you did, one way or another. We can start with tonight. Money first, and then you, Lizzie."

"The only thing you get are the drinks you've had tonight." She laughed. "On the house, for old times' sake. Now get out."

"Oh no, Lizzie girl." He started toward her, and she saw Teddy pick up the bat and move toward them. She didn't want him involved. This was *her* battle.

Her hand slipped into the pocket of her dress and withdrew the derringer, which she pointed straight at James's heart.

"Get out."

"You won't use that. You won't dare, not in front of a witness."

"Oh, but I would," she said in an icy voice. "And enjoy it. The bartender over there would swear you tried to rob me."

"Ah, Lizzie, honey. Remember how I helped you get away from your ma? You owe me," he said, desperately trying another tack.

Cat hated him so much, her hand shook. She wanted to kill him. Memories flooded back: the men who came to her room, the beatings when she protested. She had sworn never to use violence again, but now she ached to do it.

Her finger closed around the trigger, and panic filled his pale-blue eyes. "Now, Lizzie . . ."

"My name's Miss Hilliard."

He glared at her.

"Say it."

"Mi . . . Miss Hilliard."

"Do you know how much I would like to kill you?" The question was posed in a conversational tone that was much more threatening than anger. Something else Cat knew she had learned from her neighbor. *That* thought was excruciating too. She didn't want to be like him.

The man in front of her had visibly shrunk, though his hatred had not. It was pounding at her from his eyes.

"Get out," she said.

"You're my wife. . . . Any court will give me my rights."

"Another reason to kill you."

He stood, started for the door, then turned. "This isn't over, Lizzie."

"Miss Hilliard," she corrected.

"Goddamn you."

"My finger is getting tired."

James stumbled as he made for the swinging doors, pushing through them angrily.

Cat slumped down into a chair, dropping the derringer to her side. She felt as if someone had reached in and pulled her inside out, exposed every layer of her.

She sensed, rather than saw, Teddy go to the doors, close them, and lock them, then lock the windows. He came and sat down beside her, carefully avoiding the chair just occupied by their last customer.

"Cat . . . ?"

It was the first time he'd ever used that

name. It was, she knew, indicative of his worry.
She looked up through glazed eyes. They glistened not with tears—never again with tears.
Not for James, or because of him. But with the
sheen of lingering anger and frustration and the
morass of emotions invoked by this ghost from
the past.

She felt his big hand on hers, and she drank
in the comfort he silently offered. She was grateful that he didn't ask questions. She would never
be able to explain, not to him, not to anyone
about the way she'd once allowed herself to be
used.

"Did you . . . hear anything?"

He shook his head. "Will he be back?"

She shrugged wearily. "I don't know. Probably."

"Does it have . . . anything to do with
Molly?"

Cat smiled then. She knew it was probably
a very weak smile, but she was warmed by the
way he asked. It was nice to know that someone
cared about someone else.

"No. He's someone I used to know long
ago. But he's a coward. He seems so little now."
The last was said almost to herself.

"I'll keep a special eye out," he said.

She nodded, too emotionally spent to argue.
She slipped the derringer, which was sitting on
the table, back into her pocket and used the table to help her stand. Her legs were wobbly.

She had met her dragon and slain him—
temporarily. But it had taken its toll. She wondered if she would ever forget those pale-blue
eyes with all their hatred and venom. Would she

ever forget her own rage and urge to kill? She had come so close to killing him.

She remembered the cold, impersonal look in Canton's eyes after he had killed that man trying to abduct Molly. She shivered. And yet she wanted him. She wanted Canton with every fiber of her being. She wanted him to hold her, to run his long fingers over her body as if it were something fine rather than something filthy.

Go to him.

But she couldn't. What if James spread his stories throughout San Francisco? Canton would know she was exactly what he had accused her of that afternoon. He wouldn't want her then. Not in the same way. She could stand anything but his contempt.

"Catalina."

She turned toward Teddy's concerned expression. "It's all right, it really is. I'm going to bed."

She heard his rare low curse as she moved toward the stairs and dragged herself up to what used to be a sanctuary, but which, she now knew, would never be again.

Marsh had an uneasy feeling all evening. He didn't like not knowing what was going on. He didn't like the idea of Cat alone tonight. He didn't like the way she had squared her shoulders as if she had to face some kind of crucible.

He didn't like that quiet desperation he'd sensed, that had made her do something he knew she hated to do: ask him for a favor. Turn over her most precious possession to him. Trust him, for God's sake, when there was no reason to do so. Exactly the opposite, in fact.

Christ, now he knew why it had been a long time since he had cared for anyone. Caring hurt. More than that, it split open the shell he'd built around himself and made him want more than he had. Much more.

She had looked so damn gallant. He couldn't even imagine what might be plaguing a woman with her kind of strength.

He tried to distract himself, keeping an eye on the various games, helping at the bar when necessary, greeting customers. That had started to come easier; even Hugh admitted he was loosening up a bit. He didn't glower as he once did, sizing up every customer for a coffin, Hugh had added with some levity, quite unaware of how accurate he was. Still, Marsh kept glancing out across the street.

Everything seemed normal there. He had to stop himself several times from walking over. Cat had made it very clear that this was her business, and he respected that. Yet . . .

He still wore his gunbelt. Now people seemed to expect it. Part of the image of the Glory Hole, Hugh said.

Several times tonight he had found his hand going to the holster, as if in reassurance. His companion. The only friend he'd had in more years than he wished to remember. The gun was what he knew. What he depended on.

Only a few customers remained at the Glory Hole. He wandered over to the window again and looked toward the Silver Slipper. Some of the lights were out now, although the doors had not been closed. Through the windows he could see Cat, talking to a man. Just from the way she sat, he knew she was angry. Her body was tense.

It's none of your business.

But it had become his business.

He felt as tight as an overwound spring. Hugh was looking at him curiously. So was Jenny, who had finished her set of songs but had lingered. She was doing that more and more now, and he knew why, but he had no interest in Jenny.

Christ, who was that man with Cat?

He saw Cat rise, something in her hand. Small enough that he couldn't identify it. The derringer she'd said she had? The man was very angry. He stumbled slightly as he stood, leaned over the table, and then made his way to the door in a shambling, drunken gait that nonetheless hid none of his anger.

The man hesitated at the swinging doors before plunging outside, the doors to the Silver Slipper immediately closing behind him. He hesitated again in the street, looking back at the saloon, then up toward the second floor. He waited there until he saw a light go on. Cat's room, Marsh knew. Marsh felt his gut tighten.

But the man turned away then and crossed the street, making his way to the Glory Hole as Marsh moved away from the window and behind the bar. There were only five customers left in the Glory Hole now. The women dealers were gone, and so were most of the help.

He dismissed Jenny and Hugh. The man

from across the street had already entered, walking a little unsteadily toward the bar.

"Whiskey," he said in a slightly slurred voice.

Marsh poured it. "That will be two bits."

The man swore but reached into a worn pocket and pulled out a few coins, spilling them on the bar.

Marsh took a long look. His customer had probably been a handsome man once, but drink had reshaped his face into a formless thing. Every feature was reddened and sagging, his blue eyes rimmed with pink. But there also was a meanness in those eyes, a meanness he'd seen many times before in the eyes of gunslingers who actually enjoyed hurting, as well as killing. They took the jobs Marsh turned down. The taut feeling in his gut grew.

"New to San Francisco?" Marsh had never been good at small talk. He would nod at his customers, but that was about all. It was, apparently, what they expected. Hugh was the gladhander. Marsh, the mystery.

The man glared at him as he swallowed his whiskey in one gulp and slapped the glass down for a refill.

"Bitch," he said, almost under his breath.

Marsh didn't say anything, just leaned over and refilled the glass.

"Wife," the man mumbled. "She's gonna learn what it means to be a wife."

Marsh didn't like what he was hearing. It couldn't be. Not the Ice Queen.

"She owes me," the man mumbled. He looked up and met Marsh's hard gaze and downed the glass of whiskey, then grabbed one of the coins on the bar. He turned and shambled out.

Marsh told the few remaining customers the Glory Hole was closing, and locked up. A walk. That's what he needed. Fresh air. He'd put Win in his room earlier, and the damned dog needed fresh air too. Marsh hated to keep him confined, but more and more stray dogs were being killed by the police.

He didn't think the stranger posed any threat to Cat tonight. He was too drunk to do much more than sleep it off. But Marsh had seen that kind of hate in the eyes of others, and combined with the meanness in those same eyes and Cat's recent behavior, he knew he would have to keep an eye on the Silver Slipper.

If only she would confide in him. And yet there was no reason she should. He certainly had given her none. He was still a little stunned that she trusted him with the deed, but that, he'd determined, was because she had no place else to turn. Not because of an overabundance of faith.

Wife.

In all his inquiries about Cat, he'd never heard of a husband, only a lost love killed in the war. He'd seen the picture over the bar. A handsome young man with dark hair. The man who had left the Silver Slipper had blond hair. Thinning and turning gray, but blond just the same.

The very thought of this man with Cat made him ill. And itching to do something violent.

Canton released Win from the bedroom. The dog rose haughtily from a corner where he'd taken refuge and sidled along the door to get out. His tail, usually placed securely between his legs as if afraid he might lose it, lifted just a fraction of an inch before he tucked it back into its hostile, wary place.

Remembering how the dog took to Cat, Marsh just shook his head.

The night was foggy, and a cold wind swept in from the bay. All the lights were off now at the Silver Slipper, including Cat's, and it seemed peaceful. A carriage rambled down the street and disappeared around the corner, leaving the street empty except for the two of them. There was no sign of the blond stranger.

Nonetheless, his eyes kept moving as the dog paced himself next to him, as if realizing Marsh represented safety. Marsh wore only what he had in the Glory Hole, a respectable black coat, and the cold slammed through him. He welcomed it, though, for it stimulated his body and his mind.

Wife.

It made sense. Why else would she have wanted the Silver Slipper in someone else's name? She must have seen the stranger in the Silver Slipper earlier that day.

He couldn't imagine a less probable mate for Catalina Hilliard, who was always immaculately dressed. Well-spoken. Independent. This man had been slovenly, his chin weak and his face heavily veined from drinking.

Marsh was accustomed now to his late walks, usually enjoying the cool sea tang of the wind, the mists that often swirled around. But now he didn't want to go far, didn't want to stray from the vicinity of the Silver Slipper, even though he felt the man harmless enough tonight. And then, of course, there was Molly's enemy. How did he ever get tied up in so many lives? He was even worried about Hugh's Elizabeth, now that her time was near.

He'd found himself letting Hugh go home earlier and earlier. He'd even increased the man's salary. And this for a man he still didn't entirely trust.

It was all passing strange.

Yet there was no question his life had bettered, no question that he looked forward to each day when previously a new day was something merely to tolerate and survive. He even looked forward to seeing Winchester's tail wag someday with real enthusiasm. He knew how the damn dog felt. It was difficult to hope after years of expecting little.

He'd made his beginning. His past seemed behind him. No one had connected him with the gunfighter he'd left behind. If it had not been for the Molly incident, he probably would have shed his gun days ago. He had to ask about her, about Molly, and see what he could do.

Christ, he was becoming protective.

He turned back, the dog with him.

The Silver Slipper was dark. No one lurked about. Still, when he went inside, he propped a chair against a table and sat in it, his eyes fastened on the building across the street. It reminded him of other nights he'd remained awake, usually guarding people not worth guarding.

This was different. This time *he* had a

stake. Cat Hilliard was, after all, now the manager of *his* saloon.

She was under his protection.

God help anyone who tried to hurt her.

James Cahoon woke, anger burning bright through him. More than anger. Hate.

Little Lizzie thought she could outsmart him.

It was only, he told himself, that he hadn't been prepared for the new Lizzie. He merely needed to adjust. He would soon have her groveling as she had years ago.

He had the weapons. She thought she was married to him, even if she had questioned it for a moment last night. For a second he'd thought that she'd checked and really knew that the marriage was a fake, that the "minister" had been nothing of the kind.

But she had dropped the subject, and he knew she wasn't sure. That was his weapon, and as much as she claimed she didn't care what he said, he knew he could destroy her. The precious Ice Queen of San Francisco a child prostitute!

He would let her think about it a day or so, let her stew. And then he would turn up in her bedroom, when there was no bodyguard present, when he could reestablish his husbandly rights. This wasn't over, not by a long shot.

James turned over on the hard mattress. This shabby rooming house was all he could afford, while she had the Silver Slipper. Tossing him out like so much garbage.

Oh, yes, he would visit her again. He knew

which room she was in. And he would take his knife. He was damn good with a knife. It wouldn't hurt to cut her a little, teach her some manners. Too bad she was prettier than ever, although that frightened-doe look of years ago had been a prime attraction. Some men liked frightened women. It made them feel strong.

She'd changed a lot, Lizzie girl, but she was still nothing more than a girl from Natchez Under the Hill.

He might even go back there this afternoon. Just to let her know he wasn't leaving. Then again, perhaps he wouldn't. Perhaps he would just wait until tonight.

Last night he'd been too drunk to make a move. Even he knew that. He wouldn't drink today. Not a drop, he swore to himself, even though his head was pounding, and his body already cried for more.

His hand went to the scar that ran up his chest. Jagged and ugly, it reminded him of the one other time that Lizzie had rebelled. When she'd left him nearly dead.

He would have died if the hotel proprietor hadn't found him and called the none-too-competent doctor who'd taken James's last coin, sewn him up clumsily, and after a week sent him away, hardly able to walk. He'd stayed for another two weeks in the back room of a saloon he'd frequented, before he was evicted from there. It had taken him months, and a number of menial jobs, to get together a stake to start playing poker again. He could gamble when he didn't get too greedy and take wild risks; he'd had to discipline himself to do that after Lizzie left. Before that he'd always had her to fall back on. A night with young Lizzie usually satisfied a player when James couldn't come up with the money he'd wagered.

Yes, sir, he had missed little Lizzie. And he owed little Lizzie. He owed her for the scar as well as for those bad years.

And she surely had some money. She would tell him where it was with a knife against that pretty face.

His stomach crawled with expectation. God, he needed a drink. But he had to be dry for now. His hand had to be steady.

For now.

Cat didn't sleep. She was shaking with reaction. With anger. With a fury so strong, it wanted to consume her. James had brought back everything, everything she had pushed to the recesses of her mind. The men. The humiliation of waiting to see who was going to win her. The time he helped one of his "friends" tie her up for "extra fun."

Give her enough room to wriggle. I like them to wriggle. She could still hear those words in her mind.

That was when she vowed it would never happen again. She had been married for two years, believed she had to do as her husband ordered. He'd told her repeatedly that she wasn't good for anything else, that if she ever ran, he would find her and kill her. And she believed him. She had seen him use a knife. He was good with a knife, with striking when someone wasn't looking.

When James came to her two nights later, told her to dress and come to the saloon with him, she fought back, though she hadn't meant to kill him.

She'd felt so worthless. No one, not even her mother, had ever wanted anything but to use her body. Not until Ben. Not until he made her see that there was something more to Lizzie Jones.

No, she hadn't meant to kill him then. She'd suffered over the supposed killing for years. Now, as she remembered everything she'd thought she buried, she wished she'd succeeded. Lizzie hadn't the heart or guts to kill him; Cat did.

She went to the window, as she did so often now, and went stiff as she watched James Cahoon walk into the Glory Hole.

She stood there edged tight against the wall as Hugh left, but James remained.

Why was Hugh leaving early? The baby?

Then why didn't Canton close?

Canton and James. Thoughts tumbled over and over in her mind. Had James just wandered in? Then why had Hugh left? Unless there was something Canton hadn't wanted him to know or hear?

The implication was sickening. For a moment she wouldn't, couldn't even consider it. But then . . .

Years of suspicion and distrust nudged at her. She didn't want to think the worst. God help her, she didn't. But neither could she lie to herself. She'd really had no reason to trust Canton, only a gut decision. A lesser of two evils. Could she have played directly into Canton's hands? She wouldn't put it past James to skulk around, find out everything he could, let a drunken word slip.

Why hadn't she considered the possibility before? What did she really know about Canton? Had he somehow found her one weak link? It would have been easy enough if James had talked.

Why had Hugh left? That fact seemed damning in itself.

The deed was in Canton's hands, and she had placed it there. So easily. She doubled over as waves of nausea shook her, as much for her own distrust as for the thought of betrayal.

But what there was of that very fragile, budding trust exploded in a thousand pieces.

CHAPTER 21

Teddy walked over to Hugh's house for coffee—
and for information.

Molly, too, was on his mind, but foremost
was the need to get information. Something was
very wrong with Catalina, and he didn't know
what it was. He'd felt her tension all day yesterday and wondered at her trip to the Glory Hole
and then her later strange remarks. Most of all
he puzzled over the episode in the saloon with
the stranger. He had never seen her so upset.

This morning had been even worse. Catalina seldom showed her feelings, and she'd tried
this morning not to do so. But her face had been
white, her eyes rimmed with either sleeplessness

or tears. She'd tried to have breakfast with the girls as usual, but she hadn't eaten a bite before looking as if she would be sick and hurrying off with some excuse about business.

He wished she would discuss whatever was bothering her. Only once had she lowered her guard with him, and that was the night of the nightmare. Even then she'd closed up tight almost immediately, rebuffing his clumsy attempts to help.

Not until Canton came along had he seen her show a flicker of interest in a man. She was unswervingly fair, loyal to those loyal to her—and he'd never respected a person more. But she had closed the rest of herself off like a vault until Canton.

Teddy wanted to help her, but he didn't know how. Perhaps Hugh had some knowledge, though he'd be reluctant to say anything. He had become as loyal to Canton as Teddy was to Catalina, and they had silently agreed not to discuss their respective employers. But Teddy didn't know where else to turn.

Molly opened the door, and her smile was like a ray of sunshine on a foggy day. He had stayed away since their walk, afraid to want, afraid to take. He *was* too old for her. She came from a fancy background, and he was a poor ex-boxer. She was educated, and he was not, although Catalina had taught him a lot.

Molly deserved far more than he could ever offer her.

But her smile had the effect of blinding him to all those things. It was special. Just for him. He almost forgot why he came.

But then Hugh was at the door, standing behind Molly with an inquisitive look in his eyes, and Teddy nodded to him. "I was hoping I could get a cup of coffee."

Hugh opened the door wide, although there was a wariness now that didn't used to be present. "You don't like your own coffee any longer?"

"I never did," Teddy said.

Hugh grinned. "I can understand why. Now Molly here has learned to make grand coffee."

Molly blushed. Teddy had never seen anyone so pretty.

"She's doing a lot now that Elizabeth's time is near. I don't know what we would have done without her."

Molly's face went even pinker. "I'll set another place," she offered. "Breakfast is almost ready."

Hugh looked over at Teddy. "You'll stay?"

Teddy hadn't intended that. He felt he should get back, but Molly . . . "Yes, but I would like to talk to you first."

Hugh looked at him sharply. He'd already made it clear he would no longer spy on his employer.

"It's important," Teddy said.

Hugh nodded reluctantly. "We'll be back shortly," he told Molly, and followed Teddy into the yard.

Teddy looked at a rose in the garden. "Molly looks real happy."

"She's been a godsend for Elizabeth, and

the children adore her. She can stay as long as she wants."

"You haven't noticed ... anyone who shouldn't be around?"

"No, but that's not why you came," Hugh said bluntly.

Teddy hesitated. "Miss Catalina told me yesterday if I needed anything, I was to go to ... Mr. Canton."

Hugh's eyes narrowed in thought. "They were together several times yesterday."

"There's trouble, Hugh. A man came in last night and stayed after hours. I thought he was going to attack her. He would have if she hadn't pulled out a derringer."

"Do you think it had anything to do with Molly?"

Teddy shook his head. "He seemed to know Miss Catalina, and she apparently expected him. That's when she told me to see Canton if ... if I needed anything. She acted like something might happen."

"She didn't say who the man was?"

"You know Miss Catalina. She keeps things to herself. But I've never seen her like this before, so tense."

Hugh shrugged. "Mr. Canton's the same way ... doesn't say much. They seemed friendly enough yesterday."

"That's odd in itself."

"True enough, but they've always had eyes for each other. I get warm just being in their presence."

Teddy frowned. "They hate each other."

"It's not hate, cousin. It's fire, that's for sure, and it's damn scorching."

"You're crazy."

"You've just never been in love."

He had been. He *was*. And it was nothing like the battle royal that had been raging between their two bosses. It was something fine and gentle. Maybe there were two kinds of love. If there was, he would take his version anytime.

Nothing made sense. Why would Catalina go to Canton instead of to himself? He simply couldn't believe Hugh was right in his speculations. "Love? Catalina and Canton? It can't be."

"There's something there. And it isn't hate. Maybe we can give them a little push?"

"Why should we do that?"

"So we don't have to worry about what we say to each other."

But Teddy didn't like it. He didn't like anything that was happening. Canton's arrival had thrown everything in turmoil, and except for the man's rescue of Molly, he'd been nothing but trouble.

"Miss Catalina can't tolerate him," he said stubbornly, using the "Miss" as he always did in front of others.

"Then why was she in the Glory Hole twice yesterday?"

"Mother in heaven, I don't know," Teddy said, exasperated. He felt shut out, even abandoned. He had been closer to Catalina than anyone until now, even though that wasn't really close at all. He was hurt, angry, resentful.

"Ask her," Hugh suggested.

"Maybe I will," Teddy said.

"Now come have breakfast."

Teddy shook his head. "I'd better get back." No matter how much he wanted to spend time with Molly, he had a terrible feeling in his gut, the kind he used to have before a fight.

Hugh didn't try to stop him. He still felt in the middle, somewhere divided between loyalties, and he hated that feeling. If only their respective employers would . . .

But that was something they would have to decide themselves. He turned around to go inside, knowing that Molly's face was going to crumple when she saw he was alone. Teddy wasn't too bright about Molly either, Hugh thought, although he did see a little promise in that direction.

Hugh took a look around before going in, as he always did since Molly had come to stay with them. Everything looked normal. There was a stranger down the road, but he turned at about the same time Teddy did and disappeared down the road behind him.

Must have been visiting someone. Hugh went back inside.

Cat prepared for the worst. She'd already foolishly signed over the Silver Slipper to Canton. Although she had his promise in writing to sell back the saloon, that promise, she thought bitterly, probably wasn't worth the paper it occupied.

She would ask the Pinkerton detective to check it out for her and also to discover whether her marriage to James was valid.

She hated to admit to him, to anyone, that she had been such a fool. Not once, but possibly twice. First with James, then with Canton. Why had she decided to trust Canton? Still, part of her clung to the hope that she had been right in trusting him.

The image of him and James together in the Glory Hole just wouldn't leave her. Plotting together? James could have heard about the feud and talked to Canton. The feud had certainly been in all the newspapers.

The thought made her sick all over again.

How could she have been such a fool? Canton could even claim that he had already paid her the ten thousand dollars. She'd been so infernally eager to get the deed out of her possession. She'd simply panicked at the thought of James Cahoon.

Just as Canton could have surmised she would, once he knew the circumstances.

Cat fought her first urge to confront him. She would wait, check the value of the document he'd given her, and see whether he delivered the promised ten thousand dollars. Then she would determine the next move. And there was still James to deal with. He would never give up, whether or not he was in cahoots with her neighbor, she knew that. He was a vicious man, corrupt in every way, and not above a knife or bullet in the back, which was why she hadn't wanted to put Teddy in his path.

She looked at the clock on her table. The Silver Slipper opened in an hour. The Silver Slipper that now belonged to the man across the street. She looked out the window. Traffic was moving briskly along the street, like any other day. But it wasn't like any other day.

There were things to do. Precautions to take. But the old enthusiasm, the will to do battle, was gone, and she knew she was going through motions, like a person already dead. An unexpected fog of tears glazed her eyes, and she fought them back. She kept seeing Canton. Seeing him with that sudden concern in his eyes. Telling herself it was a lie. Afraid to believe otherwise, afraid to hope, afraid to trust.

Sweet Lucifer, what was happening to her? She couldn't afford this self-pity. Too many people depended on her, including Teddy and Molly, whose problems were still worse than her own. She found the derringer and put it in her reticule, along with Canton's paper. She then splashed some water on her eyes.

She would survive this, as she had survived all her life.

She would survive and win.

Somehow she would win.

Marsh counted the bills carefully, nodded to the banker, tucked them in an inside vest pocket, and left. He felt a spring in his step and marveled at it. Hell, he felt damned good.

He questioned whether Cat would be actually grateful; she was too wary, a little too much like himself to show any outward sign of gratitude. But he knew something good was happening between them. He was amazed at how good that felt, at how much he was looking forward to seeing her again.

He decided to stop at the barber's. Have a close shave, get his hair cut. He felt like a boy again, ready to attend his first ball, full of anticipation. How long since he'd felt much anticipation for anything?

He saw a shop on the corner, one he hadn't used before, and there were only a few men waiting. A piece of luck. He'd discovered there was a shortage of barbers in San Francisco.

One of the barbers nodded at him in greeting and invited him to take a chair. He did, glancing over several newspapers lying on a chair next to him. And then he saw an old, battered copy of the dime novel *Duel at Sunset*.

Marsh went still for a moment. Christ, he hated that book. In addition to being totally inaccurate, it had sent every would-be gunslinger in Colorado after him. And the damn thing kept turning up. Thank God the picture on the front of *Duel at Sunset, The True Story of the Gunfight Between Lobo and Marsh Canton* bore little resemblance to him except for the clothes he used to wear. At least the damn book had helped set Lobo free. But it had had the opposite effect on him. It had made him even more a prisoner of his own reputation.

The two barbers were busy, their customers' faces covered by hot towels. Two other men were deep in conversation with each other. Marsh slid the copy of the book between the pages of a newspaper and gave cursory attention to the news. When finally a barber signaled him, he slipped the book, newspaper and all, firmly under his arm.

Any pleasure he might have taken in the

shave and haircut was gone. The book was like
a ton of weight on his back. Maybe he was a
fool for ever thinking he could escape his past.
He had to factor it into any equation about his
future. And Cat.

She wasn't a schoolgirl. She'd obviously
seen her share of trouble and, given her general
distrust of mankind, had not had the best of experiences with men. She wouldn't shy away from
much. But a gun for hire? Not many could stomach that. Hell, he couldn't stomach himself anymore. And if his whereabouts were known,
others would come for him. Every kid seeking a
reputation. Relatives seeking vengeance. God
knew what.

He closed his eyes after the barber finished
trimming his hair and laid a hot towel across his
face. The heat felt good as it seeped through the
towel while the barber lathered the soap brush
and kept a patter of conversation going. Marsh
closed his ears as well.

He hadn't done that in years, he realized.
Day by day he was lowering his guard, living
like ordinary people. Ordinary. Did he really
want to be ordinary?

Could he be ordinary?

But then he thought of Quinn Devereux.
Marsh had sent the Devereuxs a sizable contri-
bution for their project and received a note of
thanks as well as an open invitation to visit
again soon. After that god-awful tea, they must
have a streak of masochism to want a repeat, but
there was still something about Devereux that
was familiar. An experience with violence.
Marsh had felt it through and through. If

Devereux could live so easily with civilization, perhaps he could too.

If only those damn books would disappear.

And if only Cat could understand, accept, a background like his. And a present still fraught with danger. But if anyone could, Cat could.

Christ, he was tired of walking the razor's edge. Peace. Damn, but he wanted some small measure of peace. And he wanted it with Catalina Hilliard.

The barber finished, patted Marsh's face with the towel again, and then looked expectant.

Marsh nodded and tossed him two silver dollars, earning a grin in return.

"Come back again, sir."

Marsh nodded, not explaining that part of the money was for a certain stolen article.

The newspaper firmly under his arm, he started back to the Glory Hole, the spring back in his step.

Cat ignored Teddy's anxious looks as she helped behind the bar. She needed something to do. This morning had been a complete loss.

Booth Templeton, the detective, was out on a job. Hers, she supposed. She left both Canton's agreement and instructions for him to check out a marriage between Lizzie Jones and James Cahoon in Natchez Under the Hill in Mississippi in 1857. It was a task easily checked, she thought, by other detectives in the Pinkerton Agency, which had offices all over the country.

Her doubts about Canton were stronger than ever. The image of James entering the Glory

Hole simply wouldn't go away. And so she kept busy. She wasn't going to demean herself by going over to the Glory Hole; if he had the money, he could come to her.

The Silver Slipper was now his, after all.

But how was she going to tell Teddy?

The afternoon had settled in before Canton came. Cat was turned toward the mirror in back of the bar, drawing a glass of beer when she saw him in the glass. She closed her eyes against the effect he always had on her, swallowed, then opened them as he approached her with those long, even strides.

He smelled intoxicatingly of spices, and his hair had obviously just been cut. Every other man in the place paled in comparison to Canton, but now his expression was cautious.

"Miss Cat," he said with his usual mockery, but there was a question in his face that was distinct from the surface smile. His gaze went around the room slowly, carefully, as if he were looking for someone and then turned back to her.

"Mr. Canton," she acknowledged. "The Silver Slipper is honored."

That quiet but intense storm center caught them again, holding them captive in a piece of time. Their gazes locked, both seeking information the other took pride in withholding. Pride and refuge.

Cat wanted so much to believe in him.

Marsh's heart beat faster. He wanted to lean over and kiss her. He wanted, God help him, for her to believe in him when he himself didn't know whether there was anything to believe in.

"Can we talk somewhere?"

Cat thought about her room but knew they would be the object of too much attention if they went upstairs. For the first time she wished she had a real office, but Teddy used the only available downstairs room.

"The Glory Hole?" he asked, and there was a bit of speculation in his eyes.

She hesitated. Knowing how he affected her, the last place she wanted to go was his room again. But neither did she want to risk another visit by James when she wasn't quite sure of his connection with Canton.

She nodded.

He offered his arm, but Cat pretended she didn't see it and started to move on her own. She stopped next to Teddy. "I'll be gone a few minutes." He merely nodded.

The Glory Hole had a few more customers than the Silver Slipper, probably because of the gambling. I'll have to do that soon, she thought absently, before remembering that the Silver Slipper was no longer hers.

He went directly across the room to the corridor that led to the back, and to his room.

She moved with him, her legs stiff with resolution. Her heart pounded against her ribs, and her throat was choked with a lump that was part fear, part hope. And all wariness.

Win growled as they entered, continued to growl as Cat went to him and placed a hand on his head. There was something very honest about the dog's own suspicions. She knew where

Winchester stood. Alone and hostile. She wasn't sure about the man who already dominated the room just by his presence.

"He doesn't try to go out?"

"I take him out occasionally, often at night. He seems to understand he's safe here." Canton shrugged as if the dog's survival were not of great interest, yet Cat sensed it was.

"Is he? Safe?"

He gave her a searching look. "Are you, you mean?" That soft accent was in his voice again, mellowing it.

Sweet Lucifer, no!

"I don't think anyone feels safe around you," she said softly.

She saw something flicker in his eyes. Amusement? Disappointment? She didn't know, but he stepped back and very deliberately took a cheroot from a box on the bureau.

Canton turned that dark gaze back to her as his hand went to an inside pocket of the coat he was wearing and came out with an envelope he handed to her.

Cat reached for it, her fingers touching his, searing as they did so, hesitating ever so briefly, as if the two were fused by the very heat the touch ignited. Her eyes met his again, and his were not like mirrors now. The gray, that deep, impenetrable gray, was more like a sky just before a violent thunderstorm. Roiling emotions changed the color, deepening it, like thunderclouds chasing each other across a boiling infinity.

Threatening. No peace here. No promise of peace.

The envelope fell from her hands as he moved closer. Her senses absorbed the scent of shaving soap and spices and she imagined the feel of a face so obviously newly shaved. She felt his breath, warm and quick, and the core of her fantasized, feeling him in her again, his body moving against hers.

She felt her hand tremble, quakes moving through her body as she struggled against the mesmerizing impact of him.

I always pay for services, darlin'.

Was that what he was expecting from her now? Payment?

Still, her hand went out, touching the soft, supple leather of his coat, her fingers reaching out for something else but satisfying themselves with this for a moment. Sensation. So many sensations.

She was lost in them.

His head bent, his lips covering hers enticingly. Guiding. Seducing. Ensnaring. She didn't want to respond. She didn't want to be the rabbit to his snake, or lamb to his tiger.

She didn't want . . . She didn't trust . . . She didn't . . .

Suspicion suddenly vanished as his kiss deepened, carrying her into a mindless world where only feelings ruled. Only emotions.

Only need.

Marsh's arms went around her, and he held her close as her lips met his. She felt so good. So damnably good.

He hadn't meant this to happen, not so quickly anyway. But the moment he had first seen her in the Silver Slipper, he'd known something was very wrong. She had looked at him with the old hostility, the former suspicion, and he had searched his mind for a reason. He had thought yesterday that they had laid at least part of their suspicion of each other to rest.

And yet the magnetism between them was still there, that attraction that never quite went away no matter how strong the animosity.

God, those eyes. He'd never seen anything so vividly green.

He wished they would look at him with trust, and yet part of him feared it too. He didn't know whether he could live up to trust. Nor whether she could ever accept his past.

Hell, he didn't know if *he* could ever accept it. And books like those in the barbershop would never allow him to forget it.

But now her lips yielded under his, reluctantly, but yielded just the same. He felt her growing response, felt her lips giving under his, participating in the kiss. Yet there was still a slight stiffness in her body, and he couldn't forget that silent question—almost an accusation—in her eyes.

He didn't want her like this. He wanted her without reluctance, without that distrust he still felt in her.

Marsh straightened, releasing her lips but still holding her. He tried to force her to meet his gaze through sheer will, but her will, he'd discovered, was every bit as strong as his own. Her eyes were leveled somewhere on his jacket, seemingly focused on a button, but he sensed she was seeing something else altogether.

He took one arm from around her and cupped her chin, forcing her face upward. "I'd much prefer a slap to my face," he said in a tone he tried to keep light, even mocking a little.

"I don't know what you mean."

"Yes, you do, Miss Cat. You're backing away in the most important sense. I admit you have a reason—my unforgivable behavior the other afternoon—but I'm trying to make amends."

Cat hesitated. She understood it was a difficult admission for him. Still, it was a pretty speech, one that came from a long line of fine breeding. But then she had always known that about him, ever since she first saw him in the Silver Slipper. Regardless of what had turned his eyes to ice, he had once come from something much better than her own roots. Amends or not, he couldn't help but be sickened at her own background. Any man would be.

Did he already know? Had James said anything last night?

Dear God, she wished she could trust Canton. She was so tired of lies, of holding everything to herself. But she didn't know if she could bear seeing disgust in his eyes again, as she had the other afternoon. And if he knew . . .

Damn, she had never cared before. She had overcome the past, and it had been hers to keep within herself, but now she cared desperately. She had not felt inferior for many years, only strong and independent, but now insecurity licked at everything she'd built, like a river eating away at its banks.

"Cat?"

"What do you want?" Her voice was harsher than she'd intended. "You've paid now for services rendered."

He winced. "No truce?"

"A standoff," she said.

"I deserve that," he said.

She knew that he didn't. He'd more than made amends. The envelope was on the floor, and she knew by the bulk what it was. She'd doubted him, and yet he had never lied to her, not from the beginning. Why ever James came here last night, she knew it was none of Canton's doing.

"Damn you," he whispered, his voice hoarse with frustration. His head started to lower when a knock came on the door.

Canton stiffened and then answered with a growl. "What is it?"

"Trouble out front."

Canton turned to her. "I'll be right back."

Cat nodded, relieved. A few moments and perhaps she would regain some composure. He took one more long look at her and then whirled around and disappeared out the door.

Ordinarily, Cat would be interested. Trouble for Canton was good for the Silver Slipper. But things had changed. And she had problems of her own at the moment. She didn't doubt for a moment that Canton would handle anything.

The room seemed larger now that he wasn't filling it. She steadied herself, ignoring the need that still ran through her. The dog, Win, was eyeing her speculatively. She leaned down and picked up the envelope she'd dropped earlier and looked inside. Ten large bills. She looked at it for a moment, wondered what to do with it for now, and finally put it on the bureau next to the box of cheroots.

Her glance fell on a newspaper on the bed, and she went over to it, glancing at the front page. Crime was up in San Francisco, but she didn't need a newspaper to tell her that. Almost absently she picked it up, and a paperbound book fell from it onto the floor. She reached down and picked it up.

Duel at Sunset. One of those dime novels. It didn't seem like anything Canton would read, but then, she continued to discover things about him she didn't expect. She looked at it more closely.

Then her eyes riveted to it. The cover portrayed two men facing each other, guns blazing. One of the men wore the same black suit she'd seen on Canton the first day.

Her eyes caught the words. *Notorious Gunmen Marsh Canton and Lobo in . . . Duel at Sunset: The True Story.*

Canton. How many times had she thought she should remember the name? Marsh Canton. Now she remembered. She'd heard the name mentioned in the saloon. Probably years ago.

But he'd said his name was Taylor Canton. Which meant nothing, of course. She'd said her name was Catalina Hilliard. Cat had no doubt at all that her Canton was Marsh Canton. She remembered her first impression, the coolness with which he had killed that man in the checkered suit.

She placed the book back in the newspaper exactly as it had been.

Marsh. It fit him far better than Taylor.

She'd never been able to call him Taylor for some reason. She'd told herself it was because Canton was so much more impersonal. But that wasn't it at all.

A weapon. The book was a weapon she no longer wanted. One she wouldn't use. It was his business, just as her past was her business. But it answered so many questions . . . while posing so many others.

The music. How could a killer play as he did? And there was still no denying a background of privilege.

A killer. She closed her eyes and tried to think of him that way. Maybe she could have weeks ago. But not now.

The door opened quietly, and she was reminded that he did most things quietly. Walked quietly. Drank quietly. Always with his back to the wall. Always watching.

Canton's gaze was on her.

"What was it?"

He shrugged. "A poor loser. He's gone now." Canton hesitated, then continued, "He was in here last night too. Late."

Cat felt herself tense. "Tall . . . blond?"

He raised an eyebrow. "You know him?"

"He was at the Silver Slipper last night."

"I know," Canton said in a low voice.

Cat fought down the rising suspicion and waited for him to continue.

"I saw him there," he said. "I saw you talking to him through the window. Is he why you felt you had to sell the Silver Slipper?"

Cat closed her eyes and leaned against the wall, trying to think. How much did he know?

How much did he guess? She knew James said a great deal when he'd been drinking.

"Why didn't you just put the title in your manager's name?" There was real curiosity in his voice.

She knew then that James had said something about the marriage. She thought about denying it, then dismissed the idea. She had trusted Canton this far, albeit reluctantly and not totally. "Because he would try to kill anyone who was that close to me, who tried to thwart him."

"And I was expendable?" The question was asked wryly, with that twist of the lips that gave so little away, that was neither smile nor frown.

She gave him a small, strained smile. "*You* can take care of yourself."

"Were you going to tell me about this?"

"If I thought it was necessary. As far as he knew, someone had won the Silver Slipper."

The last several questions made her uncomfortable. Posed as they were, they were like a shaft of guilt pinning her against a wall.

His steady stare did nothing to alleviate the discomfort. Those damn gray eyes seemed to penetrate every defense she had. Then he shook his head in a gesture of wonder, a chuckle starting deep in his throat.

"Not so much trust as expediency, Miss Cat?"

"A little of both," she admitted.

"Damn little of the first and a great deal of the second."

His voice was sensual with that softness that could be seduction or menace. It shifted through her consciousness like warm syrup.

"What would you have done if I hadn't paid for the Silver Slipper? I'm sure you had a plan."

Cat stood there, partially paralyzed by the power of his eyes, his very presence, by the damnable effect he always had on her. In an effort to break that hold, she told the truth. "Burn it."

"I suspected as much," he said, a rare twinkle in his eye. "And then I probably would have lost the Glory Hole."

"Probably," she admitted, "if you used it for collateral."

"So much for trust, Miss Cat."

"I didn't promise trust."

"No. You didn't promise anything," he admitted. "But a little would be nice."

"You don't seem the type of man who needs it."

"Of course not," he replied easily, but the bleakness reappeared in his eyes. Sudden and strong. Vulnerability. It seeped through every conscious part of her, melted every resolve. It was amazing. Incredible. He wanted her trust. Canton. The man she'd decided was the ultimate loner.

The gunfighter.

Cat, who'd thought herself worldly and cynical and capable of dealing with anything, couldn't deal with this side of him. Even the raw hurt stored since the afternoon they'd bedded disappeared. All the sensations she'd felt then were suddenly dwarfed by the physical response to him that had been held in check only by her anger.

But now the anger was gone, lost in that

loneliness she'd glimpsed in his eyes, a loneliness and need she understood. And, God help her, shared.

Excruciating excitement played with the most elemental of her senses. The currents running between them were stronger than ever, made more powerful by subtle messages passing between them. There was an element of trust now, despite their words. Cat knew he had given it to her when he'd asked no questions about James, and regardless of expediency she had given a measure to him when she had first come to him. She was giving him more, now that she'd seen the book, but he didn't know it.

That trust whispered between them now. Cat knew it would not be a momentous thing for most, but for her . . . and now she knew, for him—

She was suddenly in his arms, not exactly aware of how she got there . . . whether it had been he or she who had moved . . . and it didn't matter. She didn't care anymore who won or who lost, about her past or his. She only knew that she had been waiting for this, that she wanted him more than she'd ever wanted anything: the Silver Slipper, security, respectability. Safety.

Marsh Canton would never be safe for her. She knew that, and she didn't care.

Sweet explosions detonated all over her as his lips clamped down on hers. Sweet and violent. Demanding. Beseeching. All at once, until she felt like a living torch, the flame burning so deep and hot, she wondered why it didn't consume her.

She hadn't forgotten anything, not the feel of his body against hers, nor the taste of his lips. She'd thought she magnified the gentleness in her mind, but now she knew she hadn't. She felt it now in the way his hands moved along her back and along the nape of her neck.

Cat felt the intensity in him as his mouth moved downward, kissing her throat, moving along the curve of her cheek to the lobe of her ear until every nerve in her body was vibrating with eagerness.

"No reservations?" he whispered into an ear he'd just been nibbling.

"None," she said in a soft voice with a breathlessness that belied the answer.

"You and I, Cat, are like fire and gunpowder." She could barely decipher the words. "Sometimes I wonder if we won't destroy each other."

She'd wondered the same herself. So many times. But the fuse had already been lit, and there was no stopping it now. If there had ever been that possibility. As fire needed oxygen, she needed him.

She didn't even know how or when it had happened. Only that it had. And there wasn't a damn thing she could do about it, even if she wanted to.

And she didn't. Not now. She was absorbed by him, of him.

She moved slightly and felt his cheek brush lightly against hers. His breath quickened and their bodies moved closer, in unspoken tandem, hers pressing against his, feeling him respond, feeling herself respond.

"Ah, Cat . . . I . . . nee . . . want . . ."

His words were silenced by her mouth this time. He had started to say "need." He couldn't say it any more than she could, and that again touched her as little else could. They *were* like fire and gunpowder, but they were also very much, very painfully, alike. She knew she couldn't say "need" either, although she did need him.

Want and need. One word indicated something that could be controlled; the other . . . something uncontrollable.

And this was definitely uncontrollable. But Cat knew she couldn't admit it to him, just as he couldn't to her. It would be giving up a part of her.

Fire and gunpowder!

Nothing more.

Cat closed her eyes as she seemed to melt into him. She felt his arousal, and that craving inside grew as she wondered how one body could absorb so many sensations and still want more.

His lips found her mouth again, so very hungry now.

Cat was just as hungry as he picked her up and carried her to the bed, never releasing her lips. She felt his hands undressing her in sure, efficient movements and knew her own hands were fumbling with his buttons. Somehow, tangled together, they managed to undo layer after layer of clothing, and she lay there naked as he sat next to her. His fingers didn't stop, inciting new fires as his dark secret eyes probed further than she wanted him to see.

She only wanted to feel now, not to think, because she might go crazy thinking about what might have been or could be. She wanted so much more of him than he was willing to give, or, she admitted honestly, she was able to give. Her hand reached up, tracing lines in the hard angles of his chest, tangling themselves in an arrow of dark hair that ran down to his belly. Then, tentatively, they went up to the scar, as if to take it away.

She swallowed hard. She didn't want to feel tender like this, tender and loving. She didn't want him to know she cared as much as she did. She shouldn't. She shouldn't feel weak and tingling and so warm inside.

But then his hand went to the triangle at the juncture of her legs, to the most sensitive part of her, caressing and teasing until her body arched and convulsed with a series of exquisite explosions.

He positioned his own body over hers, allowing his manhood barely to touch her, causing her body to arch again in search of him. He— Canton—slowly moved down on her, entering with a deliberate slowness that created an aching, agonizing need that made her move against him in instinctive, circular movements, drawing him deeper and deeper inside her.

She felt waves of pleasure wash over her, not only the physical reaction but the unexpectedly exquisite bliss of just being with him, of having him so near, his hands caressing her with something like worship. She wanted to capture that feeling forever.

But then his strokes increased in rhythm

and power, and she wanted something even more. Her body was responding wantonly to his, moving as his did in a sensuous dance that became more and more frantic as they rode an incredible wave, a great force that rushed them headlong toward some remarkable destination, that robbed them of any sense other than feel, and she was consumed with that.

"Oh, Cat," he murmured as he plunged one last time, filling her with billows of bursting sensations, each different in its level of satisfaction and pleasure. She felt his warmth flood her and experienced a kind of contentment she'd never known before, even as her body continued to quiver with aftershocks.

He rolled over, taking her with him but removing his weight from her. She found her head on his chest, and she nuzzled the sweat-dampened hair there. All her sensations were heightened. She heard the sound of his heart beating, felt the soft whisper of his breath. She loved each of those intimate things, and she suspected that meant she loved him too.

She wanted to tell him that, but she couldn't. She was married. She had a past that would repulse him. And he was a gunfighter who would probably never linger long anywhere.

Cat felt herself touching him, running her fingers down his arms and up to his neck, playing with tufts of hair that curled around them. His eyes seemed lighter now, not so much like mirrors. There was a lazy contentment in them as his gaze followed the route of her touch.

His hand finally captured her fingers and

brought them to his mouth, where he started to nibble them.

"You're infinitely edible, you know," he said finally.

"Am I?" She was still sprawled across his body, and she could feel every nook and hard angle of it. She rested her head a little nearer his heart, thinking how fine this splendid obsession was. She could feel every movement, every tremor, every little quiver he made, right down to her bones.

"Hummmm," he said. "Want to find out how much?"

She turned her head up so she could see him. "I don't know," she said cautiously.

He chuckled, and she felt every tiny movement of his chest. "Still suspicious?"

"No," she said honestly. "I just remember that dynamite and fire don't last long together."

"We might consume each other?" he asked. "That's a very real possibility."

"We don't even like each other," she said wonderingly.

"Don't we?"

She didn't want to meet that even stare any longer. Her head turned back to rest on his chest. "You don't know anything about me."

"I know all I want to know. You're lovely and smart and mean as hell."

She giggled. She thought it was the first time she'd ever giggled. Disgusting. But she couldn't help it. She felt like giggling. Laughing. Teasing. She even found a special joyousness in it. "And edible. Don't forget edible."

"I could never forget edible."

She wanted to whisper his name. But "Canton" didn't seem right now. Neither did Taylor, which never fitted. And Marsh? It fitted him so perfectly, but then he would think she'd been snooping. More secrets. More things to hide, but then, she had never really known how to talk to a man. Small love talk. She didn't know anything about that.

And suddenly she wanted to. She wanted to be clever and enchanting.

She felt his arms go around her again, his hands caressing her back, and she knew he felt something of her despair. "I like mean as hell," he said into her ear, making the observation incredibly sensuous.

It was an absurd statement, but incredibly endearing, mainly, she thought, because it was probably true. She'd discovered he didn't lie.

"That's ridiculous," she countered.

"Everything about us is ridiculous," he said dryly, "but here we are. I tried my damnedest, but I can't seem to stay away from you."

She stared at him. She'd never suspected that. Nor that he would admit it. Her fingers played with his chest hair, not wanting that small intimacy to go away. "Me too," she admitted, wondering whether she should admit it. Yet she felt lazy and languorous and contented. And safe. So very safe at the moment.

He smiled, and it was the first real, honest-to-God smile she'd seen on his face.

"And you do trust me a little?"

"A little," she murmured.

"This isn't a thank-you?" There was the slightest doubt in his voice, and it was that hesitation again that drove a surge of tenderness through her.

"I don't give that kind of thank-you," she said. "In fact I don't give thank-yous at all."

"Why?"

She was silent for a moment. She didn't know why she had said what she had. But there was a kind of poignant honesty between them now that she didn't want to break, that seemed to compel words from her. "I never ask for anything."

Until now. But even then she had presented her offer to sell the Silver Slipper as a business proposition, as much benefit to her as to him. The purchase of something she thought he wanted; the fact that he hadn't wanted it at all didn't matter. The agreement to sell back was all his idea, presented as a fait accompli.

He understood her answer. He never asked for anything either, but somehow the simple statement from her stabbed him with a curious pain. He'd made his own lonely path, but he sensed that she had not, that it had been made for her, and he wanted to go back in her life and kill everyone who had hurt her. Starting with that blond stranger.

He didn't truly understand that overwhelming protectiveness he felt after all these years of remaining uninvolved. But it was there, deep in his gut. He wasn't uninvolved anymore. He wondered whether he ever could be again. A sense of wonder roiled in him at the knowledge.

And dread. Could he face losing again? Losing something he cared about? He'd fought against caring, but he couldn't seem to stop his heart from doing exactly that. The heart he'd thought turned to stone.

Christ!

"You don't either," she said suddenly, and he had to review their conversation to make sense of it.

"Ask for anything?" But he was. He knew he was asking for something now. He was afraid of the answer, and he realized it was the first time in years he'd been afraid of anything.

She nodded, those vivid green eyes reaching deep for an answer. He sensed she feared it as much as he.

He chuckled again, although the sound was different from before. It was wry, not amused. His hand went to her hair, running his fingers through it. "We really don't know how to talk to each other, do we?" he said ruefully.

Cat felt an infinite loneliness at the exceptional observation. She had never loved anyone before, and now she thought she did, but was afraid to express it, resorting instead to silence and awkward phrases. She didn't dare hand her heart to someone who might smash it. And although things had changed between them, she didn't think they had changed that much. She was still Lizzie Jones, and he . . . a man passing through.

But still, she took these minutes and knew she would hold them forever. This excess of feeling, of needing, of having. It was so strong, she knew it couldn't last. Nothing this powerful could last.

It hurt, dear Lucifer, how it hurt.

"Cat," he said in a very soft voice, and she

knew suddenly that she had allowed her feelings to show. She struggled to put them back in place, back in the box where she'd kept them hidden for so long.

"Don't," he commanded. "Look at me."

She did. She couldn't help it.

"Don't run away from me now."

"Why not?" She didn't intend the note of bitterness, but it was there. She was suddenly angry. Angry at herself. Angry at him. She didn't want to question anything. She wanted to leave it like this. A perfect moment, which was something grand. She didn't want to spoil it with false hopes or lies or promises that didn't mean anything. She had never expected much, and she didn't want to expect much now.

He laughed again, and again she felt those movements under her. It made crazy things happen, that brushfire building of tension deep inside, the tingling down to her toes. She loved feeling his body, loved the way their bodies melded so perfectly, as if they'd been made for each other.

"Because you don't have to," he said in a hoarse voice. "I won't hurt you. I won't let anyone else hurt you."

"I don't need your help," she said with sudden acerbic defiance, but she knew she was trying to convince herself as well as him. Part of her did need him. She was determined to restrict that need. Confine it. "I don't need anyone."

"Don't you?" he asked tauntingly as his hands moved again over the most sensitive parts of her. She felt him growing hard under her, and all the tension that came from that rumbling chuckle of his magnified. She felt her body responding, as if it had no relationship to her mind, the deep craving inside undeniable.

His hands guided her to a sitting position, pulling her legs up. She was sitting on him, unsure exactly how she had come to be there, but she found herself reacting instinctively to him as a new kind of sensation flooded her. It was even more exquisite than before as he filled her so completely, and she started to move, slowly at first, then beginning to understand as he moved against her. She was astounded as her body moved, riding him with abandon, relishing the flood of pleasure that swept over her.

She'd never known it could be like this, that a man could give as well as take, that such joy could come from an act she used to think so brutal. There was nothing brutal about Canton, about the fire-filled eyes that were no longer mirrors but through which she thought she could see a part of him hidden from the rest of the world. A kind of passion she'd heard in his music but not in his voice. A loneliness that had always been just on the edge of his mockery. A caring that he, like she, had tried to disguise. And she cared too much. She knew it, but she couldn't stop now, just as her body couldn't stop responding to him.

And then every thought disappeared as sensation after sensation rocked her and she heard his low groan and her own answering whimper. He pulled her down and his tongue licked her wet face, their sweaty bodies pressing close in a desperate embrace that partly admitted their bond and partly denied it.

I can't love him, Cat cried desperately in her mind.

She heard that low, drawling whisper. "You can't run forever, darlin'."

But she knew she could. She was better at running than anything.

And that was exactly what she planned to do.

For her life.

CHAPTER 22

Marsh knew he'd lost her again.

He knew it the minute the wonderment left her eyes, replaced by the curtain he was becoming all too accustomed to seeing there. The curtain she used to hide behind.

He eased her down, holding her tight. "Let me help, Cat. Whatever it is, let me help."

"You can't," she said. "It's something I have to do myself."

"You don't have to do everything yourself," he said with some frustration.

"I can't depend on anyone."

"Not even Teddy."

"No," she said defensively.

"Who is that man?" They both knew who he meant.

"He thinks I owe him something."

"Do you?"

"God, no," she said.

"He'll be back?"

She nodded. "I think so."

"Stay here tonight."

"I have to look after the Silver Slipper."

He grinned. "No, you don't. I'm your boss now."

"But I'm going to get it back."

His hand tangled in her hair. He still felt tremors from their lovemaking, from her proximity, but more than that, he felt as if she belonged here with him. He'd never believed in destiny until this moment.

"You belong with me, Cat, you know that."

"I don't know anything of the kind," she said. "This is . . . lust."

"Lust is a wonderful beginning," he replied lazily.

He knew he was being a fool. He couldn't promise much himself, not with those damned pulp novels and his reputation following him like shadows. Not with the death of an innocent man on his hands. There would always be a darkness in his soul because of that.

But he was willing to try. Would she even want him if she knew about his former occupation? If she knew how many dead men littered his trail? He couldn't even remember the number anymore.

He turned slightly, moving her to his side.

He raised his head, propping it on a hand so he could study her. She was so incredibly beautiful, and despite, or perhaps because, of it she looked valiant in her vulnerability with that stubborn jaw denying she needed anyone.

He felt vulnerable himself. Perhaps because it had been so long since he had reached out to anyone—it was a painfully difficult thing. He was opening himself to rejection, to denial, to loss.

But she had a right to know, first, exactly who and what he was.

"Cat, have you ever heard of Marsh Canton?"

Cat tried to hide her surprise. She nodded cautiously.

"My name is Marsh Taylor Canton." He waited for the reaction, any kind of reaction.

She had stilled completely in his arms, and he watched her face. Only her eyes showed any change, and he couldn't decipher the meaning. A warming, perhaps. He hadn't expected that. But then he didn't know what to expect. He'd never known.

"A gunfighter, Cat. A hired killer. That's what I do best." His voice was objective, although he heard the old drawl in it, the drawl that sometimes surfaced when he was . . . disturbed. It seemed to be more and more frequent since he'd met Cat.

He felt her fingers close around his hand. Acceptance. Simple acceptance, and that moment meant more to him than any they'd shared.

"I know," she finally said. "I sensed it the first time you entered the Silver Slipper, though I didn't connect the name. And then when you shot that kidnapper, I was sure. I've seen my share of gunfighters. There's something—"

"The smell of death?" He heard the bitterness in his own voice and wondered why it was there. He'd done everything by choice.

"No," she said. "Not that. It's the cautious way you view a room and always sit with your back to a wall so you can see everything. It's the way you wear that gun as if it's a part of you."

"It is, Miss Cat," he said. "A part I can't seem to let go of."

"Molly is safe because of that part."

"Aren't you repulsed?" Marsh hated the rough sound of his voice. It was, he knew, uncertainty that made it so, and he hated that too.

Cat didn't answer immediately. It was too important. Everything being said now was too important. There was a hurting honesty being given, and it deserved honesty in return.

"While you were gone, I saw the book on the bed. For a moment, perhaps, I—but then I knew it didn't make any difference."

"That damn book," he said. "It's going to follow me all my life."

"Are you retiring from that . . . business or is the Glory Hole just a diversion?" It was a question she knew had been bothering her for weeks. He had never seemed *just* a saloon owner, and she'd sensed it.

"I'm trying to retire," he replied with a wry smile. "It's a hell of a lot better than dying in a dusty street somewhere."

"And you picked the Glory Hole?"

"The Glory Hole picked me. I won it in a

poker game. When I first saw it, I wished I'd lost."

"What changed your mind?"

"You. I was told you'd chased out everyone else, and I had these visions of a real dragon. And then I saw you and knew I had to stay. I didn't realize you'd try to shanghai me, but that just made me more determined. I don't usually lose."

"No," she said. "I don't expect you do. But you know I didn't mean to have you shanghaied." She hesitated, wondering whether he would believe her. "In fact, I saved you from it. I'd just told . . . a friend of mine in the police department that a little help would be nice. I thought he would find a way to close you down. When I discovered you were headed for a long journey, I stopped it."

"So that's how I ended up in jail instead of on my way to China?"

He looked so rueful, she had to smile. "*Marsh*. I like that. 'Taylor' never did fit, so I always just called you Canton."

"Mmmmm, I like the way you say it."

"Does it stand for Marshall?"

He shook his head. "My mother's family was named Marsh."

He had cracked open a door, and Cat wanted to fling it wide. "And where are you from?"

"I was born in Georgia."

"And your family now?"

"All dead. Killed in the war."

A muscle moved in his cheek, and she knew

she had hit a vital spot, but she couldn't stop herself now. "Your mother?"

"My mother and sister were killed by some Union renegades. They were raped and left to die in a burning house." There was a hollow sound in his voice. "I didn't know about it until eight months later when I got home . . . after Lee surrendered."

"Mother" was not a word that meant much to Cat, but she heard the anguish in a voice he tried to keep hard and neutral. That he failed showed how much it had once meant to him.

"I'm sorry," she said.

"It was lifetimes ago, darlin'," he said.

"You had a plantation?"

He nodded.

"Slaves?"

"My family did. My older brother would have inherited, and I was going to be a lawyer."

"I don't think I would like owning someone else."

"You wouldn't," he said. "You're too fiercely independent, but when you're raised with slavery, are taught that it's right, even in church, you accept it as a way of life. My family was never cruel, never separated families, but I realize now how wrong it was. I probably knew it was then, which was why I never regretted the fact Rosewood wouldn't come to me. I didn't have to wrestle with the moral problem; my brother did."

"Did you wrestle with moral problems?" This was a fascinating part of him.

"Once I did. When I was a young man, when I was in law school. But then the war came, and any kind of civility or morality was lost in just trying to stay alive. There's precious little honor in war, darlin', no matter what the books say. It's killing, pure and simple. It's you or the young Yank across the stream, close enough you can see each other's eyes. You can see the fear in them. After a while your actions become reflexive. You stop thinking about it, because if you don't, you'll go insane."

Cat felt a shiver run the length of his body, and she hurt for him, hurt for that young man whose illusions died. She'd never had any illusions, and she thought perhaps that had been for the best. It didn't hurt to lose what you never had.

Is that why you became a gunfighter? Because it had become automatic? Somehow she didn't think so. She wanted to ask that question, but she couldn't. She had already pried into too many painful places.

He obviously thought so, too, because he leaned over and kissed her lazily, as if they had never had that conversation. It should have been an effective way of changing the topic. But it wasn't. Not really. Because the kiss turned desperate, as if he were trying to find something lost long ago.

And she couldn't give it to him. She couldn't give him back his past, his illusions, especially his illusions. She found herself stiffening, and his kiss stopped.

"Cat?"

She felt like crying, and she didn't want him to see her crying. So she found her mask and put it on; it hid a world of misery. Misery for him.

For her. She didn't want to be another of his lost illusions. Or hopes. "I have to go," she said in an unsteady voice.

"I want you to stay here."

The autocratic tone instinctively stopped her. She didn't want to go, but she was too emotional now. She forced her need for him, her love for him, into anger. "You want?" she asked with a dangerous edge to her voice.

"Cat . . . Catalina . . ."

My name isn't really Cat! She wanted to yell the words at him and end it all right now, but she couldn't. She merely went stiff as she'd learned to years ago, turning off everything and everyone.

She watched his eyes harden, and he shrugged, releasing her hand and rising lazily. "Of course. Of my many faults, forcing a woman is not one of them."

Cat felt sick inside. She knew him well enough now to know she had hurt him. But she would hurt him worse if she let this go further and he discovered all there was about Catalina Hilliard and Lizzie Jones.

They dressed, a still, awkward silence between them. Cat knew he had probably thought, or hoped, she would talk about herself once he had, and that he must feel a little rebuffed. He most likely wouldn't say much more, and that likelihood hurt. She fought back that pressure behind her eyes. This was best. She knew it was best.

When she had finished the last button, she darted a glance at him. He was leaning against a wall, watching her every moment with the intensity of a cat watching a mouse.

As she started to turn for the door, he picked up something from the bureau. The envelope. "Yours, I believe."

Cat looked at it. "Can . . . can I leave it here until tomorrow? The banks are closed."

"Another favor, Miss Cat?" His tone was surly, and she knew he was frustrated and trying to hide it.

She flushed. "No," she said, and reached for it.

He caught her hand. "Wait," he said steadily, and his eyes had softened a little. "Leave it here. You can pick it up in the morning." There was no apology, but then, she knew he rarely apologized. And she also knew he had no reason to do so now.

Her gaze caught his. "Can't we be friends?"

"Just friends," he mocked. "No, I don't think we can."

She knew he was right. There was something between them so strong that they could never be simply friends. Fire and dynamite. Exploding stars. Thunder and lightning and raindrops. Tears.

If only . . .

But there were no *if only*'s in this world. She was who she was: repugnant to someone of his background. A fine family. A fine education. No matter what had turned him to gunfighting, he still had the background and manners of a well-born swell. Never could their two worlds meet. She would run into someone who knew from the old days, just as James had found her.

And Marsh would become a laughingstock for being with her.

It was that simple.

But she could tell him none of it.

Her eyes met his. "Then we can't be anything."

"Try to stop it, darlin'," he taunted.

"I will. I can."

"We'll see."

She spun away on those last words, leaving the money behind. She couldn't bear for him to see on her face the effect of those words. She knew he was right, that the only way they would, could, ever remain apart for long was if she left San Francisco.

"Cat!" She heard his voice behind her, but she didn't stop, and she knew he wouldn't come after her. She knew so much about him, and so little still.

Except she loved him.

And couldn't have him.

Cat expected to see James Cahoon appear in the Silver Slipper, especially after he was tossed from the Glory Hole, but hour after nervous hour passed, and he didn't show. Her skittishness increased, and she knew that was probably what he planned.

But she wasn't sure when or where he would strike. The newspapers? The courts? Thievery in the night. It was all possible.

Her mind worked all the possibilities as she moved around the crowded saloon, using James as a shield against thinking about Canton. About Marsh.

Teddy approached her as the crowd started dwindling away. "Do you mind if I leave with Hugh tonight?" His face colored, and Cat had to smile. He wanted to see Molly; that was clear. She had become extraordinarily sensitive to that particular need lately.

Cat nodded. The girls would be upstairs; she had her derringer. And unless James had changed more than she believed, he would be dead drunk by now, just as he'd almost been last night. He'd never held his liquor well; it was one of the reasons he'd been such a poor gambler. And the dissipation she'd seen on his face told her that, if anything, his drinking had accelerated.

The Silver Slipper and Glory Hole closed at the same time, and she locked up immediately after Teddy left. She took the cash box upstairs and counted the proceeds. It had been a good night for business. But then, they were all good nights.

Cat poured herself a glass of sherry and put out the light before walking over to her window. It was closed, and she raised it. The sound of the piano again. In her mind's eye she could see him sitting there with the long elegant fingers running so easily over the keys, that disgruntled, ugly dog next to him. She wished she had asked him about that, about the music, but she'd really had no right to ask him about anything. She slid down to the floor so her ear reached the point just about the windowsill, and she leaned against the wall, listening. The gunfighter who played beautiful music and collected ugly dogs. She smiled at the thought.

She listened until the notes stopped, and then she slowly undressed, running her hands along the body he had touched and loved so well, as if she could keep a part of him by doing so.

Finally she slipped on a nightdress and crawled into a bed now unbearably lonely. Sleep, she knew, would be a long time in coming.

James Cahoon was thirsty. Very, very thirsty. His whole body craved a drink.

But he craved something even more. A measure of vengeance. No little bitch was going to get the best of him. Especially one that had stabbed him and left him for dead.

He'd spent the morning looking for an attorney. But they all wanted money in advance before they would talk to him. Only one seemed interested, and that interest died when he discovered James didn't have proof of marriage. Other individuals, the lawyer said, had tried to ruin Catalina Hilliard, and they had all been destroyed, all except the new owner of the Glory Hole.

So James had decided to return to the Glory Hole, discover what he could, maybe find an ally, a partner. Instead, he was thrown out when he'd lost what few coins he had and accused the house of cheating. When he'd asked to see the owner, the black-haired man with the deadly eyes had appeared. Before James could open his mouth, the owner had told him to get out and not come back or he'd kill him. James, who'd known men like him, had no doubt he would do exactly that. The bitch had probably gotten to the bastard.

James had gone off and licked his wounds. With no money for liquor, he sobered up, and when he was sober, he got mean. He would get something for his trouble, one way or another.

He was feeling damn mean, in fact. She had looked down on him. *Him!* After everything he had done for her, taking her from that whorehouse and all. Look at where she was now. Nice dresses. Fancy place. Everyone cozying up to her. And she wouldn't share any of it. She owed him, by God, she owed him for that wound, for those months of recuperating.

James bided his time in his room, entertaining himself with thoughts of what he would do with her. He'd couldn't believe she had changed so much; he remembered her as skinny and scared. She'd been pretty enough, he supposed. Certainly, men had been willing to pay for her. But to him the prime attraction had been her fear. It made him feel strong, powerful. He'd liked that feeling. The control. He'd liked seeing the terror.

There had been no terror last night. That was what angered him most of all. There was hate, contempt, but no fear. The little whore had looked down on *him*. He picked up the knife he often carried in a special sheath strapped around his ankle. It was razor sharp, and he had cut his share of men with it. The knife was far better than a gun. Silent. And it hurt worse. He knew how bad it hurt.

And now he would make her hurt. And take whatever proceeds she had from the evening's business. It had to be a lot, if the activity last night and today were any indication. Enough to get him someplace else, enough to give him a new stake.

It was nearly two in the morning when he strapped on the knife, pocketed a small pistol as an extra precaution, and pulled on his worn coat. Soon he would have another one. A new one. The thought brought a lift to his shoulders.

But he was still thirsty. God-awful thirsty.

Marsh felt infinitely weary. Bidding the last lingerers a good night, he closed the Glory Hole a little after Hugh left with Teddy.

He released Winchester from his room and fed him some leftover steak, watching the dog gulp it down with barely a taste. It was, he thought wryly, a little like watching a drunk gulp fine port.

He walked over to the piano, letting the fingers of his right hand move over the keys, and then as if seduced by his own tentative action, he sat down and started a Beethoven sonata.

His fingers moved into Chopin's "Heroic" polonaise. Funny, how it all came back. All the music, all the notes, all the emotion.

All the man?

His hands moved on, at first almost automatically, then with increased concentration. The polonaise was a consuming piece of music, full of emotion and pride and defiance, and he felt himself giving more and more to it, drowning his thoughts in the demands of the composition. He was drained when he finished, feeling as if he'd not only completed the polonaise but in some way had started cleansing his soul, bringing back elements that had so long been missing.

Cat had been responsible. And he had no intentions of letting her go. It might take a while, but then, he'd always been stubborn.

He looked down at Win, who sat next to the wall watching him with those baleful brown eyes. Christ, but the damn dog reminded him of himself. It was damn scary looking into those empty, watchful eyes and seeing himself.

"Come on, Win," he said. "Let's go for a walk. And then we'll keep watch over Miss Cat."

The dog ambled to its feet, still keeping a certain distance but willing enough.

"We're not going far," he warned as he opened the front door of the saloon and held it open for Win. He locked it again, and then his hand went automatically down to his pistol.

This time he didn't take Win down to the bay. He stayed within view of both the Glory Hole and the Silver Slipper, seldom taking his eyes from the latter. No matter what Cat said about taking care of herself, Marsh had seen men like Cahoon before. Cowards in many ways, they were the back-shooters, the ambushers.

And he'd had that odd premonition he sometimes got before trouble.

Noting that Win had finished his necessities, he turned back, not altogether sure the dog would follow, but he did. Perhaps they had established some kind of communication, after all.

The cool air had cleaned out the cobwebs in his head, and once back in the Glory Hole, he propped a chair in front of the window as he had before, poured himself a glass of whiskey that would last through the night. He knew a moment's satisfaction as Win stretched out next to him, settling his head between two paws, as if he too were on watch.

Marsh didn't know how long he sat there before he saw a figure starting up the stairs that led to the second floor of the Silver Slipper. Because of the shadows, he couldn't tell whether it was someone who belonged there or not. One of the ladies, perhaps? Any weariness faded, and he was instantly alert. Win was on his feet now, growling slightly as if sensing Marsh's apprehension.

Marsh rose from the chair and moved closer to the wall next to the window, watching the figure as it hesitated at the door and then leaned over, apparently opened it, and entered. A key? Someone who belonged? It seemed that way.

Damn those shadows. But he didn't wait any longer. He would check that door himself, wake the whole damn place if necessary. He left Win inside the Glory Hole and quickly moved through the door to the street and across it, going up the steps two at a time. He checked the door by feel, and it opened easily. Someone had broken the lock.

The corridor was dark. He didn't see anyone. Whoever had come in had known where he was going. He knew Cat's room, and he moved quietly to it, then leaned his ear against it. He didn't want to break it if . . .

He heard a kind of shuffling inside, a muffled noise, and then a man's voice. "You little bitch."

Marsh tried the door. It was unlocked. He took the gun from its holster and opened the door quietly, only then coming to an abrupt stop.

Cat woke, sensing immediately something was wrong. She heard the doorknob turning and knew the noise that had awakened her was probably a creak on the floor outside the door. Her first thought was the derringer. It was under her pillow, and her hand went to it, but in her haste it went skittering off the bed and clattering to the floor.

She started to reach for it, her hand frantically searching the floor, as the door opened, but the intruder reached her first and put a knife against her throat.

Even in the dark she knew who he was. A sickeningly sweet cheap cologne filled the room.

"Not so fast, Lizzie," came the hated, remembered voice. "Now, don't move or make a sound, or this knife might slip."

Cat felt rage, total rage at his latest violation. All fear vanished. She could handle him now; she just needed time.

"What do you want?"

"Want? Merely what's due me, dear wife."

"Nothing's due you," she said, and the knife tightened against her throat. She felt a trickle of blood run down her skin before she felt the burning pain.

"Didn't anyone tell you about unlocked doors, sweet Lizzie?"

Not her own bedroom in her own place. She had locked the door for years and then decided not to let fear rule her. This was her home. She clenched her teeth, wanting to pound at him, kick at him, but the knife was too close to her throat. One slip . . .

"You little bitch," he said as he felt her resistance.

He forced her to her feet and moved toward the door, apparently to lock it himself as it swung open. Even in the dark she knew from the shape that Canton stood there, and she felt the knife cut her again as James's body tensed.

"Let her go." Cat had heard many tones in his voice: mocking, cold, warm, lazy. But never before had it dripped death.

She felt a tremor run the length of James's body, but he only clutched her tighter.

"The saloon keeper," James sneered. "And the whore. How fitting, or does the saloon keeper know all about our Lizzie?"

"Let her go!"

"Oh, no. Fire that gun, and my knife might well slip."

Cat felt the bravado in his tone. And desperation. The desperation frightened her more than anything. She wasn't sure what he would do.

Canton didn't move.

"Come in and close the door," James said. "Or I'll cut her throat."

Marsh hesitated, obviously unwilling to do the other's bidding, then stepped inside and closed the door. Light from an outside street lantern filtered inside the room, enabling him to see well enough, particularly after his eyes had grown accustomed to the darkened hall.

"Now put the gun on the floor very carefully."

Again Marsh hesitated, and Cat felt the edge of the knife cut into the side of her throat again.

Marsh slowly put the gun down in a slow, graceful movement.

"Too bad you interfered with my reunion with my wife," James said. "Or didn't you know she had a husband?"

From the twisted angle of her head, Cat saw the familiar tension in Canton. She wondered whether James had any idea how dangerous Canton could be. But now, apparently, James wasn't thinking at all.

"Didn't you?"

Canton shrugged as if the announcement were of supreme indifference.

"Did she tell you I found her in a whorehouse, she and her mother? Fifteen, Lizzie was, and as good as any of 'em. Bet she didn't tell you that." James was taking pleasure in this, she knew, and he also probably thought that Canton would leave in disgust.

She knew he wouldn't. But she didn't know what he would do later. She only knew she died a little inside as she heard James's words.

"Yep, Natchez Under the Hill, that's where I found her. Dumb little thing. Couldn't read or write. I took her and married her, and the ungrateful bitch tried to kill me."

"Too bad she didn't succeed." Canton's voice was low and hard.

James's grip on her tightened. It wasn't the answer he expected. Cat wondered what Canton was really thinking, but now, as so often, it was almost impossible to decipher his reactions, particularly in the dim light.

Neither did she know what to expect of James at this moment. During their "marriage" he'd often slapped and beat her. He might well have killed her that last day so many years ago; in past years, though, when she'd thought of him, she had come to understand he was a coward.

Now he was like a rat in a trap, and rats didn't behave in rational ways. Her neck was stinging in a dozen places, and her nightdress was wet with blood. The blade of the knife was very, very sharp, and she remembered that about him, the way he had always kept that knife sharpened.

She wondered about the girls down the hall. So far the tense voices in Cat's room had been low. If only . . .

James changed his position slightly, but his knife never left her throat. Canton hadn't moved. James turned his attention back to him. "Kick that gun over toward the bed," he ordered as he took several steps backward and forced Cat to sit down on the bed with him.

Canton lazily kicked the gun a few steps, but not far enough for James to reach it. Cat heard her captor's angry growl. She was beginning to feel dizzy. She felt James move his left arm from where it had encircled her, but the relief was momentary. His fingers caught her hair and pulled her head farther back, making her neck, and the knife, more visible to Canton.

And then she knew James was going to reach for the gun. She felt his body tensing for it. In the second that he did, he would have to let go of her hair. She also knew that as long as James had the knife at her throat, Canton wouldn't endanger her. It would be up to her to make a move.

But James surprised her again. "You pick it up, Lizzie," he said. "And be very careful when you do." Keeping the knife poised at her throat, his other hand jerked her head forward by her hair until she was able to reach the Colt.

"By the barrel, Lizzie," James then ordered. "We don't want an accident, do we?"

Cat picked it up carefully. He was surprising her with his shrewdness, but then he'd always had a talent for self-preservation. Otherwise he would be dead now.

"Now I think our visitor should hear more about the life of Lizzie Jones. The way she used to help me cheat and sometimes entertain my opponents. She was very good at diverting attention, you see, and their minds were often on something more . . . interesting . . . than a game of chance."

Cat had never hated as she did now. He was destroying the one really good thing in her life, resurrecting every minute of those terrible years, every feeling of hopelessness and degradation.

He jerked on her hair. "You tell him, Lizzie," James said in the low, menacing voice she remembered so well. He apparently remembered the way she used to be paralyzed with fear, too, since his attention was wandering from Canton. He was enjoying tormenting her now. "Tell him how you used to whore. Or do you whore for him now?"

"Go to hell," she said. "Kill me, and he'll kill you."

"It might be worth it, Lizzie girl. Do you have any idea what you put me through, all the pain, the indignity?" The knife pressed against her neck again, and she felt a new stinging.

"I wish I'd killed you," she said defiantly.

"Ah, the little nit bites back." His hand was trembling slightly now. Cat didn't know whether he was getting tired, whether he was that angry, or whether it was fear. Nothing, she knew, was going the way he expected. That realization gave her courage, but she had to fight hard not to succumb to the growing numbness, the dizziness she was beginning to feel.

And then she felt James shake, and she knew that quiver in his hand *was* fear. He didn't know what to do now. That gave her power.

She tilted her head slightly, feeling the sting again of a new cut. Canton hadn't moved. The light was too dim for James to see Canton's eyes, so he wouldn't know what was going on there. But she knew. Canton didn't like not being in charge. He was waiting to spring, but he would wait patiently until he knew the time was right.

Cat had to make it right. This couldn't go on, or James's hand would slip, if he didn't cut

her on purpose. And she couldn't let him get the
gun, or he might kill Canton. She suddenly fell
against her captor, away from the knife as if
she'd fainted. He instinctively moved his hand
away from her throat, and in that moment Canton dived at James. The knife bit into her shoulder, but she twisted away from the brunt of the
intended blow as Canton's body hit James. The
two men rolled down onto the floor, and Cat
knew they were both desperately groping for the
gun.

Canton was much stronger, but James's
hand had almost landed on the weapon, and she
saw him trying to aim it at the larger man. Canton was swifter, though, his hand turning the
barrel around, and Cat heard the deafening roar
of a gun.

There was a cry of pain, and Cat knew it
belonged to James. Then there was silence. Canton was still for a moment, then moved wearily
away. He stood and went to the oil lamp, lit it,
and came over to Cat, his hands investigating the
wound on her shoulder as blood spread over her
nightdress.

There was a frantic knocking on her door,
and she heard Wilhelmina's voice. "Miss Cat?"

"Tell them to come in," she said, her voice
a whisper. She didn't want to be alone with him
now. She wanted the horror to go away. All the
horror. Including all the words that had been
said.

"Are you all right?"

No, she wasn't. She would never be all right
again. All the lies were exposed now. The world
she'd built was made of sand, and now a wave

had washed it away, all the wonderful towers and walls and bulwarks. She felt naked and exposed.

"Yes," she said in a dull tone, just as the door burst open and her eyes went to the girls, who seemed paralyzed by the sight of Canton and a blood-covered man on the floor, not to mention Cat's own somewhat battered self.

It was obvious they weren't quite sure what to do when they saw Marsh lean over her. All of them had weapons of some type, including a shotgun and a club. Wilhelmina lifted the club threateningly.

Cat forced herself to speak. "It's all right now. He . . . Mr. Canton . . . shot an intruder."

There were squeals of distress as the girls saw the cuts on Catalina, the blood-splattered gown. "Miss Catalina," one said, "you look . . ."

"Like she needs a doctor," Canton finished for her. No, not Canton—Marsh, Cat reminded herself giddily as waves of dizziness assaulted her. But that thought hurt too. She had to keep thinking of him as Canton. Less personal. Less hurtful. If anything could be less hurtful.

"I'll go," said one of the girls, and the others crowded around Cat, more or less pushing Canton aside.

Cat glanced up at him, trying to read his face, something that had never been easy and was even more difficult now. His face was again in the shadows, and his stance stiff. She looked down and saw the still body, blood pooling on the carpet. James's face looked old, but his eyes seemed to stare at her with accusation.

She felt a towel against the cuts, the hesitant gentleness of Wilhelmina's care, but all she wanted now was Canton's touch. Canton's warmth. Canton's safety. But he had given all that to someone else, to someone he thought she was.

Now he knew nearly everything. She closed her eyes to this world, wishing she were anywhere else.

Wilhelmina moved between her and Canton, as if shielding her, and glared over at the male visitor as if everything was his fault. "Can you get . . . that out of here?" she asked, looking down at the body just feet away.

Cat struggled to think. Everything had happened so fast, and she felt dizzy and weak. Her shoulder hurt as did the many cuts on her neck. Worst of all, she felt dirty and exposed. James had made her feel that way, and worse, and now for the second time he lay at her feet. This time he was really dead. She didn't know how she felt about that. Her hand trembled in Wilhelmina's. "The police . . ."

Wilhelmina grimaced. "At least give her some privacy," she said to Marsh, who was still standing. Watching. "She needs to change. . . ."

If Cat had not felt so terrible, she would have been amused. Wilhelmina didn't usually assert herself, especially to someone like Canton. It was a measure of concern Cat hadn't really expected. Perhaps she should have. Or would have if she had allowed herself to get closer to the girl. But she hadn't allowed herself to get close to anyone, not until Molly . . . and Canton.

Again her gaze went to the silent man across the room. His jaw worked slightly as he reluctantly accepted Wilhelmina's words. He nodded.

He started for the door, turned back, and strode toward her, parting the girls as Moses parted the seas. He very carefully took her chin in his hand, leaned down, and kissed her lightly. "My gallant Cat," he whispered. "I'll wait outside."

Cat was stunned. She swallowed hard, not knowing what to say. There were a lot of things she knew she should say, first of all "thank you." But any utterance was stuck in her throat, unable to fight itself through the sea of emotions. She could only stare up at him and wonder how he could accept everything James had said. Unless he hadn't believed it.

He reluctantly let go of her chin and moved away toward the door as the girls stared at him with something close to amazement. Wilhelmina shook her head for a moment and then stood up. "A fresh gown and robe?"

Cat wanted to dress properly, to feel in control again, but she couldn't, not with the growing agony of her shoulder. The pain was deeper, sharper, no longer dulled by what was happening. "Second drawer," she said.

She tried to rise but couldn't, and sat back down. She wished they could move James, wished those damn eyes didn't seem to follow her. What would this shooting mean to Canton? Especially after the last one.

She wished she could keep her thoughts from spinning from one thing to another, but she couldn't. Everything was going round and round, and she began to see double. Then the light seemed to fade, and she reached for the edge of the bed. She felt herself begin to fall.

• • •

Cat woke to the sharp odor of smelling salts.

Pain was everywhere.

Dr. MacLaren, who had treated Molly days earlier, was leaning over her.

"Miss Hilliard," he said sharply. "Do you hear me?"

She nodded.

"Good."

He held up two fingers. "How many fingers?"

"Two," she said disgustedly as she looked over the room. Marsh Canton was not there. Neither was James Cahoon's body. A policeman was. So was Wilhelmina, though the other girls were gone.

She started to sit up, but dizziness swamped her again. "You're going to have to be still awhile, Miss Hilliard," the doctor said. "You've lost a great deal of blood."

The policeman moved to her side. "Can you tell me what happened."

"An . . . intruder. He wanted the receipts. And more," she said with a small shudder that wasn't at all faked. "Mr. Canton apparently saw something and came to investigate. He . . . the intruder . . . had a knife. He would have cut my throat if it hadn't been for Mr. Canton."

The policeman nodded. "That's pretty much what he said. That Canton's a pretty busy fellow, though."

"I owe him my life."

"Well, I guess we can let him go." There was a note of reluctance in his voice. "We had to see whether his story checked out. Two dead men in a month." He shook his head. "Right in the heart, just like the other one." He hesitated. "You wouldn't know that dead fellow's name, would you?"

Cat shook her head. "He was in the Silver Slipper the other night. That's all I know."

"Paper in his pocket says he's a James Cahoon." Cat went still, She didn't want to think her name might be there, too, or any kind of connection.

She looked at the man blankly, and he nodded. "That's all, then. I might have more questions later."

"Thank you," she said, giving him what she hoped was a pitifully grateful look. She hated doing that, but she didn't want any more questions.

"I'll leave you and the doctor," he said uncomfortably, and left.

"I'm going to have to stitch some of those wounds," the doctor said, ignoring the policeman's departure, "particularly that shoulder." It was only then that Cat realized she was nearly naked. Her clean nightdress, obviously put on her by Wilhelmina, was off her shoulder, and she felt padded cloth against her shoulder and her neck. She tried to move, and pain shot through her.

"Mr. Canton?" she asked.

"He's outside with the police," said the doctor. "I thought you two were feuding," he noted with amused interest. "He sure as hell doesn't act that way. Acts more like a worried husband." He hesitated a moment, then continued as his hands gently explored the area around the shoulder wound. "I'm going to give you some chloroform," he said, "before I sew that cut. You'll sleep for a few hours, and you need that too."

Cat started to protest. She wanted to see Canton, make sure he was all right, that he was not being held by the police. She wanted to see him more than anything in the world, and yet part of her dreaded it, dreaded what she might see in his eyes once he had time to think over all of James's comments.

But most of all, she had to know he was safe.

"Not until I see Mar—Mr. Canton . . . ," she insisted. She stopped herself from saying "Marsh" just in time.

The doctor heard the determination in her voice. He'd confronted it before in other matters, and he shook his head in surrender. "Just a few moments, then. We'll wait outside."

Cat closed her eyes as she heard the steps retreat, the door open and then close again.

"Cat . . ." The voice was unusually hesitant, low.

She opened her eyes. He had stooped next to the bed so that his face was not far from hers. As usual he looked like her fallen angel, but now there was a stubble of dark beard shadowing his face. It was still the handsomest face she'd ever seen. She wanted to touch it, to know it was flesh and blood and not some dream.

She wanted to do so many things, to thank him, to ask if he had any trouble with the police, to touch him. Instead her eyes met his directly, and she blurted out what was festering inside. "Everything he said was true." She had to know how he felt about what James had said. She had to know now. Her gaze never left his face, even as she heard the tiny quiver in her voice.

A vein jumped in his temple, though his expression didn't change and his hand touched hers. Finally he said in a low voice, "Pretty Cat, I wish I could take the pain away, *all* of it."

Cat felt a rush of tears then, the only ones she'd allowed other than the first time they'd made love together. She tried to blink them back, but they wouldn't be blinked. Loss of blood, she told herself, but it wasn't. It was his tenderness, his acceptance of the unacceptable.

The tears wandered down her cheek, and she tried, as a child sometimes does, to stop them with the back of a fist. But she couldn't stem them. So many tears were back there. A lifetime of tears, held back until now by a will that no longer functioned.

"I . . . I'm . . . sorry," she whispered brokenly. She didn't want him to see her like this, and yet . . . she yearned for his presence, that quiet strength that didn't judge, just offered a comforting presence. A loved presence.

But how could he? She had been nothing but trouble for him. First the beating, then Molly. Now this. She didn't understand, but she couldn't ask, because the emotion had choked her throat.

He took a handkerchief from somewhere on him and gently, silently, dabbed at the tears, and she noted his eyes weren't like mirrors anymore at all, but were filled with a deep anguish of his own.

"Marsh . . . ," she started, hearing the trembling in her own voice, but he put a finger to her mouth.

"Not now, darlin'." The drawled "darlin'" held a new nuance now. Not mocking, as it had been the first time she'd heard it, or passion filled, or quizzical, but softly possessive. "We'll talk later. The doctor just gave me a few minutes."

"Will you . . . ?"

"I'll be here," he said quietly, and she knew he would be.

Drained of almost everything but a swelling love, she nodded, closing her eyes as he left but keeping his image in her mind.

She was barely aware of the doctor returning, of the sickly sweet smell she inhaled as she slipped off into a world that seemed truly safe for the first time in her life.

Marsh watched her sleep. The doctor had long gone, and Marsh had told Wilhelmina in a tone that brooked little disagreement that he would keep watch.

He had never seen so much pain in a person's eyes as in Cat's when Cahoon had spoken. *Found her in a whorehouse, her and her mother. Fifteen, Lizzie was, and as good as any of 'em.*

Fifteen. A child. He remembered his sister at fifteen. The sweet voice. The gentle nature. A child who still loved to run in the wet grass and marvel at sunsets. She had been the one who had made him see them in a special way. He ached for both those fifteen-year-olds now, for Cat, who apparently had never been a child, and for his sister, Melissa, who had never been an adult.

He kept hearing James's words. *Her and her mother.* Christ, what chance had she? *Dumb little thing. Couldn't even read and write.* What strength it must have taken to become what she was today! She had obviously learned to read and write, build a successful business, keep a city enthralled with personality alone.

She had built on her tragedy. Marsh knew he had done the opposite, had vented his grief and fury in destruction. Of the two, Cat had proved herself stronger, better, by far.

And she'd been so obviously afraid he would turn from her. She should be the one to turn from him, if she had any sense.

He remembered his careless words that first time he'd made love to her. *I always pay for services rendered.* Christ, he might as well have bullwhipped her or worse.

And the man who had called himself her husband? Who had apparently used her in the cruelest way possible? Marsh couldn't help thinking the man deserved to die. Still, the ugly satisfaction he had felt at killing his mother's and sister's murderers was missing. He was so damned tired of death, of living with it on such a familiar basis.

He watched Cat's now-peaceful face and wondered whether he could ever entirely put an end to that part of his life. Or whether it would haunt him forever. It just seemed to follow him, wherever he went.

Marsh didn't know how long it was before Cat stirred. A small whimper escaped as she moved, and he knew she must be hurting under that bulky bandage that covered her shoulder and neck.

Her eyes opened slightly, and something frantic darted across them before she saw him and relaxed. That small indication of trust filled him with something close to pleasure. He took her hand. "Don't move," he said.

"You're still here," she replied with wonder.

He nodded. He wanted to say he would always be there, but he wasn't sure that was possible.

"You look like a brigand," she said with an obvious attempt at lightness.

His hand went up, and he felt the bristles on his face. He had forgotten about shaving. He had forgotten about a lot of things in the past few hours. "I've been that and worse, darlin'."

Her hand went tentatively to his in the first spontaneous move on her part, and again he felt ripples of pleasure run through him. His fingers went around hers.

"Tell me."

"Do you really want to hear?" he said.

"I know you've been a gunfighter," she said simply.

"I've been a lot more than that. I was judge, jury, and executioner of an innocent man," he said in a toneless voice, then went on to tell her the whole tale.

Her eyes clear and wistful, Cat brought his hand to her mouth and kissed it.

"I wish," she said in words he remembered saying just hours earlier, "I could take away the pain, all the pain."

CHAPTER 23

Cat recuperated swiftly during the next few days. Perhaps, she thought, it was healing by happiness. Because for the first time in her life she was really happy. Ridiculously happy. Outrageously happy.

She found herself humming in the morning. Smiling for no reason.

Marsh Canton spent much of the first day with her, pampering her with meals in bed, which she'd never had before, and talking in ways she suspected were new to him. He talked about his plantation, about his family. He spoke freely, sometimes with pain, but also with affection. She suspected it was a cleansing of some kind.

She worried only about Molly and the newspapers, which ran long front-page stories about the latest shoot-out at the Silver Slipper.

"We're notorious," she said to Marsh after reading one account that Teddy had brought her. His eyes had shuttered again, and she wished she hadn't said anything. Something was bothering him, and though they had come a long way, they hadn't yet broken all the barriers.

"Darlin', I'm damned tired of being notorious."

She hesitated. "Does it have something to do with that book?"

"That book was all lies. I never fought Lobo. In fact—" He stopped suddenly. This was one secret that was not his to reveal. "—it was all fiction," he continued smoothly.

"There isn't a Lobo?"

"Oh, there was a Lobo all right. We just never fought each other. We only . . . crossed paths."

"Then why . . ."

"That damn book sent every would-be gunslinger wanting to make a reputation after me," Marsh said. "I had to kill boys no more than twenty just to stay alive." He shook his head. "That's one reason I wanted the Glory Hole. I thought San Francisco was far enough away that I could get lost."

"The newspaper stories . . ."

"At least they don't know who I am. Maybe no one will connect Taylor Canton with Marsh Canton." He didn't sound at all sure. The news stories emphasized that both killings, though apparently justified, resulted from one bullet through the heart.

In addition to that worry, there was Molly. The detective Cat had hired, Booth Templeton, had sent a report. One of his operatives was watching Molly's father's home, and Templeton himself was interviewing everyone who had been fired by Molly's father or mentioned by Molly as someone who'd tried to help her. The detective was also trying to find the fiancé of the maid who had disappeared.

Molly, in the meantime, was fine, according to Teddy, who along with Hugh had a long talk with Marsh Canton, admitting that Hugh had originally been planted as a spy. Hugh offered to quit. But Marsh apparently had chosen to believe Teddy's claim that Hugh, after the first few weeks, had switched his loyalty to Marsh and the Glory Hole. They were all on the same side now, in any event, although some awkwardness remained. There had been too much initial bitterness for it to be otherwise.

But other than those concerns, Cat felt as though she were living in a new world, one full of hope rather than dominated by the past.

She got up the second day but didn't go downstairs. Her arm was in a sling and her shoulder bulky with bandages. If she moved too suddenly, she paid for it with pain, but nothing could dim the new brightness in her life.

Because she didn't want to go into the saloon as long as her injuries were so evident, Marsh took her each afternoon for a carriage ride. They watched more than one sunset from the hill where they'd shared their first one together.

Marsh hadn't told her where they were going the first time. He'd placed a picnic basket in a carriage he'd rented and, as he'd done before, told the driver the destination in tones she couldn't hear.

Lightning and thunder still flashed between them. It would always flash between them, she sensed, but now there was none of the anger. It was an invigorating kind of storm now, the kind that Cat enjoyed viewing when she was warm and safe inside someplace. And she felt warm and safe, not frightened or threatened in any way.

This time Marsh sent the carriage away, asking that the driver return in three hours. The hillside was empty except for them, and the sunset was not far away.

There was a new ease about Marsh, although the watchfulness was still evident. Cat thought it would always be there, just as nightmares would always be with her. She loved to see him smile now, that slow, lazy smile that still held something back but was so much better than before. It held promise.

She was smiling too. Mainly because she loved looking at him. And touching him. They couldn't keep their hands off each other on the carriage ride, although he was very careful not to jolt her shoulder in any way. Her neck was also still bandaged. His hand held hers, their clasp resting on the blue skirt, and his trousered leg was snug against her.

Cat hummed one of the melodies that she'd heard him play.

When he looked at her in question, she explained, "I used to listen to you play."

He looked surprised, nonplussed, as if he'd never even considered that others might have heard him.

"I used to wonder," she added, "how such a scoundrel could play such beautiful music. Now I know."

"What do you know, darlin'?" He was honestly curious.

"That there is a fine heart buried somewhere under that fallen-angel exterior."

He grimaced. "Fallen angel?"

"I used to think of you as Lucifer . . . the fallen angel."

"And now?"

"Not so fallen."

"Just partially?" he teased.

"I don't want to give up all my illusions." She'd never bantered like this before, and she was astounded at how much she enjoyed it. Perhaps because it was part of being in love. And she was that. She knew it in every fiber of her being.

"Fallen angel," he mused. "I don't think I was ever an angel to fall."

"Me, either," she admitted.

He took her chin, a familiarly dear gesture. "I doubt that," he said, and Cat felt such an aching pleasure twist through her that she had to turn away.

Marsh spread the blanket over the ground and revealed the contents of his basket. Baked chicken, cheese, freshly baked bread, fruit. And a bottle of very fine champagne.

"For the sunset," he said.

She hugged the moment to her. "I've never been on a picnic before."

He hesitated, a flicker of something like pain moving rapidly over his face.

"We'll have one every week, if you like," he said. "To compensate."

"I think," she said slowly, "just on special occasions so it will always be . . . exceptional."

Marsh stooped as he opened the champagne, his head turned slightly. He wanted every day to be exceptional for her. He was discovering rapidly that she hadn't had many "exceptional" days. And now, when he caught sight of the child who had never been, the shy, delighted smile, he felt a jarring tenderness that ached to the marrow of his bones. He wanted to spread his early world out for her, the one that had been full of security and love; he wanted it for both of them.

It's not too late.

They nibbled at the chicken, and Marsh fed her bites of bread and cheese, but both were much more interested in each other than the food.

The sun dipped slowly, becoming a huge fiery ball just hovering over a now placid ocean. The dark-blue sky was already touched by dabs of pastel colors, the pinks that preceded the more dramatic, violent colors.

Marsh handed her a glass of champagne and watched her take it with her left hand and sip it. Her hand shook slightly, but then so did

his. He watched as she licked her lips appreciatively. It was an incredibly sensual gesture to
him, and he wanted to kiss her again, but he
knew this time it could easily, almost certainly,
develop into something else. And he didn't want
to hurt her shoulder; he knew from his own past
wounds how raw and sore it must be, and he
wished he had been the one to take the blow.
Nothing was ever going to hurt her again, dammit.

He took a sip of his own champagne, and
he thought it had never tasted so good, not even
when he'd had finer quality. He looked toward
her, and their gazes locked in sizzling union.

When the intensity was more than he could
bear, he moved over to her and carefully draped
his arm around her waist. "You're beautiful,
Miss Cat."

Her fingers trembled even more, and it was
all she could do to keep the glass from slipping
from her grasp. His proximity had always had
that effect on her, but never more so than now.
She didn't know how she could bear it, being so
close to him, wanting him so much.

In self-defense she sipped again, reveling in
the radiating warmth of his body, the comfort of
his closeness. The horizon was turning vivid
now. Brilliant gold rippled through the sky, layered by hues of vermilion, and then, as if just for
them, the sky seemed to explode into fire as the
sun slipped into the ocean, taking with it shimmering reflections of color on the water.

"My sister showed me the glory of sunsets," he said, his voice nearly a whisper in her
ear. "She used to get angry when I didn't show

proper appreciation. And then, after she died, I couldn't watch them without thinking of her."

"And now?"

"I still think of her," he said slowly, a wistful sorrow in eyes that now revealed a great deal, "but now I can think of the happy times. She had the sweetest voice, as true as the finest bell. I would often accompany her on the piano."

"How did you learn to play like you do?"

"It's just something I can do," he said. "My mother was a fine pianist, and she taught me the classics when I was a boy, but I've always been able to pick up a tune, a melody. I hadn't played in a long time until I came to the Glory Hole, and then it all came back. As if it had been sitting there like a vulture, waiting for a weak moment."

"I don't think it was a weak moment," she said. "I think it was a strong one."

He leaned over and kissed her ear. "I love you, Cat." He hadn't ever thought he would say those words, could say those words to anyone, but now they came, unplanned.

Her face clouded, even in the evening shadows, and he saw some of that brilliant light leave those green eyes.

"You have to know . . ."

"I know everything I want to know."

"No," she said, putting her finger to his mouth. "Listen first. I'll never feel safe until you do, until you know everything."

He knew what she was saying. She didn't yet trust him to accept what she had to tell him. She couldn't really believe in him until she did. The thought hurt, but he understood. How long had he carried his own dark secret and allowed it to fester and destroy?

"I was born in a brothel," she said in a toneless voice, and then she told him *her* story in *her* words. At last she got to Ben Abbott.

"Ben had come west because of his health and silver fever. But he couldn't mine, not with his bad health, and so he opened a saloon. He'd gone to Harvard, and taught back east, and he was the kindest man I'd ever met.

"I didn't trust him, not for a long time, but he ... found out I couldn't read or write, although I'd become very good at hiding it. I knew cards, because of James, and everyone just assumed I could do the other." She hesitated. "He goaded me into learning. He said I was like a sponge, and I was. Once I started, I wanted to learn and learn and learn, and he enjoyed teaching. Learning ... books ... became a key to freedom for me, to be something other than a saloon girl. But his lungs were bad, and he steadily worsened. I started managing the Silver Slipper for him.

"I was there six years when he became really sick. I ran the saloon and tried to take care of him." Her voice broke for the first time. "He wanted to leave me everything, he said. And he wanted to marry me since he had brothers and sisters back east who might try to contest a will. I didn't agree at first; it was like admitting he was going to die, but he wanted it so badly. He died seven months after the marriage," She bit her lip and looked at Marsh. "He was the first good thing that ever happened to me, and even that seems soiled now by James. I suppose I was a bigamist."

Marsh ran his hand along her arm. "You didn't know . . ."

"That I wasn't a murderess, though I left a man to die," she said sadly.

Marsh changed the subject. "How did you get to San Francisco?"

"I knew the silver mine wouldn't last, and the town was small. I wanted a fresh start, some-place where no one knew me. I knew the saloon business then, and I had always wanted to see the ocean. Everyone said San Francisco was a bustling, growing city, where money meant more than background."

"And so came the Ice Queen," Marsh said.

She shrugged. "I . . . invented a lost love. It was effective." Her eyes met his in the dusk. "I'm a good liar."

"You did what you had to do," he said softly. "I can't even imagine the strength it required to survive what you did, much less become the success you are."

"Are you sure, Marsh? Are you sure you won't look at me some day and see Lizzie Jones?"

"I'm seeing Lizzie Jones right now," he said. "and I admire her more than anyone I've ever met." He willed her to believe him.

She was silent for a moment, wondering over his words, weighing them, he knew, just as she weighed so many things. He wanted the time to come when she wouldn't have to do that.

"There's . . . something else," she said halt-ingly.

He waited.

"I was going to have a baby once. My mother drugged me and when I woke, the child had been taken from me. I was sick for a long time, and I never got pregnant again. I don't think . . . I can ever have children."

He knew from the painful way she'd said the words that she'd wanted that baby. He hated that faceless woman who had called herself a mother.

Marsh took her hand, studied it. So much strength in her. So much bottled-up love. He understood now about Molly, why Cat had been so concerned. She had started to let that love leak out, and now it was like the backwater of a dam, waiting for a breach in the confining wall. He felt a welling tenderness and wondered, for a moment, whether that analogy applied to him too. It was a startling thought. "Darlin'," he said carefully, "I think there just might be any number of people who need you, starting with those in Quinn Devereux's project." He hesitated, then continued in a rough voice. "And . . . me."

Cat's hand tightened around his fingers, and her body relaxed against his. And he knew he had said exactly the right thing. He cradled her in his arms, feeling her soft, accepting sigh as her head rested against his heart. He heard his own heartbeat slow with the exquisite tenderness he felt for her. Tenderness and a deep, fierce pride for the woman who never gave up, who defeated odds that would have buried almost anyone else.

He looked up at the sky. The moon was

pale in the darkening sky, more luminous than solid. A few stars were twinkling, and he wanted to reach up and grab one for her. A fistful.

He contented himself with pouring a glass of champagne, holding it as she drank from it. He spilled some, then licked it from her face. A sense of warm intimacy enfolded them, a kind of enchantment that closed out everything but the moment, but the discovery they were making of each other.

They remained that way until they heard the clattering of the returning carriage.

T. J. Simmons flipped through the stack of newspapers at the *Denver Post*. He had been at it all morning and was just about prepared to give up. It was the third week in a row that he had perused out-of-town newspapers. Trying to discover the whereabouts of Marsh Canton was like trying to find a needle in a haystack.

He'd had some success with the War Department. He had found records of a Colonel Marsh T. Canton, who had fought with Mosby on the Confederate side. Simmons had been just plain lucky there. The officer who'd received his query had had a special interest in General Mosby and his guerrillas. He was only too pleased to expound on the exploits of Colonel Canton. Simmons didn't know if they were true or not, and couldn't care less, but they would make great reading.

Two more papers and then he would go off and have dinner. It would be a cheap one; his money was running out. Telegrams were expensive. So was the man he'd bribed at the *Post* to let him read the newspapers.

The last paper came from San Francisco. He almost put it down without reading it. San Francisco seemed a long shot at best. His gaze wandered over the front page without much attention. He almost missed it.

San Francisco Saloon Owner Shoots Intruder.

Simmons didn't know why he continued except that anything that dealt with violence caught his attention. Excitement seeded and grew as he continued.

For the second time in a month, Glory Hole owner Taylor Canton killed a man involved in an apparent attack on the owner and an employee of the neighboring Silver Slipper saloon.

The most recent incident occurred last evening in the living quarters of the Silver Slipper, owned by Catalina Hilliard. As in the first instance, the intruder was killed with one bullet to the heart.

Four weeks earlier Mr. Canton interrupted an attempted kidnapping of a girl who worked at the Silver Slipper, and killed one of the attackers. Two other men were arrested.

The latest shooting occurred when an intruder, apparently intent on robbery, entered the bedroom of Miss Hilliard. Mr. Canton told police he was closing his own saloon when he saw someone sneak up the steps and break the lock of the upstairs level of the Silver Slipper. When he went to investigate, he found the intruder, James Cahoon, holding a knife on Miss Hilliard.

In the ensuing struggle the intruder was killed and Miss Hilliard badly cut.

Mr. Canton came to our city six months ago to open the Glory Hole. There have been rumors of a feud between the Glory Hole and Silver Slipper owners, but this reporter now believes that rift has been exaggerated.

Police were satisfied with the statements and made no charges against Mr. Canton.

Canton! Taylor Canton. And the name of the Mosby officer was Marsh T. Canton. Coincidence?

A bullet to the heart. It took a fine marksman to do that. Simmons had learned that much during his career.

He grew more and more certain that the saloon owner and his quarry were one and the same. The story was just getting better and better. *The Life and Times of a Gunman* could be the break he needed, the book that would make him famous. And rich.

In the meantime, though, he needed money. He needed to sell another dime novel, and this would give it to him. One last gunfight for Marsh Canton.

He forgot about dinner as he hurried off to the telegraph office. Tom Bailey had been waiting to hear from him. Tom Bailey would have his chance to shoot the most notorious gunman in the West.

And T. J. Simmons would be there to report it for posterity.

Molly stepped outside on the porch of Hugh O'Connell's house and looked around. Since she'd come to stay there, she had not gone out alone, on orders of both Hugh and Teddy.

But now she must. Elizabeth depended on her.

The baby was coming. Pains had started shortly after Hugh had left for work, and though Elizabeth tried to stifle her cries, they were coming frequently now. Molly had tried to make her as comfortable as possible, but now her friend needed more than what she could offer.

The older children were in school, and the others were too young to go after the doctor.

She knew that Elizabeth had had a hard time during her last delivery, that Hugh had insisted they call a doctor this time rather than a midwife. Thanks to his new job, the O'Connells could afford a good one now.

Molly took one last look around. Nothing seemed unusual. There were the customary loiterers, mostly men without jobs. She would send one of them if she thought she could trust him, but most were drinkers and like as not they would stop at some saloon once coin was in their pockets.

She found her shawl, then told five-year-old Terrence to let his mother know where she was going. She was afraid Elizabeth would try to stop her if she could. It was just a short distance after all, a few blocks, no more. She had gone to the doctor's office once with Elizabeth and Hugh.

She had almost reached the doctor's office when she heard footsteps behind her. They seemed to keep rhythm with her own.

She looked along the road. Carriages went

clattering by; people were walking alongside storefronts. Surely she was safe, but still a prickly fear gnawed at her. She hurried, darting a look backward at the man behind her. She recognized one of the loiterers, and the fear grew stronger.

Just a few more steps and she would be at the doctor's. She started to run and turned into the doorway, then, too late, remembered the empty hallway entrance. She turned back to the street where she could ask for help, but the man had already reached her. His hand went over her mouth before she could scream, his other arm locking her arms to the side.

She struggled, and he pulled her tighter against his body, pressing an elbow against her chest while his hand moved up to cover both her nose and mouth, cutting off her air. Molly struggled desperately for breath until everything went dark.

Business was brisk at the Glory Hole. The recent events had spurred even more interest in both the Glory Hole and Silver Slipper.

Notoriety, Marsh decided, had its advantages as well as disadvantages. So did the killing of James Cahoon. It had certainly lowered Cat's barriers, had been the catalyst that opened her to him.

But he would trade it all if she had not had to go through so much. He still saw that knife held to her throat, the fear in her eyes. He still recalled her humiliation as Cahoon had tried to strip her bare of dignity.

She was better now. It had been a week since her injury, and the shadows had left her eyes. He'd seen her daily since the picnic, taking her for long rides. He'd offered to take her to a concert, but she demurred, knowing the uproar that would ensue at their presence together. It would mean more publicity, she said, and neither one of them needed that now. So they usually went to their place on the cliff, or he would rent a buggy and they would drive along the shore. Several evenings he'd just stayed up in her room, talking. Touching. Her injury prevented anything else. One night she'd come over to the Glory Hole after it had closed, and he'd played, just for her.

It was a time of healing for both of them.

Marsh heard a bottle drop, and he turned toward the bar. Hugh was standing there, looking miserable and worried, staring down at a bottle seeping liquor over the floor.

"Hugh?"

Hugh shrugged and turned toward the back where they kept a mop. "It's . . . Elizabeth. She's close to her time, and I . . ."

Marsh was beginning to know what worry was. What love was. "Why don't you go home and eat dinner with her?" he said. "I'll take care of the bar."

"But . . ."

"I can't afford to lose any more bottles of whiskey," Marsh said with mock sternness. "Just go. I'll get someone else to clean this up."

Hugh turned grateful eyes on him. "Thank you."

"That's not necessary. You've been valuable to me."

"Mr. Canton . . ."

"Just get the hell out of here," Marsh said, knowing that Hugh wanted to say something about why he had first applied for the job. Marsh didn't want to hear it. He couldn't have run the Glory Hole without Hugh, and he knew it, just as he knew he now had Hugh's total loyalty.

Hugh nodded, took his coat from where he'd hung it on a peg just inside the hallway, and with another grateful nod, disappeared out the door.

Marsh kept busy the rest of the afternoon. Late in the day a carriage drew up and the driver delivered a note to one of the waiters, who hurried over with it to Marsh.

It was from Hugh. *Elizabeth in labor. Molly missing. Please inform Ted and Miss Catalina.*

"Christ," Marsh swore. Molly. He understood Cat's concern for the girl so much better now. Cat had gone through so much herself. He still remembered the afternoon when Cat had started to ask for his help, and he'd . . .

He called over the most dependable of his waiters and told him to tend bar until the evening bartenders came in. So Molly had been at Hugh's. He hadn't known that, only that Cat seemed to think she was safe.

Marsh rushed across the street. Teddy was behind the bar, Cat nowhere in sight.

He handed the note over to Teddy, watched his face flush with fury, and felt a tug of sympathy. Obviously, the man cared a great deal for

Molly. Marsh had seen it before, the time he had intercepted the kidnappers.

Teddy started to take off his apron.

"Where's Cat?" Marsh asked.

"Upstairs," Teddy said. "Will you tell her?"

Marsh put a hand on Teddy. "What are you going to do?"

"Go after her," Teddy uttered between clenched teeth.

Marsh's hand automatically went toward the gunbelt he usually wore. It wasn't there. He'd left it off since the shooting of James Cahoon, unwilling now to display the firearm publicly, to make more of the already strong speculation.

"Let's talk to Cat first," he said. "And I'll go with you."

Marsh watched Teddy struggle inwardly. It was obvious he wanted to go now. The Irishman finally nodded.

They both went up the steps two at a time. Teddy knocked on the door with panicked urgency, and Cat opened it. Books were open on the table, and it was obvious she had been working on the bookkeeping. She looked at Marsh, pleasure filling her eyes until she saw his expression and then Teddy's. "What's wrong?"

"Molly's missing from Hugh's," Teddy said.

Marsh saw Cat straighten, tense. "What happened?"

"I don't know," Teddy said. "He . . . Mr. Canton . . . just gave me this note."

Cat read it. "Dear Lucifer," she said. Then she looked up at Teddy. "The detectives. They're watching her father's house . . . if Molly's taken there, we'll know it."

Marsh looked askance.

"I hired the Pinkerton Agency to see what it could find on Molly's father," Cat explained to Marsh as she realized that Molly had not entered their recent conversations, Cat believing the girl safe, at least temporarily. "The last report indicated they might have something."

Teddy shuffled impatiently. "I think we should go to Adams's."

Marsh looked over at Cat, watching her eyes change, fascinated by the gamut of emotions they conveyed when she allowed it.

"Will you wait until I go by the Pinkerton Agency?"

Teddy shook his head. "I know where that bastard lives. I'm going there. If she isn't there, I'll find out where she is."

Cat looked pleadingly at Marsh, begging him to stop Teddy. She remembered the three men who had tried to abduct Molly earlier. If Adams had taken Molly, there would be guards. Armed guards.

Marsh hesitated. He thought of young Molly, of the fear in her eyes the first time he'd seen her, and then how young she'd looked after the attempted kidnapping. He thought of young Cat, who had also been trapped. He hadn't been able to help Cat. But Molly? "The Pinkertons are bound by the law."

Marsh said the words with such flatness that Cat knew he'd had some experience with them. But now was not the time for questions.

"I'm not bound by the law," Teddy said.

"And I won't wait." He turned around toward the stairs.

Cat looked at Marsh helplessly. She still had little use of her right shoulder: she doubted she would even be able to fire a small derringer. "Go with him," she said to Marsh, wanting desperately to go herself, knowing she would be of little assistance and could even be a hindrance. And if Molly wasn't there, they would need immediate help from the Pinkerton Agency to find her. Booth Templeton had to be alerted. She clenched her left fist, fighting every instinct to go with Marsh, forcing herself to be rational, to do the best thing for Molly.

He leaned over and kissed her. "I'll take care of him."

"And Molly."

"And Molly," he assured her.

He caught up with Teddy at the door of the Silver Slipper. "Wait here," he said, "until I get a gun."

Thoroughly frustrated with circumstances—the need to contact the detectives and the wound that made her arm useless—Cat hurried to the Pinkerton office. Templeton wasn't there, but the other man who had been in the office that first day was. She quickly told him what had happened.

He was obviously familiar with the case. "Templeton had some real luck," he said. "I think we might have damning evidence on your Mr. Adams. Templeton's at an establishment in the Barbary Coast, one that Adams seems to like to visit. Could be real embarrassing for a fine, upstanding, churchgoing banker."

"I want to go there," Cat demanded.

"It's no place for a lady," he said.

"That doesn't matter," Cat retorted. "Templeton has to know what's going on. Perhaps he can help."

"I don't think—"

"I don't care what you think. I'm paying Templeton." Cat glared at him with that icy look that had quelled so many before him. He faltered as others had. "All right. But we'll take a carriage and you wait outside."

She nodded her assent.

"Templeton will kill me for taking you to the Barbary Coast," the man mumbled.

"I'll kill you if you don't," she said.

He mumbled again, but picked up his bowler hat and escorted her out to the street, hailing a carriage for hire. "Your expense," he said with disgust.

Cat nodded. "What is this place?"

"It's called the Green Den, one of the most notorious cribs in San Francisco." He cast her a side look as if not sure how much she understood and accepted.

A lot more than he would ever know, she thought.

He looked away from her, his face reddening, as she obviously waited for more information. "I've heard . . . Templeton has heard they have . . ." He hesitated, then at the demand in her eyes, continued. ". . . real young girls."

Cat closed her eyes, barely able to breathe. She felt her throat close, a lump forming where breath should be. The image came back, that first excruciating pain so many years ago, the fear. The despair.

"Miss Hilliard?"

Cat opened her eyes again, forced them to focus on the detective. "I'm all right. How does a place like that stay open?"

The detective shrugged. "You know the corruption in this city. If rumors get out and the police feel they have to make some kind of show, there's always a tip first. The young ones disappear, move someplace else."

Cat knew, had always known, that the Barbary Coast was one of the roughest places in the world. So were certain places in Chinatown. Drugs. Shanghaiing. Prostitution. She'd been only too ready to join Quinn Devereux's project, but somehow, through some protective filter, she had not thought of children being victimized so close to her.

Her hands clenched together. First Molly. And then she would fight for the others. She would see to that. With Marsh and Quinn Devereux and his wife, she would find a way of helping young victims as she had once been. The money she'd sent to Quinn was not important; she needed to do more. She *would* do more, if she had to burn these places to the ground . . . or publicize them in some way that the police would have to do something.

The carriage came to a halt, and the detective held up a warning hand. "You promised to stay here," he said. "I'll see if Templeton is still there."

"How?"

"I'll pretend to be a customer," he said. "And you surely can't do that."

Cat peered out. "Where is it?"

"Down the block. You can see some Rangers outside," he said, using the term utilized by street toughs and enforcers who protected establishments in the rougher areas of the city.

The building was seedy looking. There were no windows. "Why is Templeton there?"

"One of our men followed Adams to this place on several occasions. We figure that if he liked his daughter, he probably liked other young girls. Booth was going to make inquiries . . . with some financial persuasion," the other man said wryly. "Now keep out of sight. This is not a safe place for a pretty woman to be."

Cat nodded. She wouldn't do anything to delay help for Molly.

Minutes passed. At long last the detective returned to the coach, got in, and straightened his bowler. "He's in there, miss, bargaining for a young girl. Trying to buy her, I heard him say. Most likely the one that Adams visited. We'll wait out here."

His breath carried the odor of poor whiskey, and he looked embarrassed when he saw she noticed. "I said none of the girls suited. Too young. Had to pay heavy for some of their rotgut, though, to get out of there with my skin intact. Very nasty place, that."

Cat shuddered. She could guess, from experience, how nasty. She wondered about the girl Templeton was trying to "buy." Did she know something that would help Molly? How old was she? Cat tried to control the rage within her. She wanted to march in and take out every girl there. But the three of them were no match for the Rangers standing outside, and she knew it.

Her thoughts were interrupted by an exclamation from the detective, who directed the driver to move up. The door opened, and a girl was almost thrown into the coach. Templeton followed.

"What in God's name . . ."

"Molly's missing." Cat said. "We think her father has her. Teddy—my manager—couldn't be stopped from going after her. He's gone to Oakland, along with Taylor Canton, to try to get her back."

Templeton rolled his eyes. "The Canton that's been in the newspaper?"

Cat nodded.

"Damn," Templeton said. "I have enough information now for some strong bargaining." He looked down at the girl. "Mr. Adams has some strange practices his banking clients might like to hear about."

The girl, sitting next to Cat, was shaking, her eyes wide with fear. She wasn't more than thirteen, if that, Cat thought. Blond like Molly, with brown eyes. The same look of fragility. Cat felt her chest tightening, and she started to reach for the girl, who flinched against the back of the coach. "It's all right," she said softly. "You're safe now." Her heart nearly broke as she saw the disbelief in the girl's eyes, and she knew this girl's life, too, must have been full of betrayals. She had known that feeling. Sweet Lucifer, how she knew it.

She looked over at Templeton. "Can you go to Oakland?"

He nodded and looked at the other detective. "We'll both go. If we're not too late, we'll see if Mr. Adams wants his secret life publicized." He told the driver to head for the waterfront.

Then Templeton turned to Cat. "You, miss?"

Cat wanted to go with them badly. But she couldn't drag this girl along with them, not after what she'd apparently been through. Again she fought those instincts of hers, her fierce need to be with Marsh, to see that Molly was safe. But then she felt the trembling of the girl next to her. She couldn't leave her alone now. No telling what the girl would do. Or where she might go. And ultimately, the girl would probably be Molly's salvation. "I'll take her to the Silver Slipper and look after her."

"Her name's Sally, or that's what they say her name is."

Cat nodded. The trip to the dock took just a few moments, and the two detectives left the carriage. Cat and Sally went on alone. The girl relaxed slightly as the two men left. Cat looked over the skimpy, gaudy red dress that showed a slender, barely developed body. Well, she could find something for the girl to wear at the Silver Slipper.

She knew not to ask questions, not yet—not until some trust was developed. So she started talking in a low, soothing voice. "I'm Catalina," she said, "and I own a saloon." She saw the girl flinch.

"Not that kind of saloon," she said, "and

you don't have to do anything, just be safe. No one will hurt you. No more. Because, you see, I . . . know how you feel. I . . . grew up in a place like that." She talked and talked as the carriage rolled along the streets. It still didn't come easily, the words. They would never come easily. Each time would be like tearing out her heart. Yet she saw some of the fear leave Sally's eyes, and the girl's body relaxed slightly, though she still kept a certain distance.

At least taking care of the girl would keep her mind away from Oakland. From Molly. From Marsh.

Molly slowly regained consciousness. She felt as she had that time of the attempted kidnapping. Her mouth was like cotton, her body like lead. She knew she had been drugged again. She tried to remember . . . the footsteps, the dirty hand on her mouth. Smothering. Thinking she was dying.

She opened her eyes and closed them immediately. Her old room. There was no light in the room, no brightness. Her room was in the back of the house, and the windows long ago had been fixed with iron decorative grating that, in effect, served as bars. For her protection, her father used to say. Now outside shutters kept out any light at all. From the cracks she knew it was still daylight, though the room was dark. Daylight was a blessing. She knew her father. No matter what happened, he would remain at the bank until the last dollar was counted from the day's business. He never varied that routine. Never!

She was alone. That, at least, was some kind of blessing. She tried to sit up and immediately felt dizzy. She shook her head to clear it. Elizabeth. The baby. She had let Elizabeth down. She clenched her fists. Teddy. Would he come after her?

Molly knew he would, and that terrified her. He was too decent to confront her father. Too many people had already been hurt because of her. She had to do something herself this time.

She sat until the dizziness faded and then tried to stand, again waiting several seconds until she could find her balance. She fought the cobwebs in her head. What would Catalina do?

Molly finally took some steps to the door. It was locked, as she knew it would be. She looked around the room. A weapon. She needed some kind of weapon. Her room was just as it had been, nothing moved. The silver comb, brush, and mirror were on the bureau, just as they always had been. An oil lamp was next to the bed and another on the bureau. She thought about breaking the mirror, but she knew she would never be able to use pieces of glass against anyone, not even her father, or Simon Parker, the butler, the jailer.

There had to be something else. If she could only knock Parker out when he came to check on her. Or her father. Then she could escape on her own.

The lamps would never work. They were too bulky to handle easily. Then her eyes found a candlestick on a table. Brass. Heavy. She swallowed, wondering whether she would ever have the courage. Then she thought of her father, of his false, hearty greeting, and then his heavy body on hers.

She took the candlestick in her two hands and huddled next to the door where she could hear footsteps. Still sick from whatever drug had been used, she kept her mind on Teddy and Catalina and Elizabeth and Hugh. She prayed that Elizabeth was all right. She kept Teddy's face in her mind. She wanted him so badly, that bearlike gentleness that always made her feel whole and alive. Even pure. He treated her that way, as if she were fine and untouched.

She loved him so, the awkward goodness that made him seem vulnerable despite his size, the intelligence and unswerving loyalty he had to Miss Catalina, the rough tenderness with which he loved Hugh's children. So many fine things.

Molly shivered. There was no fire in the fireplace, and the room was cold. Or was it fear that made her shiver?

She didn't know how long she huddled there before she heard footsteps. Parker, she knew instantly. He shuffled along, while her father's steps were commandingly sure. How long before her father was due home?

She stood, positioning herself against the wall so she wouldn't be seen as the door opened. She heard the lock turn and she raised the candlestick, fighting the instinct to let it slip through her fingers, to cower as she'd done for so many years.

The door opened and she moved farther back, hoping it wouldn't hit her and alert Parker. He hesitated a moment, apparently trying to adjust his eyes to the darkness and see the bed. He stepped toward it, away from the door, and Molly

swung the candlestick against the side of his head.
Parker moaned and dropped to his knees.

Molly didn't wait to see the damage. She
scooted around him and ran down the stairs to the
front door. It took her a moment to unlatch it, and
she heard a noise behind her. She flung the door
open and ran out, just as a carriage stopped and
Teddy stepped out, followed by Mr. Canton.

Molly flew directly into Teddy's arms, feeling them close around her, feeling him tremble
along with herself, feeling his lips against her
face. "Thank God," he whispered in her ear.
"Are you . . . ?"

She nodded. She couldn't say anything because her face was buried in his chest.

His arms tightened around her. "I'm going
to kill him," he said hoarsely.

Molly felt him stiffen and she looked
around. Parker was standing there on the steps,
blood dripping from the side of his head. Rage
suffused his face, but he was obviously stopped
by the sight of the two men, one lean and relaxed with a gunbelt that looked frequently used,
and the other the size of a bear.

A small growl came from Teddy. She felt his
arms begin to let her go, and she realized he intended to go after Parker. Teddy might well kill
him, she knew, and then he could go to jail. She
looked up. "Please . . . just let's go."

She felt his reluctance. "Please," she said
again.

Mr. Canton turned to Teddy and nodded.
"Go ahead."

Teddy still hesitated. Marsh gave him a

small push toward the carriage. "I'll have a little word with our friend there."

"It's my . . ."

"It's your responsibility to take care of Molly," he said with what Molly thought must be the strangest smile she had seen. It was even . . . sweet as he looked at her, but then a second later menacing enough to stop a lion in its tracks. She felt herself guided into the carriage, leaning on Teddy's strength, and saw that he was preparing to join Canton. "Please don't go."

He finally nodded; her hand was so tight on his, he couldn't leave without jerking away, and she knew he wouldn't do that. They watched as Canton approached the man, who started backing away. She didn't know what Canton said as Parker looked terrificd, slipped inside, and slammed the door.

Molly huddled next to Teddy, taking comfort in his warmth as Canton stepped in, elegant as always.

"He was bleeding. Did you do that to him, Miss Molly?" he asked with the courtesy he'd always used with her. But now there was admiration in it, too, and Molly felt a pride she'd never known before. She nodded, and Teddy beamed at her just before he leaned down and met her lips with his.

Canton averted his eyes and glanced out the window. He saw a man emerge from the shadows, saw him watch the carriage move down the fashionable street. The detective who was supposed to be watching the Adams home. Or one of Adams's men?

Maybe it wasn't over. Yet.

CHAPTER 24

Edwin Adams started to lock the door of the bank, when one last customer approached. He almost turned the man away. He still had another hour of work ahead, and he was anxious to get home after receiving Parker's message.

His daughter was back! Waiting for him!

The man came toward him.

"I would like to talk to you, Mr. Adams." He looked at the clerks who sat behind their desks. "Privately."

"I'm very busy," Edwin said. "Perhaps one of my assistants can help you."

"This is about your daughter."

Edwin stiffened.

"And about the Green Den," the man said quietly. "We can talk in front of these men if you prefer."

Edwin felt the blood drain from his face. He moved toward his office, waited for the man to come inside, and closed the door. "What do you want?"

"My name is Templeton. Booth Templeton. I'm with the Pinkerton Agency. I'm employed by some friends of Mary Beth Adams."

"She's my daughter. I'm her legal guardian," Edwin blustered.

Templeton sat down, relaxed. "She's made certain accusations."

"What kind of accusations?"

"Do you really want me to describe them?" The detective's voice was almost gentle, but Edwin felt a wave of fear roll through him.

"No one will believe her," Edwin said.

"You haven't asked what she said," the detective said.

"It doesn't matter. I've done nothing wrong. Mary Beth can be . . . imaginative."

The detective sighed. "I wonder if that term can also be applied to a Mr. . . ." Templeton made a show of taking a book from his pocket. "Bones. The name fits, don't you think?" The last was added conversationally. "For a price he was willing to tell me about your visits. And then there's Sally. I wonder what your customers would think about your . . . fondness for young girls?"

Edwin did not feel particularly threatened by this information. Now that his daughter was home, he could make sure she disappeared. As for the others, no one would believe a prostitute and a brothel keeper.

"Your daughter's no longer at your home," Templeton said as if he read the banker's mind. "She was ... rescued a few hours ago. One of my men saw it all. He would have helped, but it turned out to be unnecessary. It seems your daughter has a number of powerful friends in San Francisco. Friends who believe her. Friends with access to newspapers."

Edwin's hands trembled. "What do you want?" he asked again.

"That you never again approach your daughter, nor try to touch her or contact her in any way. If you do, certain information will fall into the hands of the newspapers. And the police."

"If I do as you ask?"

Templeton shrugged. "I would suggest you keep away from children. I'm still looking into the disappearance of your maid, and a few other acts of violence that somehow seemed to involve friends of your daughter's."

"Damn you."

"Oh, I don't think so, Mr. Adams. I think you're the one who's damned." Templeton rose. "You don't have to show me out." He hesitated at the door. "If anything happens to your daughter, there's a number of people who have the same information I do. If I were you, I would pray that she stays safe and healthy for a very long time." He closed the door gently behind him.

Edwin stared at the door. He watched as

one of his assistants unlocked the door to let the detective out. He felt numb.

The clerks left, one by one, bidding him good night. He was usually the last one to leave. As if by rote he finished the paperwork and then sat back in his chair. His secret was no longer safe. Even if he did what the detective said, he would never be safe. Too many people obviously knew now. And if rumor ever got started, he would be ostracized. He would lose the bank, lose his position . . .

"Mary Beth," he whispered. His daughter. His love. Gone now.

He took a pistol from the drawer in the desk and put it to his head. Slowly, he squeezed the trigger.

Oakland Banker Commits Suicide, Found Shot in Office.

The newsboy chanted the headline, and Cat snatched the newspaper, tossing the boy the first coin she found and ignoring his thanks.

She read greedily. *Prominent Oakland banker Edwin Adams was found dead in his office in the Farmers and Merchants Bank Wednesday morning.*

Mr. Adams was president of the Farmers and Merchants Bank and was well known for his civic contributions to the city. He was fifty-one at the time of his death.

His only survivor is a daughter, Mary Beth, who could not be immediately located.

The story included some speculation that

the remaining bank officials would call for an examination of the books.

So Booth Templeton had done it. She folded the newspaper. Teddy should be the one to tell Molly.

She was relieved. It was over for Molly, at least.

Cat wanted to see Marsh. She wanted to see him all the time—but particularly now. She wanted to share the news with him first. He was, after all, a part of it.

She picked up the package she had dropped to take the paper. Having only one useful arm was an infernal nuisance, especially when she could think of so many better uses for it. A few more days, the doctor had said, and she could stop using the sling. And then she planned to use what was in the treasured package, a sea-green nightdress that was all lace and silk.

They had had a party the night of Molly's return. She and Marsh and Teddy and Molly and the O'Connells. They celebrated Molly's rescue and the birth of a new daughter for Hugh and Elizabeth. Molly would stay with the O'Connells temporarily, but only because both Hugh and Teddy would be there to protect her.

Nothing could mar the future now, Cat thought. Nothing at all. A few more days and she would be in Marsh's arms again. She would be now, except he wouldn't consider it as long as her shoulder still hurt. She tried to tell him it didn't, but he just shook his head. "I've been wounded," he merely said, "and I know how long it takes to heal."

She hurried through the crowded Saturday

streets until she reached the Glory Hole. He was working every afternoon and night now that Hugh was temporarily gone, ordered to stay home by Marsh to look after Elizabeth and Molly.

Marsh looked up from the bar as she approached and favored her with that lazy smile that held so much warmth. He looked different, much more approachable, wearing a bartender's apron rather than his gunbelt. He'd told her last night he would never wear it again. Killing was too easy. He had itched, he'd said, to kill that man at the Adams's house. No more. He would let the law work now.

She handed the newspaper to him. He read it silently and then handed it back.

"Marsh?"

"I'm glad Molly's safe," he said, but no more, and Cat could only wonder what lay behind those dark eyes.

"I think she's more than safe," Cat said. "I think she loves Teddy."

"I don't think there's any doubt of it," he said with a slight grin that opened his face again.

"He's afraid it's gratitude."

"Then he didn't see her face," Marsh said. "It had love written all over it."

"Do you see mine?" she said softly.

His hand stopped, and those dark-gray eyes were suddenly smoking. "Darlin'," he drawled, "I always see your face. Christ, you've been haunting me nightly."

"Stay with me tonight?" It was shameless, but she and Marsh were past that now.

"If I did, I'm afraid I would hurt that shoulder. Nobility is hell, but let me try it once."

"The doctor takes out the stitches tomorrow."

"Tomorrow night, then," he said, his voice slightly hoarse. "If . . ."

She smiled. "I'd better get back to the Silver Slipper, now that both of our managers are occupied."

"Have a nightcap with me?"

"If you'll play some music."

"Hummm . . . you're a hard woman."

"Perfect for a hard man."

"Oh, Christ," he mumbled, thinking how absolutely apt that description was at the moment. He was very hard, indeed. He was glad the bar was between them, that his customers couldn't see beneath the apron. Apron, for God's sake. Apron for a gun. And yet it felt so right. This place. Cat. His first home in twenty years. The first place he'd ever belonged during those years. Contentment washed over him in waves as he watched her walk away, knowing she was his, knowing that they would be alone soon.

Reluctantly, he turned back to his customers.

T. J. Simmons dressed with care. This was going to be one of the great occasions in his life.

A real gunfight, and he was going to be there to witness it. He wouldn't just have to imagine it this time.

His hands shook with excitement as he fixed a string tie over the cardboard collar and carefully placed a western hat on his slicked-back hair. He only wished he had one of those cameras with him.

T.J. looked at his pocket watch. Nearly midnight now. He had advised Bailey to wait until the crowd had thinned at the Glory Hole. He didn't want anyone to get in the way. Nor did he want any other reporter there.

This was *his* story. He had already started writing his book in his head.

It really didn't matter to him who won. If Marsh Canton won, it would make a great sequel to *Duel at Sunset*. If Canton was killed, T.J. would make Bailey famous as the man who killed him. No more cheap hotel rooms like this one.

He finally tucked some paper into his pocket, made sure he had a pen and ink, and gave himself one last look. Quite dashing, he thought. And soon to be famous. He had hit pay dirt this time.

T.J. tipped his hat rakishly and left his room. He knocked on the door next to his and heard a grunt from inside, then the turn of a lock. The door opened, and he faced Bailey.

Bailey wore a double gunbelt. He was also wearing the same dirty shirt he had traveled in, and his face was thick with whiskers.

T.J. shuddered with distaste. Bailey had the meanest eyes he'd ever seen, a pale, cold blue that never seemed to blink. His hair was lanky and probably stayed in place only because of the dirt. He was unpleasant to look at, unpleasant to be with. T.J. wondered whether that was true of all gunfighters. He'd never met one before.

And Bailey stank of whiskey.

"You've been drinking," T.J. accused.

"Goddamn right," Bailey said.

"But . . ."

Bailey held out his hand. It was as steady a hand as T.J. had ever seen. "Whiskey don't affect my nerves," he said, and then sneered. "Sure you have the stomach for this?"

T.J. stiffened. "Remember who found him for you."

"At a damn steep price."

"I'm going to make you famous."

Bailey shrugged. "When I kill Canton, I won't need anyone to make me famous. The killing will do it. And that ain't the only reason I want him. He killed my only brother."

"*If* you kill him," T.J. taunted.

Bailey stared down at him. "I'm the best there is."

T.J. had tired of his companion's rude manners and arrogance. "We'll see soon enough, won't we?" he said, and turned toward the stairs leading down, knowing that Bailey would follow him.

One o'clock. Another hour before closing, Marsh thought. The crowd was already thinning out, leaving only the hard-core gamblers. Jenny had finished her performances and gone home.

Marsh was restless, impatient. Business behind the bar was slow. He thought about closing early; there were no set hours, but Cat would probably be busy for another hour anyway. Win lay on the floor behind the bar, in a corner he'd

appropriated. The dog had become more conge-
nial in recent days and had scratched at the door
of Marsh's bedroom earlier, wanting out.

Every once in a while Marsh's hand would
go down to where the gun had been. Christ, he
felt naked without it. But he'd sworn to himself
he wouldn't wear it again. Yet . . . it was still as
if a vital part of him were missing, a loss he
would have to get used to.

He knew he wanted to marry Cat. He loved
her more than he thought it ever possible to love
someone. He loved the incredible strength of her,
that indomitability that allowed her not only to
survive and succeed, but to do it with compassion. She'd opened his midnight-dark soul to
light. He enjoyed sunrises again. And he could
watch sunsets with something akin to pure joy.

He looked up at the swishing sound of the
swinging doors. Two men were entering, a
dandy, and behind him . . .

Marsh stiffened. He didn't recognize the
man's face, but he recognized everything else
about him: the cold, mean eyes, the provocative
stance, the double gunbelt. Few gunmen wore a
double gunbelt; a good gunslinger needed only
one gun. Two were usually considered a conceit,
a sign of a show-off or braggart.

Marsh watched as the two men approached. And he knew. They were looking for
him. His hand instinctively tightened into a fist
beneath the bar. There was a handgun just below
his fingers. He and Hugh kept that and a shotgun handy in case of trouble. And then Marsh
sickened. Another killing, particularly with a

gunman, would carry his name all over the country. More books. More people looking for him.

"What can I do for you?" he asked the two men as they reached the bar.

"We're looking for the owner, a man called Marsh Canton," the dandy said.

"Why?"

The dandy started to say something again, but the larger man interfered. "I have business with him."

"What kind of business?"

"My name is Bailey," the man said. "He killed my brother, and now I'm going to kill him." He looked Marsh over carefully, apparently seeing something familiar. "You Marsh Canton?"

Marsh shrugged. "My name is Canton." He heard Win growl.

The man looked down at the bartender's apron Marsh still wore and sneered. "You don't look like much."

"I don't carry a gun," Marsh said quietly, knowing suddenly that he would never do so again. He had used the gun the last two times on someone else's behalf. He wouldn't use it now on his own behalf.

The gunman stared at him. "You will, or I'll shoot you anyway."

Marsh merely stared back. He was aware that the saloon had energized, that people were moving away from a possible line of fire, but watching avidly. "No."

"A yellow belly, by God," the man said. "I never would have thought that of Marsh Canton."

The words slammed into Marsh's chest. Yellow. Coward. He kept his face impassive. "You won't get a reputation by killing an unarmed man."

"But I'll get satisfaction. You killed my brother, Mike Bailey, four years ago."

Marsh tried to think back. Bailey. But there had been too many, and he'd never wanted to know their names. Out of the corner of his eye, he saw one of his waiters slip out the door.

"A range war. Near Fort Worth," the man reminded him.

Marsh remembered the event. He'd killed several men during that dispute. All armed. All shooting back at him. He was silent.

"Goddamn you," Bailey said, "Strap on your guns."

"No," Marsh said in an almost gentle voice.

The gunman started backing away, the dandy hesitating before following him. "You can't shoot an unarmed man," the dandy said pompously. "It's against the code of the West." Marsh would have considered him a damn fool if he hadn't, at this moment, been on his side.

"To hell with the code of the West," the man said. "Either shut up or get out of here."

T. J. Simmons's face went white. This wasn't going according to plan. This would be murder, pure and simple. And he would be a part of it. "You . . . can't," he said, as he envisioned his story disappearing. How could he write a heroic tale about a coward and a murderer?

Bailey ignored him. "Last chance, Canton.

If you don't get a gun in ten seconds, I'll kill you."

Marsh kept his eyes on Bailey. He didn't want to die. Not now. "No," he said, again softly, afraid that the waiter who had slipped out had gone after Cat. He didn't want her to come in and watch.

He knew the bullet was coming. He heard the sound of the gunshot and felt the searing pain rip through him. He stumbled slightly, catching himself on the bar, feeling blood begin to drip from the hole in his white shirt. Win's growl became a howl, and Marsh knew the dog was trying to get out from behind the bar, but Marsh had blocked the entrance.

Bailey's face was red with fury, and Marsh knew he was going to fire again. Just then there was a commotion at the door, and Marsh saw Cat. He tried to say something, but the pain had spread and seemed to paralyze him.

Through a mist clouding his eyes, he saw her throw herself at Bailey. He sensed, rather than saw, Win prepare for a lunge. There was a clatter of glasses and bottles as the dog frantically jumped on the bar and hurtled forward. He heard the gun explode again, felt a new pain in his head.

Cat saw Marsh slump, and a man with the gun obviously ready to fire again. She hadn't had time to get the derringer when one of Marsh's dealers ran into the Silver Slipper. All she had was herself. She launched into the gunman.

She hit his gun arm, but it was too late. She

knew Marsh had been hit again. The gunman's hand came back and swiped across her face, the gun cutting into her cheek, knocking her down. At the same time she saw a flashing piece of furious brown fur go for the man, heard his scream, then some growls.

People were crowding in. She heard another cry of pain from the man, and she struggled to her feet. The dog was biting into the man's arm, which apparently had gone up to protect his throat. The gun was nowhere to be seen.

"Winchester!" she yelled, afraid that someone might hurt the dog. "Winchester!"

The dog stopped biting, but the growling continued, and he continued to hold the bleeding arm in his jaws. Two waiters were there then, uncertain what to do with the dog. She called the dog's name once more. It looked at her as if puzzled, then released the arm, coming over to her in a slinking walk.

"That's all right," she said. "You were wonderful."

Winchester's ears and tail went up, though he kept his eyes on the man he'd just released. Two waiters had the man now. Another had the gun and held it on him, taking the second one from the holster.

Cat ran to the bar, jerking her right arm from the sling, feeling only slight pulling from the wound. She quickly removed the barrier Marsh had put at the side entrance to keep the dog in. Marsh was lying on the floor, blood pouring from a wound in his chest and trickling from a graze on his head.

"Get a doctor!" she screamed. "Dr. MacLaren!"

She knelt at Marsh's side, cradling his head in her arms. He was unconscious, blood dripping from a wound alongside his head and chest area. "Marsh," she whispered. "You can't leave me now."

One of the waiters came over to her. "What should we do with . . ."

"Find a policeman somewhere," she said. "But go after the doctor first."

She grabbed one of the towels from behind the bar and unbuttoned Marsh's shirt, pressing the cloth against the wound in his chest. That wound was by far the more serious, she knew. "You can't die," she ordered him. "I won't let you."

She ran her hand along his cheek. His breathing was labored. She leaned down and kissed him enticingly, as if to bring him back from someplace else. Cat wanted to talk to him, but the lump in her throat was too thick. She could only keep running her fingers over his face, along his arms, telling him she was there, she would always be there, while her other hand held the towel tight against the wound.

Cat saw that his face was wet, and it took her a moment to realize it was from her tears. "I never cried until I met you," she whispered achingly. "I never knew I could."

She bent down until her cheek touched his, her wet one against his damp one, fallen tears mingling with new ones.

The dog whined. He had followed her into the bar area, and now he lay with his head on one of Marsh's legs. "He wants you back too," she said to Marsh, forcing the words through her choked throat.

If only she could stop the bleeding. If only she had arrived a few minutes earlier. If only she could give him her life.

Why, dear God, didn't he have a gun? The waiter who came after her said the gunman had challenged him, that Marsh had refused to get one. Why? "Oh, Marsh," she whispered. "Why now?" It seemed like hours before Dr. MacLaren appeared and stooped down next to her in the crowded area. She had to move away from Marsh then, and she felt as if her soul were being torn from her.

The doctor quickly examined the wounds, then looked at her. "Where can we take him?"

"His room is through that door, down the hall on the left," she said.

He nodded, standing up and asking for several volunteers. Several men crowded inside while Cat was pushed farther and farther back. Win bared his teeth and emitted a low warning growl. "Let them go, Win," she said. "It's all right."

Her voice apparently soothed the dog, although he stood stiffly, watching every move as Marsh was picked up and carried into his room. Cat followed.

The doctor looked at her. "You two are sure keeping me busy. Why don't you wait outside?"

"No," she said flatly.

MacLaren sighed. "I won't waste time arguing with you, but if you won't leave, you do exactly as I say."

Cat nodded.

"We need hot water. Towels."

There was a crowd outside. Marsh's employees. All with worried faces, and Cat knew they cared. They obviously cared very much despite the short time they had been with him. She told one what was needed, and he disappeared. Another stepped up. "The police have that fellow."

"Thank you," she said, another well of tears beginning to fall. Win, who had been shut out before, gave her a beseeching look. She started to close the door on him, heard the low wail, and opened it. "In the corner," she said. To her surprise the dog found a corner, laid down, and put his head on his paws, his eyes remaining intent on the silent figure on the bed.

The doctor had Marsh's shirt unbuttoned and was feeling around the wound. "The head wound isn't serious," he said. "That can wait."

The doctor finally turned to her. "Help me turn him and get the damn shirt off. I hope to God that bullet went through. It's hard to tell with all the blood." Cat moved over to the bed, removing the shirt as the doctor turned Marsh's unconscious body, wincing to see the amount of blood he'd lost.

"Ahhhh," the doctor said. He looked up at Cat. "The bullet went straight through and apparently missed the heart and lungs. If we can stop the bleeding and there's no infection . . ."

He stopped speaking then, his hands pressing a towel to the wound. He handed the bloody

towel to Cat and held out his hand for a fresh
one. To Cat it looked as if all Marsh's blood
were drenching the bed.

There was a knock on the door and the
waiter appeared, two pails of boiling water in his
hands. Another man held a stack of towels, and
Cat took them gratefully, setting them down on
the floor of the bare room. "Go tell Hugh," she
told the men. "He'll want to know. Close the
Glory Hole, and then you can all go home."

"If you don't mind," came the voice of one
of the women dealers who was standing outside,
"we would rather stay."

Another lump formed in her throat. She
wondered whether Marsh knew the kind of loyalty he'd inspired. Probably not, from what he'd
said in the past. She nodded—"Of course"—and
turned back to the doctor leaning over the bed.

"I think the bleeding has slowed," the doctor said. "I'll sew the wound and then . . . we'll
just have to wait."

Cat shuddered. She couldn't bear to think
of that body, already marked by scars, under-
going any more pain.

"Miss Hilliard," the doctor said sharply.

"I'm all right," she said, forcing strength
into her voice.

"You keep the area clean of blood," the
doctor said as he prepared the needle and started
working. Marsh's body twitched, even in unconsciousness, at the additional violation of his
body. Cat held a towel, wiping away blood at
the doctor's direction, praying for the first time
in her life.

There was a triumphant cry from the doctor as he finished. "That is the luckiest man I've ever seen," he said again. "Didn't hit anything vital, though it came damn close to the heart."

"He'll be all right, then?"

"Well, he's bled a lot, and you can't always tell about head wounds, but right now I'd say the prognosis is good. I'm leaving a little laudanum for pain. I 'spect you know how to use it. How's your shoulder, by the way?" he added, looking disapprovingly at the empty sling.

Cat smiled wanly. "I barely feel it."

He shook his head. "You two must have guardian angels someplace."

Maybe, she thought ruefully, they had been lurking somewhere in the past, ready to rally at the right time. Or perhaps Marsh and she were each other's guardian angels. It was a wistful idea. Foolish. And yet it wouldn't go away.

The doctor finished sewing up the wounds. "If he doesn't wake by first light, call me," he said. "And next time mayhem strikes . . . for God's sake . . . try to arrange it at a respectable hour."

She smiled weakly. "No more, I promise," she said to his skeptical look. "I'll stay here with him," she added.

"I thought you would," he said irascibly, but his hand was gentle as he touched the cut on her cheek from the swing of gun. She had forgotten about it in her concern for Marsh.

"I don't think we need any stitches," the doctor said, "but I'm going to clean and bandage it."

The doctor departed moments later, and she took his chair. He was right, she thought. They must have guardian angels, after all, or perhaps her prayer had been answered. Her fingers clasped his. How strong and capable that hand was. She lifted it to her mouth and kissed it. She wanted to be as close to Marsh as possible, to give to him the love she felt. So poignantly deep. So hurtful. She had been afraid of that, of feeling, of being hurt, but now the glow of loving, still so very painful, was a part of her, a part so real, so glorious, she knew she would never, ever give it up for safety.

"I love you," she whispered in a choked voice. That damn lump wouldn't go away, nor would the tears.

Marsh woke slowly to burning pain and a terrible headache. He fought back a groan and opened his eyes. The room was dark, but he saw a still figure in a chair next to him. Cat. Sleeping. She looked so weary, slumped slightly in the chair. How long had she been there?

The sight of her triggered something else. An impression. A cool cloth against his face, and the light caress of fingers. Her fingers. Cat's fingers. No others would be that loving.

Or was it a dream?

He tried to remember what had happened, and it came back slowly, in jumbled pieces like a puzzle he had to solve. And when he did, he wanted to reach out and scatter them again.

The gunman. The shots. And the terrible knowledge that he would never be free of his past. There would be others, trying to goad him, trying to earn a reputation. *Yellow belly*. That would follow him now too.

Any hope he'd had of marrying Cat disappeared, leaving him hollow and more alone than he'd ever been. But he couldn't endanger her. She'd had enough grief in her life without sharing a name synonymous with death, and now with cowardice.

Unlike Cat, he'd made his own path. He remembered a poem by Samuel Butler: "For as you sow, ye are like to reap." He didn't want Cat to share his deadly harvest.

But giving her up would be like tearing his heart out, just when he found he had one. The fact that his love was so new should make it easier, but it wasn't. He'd discovered how empty his life had been, how bleak, and he'd had a glimpse of sun, and he didn't know how he could survive without its rays.

He would have to leave. They couldn't stay away from each other, he and Cat, otherwise. Christ knew he'd tried. She'd certainly tried. But they were like magnets to each other. He watched her, ignoring the pain that gnawed at him; it was small compared to the larger pain of losing Cat, of losing the one place he'd felt he belonged.

The dark started to surrender to thin streams of daylight, and still he couldn't take his eyes from her, from that fine face and the dark hair, fallen now, that so softly framed it. He hadn't thought it possible to love like this, to feel with every fiber of his being. To love enough to turn away from what he wanted most in the world.

The light was just touching her when she woke. Even in that, she was enchanting. First the sleep-shaded eyes opened slightly, then flew open as she apparently realized where she was. They were slightly red, and he sensed she had been crying. The thought was humbling, and it made him ache. He wasn't worth hurting for, yet it warmed him in ways he couldn't completely understand.

A hand went to her hair, pushing it back in a completely feminine gesture, but one he'd never really identified with her: a kind of uncertainty. "How long have you been awake?" she asked.

"Not long."

"How do you feel?"

"Like I've been shot."

She smiled at that. "Foolish question?"

"Nothing you do is foolish, except maybe leaping at armed men."

"Winchester did better than I, and then your waiters held him until the police came. He's in jail. He'll be there for a long time."

At his name Winchester stood up, stretched, and went over to the bed, glaring at Marsh. "He really went after Bailey, did he?" Marsh asked with a slight, whimsical smile.

"I think he's decided he owns you."

"I know it's not the other way around," Marsh said with a chuckle, which ended abruptly as a wave of pain obviously swept over him. When he'd apparently conquered it, he lifted his hand to her face, carefully touching the bandage there. "Are you . . . ?"

"It's nothing," she said. "Not even deserving of a stitch, the doctor says."

"There won't be a . . . scar?"

She shook her head.

"I would never forgive myself. . . ." His voice trailed off, and Cat hated the guilt she saw in his eyes. She decided to change the subject.

"Marsh . . ."

"Yes?"

"Why didn't you fight that man?" She'd given Hugh an explanation, but she wanted to hear it from him. "You would have won."

"Perhaps," he said, "in a way." His eyes fixed on hers. "Do you think I'm a coward?"

Her hand went to his and squeezed it. "I think what you did was the most courageous thing anyone could do. It took a different kind of strength, a more difficult kind of strength."

"It had to stop, Cat. The killing had to stop somewhere. But that won't make a difference. Now that my whereabouts are known, they'll keep coming. Every man with a grudge. Every kid wanting a reputation." He heard the hopelessness in his own voice and saw her face change. She used to be so good at hiding feelings. He wondered whether he was becoming as transparent. A fatal flaw for someone like him.

Cat stared at him uncomprehendingly. "They won't come now, will they? Now that you've made it clear you've taken off your guns."

"Some probably will. I've made a number of enemies, Cat, which is why I must leave."

"Where will we go?"

"Not we, Cat." His voice was flat. Almost dead.

"No!" That fury he once so admired came back into her eyes.

"I tried, Cat. I tried to put it behind me, but that kind of life won't stay behind. I won't endanger you. I won't have you called a coward's wife."

There it was. The word. "Wife." A word neither of them had mentioned before. He knew why he hadn't. It had been too fine a dream.

"Dear Lucifer, that's one thing you could never be."

"But there are those who will believe . . ."

"I don't care. I know what you are. So do others. Do you know that no one would leave here last night until they knew how you were, that Hugh has been here all night despite the fact that his wife probably needs him? Do you have any idea how many people care about you?"

He started to say something, but she didn't give him the chance. "Are you going to start running, like I ran? Like I was still running until I met you?"

"You don't realize . . ."

She was furious. "And me. What about me? You . . . you made me care. For the first time I really learned how to care, and now you want to take it away. Like everyone else, you just use . . ."

"Cat!" His voice was hoarse with emotion. "Oh, God, Cat, you can't believe that."

"I can believe anything I want," she replied bitterly. "Go ahead. Run. Run like a rabbit."

"Don't you understand . . . I'm thinking of you."

"No, you're not," she retorted. "You're thinking about what's easiest for you. If you thought anything about me, you would know that I might as well be dead if you left. Damn you, I was doing just fine before you came, and then you opened a new world for me. I can't go back to the old one again, and the new one goes with you. So where am I?"

"You'll make one of your own."

"No. I'll just die a little day after day, worrying about you, wondering about you, missing you. I'll never be whole again. I was never whole until I met you. Don't take that away."

Cat had never begged before, but now she was fighting for her life. For his life.

She saw him swallow, saw the raw agony in his eyes, and she knew it wasn't from the wounds. She also knew she wouldn't have the courage to say what she was saying unless she felt to the marrow of her bones that he loved her. They had been at cross purposes too long.

She attacked again. "Are you afraid people will think you a coward?"

Marsh shook his head. He'd never cared much about what people said. It had been Cat he worried about.

"Do you think I'm so stupid that *I* care what people think?"

His lips twisted slightly upward. She knew how to phrase a question. "Ah, Cat. Don't make it so hard. I'm out of practice being decent."

"I like you when you're indecent," she said with a slight smile of her own.

He released a long breath of air that had been lodged in his throat. "You're the most . . . difficult woman I've ever met."

"You've said that before."

"I think I like difficult." The words came out before he could stop them.

Now Cat held her breath. "You'll stay?"

He wanted to. Christ, how he wanted to. She was right about one thing. If he left her behind, he would never be whole, just as she said she wouldn't. They were part of each other now.

He closed his eyes, thinking. He had to close them against those green eyes, against that impassioned lovely face. He couldn't think when he was with her.

"Marsh?" Her voice had softened with emotion. So tender. So caring. He had forgotten how good it was when someone cared.

His eyes opened, and he tried to move. Pain enveloped him, and he couldn't say anything. He could only let it roll through him, one wave after another, almost blinding him with its intensity.

He heard a small whimper from the dog. He tried to focus on Winchester, on anything but the pain. The different kinds of pain. What would he do with Winchester? And Hugh? And his agreement to help Devereux?

He couldn't think with the pain. He couldn't think with Cat there. He heard the rustling of her dress, the light footsteps as she left his bedside, and then he knew from the light fragrance that she was back. She lifted his head with gentle fingers, urging him to drink a milky liquid.

A kind of numbness started to seep into his

body, expelling the worst of the pain. Expelling thought. He closed his eyes again, feeling them weighed down by the drug, but he still felt her presence, and just before he slipped into oblivion, he heard her soft words. "You are my life now. I won't let you go. Where you go, I will go."

Light streamed through a window when Marsh woke again. He felt groggy, and pain was still burning his insides. Christ, but he was thirsty. He looked around. Someone had placed a table next to his bed and there was a cup of water on it. He drank greedily, even as the pain increased with every movement.

Marsh wondered how long he'd been asleep. Or when she had left. Even the momentary loss of her was staggering, reducing his physical pain to nothing. The emptiness of the room was overwhelming.

He remembered their conversation. Every sentence. Every nuance. *You are my life now. I won't let you go. Where you go, I will go.*

And he knew she would. He knew she would follow him. Because that was Cat. She didn't know the meaning of the word "defeat."

Go ahead. Run. Run like a rabbit. You're thinking about what's easiest for you.

Perhaps he was. Perhaps that was what he'd always done. He'd run from memories. He'd run from his own acts. And if he didn't stop now, he never would.

Marsh felt humbled. Despite fears he knew were overwhelming, Cat had stayed to fight

Cahoon. How could he do less? Someone might come for him again. He might be called coward and worse. But he had been given a chance most men didn't get: an extraordinary woman, an extraordinary love. He knew he couldn't throw it away.

And he knew he couldn't ask Cat to give up everything she had built here in San Francisco.

Elation suddenly flooded him as he knew he would stay. Any consequence would be small compared to the pain of losing Cat, of watching her lose that wonderful new light in her eyes. Just the thought of her made him feel . . . invincible, and he knew he could not face living without her.

Cat. Cat would be here soon. Cat would always be there. He swallowed, thinking about it all, feeling pleasure and an aching kind of joy.

"Marsh?" Her soft voice came from the doorway. He looked up and smiled. He didn't have to do anything else as her face lit with understanding, happiness sparking her green eyes as she leaned down, her lips touching his with such love and promise that he thought his heart would swell so large it would explode.

"I love you, Miss Catalina."

"I love you, Marsh Taylor Canton."

Her fingers brushed the bristles on his cheek.

"Do you want to marry a notorious gunfighter?"

"Ex-gunfighter," she corrected as she slid beside him in the bed. "If you want to marry a notorious saloon owner."

He grimaced. "I suppose we could be notorious together."

"Oh, we'll become so staid and upright that no one will remember."

His face expressed doubt.

"We could always leave San Francisco," she ventured.

"You would give up the Silver Slipper?"

"I would give up anything but you," she said as she started to nibble on his ear.

"Remember what you said about running away?"

"Hummmmmm . . ."

"Why don't we stay here awhile?"

"Hummmmmm . . ."

"Cat?"

"Hummmmmm?"

"You didn't answer when I asked you to marry me."

She stopped nibbling, and he realized suddenly that she had been avoiding that answer.

Her eyes met his. They were shimmering now, and he didn't know whether it was tears or happiness. "Don't run away from me now," he said softly, realizing that she still wasn't sure he could totally accept her past. She was obviously willing to give him everything while afraid to take anything.

"I want you as my wife, Cat. I want everything you are. Everything. I won't take any less."

She smiled, the most beautiful, breathtaking smile he'd ever seen. There wasn't a shadow in it.

Her hand touched his face. "I love you so,

Marsh Canton. It's just so . . . hard to be this happy."

And painful. He knew. The fear of losing was part of it. But there was more. When you loved so deeply, so much, there was a kind of ache that went with it, a feeling that it was undeserved . . . too magical.

"I know," he said softly, his mouth now moving along her cheek, fighting his own rampaging emotions. "Pretty Cat, I wonder if you'll ever realize how much you've given me. I couldn't even look at a sunset before. Everything was dark, bleak. You're like the sun to me, the giver of life. When I thought I had to leave you, I . . ."

Her lips touched his. Caressed and loved. Comforted. And more. If he wasn't so damn . . .

A shudder went through his body, and she misunderstood, moving quickly away from him. "I'm . . . sorry . . ."

"Don't ever be sorry for that," he said with a wry grin. "It wasn't the wound."

She started to smile, a sweet, wondrous smile that made his heart ache.

"You still haven't answered," he complained with a grin of his own. She had given him an answer of sorts.

"I would be delighted to be your wife," she said, a sound of giddy happiness creeping into her voice.

"As soon as possible?" he said.

She nodded. "A quiet wedding."

"Small," he agreed.

"The newspapers . . ."

He winced. "Our . . . notorious feud."

"I hope you don't think it's ending," she said with mischief in her eyes. "I have every intention of keeping the Silver Slipper . . . at least for a while."

His eyes met hers. She could see straight into his soul now, and she loved everything she saw.

He grinned. "A gentle feuding."

The mischief in her eyes turned challenging. "At times," she warned. "And then at others . . ."

"At others?" he asked suggestively.

But she just smiled, allowing the magic between them, the thunder and lightning that was always there, to finish the thought.

Epilogue

Just after sunrise ...

EARLY AUTUMN 1879

T. J. Simmons caught the evening train for Denver. He couldn't afford San Francisco, and he had no interest in staying there. He picked up the *Globe* at the train station and read the story that ran at the bottom of the front page.

San Francisco businessman Taylor Canton, who opened the Glory Hole in this city a few months ago, was badly wounded during an altercation in his saloon Wednesday night.

The police arrested Tom Bailey of Texas for the attack.

According to police, Bailey entered the Glory Hole with an unknown second man, apparently falsely identified Mr. Canton as Marsh Canton, a known gunfighter, and challenged him to a gunfight. Mr. Canton, who was unarmed, refused to arm himself and was shot twice. He is expected to live.

One onlooker called Mr. Canton's refusal to fight "an act of courage." Mr. Canton's bravery was unquestioned since he recently prevented a kidnapping and theft at the neighboring Silver Slipper saloon.

The gunman was apparently mistaken in identifying Taylor Canton, a Texas businessman, as Marsh Canton, a gunfighter in Colorado. Witnesses said Bailey had indicated he'd never met the gunfighter before and had merely assumed from the last name that the two men were the same. The outcome proved the opposite.

This newspaper agrees with the conclusion that Mr. Canton's refusal to fight was indeed an act of courage, another demonstration that civilization has reached San Francisco, and the gun no longer rules here.

T.J. crushed the newspaper in his hand. His story was gone. Bailey had shot an unarmed man. Canton had refused to fight. And now that Simmons thought about it, the man might not have been Marsh Canton after all. He had said merely that his name was Canton.

Marsh Canton would have fought. No

doubt about that. The Colorado gunman hadn't been afraid of anyone, and no one had ever accused him of having scruples. *Marsh* Canton wouldn't have stood there and allowed someone to shoot him down. To say otherwise would even cast doubt on the authenticity of his book, *Duel at Sunset*.

Hell, he must have made a mistake. Almost got an innocent man killed.

And he was near broke. He had only a few dollars left of the fee he'd charged Bailey to find Canton, most of which he'd spent on the trip.

Muttering low curses, he boarded the train. He would have to find another gunfighter now. Or maybe he would go back to the newspaper. Maybe civilization was coming. Maybe the day of the gunfighter was over.

"I thought you might like to read a newspaper account of what happened," Hugh said, striding over to Marsh and putting the paper on the bed.

Marsh didn't. The name Marsh Canton spread all over the papers? The fact that he refused to fight, that he'd allowed himself to be shot like a dog? He heard a low growl and wondered whether Winchester had become a mind reader was well as defender these days. Or perhaps he was just growling at the approach of Hugh. Marsh believed he liked the first explanation better. The whimsical thought delayed his glance at the newspaper, one of San Francisco's many.

He might as well know the worst. He looked down and started reading, an unexpected warmth spreading through him, damping the pain, erasing the emptiness. "Are the others like this?"

Hugh nodded. "Cat made a few trips to the newspapers. With Mr. Devereux."

Falsely identified. Marsh Canton was as dead now as Lobo.

San Francisco businessman wounded. The city had claimed him as one of its own.

Hugh stood, grinning. Winchester sat with his head on his bed. Cat was expected back any minute. Marsh chuckled. It hurt, but he couldn't help it. Cat. His Cat. Cat, who almost had him shanghaied. Cat who was unlike any other woman in the world. He should have known that somehow his Cat would manage to make things right.

About the Author

PATRICIA POTTER has become one of the most highly praised writers of historical romance since her impressive debut in 1988, when she won the Maggie Award and a Reviewer's Choice Award from *Romantic Times* for her first novel. She recently received the *Romantic Times* Career Achievement Award for Storyteller of the Year for 1992 and Reviewer's Choice nominations for her novel LIGHTNING (Best Civil War Historical Romance), and the hero, Lobo, in LAWLESS (Knight in Shining Silver). She has worked as a newspaper reporter in Atlanta and was president of the Georgia Romance Writers Association.

Look for Patricia Potter's next historical romance
Relentless
coming in May 1994 from Bantam Books

Beneath the outlaw's smoldering gaze Shea Randall felt a stab of pure panic ... and a shiver of shocking desire. Held against her will by the darkly handsome bandit, she knew that for her father's sake, she must find a way to escape. Only later, as the days of her captivity turned into weeks, and Rafe Tyler's fiery passion sparked her own, did Shea fully realize her perilous position—locked in a mountain lair with a man who could steal her heart. . . .

Framed for an act of treachery he never committed, Rafe Tyler survived ten years in prison, sustained only by his dreams of getting even with the man who put her there. But kidnapping Jack Randall's spitfire of a daughter had never been part of the Texan's scheme. Now Rafe must deal with an unwilling hostage who fears him—and fills with him an explosive hunger, the kind of white-hot passion that could shake a man's convictions and threaten everything he's lived for. . . .

Immediately following is a sneak peek at this fabulous romance.

Rafe hesitated at the door of the cabin. He wished the woman had screamed or cried, or even fainted. He could handle that easily. He could handle anything but that quiet dignity that was so unnerving.

Despite himself, despite the fact that she may be Randall's daughter, he felt a glimmer of admiration. She had a hell of a lot more guts than her father.

But that didn't mean she wasn't every bit as devious and treacherous as her father.

Still, Rafe's quarrel was with Jack Randall, not a woman. He wouldn't use substitutes. Not the way Randall did.

He wished it hadn't been so damn long since he'd been with a woman. In prison, he'd blocked out those kind of memories, those kind of wants, and thought he'd brought them under control. But now they were tormenting him, like tiny devils stabbing his lower region with pitchforks.

Not that the woman was that pretty. Actually, she was not his type at all. Allison had been strikingly beautiful with black hair and green eyes and a figure that was all curves. This woman was tall and slender, her light brown hair carelessly bound in a loose braid that hung halfway down her back. Her eyes were calm, even restful, except for those few times when sparks seemed to ignite in them. Mainly when he had said something about Jack Randall.

Loyalty? In a Randall? That was absolutely incomprehensible to him. Any decent quality must be foreign to a Randall. She could, for all he knew, even be a spy. Hell, he wouldn't put anything past Randall. The thought stoked his anger and lowered his admiration to a controllable level. It made things a hell of a lot easier.

He opened the door and strode in, noting that she was sitting on the cot. He suspected she hadn't been sitting there long. The bottom of her dress was edged with dust that had settled on the floor. His eyes swept the rest of the room. Nothing seemed to have been disturbed.

"Stand up," he ordered curtly as he moved toward her.

She shied away from him.

He shrugged. "All right, stay tied the rest of the day."

She bit her lip for a moment, looking vulnerable, and finally stood, presenting her back to him. His fingers deftly untied the knot that bound her wrists, and he watched as she rubbed them together once they were free.

She turned and looked at him, and seemed to flinch at the expression in his face. But her back straightened and her chin lifted as she met his gaze straight on. "Have the others gone?"

It was clear that she hoped they had not. That bothered him for some reason, and his eyes narrowed as he studied her again. Either she had lied about being Randall's daughter, or she *was* Randall's daughter, which was worse. Either way, he wouldn't trust her farther than he could toss her.

Rafe chose to ignore her inquiry and made one of his own.

"What's your name?"

She didn't answer. He was getting accustomed to her silence. Hell, he undestood it. How many times had he used silence as a tool, especially when he knew insults or curses would only result in punishment? She learned a hell of a lot faster than he had. "All right, I'll call you Joe," he finally said.

She searched his face, and he knew she was looking for a flash of humor. There was none.

"I've got to call you something," he said, surprised at himself for explaining anything to her.

"Shea," she said finally.

"Shea Randall?"

She fell silent once more.

"Let's try something else," he said. "Where did you come from?"

She searched her mind for reasons not to tell him and could find none, except she didn't want to cooperate with him. She didn't want to give him that satisfaction. So she turned away and went to the door, looking out, hoping to see the man called Clint. But there was only an empty clearing and she knew she was alone with this . . . outlaw.

"It won't work," he said from behind her. His voice was hoarse, deep and insistent. "I'll find out everything."

She whirled around, the anger she had been trying to hold in check threatening to spill over. She didn't want that to happen. She couldn't let that happen. She suspected he would enjoy it, that he was trying to provoke it.

"Why are you keeping me here?"

"Not for your charm," he said. "So rest easy in that regard. Ten years of prison or not, I'm not desperate enough to take Randall's get. Or his leavings, whichever you are." He uttered the last sentence in that taunting low voice that was almost a whisper.

She hated his mockery, the open contempt he didn't bother to hide. It was the last insult she was going to tolerate. Despite her vow that she would pretend obedience for the moment, she found her left hand starting to swing, only to be caught in a vise-like grip.

"So the lady does have a temper," he observed. "What else are you? A liar? A spy?"

"Let me go," she demanded, looking down at her wrist.

He laughed bitterly but loosened his hold. "You

should know the bite of iron, Miss Shea. Cold. Hard. Cutting. My hand can't come close to that feel."

"I would prefer it to you," she spat at him.

"Behave, or you'll have the opportunity to find out," he retorted.

She felt the blood drain from her face. "You wouldn't?"

"I'll do whatever I must to finish what I've started."

"And what's that?"

"Your father, or whatever he is to you, has a certain debt to pay."

"Because he testified against you?"

"Oh, that's just one of the reasons," Rafe said.

"He was just doing his duty."

"Was he?"

His cold green eyes suddenly blazed and she felt the heat of his anger. But there was something else altogether. Something very frightening. She stepped away. "What are you planning?"

"That, Miss Shea, is none of your business."

"It is," she insisted.

"No," he said flatly. "And you'll stay here. In this cabin."

"And you?" Shea tried to keep her apprehension from showing.

"Lady, I don't want to be any place close to you."

"I can't stay here." She hated the plea in her voice.

"You don't have any choice. And if you're smart, you'll do as you're told."

"I'm obviously not, since I was foolish enough to trust . . . Ben Smith or whatever his name is."

"Let's see if you're a fast learner then," he said, glancing around the cabin and then picking up all the weapons she'd noticed earlier. He stopped midway to the door and turned back to her. "I don't make war on women. But be clear on this—I'll do what I must to finish what I started. If it means confining you in here, even chaining you, I'll do it. I won't like it, but I'll do it. In the meantime, you don't have to worry about your safety. I have no interest in you, other than to ensure you don't interfere with my plans. Do you understand?"

She defied him silently, her hands clenched at her side. Her wrists still bore the print of his hand, her skin its heat. She couldn't take back anything, not that foolish trust in Ben Smith, or the words that gave Rafferty Tyler a weapon against her father. She could only try to escape, to get to her father, to warn him.

Outlaws, they'd said in Boulder City. She wondered whether her father knew who led the outlaws, or the hate that drove them. It was like a live thing, that hate. She could feel it in the room, and it made her shiver.

"Do you understand?" he said again.

She nodded without accepting. She wanted him to leave although she'd lost some of her fear of him. She believed what he'd said, that she was in no physical danger of him, at least not at the moment.

He didn't say anything else, just turned toward the door without giving her another glance. He kicked the door shut behind him, and the cabin dimmed accordingly. After several seconds, she heard metal against metal, and knew he had placed a padlock on the door. There was one window, through which light filtered, and with a sinking feeling, she waited for him to rob her of that too. She didn't have to wait long. Shutters closed, and she heard the slam of a bar holding them in place.

She was alone in darkness now, alone in these forested mountains with an outlaw who hated her father, a man she didn't even know. She didn't understand Tyler's hatred, and she couldn't minimize it. Or her own danger. No matter what he said, he couldn't help but see her as a weapon. She tried to keep the rising terror at bay, to submerge it under other thoughts.

She searched for a weakness in Rafferty Tyler, and the artist in her recalled every feature of his face, every harsh line. She wondered what his face would look like at ease, if it had ever been that way. And she remembered the way he'd spoken of the ten years in prison, of the feel of iron. There had been tightness in his voice and tension in his body. She relived that moment when anger radiated from him as he'd showed her his scarred hand.

And she knew he blamed it all on Jack Randall.

Unjustly. Rafferty Tyler had brought on his own problems by stealing Army payrolls, even if the punishment did seem barbaric. But it was his own fault, she told herself, trying to dismiss her sympathy for him. That she could have any soft feelings toward him made it even more essential that she escape.

She just had to.

Rafe prowled the woods like a wounded panther.

He felt cut to the core and knew his soul was as mutilated as his hand.

He kept seeing those soft blue gray eyes: widened with terror, filled with bravery, glinting with defiance. When he'd locked the door, they must have reflected the feeling he'd had when a cell door first closed on him.

What kind of a man had he become?

Damn Ben. And yet, Rafe knew he would have done the same thing Ben had, given the opportunity.

Randall's daughter. He still couldn't believe it was true, but part of him was willing to admit it was a possibility.

Could he really trade the daughter for a confession, instead of going through with the current plan:

forcing Randall against a wall, bankrupting him until he did something stupid?

But no one knew about a daughter, so she couldn't mean much to his enemy, certainly not enough to go to prison. Dammit all to hell. What was he going to do with her?

If only she hadn't seen Ben and Clint . . .

But she had, and now their lives and futures were at risk, particularly Clint, who was working at her father's ranch and was in too deep to unravel himself. It had been Clint who brought the men together, who had helped with the first robbery a month ago.

An eye for an eye. The woman shouldn't bother him. He wasn't going to hurt her. And God knew he would keep her only as long as necessary, certainly nothing like the months and years he'd spent in prison because of her father. Just a few weeks. Perhaps months.

Christ, how could he handle that?

How could *she* handle that, despite her . . . gallant attempt at bravery? She had to fear the worst, that he would rape or kill her. There was no reason for her to think otherwise.

He'd thought he'd lost all emotions except the need for revenge, and he bitterly resented the guilt that now nibbled at him.

But it was not enough to change his mind. He had survived mutilation, the worst kind of abasement in prison, and incarceration for nearly one third of his life only by promising himself that Randall would pay for every moment in kind. It had been the only thing that had kept him going when every remnant of pride and manhood had been systemically stripped from him, and now when he looked at his hand and knew that any chance he'd ever had for any kind of life was gone.

He couldn't let it go. The need for revenge was too much a part of him, had been for too many years. He would do what was required to satisfy it.

And then? He couldn't think beyond then. The beyond didn't exist. Desolation wrapped around him as if he were whirling down a black bottomless hole, speeding toward a nothingness that was more frightening than any kind of physical pain.

He reached out, anchoring himself by touching a tall pine, forcing his mind back to the woman. He had no idea how to alleviate her fears. Christ, he didn't know how to talk to anyone anymore.

Except perhaps Abner, who demanded little. His hand went into his pocket, and then he remembered he'd left the mouse in the cabin. It had been eating a cracker when Clint appeared. He wondered how Miss Randall felt about mice.

He knew he should go back. But couldn't force himself yet. He had wanted to touch her, to wipe away that fear. That feeling had surprised him. It had been so damn long since he'd touched anyone with . . . human feeling.

But the woman in the cabin had stirred something in him, something he couldn't bear to contemplate. He had no soft feelings left, no pity, dammit. He would never be used again, not by anyone.

His body shuddered as he thought of his imprisonment. He wished he could let that go, but he couldn't. There were so many things he would have to live with alone, those first months in jail when he'd been stripped and thrown in the box without so much as a bucket. He'd turned into an animal, living in darkness in his own waste. He'd lost something then he would never regain, just as his keepers planned. They broke spirits because then prisoners were easier to handle. They would do anything, say anything, be anything to keep from going back there, and he'd hated himself for being one of them. He could never regain his self-respect, not totally, but perhaps vindication might mend it a little.

Shea. An unusual name, soft and quiet sounding.

It suited her. He cursed himself. He couldn't think of her that way. She was Randall's daughter, nothing more. He had to keep telling himself that. The get of a viper was still a viper.

He started back, moving with caution. The trapper who'd once lived in the cabin had set traps throughout these woods, and Rafe had already found several with animals caught in the teeth. He'd sprung the live ones, and for those already dead he'd felt an infinite sadness, aware of a certain kinship with them.

The last thing Rafe needed was to be caught in another trap.

Or maybe he thought dryly, he already was.

Tears had dried on Shea's face. Useless, foolish tears that didn't accomplish anything. She was angry at herself for expending that energy, and even more so at the thought that her captor might see evidence of her having cried.

She was thirsty and hungry and dirty. And so alone.

She'd never been alone like this before. There had always been her mother and friends, customers at the shop who'd oohed and aahed over her hat designs. There had even been the occasional young man.

But all that was gone. She didn't even know who and what she was anymore.

The fact that her world had proved false deepened her uncertainty. The one person she had trusted had lied to her, had lied about the most important, most essential, part of her life: the fact that her father was alive.

She tried to push her confusion aside. Escape! Think about escaping. Concentrate on escaping. She would have to plan carefully, if she were to be successful. The best way was to disarm her captor, make him think she had accepted her situation. She had to get a horse. She'd have no chance without one, not up here, where she could well be in more danger from nature than from the man who held her.

She wondered where Rafferty Tyler had gone. At first, she had hoped fervently he wouldn't come back, but now she worried just the opposite. In the darkness she had searched the cabin and found matches and a few candles. She could try to burn the place down, but she might kill herself in the process. Yet that remained an option if he didn't return.

She lit a candle and peered around. There was a box in a corner, which she opened. A tin of crackers. Canned fruits. She had no way of opening the cans, so she opened the cracker tin and ate half of one. It tasted like chalk.

Shea swallowed, feeling the dryness of her mouth. If only he had left something she could use as a weapon. In disgust, she went back to the cot, taking the candle with her, wondering whether she should put it out or not. But she didn't like the darkness. It increased her fear. Somehow she could cope if she had light.

Something moved at the end of the bed, and she flinched. There was no telling what creatures inhabited the cabin. She moved the candle and saw a mouse sitting on the end of the cot, regarding her as curiously as she watched him.

It sat up on his haunches and put its two front legs together as if begging. It obviously had no fright of her.

She'd seen rats before in the streets of Boston, big ugly rodents, but this small mouse was appealing.

Shea remained still, wondering whether it would come closer, or scamper off. She wished she had her sketch pad, but that had been left outside, on the tree stump. Instead, she concentrated on the tiny animal, willing it to come to her.

She tried talking to it. "You don't know a way out, do you?" she asked. "Of course you do, or you wouldn't be here, but I suspect it would be much too small for me."

The mouse came a few inches closer. Shea reached out her hand, surprised when the mouse crept forward and then investigated her fingers with its tiny mouth. It flicked its tail and sat back on its haunches again with what Shea thought was disappointment. Fascinated, she wondered if she should fetch a cracker. What if the mouse disappeared while she was getting the tin? Somehow the thought was excruciating.

She heard a noise at the door, and tensed. The mouse didn't move, and she knew she had to protect it. She picked it up, surprised that it didn't flee from her, and thrust it underneath the cot. She hoped it would stay there.

The door opened, and the bright light of the afternoon sun almost blinded her. Her eyes were drawn to the large figure in the doorway. Silhouetted by the sun behind him, Tyler seemed even bigger, stronger, more menacing. She had to force herself to keep from backing away.

He hesitated, his gaze raking over the cabin, raking over her. He frowned at the candle.

She stood. It took all her bravery, but she stood, forcing her eyes to meet his, to determine what was there. There seemed to be nothing but a certain coolness.

"I'm thirsty," she said. It came out as more of a challenge than a request, and she saw a quick flicker of something in his eyes. She hoped it was remorse, but that thought was quickly extinguished by his reply.

"Used to better places?" It was a sneer, plain and simple, and Shea felt anger stirring again.

"I'm used to gentlemen and simple . . . humanity."

"That's strange, considering your claim that you're Randall's daughter."

"I haven't claimed anything to you."

"That's right, you haven't," he agreed in a disageeable voice. "You haven't said much at all."

"And I don't intend to. Not to a thief and a traitor."

"Be careful, Miss Randall. Your . . . continued health depends on this thief and traitor."

"That's supposed to comfort me?" Her tone was pure acid.

His gaze stabbed her. "You'll have to forgive me. I'm out of practice in trying to comfort anyone. Ten years out of practice."

"So you're going to starve me?"

"No," he said slowly. "I'm not going to do *that*."

The statement was ominous to Shea. "What are you going to do?"

"Follow my rules, and I won't do anything."

"You already are. You're keeping me here against my will."

He was silent for a moment, and Shea noted a muscle moving in his neck, as if he were just barely restraining himself.

"Lady, because of your . . . father, I was 'held' against my will for ten years." She wanted to slap him for his mockery. She wanted to kick him where it would hurt the most. But now was not the time.

"Is that it? You're taking revenge out on me?"

The muscle in his cheek moved again. "No, Miss Randall, it's not that. You just happened to be in the wrong place at the wrong time. I don't have any more choices than you do." He didn't know why in the hell he was explaining, except her last charge galled him.

"You do."

He turned away from her. "Believe what you want," he said, his voice indifferent. "Blow out that candle and come with me if you want some water."

She didn't want to go with him, but she was desperate to slake her thirst. She blew out the candle, hoping that once outside he wouldn't see dried streaks of tears on her face. She didn't want to give him that satisfaction.

Shea didn't have to worry. He paid no attention to her, and she had to scurry to keep up with his long-legged strides. She knew she was plain, especially so in the loose-fitting britches and shirt she wore and with her hair in a braid. She also knew she should be grateful that he was indifferent to her, but a part of her wanted to goad him, confuse him . . . attract him.

Shea felt color flood her face. To restrain her train of thought, she concentrated on her surroundings.

Her horse was gone, although her belongings were propped against the tree stump. There was a shack to the left, and she noticed a lock on the door. That must be where he'd taken the weapons and where he kept his own horse. The keys must be in his pockets. He strode over to the building and picked up a bucket with his gloved hand.

She tried to pay attention to their route, but it seemed they had just melted into the woods and everything looked alike. She thought of turning around and running, but he was only a couple of feet ahead of her.

He stopped abruptly at a stream and leaned against a tree, watching her.

Shea had never drunk from a stream before, yet that was obviously what he expected her to do. The dryness in her mouth was worse, and she couldn't wait. She moved to the edge of the stream and kneeled, feeling awkward and self-conscious, knowing he was watching and judging. She scooped up a handful of water, then another, trying to sip it before it leaked through her fingers. She caught just enough to be tantalized.

She finally fell flat on her stomach and put her mouth in the water, taking long swallows of the icy cold water, mindless of the way the front of her shirt got soaked, mindless of anything but water.

It felt wonderful and tasted wonderful. When she was finally sated, she reluctantly sat up, and her gaze went to Tyler.

His stance was lazy but his eyes, like fine emeralds, were intense with fire. She felt a corresponding wave of heat consume her. She couldn't move her gaze from him, no matter how hard she tried. It was as if they were locked together.

He was the first to divert his gaze and his face settled quickly into its usual indifferent mask.

She looked down and noticed that her wet shirt clung to her, outlining her breasts. She swallowed hard and turned around. She splashed water on her face, hoping it would cool the heat suffusing her body.

She kept expecting Tyler to order her away, but he didn't. And she lingered as long as she could. She didn't want to go back to the dark cabin. She didn't want to face him, or those intense emotions she didn't understand.

She felt his gaze on her, and knew she should feel fear. He had been in prison a very long time. But she was certain he wouldn't touch her in a sexual way.

Because he despises you.

Because he despises your father.

She closed her eyes for a moment, and when she opened them, a spiral of light gleamed through the trees, hitting the stream. She wanted to reach out and catch that sunbeam, to climb it to some safe place.

But there were no safe places any longer.

She watched that ray of light until it slowly dissipated as the sun slipped lower in the sky, and then she turned around again. She hadn't expected such patience from Tyler.

"Ready?" he asked in his hoarse whisper.

The word held many meanings.

Ready for what? She wasn't ready for any of this. But she nodded.

He sauntered over and offered his hand.

She refused it and rose by herself, stunned by how much she suddenly wanted to take his hand, to feel that strength again.

And Shea realized her battle wasn't entirely with him. It was also with herself.

Photoshop Elements 4

POUR LES NULS

Deke McClelland et Galen Fott

FIRST
Interactive

Photoshop Elements 4 pour les Nuls

Titre de l'édition originale : Photoshop Elements For Dummies
Publié par Wiley Publishing, Inc.
111 River Street
Hoboken, NJ 07030-5774
USA

Edition française publiée en accord avec Wiley Publishing, Inc.
© 2006 Éditions First Interactive
27, rue Cassette
75006 Paris - France
Tél. 01 45 49 60 00
Fax 01 45 49 60 01
E-mail : firstinfo@efirst.com
Web : www.efirst.com
ISBN : 2-84427-841-8
Dépôt légal : 2ᵉ trimestre 2006

Collection dirigée par Jean-Pierre Cano
Edition : Pierre Chauvot
Maquette et mise en page : Edouard Chauvot
Traduction : Bernard Jolivalt

Imprimé en Italie

Sommaire

Introduction

. . . .

*P*hotoshop Elements 4.0 a pour objectif principal d'améliorer vos
photos. Poussant cette logique toujours plus loin, vous disposez
désormais d'un logiciel convivial, issu de Photoshop, le programme de
référence en matière de retouche d'image. Comme ce grand frère est
d'une puissance et d'une complexité affichées, Adobe en a extrait les
fonctionnalités majeures afin de les mettre à la portée de tous, laissant
les plus sophistiquées à ceux dont le métier est de retoucher quotidiennement des photographies.

Photoshop Elements, c'est Photoshop.

Que voulons-nous dire exactement quand nous affirmons, sans honte,
que Photoshop Elements est une version plus simple à utiliser que
Photoshop ? Elements, diminutif affectif de Photoshop Elements,
propose de nombreuses aides qui évitent les affres d'un apprentissage
souvent long des possibilités intrinsèques de tout logiciel graphique
affichant une certaine puissance de traitement des images. Mais ce
n'est pas pour cela que Photoshop Elements doit échapper à un
ouvrage *Pour les Nuls*. Peut-être même au contraire, dans la mesure où
ce programme est livré avec quantité de scanners, imprimantes ou
appareils photo numériques. N'oubliez jamais qu'en matière de
traitement des images, même quand un logiciel est dit "facile", le
nombre impressionnant de ses fonctions nécessite une aide comme
celle prodiguée par ce merveilleux ouvrage.

Vous voulez des exemples ? Commencez par jeter un œil sur la
photographie suivante :

Ce cliché pourrait être intéressant, drôle, et pour le moins sympathique, s'il n'était pas entaché d'un manque évident de contraste et de
luminosité. Dans un programme de traitement d'image, votre premier
réflexe serait d'utiliser une fonction communément appelée Lumino-
sité/Contraste, exactement comme vous le feriez pour régler empiri-
quement les faiblesses de votre téléviseur. Vous croyez qu'il suffit de

Figure 1 : Un chat bien pantouflard !

tourner deux boutons, ou en l'occurrence de faire glisser deux curseurs, pour régler définitivement et précisément le problème. Comme vous êtes naïf ou ignorant !

Vouloir contrebalancer les faiblesses d'une photographie aussi sombre que celle-ci avec une fonction Luminosité/Contraste est une erreur fondamentale. Nous convenons qu'elle est très simple à mettre en œuvre, mais corriger des photos sur un ordinateur ressemble à bien des choses de notre vie quotidienne : le résultat est à la hauteur des moyens que vous utilisez. Que ce soit dans Photoshop ou dans Photoshop Elements, le meilleur moyen de corriger l'absence de luminosité d'une image est d'utiliser la commande Niveaux. Vous accédez alors à une boîte de dialogue disposant de nombreux réglages. La précision est de mise. La correction sera alors à la hauteur de *nos*, pardon, de *vos* espérances.

Nous sommes conscients que ces "montagnes", ces curseurs, ces pipettes, ces valeurs troublent votre esprit qui vous fait réagir aussi promptement qu'une poule face à un couteau.

Nous sommes bien d'accord avec vous, l'utilisation de la boîte de dialogue Niveaux n'est pas aussi intuitive que Luminosité/Contraste, mais c'est le prix à payer pour corriger des images mal photographiées, mal numérisées ou les deux à la fois. Niveaux est un fantastique outil qui permet de rehausser intelligemment la luminosité

Figure 2 : Histogramme de la photographie du chat montrant une grande quantité de données graphiques trop sombres.

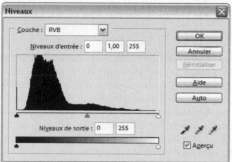

défaillante des images. La bonne nouvelle dans tout cela est que tous deux fonctionnent de la même manière dans Photoshop et Elements.

Les conventions de ce livre

Elles sont simples et traditionnelles dans un ouvrage *Pour les Nuls*. Tout au long de votre lecture, nous vous demanderons d'appuyer sur des touches de votre clavier. Ces combinaisons, appelées *raccourcis*, demandent à Photoshop Elements d'exécuter une tâche. Nous les mentionnons sous cette forme :

Ctrl+Maj+P

Cela signifie que vous devez appuyer sur la touche Ctrl puis, sans la relâcher, appuyer sur Maj, et enfin sur P. En d'autres termes, pour exécuter l'action correspondant à cette combinaison, vous devez maintenir enfoncées trois touches simultanément : Ctrl, Maj, et P.

A l'heure où ces lignes étaient écrites, la version 4.0 pour Macintosh était "en cours de développement", selon Adobe, et devait sortir "dans un futur proche". On se saurait être plus affirmatif et précis... C'est pourquoi cet ouvrage ne traite que de la version Windows du produit.

Contenu de ce livre

Les sections suivantes font le tour des cinq parties qui composent cet ouvrage.

Première partie : Cours élémentaire première année

Le bon ordre veut que nous commencions par le commencement en répondant à la question : "Qu'est-ce que l'édition ou la modification d'images ?" La réponse se trouve dans une étude de l'interface de Photoshop Elements, avec ses outils, ses palettes, et leur disposition à l'écran. Nous expliquerons l'ouverture d'une image (oui, nous savons, on ouvre un sac, une portière, mais une image ?) et la notion de pixel sans laquelle il n'y aurait jamais rien sur votre splendide moniteur (écran). Enfin, nous terminerons avec la couleur, notion souvent difficile à comprendre pour le néophyte qui se perd dans les espaces colorimétriques comme un satellite d'exploration dans les espaces intersidéraux. Rassurez-vous, tout a été mis en œuvre pour faire passer la chose sans que vous deveniez vert de peur ou rouge de colère.

Deuxième partie : Apprendre à travailler

C'est la partie que vous ne lirez pas car vous pensez pouvoir utiliser immédiatement Photoshop Elements pour améliorer vos photos ou y perpétrer quelques manipulations dignes du docteur Frankenstein. Vous y reviendrez vite en constatant que la maîtrise d'outils pointus ne s'improvise pas. Le Chapitre 6 présente la nouvelle fonction d'organisation des photos avec l'utilitaire intégré Organiseur. Le Chapitre 7 montre comment enregistrer les fichiers dans un format approprié. Le Chapitre 8 dévoile la façon de corriger vos erreurs et d'imprimer vos images une fois cette correction réalisée. Le Chapitre 9 se focalise sur les sélections, c'est-à-dire l'isolement d'une partie d'une image qui subira, elle seule, l'effet de vos modifications. Enfin, le Chapitre 10 aborde l'un des sujets essentiels du travail sous Photoshop Elements : les calques.

Troisième partie : Plus vrai que nature

Cette partie de l'ouvrage traite de l'amélioration des images avec Photoshop Elements 4.0. Au Chapitre 11, nous apprenons à nettoyer les photos. Au 12, nous passons en revue les différents outils de modification de Photoshop Elements. Au 13, nous apprécions la puissance des outils qui permettent d'améliorer l'exposition d'une photographie, y compris l'extraordinaire commande Niveaux.

Quatrième partie : L'art et la manière

Les précédentes parties montrent comment améliorer les images.
Cette quatrième partie, quant à elle, aborde les techniques de déformation de Photoshop Elements. Elles permettent d'explorer les
univers de la peinture et de la colorisation numérique.

Cinquième partie : Les dix commandements

Traditionnelle partie de la collection *Pour les Nuls*, vous y trouverez
des trucs, des astuces, des conseils, pour travailler plus rapidement et
plus facilement avec Photoshop Elements. Vous y découvrirez
également dix raisons susceptibles de vous faire passer de Photoshop
Elements à Photoshop... un de ces jours.

Les icônes de ce livre

Une étude scientifique a démontré qu'une majorité de lecteurs d'un
livre de la collection *Pour les Nuls* apprenait beaucoup de choses et
qu'une minorité était perturbée par les pictogrammes qui apparaissent
çà et là dans la marge. Nous pouvons affirmer qu'avec *les Nuls*, un
véritable système est né et qu'il perdure d'année en année. Donc, ce
livre ne déroge pas à la tradition. Des icônes surgissent dans nos
pages pour attirer votre attention sur des points précis.

Cette icône signale une nouvelle caractéristique de Photoshop
Elements 4.0. Les utilisateurs expérimentés peuvent survoler le livre à
la recherche de cette icône pour connaître les nouveautés, mais
sachez que des fonctions nouvelles ont été ajoutées, et que d'autres
ont disparu ou changé de nom. Autrement dit : il est préférable de tout
lire.

Voici une astuce qui vous permettra de gagner du temps dans
Photoshop Elements. Il s'agit d'un gain d'expérience exceptionnel qui
vous servira toute votre vie. Lisez ces paragraphes et n'oubliez pas de
nous remercier.

Cette icône met le doigt sur un point spécifique qu'il est judicieux de
retenir.

Cette icône ne veut pas dire que votre ordinateur risque d'exploser
mais elle attire votre attention sur un danger potentiel. À lire attenti-
vement !

Que faire ?

Maintenant, à vous de jouer avec vos images pour devenir la référence familiale en matière d'amélioration de photos, de trucages, voire de publication Web de clichés qui raviront petits et grands de votre famille. Cette constatation n'exclut pas le fait que vous deveniez un véritable mordu de l'imagerie numérique au point de vouloir l'élever au rang artistique qu'elle mérite.

Première partie

Cours élémentaire première année

Dans cette partie...

ans l'univers de la conception numérique graphique, considérez *Photoshop Elements pour les Nuls* comme un manuel de survie. C'est le vôtre ! Ne le prêtez à personne ! Inscrivez votre nom dessus, car chaque élève doit posséder son propre exemplaire. Non mais ! Puisque vous débutez, nous sommes conscients que l'apprentissage d'une nouvelle technique est aussi intimidant qu'un premier jour d'école maternelle. Par conséquent, nous vous invitons à lire le premier chapitre.

Il permet de bien comprendre la philosophie de Photoshop Elements. Il répondra sans nul doute à cette obsédante question : "Mais Photoshop Elements, c'est quoi exactement ?" Le chapitre suivant disséquera l'interface pour mieux reprendre certains réflexes élémentaires qu'il faut avoir dans la quasi-totalité des logiciels. Une fois l'apprentissage de l'ouverture d'une image effectué, nous verrons comment s'y déplacer. Ensuite, viendra l'heure d'étudier le pixel, ce petit point dont la juxtaposition de nombre d'entre eux forme une image. Enfin, vous saurez presque tout sur le monde merveilleux de la couleur et les risques de la publication d'une image sur le Web quand on ne prend pas les précautions indispensables à ce genre d'opération.

À la fin du Chapitre 5, nous vous assurons que vous en saurez assez pour répondre à bien des questions sur Photoshop Elements en particulier et l'imagerie numérique en général.

Chapitre 1
Braver les éléments

. . . .

Dans ce chapitre :

▶ Présentation de Photoshop Elements.

▶ Les outils de peinture.

▶ Les outils d'édition.

▶ Les fonctions d'aide d'Elements.

. . . .

L a plupart d'entre vous ont obtenu Photoshop Elements en achetant un scanner, une imprimante ou un appareil photo numérique. De prime abord, ce logiciel paraît simple, convivial, et suscite une confiance qui pousse à la fainéantise. On suit des guides, des assistants, et on se prend pour le nouveau Robert Doisneau. Pourtant, à y regarder de plus près, on s'aperçoit qu'Elements est un programme aux profondeurs insondables, dont l'inimitié est capable de vous déchirer le cœur. Sigmund Freud verrait en Photoshop Elements un cas clinique de dédoublement de la personnalité ; mi-ange mi-démon, Laurel et Hardy, King et Kong, mais pire peut-être : Dr. Jekyll et Mr. Hyde. De quoi vous effrayer !

Ce chapitre explore les deux facettes de ce caractère bien spécial, en distinguant le bien et le mal dans Photoshop Elements.

Ce bon docteur Jekyll

Le bon côté de Photoshop Elements réside dans sa palette d'outils que montre la Figure 1.1. Elle a été détachée du bord en la tirant par la languette supérieure et elle flotte maintenant librement à l'écran. Tous ces outils sont tellement simples que votre grand-mère pourrait les utiliser sans avoir jamais touché une souris – on ne parle pas du rongeur – de sa vie. La Gomme efface, le Crayon dessine des traits aux bords nets, le Pinceau peint, et ainsi de suite. Ces outils magiques séduisent les novices, mais attention : "Tout ce qui brille n'est pas or."

Figure 1.1 :
La palette
d'outils
d'Elements 4.

Vous constaterez rapidement que ces outils en promettent bien plus qu'ils n'en font réellement. Par exemple, une ligne tracée avec l'outil Crayon n'est pas plus originale qu'une ligne tracée avec un crayon traditionnel sur une feuille de papier. On ne peut pas vraiment parler de travail ou d'édition numérique. Il faudra une grande perspicacité et un sens pointu de la multiplicité des outils pour obtenir des résultats probants dignes de ce que permettent les logiciels de création graphique.

Ce puissant mais inquiétant Mister Hyde

Quand vous n'en avez pas pour votre argent avec les outils de création et d'édition numériques, ajustez leurs performances et dynamisez leur expérimentation pour un contrôle optimum de vos images numériques dans Photoshop Elements. C'est le côté Mr. Hyde du programme. Une puissance certes, mais pas évidente à mettre en œuvre. Vous buterez sur des options aussi incompréhensibles que Fondu, Produit et Différence. Vous découvrirez des commandes comme Luminosité/ Contraste et Taille de l'image qui, mal employées, pourraient endommager votre image. De plus, cliquer sur des icônes ne déclenchera souvent aucune action. Bref, suffisamment de contradictions laborieuses pour porter atteinte à la santé mentale d'un artiste numérique déjà réticent.

Photoshop Elements a heureusement un côté Mr. Hyde, sans quoi il serait une pâle copie de logiciels miteux qui accomplissent bien peu de choses dans le domaine de l'expression numérique artistique. Alors, plutôt que de se lamenter sur un sort funeste, partez à l'apprentissage des deux aspects d'un programme plein de promesses.

La double personnalité de Photoshop Elements

Ces deux aspects de Photoshop Elements poursuivent des objectifs différents. La rigidité du Dr. Jekyll se concentre uniquement sur la *peinture*, tandis que la complexité de Mr. Hyde se développe dans l'*édition d'image* pure et dure. Par conséquent, pour bien appréhender ce programme génial, il faut comprendre la différence entre les deux personnalités qui l'habitent.

La peinture sans se salir

Peindre dans un univers numérique revient à prendre un pinceau et à étaler la couleur sur une toile. Ici, la toile n'est rien d'autre que l'écran de votre moniteur. Il est possible de peindre sur une toile vierge, c'est-à-dire un fond blanc, ou directement sur une photographie. La première hypothèse exige du talent. Il faut savoir manier la souris ou le stylet avec la dextérité d'un peintre. Les mieux lotis en la matière sont les dessinateurs patentés, qu'ils soient autodidactes ou qu'ils sortent d'une école d'art. La seconde hypothèse est à la portée de tous dans la mesure où vous partez d'une image existante sur laquelle vous appliquez des couleurs. Remarquez la charmante jeune femme sur la Figure 1.2. Nous l'utiliserons pour démontrer les impressionnantes fonctions d'Elements.

En quelques coups de pinceau numérique, vous obtenez l'image représentée sur la Figure 1.3. Toutes ces modifications ont été réalisées avec un seul outil – le Pinceau – et deux couleurs, le noir et le

Figure 1.2 :
Êtes-vous
une bonne ou
une
mauvaise
fée ?

blanc. Sans talent particulier, nous avons peint des traits sur la photographie. Malgré ces coups de pinceau, l'image d'origine demeure intacte, contrairement au résultat indélébile que vous obtenez en peignant directement sur une "vraie" photographie avec un "vrai" pinceau. En effet, tant que l'image n'a pas été enregistrée sous le même nom de fichier, l'original ne subit aucune altération, comme cela est expliqué au Chapitre 7.

Édition (ou modification) d'une image existante

La jeune femme à gauche sur la Figure 1.3 n'a subi l'assaut que de quelques coups de pinceau. Elle est grimée mais loin d'avoir subi les affres de l'édition graphique pure et dure. Ce qui distingue cette dernière de la peinture numérique est que vous pouvez distordre une image et grossir ses détails. En d'autres termes, vous peignez avec l'image elle-même.

Figure 1.3 :
A gauche,
quelques
coups de
pinceau et de
crayon
modifient
l'image. À
droite, le
trucage est
encore plus
sophistiqué.

La photo de la jeune femme à droite sur la Figure 1.3 démontre nos propos. Pour arriver à cette image bizarre, nous avons démarré par un peu de chirurgie plastique sur notre sujet. Nous avons exploité le filtre Fluidité pour créer la coiffure. Nous avons sélectionné sa couronne avec l'outil Lasso et l'avons replacée sur sa tête avec une inclinaison espiègle. Sa robe a été transformée en sorte de queue d'hippocampe par le filtre Tourbillon. Nous avons remplacé ses pauvres petites ailes de fée par une paire d'ailes d'aigle provenant d'une autre image. Nous avons ensuite coupé l'ensemble afin de le placer sur un nouvel arrière-plan. Enfin, nous avons utilisé l'outil Forme personnalisée pour dessiner le symbole du yin et du yang au bout de sa baguette magique, et appliqué deux styles de calque pour lui donner de la dimension et une lueur agréable.

Votre apprentissage n'impose pas que vous réalisiez immédiatement semblable tour de force. Par ailleurs, votre volonté n'est peut-être pas de caricaturer les modèles de vos photographies mais simplement d'en améliorer l'aspect ou de donner des effets plus subtils. La Figure 1.4 montre des réglages très discrets qui affectent l'aspect général de la photographie sans donner l'impression qu'elle a subi une mutation génétique. Ces modifications accentuent légèrement les détails ou atténuent certains défauts de l'image. Dans les deux cas, vous obtenez un autre type de photographie impossible à réaliser au moment de la prise de vue ou au développement.

Figure 1.4 :
Accentuez la
netteté et
corrigez les
couleurs.

Assistance psychiatrique (le docteur est fourni)

Pauvre Dr. Jekyll... Il a passé sa vie à tenter de mettre au point un antidote pour en finir avec ses problèmes de double personnalité sans jamais y parvenir, alors que la solution relevait d'une psychothérapie. Heureusement, Photoshop Elements n'est pas schizophrène ; il dispose de nombreuses fonctions d'aide permettant aux utilisateurs de faire la part des choses et d'éviter de prendre des vessies pour des lanternes. En d'autres termes, pour s'égarer et pire, se tromper de personnalité dans Elements, il faut vraiment le faire exprès.

L'écran de bienvenue

L'écran de bienvenue est la première chose que vous voyez en ouvrant Photoshop Elements (si vous ne savez pas comment démarrer

Photoshop Elements, consultez le chapitre suivant. Pour le moment, nous vous expliquons ce que vous rencontrerez si, dans l'exaltation, vous brûlez certaines étapes et ouvrez immédiatement le programme.)

La Figure 1.5 montre l'écran de bienvenue. Il propose de nombreuses activités réparties dans sept icônes :

- ✔ **Présentation du produit :** Cliquez ici pour obtenir une présentation générale de Photoshop Elements. Un lien explique comment mettre à niveau une ancienne version du logiciel.

- ✔ **Afficher et organiser les photos :** Cliquez sur ce lien pour accéder instantanément au module Organiseur que nous étudions au Chapitre 6.

- ✔ **Retoucher rapidement les photos :** Bascule le programme en mode Retouche rapide qui donne accès à des réglages sommaires améliorant sensiblement vos clichés.

- ✔ **Retoucher et corriger les photos :** Permet d'afficher le mode d'édition classique de Photoshop Elements.

- ✔ **Créer avec vos photos :** Ouvre la fenêtre Configuration de la création qui est un des éléments du module Organiseur.

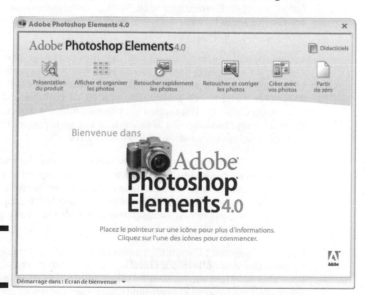

Figure 1.5 :
L'écran de
bienvenue.

> ✔ **Partir de zéro :** Ouvre la fenêtre Nouveau, boîte de dialogue où vous configurez votre zone de travail. Nous en expliquerons les tenants et les aboutissants dans quelques chapitres.
>
> ✔ **Didacticiels :** Cliquez sur ce bouton pour ouvrir la fenêtre du navigateur Web et accéder à la page Web Adobe consacrée au support de Photoshop Elements.

Le menu Démarrage, situé dans le coin inférieur gauche de l'écran de bienvenue, permet de choisir la session d'Elements à démarrer. L'option Écran de bienvenue est sélectionnée par défaut. Cela signifie que l'écran s'affiche au démarrage du programme. Si vous sélectionnez Éditeur ou Organiseur, Elements s'ouvrira dans l'interface choisie jusqu'à ce que vous en sélectionniez une autre dans ce menu.

L'aide Adobe

Cliquer sur Aide/Aide de Photoshop Elements donne accès à l'aide en ligne. Elle est répartie sous quatre onglets : Sommaire, Index, Rechercher et Signets. Cliquez sur l'onglet qui vous permettra d'obtenir l'aide appropriée. Vous pouvez également obtenir une aide depuis le site Web d'Adobe. Pour cela, cliquez sur Aide/Support en ligne, ou encore Aide/Photoshop Elements en ligne. Vous y trouverez de nombreuses informations, des forums, des astuces, et accéderez à une véritable communauté d'utilisateurs.

Les avertissements, les messages et les boîtes de dialogue qui s'affichent tout au long d'un travail dans Photoshop Elements peuvent venir troubler votre esprit tranquille, déjà perturbé par l'apparition dans votre vie d'un ordinateur, d'un appareil photo numérique et de Photoshop Elements. Les termes qui posent problème sont soulignés en bleu. Ils représentent des liens sur lesquels vous pouvez cliquer pour obtenir des informations complémentaires.

Le système d'aide peut également être sollicité depuis l'interface du programme, en cours d'édition d'une image. Le champ est situé dans la barre des menus. Par défaut, il affiche cette phrase : "Entrez un terme ou une expression". Remplacez ces mots par une phrase simple concernant le problème qui vous perturbe. Validez-la en appuyant sur la touche Entrée. Une fenêtre intitulée Adobe Help Center apparaît.

L'aide est également disponible en plaçant le pointeur de la souris sur un outil. Une info-bulle décrit l'outil sous forme d'un lien hypertexte. Si vous avez un doute sur l'utilisation de cet outil, cliquez sur le lien. L'aide d'Adobe s'ouvre à la rubrique concernant cet outil.

Dans de nombreuses boîtes de dialogue, une option En savoir plus, suivie d'un lien (voir Figure 1.6), permet d'accéder directement à l'aide. Cette fonction, qui existait déjà dans la version précédente d'Elements, est généralisée à un plus grand nombre de panneaux.

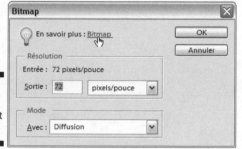

Figure 1.6 :
Une aide est
fournie à tout
moment.

La palette Utilisation

La palette Utilisation explique comment exécuter facilement certaines tâches. Il suffit de cliquer sur le lien de la tâche qui vous intéresse pour obtenir des instructions détaillées sur la procédure à suivre.

Chapitre 2

Utilisation de votre environnement de travail

S i vous êtes nouveau venu dans Photoshop Elements en particulier, ou dans l'univers informatique en général, ce chapitre est fait pour vous. Vous allez acquérir les réflexes indispensables à toute bonne utilisation d'un programme.

Même si l'interface d'Elements ne vous est pas totalement inconnue, lisez ce chapitre pour que nous soyons tous certains de parler de la même chose avec les mêmes mots.

Donner vie (électronique) à Elements

Pour découvrir l'interface d'un programme, il faut préalablement l'ouvrir en procédant comme suit :

1. **Cliquez sur le bouton Démarrer de la Barre des tâches.**

2. **Cliquez sur Tous les programmes.**

3. **Cliquez sur Adobe Photoshop Elements 4.0.**

   L'écran de bienvenue apparaît.

4. **Cliquez sur Retoucher et améliorer des photos.**

   La Figure 2.1 montre l'interface de Photoshop Elements 4.0.

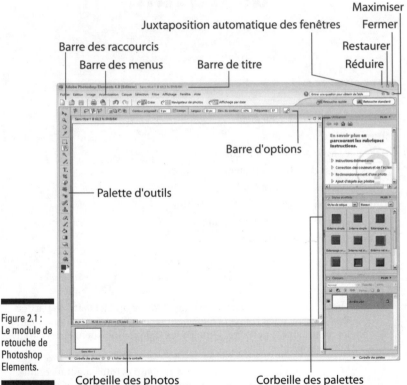

Figure 2.1 :
Le module de
retouche de
Photoshop
Elements.

Travailler avec des fenêtres

Dans tous les programmes fonctionnant sous Windows, vous avez
affaire à deux types de fenêtres : celle du programme, qui contient la

zone de travail principale d'Elements ; et la fenêtre de l'image, qui se trouve dans l'interface de Photoshop Elements. La Figure 2.2 montre la fenêtre du programme ; reportez-vous au Chapitre 3 pour voir celle de l'image.

Ces deux types de fenêtres contiennent les mêmes éléments de base que tout autre programme.

Naviguer dans les menus

Photoshop Elements dispose de menus. Cet élément est présent dans la quasi-totalité des applications. En revanche, Elements possède deux choses que de nombreux autres programmes n'ont pas : une barre de raccourcis et une barre d'options. La barre de raccourcis, souvent appelée barre d'outils standard dans les applications fonctionnant sous Windows, permet d'exécuter une tâche en un clic de souris alors qu'il faudrait normalement dérouler plusieurs menus et sélectionner diverses commandes.

La barre d'options sert à contrôler le fonctionnement des outils sélectionnés. Il est possible de placer ces deux barres où bon vous semble sur l'interface d'Elements. Lorsque vous modifiez les options d'un outil, il est parfois difficile de retrouver exactement ses paramètres initiaux. Dans ce cas, cliquez sur l'icône de l'outil située dans le coin gauche de la palette des options. Dans le menu local qui apparaît, choisissez Réinitialiser cet outil ou Réinitialiser tous les outils. Le libellé de ces deux commandes est assez éloquent.

Chacun des mots présents sur la barre de menus identifie un menu déroulant : Fichier, Édition, Image, Accentuation, etc. Un *menu* est une liste de commandes que vous utilisez pour ouvrir, fermer des images, manipuler des sections de certaines photographies, afficher et masquer des palettes, et entreprendre de nombreuses autres tâches très sophistiquées.

Nous expliquons les commandes essentielles de Photoshop Elements tout au long de cet ouvrage.

Discuter avec des boîtes de dialogue

Elements réagit spontanément à certaines commandes. D'autres ouvrent des boîtes de dialogue qui exigent de définir les paramètres devant être appliqués à des images. Le nom des commandes ouvrant des boîtes de dialogue est suivi de points de suspension.

La Figure 2.2 affiche une boîte de dialogue. Comme le montre cette illustration, les boîtes de dialogue peuvent contenir plusieurs types d'options. Elles fonctionnent de la manière suivante :

- Une zone où vous pouvez saisir des chiffres ou du texte est appelée un *champ*. Double-cliquez dedans pour en sélectionner le contenu. Remplacez-le par une valeur saisie au clavier.

- Certains champs ont des *glissières*. Actionnez le curseur vers la gauche ou la droite pour diminuer ou augmenter la valeur affichée.

- Vous ne pouvez sélectionner qu'un seul *bouton d'option* (circulaire) dans une boîte de dialogue. Ce sont des sélections exclusives. Choisir une option exclut les autres et réciproquement. Un point noir apparaît dans le cercle du bouton sélectionné, c'est-à-dire de l'option active.

- En revanche, vous pouvez cocher plusieurs cases à la fois donc définir plusieurs options. Le fait de cliquer dans une *case à cocher* désactive l'option (la coche disparaît).

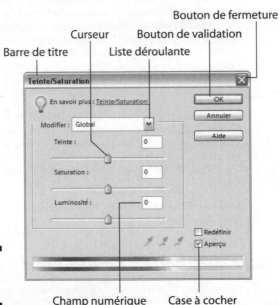

Figure 2.2 :
Une boîte de
dialogue.

🖊 Pour gagner de la place et ne pas se retrouver avec des boîtes de dialogue gigantesques, des *listes déroulantes* proposent plusieurs options. Cliquez sur la flèche de la liste, puis sur l'option à utiliser. Vous ne pouvez sélectionner qu'une seule option à la fois.

🖊 Les boutons des boîtes de dialogue permettent généralement d'appliquer les options sélectionnées (*bouton OK*), de fermer la boîte de dialogue sans appliquer les options (*bouton Annuler*), d'obtenir de l'aide (*bouton Aide*). D'autres boutons affichent une nouvelle boîte de dialogue. Vous comprenez la difficulté pour le profane à comprendre toutes les possibilités des options proposées dans une boîte de dialogue.

À l'instar des menus, vous pouvez sélectionner des options et exécuter des actions dans les boîtes de dialogue sans quitter votre clavier. Voici les raccourcis clavier les plus utilisés dans les boîtes de dialogue :

🖊 Pour passer à l'option suivante ou sélectionner le contenu d'un champ, appuyez sur la touche Tab. Pour revenir à l'option ou au champ précédent, appuyez sur Maj+Tab.

🖊 Appuyez sur la touche Entrée pour sélectionner l'option entourée par des pointillés (comme le bouton OK sur la Figure 2.2). Appuyez sur Echap pour fermer la boîte de dialogue sans appliquer les paramètres.

🖊 Appuyez sur la touche ↑ du pavé directionnel pour augmenter d'une unité la valeur affichée dans un champ, ou sur la touche ↓ pour la diminuer d'une unité. Pour augmenter ou diminuer les valeurs par tranche de dix unités, maintenez la touche Maj enfoncée tout en appuyant sur la flèche adéquate du pavé directionnel.

🖊 Quand vous souhaitez retrouver les valeurs initiales d'une boîte de dialogue, maintenez enfoncée la touche Maj afin que le bouton Annuler devienne Réinitialiser. Cliquez dessus sans relâcher la touche Maj pour récupérer les paramètres par défaut.

Faire connaissance avec les palettes

Elements dispose de palettes que vous pouvez déplacer librement ou fermer. Les palettes sont des boîtes de dialogue spéciales dont les options permettent de modifier l'apparence des images ou vous assistent dans vos aventures numériques.

Apparue dans la version précédente d'Elements, la Corbeille des palettes est un grand volet vertical, placé sur le côté droit de l'interface du programme, contenant par défaut des palettes. Si vous estimez qu'elle prend trop de place, réduisez sa taille. Pour cela, placez le pointeur de la souris sur la fine barre verticale, cliquez et, sans relâcher le bouton de la souris, faites glisser la barre vers la droite. Vous pouvez même masquer la Corbeille des palettes en cliquant sur le triangle de la barre verticale en question, ou sur celui placé à gauche des mots "Corbeille des palettes" affichés dans le coin inférieur droit de la fenêtre d'Elements. Vous pouvez également masquer et afficher cette corbeille via Fenêtre/Corbeille des palettes.

Par défaut, trois palettes sont ancrées dans cette corbeille : Utilisation, Styles et effets, et Calques.

Une palette de la corbeille peut devenir une palette flottante. Pour ce faire, cliquez sur le titre de la palette et, sans relâcher le bouton de la souris, faites glisser la palette vers un autre emplacement de l'interface du programme. Une fois l'emplacement trouvé, relâchez le bouton de la souris. La Figure 2.3 montre la palette flottante Calques *extraite* de la Corbeille de palette.

Figure 2.3 :
Une palette
flottante.

Ouvrir la boîte à outils

La boîte à outils se trouve par défaut sur le bord gauche de l'interface, sous la forme d'une étroite colonne d'outils. Si vous cliquez sur la ligne pointillée située en haut de la boîte à outils et que vous la faites glisser vers la droite, la palette se désolidarise de l'interface. Dès que vous relâchez le bouton de la souris, la boîte à outils devient plus compacte, affichant les outils sur deux colonnes. Pour repositionner la boîte à outils sur le bord gauche de l'interface, faites-la glisser jusqu'à ce bord. Un cadre noir hachuré indique si la boîte à outils est ou non de nouveau ancrée à l'interface.

Qu'elle soit affichée sur une ou deux colonnes, les outils proposés sont les mêmes. Ses composants se répartissent en deux catégories de base : les outils et les contrôles de la couleur. Les prochains chapitres expliquent en détail l'utilisation de ces éléments ; en voici une rapide présentation :

✔ Les cinq parties de la boîte à outils, divisées par un petit séparateur, sont des outils au sens propre du terme. Ils permettent d'effectuer des modifications sur les images. Pour les activer, il suffit de cliquer dessus ou d'appuyer sur la lettre du clavier correspondant à l'outil à sélectionner.

✔ Le petit triangle en bas à droite de certaines icônes indique la présence d'autres options. Maintenez le bouton de la souris enfoncé pour accéder à ces options cachées, assimilées à des sous-outils. Faites glisser le pointeur dans ce menu local et cliquez sur l'outil à utiliser.

✔ Vous pouvez également cliquer successivement sur une même icône en maintenant la touche Alt enfoncée pour sélectionner un de ses sous-outils.

✔ La partie inférieure de la boîte à outils contient deux nuanciers qui permettent de choisir deux couleurs de travail.

✔ Vous ne pouvez utiliser un outil que si une image est ouverte. Vous ne savez pas ouvrir une image ? Alors, rendez-vous au Chapitre 3.

✔ Vous pouvez activer des outils et contrôler deux couleurs avec le clavier. Par exemple, pour sélectionner l'outil Pinceau, appuyez sur la touche B. Pour sélectionner l'outil Forme impressionniste, qui se trouve au même endroit, appuyez sur Maj+B.

Les raccourcis ne sont pas faciles à mémoriser car ils reprennent la première lettre du nom de l'outil exprimé en anglais. Ainsi, l'outil Gomme (*Eraser*). Appuyer sur la touche G activera le Dégradé (*Gradient*). Vous comprenez alors que pour activer la gomme, vous devez appuyer sur la touche E (pas évident !). Ceux qui sont familiarisés avec l'anglais ou qui ont une bonne mémoire se souviendront assez facilement du nom des touches. En revanche, les autres gagneront du temps en cliquant sur l'outil plutôt que de rechercher la touche appropriée.

✔ Si appuyer sur la touche Maj pour changer d'outil vous agace, choisissez Édition/Préférences/Général et décochez la case Touche Maj pour changer d'outil. Vous changez alors d'outils en appuyant répétitivement sur la même lettre.

> ✔ Si vous oubliez la touche de raccourci d'un outil, placez le
> pointeur sur son icône. Une info-bulle indique la touche à
> utiliser. En cas de doute sur la fonction de l'outil, cliquez sur son
> nom qui, en fait, est un lien hypertexte ouvrant l'aide en ligne
> Adobe sur la rubrique traitant de l'utilisation de l'outil sélec-
> tionné.

La Corbeille des photos

Vos prouesses infographiques ne manqueront pas de s'améliorer. Un
jour, vous serez surpris de travailler avec plusieurs images ouvertes
simultanément. Elements 4.0 dispose d'un nouvel outil de gestion des
images : la Corbeille des photos. Elle se situe tout au long de la partie
inférieure de l'interface, comme vous pouvez le voir sur la Figure 2.1.
Lorsqu'une image est ouverte dans Elements, sa vignette s'affiche dans
la Corbeille des photos. Et quand vous en ouvrez d'autres, leurs
vignettes s'ajoutent à celles déjà présentes. Pour afficher une image
afin de la modifier, cliquez sur sa vignette dans la Corbeille des
photos. L'image correspondante apparaît au premier plan. Pour passer
d'une image à l'autre, il est également possible de cliquer sur l'une des
flèches situées à gauche de l'indicateur du nombre d'images présentes
dans la corbeille, dans le coin inférieur droit de l'interface, à côté du
nom Corbeille des photos. Vous pouvez masquer la corbeille soit en
cliquant sur le triangle dirigé vers le bas situé au centre de sa ligne
horizontale, soit en choisissant Fenêtre/Corbeille des photos. Même
masquée, les boutons de défilement des photos en bas de la corbeille
restent accessibles, permettant de passer en revue les images
ouvertes et choisir celle sur laquelle vous désirez travailler.

La fenêtre est redimensionnable en plaçant le pointeur de la souris sur
la barre horizontale verticale qui sépare la corbeille de la zone de
travail. Cliquez et, sans relâcher le bouton de la souris, tirez cette
barre vers le haut pour agrandir l'espace occupé par la corbeille, ou
vers le bas pour le réduire. Pour masquer rapidement la corbeille,
cliquez sur la flèche située à gauche de son nom dans le coin inférieur
gauche de la fenêtre. Pour l'afficher de nouveau, cliquez sur cette
même flèche.

Chapitre 3

"Ouvrez-nous !" qu'ils disaient !

- -

Dans ce chapitre :

▶ Ouvrir et fermer des images.

▶ Utiliser l'Explorateur de fichiers.

▶ Créer une nouvelle image.

▶ Maîtriser les fenêtres de vos images.

▶ Se déplacer dans une image.

▶ Grossir et maigrir à volonté (le régime du zoom).

▶ Travail de précision sur les images.

- -

C e chapitre explique comment ouvrir des images existantes et comment en créer de nouvelles. Ensuite, nous vous distillerons un cours de navigation au sein des diverses images ouvertes dans Photoshop Elements.

Ne restez pas à rien faire, ouvrez quelque chose !

L'interface de Photoshop Elements propose une bonne dizaine de méthodes d'ouverture d'un fichier... moins une ! L'Explorateur de fichiers, qui avait fait une unique apparition dans la version 3.0, a disparu, tout comme il a disparu dans la dernière version de Photoshop où il est remplacé par un programme autonome appelé Bridge. Pas de Bridge toutefois dans Photoshop Elements 4, où les fonctions de l'Explorateur de fichiers ont migré vers d'autres emplacements dans le logiciel.

Ouvrir un fichier d'image

Nous avons vu au Chapitre 1 l'option Connexion à l'appareil photo ou scanner, visible dans l'écran de bienvenue, de même que la nouvelle option Image à partir de la vidéo. Ces mêmes options sont accessibles dans le sous-menu Fichier/Importation ou en cliquant sur le bouton Importer dans la barre de raccourcis.

La Figure 3.1 montre qu'un bouton Ouvrir bien pratique est également disponible dans la barre de raccourcis ; c'est la deuxième icône à partir de la gauche. Néanmoins, si vous préférez manœuvrer par le biais de menus, choisissez Fichier/Ouvrir. Pour ouvrir un fichier à l'aide d'un raccourci clavier, cliquez sur Ctrl+O. La boîte de dialogue Ouvrir apparaît comme à la Figure 3.2.

Figure 3.1 :
Maniaque de
la souris, la
barre de
raccourcis
est faite pour
vous !

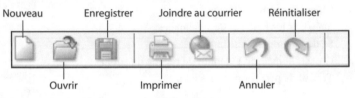

Trouver un fichier via la boîte de dialogue Ouvrir ressemble beaucoup à la navigation avec l'Explorateur Windows. Il suffit de parcourir les disques durs et les dossiers jusqu'à trouver le dossier contenant l'image désirée. Si vous n'êtes pas sûr que c'est la bonne, sélectionnez-la en cliquant dessus : un petit aperçu de l'image s'affichera en bas de la boîte de dialogue. Lorsque vous l'avez trouvée, double-cliquez dessus, ou cliquez dessus et appuyez sur Entrée, ou encore, cliquez dessus puis sur le bouton Ouvrir.

Si vous avez ouvert récemment une image, vous la retrouverez dans le sous-menu Fichier/Ouvrir un fichier récemment modifié. Vous pouvez régler le nombre de fichiers affichés dans ce sous-menu, via le panneau Enregistrement des fichiers des préférences d'Elements.

Création d'une nouvelle image

Pour créer une nouvelle image au lieu d'en ouvrir une, passez par l'écran de bienvenue à l'ouverture de Photoshop Elements. Vous pouvez utiliser la fonction Partir de zéro de l'écran de bienvenue (voir

Figure 3.2 :
Cette boîte
de dialogue
permet de
localiser et
d'ouvrir des
images
présentes sur
vos divers
lecteurs.

le Chapitre 1), cliquer Fichier/Nouveau/Fichier vide, ou appuyer sur
Ctrl+N.

Dans la boîte de dialogue Nouveau, vous pouvez : nommer votre
fichier ; spécifier la largeur, la hauteur et la résolution (voir le Chapitre 4) ; définir le mode de couleurs (voir le Chapitre 5) ; et déterminer
si le fichier sera rempli avec du blanc ou avec la couleur d'arrière-
plan actuelle ou s'il sera transparent. Il existe une possibilité bien
pratique dans Elements pour régler les dimensions et la résolution
d'un fichier : le menu Paramètre prédéfini. Vous avez le choix entre
plusieurs tailles standard pour l'impression, le Web ou le travail sur la
vidéo numérique.

Comprendre la fenêtre de l'image

Une fois que vous avez ouvert une image, Elements l'affiche dans une
fenêtre placée dans l'interface générale du programme. Cette dernière
affiche de nouvelles informations, comme le montre la Figure 3.3.

Barre de titre   Zone de travail   Barre de défilement

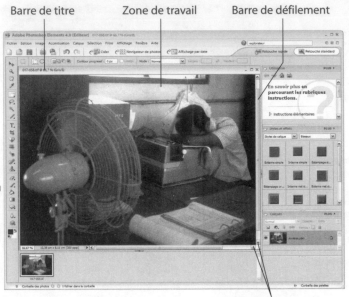

Figure 3.3 :
Une image
affichée dans
sa propre
fenêtre
modifie
quelque peu
l'interface.

Flèche de défilement

En voici un bref aperçu :

✔ La barre de titre de la fenêtre de l'image indique le nom du
fichier, son format (voir le Chapitre 7), son facteur d'agrandissement (ce facteur est 100 % par défaut) et l'espace colorimétrique
utilisé (par exemple RVB ou Gris). Ces éléments sont encore
incompréhensibles pour la majorité d'entre vous, mais la lecture
de cet ouvrage va vite gommer ces lacunes.

✔ Pour fermer une image, choisissez Fichier/Fermer ou appuyez
sur Ctrl+W. Quand vous fermez une image, Elements propose
d'enregistrer les dernières modifications que vous y avez
apportées. Cette procédure est expliquée au Chapitre 7.

✔ Pour modifier la taille de la fenêtre de l'image, placez le pointeur
dans son coin inférieur droit (boîte de redimensionnement).
Quand il prend la forme d'une double flèche, maintenez le
bouton de la souris enfoncé et faites glisser le pointeur vers
l'extérieur pour agrandir la fenêtre, ou vers l'intérieur pour la
réduire. L'image reste intacte, seule la fenêtre est
redimensionnée.

✔ Les barres de défilement permettent de naviguer dans une image dont la fenêtre est trop petite pour l'afficher en intégralité, ou si vous avez effectué un zoom avant pour travailler sur des détails. Agissez sur les curseurs ou les flèches de défilement pour afficher les parties masquées de l'image.

Si vous cliquez sur une flèche de défilement, vous accédez à la partie de l'image masquée, dans la direction indiquée par la flèche. Par exemple, si vous cliquez sur la flèche dirigée vers la droite, vous affichez la partie droite de l'image. Lorsque vous cliquez sur une partie vide d'une barre de défilement, vous effectuez un déplacement très rapide dans l'image.

Naviguer dans une image avec les barres de défilement est la technique la moins efficace. Vous en découvrirez d'autres dans la prochaine section.

✔ La zone entourée par la barre de titre et les barres de défilement est la zone de travail. C'est ici que vous modifiez vos images.

Vous pouvez ouvrir autant d'images que le permet la mémoire de votre ordinateur et la taille de votre écran. En revanche, une seule image est active à la fois. Pour activer une image, cliquez dessus ou choisissez son nom en bas du menu Fenêtre.

Les commandes du sous-menu Fenêtre/Images permettent de gérer plusieurs fenêtres d'images ouvertes simultanément. La meilleure d'entre elles est l'option Juxtaposer. Vous pouvez également l'exécuter en cliquant sur le bouton Juxtaposition automatique des fenêtres, à l'extrême droite de la barre de menus. Cela permet de redimensionner automatiquement les fenêtres de plusieurs images pour les afficher simultanément. L'espace de travail est alors rempli de fenêtres d'images.

L'écran, votre toile numérique

La boîte à outils de Photoshop Elements comporte deux outils de déplacement respectivement nommés Main et Zoom. Le premier translate le contenu de l'image dans sa propre fenêtre ; le second permet d'agrandir ou de réduire une partie de l'image. Dans les deux cas, vous ne modifiez pas "physiquement" l'image, mais simplement son affichage à l'écran. Certaines modifications sont plus faciles à réaliser lorsque vous avez une vue rapprochée d'une partie de l'image.

Outre ces deux outils, Photoshop Elements met à votre disposition une palette très utile : Navigateur. Elle permet de zoomer sur l'image et de s'y déplacer. Dès que vous serez familiarisé avec cette palette, parions que vous n'utiliserez plus les outils Main et Zoom.

Utilisation de l'outil Main

Si vous connaissez bien les programmes conçus pour Windows, vous savez que les barres de défilement sont relativement peu utilisées. Donc, nous vous en conjurons, ne les touchez pas. Choisissez plutôt l'outil Main ou la palette Navigateur.

L'image de gauche sur la Figure 3.4 montre une fillette assise sur une balancelle parlant visiblement à quelqu'un. Le problème est que cette image est plus grande que ce que peut en afficher la fenêtre. Impossible alors de savoir à qui cette fillette s'adresse.

Pour voir les éléments de cette image, masqués à cause d'une fenêtre trop étroite, activez l'outil Main en cliquant dessus. Placez le pointeur de la souris sur l'image. Il prend la forme d'une main. Maintenez le bouton gauche de la souris enfoncé et faites glisser le pointeur (la main) vers la gauche. Comme l'illustre la seconde image de la Figure 3.4, vous découvrez à qui s'adresse la fillette.

Figure 3.4 :
Le cliquer-glisser avec l'outil Main révèle qu'un dialogue est plus intéressant qu'un monologue.

Faire glisser la main sur une image revient à tourner la tête pour découvrir les éléments de votre environnement qui se trouvent à votre gauche ou à votre droite, mais qui n'entrent pas dans votre champ de vision. Comme le déplacement peut également s'effectuer verticalement, cela revient aussi à lever et baisser la tête pour mieux voir les objets placés plus haut ou plus bas.

Utilisation des raccourcis clavier

Comme dans la plupart des programmes, les touches du clavier permettent de se déplacer dans un document. On parle alors de *raccourcis clavier*. Ainsi, pour faire défiler le contenu d'une image de la valeur d'un écran vers le haut ou le bas, appuyez sur la touche Page Haut ou Page Bas. Pour que le déplacement soit moins important, appuyez sur Maj+PageHaut et Maj+PageBas. Appuyez sur la touche Origine pour afficher le coin supérieur gauche de l'image, et appuyez sur Fin pour afficher le coin inférieur droit.

Pour être complet, Photoshop Elements offre des raccourcis clavier afin de se déplacer vers la droite et la gauche de la fenêtre de l'image. Appuyez sur Ctrl+PageHaut ou Ctrl+PageBas pour vous déplacer d'un écran. Appuyez sur Ctrl+Maj+PageHaut ou Ctrl+Maj+PageBas pour vous déplacer moins radicalement dans ces deux directions.

Zoomer sur votre travail

Quand vous ouvrez une image, Photoshop Elements l'affiche dans la totalité de la fenêtre. Selon la résolution d'affichage de votre moniteur, certains détails peuvent vous échapper. Pour approfondir l'affichage d'une image, vous devez vous en approcher. Inutile de plaquer votre visage sur l'écran ! Vous risquez de vous abîmer les yeux sans mieux voir pour autant ! Lisez plutôt ce qui suit.

Elements permet de zoomer sur votre travail de différentes manières.

Le zoom avant effectué sur une image n'en modifie pas la taille. Il s'agit simplement d'une modification de son affichage pour mieux travailler dessus. L'image ne pèse pas plus lourd. C'est comme si vous la placiez sous un microscope. Ses différentes parties sont grossies, mais la taille d'origine ne subit aucune altération.

L'outil Zoom

L'outil Zoom va changer votre vie naissante de retoucheur d'images numériques. Dès que vous cliquez sur l'image, elle grossit. La conséquence est que vous voyez davantage de détails d'une portion de l'image au détriment de l'affichage de l'image entière. Mais l'outil Zoom est fait pour cela : isoler une partie de l'image pour mieux travailler sur ses détails. Voici comment l'utiliser :

1. **Sélectionnez l'outil Zoom.**

Il suffit de cliquer sur son icône dans la boîte à outils. Une autre méthode consiste à appuyer sur la touche Z.

2. Cliquez sur une partie de l'image.

Elements grossit l'image en appliquant le facteur de zoom prédéfini, comme le montre la Figure 3.5. Le programme centre l'image par rapport au point où vous avez cliqué, comme en témoigne la seconde image de la Figure 3.5. Vous constatez que l'on a cliqué sur le nez de la petite fille.

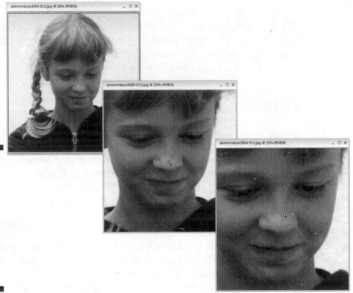

Figure 3.5 : L'outil Zoom opère un grossissement de l'image en appliquant les facteurs de zoom prédéfinis.

3. Recommencez.

Pour grossir davantage l'image, cliquez de nouveau dans sa fenêtre avec l'outil Zoom.

Voici d'autres considérations qui permettront de mieux utiliser l'outil Zoom :

✔ Pour effectuer un zoom arrière, vous devez changer l'état de l'outil Zoom. Il suffit pour cela de maintenir enfoncée la touche Alt tout en cliquant à l'aide de l'outil Zoom. Au lieu d'effectuer un zoom avant, il réalise un zoom arrière, réduisant ainsi l'affichage de l'image dans sa fenêtre.

✔ Quand vous zoomez, Elements affiche le facteur dans la barre de titre de l'image. Quand il est de 100 %, vous voyez la totalité des pixels de la portion de l'image affichée. En fonction de la résolution d'affichage de votre moniteur et de la taille de l'image, 100 % permet de voir la totalité de l'image et pas seulement une partie. Nous pouvons dire qu'un facteur de zoom de 100 % affiche la taille réelle de l'image. Vous en saurez davantage sur les pixels au Chapitre 4.

N'oubliez jamais qu'il existe une différence énorme entre la taille d'affichage d'une image et sa taille d'impression. Un affichage de 100 %, même s'il permet de voir la totalité de l'image sur votre écran, ne donnera pas du tout une taille identique une fois l'image imprimée sur papier. Elle pourra être plus grande ou plus petite. La commande Taille d'impression, expliquée dans la prochaine section, permet d'avoir une idée précise sur ce que sera la taille d'impression de l'image affichée.

✔ Pour ne grossir qu'une partie de l'image, formez avec l'outil Zoom un cadre de sélection entourant la zone à grossir. Des pointillés délimitent la zone qui sera agrandie. Celle-ci occupe ensuite la totalité de la fenêtre de l'image.

✔ Pour utiliser momentanément l'outil Zoom alors qu'un autre outil est sélectionné, appuyez sur Ctrl+Barre espace. Pour effectuer un zoom arrière sans changer d'outil, appuyez sur Ctrl+Alt+Barre espace et cliquez sur l'image. Quand vous relâchez les touches ainsi appuyées, vous retrouvez immédiatement l'usage de l'outil sélectionné avant l'utilisation momentanée de l'outil Zoom.

✔ Il est possible d'effectuer rapidement un zoom avant en appuyant sur Ctrl+"+" et un zoom arrière avec Ctrl+"-". Ces raccourcis fonctionnent même si l'outil Zoom n'est pas sélectionné.

✔ Pour afficher instantanément une image à 100%, double-cliquez sur l'outil Zoom, dans la boîte à outils.

Les commandes d'affichage

Le menu Affichage contient des commandes qui modifient l'agrandissement de l'image dans sa fenêtre. Les deux premières commandes du menu sont Zoom avant et Zoom arrière. Elles n'apportent rien de plus que l'outil Zoom. En revanche, vous trouverez un intérêt certain dans les autres commandes :

✔ Choisissez Affichage/Taille écran ou appuyez sur Ctrl+0 (zéro du pavé numérique) pour que l'image s'affiche intégralement dans sa fenêtre.

✔ Choisissez Affichage/Taille réelle des pixels ou appuyez sur Ctrl+Alt+0 (zéro du pavé numérique) afin de revenir à un facteur de zoom de 100 %. Ce mode d'affichage utilise un pixel de votre moniteur pour afficher un pixel de l'image. Par conséquent, c'est le mode d'affichage le plus précis.

✔ Vous pouvez appliquer l'affichage en mode écran en double-cliquant sur l'outil Main. Si vous double-cliquez sur l'outil Zoom, vous appliquez le mode d'affichage Taille réelle des pixels.

✔ Choisissez Affichage/Taille d'impression pour afficher la taille de l'image telle qu'elle sera imprimée. Cet affichage est approximatif.

✔ Quand vous sélectionnez les outils Main ou Zoom, cliquez directement sur les boutons Taille réelle des pixels, Taille écran et Taille d'impression, de la barre d'options.

✔ Choisissez Affichage/Nouvelle fenêtre pour créer un second affichage de la même image. Cela ouvre une nouvelle fenêtre d'image. Attention, cette commande ne crée pas un nouveau fichier. Ne la confondez pas avec la commande Dupliquer l'image qui crée un autre fichier de la même image. Ici, vous obtenez une copie conforme à des fins d'édition et de comparaison. Vous effectuez vos modifications sur une image agrandie tout en voyant le résultat sur une image en taille réelle sans être obligé d'effectuer constamment des zooms avant et arrière.

La boîte d'agrandissement

Utiliser l'outil Zoom et les commandes du menu Affichage est parfait si vous souhaitez appliquer un facteur de zoom prédéfini, mais qu'en est-il lorsqu'il doit être personnalisé ? Sur la version précédente d'Elements, les utilisateurs d'un Mac avaient une réponse toute trouvée sous la forme d'une zone d'agrandissement située dans le coin inférieur gauche de la fenêtre de l'image. Espérons qu'elle figurera encore dans la version 4.0, lorsque Adobe aura décidé de la sortir.

Pour saisir directement un facteur d'agrandissement, double-cliquez dans la boîte affichant un pourcentage. Une fois le facteur de zoom saisi (qu'il soit inférieur ou supérieur à 100), appuyez sur la touche Return. Pour tester plusieurs pourcentages d'agrandissement/ réduction, saisissez la valeur et appuyez sur Maj+Return. Vous constatez alors que la valeur saisie reste sélectionnée. Si le résultat ne

vous convient pas, saisissez une nouvelle valeur et appuyez de
nouveau sur Maj+Return. Dès que le facteur de zoom vous satisfait,
appuyez sur Return pour le valider.

Naviguer avec une palette

La palette Navigateur de Photoshop Elements est le meilleur outil de
déplacement dans un document car elle cumule les fonctions des
outils Zoom et Main. Il suffit de regarder la Figure 3.6 pour s'en
convaincre. Généralement, la palette Navigateur est l'avant-dernier
onglet de la barre des palettes située à droite de la barre de raccourcis. Cliquez dessus pour l'activer ou choisissez Fenêtre/Navigateur.
Vous pouvez l'agrandir ou la réduire en plaçant le pointeur de la souris
dans la boîte de redimensionnement. Quand il prend la forme d'une
double flèche diagonale, maintenez le bouton de la souris enfoncé et
faites glisser le pointeur vers l'extérieur pour agrandir la palette, ou
vers l'intérieur pour en réduire la taille.

Curseur de zoom

Zone d'agrandissement

Zoom arrière   Zoom avant

Figure 3.6 :
La palette
Navigateur
cumule les
fonctions des
outils Zoom
et Main.

Zone d'aperçu

Boîte d'agrandissement du navigateur

La palette Navigateur est indispensable quand vous travaillez sur une
grande image. Voici comment l'utiliser à bon escient :

✔ Au centre de la palette s'affiche une miniature de l'image sur
laquelle vous travaillez, comme le montre la Figure 3.6.

La palette affiche toute l'image même si vous ne la voyez pas entièrement dans la fenêtre de l'image elle-même.

✔ Un cadre rouge entoure une partie de la miniature ? C'est la zone d'aperçu. Ce qu'elle contient est affiché dans la fenêtre de l'image. Quand vous déplacez ce cadre rouge, vous modifiez simultanément ce qui est affiché dans la fenêtre de l'image. Dans la palette Navigateur, vous pouvez directement cliquer sur la partie de l'image à afficher dans la fenêtre de l'image. Le cadre d'aperçu s'y place immédiatement, et la zone concernée apparaît dans la fenêtre de l'image.

✔ Lorsque le pointeur de la souris se trouve sur la miniature, il prend la forme d'une main. Appuyez sur la touche Ctrl pour qu'il prenne la forme de l'outil Zoom (c'est-à-dire une loupe). Cliquez sur la miniature pour effectuer un zoom avant.

✔ La palette contient également une boîte d'agrandissement légendée sur la Figure 3.6. Elle fonctionne comme celle de la barre d'état de la fenêtre principale de Photoshop Elements. Il vous suffit d'y saisir la valeur du zoom et d'appuyer sur la touche Entrée.

✔ Pour appliquer les facteurs d'agrandissement et de réduction prédéfinis de Photoshop Elements, cliquez sur les boutons Zoom arrière et Zoom avant, légendés sur la Figure 3.6.

✔ Vous pouvez réaliser des zooms ultra précis en agissant sur le curseur de la palette Navigateur. Faites-le glisser vers la droite pour agrandir l'image et vers la gauche pour la réduire.

Si vous avez des difficultés pour voir le cadre délimitant la zone d'aperçu, cliquez sur le menu Plus et choisissez Options de palette. Dans la liste Couleur de la boîte de dialogue du même nom, choisissez une autre teinte prédéfinie. Ou cliquez sur la nuance pour ouvrir le Sélecteur de couleurs, où vous pourrez choisir exactement la teinte désirée. Pour plus d'informations sur le Sélecteur de couleurs, reportez-vous au Chapitre 5.

Des outils d'une précision diabolique

Comme le montre la Figure 3.7, une *grille* est un quadrillage qui permet d'aligner précisément des objets. Par exemple, sur cette figure, le texte a été aligné verticalement et horizontalement.

Règles   Grille

Figure 3.7 :
Notre ami le
tigre n'est
pas en cage
mais
simplement
couvert par
la grille.

Outre les grilles, Photoshop Elements affiche des règles. Elles se
trouvent dans la partie supérieure et gauche de la fenêtre de l'image.
Le couple grille-règles est indispensable à la composition d'images
précises. Cette précision est assistée par une palette indispensable,
j'ai nommé : la palette Infos.

Les règles

Pour afficher les règles, cliquez sur le bouton Règle de la barre de
raccourcis. Cette icône ressemble à... une règle. Ça tombe bien ! Vous
pouvez également choisir Affichage/Règles. Pour les masquer, cliquez
de nouveau sur le bouton Règles ou choisissez Affichage/Règles. Une
dernière méthode consiste à appuyer sur Ctrl+R aussi bien pour les
afficher que pour les masquer.

L'unité de mesure par défaut des règles est le centimètre. Pour utiliser
une autre unité, double-cliquez sur la règle ou choisissez Édition/
Préférences/Unités et règles. Dans la section Unités de la boîte de
dialogue Préférences, sélectionnez une nouvelle unité de mesure dans
la liste Règles. Une méthode bien plus rapide consiste à cliquer sur la
règle avec le bouton droit de la souris. Dans le menu contextuel,
sélectionnez l'unité de mesure à utiliser. Facile !

La grille

Les lignes de la grille sont réparties à intervalle régulier. Cet intervalle est prédéfini. Bien que vous ne puissiez pas déplacer les lignes de la grille, vous pouvez les afficher ou non, modifier leur espacement et leur couleur.

Pour activer la grille, choisissez Affichage/Grille. Pour modifier l'espacement des lignes de la grille, choisissez Édition/Préférences/ Grille. Elements affiche la boîte de dialogue Préférences. Dans le champ Pas, spécifiez l'espacement des lignes. L'unité de mesure utilisée est celle définie par défaut, en l'occurrence le centimètre. Par exemple, si vous saisissez **5**, chaque ligne sera espacée des autres de 5 centimètres. Ensuite, dans le champ Subdivisions, indiquez en combien de parties doit être divisé l'espace séparant deux lignes. Par exemple, si vous saisissez **2**, chaque ligne espacée de 5 cm sera subdivisée tous les 2,5 cm. La subdivision permet d'augmenter la précision du placement des objets sur une image. Attention car, plus la subdivision est importante, moins l'image est visible. Enfin, en fonction des couleurs de votre image, la grille est plus ou moins visible. Pour modifier la couleur de la grille, soit vous sélectionnez une couleur prédéfinie dans la liste Couleur, soit vous cliquez sur Autre, soit vous cliquez sur le carré de couleur. Dans ces deux derniers cas, vous accédez à la boîte de dialogue Sélecteur de couleurs, vaste nuancier qui met à votre disposition un maximum de 16 millions de couleurs.

Les lignes de la grille ont des pouvoirs magnétiques que vous pouvez activer ou désactiver. Le Magnétisme signifie que, dès qu'un objet se trouve à proximité d'une ligne, il vient s'y plaquer sans autre intervention de votre part. Vous obtenez alors un alignement très précis. Pour activer ou désactiver cette fonction, choisissez Affichage/Magnétisme de la grille. Une coche placée à gauche de la commande indique qu'elle est active. Sinon, elle est inactive.

Les informations

La palette Infos (Fenêtre/Infos) est d'une aide précieuse quand vous désirez connaître des valeurs exactes relatives à votre image. Par défaut, la palette Infos est divisée en quatre parties : les deux sections supérieures donnent les valeurs exactes de la couleur du pixel sur lequel se trouve le pointeur de la souris. La section inférieure gauche indique la position exacte du pointeur et la section inférieure droite affiche les dimensions d'une sélection active.

Vous pouvez modifier les unités de mesure de deux manières. Cliquez sur la petite pipette de la section supérieure gauche. Dans le menu local, choisissez le type de valeurs de couleur à afficher. Le mode colorimétrique par défaut est celui de l'image ouverte. Cliquez sur la croix de la section inférieure gauche pour choisir l'unité de mesure des axes x et y. Une autre méthode consiste à utiliser le menu local de la palette Infos en cliquant sur la flèche Plus située dans le coin supérieur droit. Choisissez-y Options de palette.

La palette Infos communique des informations relatives à l'outil utilisé. Si votre moniteur est suffisamment grand – ou si vous avez le privilège de travailler avec deux écrans –, nous vous recommandons de garder cette palette constamment ouverte. Dans notre société où l'information prédomine, afficher cette palette est un réflexe conditionné.

Chapitre 4

Pixels : c'est trop bien d'être un carré

C e chapitre explique tout ce qu'il faut savoir pour travailler convenablement avec des pixels. Un des problèmes fréquemment rencontrés par les artistes graphiques en herbe est l'incidence des pixels sur la qualité des images, la taille d'impression, la taille écran, et l'espace qu'ils occupent sur le disque, c'est-à-dire le poids ou la taille de l'image. (Oui ! Nous savons ! Le terme "taille" est employé à toutes les sauces en informatique, mais il va falloir vous y faire très vite car l'infographie est un domaine particulièrement friand en la matière.) Vous verrez également comment agrandir et réduire la taille écran de votre espace de travail, communément nommé "la *toile*".

Bienvenue à Pixelville

Imaginez que vous soyez victime d'une expérience scientifique terrifiante à l'issue de laquelle vous ne mesurez plus qu'un millimètre de haut (comme dans le film *L'homme qui rétrécit* de l'excellent Jack Arnold). Une fois remis de ce traumatisme bien normal, vous faites connaissance avec votre environnement. C'est une incroyable découverte : vous êtes assis sur un carré bleu. Ce carré est en fait une dalle de carrelage. Vous remarquez qu'au-delà de votre dalle, il y en a huit autres. Un à droite, un à gauche, un devant, un derrière, et les quatre autres aux coins. En d'autres termes, les carreaux sont parfaitement alignés sur une grille, comme le carrelage de votre cuisine. Mais, en y regardant de plus près, vous observez que chaque carreau bleu a une teinte légèrement différente des autres. C'est toujours du bleu mais pas tout à fait le même d'un carreau à l'autre.

Au bout de quelques minutes, l'expérience scientifique prend fin et vous reprenez progressivement votre taille normale. Dans un premier temps, vous mesurez 5 cm. Vous constatez alors que vous êtes dans un vaste auditorium carrelé de toutes parts. Les couleurs vont progressivement du bleu au vert, au rouge et au jaune. Votre croissance se poursuit : 10 cm, 20, 50, et un mètre. Les carreaux commencent à se mélanger dans la mesure où, si vous grandissez, eux deviennent de plus en plus petits. Ce mélange produit un motif. 2 mètres, puis 5, puis 10. Vous êtes comme *Alice au pays des merveilles*. Vous faites maintenant huit fois votre taille normale.

Quand vous êtes aussi grand qu'un immeuble de cinquante étages dont vous avez royalement détruit le toit, vous constatez en regardant vos pieds que vous n'êtes pas sur un carrelage de cuisine, mais sur une image, riche de détails et de couleurs, impossibles à distinguer quand on est un être humain de petite taille. Les grands carreaux apparaissent comme des points juxtaposés pour donner l'illusion d'un mélange de couleurs sans aucun raccord visible. C'est la magie de la petitesse et des limites de la résolution de l'œil humain. Plus les points juxtaposés sont petits, plus ils produisent l'impression de continuité des couleurs. C'est ainsi qu'il est possible de représenter tous les tons d'une photographie sur un ordinateur.

Quel rapprochement faire entre cette expérience scientifique et le travail dans Photoshop Elements ? Eh bien, il est énorme ! Comme les motifs de cet auditorium, vos images dans Photoshop Elements sont constituées d'une grille de carrés colorés. Ici, les carrés sont appelés des *pixels*.

Pixels de l'écran et pixels de l'image

Comme le carrelage de la petite histoire précédente, chaque pixel d'une image numérique est parfaitement carré, arrangé sur une grille, et uniformément coloré. Vous comprenez alors que chaque pixel ne représente qu'une seule couleur. Regroupez ces pixels et votre cerveau reconstitue instantanément une photo.

L'affichage de votre moniteur, c'est-à-dire l'écran de votre ordinateur, est également fait de pixels. Comme ceux des images, les pixels de l'écran sont carrés et organisés sur une grille. Par exemple, un moniteur typique mesure au moins 1024 pixels de large et 768 pixels de haut.

Pour comprendre la relation entre les pixels de l'écran et ceux de l'image, ouvrez une image. Ceci fait, double-cliquez sur l'outil Zoom ou choisissez Affichage/Taille réelle des pixels. La boîte de redimensionnement de la barre d'état affiche 100% tout comme la barre de titre de l'image. Cela signifie qu'un pixel de l'image correspond exactement à un pixel de l'écran.

Pour voir les pixels de plus près, saisissez la valeur **200 %** dans la boîte de redimensionnement. Cette fois, les pixels de l'image sont deux fois plus gros que ceux de l'écran. Si vous appliquez un facteur d'agrandissement de 400 %, Elements affiche un total de 16 pixels écran pour chaque pixel de l'image (4 pixels écran de haut par 4 pixels écran de large). La Figure 4.1 montre comment les différents facteurs de zoom affectent l'apparence des pixels de votre image à l'écran.

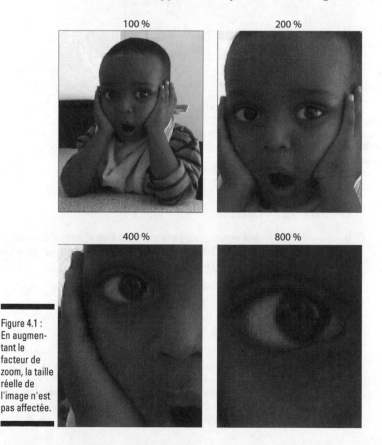

Figure 4.1 : En augmentant le facteur de zoom, la taille réelle de l'image n'est pas affectée.

Taille, résolution de l'image et autres éléments impliquant des pixels

Une image de Photoshop Elements possède trois caractéristiques primaires qui dépendent des pixels : la *taille du fichier*, la *résolution* et les *dimensions physiques*. Vous contrôlez ces attributs dans la boîte de dialogue Taille de l'image, illustrée sur la Figure 4.2. Pour afficher cette boîte de dialogue, choisissez Image/Redimensionner/Taille de l'image.

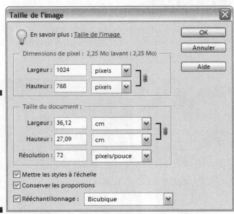

Figure 4.2 : Ici, vous contrôlez la taille du fichier, les dimensions de l'image et la résolution.

Bonne résolution

Bien que la résolution semble une option parmi tant d'autres dans la boîte de dialogue Taille de l'image, c'est la valeur la plus importante pour la qualité de votre image.

La valeur Résolution détermine la précision d'impression des pixels. C'est un peu comme la densité de la population. Prenez Lagos par exemple, une ville nigériane de presque 15 millions d'âmes, avec environ 267 000 habitants au kilomètre carré.

Pour augmenter la densité de la population, vous devez soit augmenter le nombre d'habitants, soit diminuer la superficie de la ville. C'est la même chose avec la résolution. Pour une résolution plus élevée (c'est-à-dire pour avoir plus de pixels par pouce), vous pouvez soit diminuer la taille de document de l'image, soit augmenter les dimensions en pixels en ajoutant des pixels à l'image. Par exemple, les deux images de la Figure 4.3 ont les mêmes dimensions en pixels mais l'image du haut a une taille de document plus petite, ce qui lui donne une résolution deux fois plus importante que l'autre – 180 ppp contre 90 ppp.

Figure 4.3 :
Deux images
en deux
résolutions
différentes.

Modifier les dimensions des pixels

Les deux premières options de la boîte de dialogue Taille de l'image permettent de modifier les dimensions exprimées en pixels. Sauf si vous savez parfaitement ce que vous faites, évitez de toucher à ces deux options.

Diminuer les valeurs de dimension des pixels est risqué car vous supprimez un certain nombre de pixels. Par conséquent, plus vous ôtez de pixels, plus vous enlevez de détails à l'image, comme l'illustre la Figure 4.4. La taille de document des trois images est la même, mais vous voyez nettement que leur qualité varie de l'une à l'autre. La première image contient 64 000 pixels et est imprimée dans une résolution de 140 ppp ; la deuxième contient 16 000 pixels avec une résolution d'impression de 70 ppp ; la troisième contient 4 000 pixels dans une résolution d'impression de 35 ppp. Vous constatez que la précision de l'image va en diminuant. Plus le nombre de pixels diminue, plus il est difficile de distinguer nettement les cheveux, les yeux et les oreilles.

Figure 4.4 :
Trois images
contenant
progressive-
ment de
moins en
moins de
pixels et une
résolution
d'impression
chaque fois
inférieure à
la précé-
dente.

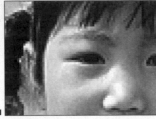

Augmenter les dimensions en pixels n'est pas une très bonne idée dans la mesure où Photoshop Elements est obligé d'ajouter artificielle-ment des pixels, donc des détails. Pour cela, il opère un savant calcul entre les pixels qui se juxtaposent pour en générer de nouveaux. Cette procédure se nomme *interpolation*. Le résultat obtenu est souvent décevant car Photoshop Elements ne peut inventer des détails là où il n'y en a pas. L'image s'estompe, devient floue, avec des zones de couleurs pâles ou pixellisées. La qualité de l'image en souffre.

Si toucher aux options de taille détériore l'image, pourquoi Photoshop Elements propose-t-il ces options ? Bien que nous recommandions de ne pas augmenter la taille des pixels, c'est-à-dire ajouter des pixels à une image, vous pouvez parfois en diminuer les dimensions. Si la taille de votre fichier est très importante, c'est-à-dire que votre image est composée de dizaines de millions de pixels, vous serez parfois amené à en éliminer un certain nombre.

Dans un monde idéal, plus il y a de pixels, plus l'image est détaillée. Mais, si vous la publiez sur Internet, sa taille est un facteur essentiel de temps. Plus l'image met de temps à se télécharger dans le naviga-teur de l'internaute, moins celui-ci aura la patience d'attendre son affichage. En conséquence, on ne prépare pas de la même façon une image destinée à l'impression et une image destinée au Web ou à un envoi par courrier électronique. À cela s'ajoute une constatation incontournable : plus l'image contient de pixels dans une résolution d'impression importante, plus sa taille est grande. En moyenne, une image au format A4 dans une résolution d'impression de 300 ppp "pèse" 40 méga-octets. Dans Photoshop Elements et Photoshop, cela pénalise les petites configurations qui disposent de 64 ou 128 Mo de mémoire. En effet, au fur et à mesure que vous y ajoutez des calques, la taille de l'image, en terme de pixels, devient gigantesque. L'applica-tion du moindre filtre exige plusieurs minutes de calcul. Le travail est alors considérablement ralenti et devient très fastidieux.

Modifier les dimensions physiques de l'image

Les champs Largeur et Hauteur de la zone Taille du document affichent les dimensions d'impression de votre image. Les listes à proximité de ces deux champs permettent de sélectionner l'unité de mesure. Par exemple, si vous sélectionnez picas dans la liste Largeur, Elements convertit la valeur affichée en picas. (Un *pica* est une unité de mesure, datant de nos bonnes vieilles machines à écrire, et est égal à 1/6 de pouce, soit environ 5 mm.) L'option % de ces deux listes permet d'exprimer la taille d'impression en pourcentage des valeurs originales. Si vous saisissez une valeur supérieure à 100, vous augmen-tez la taille d'impression ; si vous saisissez une valeur inférieure à 100, vous la réduisez.

Les bonnes proportions

Les paires de champs Largeur et Hauteur de la boîte de dialogue Taille de l'image listent les dimensions de votre image. Si vous saisissez une autre valeur dans l'un de ces champs et que vous cliquez sur OK, Elements redimensionne l'image en conséquence.

Mais étrangement, quand vous modifiez la valeur de hauteur ou de largeur, les autres changent aussi. Cela tient au fait que la case Conserver les proportions est cochée. Donc, les valeurs sont liées pour ne pas déformer l'image. Ainsi, en modifiant la largeur, la hauteur s'adapte pour conserver l'image dans ses proportions originales. Une image rectangulaire agrandie ou réduite reste rectangulaire. Si cela ne vous convient pas, décochez la case Conserver les proportions. Dès que vous saisissez une valeur dans un champ et que vous la validez en appuyant sur la touche Tab, vous constatez que les valeurs des autres champs ne bougent pas. C'est le résultat obtenu sur la Figure 4.5. Dans la première image, la valeur de la largeur a été réduite, mais la hauteur n'a pas bougé (normal puisque la case Conserver les proportions a été décochée). Dans la seconde image, la valeur de la hauteur a été réduite, laissant intacte la valeur de la largeur.

Pour désélectionner Conserver les proportions, vous devez activer Rééchantillonnage. Comme expliqué dans la section suivante "Utilisation sécurisante de la boîte de dialogue Taille de l'image", lorsque vous changez la largeur ou la hauteur de votre image alors que la case à cocher Rééchantillonnage est sélectionnée, Elements ajoute ou supprime des pixels de l'image. À l'évidence, pour étirer une image comme sur la Figure 4.5, des pixels doivent être ajoutés ou supprimés. Par conséquent, si vous désactivez Conserver les proportions, vous devez valider Rééchantillonnage.

Utilisation sécurisante de la boîte de dialogue Taille de l'image

Comme cela est indiqué dans la section "Taille, résolution de l'image et autres éléments impliquant des pixels", vous disposez de trois attributs d'image – taille, résolution et dimension – suspendus à vos désirs et interférant les uns avec les autres. En fait, ces attributs sont comme les trois points d'un triangle. Modifiez n'importe quel point et les autres se modifient proportionnellement. Si vous réduisez les dimensions en pixels, la taille du document ou la résolution (nombre de points par pouce) doivent aussi diminuer. Pour augmenter la taille de document, vous devez augmenter les dimensions en pixels – ajouter des pixels – ou diminuer la résolution.

Figure 4.5 :
En désac-
tivant l'option
Conserver les
proportions,
l'image est
déformée.

Il y a de quoi s'y perdre dans toutes ces possibilités. Retenez simplement ce que vous pouvez faire avec la boîte de dialogue Taille de
l'image, et surtout les erreurs à éviter. Voici les conseils à garder dans
un petit coin de votre tête :

N'OUBLIEZ PAS

✔ La première question à vous poser lors de l'emploi de la
commande Taille de l'image est : "Dois-je changer le nombre de
pixels dans mon image ?" Si l'image est destinée à l'impression,
la réponse est presque certainement "Non". Dans ce cas, la
première chose à faire est de désélectionner la case à cocher
Rééchantillonnage. La désélection de cette case vous permet
uniquement de changer la taille de document, qui affecte les
dimensions de l'image lorsqu'elle est imprimée. Cependant, tout

en réglant la largeur ou la hauteur, gardez un œil sur la résolution pour être sûr qu'elle ne tombe pas au-dessous d'une valeur acceptable (pour quelques chiffres clés, voir l'encadré "Bon, d'accord, mais quelle résolution dois-je utiliser ?").

✔ Si cependant votre document est destiné au Web, il peut être nécessaire de modifier le nombre de pixels dans l'image. Même un appareil photo numérique à un mégapixel produit des images contenant trop de pixels pour être vues dans leur intégralité sur la plupart des écrans d'ordinateur. Dans ce cas, assurez-vous que Rééchantillonnage est sélectionné. Vous pouvez ignorer totalement la portion Taille du document de la boîte de dialogue Taille de l'image ; lors de la préparation d'images destinées à l'affichage sur écran d'ordinateur, la seule chose qui importe est la taille en pixels.

Voici quelques autres aspects à garder à l'esprit :

✔ Lorsque vous désélectionnez la case à cocher Rééchantillonnage, la boîte de dialogue Taille de l'image change, et les options Largeur et Hauteur dans la portion Dimensions en pixels de la boîte de dialogue deviennent indisponibles. Une icône de lien connecte par ailleurs les cases des options Taille du document, c'est-à-dire Largeur, Hauteur et Résolution, montrant que la modification d'une valeur affectera les deux autres valeurs.

✔ Si vous modifiez trop de paramètres au point d'être totalement perdu dans le redimensionnement, restaurez les valeurs d'origine en appuyant sur la touche Alt. Vous constatez que le bouton Annuler bascule en Réinitialiser. Cliquez dessus sans relâcher la touche Alt bien entendu !

✔ Dans la liste Rééchantillonnage, vous trouverez notamment les options Bicubique plus lisse et Bicubique plus net. Lorsque vous diminuez le nombre de pixels d'une image, vous perdez un peu de netteté. Pour compenser cette dégradation, choisissez le mode de rééchantillonnage Bicubique plus net. En revanche, si vous augmentez le nombre de pixels de l'image, optez pour le mode de rééchantillonnage Bicubique plus lisse.

✔ Pour changer l'unité de mesure par défaut de la boîte de dialogue Taille de l'image, choisissez Édition/Préférences/Unités et règles. Dans la liste Règles, choisissez une nouvelle unité de mesure.

Que fait la commande Taille de la zone de travail ?

Quand vous choisissez Image/Redimensionner/Taille de la zone de travail, vous ouvrez la boîte de dialogue représentée sur la Figure 4.6. Voici ce que vous pouvez en faire :

✔ Saisissez de nouvelles valeurs dans les champs Largeur et Hauteur. Vous pouvez également changer l'unité de mesure en cliquant sur la flèche d'une des listes, comme avec la boîte de dialogue Taille de l'image.

✔ Quand la case Relative est cochée, la Taille de la zone de travail *ajoute* automatiquement, aux dimensions actuelles, les valeurs saisies dans les champs Largeur et Hauteur. Ceci est génial pour ajouter quelques pixels autour d'une image afin de créer un cadre (une bordure). Ainsi, pour ajouter 20 pixels tout autour de l'image, vous saisissez **40** dans les champs Largeur et Hauteur. Relative est une option qui permet aussi de recadrer une image. Par exemple, si vous désirez enlever 20 pixels tout autour d'une photo, saisissez **-40** dans les deux champs Largeur et Hauteur.

✔ La section Position affiche un diagramme. Il permet de définir la direction du redimensionnement. Par défaut, l'image se trouve au centre de ce diagramme. Mais, vous pouvez la déplacer dans n'importe quel autre carré en cliquant dessus.

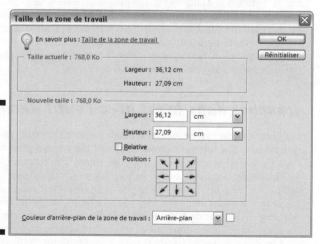

Figure 4.6 : Cette boîte de dialogue permet de changer les dimensions de la page virtuelle de l'image.

> ✔ L'option Couleur d'arrière-plan de la zone de travail permet de spécifier la couleur des pixels ajoutés. Vous avez le choix entre les couleurs de premier plan, d'arrière-plan, le blanc, le noir, le gris, ou autre. Si vous choisissez Autre ou que vous cliquez sur le nuancier situé à droite de la liste, vous ouvrez le Sélecteur de couleurs, lieu de prédilection pour la définition d'une teinte.

> ✔ Si vous réduisez la largeur ou la hauteur et que vous appuyez sur Entrée, Elements demande si vous désirez vraiment rogner l'image (on parle aussi de *recadrer l'image*). Si vous acceptez en cliquant sur Continuer et que le résultat ne vous satisfait pas, cliquez sur le bouton Aller vers l'arrière de la barre de raccourcis ou appuyez sur Ctrl+Z pour restaurer la taille originale du document.

> ✔ Comme avec Taille de l'image, si vous voulez changer l'unité de mesure exploitée par défaut dans la boîte de dialogue Taille de la zone de travail, choisissez Édition/Préférences/Unités et règles, puis sélectionnez une autre option dans la liste déroulante Règles.

Bien dégagé sur les côtés

Bien que vous puissiez utiliser la commande Taille de la zone de travail dans le but de recadrer une image, il y a de bien meilleurs outils pour cela à votre disposition dans Photoshop Elements. Nous savons que la commande Taille de l'image peut transformer une photo de mariage en une minuscule vignette sans enlever le moindre membre de votre famille. Mais supposons que, justement, vous souhaitiez y supprimer tante Henriette, là sur le côté gauche, qui vous a offert un moulin à café alors que vous détestez le café ! Comment la supprimer (virtuellement, entendons-nous bien !) ?

Trancher dans le vif avec l'outil Recadrage

Les photographes en herbe ont tendance à photographier plus large qu'il ne faut. Une fois la photo développée, il n'y a plus grand-chose à faire. Ce qui est en trop est en trop. Que nenni ! Photoshop Elements est là ! Il suffit de numériser ou de télécharger l'image dans votre ordinateur, de l'ouvrir dans Elements et de recadrer l'image pour supprimer tous les éléments superflus. Cette technique se nomme *recadrage*. À l'instar de la commande Taille de la zone de travail, le recadrage modifie les dimensions de pixel et la taille du document sans modifier la résolution de l'image. (Bien évidemment le contenu de votre image subit quelques modifications.)

Dans Elements, sortez vos ciseaux virtuels pour couper tout ce qui est en trop. Ces ciseaux prennent la forme de l'outil Recadrage. Pour l'utiliser, cliquez dessus dans la boîte à outils ou appuyez sur la touche C.

Voici comment fonctionne l'outil Recadrage :

1. **Avec l'outil, tracez un cadre autour de la zone de l'image que vous désirez conserver.**

   Sur la Figure 4.7, il s'agit de la promeneuse et de son chien. Un rectangle de délimitation apparaît autour de la zone à conserver. Vous constatez que tout ce qui se trouve à l'extérieur est plus sombre. Utilisez les paramètres de la barre d'options de l'outil Recadrage pour spécifier la couleur et l'opacité de la zone à supprimer. Rien ne vous empêche de désactiver l'option d'opacité des parties exclues de la sélection. Ce n'est pas grave si la zone de recadrage n'est pas parfaitement bien délimitée. Les bords du cadre peuvent être redimensionnés comme cela est expliqué à l'Étape 2.

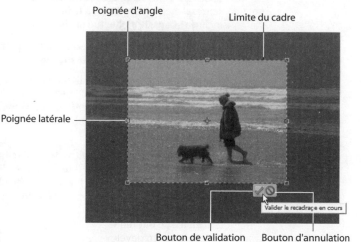

Figure 4.7 :
Le cadre peut être redimensionné et déplacé.

2. **Faites glisser les bords du cadre.**

   Après avoir relâché le bouton de la souris, Elements affiche huit poignées, une dans chaque angle et au milieu de chaque bord du contour (regardez la Figure 4.7). Si le cadre n'est pas à la bonne taille, faites glisser une poignée pour la redimensionner.

Le pointeur de la souris prend la forme d'une flèche à deux pointes dès qu'il se trouve correctement placé sur la poignée. Vous pouvez faire glisser autant de poignées que vous le désirez – mais une à la fois – avant de procéder au recadrage. Si vous maintenez la touche Maj enfoncée tout en faisant glisser la poignée, vous conservez les proportions du cadre. Si vous maintenez la touche Alt enfoncée, le redimensionnement s'opère à partir du centre du cadre.

Si vous avez créé une zone de recadrage et que vous ne parvenez pas à la redimensionner convenablement, cliquez sur le bouton Annuler le recadrage en cours, en bas à droite du cadre. Procédez à un nouveau recadrage. Pour recadrer convenablement des images, consultez la prochaine section "De bonnes nouvelles sur le recadrage".

Si vous placez le pointeur légèrement en dehors du cadre mais à proximité d'une poignée, il prend la forme d'une double flèche incurvée. Tirez pour pivoter le cadre de sélection. Vous pourrez ainsi mettre à l'horizontale une photo qui était mal cadrée. Sachez cependant qu'il existe un outil spécifique pour cela, nommé Redressement. Il est décrit à la fin de ce chapitre. Le cadrage incliné est aussitôt effectué et l'image remise d'aplomb.

3. **Le cadrage défini, double-cliquez dedans ou cliquez sur le bouton de validation, en bas à droite du cadre.**

   Vous pouvez également appuyer sur la touche Entrée, ou cliquer du bouton droit dans le cadre et choisir Recadrer. Elements supprime tous les pixels situés à l'extérieur du cadre. Si vous avez fait pivoter le cadre à l'Étape 2, Elements redresse l'image comme en témoigne la Figure 4.8.

Quand vous pivotez une image par cette méthode, Elements la *rééchantillonne,* c'est-à-dire qu'il réorganise tous les pixels de l'image. Pour obtenir le meilleur résultat, évitez de pivoter l'image plusieurs fois de suite. Quand vous pivotez une image de 90 degrés, Elements n'a pas besoin de la rééchantillonner.

De bonnes nouvelles sur le recadrage

Une application aussi généreuse que Photoshop Elements propose bien d'autres techniques de recadrage.

✔ Après avoir sélectionné l'outil Recadrage, mais avant de tracer le cadre, regardez les paramètres de la barre d'options. Les

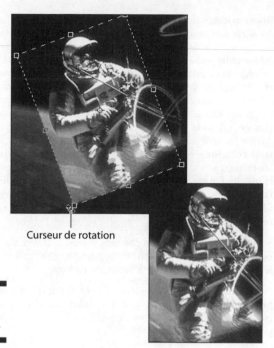

Curseur de rotation

Figure 4.8 :
Recadrez
votre image.

champs Hauteur, Largeur et Résolution permettent de définir un recadrage ultra précis.

✔ Le nouveau paramètre Options des paramètres prédéfinis propose plusieurs types de recadrage standard. Le problème est que les valeurs sont exprimées en pouces, ce qui vous oblige à multiplier les dimensions proposées par 2,54 pour obtenir des centimètres. Si vous choisissez Recadrage 6x4 pp, ces deux valeurs s'affichent respectivement dans les champs Largeur et Hauteur de la barre d'options. Ainsi, lorsque vous faites glisser l'outil Recadrage sur votre image, vous êtes contraint à cette proportion. Pour inverser ces valeurs, cliquez sur les deux flèches situées entre les champs Largeur et Hauteur. Pour annuler l'utilisation des Options des paramètres prédéfinis, cliquez sur le bouton Effacer de la barre d'options.

✔ Dans le menu déroulant Proportions, l'option Utiliser le rapport photo affiche les valeurs en centimètres. Hélas, un seul et unique format est proposé : le classique 13 x 18 bien connu des photographes amateurs.

TRUC

L'option Image de premier plan est très utile. Elle permet de recadrer une image de manière qu'elle soit à la même taille qu'une autre image. Supposons que l'image B doive être à la même taille que l'image A. Commencez par ouvrir les deux images. Assurez-vous que l'image A est l'image de premier plan, en cliquant sur sa barre de titre. Activez l'outil Recadrage et cliquez sur le bouton Image de premier plan dans la barre d'options. Elements charge les paramètres du recadrage de l'image A dans la barre d'options. Sélectionnez l'image B. Faites-y glisser l'outil Recadrage pour définir une zone de sélection ; vous remarquerez que le cadre de sélection conserve toujours les mêmes proportions que l'image A. Quand vous appuyez sur la touche Entrée, Elements redimensionne automatiquement l'image B afin que sa taille corresponde à celle de l'image A. Cliquez sur le bouton Effacer pour sortir de ce mode de recadrage.

- ✔ Si, après avoir cadré, vous changez d'avis, appuyez sur la touche Echap. Le contour disparaît. Vous pouvez également cliquer sur le bouton Annuler, en bas à droite du cadrage.

- ✔ Pour déplacer le cadrage, placez-y le pointeur de la souris. Il prend la forme d'une grosse flèche. Maintenez alors le bouton de la souris enfoncé, puis faites glisser le cadre jusqu'à la nouvelle position.

- ✔ Il est également possible de recadrer l'image après délimitation d'une zone de recadrage en choisissant Image/Recadrer (voir le Chapitre 9). Dans ce cas, une sélection irrégulière est acceptée. Mais, Photoshop Elements ne cadre pas en fonction de cette forme. Tout en s'en rapprochant au plus près, il n'effectue qu'un recadrage rectangulaire. Dommage...

- ✔ Comme nous l'avons déjà mentionné, il est possible de recadrer une image avec la commande Taille de la zone de travail. Envisagez cette méthode pour découper une image en fonction d'un ou plusieurs de ses côtés mais en définissant un nombre précis de pixels. L'option Relative est particulièrement utile dans cette circonstance.

L'outil Emporte-pièce peut recadrer une image en définissant une forme graphique comme un cœur, un papillon, une flèche, j'en passe et des meilleures. Si vous activez son option Recadrage, la découpe va également recadrer l'image, c'est-à-dire en réduire les dimensions physiques. Cet outil est étudié au Chapitre 15.

L'outil Redressement

Outre la tendance à cadrer trop large, que nous avions mentionnée à propos du cadrage, les photographes amateurs ont aussi tendance à produire des images inclinées. Par exemple, à la Figure 4.9, le photographe a respecté la verticalité du personnage... oubliant que la ligne d'horizon doit être horizontale.

Figure 4.9 : Cette photo doit absolument être redressée.

Qu'à cela ne tienne, nous allons corriger cela grâce à un nouvel outil de Photoshop Elements extrêmement commode et facile à utiliser : j'ai nommé l'outil Redressement.

1. **Activez l'outil Redressement, dans la boîte à outils.**

2. **Dans la barre d'options, déroulez le menu Options de zone de travail et sélectionnez Détourer l'arrière-plan.**

   Les deux autres options, Etendre la zone de travail (par défaut) et Recadrer selon la taille d'origine produisent une image penchée sur le côté qu'il faut ensuite recadrer manuellement. L'option que nous préconisons, Détourer l'arrière-plan, se charge de cette opération.

3. **Tirez une droite le long de la ligne d'horizon, comme à la Figure 4.9, puis relâchez le bouton de la souris.**

Après avoir relâché le bouton, Elements rééchantillonne l'image – l'opération peut exiger un peu de temps – puis il affiche la photo redressée, comme à la Figure 4.10.

Figure 4.10 :
La photo est
maintenant à
l'horizontale.

Remarquez la réduction des dimensions, indiquées en bas à gauche : Elements a taillé dans l'image comme si vous aviez recadré un tirage photo avec une règle et un cutter. En réalité, cet outil inscrit un rectangle dans l'image penchée et élimine ce qui dépasse.

Lorsque vous utilisez l'outil avec l'option Etendre la zone de travail ou Recadrer selon la taille d'origine, l'image est redressée sans être rognée ; ce sera à vous de le faire manuellement.

Le plus souvent, l'inclinaison d'une photo n'est pas aussi importante que dans notre exemple. Dans ce cas, la partie coupée est minime. Cet outils dépannera les porteurs de lunettes, qui distinguent parfois mal les bords du viseur de l'appareil photo, et sont de ce fait plus exposés à incliner légèrement une image.

Chapitre 5

Arc-en-ciel numérique

- -

Dans ce chapitre :

▶ Comprendre la théorie des couleurs.

▶ Gérer la couleur dans Photoshop Elements.

▶ Prélever vos couleurs.

▶ Convertir une image en couleurs en image à niveaux de gris.

- -

*F*orce est de constater que la production des images en couleurs coûte cher, qu'il s'agisse d'une impression professionnelle ou avec une simple imprimante à jet d'encre. En revanche, le noir et blanc est bien plus abordable. Vous obtiendrez de superbes images avec une imprimante laser en noir et blanc, et il est plus facile de photocopier un document imprimé en noir et blanc pour en tirer des centaines d'exemplaires à prix réduit. De plus, vous pouvez envoyer facilement vos images par télécopie, et vous constaterez rapidement qu'une image en noir et blanc occupe bien moins d'espace disque qu'une image en couleur de taille équivalente.

Que vous choisissiez le noir et blanc ou la couleur, ce chapitre montre comment travailler dans ces deux formes d'imagerie numérique. Vous apprendrez à créer et utiliser des couleurs que vous appliquerez avec des outils de peinture.

Regarder les couleurs sous un autre angle

Pour bien comprendre la couleur dans Elements, vous devez en connaître la théorie. Si une image en couleur est ouverte dans Elements, vous constatez que les lettres RVB (c'est-à-dire rouge, vert, bleu) sont inscrites entre parenthèses dans la barre de titre de la fenêtre de l'image. Cela indique que l'image a été créée dans l'espace colorimétrique RVB, traditionnellement utilisé pour les images affichées à l'écran (multimédia, Web, vidéo, etc.). Dans cet espace (appellé également *mode* dans toutes les versions de Photoshop), les couleurs sont créées à partir d'un dosage des couleurs rouge, vert et bleu.

Une autre appréciation des couleurs se fait au travers des couches, comme l'illustre la Figure 5.1. Bien qu'elle soit en noir et blanc, distinguez les trois couches Rouge, Vert et Bleu (de gauche à droite) qui, superposées, produisent une image en couleurs. Vous remarquez que la couche Rouge est plus claire que les deux autres. Vous en déduisez alors que l'image contiendra moins de nuances de rouge que de nuances de vert et de bleu.

Figure 5.1 :
Les couches
monochro-
mes des
composantes
Rouge, Vert
et Bleu
permettent
d'obtenir une
image en
couleurs.

Les paragraphes suivant expliquent comment le mélange de ces divers pixels produit des pixels colorés. Dans cette explication, blanc indique un pixel illuminé, noir un pixel éteint.

- Un pixel blanc d'une couche qui se mélange avec les pixels noirs des autres couches produit la couleur de la première couche. Par exemple, si le rouge est blanc, et que le vert et le bleu sont noirs, vous obtenez un pixel rouge.

- Le mélange des pixels blancs des couches rouge et vert plus un pixel noir de la couche bleu produit du jaune. Comme vous mélangez des couleurs projetées depuis votre moniteur, ces deux couleurs projetées simultanément produisent une teinte plus lumineuse.

Est-ce que vous suivez ? Non ? Eh bien, supposons que vous ayez un projecteur de lumière recouvert d'un filtre rouge, et qu'un de vos amis ait le même mais recouvert d'une membrane verte ; admettons que ce soit Noël et que le sol soit recouvert de neige. Si vous braquez votre projecteur vers le sol, une tache de lumière rouge apparaît. Pour le moment, rien d'étonnant. Maintenant, si votre ami pointe son projecteur au même endroit que le vôtre, c'est-à-dire envoie sa lumière verte sur votre lumière rouge, vous obtenez une couleur plus claire, jaune.

✔ Le mélange des pixels blancs des couches vert et bleu plus un pixel noir de la couche rouge produit un bleu turquoise clair appelé cyan. Le mélange des pixels blancs des couches rouge et bleu plus un pixel noir de la couche verte donne du magenta (une sorte de fuchsia).

Votre moniteur génère du blanc en mélangeant les quantités les plus claires de rouge, de vert et de bleu – l'inverse de ce qui se passe en impression où les encres de couleurs primaires – cyan, magenta et jaune –sont des *filtres colorimétriques*. Quand la lumière blanche atteint l'encre cyan imprimée sur une feuille, cette encre absorbe toutes les traces de rouge et ne renvoie que le vert et le bleu, dont le mélange produit le cyan. Identiquement, le magenta est un filtre vert clair, et le jaune un filtre bleu clair. Cela, et bien d'autres facteurs, comme la pureté des encres, la variation des teintes, la texture du papier et les conditions lumineuses sont caractéristiques du procédé CMJN (cyan, magenta, jaune et noir). Le mélange des encres cyan, magenta et jaune produit un vilain marron foncé, c'est pourquoi l'encre noire est ajoutée pour obtenir un noir franc et profond.

✔ Le mélange des pixels blancs des trois couches tend à produire du blanc et les pixels noirs du noir. Un dosage égal de chaque couche produit un gris.

Gérer la couleur sous Photoshop Elements

Maintenant que vous en savez un peu plus sur la théorie des couleurs, passons à la gestion des couleurs. Aujourd'hui, les utilisateurs d'un ordinateur sont habitués au WYSIWYG, le fameux concept du *What You See Is What You Get*, ce qui signifie en gros *Vous obtenez ce que vous voyez* ou *tel écrit tel écran*. Ce concept s'étend à l'imagerie numérique. L'utilisateur veut que ce qu'il voit à l'écran s'affiche ou s'imprime exactement de la même manière, quel que soit le support final de l'image.

Donne-moi un bon gamma

Obtenir une couleur exacte est quasiment impossible. Cependant, des matériels et des logiciels d'étalonnage permettent d'y parvenir. Autrefois très onéreux, cet équipement est désormais à la portée de l'amateur (comptez une centaine d'euros). Cependant, Photoshop Elements est livrée avec le Panneau de configuration Adobe Gamma.

1. **Choisissez Démarrer/Panneau de configuration. Dans le volet d'exploration, cliquez sur Basculer vers l'affichage classique. Double-cliquez ensuite sur Adobe Gamma.**

2. **Pour une assistance complète, activez l'option Étape par étape et laissez-vous guider ; pour une méthode plus rapide, choisissez l'option Panneau de configuration et cliquez sur le bouton Suivant.**

   Le Panneau de configuration apparaît comme sur la Figure 5.2, mettant à votre disposition tous les paramètres nécessaires à un bon étalonnage.

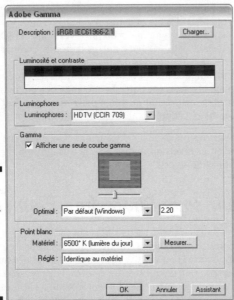

Figure 5.2 : Le Panneau de configuration Adobe Gamma permet d'étalonner votre moniteur.

3. **Donnez à votre profil écran un nom distinctif et cliquez sur Suivant.**

Vous créez ici un *profil colorimétrique*, c'est-à-dire un fichier de paramètres qui décrit comment votre écran affiche la couleur.

4. **Réglez la luminosité et le contraste de votre écran, et cliquez sur Suivant.**

   Il est probable que ces commandes se trouvent à l'avant de votre moniteur, ou dessous. Suivez les instructions à l'écran.

5. **Choisissez une valeur pour les luminophores (canaux rouge, vert ou bleu d'un pixel) de votre écran, puis cliquez sur Suivant.**

   Il se peut que vous ne connaissiez pas cette information. Si vous ne trouvez rien à propos de luminophores dans la documentation fournie avec votre écran, acceptez la valeur par défaut. Il ne s'agit pas encore là de l'aspect réellement important.

6. **Désélectionnez la case à cocher Afficher une seule courbe gamma, réglez les trois curseurs et cliquez sur Suivant.**

   Il s'agit de fusionner au maximum les rectangles du milieu avec les rectangles externes. Cela vous aidera éventuellement de reculer le plus possible de votre écran, de loucher ou de regarder au-dessus des rectangles et d'utiliser votre vision périphérique. C'est assez bizarre, nous en convenons, mais ça vaut la peine d'essayer. Laissez le paramètre Optimal sur Par défaut.

7. **Mesurez le point blanc matériel et cliquez sur Suivant.**

   Vous définissez ainsi la dominante de couleur générale de votre écran. Là encore, vous ne connaissez probablement pas ce paramètre. Il existe heureusement un moyen de le mesurer : cliquez sur le bouton Mesurer et suivez les instructions affichées.

8. **Utilisez ce réglage pour Point blanc réglé, puis cliquez sur Suivant.**

   Il suffit pour cela de garder Identique au matériel.

9. **Comparez l'affichage Avant et Après si désiré, puis cliquez sur Terminer.**

   Vous pouvez comparer l'aspect de l'affichage avant les réglages via Adobe Gamma avec l'aspect qu'il a désormais.

10. **Enregistrez le profil colorimétrique.**

L'emplacement par défaut est parfait ; Elements saura ainsi où trouver votre profil. Cliquez sur OK.

Définir les paramètres colorimétriques

Obtenir une homogénéité des couleurs est incontestablement l'aspect le plus complexe du travail sur les images numériques. Dans Photoshop, la boîte de dialogue des paramètres des couleurs est impressionnante. Comme vous n'êtes pas un professionnel de l'image, tout a été amplement simplifié dans Photoshop Elements. Voyons de quoi il retourne.

1. **Choisissez Édition/Couleurs.**

   Une boîte de dialogue simplifiée, illustrée sur la Figure 5.3, apparaît. Quatre options sont proposées.

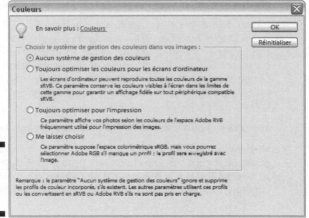

Figure 5.3 : Les paramètres de couleurs.

2. **Décidez de la manière dont vous allez gérer les couleurs :**

   Si la couleur telle qu'elle apparaît vous satisfait, conservez le paramètre par défaut, c'est-à-dire Aucun système de gestion des couleurs.

   Après tout, si les couleurs imprimées depuis Elements vous conviennent, pourquoi se compliquer l'existence ?

   Si vous envisagez de travailler sur des images destinées au Web, choisissez l'option Toujours optimiser les couleurs pour les écrans d'ordinateur. Il utilise l'espace de travail sRVB.

Ce paramètre permet de travailler dans un espace colorimétrique appelé sRVB, qui prend en considération l'aspect des images une fois affichées sur un écran de PC standard, utilisé par la plupart des internautes. Le profil sRVB est un standard généralement accepté, reconnu par de nombreux fabricants de matériel et éditeurs de logiciels.

Notez que si l'image contient déjà un profil colorimétrique, l'option Toujours optimiser les couleurs pour les écrans d'ordinateur supprime le profil et le remplace par le profil sRVB.

Si vos images sont destinées à l'impression, choisissez Toujours optimiser pour l'impression.

Quand nous parlons d'"impression", nous envisageons l'*impression professionnelle*. Dans ce secteur, Photoshop est bien plus puissant que Photoshop Elements. Il incorpore un profil masqué dans le code de vos images lorsque vous les enregistrez. Ce profil donne à l'utilisateur suivant une idée de l'aspect qu'avait votre image la dernière fois que vous y avez travaillé.

L'option Me laisser choisir propose de sélectionner le profil sRVB ou le profil RVB.

3. **Cliquez sur OK.**

Sincèrement, tout cela n'est pas si compliqué ?

Prélever des couleurs et les mélanger

Merci de votre patience. Car avec autant de théorie sur les couleurs, vous n'êtes pas encore passé à la pratique. Nous supposons même que certains d'entre vous se sont endormis. Eh ! Réveillez-vous ! Tout ce discours soporifique sur la couleur est important à comprendre, mais il est maintenant nécessaire d'agir. Pensez à des choses aussi simples que "Comment vais-je choisir des couleurs ?" et "Comment puis-je les conserver ?" Alors, lisez !

Jongler avec les couleurs de premier et d'arrière-plan

Dans la boîte à outils d'Elements, vous travaillez avec deux couleurs en même temps : une *couleur de premier plan* et une *couleur d'arrière-plan*. La plupart des outils et des commandes appliquent la couleur de premier plan, mais quelques-uns s'appuient d'abord sur la couleur d'arrière-plan.

La boîte à outils affiche deux couleurs (en bas). Comme le montre la Figure 5.4, la couleur de premier plan chevauche la couleur d'arrière-plan. Voici comment fonctionnent ces couleurs :

- ✔ La couleur de premier plan est appliquée par les outils de peinture, comme le Pinceau et le Crayon.

- ✔ Quand vous utilisez l'outil Gomme, vous peignez avec la couleur d'arrière-plan, sauf si vous travaillez sur un calque où vous utilisez la transparence pour effacer. Pour en savoir plus sur les calques, reportez-vous au Chapitre 10.

- ✔ L'outil Dégradé, par défaut, crée un arc-en-ciel entre les couleurs de premier et d'arrière-plan.

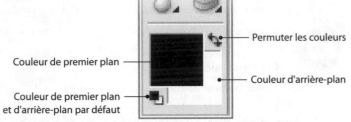

Figure 5.4 :
Les icônes de couleurs en bas de la boîte à outils.

Couleur de premier plan

Couleur de premier plan et d'arrière-plan par défaut

Permuter les couleurs

Couleur d'arrière-plan

La boîte à outils de Photoshop Elements comprend des icônes qui permettent de changer les couleurs de premier et d'arrière-plan, de les permuter, et bien d'autres choses encore. Faisons un petit tour d'horizon de ces possibilités :

- ✔ Cliquez sur le petit nuancier des couleurs de premier et d'arrière-plan pour ouvrir le Sélecteur de couleurs. Appuyez sur Echap ou cliquez sur Annuler pour fermer cette boîte de dialogue.

- ✔ Cliquez sur l'icône des couleurs par défaut (appelées aussi des couleurs courantes) pour restaurer le noir comme couleur de premier plan, et le blanc comme couleur d'arrière-plan.

- ✔ Cliquez sur la double flèche incurvée afin de permuter les deux couleurs.

📌 Vous pouvez rétablir les couleurs par défaut et les permuter avec le clavier. Appuyez sur la touche D pour rétablir les couleurs par défaut. Appuyez sur la touche X pour permuter les couleurs.

Définir des couleurs

Les couleurs de premier et d'arrière-plan peuvent être définies de trois manières différentes :

- Cliquez sur l'icône de la couleur de premier plan et d'arrière-plan de la boîte à outils pour ouvrir le Sélecteur de couleurs.

- Utilisez l'outil Pipette pour prélever une couleur dans une image.

- Utilisez la palette Nuancier.

Utilisation du Sélecteur de couleurs

Pour accéder au Sélecteur de couleurs représenté sur la Figure 5.5, cliquez sur l'icône de la couleur de premier ou d'arrière-plan. Une chose vous saute aux yeux : l'immense zone colorée située sur la partie gauche de la boîte de dialogue. À droite de cette zone, vous voyez un étroit rectangle vertical rempli d'un dégradé de couleurs. En bas de ce rectangle se trouve le curseur de couleur. Le rectangle situé dans le coin supérieur droit affiche la couleur que vous sélectionnez dans le vaste nuancier (grand carré de couleurs). Vous découvrez également de nombreux champs ornés de boutons radio. Tous ces éléments permettent de contrôler la couleur depuis ce Sélecteur de couleurs.

Voici comment définir une couleur depuis cette boîte de dialogue :

1. **Dans la boîte à outils de Photoshop Elements, cliquez soit sur l'icône de couleur de premier plan, soit sur celle d'arrière-plan.**

2. **Vérifiez que le bouton d'option T (Teinte) est actif. Faites alors glisser le curseur de couleur pour définir la nouvelle teinte.**

3. **Activez les champs Saturation puis Luminosité pour parfaire la couleur.**

4. **Cliquez sur OK.**

Pour un utilisateur qui n'est ni photographe ni peintre, le mélange des couleurs RVB est déconcertant. Il lui est difficile d'évaluer, par exemple, le savant mélange de rouge et de vert qui produira du jaune

Curseur de couleur   Couleur courante

Champ de couleurs   Couleur Web sécurisée

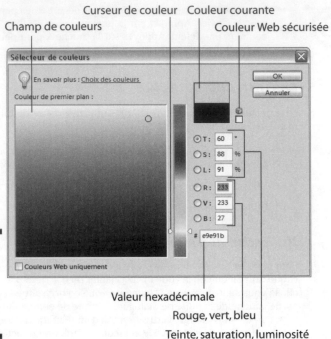

Figure 5.5 :
Le Sélecteur
de couleurs
invite
cordialement
à définir une
couleur.

Valeur hexadécimale

Rouge, vert, bleu

Teinte, saturation, luminosité

ou de l'orange. C'est pourquoi nous vous encourageons à tester et tester encore le Sélecteur de couleurs.

En définissant la couleur orange comme nous venons de le faire dans le Sélecteur de couleurs, vous remarquez que seul le carré de couleur supérieur affiche cette teinte. Le carré situé juste en dessous affiche la couleur initiale du nuancier sélectionné dans la boîte à outils de Photoshop Elements. Il est ainsi très facile de comparer l'ancienne et la nouvelle couleur.

Le mode colorimétrique TSL est une autre représentation des couleurs. Plutôt que de travailler sur les couches primaires des couleurs vidéo, vous insistez sur la Teinte (que l'on peut tout simplement assimiler à la "couleur"), sur la Saturation (c'est-à-dire la densité de la couleur) et sur la Luminosité.

Prélever des couleurs avec l'outil Pipette

Vous pouvez changer la couleur de premier et d'arrière-plan en la prélevant dans l'image à l'aide de l'outil Pipette (il se trouve juste sous l'outil Main). La couleur peut être prélevée dans n'importe laquelle des images ouvertes dans Photoshop Elements.

Voici quelques précisions sur cet incroyable outil :

- ✔ Vous pouvez appuyer sur I pour sélectionner l'outil Pipette depuis le clavier de votre ordinateur.

- ✔ Par défaut, la pipette détermine la couleur de premier plan. Pour définir la couleur d'arrière-plan, maintenez la touche Alt enfoncée et cliquez sur la teinte à prélever.

- ✔ En appuyant sur la touche Alt, vous pouvez temporairement utiliser la pipette sans désactiver l'outil en cours d'utilisation. Cette astuce fonctionne avec le Pot de peinture, le Dégradé, le Crayon, le Pinceau, la Gomme d'arrière-plan, la Gomme magique et Forme.

- ✔ Elements permet de prélever une couleur n'importe où sur votre écran, même en dehors du logiciel ! Pour cela, activez l'outil, appuyez sur le bouton de la souris et faites glisser la pipette jusqu'à la zone de l'écran où vous désirez prélever une couleur. Dès que la pipette est dessus, relâchez le bouton de la souris. La couleur est prélevée !

- ✔ Utilisez l'outil Pipette avec l'onglet Info afin de connaître les valeurs RVB de la teinte prélevée.

- ✔ L'option Taille de la barre d'options de l'outil Pipette détermine la précision de la sélection de la couleur. Quand vous choisissez Échantillon ponctuel, la pipette prélève la couleur du pixel sur lequel vous cliquez. Avec Moyenne 3 x 3, la pipette établit la moyenne colorimétrique des 3 pixels carrés qui entourent le pixel sur lequel vous cliquez. L'option Moyenne 5 x 5 travaille de la même manière mais en prenant en compte 5 pixels au carré, soit la moyenne des 25 pixels entourant celui sur lequel vous cliquez. Cela est très utile pour prélever une couleur impossible à sélectionner en cliquant sur un seul pixel, comme ce peut être le cas avec un ciel bleu.

Utilisation de la palette Nuancier

À cet instant précis, vous pensez que l'on ne peut définir que deux couleurs – celles de premier et d'arrière-plan –, ce qui est très limité.

La palette Nuancier est une sorte de conteneur de teintes, ou encore un marchand de couleurs (Figure 5.6).

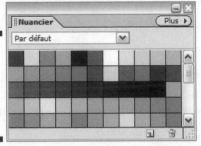

Figure 5.6 :
Les carrés
sont en
couleurs
mais ce livre
est en noir et
blanc...

Activez la palette Nuancier en cliquant sur son onglet dans la barre des palettes ou en choisissant Fenêtre/Nuanciers. Vous pouvez également l'isoler de la barre. Il suffit de maintenir le bouton de la souris enfoncé sur l'onglet et de le faire glisser jusqu'à un nouvel emplacement de la fenêtre de Photoshop Elements. Comme vous le constatez, la palette Nuancier contient un certain nombre de couleurs prédéfinies. Pour en obtenir d'autres, cliquez sur le bouton Plus dans le coin supérieur droit. Diverses options permettent de changer de mode colorimétrique, de charger ou d'enregistrer des nuanciers, ou encore d'afficher une petite liste de couleurs.

Pour définir une de ces couleurs comme couleur de premier plan, placez le curseur sur un des carrés du nuancier – comme par magie le pointeur de la souris prend la forme d'une pipette. Cliquez ! C'est fait ! Pour définir la couleur d'arrière-plan, maintenez la touche Alt enfoncée et cliquez sur la couleur appropriée du nuancier. Simple, n'est-il pas ?

Elements est livré avec plusieurs nuanciers accessibles via la commande Charger un nuancier du menu Plus de la palette. Mais, la vraie puissance de la palette Nuancier réside dans sa capacité à créer et enregistrer des nuanciers. Pour ajouter la couleur de premier plan à la palette Nuancier, placez le pointeur de la souris dans un endroit vide de la palette. Le pointeur prend la forme d'un pot de peinture. Cliquez. Elements ouvre une boîte de dialogue dans laquelle vous pouvez saisir le nom de votre nuance. Pour accepter directement le nom par défaut, maintenez la touche Alt enfoncée tout en cliquant. La boîte de dialogue de dénomination de la nuance ne s'ouvre pas. Vous pouvez également passer par le menu Plus de la palette. Choisissez-y Nouvelle nuance. Cette méthode évite de recourir à l'utilisation du Pot de peinture et du clic.

Lorsque vous ajoutez une nouvelle nuance au nuancier Par défaut, un astérisque apparaît avant ce terme dans la palette Nuancier. Cela indique que le nuancier par défaut a subi des modifications. Si vous sélectionnez un autre nuancier dans la liste, Elements affiche un message vous demandant s'il faut ou non enregistrer les modifications apportées au nuancier. Si vous répondez Non, la nuance ajoutée au nuancier Par défaut est à tout jamais perdue.

Pour conserver cette nuance, répondez Oui. La boîte de dialogue Enregistrer apparaît afin que vous sauvegardiez ce nuancier sous un nouveau nom. Par défaut, Elements propose Nuancier sans titre. Quel que soit le nom donné, ne choisissez pas un autre dossier de stockage. En effet, il sera plus facile de retrouver ce nuancier à son emplacement par défaut, quand vous utiliserez la commande Charger pour récupérer un nuancier à partir du menu local Plus.

Pour charger un nuancier, déployez le menu local Plus et cliquez sur Charger un nuancier. Dans la boîte de dialogue Charger qui s'ouvre sur le dossier des nuanciers d'Elements, cliquez sur le nom du nuancier que vous venez de sauvegarder, puis sur le bouton Charger. Il remplace le nuancier affiché et devient accessible en bas de la liste des nuanciers de la palette.

Pour vérifier tous les nuanciers prédéfinis, les formes, les dégradés et les motifs, choisissez Édition/Gestionnaire des paramètres prédéfinis. Toutes les catégories sont stockées dans la liste Type. Le bouton Plus à droite de cette liste donne accès à un menu. Il permet d'afficher des catégories spécifiques inhérentes à chaque type de paramètres. Vous disposez également de boutons pour Charger, Enregistrer, Renommer et Supprimer des groupes.

Les niveaux de gris

Tout ce qui a été dit précédemment pour la couleur vaut pour les images en niveaux de gris. Vous disposez d'une couleur de premier et d'arrière-plan. Vous pouvez définir des couleurs avec le Sélecteur de couleurs. Quelle que soit la couleur choisie dans le Sélecteur de couleurs, la couleur apparaîtra sous forme de nuances de gris dans l'échantillon de couleur de premier plan ou d'arrière-plan. Les nuances d'une image en niveaux de gris peuvent être prélevées à l'aide de l'outil Pipette.

Destination niveaux de gris

La plupart de vos images seront en couleurs. Cela sous-entend qu'il faudra les convertir en niveaux de gris pour travailler dans ce mode.

Contrairement aux trois couches RVB, une image en niveaux de gris n'en contient qu'une seule. Si vous envisagez d'imprimer en noir et blanc, vous devez neutraliser les données chromatiques pour deux raisons majeures. La première est qu'il est plus facile à Elements de gérer une seule couche plutôt que trois. En fait, passer de trois à une couche lui permet de travailler plus vite. La seconde est qu'il est plus facile de voir à quoi ressemble l'équivalent noir et blanc d'une image en couleur. Quand vous concevez une image destinée à une impression noir et blanc, supprimez purement et simplement la couleur.

Pour convertir une image en couleur en image en noir et blanc, choisissez Image/Mode/Niveaux de gris. Elements demande confirmation de la suppression des informations de couleur de l'image. Cliquez sur OK pour convertir l'image en niveaux de gris. Aussitôt, vous réduisez l'image à une seule couche.

Avant de convertir une image en couleurs en une image à niveaux de gris, faites une copie de l'original. Vous pourrez ainsi récupérer l'image en couleurs. Pour en savoir plus sur la sauvegarde des images, consultez le Chapitre 7.

Si l'image contient plusieurs calques et que vous désirez ne supprimer la couleur que sur un seul calque, choisissez Accentuation/Régler la couleur/Supprimer la couleur, ou appuyez sur Ctrl+Maj+U. La couleur est supprimée, mais l'image reste en couleurs. Cela signifie qu'Elements ne modifie pas le mode colorimétrique de l'image. Par exemple, elle restera en RVB.

Apprendre à travailler

"Et si on mettait un peu de fraîcheur
sur nos photos pour attirer les clients ?"

Dans cette partie...

Nous savons que, comme tout utilisateur de logiciel graphique, vous êtes impatient de passer à l'action, et dépasser ainsi le simple cadre théorique de la première partie.

Mais nous savons aussi qu'avant de passer à la retouche des images, vous devez apprendre de nouvelles choses, comme maîtriser l'excellent module d'organisation des fichiers de Photoshop Elements ou apprendre à enregistrer un fichier. Photoshop Elements propose plusieurs techniques d'enregistrement. De plus, il existe une bonne douzaine de formats de fichier d'image, et il est préférable de ne pas se tromper en fonction de l'utilisation finale. Et, que faire si vous commettez une erreur dans la modification d'une image de vacances à laquelle vous tenez ? Comment respecter les proportions des images ? Comment rétablir votre image telle quelle était à un moment précis lors de la retouche ? Sans doute savez-vous utiliser la fonction d'annulation Ctrl+Z, mais connaissez-vous les extraordinaires possibilités de la palette Annuler l'historique ? Et comment imprimerez-vous l'image ? Tout cela n'est rien à côté de la puissance des sélections et de l'utilisation des calques, qui fait d'Elements un logiciel de retouche d'images n'ayant que quelques fonctions à envier à son aîné Photoshop.

Alors patience, gentil lecteur. Nous allons aborder toutes les fonctionnalités promises. Consultez cette partie au même rythme que nous l'avons écrite. Les autres parties de l'ouvrage traitent de la modification des images. Croyez-nous, votre superbe photo de vacances peut attendre encore quelques pages d'une lecture indispensable à la pérennité de vos fichiers graphiques.

Chapitre 6

Soyez organisé !

*A*près avoir étudié le module Éditeur, examinons l'application Organiseur qui permet de créer des collections d'images et de retrouver facilement vos clichés.

Si vous connaissez Photoshop Album 3.0, l'interface de l'Organiseur vous sera familière, comme le montre la Figure 6.1. Il y a quelques années, ce module était un programme d'organisation et d'archivage indépendant appelé Photoshop Album. Mais, pour satisfaire ses clients, Adobe a décidé de l'intégrer à Elements sous le nom d'Organiseur.

Dans ce chapitre, vous apprendrez à utiliser ce module de catalogage des photos. Ensuite, nous verrons comment marquer des clichés et créer des collections, deux fonctions clés du programme qui aident à grouper et à structurer vos images. Le marquage des photos avec des étiquettes est une opération essentielle car elle permet de retrouver rapidement des images. L'Organiseur sert aussi à sauvegarder vos collections de photos sur CD et DVD.

Valeur hexadécimale

Corbeille de l'organiseur

Bande de montage   Barre des raccourcis

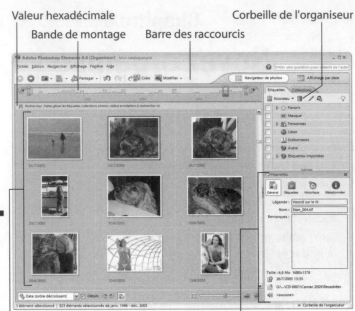

Figure 6.1 :
L'interface
de
l'Organiseur
est un
modèle de
simplicité et
d'élégance.

Navigateur de photos

Panneau Propriétés

Importer des photos dans l'Organiseur

Il est impossible d'organiser des photos sans l'aide d'un programme spécialisé. Bien sûr, vous pouvez créer un dossier nommé "2006" sur votre disque dur et y placer toutes les photos prises durant cette année. Toutefois, vous vous apercevrez rapidement que la gestion de centaines de clichés devient vite un pensum. Alors, vous créerez des sous-dossiers mensuels. Mais là aussi, des centaines de photos prendront place en fonction des mois où les prises de vues ont été effectuées. Le plus organisé des photographes ne peut rivaliser avec l'intelligence d'un module comme l'Organiseur de Photoshop Elements 4.0. Il simplifie la tâche de gestion et d'organisation des images, que vous en ayez une dizaine ou des milliers.

Par défaut, l'Organiseur crée un catalogue et lui attribue le nom fort original de "Mon Catalogue". Bien entendu, vous pouvez en créer autant que vous le souhaitez via la commande Fichier/Catalogue. Il est impossible de voir simultanément les photos de plusieurs catalogues.

L'Organiseur permet d'afficher et de trier les images de multiples
façons. Ces possibilités font que, objectivement, il n'y a aucune raison
de créer des groupes isolés de photos puisque l'Organiseur sait gérer
et cataloguer tous les clichés placés à un seul endroit de votre disque
dur.

Comment importer des photos dans un catalogue ? La réponse dépend
de l'endroit où se trouvent vos images.

Importer des photos

La première étape de l'importation consiste à gérer les photos
présentes sur votre disque dur. Il suffit de cliquer sur Fichier/Obtenir
des photos/Par recherche. Ceci ouvre la boîte de dialogue Obtenir des
photos en cherchant des dossiers (voir la Figure 6.2). Si plusieurs
disques durs sont installés dans votre ordinateur, vous pouvez
sélectionner le ou les disques ciblés par la recherche dans la liste
Dans de la section Options de recherche. Toutefois, comme vous ne
savez peut-être pas très bien où vous avez stocké toutes vos photos,
nous vous conseillons de laisser l'option par défaut Tous les disques
durs.

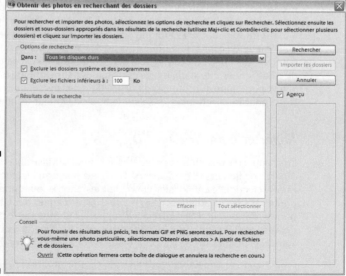

Figure 6.2 :
Première
étape d'une
organisation
contre
laquelle il
serait vain de
résister.

Les options définies, cliquez sur le bouton Rechercher. L'Organiseur analyse vos lecteurs pour trouver les images répondant à vos critères. Les chemins d'accès aux fichiers s'affichent dans la liste Résultats de la recherche. Vous pouvez sélectionner les dossiers un à un, ou plus simplement cliquer sur Tout sélectionner, puis sur Importer les dossiers.

Il en résulte une succession de boîtes de dialogue :

- Obtention de photos montre la progression de la recherche avec création de vignettes des images importées dans le catalogue.

- Ensuite, vous verrez probablement la fenêtre Éléments non importés. Il y est fait référence aux fichiers dont la taille est inférieure à celle spécifiée dans le champ Exclure les fichiers inférieurs à. Vérifiez les fichiers puis cliquez sur OK.

- Enfin, un message vous informe que les éléments affichés dans le catalogue sont ceux que vous venez d'importer. Cliquez sur OK pour valider l'importation.

La méthode Par recherche est celle que vous devez exécuter quand vous utilisez l'Organiseur pour la première fois. Par la suite, vous importerez des images avec la commande Fichier/Obtenir des photos/ À partir de fichiers et de dossiers, ou en appuyant sur Ctrl+Maj+G, ou encore en cliquant sur l'icône de l'appareil photo et en exécutant la commande précitée dans son menu local. L'option Obtenir des photos à partir de sous-dossiers indique que l'Organiseur va analyser le contenu du dossier sélectionné et celui des sous-dossiers qu'il contient. Rien ne vous empêche d'ouvrir une succession de dossiers, de sélectionner une seule image et de cliquer sur Obtenir les photos. Sinon, pour importer toutes les images d'un dossier, cliquez sur son icône pour le sélectionner, puis sur le bouton Obtenir les photos.

Importer à partir d'un CD

Pour importer des photos présentes sur un CD, utilisez la commande À partir de fichiers et de dossiers. Naviguez jusqu'au lecteur de CD-ROM, sélectionnez le dossier contenant les photos, ou toutes les photos si elles ne sont pas dans un dossier, et cliquez sur Obtenir les photos. Par défaut, l'Organiseur va copier les photos sur le disque dur. Ce n'est peut-être pas ce que vous souhaitez. En général, vous stockerez des photos sur un CD pour éviter d'encombrer votre disque dur.

Pour éviter cette copie, activez l'option Garder photo(s) originale(s) hors ligne. L'Organiseur va générer une version en basse résolution, appelée "proxy", des fichiers et créer un lien de ce proxy vers la version en pleine résolution du CD. Si vous souhaitez modifier les images, l'Organiseur vous invitera à insérer le CD d'origine. Surtout, et nous disons bien "surtout", libellez correctement vos CD et saisissez le même nom dans le champ Note de référence facultative pour le CD. Ainsi, vous saurez quel CD insérer à la demande de l'Organiseur.

Importer des photos d'un appareil photo numérique ou d'un lecteur de carte

Une fois l'appareil ou le lecteur connecté à l'ordinateur, téléchargez vos photos à l'aide de l'Organiseur. Dès que vous allumez l'appareil photo numérique, l'interface du Téléchargeur de photos se met immédiatement en route.

Lorsque l'Organiseur est ouvert, la boîte de dialogue Téléchargeur de photos apparaît, comme à la Figure 6.3.

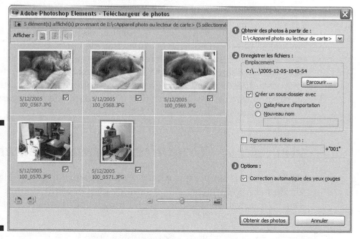

Figure 6.3 :
Cette boîte
de dialogue
vous guide
dans
l'importation
des photos.

Dans la partie gauche de cette fenêtre, les photos présentes dans la carte mémoire de l'appareil photo numérique, le lecteur de carte ou, depuis la version 4.0, une clé USB, s'affichent sous forme de vignettes. Par défaut, toutes sont cochées, c'est-à-dire qu'elles seront toutes importées. Si ce n'est pas ce que vous souhaitez, décochez les photos à ne pas transférer. Pour importer les photos dans un autre dossier que celui proposé par défaut, cliquez sur le bouton Parcourir. Dans la boîte de dialogue qui apparaît, sélectionnez le disque dur et le dossier de destination. Vous pouvez même créer un nouveau dossier en cliquant sur le bouton du même nom. Une fois l'emplacement indiqué, cliquez sur OK. Ensuite, vérifiez que le chemin d'accès à ce dossier est bien affiché dans l'Étape 2 Enregistrer les fichiers de l'interface d'importation.

Pour donner un autre nom aux fichiers, cochez Renommer les fichiers en. Dans le champ situé en dessous, saisissez un nom pour identifier les photos comme appartenant à la même catégorie ou au même thème. Par exemple, saisissez **vacances** et l'Organiseur les renommera "vacances001", "vacances002", et ainsi de suite. Dès que vous cliquez sur le bouton Obtenir les photos, l'Organiseur les télécharge dans le dossier spécifié et, éventuellement, les renomme. Si nécessaire, l'Organiseur importe les photos dans votre catalogue.

L'option Correction automatique des yeux rouges, cochée par défaut, élimine automatiquement l'effet de yeux rouges, si Elements détecte la couleur caractéristique de ce défaut. Le rouge est remplacé par une couleur plus naturelle aussi sûrement qu'avec l'outil Retouche des yeux rouges décrit au Chapitre 11.

La dernière étape demande de supprimer ou non les photos de l'appareil photo numérique ou du lecteur de carte. Bien que la fonction soit séduisante, nous ne la recommandons pas. En effet, vous effacerez les originaux sans être certain que les clichés ont été correctement importés. Il est toujours préférable de ne supprimer les photos d'une carte mémoire qu'après avoir effectué une copie de sauvegarde des fichiers importés.

Accéder à l'Organiseur depuis Elements

Rien n'est plus simple que d'accéder à l'Organiseur depuis l'interface de Photoshop Elements 4.0 : il suffit de cliquer sur le bouton Navigateur de photos, dans la barre de boutons supérieure.

Numériser des photos

Bien que votre programme de numérisation joue un rôle prépondérant dans la capture de photos à importer dans votre catalogue, l'Organiseur pose quelques questions avant de lancer la procédure. Choisissez Fichier/Obtenir des photos/À partir d'un scanner. Générale- ment, la boîte de dialogue apparaît d'elle-même à la mise en route du scanner. Vous pouvez aussi cliquer sur l'icône de l'appareil photo et choisir cette commande dans le menu local. Dans la boîte de dialogue Obtenir des photos à partir d'un scanner, cliquez sur le bouton Parcourir pour indiquer l'emplacement de stockage de l'image numérisée. Si vous n'êtes pas un as des chemins d'accès, conservez celui proposé par défaut.

La liste Enregistrer sous permet de sélectionner le format du fichier numérisé. JPEG est un format compressé qui dégrade l'image proportionnellement à la qualité de la compression. Plus cette qualité est faible, plus l'image est détériorée. Si vous placez le curseur Qualité au maximum (à droite), vous ne constaterez, à l'œil, aucune détérioration de l'image numérisée. TIFF et PNG sont des formats sans pertes de données. Une fois les paramètres définis, cliquez sur OK. Votre programme de numérisation démarre. Suivez ses instructions.

Organiser les photos prises avec un téléphone mobile

Cliquez sur Fichier/Obtenir des photos/À partir d'un téléphone mobile, ou appuyez sur Ctrl+Maj+M. Dans la boîte de dialogue qui apparaît, cliquez sur le bouton Parcourir pour spécifier un dossier dans lequel télécharger les photos de votre téléphone.

Organiser les photos

Une fois les photos dans l'Organiseur, vous devez les organiser. Vous disposez de nombreuses méthodes qui vont de procédures automatiques à des fonctions plus manuelles très amusantes. Mais avant d'en arriver là, nous devons faire quelques suppositions sur vos images pour éviter tout problème.

Corriger la date

Une photo numérique contient bien plus d'informations que l'image qu'elle nous montre. Elles sont stockées sous la forme de *métadonnées* qui indiquent la date, les réglages de l'appareil, etc. Elles sont au format EXIF (EXchangeable Image File). Lorsque vous regardez une image sur l'écran de votre ordinateur, vous ne voyez pas ces informations. Cependant, certaines applications, comme Photoshop Elements, peuvent les révéler.

Les données EXIF contiennent la date et l'heure auxquelles les photos ont été prises. Ces deux informations viennent des fonctions d'horodatage de l'appareil photo numérique. Elles ne sont valables que si elles sont correctement configurées. Si la date est erronée – à cause de batteries déchargées ou parce que vous ne l'avez jamais réglée –, cette date incorrecte est néanmoins inscrite sous forme de métadonnées EXIF.

Pour modifier la date et l'heure d'une ou plusieurs photos, sélection-nez-les dans le navigateur de photos. Ensuite, cochez la case Détails située en bas de l'Organiseur. Cliquez sur la date et l'heure affichées sous la photo. La boîte de dialogue Régler la date et l'heure apparaît. Vous pouvez également afficher cette boîte de dialogue via Édition/ Régler la date et l'heure.

Voici les trois options de la boîte de dialogue :

- La première option, Remplacer par une date et une heure spécifiées, ouvre la boîte de dialogue Définir la date et l'heure. Ici, vous indiquez l'année, le mois, le jour et l'heure. Si vous ne connaissez pas cette dernière, optez pour Indéterminée.

- La deuxième option, Changer pour faire correspondre la date et l'heure du fichier, aligne la date sur celle de la métadonnée EXIF. Choisissez cette option pour les images numérisées.

- La troisième option, Décaler du nombre d'heure défini (réglage du fuseau horaire), permet d'appliquer une heure en fonction des différents fuseaux horaires de la planète. Par exemple, si votre appareil photo numérique est réglé sur l'heure de Paris et que vous allez à Orlando en Floride, la photo de Disney World prise à telle heure sera enregistrée à l'heure de Paris. En corrigeant le décalage horaire dans la boîte de dialogue Réglage de fuseau horaire, l'heure de la prise de vue sera rétablie.

Étiquettes

Les étiquettes sont des sortes de mots-clés visuels applicables aux images afin de les retrouver plus rapidement dans vos collections de photos. Supposons que vous possédiez une photo de votre enfant Julien jouant avec votre chat Loupiot le jour d'Halloween. Vous pouvez appliquer trois étiquettes à l'image : une pour Julien, une pour Loupiot, une pour Halloween. Après avoir étiqueté des milliers d'images, vous pouvez les trier plus facilement. Dans la Corbeille de l'Organiseur, double-cliquez sur l'étiquette Julien. L'Organiseur affichera certainement des centaines de photos auxquelles vous avez appliqué l'étiquette Julien. Maintenant, ajoutez l'étiquette Loupiot pour que la fenêtre de l'explorateur n'affiche que les quelques dizaines de photos réunissant Julien et le petit chat. Enfin, en ajoutant l'éti-quette Halloween, l'Organiseur ne montre qu'une seule photo : celle représentant Julien et Loupiot le soir d'Halloween.

Bien que l'Organiseur propose plusieurs manières pour grouper, arranger et afficher vos photos, les étiquettes nous paraissent vraiment indispensables. Prenez le temps d'en comprendre le fonctionnement.

Créer des étiquettes

En haut de la Corbeille de l'Organiseur, un onglet Étiquettes se trouve à côté de l'onglet Collections. Il s'agit d'une petite interface de gestion des étiquettes. Par défaut, il en existe déjà quelques-unes : Favoris qui permet d'organiser les images en fonction de leur qualité ; Masqué qui empêche d'afficher des images de votre collection (mais que vous ne souhaitez pas supprimer) ; et quelques catégories et sous-catégories comme Personnes, Lieux, Événements, Autre et Etiquettes importées.

Pour créer une étiquette, cliquez sur le bouton Nouveau situé en haut de l'onglet. Dans le menu local qui apparaît, choisissez Nouvelle étiquette (Ctrl N). Dans la boîte de dialogue Créer une étiquette, choisissez la catégorie à laquelle l'étiquette devra appartenir. Dans le champ Nom, assignez un nom à l'étiquette, puis ajoutez une note dans la zone Remarque si vous en ressentez la nécessité. Vous pouvez définir une icône pour la photo correspondant à votre étiquette en cliquant sur le bouton Modifier l'icône. Sachez qu'il est toujours plus facile de définir une icône une fois l'étiquette créée (nous en expliquons la procédure dans une minute). Cliquez sur OK pour créer l'étiquette.

Vous pouvez modifier à votre convenance une étiquette, y compris son icône, en sélectionnant et en cliquant sur l'icône du crayon située en haut du panneau Étiquettes. Cette action ouvre la boîte de dialogue Modifier l'étiquette.

Cliquez sur le bouton Modifier l'icône pour ouvrir la boîte de dialogue Modifier l'icône de l'étiquette. Dans cette boîte de dialogue, vous pouvez choisir une icône parmi les images affichées. Pour naviguer dans ces images, cliquez sur les flèches gauche et droite. Si vous ne trouvez pas votre bonheur, ou si la boîte de dialogue n'affiche aucune image, cliquez sur le bouton Importer. Dans la boîte de dialogue d'importation, parcourez vos lecteurs pour localiser l'image à utiliser en tant qu'icône de l'étiquette. Sélectionnez l'image et cliquez sur Ouvrir. Validez l'icône en cliquant sur le bouton OK. Pour voir toutes les images des étiquettes, cliquez sur le bouton Rechercher.

Comme les étiquettes sont de petite taille, il est recommandé de les recadrer pour afficher un détail plutôt qu'une vue d'ensemble. Lorsque vous avez terminé, cliquez sur OK, puis fermez la boîte de dialogue

Modifier l'étiquette. L'icône s'affiche dans la catégorie sélectionnée lors de la création de l'étiquette.

Créer des catégories et des sous-catégories

Pour créer des catégories et des sous-catégories, il suffit de cliquer sur le bouton Nouveau et de choisir Nouvelle catégorie ou Nouvelle sous-catégorie. Les catégories et les sous-catégories ne sont utiles que dans l'organisation hiérarchique de vos étiquettes, mais elles sont elles-mêmes considérées comme des étiquettes.

Lorsque vous créez une catégorie, vous pouvez choisir l'icône qui la représentera. Il suffit de la sélectionner dans la boîte de dialogue Créer une catégorie. Vous pouvez également assigner une couleur à cette catégorie. Cette couleur ne s'affichera pas dans l'étiquette de la catégorie elle-même mais dans ses sous-catégories et dans les étiquettes que vous y placerez.

Vous pouvez glisser-déplacer les étiquettes, les sous-catégories et les catégories dans le panneau Étiquettes. Ceci permet un tri hiérarchique des éléments et des sous-catégories incorporées.

Étiqueter des photos

Pour appliquer des étiquettes sur des photos, il suffit de les faire glisser de l'onglet Étiquettes jusqu'à la photo affichée dans l'Explorateur. Pour appliquer une même étiquette à plusieurs photos, appuyez sur la touche Maj ou Ctrl et cliquez sur les photos à sélectionner. Glissez-déposez ensuite l'étiquette sur une seule de ces photos.

Il suffit de regarder dans le navigateur de photos pour identifier instantanément les images étiquetées. En effet, une petite icône correspondant à la catégorie des étiquettes s'affiche sous le coin inférieur droit de la photo. L'icône de la catégorie révèle d'autres détails lorsque vous optez pour un affichage plus grand des vignettes comme le montre la Figure 6.4. Dans ce cas, vous voyez l'icône, le nom de l'étiquette, la date et l'heure de la prise de vue, ainsi qu'une zone de saisie de texte où vous pouvez ajouter une description à l'image. Par défaut, cette zone de texte affiche le nom de votre appareil photo numérique. Pour masquer tous ces éléments, décochez la case Détails. Pour afficher les propriétés de la photo sélectionnée, cliquez sur le bouton homonyme situé en bas du navigateur. Ceci ouvre le panneau Propriétés. Le bouton Étiquettes de ce panneau permet de voir toutes les étiquettes assignées à l'image.

Figure 6.4 :
Les
étiquettes
s'affichent
dans le
navigateur de
photos quand
l'option
Détails est
active.

Si vous avez un groupe de photos sur votre disque dur réunies dans un dossier spécifique – certainement un reliquat d'une ancienne version de Photoshop Elements – vous pouvez rapidement créer une étiquette à partir du nom de ce dossier et marquer de cette manière toutes les photos qu'il contient.

Pour cela, sélectionnez Emplacement du dossier dans la liste Organisation du navigateur de photos (dans le coin inférieur gauche de l'interface). Vous constatez l'apparition d'un séparateur. Le nouveau volet situé à gauche affiche la hiérarchie de vos dossiers. Dans le volet affichant les images, c'est-à-dire le navigateur de photos, cliquez sur le bouton Étiquette instantanée. La boîte de dialogue Créer et appliquer une nouvelle étiquette apparaît. Elle utilise, par défaut, le nom du dossier. Effectuez toutes les modifications nécessaires, puis cliquez sur OK. Toutes les images du dossier sont désormais marquées. C'est une méthode très rapide pour étiqueter des images dont l'organisation initiale n'est pas l'œuvre de Photoshop Elements.

Reconnaître les visages

Photoshop Elements est devenu physionomiste : il est désormais capable de reconnaître automatiquement les visages qui se trouvent sur vos photographies, vous permettant de les étiqueter pour les retrouver rapidement par la suite. Entendons-nous bien : Eléments n'identifie pas les gens. Il ne sera pas capable de faire la différence entre Tatie Danièle et la tante Jeanne, mais au moins, il ne les confondra pas avec des tentes canadiennes.

La fonction de reconnaissance des visage d'Elements 4.0 repose sur un puissant algorithme de reconnaissance des formes. Procédez comme suit pour découvrir toutes les photos comportant des visages :

1. **Dans l'Organiseur de Photoshop Elements, choisissez Rechercher/Rechercher des visages pour l'ajout d'étiquette.**

   L'organiseur affiche une boîte de dialogue demandant si vous voulez vraiment rechercher les visages dans toutes les photos affichées.

2. **Cliquez sur OK pour confirmer la recherche.**

   Si d'autres fichiers que des images – texte, vidéo... – se trouvent dans les dossiers, Elements le signale et prévient que les visages n'y seront pas recherchés. Cliquez sur OK.

   Ne vous souciez pas de la mention Aucun élément sélectionné, en bas à droite de l'Organiseur. Patientez un moment, le temps qu'Elements commence à traiter les images, ce qui peut durer plusieurs minutes, si la photothèque est fournie.

   Peu à peu, des visages apparaissent dans des petites vignettes carrées, comme le révèle la Figure 6.5. Pour une photo de groupe, il y aura autant de vignettes que de visages reconnus. Une barre de progression, en bas à droite de l'interface, indique l'avancement de l'analyse.

   Elements parvient à détecter même des visages très flous et parfois – rien n'est parfait – il se trompe, intégrant l'oreille du chien ou un vol de mouettes dans lesquels il a cru reconnaître quelque chose d'humain. Contentez-vous d'ignorer ces erreurs.

   Pour voir la photo à laquelle appartient un portrait, cliquez sur la vignette. La photo complète apparaît en bas à droite de l'interface.

3. **Pour étiqueter un visage, procédez comme nous l'avons expliqué précédemment à la section "Etiqueter des photos", en faisant glisser une étiquette jusque sur la vignette.**

   Une vignette étiquetée disparaît aussitôt.

   Les étiquettes utilisées s'accumulent dans la zone Etiquettes récemment utilisées, ce qui facilite leur réutilisation ultérieure.

Figure 6.5 :
Photoshop
Elements
détecte tous
les visages
qui se
trouvent dans
votre
photothèque.

4. **Cliquez sur Terminer pour quitter la fonction de reconnaissance des visages.**

Collections

L'organisation des photos peut se faire sous forme de collection. Les collections se comportent un peu comme les étiquettes. Vous les créez et les appliquez de la même manière, vous leur assignez des icônes, et vous les hiérarchisez dans des groupes de collections. La grande différence est qu'une collection doit être utilisée comme première étape d'une création. Ainsi, lorsque vous affichez une collection de photos, chacune d'elles est numérotée. Ce numéro apparaît dans le coin supérieur gauche de l'image. Vous pouvez déplacer les photos dans une collection pour les réorganiser.

Pour travailler avec des collections, il suffit de cliquer sur l'onglet Collections situé en haut de la Corbeille de l'Organiseur. Ici, vous appliquez les mêmes règles de création qu'aux étiquettes. Cliquez sur le bouton Nouveau et optez pour la création d'une nouvelle collection ou d'un nouveau groupe de collections. Pour modifier la collection ou le groupe, cliquez sur l'icône du crayon. Pour supprimer une collection ou un groupe, cliquez sur le bouton de la poubelle. Pour insérer une photo dans une collection, glissez-déposez l'icône de la collection depuis la Corbeille de l'Organiseur jusqu'à la photo, exactement comme vous le faites avec les étiquettes. Contrairement aux catégories et aux sous-catégories d'étiquettes, les groupes de collections ne peuvent pas être appliqués aux photos.

Piles et jeux de versions

Nous allons vous demander un petit effort de mémoire. Au début de notre discussion sur les étiquettes, nous avons abordé le sujet de l'étiquette Masqué. Elle permet de ne pas afficher certaines photos dans la fenêtre du navigateur. Toutefois, l'Organiseur propose plusieurs méthodes pour empêcher l'affichage de certaines des images. Si vous avez une série d'images à peu près identiques – par exemple plusieurs clichés du même sujet, cadrés différemment –, vous souhaiterez certainement n'afficher que les meilleures photos de cette série. La fonction Pile de l'Organiseur permet "d'empiler" une série de photos qui n'utilisera qu'une seule vignette dans la fenêtre du navigateur.

Piles

Pour empiler des photos, sélectionnez un ensemble d'images similaires en appuyant sur la touche Ctrl ou Maj. Nous rappelons que ces deux touches permettent d'effectuer une multisélection. Cliquez ensuite sur Édition/Pile/Empiler les photos sélectionnées, ou bien appuyez sur Ctrl+Alt+S. L'icône d'une pile de photos apparaît dans le coin supérieur droit de la vignette pour indiquer que d'autres photos non visibles sont empilées sous elle. Pour afficher toutes les photos de la pile, cliquez sur Édition/Pile/Faire apparaître toutes les photos de la pile, ou appuyez sur Ctrl+Alt+R. Vous pouvez alors sélectionner une des photos affichées, puis cliquer sur Édition/Pile/Supprimer la photo de la pile pour retirer cette unique photo de la pile d'images. En revanche, si vous souhaitez que cette image apparaisse en haut de la pile, c'est-à-dire qu'elle soit affichée dans le navigateur de photos, exécutez la commande Définir comme photo au-dessus de la pile.

Vous pouvez définitivement désempiler des photos de deux manières. La commande Édition/Pile/Désempiler les photos affiche toutes les photos empilées dans le navigateur. *De facto*, la pile n'existe plus. La commande Édition/Pile/Aplatir la pile supprime toutes les photos de votre catalogue à l'exception de la première photo de la pile. Si vous souhaitez également effacer les photos de votre disque dur, cochez l'option Supprimer aussi les photos du disque dur dans la boîte de dialogue de confirmation de la suppression.

Jeux de versions

Les jeux de versions sont similaires aux piles mais ils se basent sur différentes versions de la même photo. Pour créer un jeu de versions :

1. **Dans le navigateur de photos, sélectionnez une image.**

   Choisissez une image JPEG qui a besoin d'être modifiée.

2. **Dans la barre des raccourcis de l'Organiseur, cliquez sur le bouton Modifier. Dans le menu local, sélectionnez Aller à la retouche rapide.**

   La photo sélectionnée s'ouvre dans la fenêtre que montre la Figure 6.6. Elle contient une version abrégée de Photoshop Elements 4.0. Elle ne contient que les outils Zoom, Main, Sélecteur magique (une nouveauté que nous étudierons au Chapitre 9), Recadrage et Correction des yeux rouges. A gauche, un panneau contient les commandes les plus couramment utilisées.

Figure 6.6 :
La retouche rapide sert à effectuer les corrections les plus courantes.

3. **Effectuez les modifications nécessaires.**

   Faites de votre mieux ! Ou de votre pire ! Nous étudierons les fonctions de retouche automatique un peu plus tard. Pour l'instant, faites ce que vous pouvez avec les quatre commandes disponibles dans cette fenêtre. Toutefois, ne cliquez pas sur le bouton Retouche Standard. Cette action ouvrirait L'Editeur habituel de Photoshop Elements.

4. Cliquez sur OK.

Un message vous avertit que votre image a été sauvegardée avec le suffixe _modifiée-1 ajouté à la fin de son nom.

5. Cliquez de nouveau sur OK.

De retour dans l'Organiseur, vous notez que la vignette reflète les modifications apportées. L'icône d'un jeu de versions s'affiche dans le coin supérieur droit de la vignette. Si la photo est toujours ouverte dans l'Editeur, une bandeau horizontal rouge, avec la mention Modification en cours, barre la vignette. Le sous-menu Édition/Jeu de versions dispose de commandes identiques aux piles. Vous pouvez faire apparaître, aplatir et définir comme photo au-dessus.

Légendes et remarques

L'Organiseur permet de saisir des légendes pour chaque photo de votre catalogue, ainsi que des remarques sur l'image en cours d'enregistrement. Ces légendes sont utilisables pendant des créations. Pour saisir remarques et légendes, sélectionnez une photo et cliquez sur le bouton Ouvrir Propriétés, en bas à droite du navigateur de photos, ou appuyez sur Alt+Entrée. Dans la section Général du panneau Propriétés se trouvent les champs Légendes, Nom et Remarques.

Vous pouvez également attribuer une légende à une photo en choisissant Édition/Ajouter une légende ou en appuyant sur Ctrl+Maj+T. Si plusieurs images sont sélectionnées, cette commande ajoute la même légende à toutes les photos. Si vous affichez les photos en Mode une seule photo (taille maximale des vignettes), vous pouvez cliquer directement dans la zone Cliquez ici pour ajouter une légende. Le texte saisi servira de légende.

L'Organiseur permet d'enregistrer des légendes audio. Ces légendes serviront de narration à un futur diaporama. Pour y parvenir, cliquez sur l'icône du haut-parleur située en bas du panneau Propriétés. Vous accédez à la boîte de dialogue Sélectionner un fichier audio. Là, vous pouvez importer un fichier préenregistré en cliquant sur Fichier/ Parcourir, ou bien enregistrer une voix en cliquant sur le bouton Enregistrement de la boîte de dialogue. Dans cette circonstance, vous enregistrerez une voix en direct, ce qui nécessite qu'un micro soit connecté à votre ordinateur et que tous les paramètres de votre carte

son soient correctement définis. Une fois la légende enregistrée,
cliquez sur Arrêt. Si la légende ne vous plaît pas, cliquez sur Édition/
Effacer et recommencez l'opération. Dès que la légende vous satisfait,
fermez la fenêtre d'enregistrement. L'Organiseur vous invite à sauvegarder la légende audio.

Afficher et rechercher des photos

Vous connaissez les grandes lignes de l'affichage des photos dans
l'Organiseur. Voici quelques informations complémentaires :

- ✔ Il est possible de basculer du navigateur de photos à l'affichage
  en mode Date par un simple clic sur le côté droit homonyme de
  la barre des raccourcis, ou en appuyant sur Ctrl+Alt+O et
  Ctrl+Alt+C.

- ✔ La liste Organisation du navigateur de photos, située dans le
  coin inférieur gauche, permet d'opter pour un affichage des
  photos par Date (ordre croissant), Date (ordre décroissant), Lot
  importé et Emplacement du dossier.

- ✔ Le curseur d'affichage des vignettes, situé dans le coin inférieur
  droit, détermine la taille des miniatures affichées dans le
  navigateur de photos. Plus vous glissez le curseur vers la droite,
  c'est-à-dire vers l'icône la plus grande, plus les vignettes seront
  grandes et moins le navigateur pourra en afficher simultanément. En revanche, plus vous déplacez ce curseur vers la
  gauche, plus vous réduisez la taille des vignettes, permettant
  ainsi au navigateur d'en afficher un maximum.

- ✔ Lorsque vous affichez une vignette à sa taille maxi, une seule
  photo s'affiche dans le navigateur. La légende apparaît sous
  l'image avec la date et l'heure. Vous pouvez naviguer par les
  vignettes affichées en Mode une seule photo en glissant la barre
  de défilement vertical, ou en appuyant sur les flèches Haut et
  Bas du pavé directionnel.

- ✔ En haut du navigateur de photos se trouve la barre Rechercher.
  Vous pouvez l'utiliser pour effectuer des recherches et en afficher les critères. Pour rechercher des photos étiquetées ou des
  photos dans une collection, glissez l'étiquette ou la collection
  depuis la Corbeille de l'Organiseur jusqu'à cette barre de
  recherche.

- ✔ La case à cocher Correspondance, qui apparaît lorsque vous
  avez placé des étiquettes dans la barre de recherche, permet de
  contrôler l'importance de cette recherche. Par exemple, si vous

placez deux étiquettes dans cette barre, l'Organiseur affichera
les photos auxquelles ces étiquettes sont attachées. Si vous
cochez la case Correspondance, seules les photos possédant
ces deux étiquettes (et non pas l'une ou l'autre) seront affichées.

Mode Plein écran et comparaison de photos

Regarder des photos sous forme de vignettes ne permet pas d'en saisir
les détails. Lorsque vous utilisez l'Organiseur pour afficher des photos
et pas seulement pour les classer, vous déterminez plus facilement
celles à imprimer ou à envoyer par e-mail. Parfois, vous souhaiterez
zoomer sur une image ou en comparer deux côte à côte. Pour y
parvenir, utilisez les modes d'affichage Plein écran et Comparaison des
photos.

Le mode Plein écran

Le mode Plein écran, accessible par Affichage/Afficher les photos en
plein écran, ou en appuyant sur la touche F11, affiche toutes les
photographies, sauf si vous n'en sélectionnez que quelques-unes.

Dans ce mode, une boîte de dialogue Options de la vue plein écran
apparaît. Vous pouvez personnaliser votre diaporama en réglant les
options de présentation comme ceci :

- Pour entendre de la musique pendant l'affichage des photos,
cliquez sur le bouton Parcourir de la liste Fond musical. Ou
alors, parcourez vos lecteurs pour sélectionner le fichier audio
au format MP3, WAV ou WMA qui fournira l'accompagnement
musical.

- Si vous avez enregistré des légendes audio, cochez la case Lire
les légendes audio.

- L'option Fréquences des pages permet de définir la durée
d'affichage de chaque photo. Vous pouvez choisir une option
dans la liste ou saisir directement la durée au clavier.

- Pour afficher les légendes sous les photos, cochez la case
Inclure les légendes.

- L'option Autoriser le redimensionnement des photos permet aux
images en basse résolution de remplir la totalité de l'écran.
Toutefois, cet agrandissement forcé réduit la qualité d'affichage.
Pour obtenir le même résultat avec les vidéos, cochez la case
Autoriser le redimensionnement des vidéos.

✔ Pour lancer un diaporama en continu, cochez l'option Répéter le diaporama.

✔ Pour afficher les vignettes des images dans un bandeau à droite de l'écran, cochez la case Afficher le film fixe.

Une fois les paramètres du diaporama (ou de la présentation, si vous préférez) définis, cliquez sur OK. Si certaines photos sont inaccessibles, une boîte de dialogue vous invite à insérer le CD approprié. Si vous ne désirez pas le faire, vous pouvez choisir l'option qui occulte les photos "hors ligne".

Le mode Plein écran comporte trois éléments : l'image affichée, une barre de commandes et, à droite, un bandeau défilant contenant les vignettes des images (s'il n'est pas visible, cliquez dans l'image du bouton droit et choisissez l'option Afficher le film fixe).

Lorsque vous lancez le diaporama, la première photo qui apparaît est celle dont vous avez sélectionné la vignette. Pour lancer la lecture automatique, cliquez sur le bouton Lecture ou appuyez sur F5. Le diaporama affiche chaque image pendant la durée indiquée puis passe à la suivante en fondu enchaîné. Vous pouvez également parcourir le diaporama image par image ou cliquer directement sur la vignette à afficher. Dans ce cas, la lecture du diaporama s'interrompt. Pour la relancer depuis cette image, cliquez sur Lecture.

La barre de contrôle (ou de transport) permet d'effectuer les actions suivantes :

✔ Sur la gauche de la barre de contrôle, vous disposez de boutons de lecture. Vous pouvez revenir à l'image précédente, lancer la lecture ou la mettre en pause, passer à l'image suivante, ou quitter la révision.

✔ À droite de ces contrôles de lecture, vous disposez de boutons pour pivoter la photo affichée ou la supprimer.

✔ Le menu Actions permet d'exécuter diverses tâches sur l'image affichée comme l'étiqueter, l'ajouter à des collections et exécuter une retouche automatique. Vous retrouvez la majorité de ces commandes dans le menu contextuel qui s'affiche quand vous cliquez sur la photo avec le bouton droit de la souris. Si vous indiquez vouloir imprimer une photo, un message s'affiche quand vous quittez le diaporama. Vous pouvez immédiatement imprimer la photo en question.

✔ Vous pouvez basculer du mode Révision au mode Comparaison en cliquant sur le bouton Côte à côte.

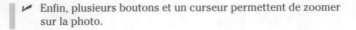

✔ Enfin, plusieurs boutons et un curseur permettent de zoomer sur la photo.

Comparer des photos

Comme vous pouvez le voir sur la Figure 6.7, le mode Comparaison des photos permet de juxtaposer deux images. Pour accéder à ce mode, cliquez sur Affichage/Comparer des photos côte à côte, ou appuyez sur F12. Une autre technique consiste à cliquer sur le bouton Mode Côte à côte, dans la barre de commandes, depuis le mode Plein écran.

Commandes de navigation

    Rotation   Vue Plein écran

      Supprimer   Mode Côte à côte

        Menu Actions   Zoom et synchronisation

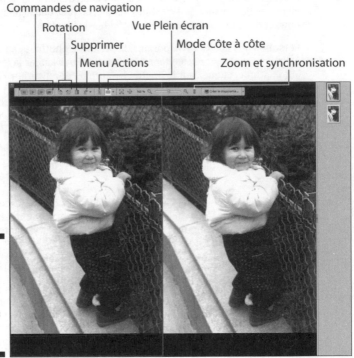

Figure 6.7 : Comparer des photos permet d'examiner deux images en même temps.

Le mode Côte à côte affiche un écran coupé en deux horizontalement ou verticalement selon que vous optez pour l'option Côte à côte ou pour l'option Au-dessus et au-dessous. Pour charger une image dans une des deux zones, cliquez dans la zone en question puis sur l'image dans les vignettes situées à droite. Procédez à l'identique pour la seconde photo.

La comparaison dispose des mêmes contrôles de navigation que le mode Révision. Vous disposez d'un bouton supplémentaire qui prend la forme d'un chaînon situé à droite de l'échelle du zoom. Si vous cliquez dessus, les facteurs de zoom des deux images sont liés. En d'autres termes, si vous zoomez en avant ou en arrière sur une image, l'autre sera agrandie ou réduite dans les mêmes proportions.

Rechercher par date

Si vous cherchez une photo et que vous connaissez la date à laquelle elle a été prise, vous pouvez parcourir le navigateur de photos jusqu'à ce que vous la trouviez. Mais, nous pensons, et surtout nous savons, qu'il existe une méthode bien plus rapide. Sous la barre des raccourcis, se trouve la bande de montage, une aide visuelle essentielle pour retrouver des photos.

La bande de montage

Comme vous pouvez le voir sur la Figure 6.8, l'Organiseur représente le temps sous la forme d'une bande horizontale. On peut parler de *frise chronologique*. Lorsque vous déplacez le curseur, vous passez sur les diverses périodes couvertes par l'ensemble des photos affichées dans le navigateur. Vous y voyez des bandes verticales. Plus elles sont hautes, plus il y a de photos concernant la période correspondante.

Curseur de délimitation de période

Figure 6.8 :
La bande de
montage.

Pour limiter vos recherches, la bande de montage permet de réduire l'étendue de temps. Faites glisser les curseurs de droite et/ou de gauche pour réduire la période de recherche. Vous pouvez également le faire moins intuitivement via Rechercher/Définir la période, ou en appuyant sur Ctrl+Alt+F. Vous accédez à la boîte de dialogue Définir la période qui permet d'indiquer une date de début et de fin de la recherche. Pour afficher de nouveau toutes vos photos, cliquez sur Rechercher Effacer la période, ou appuyez sur Ctrl+Maj+F.

Afficher par date

L'Organiseur dispose d'une fonction qui permet d'afficher les photos par leur date de prise de vue. Pour cela, cliquez sur le bouton Affichage par date de la barre des raccourcis. Un superbe calendrier apparaît. Les trois boutons situés en bas de l'écran (voir la Figure 6.9) donnent le choix entre l'affichage de l'année entière, d'un mois ou d'un jour.

Figure 6.9 : L'affichage par date permet de situer les photos selon une période de l'année ou un événement.

Petit aperçu de son fonctionnement :

- ✔ En mode Année, vous naviguez d'année en année avec les boutons situés en haut du calendrier. Lorsqu'une date d'un des mois est bleue, cela indique qu'il y a des photos.

  Pour marquer des dates spéciales, comme des périodes de vacances, cliquez sur Édition/Préférences/Calendrier. Vous pouvez supprimer certains événements ou ajouter les vôtres.

  Cliquez sur une de ces dates pour afficher une miniature de la photo dans la partie droite de l'interface. Toute date de couleur rouge indique un jour férié ou une fête particulière.

- ✔ En mode Mois, vous affichez le mois qui vous convient. Cette fois, une vignette identifie la photo prise tel jour. Le nom de la fête correspond à un jour férié, et/ou l'événement que vous avez créé apparaît sous la date ou sous la vignette de la photo.

✔ Le mode Jour affiche toutes les photos qui ont été prises le jour en question. Vous pouvez également y accéder en double-cliquant sur la vignette du jour sélectionné dans le calendrier.

Pour changer la photo qui s'affiche sous forme de vignette sur le calendrier, cliquez avec le bouton droit de la souris sur une des photos affichées à droite en mode Jour. Là, cliquez sur Définir comme priorité du jour. En mode Année et Mois, il est possible de faire défiler toutes les photos du jour en cliquant sur les boutons Elément précédent ou Elément suivant, sous l'aperçu de la photo en haut à droite.

Rechercher par étiquette et par collection

Pour retrouver des photos en fonction des étiquettes que vous leur avez assignées, il suffit d'afficher le panneau Étiquettes et de cliquer dans la case vide qui précède de nom de l'étiquette. L'icône d'une paire de jumelles apparaît, affichant toutes les photos étiquetées. Pour filtrer le résultat de cette recherche, activez une seconde étiquette. Dans ce cas, le navigateur n'affichera que les images qui ont les deux étiquettes en question. Ceci réduit généralement le nombre de photos trouvées.

Vous pouvez aussi étiqueter des photos à *exclure*. Supposons que vous souhaitiez trouver toutes les photos de Julien où il n'est pas avec le chat Loupiot. Commencez par double-cliquer sur l'étiquette Julien puis cliquez sur l'étiquette Loupiot avec le bouton droit de la souris. Dans le menu contextuel, choisissez Exclure les photos avec la catégorie Loupiot. Les photos sont alors filtrées, ne montrant que celles de Julien.

La recherche par collection fonctionne de la même manière. Double-cliquez sur la collection dans la Corbeille de l'Organiseur pour afficher ses photos dans le navigateur. La seule différence ici est que vous ne pouvez pas ajouter ou redéfinir une recherche comme vous le faites avec une étiquette.

Rechercher par légende ou par remarque

Une autre recherche peut se faire sur les mots d'une légende ou d'une remarque. Cliquez sur Rechercher/Par légende ou remarque (ou appuyez sur Ctrl+Maj+J) pour afficher la boîte de dialogue Rechercher par légende ou remarque. Dans le champ de saisie, tapez le texte de la recherche. Bien évidemment, il doit contenir des termes que vous avez réellement saisis lors de sa définition. La boîte de dialogue contient deux boutons radio qui limitent, d'une certaine manière, la portée de la recherche : "Le début des mots dans les légendes et les remarques" et "Une partie quelconque d'un mot dans les légendes et les remarques". Avec la première option, si vous saisissez **photo**, le résultat de la recherche englobera *photographie*, *photographe*, *photocopie*, *Photoshop*, etc. Si vous choisissez la seconde option, le résultat de la recherche n'inclura que des termes où *photo* n'est pas au début du mot, comme dans *téléphotographie*.

Rechercher par nom de fichier

Cliquez sur Rechercher/Par nom de fichier, ou appuyez sur Ctrl+Maj+K, pour ouvrir la boîte de dialogue homonyme. Saisissez le texte que l'Organiseur devra trouver dans les noms de fichiers de vos photos.

Rechercher par l'historique

Comme l'Organiseur conserve une trace de l'histoire de chaque photo – quand vous l'importez, vous l'imprimez, ou l'envoyez à quelqu'un par e-mail –, la recherche fondée sur l'historique est très puissante. Cliquez sur Rechercher/Par historique pour afficher une série de commandes correspondant à des événements bien précis correspondant à vos clichés.

Par exemple, si vous choisissez Rechercher/Par historique/ Importée(s) le, une boîte de dialogue liste chaque session d'importation des photos dans votre catalogue. Sélectionnez une session et cliquez sur OK. Le navigateur de photos affiche alors les photos qui ont été importées lors de cette session.

L'historique d'une photo s'affiche dans le panneau Propriétés, section Historique.

Rechercher par type de support

L'Organiseur ne catalogue pas uniquement les photographies avec la commande Rechercher/Par type de support. Dans le sous-menu, choisissez le type de support convoité : Photos, Vidéos, Audio, Créations, Éléments et, nouveauté, PDF.

Photoshop Elements 4.0 reconnaît désormais les fichiers PDF, qu'il
gère à l'instar de n'importe quel fichier d'image. Comme eux, les
fichiers PDF peuvent être étiquetés.

Rechercher autrement

Il existe d'autres commandes disponibles dans le menu Rechercher :
date et heure indéterminées, éléments sans étiquettes, éléments
absents dans les collections. La quatrième possibilité permet d'effectuer une recherche sur la Similarité chromatique. Ceci demande
quelques explications.

Dans le navigateur de photos, sélectionnez plusieurs clichés. Ensuite,
cliquez sur Rechercher/Par similarité visuelle avec les photos sélectionnées. À la différence des autres recherches, l'Organiseur n'affiche
pas uniquement les photos qui répondent à des critères particuliers.
Non ! Il les organise en fonction des similitudes de couleurs.
L'Organiseur analyse rapidement le contenu des photos qui ont des
couleurs majoritairement identiques. Les autres photos sont occul-
tées. Pour réduire le nombre d'images trouvées, nous conseillons de
sélectionner, comme le suggère l'Organiseur, quatre photos sensiblement identiques.

Modifier vos photos

Nous savons que Photoshop Elements 4.0 dispose d'un module d'accès
direct aux fonctionnalités d'édition des clichés. Mais il permet
également d'y apporter des corrections depuis l'Organiseur. Il suffit de
sélectionner une des deux commandes du bouton Modifier :

- **Aller à Retouche rapide :** Donne accès, comme nous l'avons vu
  précédemment, à un nombre limité de paramètres. Une fois la
  correction effectuée, cliquez sur Enregistrer sous. Donnez un
  nouveau nom au fichier pour ne pas remplacer l'original, puis
  cochez l'option Enregistrer dans un jeu de versions avec
  l'original.

- **Aller à Retouche standard :** Ceci ouvre l'Éditeur standard de
  Photoshop Elements 4.0. Vous modifiez puis enregistrez les
  images en respectant les indications du précédent paragraphe.

Sauvegarder

Vous connaissez certainement l'adage "mieux vaut prévenir que guérir". Si vous perdez vos photos à cause d'une panne de disque dur ou de toute autre mésaventure informatique, vous n'aurez aucun recours. C'est pourquoi vous avez intérêt à utiliser la fonction de sauvegarde de l'Organiseur.

L'Organiseur est prévenant. Il avertit régulièrement l'utilisateur d'une perte potentielle de ses images après telle ou telle action. Puis, il met à sa disposition deux commandes de sauvegarde dans le menu Fichier – Graver et Sauvegarder. Ces deux commandes ouvrent la même boîte de dialogue. Là, vous décidez de copier ou de déplacer les fichiers sélectionnés sur un CD ou un DVD, pour libérer de l'espace sur votre disque dur, ou alors de sauvegarder le catalogue (fichiers compris). Nous nous intéresserons plutôt à cette seconde possibilité.

Sauvegarder le catalogue

Après avoir sélectionné l'option Sauvegarder le catalogue, cliquez sur le bouton Suivant. Le message "Vérification des fichiers manquants avant sauvegarde" apparaît. Il permet de rétablir la connexion entre des vignettes et les fichiers correspondants qui auraient été déplacés voire supprimés. Le bouton Reconnecter lance une analyse des fichiers afin que l'Organiseur puisse retrouver la trace des disparus. Nous conseillons fortement de ne pas omettre cette phase sous peine de perdre des références essentielles à la cohérence de votre catalogue.

Les fichiers retrouvés, l'Organiseur tente de les reconnecter en les affichant dans une nouvelle boîte de dialogue. Comparez la vignette identifiée par l'Organiseur avec celle de l'image. Si les deux correspondent, effectuez la connexion en cliquant sur le bouton Connecter. Si l'image ne correspond pas ou si l'Organiseur n'en trouve pas, parcourez vos lecteurs pour localiser le fichier. Dès que c'est fait, cliquez sur Connecter. Une fois toutes les connexions établies, cliquez sur Fermer.

La deuxième étape consiste à choisir entre une Sauvegarde complète ou une Sauvegarde incrémentielle. Lisez les explications sous chaque option pour bien comprendre de quoi il s'agit. La sauvegarde incrémentielle permet d'enrichir un catalogue, surtout quand vous n'avez pas suffisamment d'images pour remplir tout un CD, avec les nouvelles photos – et uniquement elles – que vous y ajoutez. Toutefois, comme vous sauvegardez peut-être pour la première fois, optez pour "complète" et cliquez sur Suivant.

Vous voici dans l'étape des Paramètres de destination. Choisissez
votre graveur de CD ou de DVD dans la liste Sélectionner le lecteur de
destination. En fonction de ses capacités, la vitesse de gravure est
automatiquement sélectionnée. En bas de la boîte de dialogue, vous
voyez l'espace qui sera utilisé sur le CD et le temps de gravure. Cliquez
sur Fermer. Photoshop Elements prépare la gravure. Il vous demande
d'insérer un disque. Annulez si vous n'avez pas de CD sous la main, ou
bien insérez le disque compact et cliquez sur OK. La gravure commence et se poursuit jusqu'à la fin.

Vérifier ou ne pas vérifier ? L'Organiseur demande si vous désirez ou
non vérifier les données gravées. Nous vous conseillons de le faire.
Bien sûr, cela double la durée de la gravure, mais il serait dommage
qu'un incident technique vous fasse perdre vos belles images.

Copier ou déplacer des fichiers

Pour copier des images sur un CD ou un DVD afin de les partager avec
des amis, ou transférer quelques photos hors de l'ordinateur pour
libérer de l'espace disque, sélectionnez les photos concernées, puis
cliquez sur Fichier/Graver. Dans la boîte de dialogue qui s'ouvre, optez
pour Copier/déplacer des fichiers, puis cliquez sur Suivant.

Pour libérer de l'espace disque, activez Déplacer les fichiers. Ainsi,
une fois que les fichiers auront été copiés sur le CD ou le DVD, ils
seront supprimés du disque dur. Elements les remplacera par une
version hors ligne, c'est-à-dire des images "proxy" en basse résolution.
Pour accéder aux originaux, c'est-à-dire aux versions haute résolution,
vous devrez insérer le CD. Toutefois, si votre objectif est de copier des
images sur un disque pour les donner à votre famille ou à vos amis,
décochez Déplacer les fichiers. Vous pouvez également inclure tous
les fichiers d'une pile ou d'un jeu de versions en cochant la case
appropriée.

Cliquez sur Suivant pour indiquer la destination de la copie ou du
déplacement, c'est-à-dire pour choisir le graveur. Insérez un CD ou un
DVD vierge (ou non fermé) et lancez la gravure par un clic sur OK.

Imprimer les photos

La majeure partie du Chapitre 8 est consacrée à l'impression depuis
l'Éditeur d'Elements. Cependant, il est possible d'imprimer depuis
l'Organiseur. Sélectionnez la ou les photos à imprimer. Puis, cliquez
sur le bouton de l'imprimante, ou appuyez sur Ctrl+P. Dans les deux

cas, vous ouvrez la boîte de dialogue Imprimer les photos sélectionnées. Trois étapes numérotées, dans le volet droit de l'interface, vous
guident dans l'impression.

Étape 1 : Choisissez l'imprimante dans la liste. Ensuite, sélectionnez ou
non les technologies d'impression PIM et/ou EXIF d'Epson qui permettent d'obtenir une image aussi fidèle que possible à l'originale affichée
sur votre écran. Si votre appareil photo numérique gère ces technologies, vous pouvez cocher la ou les cases appropriées.

Étape 2 : Choisissez la manière dont les photos seront imprimées :
Tirages individuels, Planche contact, Collection d'images ou Libellés.

Étape 3 : Définissez la taille des tirages et choisissez ou non d'imprimer des étiquettes (date, légende, nom de fichier).

Chapitre 7

Enregistrer avec élégance

Si vous avez déjà utilisé d'autres applications informatiques, nous pensons que l'enregistrement de vos fichiers n'a plus de secret pour vous. Le réflexe du raccourci Ctrl+S est un classique que vous utilisez dans la plupart de vos applications. Photoshop Elements répond au même principe et il met à votre disposition une icône Enregistrer sur la barre de raccourcis.

Ce chapitre fournit des explications détaillées sur l'enregistrement des fichiers et le choix du format approprié. "Formats ?" Oui, c'est une notion abstraite pour le débutant, mais que vous comprendrez en lisant les quelques sections d'un chapitre essentiel à la bonne conduite de vos travaux.

Une image sauve, une image gardée

Comme tout bon utilisateur d'un ordinateur, vous faites partie de ces gens qui n'apprécient pas de travailler des heures sur une image pour la contempler uniquement quand l'ordinateur est allumé, et de la voir s'évanouir à tout jamais dès qu'elles éteignent leur machine ou qu'intervient une panne électrique... ou de leur ordinateur. Pour ne pas être menacé d'une terrible déprime en perdant l'intégralité de votre labeur numérique, sans équivalent au monde puisque c'est le vôtre, l'enregistrement des images devient une phase incontournable de votre travail sous Photoshop Elements. La sauvegarde régulière de vos travaux vous prémunit contre bien des désillusions.

Enregistrer pour la première fois

Voyons la procédure générale d'enregistrement d'une image pour ne pas détruire la photo originale qui pourrait bien vous resservir en cas de malheur :

1. **Choisissez Fichier/Enregistrer sous.**

   La boîte de dialogue représentée sur la Figure 7.1 apparaît. Utilisez cette boîte de dialogue pour nommer votre image et décider de son stockage sur votre disque dur.

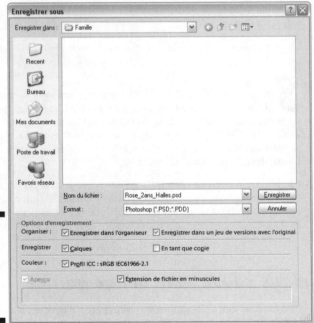

Figure 7.1 : La boîte de dialogue Enregistrer sous de Photoshop Elements.

Vous pouvez ouvrir cette boîte de dialogue en appuyant sur Ctrl+Maj+S.

2. **Saisissez un nom.**

Entrez un nom de fichier descriptif. Si vous enregistrez une copie d'un fichier, le nom doit être suivi d'un point et d'une extension à trois caractères qui détermine le format du fichier. Pour assurer la compatibilité avec d'autres systèmes d'exploitation, n'utilisez ni espace ni caractères spéciaux comme les signes accentués ou le "&". Cantonnez-vous aux lettres et aux chiffres standard. Inutile de saisir l'extension du fichier car Elements le fait à votre place. Pour assurer la compatibilité avec d'autres programmes, cochez la case Extension de fichiers en minuscules.

3. **Dans la liste Format, sélectionnez un format de fichier.**

   Comme vous vous en doutez, il s'agit d'un format d'image numérique, et non de dimensions du genre "format A4" ou "format A5".

4. **Dans la liste Enregistrer dans, sélectionnez le dossier dans lequel vous désirez stocker l'image.**

5. **Sélectionnez une ou plusieurs des options suivantes. Chaque possibilité dépend du type de l'image et de la présence ou non de calques dans l'image (vous en saurez davantage au sur les calques au Chapitre 10).**

   Enregistrer dans l'Organiseur. Cette option permet d'envoyer l'image enregistrée dans le catalogue actuellement ouvert.

   Calques. Avec cette option, l'image conserve tous les calques qui la composent. Dans le cas contraire, l'image est *aplatie*, c'est-à-dire que les calques sont fusionnés pour former une image sans calque.

   Enregistrer dans un jeu de versions avec l'original. Si vous venez de modifier une image qui se trouve dans un catalogue de l'Organiseur, cette option crée un jeu de versions contenant l'image d'origine plus cette version modifiée. Pour plus d'informations sur les jeux de versions, reportez-vous au Chapitre 6.

   En tant que copie. Plutôt que de donner un autre nom à votre image, cochez la case Enregistrer en tant que copie. Cette option ajoute automatiquement le mot "copie" après le nom original du fichier. Vous êtes alors certain que l'image d'origine restera intacte.

   Profil ICC : Cette option incorpore le profil de couleurs défini dans la boîte de dialogue Adobe Gamma.

6. **Cliquez sur le bouton Enregistrer ou appuyez sur la touche Entrée.**

7. **Si une autre boîte de dialogue apparaît, choisissez les options et appuyez sur Entrée.**

   Certains formats ont besoin d'informations supplémentaires que vous devez indiquer dans une boîte de dialogue particulière. Nous verrons cela en temps utile.

Votre image est sauvegardée !

Pour qu'Elements enregistre systématiquement des aperçus, ouvrez la boîte de dialogue Préférences (rubrique Enregistrement des fichiers) puis, dans le menu déroulant Aperçus d'image, sélectionnez Toujours enregistrer.

L'enregistrement d'un aperçu est préjudiciable pour les images destinées au Web. En effet, cette miniature augmente le volume de l'image finale, d'où un téléchargement plus long. Si vous enregistrez des images pour le Web, employez la commande Enregistrer pour le Web, étudiée plus loin dans ce chapitre.

Le réflexe qui sauve

Lorsque votre image a été enregistrée, appuyez sur Ctrl+S chaque fois que vous apportez une modification essentielle. Usez et abusez de ce raccourci. Dans ce cas, aucune boîte de dialogue ne s'affiche puisque Elements sait exactement où vous avez stocké l'image. Il remplace l'ancienne version de l'image par la nouvelle. Ainsi, en cas d'incident, vous ne perdez que les dernières interventions (ce réflexe est vivement recommandé dans toutes vos applications, pas seulement dans Photoshop Elements).

Guide des formats de fichiers

Le choix d'un format d'image est délicat. C'est pourquoi, soyez attentif à la section qui suit, même si le sujet vous semble rébarbatif.

Qu'est-ce qu'un format de fichier ?

Un *format de fichier d'image* est la structure informatique de l'image, autrement dit, la manière dont des données graphiques (lignes et colonnes de pixels, nombre de couleurs, caractéristiques chromatiques...) sont organisées. Il existe des centaines de formats d'image, mais seuls une douzaine sont largement utilisés.

Cette multiplicité peut prêter à confusion d'autant que chacun dispose d'options qui lui sont propres. Heureusement, dans la plupart des circonstances, vous n'avez pas à vous soucier de ces options. Le format Photoshop Brut (RAW), par exemple, sacrifie les couleurs d'impression et d'autres données graphiques ; par conséquent, évitez-le. En revanche, ne le confondez pas avec le format photographique RAW géré par le module Camera Raw, étudié au Chapitre 13. Les formats TARGA (TGA) et Scitex CT (SCT) sont très sophistiqués. Comme on les rencontre rarement, vous n'aurez sans doute jamais à les utiliser.

En fait, vous vous servirez principalement des formats suivants : TIFF, PDF, JPEG (ou JPEG 2000), GIF et, peut-être le plus important, PSD qui est le format natif de Photoshop Elements, mais aussi de son grand frère Photoshop. Les sections suivantes présentent les formats les plus répandus en imagerie numérique, que vous rencontrerez tout au long de votre existence d'infographiste. Nous aborderons les formats JPEG, GIF et PNG dans la section "Enregistrer pour le Web" plus loin dans ce chapitre.

TIFF : le grand communicateur

L'un des meilleurs et des plus répandus formats de fichiers est TIFF. C'est l'acronyme de *Tagged Image File Format*. Il a été développé pour faciliter l'échange des fichiers graphiques entre les plates-formes Mac et PC. Il est également employé dans le domaine de l'impression professionnelle. On l'utilise dans les programmes de PAO et la majorité des applications de dessin.

Lorsque vous sélectionnez le format TIFF dans la boîte de dialogue Enregistrer sous, Elements affiche une autre boîte de dialogue dès que vous cliquez sur le bouton Enregistrer, comme le montre la Figure 7.2. Puisque nous supposons que vous travaillez sur un PC, activez l'option IBM PC et éventuellement la Compression LZW.

La boîte de dialogue Options TIFF propose plusieurs techniques de compression : LZW, JPEG et ZIP. La compression LZW ne sacrifie aucune donnée pour réduire la taille du fichier. On parle d'un schéma de compression *sans perte de données*. La compression ZIP est du même type et fonctionne très bien avec des images contenant de vastes zones d'une seule couleur. La compression ZIP est un classique sous Windows. Enfin, la dernière compression, JPEG, *à pertes de données*. Cela signifie que plus le taux de compression est élevé, plus

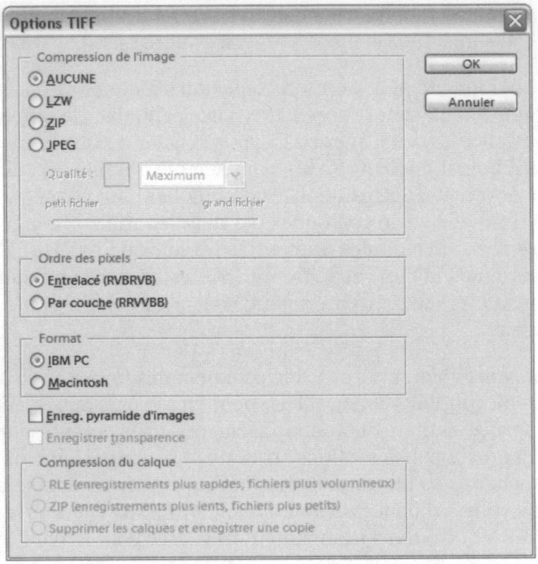

Figure 7.2 :
Les options
avancées du
format TIFF.

votre image perd de détails. Elle est certes beaucoup moins volumineuse, mais parfois nettement dégradée. Vous trouverez davantage d'informations sur le format JPEG dans la section "Enregistrer pour le Web", dans ce chapitre.

Vous avez tout intérêt à utiliser la compression LZW des fichiers TIFF. En effet, toutes les applications qui supportent ce format supportent également cette compression. Par exemple, vous pouvez importer une image TIFF compressée dans des applications comme InDesign, PageMaker ou QuarkXPress qui sont des références dans le domaine de la publication assistée par ordinateur (PAO). La compression LZW ralentit l'enregistrement et l'ouverture du fichier, mais économise beaucoup d'espace disque pour son stockage.

Le format TIFF supporte les calques. Si ce terme ne vous dit rien, reportez-vous au Chapitre 10.

Photoshop PDF

PDF est un format puissant d'une grande polyvalence qui permet d'échanger facilement des fichiers entre les différentes plates-formes informatiques (Windows, Mac, Linux, etc.). PDF est l'acronyme de *Portable Document Format*, une invention de l'éditeur Adobe. Il est, sans surprise, supporté par les applications Adobe comme Illustrator, InDesign et PageMaker. Au fil des années, PDF est devenu un format d'échange et de présentation universellement accepté. Mais pour lire le contenu d'un fichier PDF, il faut installer un logiciel gratuit appelé Adobe Acrobat Reader. Cette application est présente sur tous les CD d'installation des produits Adobe et vous pouvez le télécharger sur le site Adobe à l'adresse www.adobe.fr.

Dans la boîte de dialogue Enregistrer ou Enregistrer sous, choisissez Photoshop PDF dans la liste Format, puis cliquez sur Enregistrer. Ou encore cliquez sur le bouton Enregistrer au format PDF dans la barre de raccourcis, puis sur Enregistrer. Une nouvelle boîte de dialogue apparaît. Choisissez-y le codage ZIP pour une compression sans perte, ou le codage JPEG pour une compression dont la perte dépend du paramètre Qualité. Si votre image contient des zones de transparence, cochez la case Enregistrer les zones de transparence. L'option Interpolation de l'image signifie que les images basse résolution de votre document PDF seront lissées : de nombreuses zones pixelisées seront supprimées du fait de la basse résolution. N'activez pas cette option car l'interpolation n'améliore pas sensiblement la qualité des images affichées en basse résolution.

BMP : la colle à papier du PC

BMP est le format par excellence de l'univers PC. Il fait partie intégrante du système d'exploitation Windows et le papier peint du Bureau a longtemps été à ce format avant que le JPEG l'évince. Les programmeurs utilisent volontiers le format BMP pour les images de leurs fichiers d'aide.

Quand vous enregistrez un fichier au format BMP, ne vous occupez pas des options de la boîte de dialogue qui apparaît. Laissez faire Photoshop Elements.

À propos du format natif de Photoshop Elements

Une preuve supplémentaire que Photoshop Elements est très proche de Photoshop : le format natif d'Elements est celui de Photoshop. Les trois lettres de l'extension sont PSD.

PSD, TIFF et PDF sont les seuls formats de fichiers capables d'enregistrer les calques d'une image ; tous les autres les aplatissent (fusionnent) en une seule image (dépourvue de calque donc).

Quand utiliser quel format ?

Sans complexe, vous avez sauté les sections consacrées aux formats.
Vous êtes du genre rapide et voulez une information utile sans théorie
superflue.

Parfait ! Considérez la liste qui suit comme un mémo indiquant
succinctement quand choisir tel format de fichier plutôt que tel autre
mais sans en connaître la raison.

- ✔ Si vous devez faire et refaire du montage avec des calques,
  enregistrez-la au format natif Elements, c'est-à-dire PSD.

- ✔ Si votre image contient des calques que vous souhaitez conserver, enregistrez l'image au format PSD, TIFF ou PDF.

- ✔ Pour importer votre image dans un autre programme, enregistrez-la au format TIFF, qui est universellement reconnu.

- ✔ Pour importer votre image dans un autre programme tout en
  économisant de l'espace disque, et si la compression LZW du
  format TIFF est insuffisante, utilisez la compression JPEG.

- ✔ Si vous travaillez sur une photographie à envoyer par courrier
  électronique ou à publier sur le Web, utilisez le format de fichier
  JPEG. Pour des images fortement contrastées (au trait) ou
  contenant des transparences, utilisez le format GIF. Pour en
  savoir davantage sur ces deux formats, lisez la prochaine
  section.

Enregistrer pour le Web

Oui, JPEG et GIF sont les deux formats les plus utilisés pour publier
des images sur le Web. Vous pouvez choisir Fichier/Enregistrer sous
et sélectionner soit JPEG, soit GIF. Cependant, Photoshop Elements
dispose d'une commande appropriée pour l'Internet : Enregistrer pour
le Web. Une boîte de dialogue apparaît, affichant à gauche l'image
d'origine et à droite l'image optimisée pour Internet. En fonction des
différents réglages définis dans la zone de droite, vous choisissez GIF
ou JPEG, le nombre de couleurs, le taux de compression, etc.

Qu'est-ce que le format PNG ?

Outre les formats GIF et JPEG, un autre format se développe sur le
Web : PNG (*Portable Network Graphic*). Il est destiné à remplacer le
très populaire GIF. PNG est plus sophistiqué que le format GIF. Il gère

des millions, voire des milliards de couleurs, alors que GIF est limité à
256 couleurs. Le format PNG supporte le mode RVB, les niveaux de
gris ou ce que l'on appelle des couleurs indexées ainsi que, cerise sur
le gâteau, la transparence. Pour résumer, on peut dire que PNG
présente tous les avantages des formats JPEG et GIF. Mais PNG
présente un inconvénient majeur : il n'est pas reconnu par tous les
navigateurs Web. Si vous êtes certain que votre image sera affichée
dans un navigateur récent, essayez PNG ; dans le cas contraire, il est
préférable de s'en tenir aux formats JPEG et GIF.

Si, malgré ces recommandations, vous persistez à utiliser le PNG, vous
aurez le choix entre le PNG-8 et le PNG-24. Codé sur 8 bits, le PNG-8
sauvegarde les fichiers comme le format GIF, en 256 couleurs maximum. En revanche, le PNG-24, codé sur 24 bits enregistre plus de
16,7 millions de couleurs. Reportez-vous à la section consacrée au
format GIF pour en savoir plus à ce propos.

La commande Enregistrer pour le Web

La commande Fichier/Enregistrer pour le Web ou son raccourci,
Ctrl+Maj+Alt+S, ouvre la boîte de dialogue représentée sur la Figure 7.3. Elements affiche l'image d'origine à gauche et la copie
compressée à droite. Vous voyez l'image exactement comme elle
apparaîtra dans un navigateur Web. Modifiez les paramètres affichés
dans la partie droite de la boîte de dialogue.

Pour voir l'image de plus près, vous pouvez zoomer et faire défiler le
contenu de la fenêtre. Pour prévisualiser le résultat de vos paramètres
dans votre navigateur Web favori, cliquez sur le bouton Aperçu dans.
L'image s'affiche alors dans la fenêtre du navigateur.

Si vous comptiez réduire l'image afin de la publier sur le Web en
utilisant Image/Redimensionner/Taille de l'image, mais que vous ayez
oublié de le faire, Elements 4.0 permet de le faire dans la boîte de
dialogue Enregistrer pour le Web. C'est dans la zone Nouvelle taille
que cela se passe : entrez les nouvelles dimensions en pixels ou en
pourcentage. À moins de vouloir écraser ou étirer votre image, laissez
cochée la case Conserver les proportions. Après le réglage, cliquez sur
le bouton Appliquer.

La liste Paramètres prédéfinis contient des réglages relativement
standard pour un affichage dans une page Web ou pour un envoi par
courrier électronique. Dans les sections suivantes, nous examinerons
les options des formats d'optimisation GIF et JPEG.

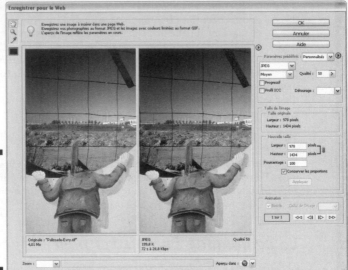

Figure 7.3 :
Comparez
l'image
originale
avec celle
que vous
optimisez
pour le Web.

Cliquez sur la flèche située à droite de la section Paramètres prédéfinis. Dans le menu local, choisissez Optimiser pour la taille du fichier. Dans la boîte de dialogue qui apparaît, saisissez le poids que doit faire votre image après l'optimisation. En fonction de la taille d'origine de l'image et de la valeur saisie ici, Elements effectue lui-même la compression au bon format. Pour imposer le choix du format, activez l'option Paramètres actuels. N'utilisez cette commande que si le poids de l'image est une priorité. En effet, plus vous réduisez ce poids plus l'image sera compressée donc dégradée.

Dans la section Démarrer avec de la boîte de dialogue Optimiser pour la taille du fichier, l'option Paramètres actuels crée un fichier avec le format spécifié dans la boîte de dialogue Enregistrer pour le Web. Si vous choisissez Sélection automatique GIF/JPEG, Elements analyse l'image et détermine le meilleur format selon la compression qu'il doit appliquer.

JPEG : le meilleur choix pour les photos

JPEG signifie *Joint Photographic Experts Group* (groupement commun des experts en photographie), mais qui s'en soucie ? L'important est de savoir que JPEG est le format le plus efficace pour la compression des images. Cependant, cette compression entraîne des pertes de données : un algorithme complexe supprime les détails qui ont de fortes chances de ne pas être perçus par l'œil. En réalité, cette suppression est souvent très discernable. Elle se manifeste par un moutonnement peu esthétique aux limites entre deux couleurs. Il en résulte une image de moins bonne qualité que l'original, bien que d'un "poids" bien moins élevé.

Voici une description des paramètres :

✔ **Qualité de la compression (Bas, Moyen, Haut, Supérieur, Maximum) :** Sélectionnez une option dans la liste située juste en dessous de JPEG. L'option Maximum est la meilleure car elle préserve la plupart des données de l'image, mais les paramètres Haut et Supérieur produisent également d'excellents résultats. Notez que le curseur Qualité permet de régler la compression à une valeur supérieure à 80, qui est celle associée par défaut à Haut, et à une valeur inférieure à 10, associée par défaut au paramètre Bas.

✔ **Progressif :** Cette option autorise l'affichage graduel de l'image par étapes – d'abord grossière puis de plus en plus nette – pendant son téléchargement dans le navigateur Web de l'internaute. C'est le moyen idéal de le faire patienter lorsqu'il surfe en bas débit. Dans la mesure où tous les navigateurs ne supportent pas cette option, ne la cochez pas.

En utilisant la commande Enregistrer sous et en choisissant le format JPEG, vous pouvez spécifier le nombre d'étapes nécessaires à l'image pour se charger totalement.

✔ **Profil ICC :** Cette option incorpore un profil de couleurs dans l'image JPEG. Ce profil augmente le fichier d'environ 3 kilo-octets. Sachez que peu de navigateurs gèrent les profils ICC. Vous ajoutez donc 3 Ko de données pour rien. Ne cochez pas cette case.

✔ **Qualité :** Cette option contrôle le taux de la compression JPEG, et par conséquent la qualité finale. Plus la valeur est élevée, meilleure est l'image, mais moins importante est la compression. Plus la valeur de la qualité est faible, plus la compression est importante mais moins bonne est la qualité de l'image. Les options JPEG de la boîte de dialogue Enregistrer sous autorisent des valeurs comprises de 0 à 12, tandis que celles de la boîte de dialogue Enregistrer pour le Web s'étendent de 0 à 100.

✔ **Détourage :** Cette option ne s'applique que si l'image contient des zones transparentes. Comme la compression JPEG ne reconnaît pas la transparence, vous devez choisir une couleur qui s'affichera dans les zones transparentes. Par exemple, si le bleu est sélectionné et que cette même teinte est utilisée comme couleur d'arrière-plan de la page Web, les bords de l'image donneront l'impression de se fondre doucement dans l'arrière-plan.

Vous pouvez sélectionner une couleur de Détourage avec l'outil Pipette, situé dans le coin supérieur gauche de la boîte de dialogue Enregistrer pour le Web. Vous pouvez également cliquer sur le nuancier situé sous la pipette pour accéder au Sélecteur de couleurs représenté sur la Figure 7.4. Cochez la case Couleurs Web uniquement pour sélectionner les couleurs dans la palette sécurisée Web de 216 teintes. Sinon, cliquez sur le cube pour remplacer la couleur sélectionnée par l'équivalent le plus proche de la palette sécurisée Web. Si vous êtes un pro de l'HTML, le langage de programmation du Web, saisissez directement une valeur hexadécimale dans le champ # de la boîte de dialogue.

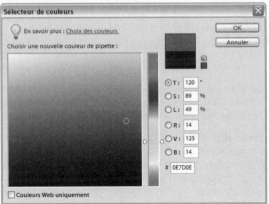

Figure 7.4 : Le Sélecteur de couleurs d'Elements possède trois options spécifiquement destinées aux concepteurs Web.

GIF : l'origine des graphiques sur le Web

Il ne faut pas rester *nul* toute sa vie. La première chose à connaître en infographie est la manière de prononcer GIF. Ici *G* équivaut à *J*, rien de bien surprenant en français. Prononcez GIF comme vous prononcez *Givrer*. Vous venez de faire un grand pas en avant. Le format GIF est idéal pour les images à fort contraste. Ici, une petite précision s'impose. Par *fort contraste*, on entend des images sans transition progressive de teintes. Par exemple, la juxtaposition de deux couleurs unies, comme un rouge et un bleu, c'est-à-dire de deux aplats, représente une image à fort contraste. Il est donc recommandé d'utiliser le format GIF pour des dessins au trait, du texte, des fonds unis, etc. L'inconvénient majeur du GIF est sa palette de couleurs limitée à 256 teintes (toutes numérotées de 0 à 255, d'où l'appellation de "couleurs indexées"), soit une profondeur de 8 bits. Aujourd'hui, ce format est surtout utilisé pour créer ces animations rudimentaires qui égayent les pages Web.

Voici les options GIF :

✔ **Algorithme de réduction des couleurs [Perception, Sélective, Adaptive, Restrictive (Web)]** : Ce menu permet de réduire le nombre de couleurs d'une image de 16 millions de teintes à 256 ou moins. L'algorithme de réduction des couleurs produit une palette contenant les couleurs utilisées dans l'image.

  • **Adaptative** sélectionne les couleurs les plus fréquemment utilisées. Si une image contient peu de couleurs et que vous désiriez retrouver des nuances aussi exactes que possible, choisissez cette palette.

  • **Perceptive** est une variante de la palette Adaptative. Perceptive est plus intelligente qu'Adaptative. Elle analyse l'image afin de rééchantillonner les couleurs et donner les meilleures transitions. Utilisez cette palette avec les photographies – si vous ne savez pas ou ne voulez pas utiliser la compression JPEG –, dans lesquelles les transitions entre les couleurs sont généralement subtiles.

  • **Sélective** est aussi une variante de la palette Adaptative, mais elle préserve bien mieux les couleurs dans l'optique d'une utilisation des images pour le Web. Utilisez cette palette lorsqu'une image contient des teintes lumineuses ou parfaitement délimitées les unes par rapport aux autres.

  • **Restrictive (Web)** utilise les 216 nuances sécurisées du Web qui s'affichent par défaut dans tous les systèmes codés sur 8 bits. A vrai dire, il existe de bien meilleures palettes que celle-ci.

✔ **Transparence** : Si une image composée de plusieurs calques contient des zones transparentes, conservez-les en cochant cette option. N'oubliez pas que la transparence GIF n'est pas progressive comme dans les calques d'Elements.

✔ **Animer** : Ne s'applique que si vous créez des animations GIF.

↙ **Entrelacé :** Cette option produit un fichier GIF entrelacé. Dans ce cas, l'image s'affiche progressivement dans le navigateur Web pendant toute la durée de son téléchargement. Cette option est formidable quand elle fonctionne correctement, mais il y a malheureusement des problèmes de compatibilité. À utiliser avec précaution.

↙ **Couleurs :** C'est ici que vous spécifiez le nombre de couleurs utilisées dans une image convertie pour le Web. Commencez avec un nombre de couleurs assez faible, comme 64. Observez s'il y a ou non dégradation de l'image. Si le résultat ne vous convient pas, choisissez 128. Essayez d'obtenir le nombre de couleurs le plus faible sans trop nuire à la qualité de l'image sur le Web. Avec des photographies, vous constaterez que le nombre de couleurs doit être très élevé. Mais, "très élevé" signifie en GIF 256 couleurs maximum. Pour cette raison, il est préférable d'opter pour le format JPEG, qui affiche plus de 16,7 millions de couleurs.

↙ **Tramage :** Cette magnifique option contrôle le tramage appliqué à une image, c'est-à-dire l'utilisation de pixels colorés adjacents pour produire, par confusion, une couleur qui n'existe pas dans la palette choisie. Vous pouvez modifier l'incidence du tramage en augmentant ou en diminuant sa valeur. Les valeurs les plus faibles produisent des transitions franches, tandis que les valeurs les plus élevées produisent des transitions faibles. Cette option est délicate à maîtriser. Ne quittez jamais l'aperçu des yeux quand vous l'utilisez.

↙ **Détourage :** Cette option est comparable à l'option Détourage de la compression JPEG. Quand la Transparence est désactivée, la couleur Cache est mélangée avec les pixels translucides, tandis que les pixels transparents restent transparents. Ce paramètre est très utile pour créer une image mélangée avec la couleur d'arrière-plan de la page Web.

Lorsque vous choisissez le format CompuServe GIF dans la boîte de dialogue Enregistrer sous, la boîte de dialogue représentée sur la Figure 7.5 propose quelques options supplémentaires :

↙ **Palette :** C'est la même option que celle rencontrée dans l'algorithme de réduction de couleurs de la boîte de dialogue Enregistrer pour le Web. Vous y trouvez quelques autres choix :

  Exacte : Si une image contient moins de 256 couleurs, la palette Exacte apparaît par défaut. N'y touchez pas.

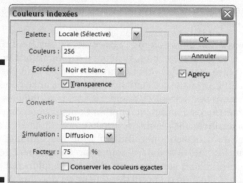

Figure 7.5 :
La boîte de
dialogue
Couleurs
indexées
contrôle
l'aspect des
images GIF.

Système : Utilisez cette palette si vous désirez ajouter un graphisme à votre système (comme un motif de Bureau ou un fichier d'icône pour le Bureau).

Web : Cette option convertit les couleurs de votre image dans la palette sécurisée Web de 216 couleurs.

Uniforme : La pire de toutes les palettes. Elle génère un échantillonnage uniforme du spectre des couleurs. Ne l'utilisez jamais !

Précédente : Cette palette se base sur la dernière table de couleurs créée par la commande Couleurs indexées. On s'en sert généralement pour créer une série de graphismes à hauts contrastes sans porter préjudice à l'harmonie de l'ensemble des images ainsi affichées.

Le menu Aperçu

Avant de quitter la fenêtre Enregistrer pour le Web, étudions un dernier jeu d'options. En haut à droite de la fenêtre, vous découvrez une flèche. Cliquez dessus pour accéder à un menu local. Les commandes de ce menu contrôlent l'apparence de l'affichage et renvoient des informations sur la vitesse de téléchargement de l'image en fonction d'une vitesse de modem sélectionnée.

Les commandes sont divisées en trois sections :

- **Navigateur de tramage :** Sélectionnez cette option pour simuler l'aspect de l'image sur un moniteur à 256 couleurs (une antiquité, vous aurez bien du mal à en trouver un...). Cette technique est parfaite pour savoir si vous devez ou non utiliser la palette Web sécurisée.

✔ **Compensation des couleurs :** Les couleurs changent d'un moniteur à un autre et d'un système d'exploitation à un autre (c'est-à-dire entre Mac OS et Windows). On ne peut pas savoir comment une image sera affichée, mais les quatre commandes de couleurs permettent d'anticiper certains problèmes colorimétriques. Par défaut, l'option Couleur non compensée est active. Ici, Elements n'anticipe aucun comportement d'affichage des couleurs. Sélectionnez Couleur Windows standard ou Couleur Macintosh standard pour apprécier l'aspect des couleurs affichées sur une autre plate-forme informatique. L'option Utilisation du profil de couleur du document exploite le profil incorporé dans le document, s'il existe (Voir le Chapitre 5 pour plus d'informations sur les profils de couleur).

✔ **Taille/Durée du téléchargement :** Les douze dernières commandes permettent d'estimer la durée de téléchargement d'une image selon le taux de transfert des modems.

Chapitre 8

C'est parfait ! Non, attends ! OK, imprime !

C e chapitre est consacré à l'impression d'une image numérique. La procédure n'est pas facile à expliquer dans la mesure où elle varie d'une imprimante à une autre. Diverses variables entrent en jeu : la qualité du papier, le type de raccordement du périphérique d'impression, une éventuelle mise en réseau de l'imprimante, etc. En bref, nous entrons dans un univers un peu compliqué. Soyez indulgent à notre égard si les procédures indiquées ici diffèrent sensiblement de celles imposées par votre imprimante. Mais auparavant, voyons comment annuler des actions avec une extraordinaire souplesse.

Voyager dans le temps

Plus vous travaillez sur une image, plus vous vous exposez à des erreurs difficiles à rattraper. Une succession de mauvais gestes, et tout votre travail est compromis.

La palette Annuler l'historique

Photoshop Elements est heureusement capable de revenir en arrière, vous permettant de repartir sur des bases nouvelles. Voici comment

utiliser une des fonctions les plus souples et les plus utiles de
Photoshop Elements, nous avons nommé la palette Annuler l'historique :

1. **Ouvrez la palette Annuler l'historique.**

2. **Créez une nouvelle image.**

   La taille importe peu ; créez une image suffisamment grande
   pour y donner des coups de pinceau. Ceci fait, vous remarquez
   que la palette Annuler l'historique affiche une première étape :
   Nouveau. Une étape représente une action, ici la création d'une
   nouvelle image. Vous ne pouvez rien en faire. C'est le début de
   votre travail, ou plus exactement son *point de départ*.

3. **Sélectionnez l'outil Pinceau et faites-le glisser sur l'image.**

   Appuyez sur la touche B pour activer le Pinceau. Ensuite
   appuyez sur D pour restaurer les couleurs de premier et
   d'arrière-plan par défaut, c'est-à-dire le noir et le blanc. Appliquez un seul coup de pinceau, pas plus. Regardez la palette
   Annuler l'historique : une nouvelle étape y apparaît, appelée
   Pinceau.

4. **Faites une pause.**

5. **Cliquez sur l'icône Annuler de la barre de raccourcis (la
   flèche incurvée vers la gauche).**

   Vous observez deux choses : votre coup de pinceau disparaît de
   la zone de travail (la toile) et l'état Pinceau de la palette Annuler
   l'historique est en grisé, c'est-à-dire impossible à sélectionner.

6. **Cliquez sur l'icône Réinitialiser de la barre de raccourcis (la
   flèche courbée vers la droite).**

   Le coup de pinceau réapparaît et l'état Pinceau de la palette
   Annuler l'historique redevient disponible. Remarquez qu'il
   existe un lien ténu entre les deux icônes Annuler et Réinitialiser
   de la barre de raccourcis et la palette Annuler l'historique.

7. **Donnez trois autres coups de pinceau.**

   Séparez bien chaque coup de pinceau des autres. Dans la palette
   Annuler l'historique, trois étapes supplémentaires apparaissent.
   La palette en contient désormais quatre, c'est-à-dire quatre
   actions distinctes.

8. **Maintenant, appuyez trois fois sur Ctrl+Z.**

Vous revenez à la première étape. Restaurez alors les coups de pinceau en appuyant trois fois sur Ctrl+Y.

9. **Cliquez sur le premier état Pinceau de la palette Annuler l'historique.**

C'est la manière la plus directe pour voyager dans l'Historique.

Annuler (Ctrl+Z) permet d'annuler jusqu'à ce qu'il n'y ait plus rien à annuler. Rétablir (Ctrl+Y) fait exactement le contraire, permettant de rétablir les actions jusqu'à ce qu'il n'y en ait plus.

Annuler et Rétablir fonctionnent même quand la palette Annuler l'historique n'est pas ouverte.

Les restrictions du voyage

Annuler et Rétablir procurent une grande flexibilité dans le travail. Cependant, voici quelques points fondamentaux à garder à l'esprit quand vous utilisez ces outils :

✔ Les seules actions susceptibles d'être annulées ou sélectionnées, dans la palette Annuler l'historique, sont celles qui modifient l'image. L'utilisation d'outils comme Zoom et Main n'est pas réversible car elle n'affecte que l'affichage d'une partie de l'image et n'est que temporaire.

✔ Vous ne pouvez pas inverser les couleurs de premier et d'arrière-plan par ces méthodes, ni un paramètre que vous auriez défini dans la boîte de dialogue Préférences, ni masquer ou afficher des palettes, ni même modifier les options de la barre d'options ou la sélection d'un outil.

✔ Dès que vous fermez une image, vous perdez toutes les étapes de l'historique car Photoshop Elements ne les mémorise pas.

La palette Annuler l'historique

Voyons de plus près la palette Annuler l'historique illustrée sur la Figure 8.1. Elle enregistre toutes les interventions sur une image et produit une liste d'étapes correspondant à chaque action. Chaque fois que vous exécutez une tâche, l'Historique ajoute une étape. Elements nomme chaque étape et affiche son icône afin de mieux l'identifier.

Voici la liste des caractéristiques et des fonctions de la palette Annuler l'historique et la façon d'en tirer profit :

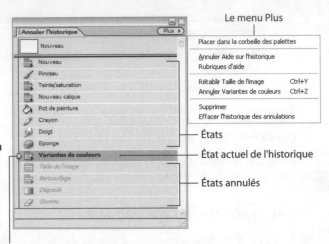

Le menu Plus

États

État actuel de l'historique

États annulés

Figure 8.1 :
La palette
Annuler
l'historique
enregistre
chaque
étape.

Curseur des états d'annulation de l'historique

- Pour revenir à un état précédent, cliquez dessus. Vous remarquez qu'Elements annule temporairement les effets des autres étapes.

- Les états estompés sont les *états annulés*. Un état annulé peut être rétabli en cliquant dessus. Si vous réalisez une nouvelle opération après avoir annulé des états dans la palette Annuler l'historique, ces états annulés disparaissent.

- Pour remonter dans la palette état par état, appuyez sur Ctrl+Z. Pour avancer étape par étape, appuyez sur Ctrl+Y. Ces commandes sont également accessibles par le menu de la palette Annuler l'historique.

- Les équivalents clavier pour Annuler et Réinitialiser peuvent être personnalisés via Édition/Préférences/Général. Notez que dans cette boîte de dialogue, les termes sont Aller vers l'arrière/ avant.

- Faites glisser le curseur de la palette Annuler l'historique pour afficher les états masqués. Vous pouvez rapidement afficher les premiers et les derniers états.

- Elements permet de consigner jusqu'à 1 000 états d'historique. Via Édition/Préférences/Général, vous pouvez fixer le nombre maximum d'étapes de la palette Annuler l'historique. Si votre ordinateur dispose d'une quantité insuffisante de mémoire vive (RAM), diminuez le nombre d'étapes. Sachez que lorsque vous dépassez le maximum admis, les étapes les plus anciennes ⸱ (c'est-à-dire en partant du haut de la liste des états) disparaissent.

✔ Si l'image vous satisfait totalement et que votre ordinateur donne des signes de faiblesse à cause d'un manque certain de mémoire, choisissez Effacer l'historique des annulations dans le menu de la palette Annuler l'historique. Si vous estimez que cela est une erreur, choisissez immédiatement Édition/Annuler Effacer l'historique ou appuyez sur Ctrl+Alt+Z. Si plusieurs fichiers sont ouverts, effacez tous les historiques en choisissant Édition/Effacer/Annuler l'historique.

✔ Si vous voulez gérer le nombre d'états disponibles dans la palette Annuler l'historique et que vous avez déjà commencé à travailler dans Elements, il est préférable de supprimer les derniers états que vous avez créés. Pour ce faire, sélectionnez l'état le plus ancien à supprimer et choisissez Supprimer dans le menu Plus. Elements supprimera l'état sélectionné ainsi que tout état subséquent.

✔ Chaque fichier a sa propre histoire ; par conséquent, vous pouvez travailler sur plusieurs images indépendamment les unes des autres.

✔ Après avoir fermé votre image, son historique disparaît à tout jamais. Les états de la palette Annuler l'historique ne sont pas enregistrés dans le fichier.

Renoncer à une multitude d'éditions

Parfois vos erreurs sont minimes, parfois elles sont grossières. Si après quelques minutes d'un travail approximatif, vous détestez le résultat obtenu, récupérez l'aspect de l'image dernièrement enregistrée. Pour cela, deux actions sont possibles. Vous pouvez cliquer sur le premier état de la palette Annuler l'historique. Mais attention ! N'oubliez pas que si vous avez dépassé le nombre maximum d'actions acceptées par l'Historique, il n'est plus possible de récupérer l'image telle qu'elle apparaissait au moment de son ouverture. Ce nombre d'annulations est défini dans la boîte de dialogue Préférences. Si cela se produit, et nous dirions même pour plus de sûreté, choisissez Fichier/Version enregistrée. Elements recharge l'image, annulant ainsi toutes vos modifications.

La commande Imprimer

Si cela ne vous est jamais arrivé, car vous débutez dans l'univers de l'infographie, il y a fort à parier que l'impression vous réserve de mauvaises surprises. La première est qu'il faut s'habituer aux caractéristiques de son imprimante avant d'obtenir des images parfaites. La seconde mauvaise surprise, découlant de la première, est que vous gâchez beaucoup d'encre et de papier, des consommables terriblement onéreux. Si, au début d'une impression, vous constatez que l'image est ratée, cliquer sur le bouton Annuler de la barre de raccourcis n'aura pas pour effet d'interrompre l'impression et ramener la feuille de papier dans le bac de l'imprimante, tout en pompant l'encre pour la restituer dans les cartouches d'où elle était sortie. Ce qui est gâché est irrémédiablement perdu. Alors examinons de plus près la procédure d'impression pour se mettre à l'abri de ces mauvaises surprises.

Tout ce qu'il faut savoir sur l'impression

Quand tout baigne (dans l'encre, bien sûr), l'impression n'est pas une procédure complexe. Les étapes suivantes expliquent comment cela se passe :

1. **Allumez votre imprimante.**

2. **Choisissez Fichier/Enregistrer ou appuyez sur Ctrl+S.**

   Cette étape n'est qu'une sage précaution. Il est toujours préférable d'enregistrer son travail avant de lancer l'impression, au cas où les événements tourneraient mal. Il arrive qu'un bogue surgisse, bloquant l'ordinateur. Adieu les dernières modifications non enregistrées avant de lancer l'impression ! Alors, pas de blague... Prenez l'habitude d'enregistrer préalablement.

3. **Vérifiez que l'image correspond aux dimensions de votre feuille.**

   Cliquez sur l'icône Aperçu avant impression de la barre de raccourcis, ou choisissez Fichier/Imprimer. Une dernière précaution consiste à appuyer sur Ctrl+P : Elements affiche un aperçu de l'image avant impression qui montre exactement comment le document apparaît sur la page. Si l'image n'excède pas les limites de la feuille, elle sera correctement et intégralement imprimée. Dans le cas contraire, cochez la case Ajuster au support, dans la partie Zone d'impression mise à l'échelle de la boîte de dialogue Aperçu avant impression. L'image sera alors réduite pour s'assujettir aux dimensions de la feuille. Cela n'affecte en rien l'image sur le disque, seulement son impression.

4. **Sélectionnez une imprimante, une taille de papier et une orientation de la page.**

   Tous ces choix sont effectués dans la boîte de dialogue Mise en page que vous ouvrez en cliquant sur le bouton Format d'impression de la boîte de dialogue Aperçu avant impression. Vérifiez la conformité de vos paramètres et validez le tout en cliquant sur OK.

   Vous pouvez directement ouvrir la boîte de dialogue Mise en page en appuyant sur Ctrl+Maj+P. Les paramètres définis, cliquez sur OK pour quitter la boîte de dialogue Mise en page.

   Cliquez éventuellement sur les boutons d'orientation pour modifier la position de l'image sur la page.

5. **Cliquez sur le bouton Imprimer de la boîte de dialogue Aperçu avant impression.**

   Elements affiche la boîte de dialogue Impression. Vous y spécifiez notamment le nombre de copies à réaliser, ainsi que les propriétés d'impression selon le papier utilisé et la qualité recherchée.

6. **Appuyez sur la touche Entrée.**

   Les spécialistes considèrent que vous entrez à présent dans la phase la plus sereine de l'impression, tandis que les statistiques montrent que nombre d'utilisateurs angoissent en attendant la sortie du tirage.

Choisir une imprimante

Cette section est consacrée aux utilisateurs ne possédant qu'une seule imprimante. En revanche, si votre ordinateur est connecté à un réseau ou si vous disposez de plusieurs imprimantes, vous devez indiquer à Elements celle qu'il doit mettre en œuvre.

Pour sélectionner une imprimante, ouvrez la boîte de dialogue Mise en page, soit en choisissant Fichier/Format d'impression, soit en appuyant sur Ctrl+Maj+P, soit encore en cliquant sur le bouton Format d'impression de la boîte de dialogue Aperçu avant impression. En fonction de votre imprimante et de votre système d'exploitation, la boîte de dialogue ressemble plus ou moins à celle de la Figure 8.2.

Figure 8.2 :
Vous
sélectionnez
une
imprimante
dans cette
boîte de
dialogue.

Pour sélectionner une imprimante, choisissez-la dans la liste Nom. Cliquez sur OK pour fermer la boîte de dialogue.

Image et papier

La boîte de dialogue Aperçu avant impression, immortalisée sur la Figure 8.3, fournit bien plus qu'un simple aperçu de votre image sur la feuille de papier. Voici tous les paramètres qu'elle permet de définir :

- ✔ **Taille d'impression :** Cette nouvelle option permet de choisir parmi des dimensions standard de papier. Si vous n'y trouvez pas celle que vous utilisez, créez-la !

- ✔ **Zone d'impression mise à l'échelle :** Les options de cette partie de la boîte de dialogue permettent d'agrandir ou de réduire la taille de l'image pour l'impression uniquement. Entrez un pourcentage inférieur à 100 pour réduire les dimensions de l'image imprimée. Tous les pixels de l'image sont imprimés, mais à une taille réduite. Vous pouvez également saisir des valeurs dans les champs Hauteur et Largeur, ou activer l'option Afficher le cadre de sélection pour définir manuellement la taille dans la zone d'aperçu en agissant sur les poignées de redimensionnement. Vous notez que les paramètres Échelle, Hauteur et Largeur sont liés. La modification d'une des valeurs se répercute sur les deux autres.

Si vous sélectionnez une partie de votre image avant d'afficher l'Aperçu avant impression (via les outils étudiés au Chapitre 9), vous pouvez limiter l'impression à cette sélection en cochant la case Imprimer la sélection. Ceci est excellent pour effectuer un test, évitant ainsi de gaspiller encre et papier.

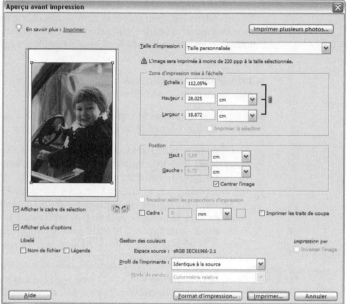

Figure 8.3 :
Prévisualisez
la taille de
l'image en
utilisant la
boîte de
dialogue
Aperçu avant
impression.

✔ **Position :** Cochez l'option Centrer l'image pour qu'elle s'imprime
au centre de la page. Pour saisir de nouvelles valeurs de
positionnement, désélectionnez Centrer l'image et tapez des
valeurs dans les cases Haut et Gauche, ou activez Afficher le
cadre de sélection. Dans la fenêtre d'aperçu, faites glisser les
poignées, afin de réduire ou d'augmenter la taille d'impression
de l'image, et déplacez le cadre de sélection à l'endroit où vous
désirez imprimer la page.

✔ **Afficher le cadre de sélection :** Cette option fait apparaître un
cadre autour de l'image dans la zone d'aperçu. Vous voyez les
limites de l'image et pouvez agir sur sa position et ses dimensions.

✔ **Rotation :** Cliquez sur l'icône affichée sous l'aperçu pour faire
pivoter l'image de 90 degrés à chaque clic.

✔ **Recadrer selon les proportions d'impression :** Si vous avez
choisi une taille de page dans la liste Taille d'impression, l'image
est recadrée en conséquence avec un respect total des proportions qui existent entre la hauteur et la largeur.

✔ **Cadre :** Pour imprimer un contour, cliquez sur cette option. La taille du cadre s'exprime en pouces, millimètres, ou points. Pour définir la couleur du cadre, cliquez sur le carré blanc par défaut. Définissez une teinte dans le Sélecteur de couleurs qui apparaît, et cliquez sur OK.

✔ **Imprimer les traits de coupe :** Cette option affiche et imprime des traits de coupe dans chaque angle de l'image.

✔ **Afficher plus d'options :** Vous pouvez accéder aux options Libellé et Gestion des couleurs. Voyons de quoi il retourne.

• **Libellé :** Imprime un texte sous l'image. Pour saisir ce texte, vous devez d'abord cliquer sur Annuler dans la boîte de dialogue Aperçu avant impression, puis choisir Fichier/ Informations. Dans le champ Légende, saisissez le texte à imprimer sous l'image, puis cliquez sur OK. Quand vous revenez dans la boîte de dialogue Aperçu avant impression, vous voyez dans l'aperçu le texte qui s'imprimera sous l'image. Si vous cochez Nom de fichier, le nom sous lequel l'image est enregistrée s'imprime au-dessus.

• **Gestion des couleurs :** Ces options sont basées sur le concept d'*espaces colorimétriques*. Les divers équipements d'une chaîne d'impression opèrent dans différents espaces colorimétriques. Les moniteurs, les imprimantes de bureau et les imprimantes professionnelles ont un espace colorimétrique unique. Les options de Gestion des couleurs permettent de convertir l'espace colorimétrique au moment de l'impression. Par exemple, si vous créez une image RVB dans le profil Adobe RGB (1998), vous pouvez convertir l'image dans l'espace colorimétrique des imprimantes Epson si vous en utilisez une (pour plus d'informations sur la gestion des couleurs, consultez le Chapitre 5).

✔ **Impression par transfert :** Ici, l'option Inverser l'image permet d'imprimer l'image comme si vous la placiez devant un miroir. De ce fait, quand l'image est imprimée sur du papier transfert par exemple, elle sera correctement imprimée sur le vêtement de destination. (Qui n'a jamais voulu créer un joli tee-shirt à son effigie ?)

La boîte de dialogue Mise en page permet de faire d'autres choix qui affectent la sortie de l'image sur papier. Pour ouvrir cette boîte de dialogue, choisissez Fichier/Format d'impression ou appuyez sur Ctrl+Maj+P, ou bien encore cliquez sur le bouton Format d'impression de la boîte de dialogue Aperçu avant impression.

Dans les propriétés de l'imprimante, vous pouvez choisir une impression en mode Paysage ou Portrait, c'est-à-dire horizontal ou vertical (ou encore, "à l'italienne" ou "à la française", comme on dit de par chez nous). Si, dans l'un des deux modes, l'image ne peut pas s'imprimer correctement, Elements la pivote de manière à ce qu'elle occupe correctement la page.

Transmettre l'image à l'imprimante

L'épreuve des options d'impression surmontée, vous êtes presque tiré d'affaire. Il ne reste plus qu'à indiquer des informations de dernière minute, comme le nombre de tirages, ou copies, à effectuer. Cliquez sur le bouton Imprimer de la boîte de dialogue Aperçu avant impression pour accéder à la boîte de dialogue Impression représentée sur la Figure 8.4.

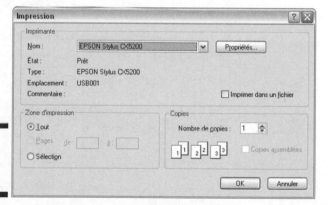

Figure 8.4 :
La boîte de
dialogue
Impression.

Si l'image est plus grande que la page, Elements affiche un message signalant que certaines zones seront tronquées. Si vous décidez de ne pas imprimer l'image dans ces conditions, vous devrez par la suite modifier sa taille. L'impression peut néanmoins être lancée avec les conséquences indiquées par le message d'Elements.

Si vous avez totalement confiance dans les proportions de votre image et de la taille de votre papier, mais qu'Elements indique que l'image sera tronquée, vérifiez l'orientation de la page dans la boîte de dialogue Mise en page. Dans bien des cas, changer son orientation arrange les choses.

Cliquez sur le bouton OK ou appuyez sur la touche Entrée. L'impression sera plus ou moins longue selon la résolution d'impression, la taille de l'image, la qualité du papier et de l'imprimante.

Chapitre 9

Sélection de pixels

● ●

Dans ce chapitre :

▶ Sélectionner au Lasso, au Rectangle de sélection et avec la Baguette magique.

▶ La Forme de sélection.

▶ Enregistrement de sélections.

▶ Masquer des sélections.

▶ Modifier les sélections.

● ●

Si vous avez déjà vu un rodéo, vous savez ce qu'est un lasso. Dans Elements, vous attrapez les pixels comme les vaches dans une arène. L'avantage ici est que vous ne risquez pas de prendre un coup de cornes ou d'être victime d'une ruade.

Il existe quelques moyens pour sélectionner des pixels autrement qu'avec le lasso : on trouve dans Elements une baguette magique, deux outils de sélection géométrique et, peut-être le meilleur de tous, un outil appelé Forme de sélection. Ce chapitre traite des techniques de sélection des parties d'une image. Avec un peu de pratique, vous pourrez sélectionner précisément des pixels, alors que, pour attraper une vache au lasso, des années d'entraînement sont souvent nécessaires.

Manipuler le Lasso avec dextérité

Photoshop Elements met à votre disposition plusieurs outils de sélection qui sont identifiés sur la Figure 9.1. Ces outils comprennent le Lasso, le Lasso polygonal, le Lasso magnétique, des outils de sélection géométrique, un sélecteur automatique des couleurs appelé Baguette magique et la nouvelle Forme de sélection. Voici comment ils fonctionnent :

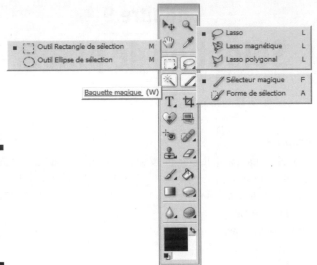

Figure 9.1 :
Utilisez ces
outils pour
sélectionner
la partie de
l'image que
vous désirez
modifier.

✔ L'outil Rectangle de sélection permet de sélectionner une zone rectangulaire. Il suffit de cliquer et tirer pour former un contour de sélection rectangulaire. Il se présente sous forme de tirets animés.

✔ L'outil Ellipse de sélection, qui partage l'emplacement dans la boîte à outils avec l'outil Rectangle de sélection, trace des sélections ovales.

✔ Promenez le Lasso sur l'image pour sélectionner des formes à main levée, aux contours irréguliers.

✔ Utilisez le Lasso polygonal, qui partage son menu avec le Lasso classique et le Lasso magnétique, pour tracer, point par point, un contour constitué d'une succession de segments rectilignes.

✔ L'outil Lasso magnétique place le contour entre deux zones de l'image bien contrastée, en fonction de la luminosité et d'un seul de tolérance. Cela vous paraît confus ? Vous comprendrez mieux un peu plus loin dans ce chapitre.

✔ L'outil Baguette magique sélectionne des plages de couleur. Par exemple, pour sélectionner un ciel bleu sans les nuages blancs, cliquez dans le ciel. Nous vous donnons ici la version idyllique d'une utilisation de la Baguette magique car sa maîtrise exige un peu de pratique. Disons que la Baguette magique n'est pas aussi magique que vous le supposez.

✔ Avec l'outil Sélecteur magique, vous griffonnez dans la partie de l'image à sélectionner. Elements définit ensuite les contours précis de la plage de couleur correspondante.

✔ La Forme de sélection permet de "peindre" la zone à sélectionner. En mode Sélection, le travail avec la Forme de sélection est très semblable au travail avec les autres outils de sélection. C'est en mode Masque que la réelle puissance de l'outil devient apparente.

Dans Elements, une sélection active est représentée par un contour fait de tirets en déplacement constant que les anglophones appellent affectueusement "colonne de fourmis en marche. Tout ce qui se trouve dans le contour est sélectionné ; tout ce qui est en dehors du contour ne l'est pas. Bien que ce soit un moyen plutôt efficace de matérialiser la sélection active, le contour n'est parfois pas souhaitable. La section "Masquer les fourmis" ci-après indique comment rendre temporairement invisibles ces inlassables fourmis qui distraient l'attention. Par ailleurs, l'outil Forme de sélection offre une autre possibilité très efficace. Nous y reviendrons.

Maintenant que vous savez comment fonctionnent les outils de sélection, voyons comment les activer. La petite flèche située en bas à droite de l'icône d'un outil de sélection ouvre un menu local permettant d'accéder à d'autres outils de sélection – parfois appelés "sous-outils" – qui sont des variantes de l'outil auquel ils se rapportent. L'ensemble de ces outils est également affiché dans la barre d'option, ce qui permet de passer directement du Lasso normal au Lasso magnétique ou polygonal.

Pour sélectionner rapidement un autre outil situé dans ce type de menu, maintenez la touche Alt enfoncée et cliquez sur l'outil. Chaque clic change d'outil. Quand vous arrivez au dernier, il suffit de cliquer dessus pour activer le premier outil du menu. Vous pouvez également employer les boutons d'outils disponibles à gauche de la barre d'options ou encore sélectionner des outils avec un raccourci clavier :

✔ Appuyez sur la touche M pour activer un outil de sélection géométrique. Pour activer l'autre outil, appuyez de nouveau sur M.

✔ Appuyez sur L pour activer l'outil Lasso. Pour changer d'outil Lasso, pressez de nouveau L. Ainsi, vous passez du Lasso au Lasso polygonal, et du Lasso polygonal au Lasso magnétique.

✔ Appuyez sur W pour activer la Baguette magique.

✔ Appuyez sur F pour activer le Sélecteur magique.

✔ Appuyez sur A pour activer la Forme de sélection.

NdT : Les raccourcis ne sont pas faciles à mémoriser car les lettres correspondent à la première lettre du nom de l'outil en anglais. "L" pour Lasso est une des rares exceptions des raccourcis de cette barre d'outils.

Faire tournoyer les lassos

Le Lasso normal et le Lasso polygonal sont faciles à utiliser. En revanche, l'outil Lasso magnétique est un peu plus subtil donc délicat, mais très efficace.

Utilisation du Lasso normal

Voici comment utiliser convenablement le Lasso normal :

✔ **Tracez un contour autour de la partie de l'image à sélectionner.**

C'est ce que nous avons fait sur la Figure 9.2 pour la grenouille. Comme vous le constatez le contour de sélection est visible en pointillé. Il représente le tracé que vous avez dessiné. Si vous relâchez le bouton de la souris avant de connecter le point d'arrivée avec le point de départ, Elements les connecte automatiquement par une droite.

Il est très difficile, surtout avec une souris, de tracer un contour précis avec l'outil Lasso. Si vous possédez une tablette graphique, comme celles fabriquées par Wacom, il vous sera peut-être plus facile de sélectionner avec le stylet plutôt qu'à la souris. Mais, si la sélection n'est pas aussi précise que vous le souhaitez, sachez qu'il existe plusieurs moyens de la corriger.

Tracer des sélections avec des segments de droite

Supposons que vous désirez sélectionner un cube situé au centre d'une image. Vous pouvez tracer la sélection avec l'outil Lasso, mais il est à craindre qu'elle soit approximative. L'idéal ici est de recourir à l'outil Lasso polygonal qui ne trace que des segments de droite.

Marque de sélection   Curseur du Lasso

Figure 9.2 :
La grenouille
a été
sélectionnée
en traçant un
contour avec
le Lasso.

Pour sélectionner un objet de cette manière, cliquez avec l'outil Lasso polygonal pour définir le début du premier segment de la sélection. Ensuite, sans appuyer sur le bouton de la souris, déplacez le pointeur du Lasso puis cliquez pour définir l'extrémité du segment suivant. Tracez un autre segment de la même manière. Ainsi, de segment de droite en segment de droite, vous formez une sélection parfaite autour du cube. De retour au point de départ (un cercle apparaît près du pointeur), cliquez pour fermer la sélection.

Le Lasso polygonal sert aussi à sélectionner des objets aux formes courbes. Vous pouvez, en atteignant la courbe, basculer en mode Lasso normal. Pour cela, il suffit d'appuyer sur la touche Alt. Sans la relâcher, suivez la courbe, puis lâchez la touche Alt et poursuivez la sélection avec l'outil Lasso polygonal. Une autre technique consiste à cliquer plusieurs fois dans la courbe à intervalles rapprochés. Ce sont alors de minuscules segments de droite qui définissent au mieux la courbe de l'objet à sélectionner.

Le recours à la touche Alt est valable pour tous les lassos pour basculer en mode Lasso polygonal. Lorsque vous appuyez dessus, ne la relâchez surtout pas quand vous passez d'un outil à un autre. En effet, sans la touche Alt enfoncée, si vous relâchez le bouton de la souris, vous terminez la sélection. La touche Alt enfoncée garantit un changement d'outil de sélection dès que vous relâchez le bouton de la souris pour poursuivre votre tâche.

Sélectionner avec l'outil Lasso magnétique

Cet outil Lasso est plus subtil que les deux autres et permet des solutions précises avec un minimum d'effort quand il est bien paramétré.

L'outil Lasso magnétique fonctionne bien avec des images fortement contrastées. C'est le cas pour sélectionner un objet reposant sur un fond uni. Grâce aux paramètres de la barre d'options, vous définissez le niveau d'analyse des pixels. Voici comment fonctionne l'outil Lasso magnétique :

1. **Activez l'outil Lasso magnétique.**

2. **Cliquez sur l'un des bords de l'objet à sélectionner.**

3. **Déplacez le pointeur de l'outil tout autour de l'objet, sans maintenir le bouton de la souris enfoncé.**

    Faites simplement glisser le pointeur autour de l'objet. Le Lasso magnétique crée un contour en plaçant des points d'ancrage aux endroits stratégiques de la sélection. Si le tracé s'écarte de l'objet, revenez vers un des points d'ancrage pour rectifier la progression de la sélection. Si un point d'ancrage est mal placé, appuyez sur la touche Suppr ou Retour arrière. Pour créer vos propres points d'ancrage, cliquez. L'ajout manuel de points d'ancrage est appréciable quand la sélection s'avère quelque peu ardue, c'est-à-dire lorsque le Lasso a tendance à perdre le contour de l'objet.

4. **Continuez d'entourer l'objet, en revenant finalement au point de départ de la sélection.**

    Un petit cercle apparaît à côté du pointeur indiquant qu'il est prêt à fermer la sélection.

5. **Pour fermer le contour, cliquez sur le point d'ancrage de départ.**

    Dès que vous relâchez le bouton de la souris, le contour de sélection apparaît.

6. **Appuyez sur Echap pour annuler l'outil Lasso magnétique en cours de sélection.**

Pour créer un segment de droite lorsque vous utilisez l'outil Lasso magnétique, appuyez sur la touche Alt et cliquez sur le bouton de la souris. Vous observez que l'icône de l'outil se change temporairement en Lasso polygonal. Relâchez la touche Alt et faites glisser le pointeur pour utiliser de nouveau l'outil Lasso magnétique.

Les options du Lasso

Si vous utilisez le Lasso normal, polygonal ou magnétique, vous pouvez modifier leur fonctionnement avec les paramètres de la barre d'options. Peu nombreux, ils n'en sont pas moins essentiels :

✔ En règle générale, les sélections opérées avec les outils Lasso doivent être lisses et suivre naturellement les contours des objets. Ce lissage des pixels est appelé *anticrénelage*. Pour le désactiver, décochez l'option Lissé. Des effets d'escalier risquent d'apparaître le long de la sélection.

✔ Les options Contour progressif et Lissé affectent le contour de la future sélection dessinée avec l'outil Lasso, mais pas la sélection actuelle. Ce paramètre atténue les bords en créant une transition entre la sélection et les pixels situés autour de celle-ci. Cet effet de flou peut provoquer la perte de détails sur le contour de la sélection. De son côté, Lissé lisse les bords crénelés d'une sélection en adoucissant la transition de couleur entre les pixels du bord et ceux de l'arrière-plan. Dans la mesure où seuls les pixels du bord changent, aucun détail n'est perdu.

✔ La Figure 9.3 montre une même sélection effectuée avec des options différentes. Dans l'image de gauche, l'option Lissé a été désactivée, tandis que, dans celle de droite, les contours sont plus doux, c'est-à-dire lissés. Le Chapitre 10 explique toutes les techniques de déplacement des sélections. Si vous souhaitez déplacer une sélection dès maintenant, faites-la glisser avec l'outil Déplacement. Il se trouve tout en haut de la barre d'outils, ou en haut à droite lorsque cette barre est flottante (sur deux colonnes).

✔ Dans la plupart des cas, activez l'option Lissé. Ne la désactivez que si vous devez sélectionner des parties irrégulières.

✔ Saisissez une valeur dans le champ Contour progressif pour augmenter l'effet d'atténuation de la prochaine sélection et la rendre plus estompée. Par exemple, si vous entrez **3**, la zone d'atténuation est de trois pixels. Comme vous le constatez sur le premier exemple de la Figure 9.4, l'atténuation de la sélection est faible. Dès que la valeur est portée à **10**, l'atténuation est plus importante, comme on le constate sur le second exemple de la Figure 9.4.

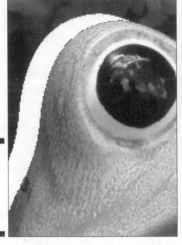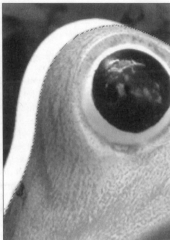

Figure 9.3 :
Sélection
crénelée (à
gauche) et
lissée (à
droite).

3 pixels   10 pixels

Figure 9.4 :
Une valeur
de contour
progressif
plus
importante
adoucit la
sélection.

Un œil sur les options propres au Lasso magnétique

L'outil Lasso magnétique possède des options uniques concernant sa sensibilité :

- **Largeur :** Détermine la distance à laquelle doivent se trouver les bords de l'objet pour que le magnétisme agisse correctement. La plage s'étend de 1 à 256 pixels.

- **Déviation du contour :** Indique le niveau de contraste, c'est-à-dire de différence entre la couleur de la zone à sélectionner et les autres éléments de l'image, nécessaire pour que le magnétisme agisse. La plage de valeurs s'étend de 1 à 100 %. Si la zone où s'opère la sélection est claire, il est recommandé d'utiliser des valeurs plus élevées. Si l'image est faiblement contrastée, diminuez la déviation du contour.

- **Fréquence :** Indique la fréquence d'insertion des points d'ancrage sur la sélection, de 0 à 100. Si vous souhaitez plus de points, saisissez une valeur supérieure ; pour moins de points, entrez une valeur plus faible. Les valeurs élevées sont idéales pour des bords irréguliers, alors que les valeurs les plus faibles sont recommandées pour les contours de sélection lissés. N'oubliez pas que pour ajouter vos propres points d'ancrage, il suffit de cliquer.

Commencez avec les paramètres par défaut. Voyez comment cela se passe. En cas de problème, n'hésitez pas à tester de nouvelles valeurs. Si votre image contient de faibles contrastes, optez pour une Déviation des contours de 5 %. Si les contours sont crénelés, essayez une Fréquence de 70 et une Largeur de 5 pixels. Si jamais l'outil Lasso magnétique ne produisait pas un résultat satisfaisant, préférez le Lasso normal ou polygonal. Ils ne sont techniquement pas très puissants, mais cependant utilisables.

Utilisation des outils de sélection géométrique

Les outils Rectangle de sélection et Ellipse de sélection sont très faciles à utiliser. Pour tracer un rectangle ou une ellipse de sélection, cliquez dans l'image puis, tout en maintenant le bouton de la souris enfoncé, faites glisser le pointeur dans le coin inférieur opposé. Un contour s'affiche afin que vous puissiez apprécier exactement les dimensions du rectangle ou de l'ellipse en cours de création.

Si l'utilisation d'un outil géométrique de sélection ne donne pas entière satisfaction alors que vous avez déjà commencé à tracer, appuyez sur la barre d'espace tout en maintenant le bouton de la souris enfoncé. Vous déplacez ainsi la totalité de la sélection. Dès que le positionnement du rectangle ou de l'ellipse vous convient, relâchez la barre d'espace. Le bouton de la souris étant toujours enfoncé, poursuivez la création de la sélection.

Carré et cercle de sélection

Il est possible d'opérer des sélections carrées et circulaires parfaites avec les outils Rectangle de sélection et Ellipse de sélection.

✔ Pour dessiner un carré, maintenez la touche Maj enfoncée tout en utilisant l'outil Rectangle de sélection. Faites de même avec l'outil Ellipse de sélection pour obtenir un cercle.

✔ Pour obtenir un carré ou un cercle, vous pouvez appuyer sur la touche Maj à n'importe quel moment de la création de la sélection, à condition que ce soit avant de relâcher le bouton de la souris.

✔ Si vous appuyez sur la touche Maj avant de commencer à tracer la sélection, vous risquez d'ajouter une sélection à une sélection existante. Si une portion de l'image est déjà sélectionnée, l'enfoncement préalable de la touche Maj avant le cliquer-glisser ajoute la nouvelle sélection à la précédente au lieu de contraindre la nouvelle sélection à une forme carrée ou circulaire. Si cela vous arrive, désélectionnez tout et recommencez. Cependant, si vous désirez réellement ajouter une sélection carrée ou circulaire à une sélection existante, voici comment procéder : maintenez la touche Maj enfoncée, commencez à faire glisser, puis gardez le bouton de la souris enfoncé tout en relâchant et enfonçant de nouveau la touche Maj. C'est bizarre mais cela fonctionne.

Toujours plus de contrôle sur les sélections

Vous êtes un fou du contrôle sur les événements et ce que vous venez d'apprendre sur les sélections ne permet pas d'assouvir totalement votre désir de domination ?

Supposons, par exemple, que vous tenez à obtenir un rectangle ou un ovale de sélection deux fois plus large que haut. L'outil de sélection actif, choisissez Proportions fixes dans la liste Style de la barre d'options. Les champs Hauteur et Largeur apparaissent. Saisissez les valeurs de votre "disproportion". Ainsi, pour obtenir une sélection plus large que haute, saisissez **2** dans le champ Largeur et **1** dans le champ Hauteur.

Pour une sélection de taille précise et imposée, choisissez Taille fixe dans la liste Style et saisissez une dimension exprimée en pixels dans les champs Largeur et Hauteur.

L'icône des deux flèches séparant les champs Hauteur et Largeur permute les valeurs affichées. En d'autres termes, cliquer sur ce bouton remplace la valeur de Largeur par celle de Hauteur et réciproquement.

Comme l'outil Lasso, les marques de sélection géométriques ont des options de contour progressif et de lissage. Cette dernière option est indisponible avec l'outil Rectangle de sélection, car les angles d'un rectangle ou d'un carré sont droits, inutile de chercher à les lisser.

Dessiner à partir du centre

Comme mentionné précédemment, vous dessinez généralement un rectangle ou une ellipse de sélection en partant d'un de ses angles (dans le cas de l'ellipse, l'angle est celui du quadrilatère dans lequel elle s'inscrit).

Cependant, il est possible de tracer une sélection depuis son centre. Ainsi, la sélection s'étend vers l'extérieur. Pour cela, commencez à tracer la sélection et maintenez enfoncées les touches Maj et Alt. Si, en cours de traçage, vous décidez de ne plus partir du centre, relâchez la touche Alt et continuez de dessiner la sélection.

Baguette magique

La Baguette magique est l'outil de sélection en principe le plus facile d'emploi. Mais, pour sélectionner exactement ce que l'on désire, ce n'est pas aussi simple que cela. Pour utiliser cet outil, cliquez dessus dans la boîte à outils d'Elements. Cliquez ensuite, dans l'image, sur la couleur que vous désirez sélectionner.

Mince ! J'ai cliqué dans le ciel !

La Figure 9.5 montre le fonctionnement de la Baguette magique. Sur la première image, nous avons cliqué sur le ciel avec cet outil, juste au-dessus de ce dinosaure virtuel. Elements sélectionne automatiquement toutes les teintes les plus proches de celle sur laquelle nous avons cliqué. En l'occurrence, il s'agira de tous les bleus clairs. La seconde image montre ce qu'il résulte après avoir appuyé sur la touche Ctrl+Retour arrière. La couleur sélectionnée est remplacée par la couleur d'arrière-plan. Sur cette image, vous ne voyez plus la marque de sélection car elle a été masquée.

Figure 9.5 :
Le contenu est remplacé par la couleur d'arrière-plan.

Notez que la baguette ne sélectionne par défaut que les zones de couleurs continues. Par conséquent, la partie du ciel qui se trouve sous la queue du dinosaure est intacte. Vous devez cliquer dedans, puis appuyer sur la touche Retour arrière pour supprimer cette partie du ciel.

Comprendre la tolérance de la baguette

Vous pouvez changer le comportement de la Baguette magique en agissant sur le paramètre Tolérance, dans la barre d'options. Trois autres paramètres s'y trouvent : Lissé, Pixels contigus et Utiliser tous les calques.

Nous avons présenté l'option Lissé dans la section "Les options du Lasso" précédemment dans ce chapitre. L'option Utiliser tous les calques entre en jeu quand votre image contient plusieurs calques (consultez le Chapitre 10). Lorsqu'elle est désactivée, la Baguette magique ne sélectionne que les couleurs du calque sélectionné. Pour sélectionner cette même couleur sur les autres calques, l'option Utiliser tous les calques doit être activée.

Quand la case Pixels contigus est cochée, la Baguette magique ne sélectionne que les pixels adjacents. Sinon, elle recherche tous les pixels de la même couleur contenus dans l'image, compris dans le seuil de tolérance défini pour la baguette.

Cela nous conduit à l'option Tolérance (NdT : comme disait le dramaturge Paul Claudel "La tolérance ? Il y a des maisons pour cela") qui détermine la puissance et l'efficacité de la Baguette magique. Elle indique à Elements les couleurs à sélectionner et celles à ne pas sélectionner. Plus la valeur de Tolérance est faible, moins vous sélectionnez de pixels ; plus elle est élevée, plus vous sélectionnez de couleurs.

La Figure 9.6 démontre ce comportement. Chaque paire d'images dénote les effets d'une valeur de tolérance différente. Nous commençons avec la valeur 32 par défaut, pour atteindre 180 sur la dernière image. Nous avons chaque fois cliqué au même endroit pour ne pas fausser la démonstration. Sur cette figure, l'image de gauche montre la sélection et celle de droite le remplacement de son contenu par la couleur d'arrière-plan. Dans l'image de droite, le contour de sélection a été masqué.

Le problème de l'outil Baguette magique est qu'il est difficile de trouver le bon seuil de tolérance. Il est parfois impossible d'effectuer une sélection précise avec cet outil, même en procédant en plusieurs étapes. Faites des essais et modifiez la valeur de la tolérance.

Tolerance : 32

Tolerance : 90

Tolerance : 180

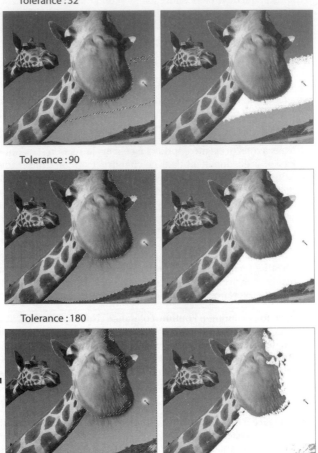

Figure 9.6 :
Une
Tolérance 90
semble
idéale.

D'autres paramètres affectent le comportement de la Baguette magique, mais ils ne se trouvent pas sur la barre d'options. Pour y accéder, vous devez activer l'outil Pipette et déterminer le nombre de pixels qu'il doit analyser afin de prélever une couleur. Échantillon ponctuel signifie que la Pipette prélève la couleur du pixel sur lequel vous cliquez. Moyenne 3 x 3 établit une moyenne des teintes contenues par les 8 pixels entourant celui sur lequel vous cliquez. Moyenne 5 x 5 opère de la même manière, mais en prenant en compte 24 pixels autour de celui sur lequel vous cliquez.

Nous atteignons la fonction la plus difficile à mémoriser dans Photoshop Elements : l'option Taille de l'outil Pipette, qui affecte le comportement de la Baguette magique. Si l'outil Pipette est défini sur Moyenne 3 x 3, sachez alors que la Baguette magique effectuera une sélection basée sur la moyenne des 8 pixels entourant celui sur lequel vous cliquez. Il en va de même avec Moyenne 5 x 5 mais en faisant la moyenne des 24 pixels entourant celui sur lequel vous cliquez. Par conséquent, avant d'utiliser l'outil Baguette magique, vérifiez toujours le paramètre de l'outil Pipette.

Le Sélecteur magique

Le nouvel outil Sélecteur magique sert à sélectionner rapidement une plage de couleur en griffonnant dedans pour indiquer à Elements la partie à prendre en compte. A l'instar de la Baguette magique, sa maîtrise exige un peu de pratique.

Dans l'exercice suivant, nous sélectionnerons une des statues :

1. **Activez l'outil Sélecteur magique.**

   Photoshop Elements affiche une boîte de dialogue décrivant très succinctement, et propose d'accéder à son aide. Cliquez sur OK.

2. **Dans la barre d'options (voir Figure 9.7), réglez le diamètre du sélecteur.**

   Si la zone est vaste, choisissez un sélecteur de grand diamètre. Au contraire, pour sélectionner dans des parties étroites, réduisez le diamètre de la forme.

3. **Griffonnez dans la zone à sélectionner. Dans la Figure 9.7, il s'agit de la sculpture au premier plan. Relâchez le bouton de la souris.**

   Sitôt le bouton relâché, Elements calcule la sélection en se basant sur le griffonnage. Selon la complexité de la sélection et la taille de la zone, l'opération peut durer d'une à plusieurs dizaines de secondes.

   Dans la majorité des cas, la sélection est décevante. Comme le révèle la Figure 9.8, elle est beaucoup trop étendue : toutes les statues ainsi que les piliers ont été sélectionnés.

   L'outil Sélecteur magique ne comporte aucun réglage de la tolérance. Pour réduire la zone excédentaire, nous devrons nous y prendre autrement.

Figure 9.7 :
Dès que le
bouton de la
souris a été
relâché,
Elements
calcule la
sélection.

4. **Dans la barre d'options, cliquez sur le bouton Arrière-plan. Il est orné du symbole de l'outil accompagné du signe "moins".**

A l'instar du bouton Premier-plan qui le précède, Arrière-plan est bien mal nommé. Il aurait dû s'appeler "soustraire de la sélection" et l'autre, en toute logique, "ajouter à la sélection". Remarquez que dans l'indicateur de couleur, la teinte change. L'outil Sélection magique, qui peignait en rouge, peindra à présent en bleu.

5. **Peignez dans la ou les parties de la sélection à supprimer. Dès que le bouton de la souris est libéré, Elements recalcule la sélection. Cette fois, elle est correcte, comme en témoigne la Figure 9.9.**

Un examen détaillé du résultat montre qu'une petite zone a échappé à la sélection au coin supérieur gauche du socle. Ce détail pourra être facilement corrigé avec l'outil Baguette magique, en maintenant la touche Maj enfoncée pour ajouter à

Figure 9.8 :
La sélection
est manifes-
tement trop
étendue.

Figure 9.9 :
La sélection
excédentaire
a été
supprimée.

la sélection (l'ajout et la soustraction à une sélection sont décrits un peu plus loin dans ce chapitre).

Le fonctionnement de l'outil Sélection magique s'apparente à la Baguette magique. Son avantage sur cette dernière est la possibilité de soustraire facilement une zone à la sélection, comme nous l'avons vu.

Retenez aussi qu'après avoir défini une première sélection, l'option Premier plan est automatiquement activée : vous pouvez ainsi ajouter d'autres zones à inclure dans la sélection. Pour refaire une sélection à partir de zéro, vous devez cliquer sur le bouton Nouvelle sélection.

La grâce de la Forme de sélection

Le principe de l'outil Forme de sélection est très simple : vous peignez dans l'image avec la Forme de sélection pour créer une sélection. Lorsque le menu Mode dans la barre d'options est sur Sélection, la Forme de sélection utilise la colonne de fourmis, désormais familière, pour matérialiser la sélection. La permutation en mode Masque change un certain nombre de choses. La Forme de sélection recouvre à présent l'image avec une étrange teinte rouge. Les zones recouvertes par ce film ne sont pas sélectionnées ; ce sont les zones claires qui sont sélectionnées. Par conséquent, en mode Masque, la Forme de sélection devient en fait une Forme de *dé*sélection, masquant les zones de l'image que vous voulez protéger des modifications.

Vous découvrirez dans la suite ce qui rend si intéressant le mode Masque.

1. **Activez l'outil Ellipse de sélection.**

2. **Choisissez une forte valeur de Contour progressif dans la barre d'options.**

   Par exemple, 30.

3. **Tracez une sélection.**

   La progressivité n'est pas forcément évidente. Le problème est que le contour de sélection n'a aucun moyen de matérialiser la progressivité de la sélection.

4. **Sélectionnez l'outil Forme de sélection.**

   Ne désélectionnez pas le contour de sélection ; gardez-le actif.

5. **Dans la barre d'options, passez en mode Masque et observez la sélection.**

La progressivité de la sélection est maintenant évidente ! Le recouvrement est rouge là où l'image est totalement non sélectionnée, transparent là où l'image est totalement sélectionnée, et se présente sous forme d'un fondu progressif entre le rouge et le transparent pour les niveaux intermédiaires. Par conséquent, lorsqu'il est important de travailler avec des bords flous, la Forme de sélection est clairement l'outil à exploiter.

Voici les réglages dans la barre d'options de la Forme de sélection :

- **Forme :** Sélectionnez ici le type de forme à employer pour peindre votre sélection. (Pour en savoir plus sur les formes, voir le Chapitre 15.)

- **Épaisseur :** Pour choisir les dimensions de la forme, tapez une valeur en pixels ou cliquez sur la flèche et faites glisser le curseur.

- **Mode :** Permutez entre le mode Sélection (colonne de fourmis) et le mode Masque (recouvrement rouge).

- **Dureté :** Ce paramètre détermine la progressivité de la sélection obtenue. Une faible valeur produit un bord très flou ; une valeur élevée crée un bord net. Pratiquez un peu le mode Masque et vous en saisirez l'idée.

- **Opacité d'incrustation (mode Masque uniquement) :** Ce paramètre détermine la transparence du recouvrement. Une valeur de 100 % occulte totalement l'image sous-jacente et il est probablement préférable de l'éviter ; de même, une valeur de 0 % fait disparaître le recouvrement complètement, ce qui est inutile.

- **Couleur (mode Masque uniquement) :** S'il existe une forte quantité de rouge dans l'image sous-jacente, il se peut qu'un recouvrement rouge ne soit pas le plus judicieux. Cliquez sur l'échantillon pour accéder au Sélecteur de couleurs et choisissez une couleur présentant plus de contraste.

Autre chose à savoir à propos de la Forme de sélection : maintenir la touche Alt enfoncée indique à l'outil de se comporter de manière inverse. Par conséquent, maintenir la touche enfoncée en mode Sélection provoque la désélection des zones sélectionnées sur lesquelles vous passez l'outil ; l'emploi de Alt en mode Masque force la Forme de sélection à peindre de la transparence, effaçant le recouvrement et donc sélectionnant les zones où vous passez l'outil.

Tout sélectionner

Quand aucune partie de l'image n'est sélectionnée, vous pouvez la modifier dans son intégralité. Il est également possible de modifier la totalité d'une image en la sélectionnant intégralement via Sélection/ Tout sélectionner ou Ctrl+A.

Je sais, ce comportement est assez incompréhensible. Pourquoi se casser la tête à sélectionner toute une image pour la modifier quand on peut le faire sans rien sélectionner ? Cela permet d'effectuer une copie de l'image. Choisissez Ctrl+A, puis Ctrl+C (pour en savoir plus sur copier et coller, consultez le Chapitre 10).

Tout désélectionner

Supposons que vous ayez sélectionné une partie de votre image. Vous changez d'avis et décidez d'en sélectionner une autre partie. La première chose à faire est de désélectionner la sélection existante. Plusieurs méthodes sont à votre disposition :

✔ Cliquez n'importe où dans l'image avec un des outils de sélection.

✔ Pour supprimer une sélection existante et en créer une nouvelle en même temps, créez directement la nouvelle sélection avec l'outil de votre choix. Créer une sélection dans une sélection existante a pour effet de supprimer la première sélection. Notez que la Forme de sélection est une exception à cette règle ; l'emploi de la Forme de sélection conserve toujours toute sélection déjà active.

✔ Cliquez dans la sélection avec la Baguette magique. (Si vous cliquez en dehors de la sélection existante, non seulement vous la désélectionnez mais en plus, vous en créez une nouvelle.)

✔ Choisissez Sélection/Désélectionner ou appuyez sur Ctrl+D. L'emploi de Sélection/Resélectionner ou de Ctrl+Maj+D récupère votre dernière sélection désélectionnée. Vous pouvez utiliser cette commande même après avoir exécuté d'autres actions entre-temps.

✔ Cliquez sur l'avant-dernier état dans la palette Annuler l'historique.

Enregistrement et chargement de sélections

Selon sa complexité, effectuer une sélection est une tâche plus ou moins difficile que vous n'aurez peut-être pas envie de recommencer plusieurs fois. Pour éviter cela, il est possible de mémoriser la sélection dans le fichier d'image, de sorte que même si vous fermez et rouvrez l'image, vous conservez la possibilité de charger la sélection.

Pour ce faire, tracez une sélection et choisissez Sélection/Mémoriser la sélection. Vous avez ici juste à saisir un nom pour la sélection ; ceci fait, cliquez sur OK. Désélectionnez maintenant la sélection. Fermez carrément l'image après avoir enregistré les changements. Rouvrez l'image et choisissez Sélection/Récupérer la sélection. Le nom de la sélection enregistrée sera visible dans le menu Sélection ; cliquez sur OK. Vous retrouverez votre ancienne sélection. Vraiment pratique.

Les autres options Mémoriser la sélection entrent en jeu lorsque vous gérez plusieurs sélections. Si vous actionnez la commande Mémoriser la sélection lorsqu'une sélection est déjà mémorisée, le choix d'un nom de sélection dans le menu Sélection (au lieu de choisir Nouveau) indique que vous voulez écraser cette sélection. Les boutons radio Résultat proposent quatre options pour combiner la nouvelle sélection avec l'ancienne. Vous pouvez remplacer complètement l'ancienne sélection, ajouter la nouvelle sélection à l'ancienne, soustraire la nouvelle sélection à l'ancienne ou conserver uniquement l'intersection des deux sélections.

Quand vous récupérez une sélection, vous disposez d'une case à cocher Inverser. Lorsque vous cochez cette case, la sélection est inversée avant d'être chargée. Dans la boîte de dialogue Récupérer la sélection, vous disposez aussi d'une liste Sélection pour choisir la sélection enregistrée à récupérer. Les boutons radio Résultat fonctionnent comme ceux de la boîte de dialogue Mémoriser la sélection. Vous déterminez ici de quelle façon la sélection chargée doit interagir avec une éventuelle autre sélection active dans le document.

Enfin, la commande Sélection/Supprimer la sélection sert à choisir une sélection à supprimer dans le menu Sélection.

Masquer les fourmis

Voici une chose très importante à connaître concernant les contours de sélection dans Elements. Dans le menu Affichage, vous disposez d'une commande Sélection. La commande Sélection masque la "colonne de fourmis" du contour de la sélection active. Cela permet de voir plus facilement ce que vous faites, particulièrement sur les bords de la sélection ; cette troublante colonne de fourmis devient invisible. Le résultat n'est cependant pas le même que lorsque vous désélectionnez la sélection. Quand vous choisissez Affichage/Sélection, la sélection reste active ; elle est simplement masquée.

Bien que le masquage de contours de sélection soit un outil crucial, il mène également à l'erreur courante numéro un. Vous créez une sélection, appuyez sur Ctrl+H pour masquer la sélection, travaillez dans votre sélection, puis commencez à travailler en dehors de la sélection – et rien ne se passe. Impossible de modifier l'image. Vous êtes contrarié, commencez à pester, décidez que le problème est simplement que vous n'appuyez pas assez fort sur le bouton de la souris, jusqu'à vous persuader qu'Elements et votre ordinateur conspirent contre vous. Prenez une profonde inspiration et demandez-vous calmement si vous n'avez pas masqué votre contour de sélection ; répondez oui, puis appuyez sur Ctrl+D.

Modification des sélections

La première sélection que vous faites n'est jamais parfaite (sauf un miracle ou une maîtrise exceptionnelle de ces outils). Par exemple, vous englobez un doigt, un cheveu, un cil, dans votre sélection alors que vous ne le souhaitez pas. Quel que soit le problème qui apparaît avec une sélection, remédiez-y en ajoutant ou ôtant des éléments à la sélection.

Ajouter et soustraire d'une sélection

Lorsque vous avez créé une sélection avec un outil Lasso, le Rectangle de sélection, la Baguette magique ou le Sélecteur magique, et que vous voulez la compléter ou en retirer une partie avec la Forme de sélection, cela ne pose aucune difficulté. La Forme de sélection respecte systématiquement la sélection active, elle ne la supprime pas lorsque vous commencez à appliquer l'outil. Et quel que soit le réglage du Mode, vous gardez constamment la possibilité de permuter le comportement de la Forme de sélection en enfonçant la touche Alt.

Cependant, si vous voulez employer un outil Lasso, l'outil Rectangle de sélection, la Baguette magique ou le Sélecteur magique pour compléter ou retirer une partie d'une sélection existante, vous devez vous y prendre différemment. Les quatre boutons de modification de la sélection de la barre d'options sont parfaits pour cette entreprise. Jetez un œil sur la Figure 9.10. Vous pouvez créer une nouvelle sélection, ajouter à la sélection, soustraire à la sélection ou sélectionner l'intersection. Par exemple, si vous avez réalisé une sélection rectangulaire avec l'outil Rectangle de sélection et que vous avez également besoin d'une sélection circulaire, commencez par activer l'outil Ellipse de sélection. Cliquez sur le deuxième modificateur de sélection, c'est-à-dire Ajouter à la sélection. Dès que vous tracez cette nouvelle sélection, le rectangle reste en place. Vous ajoutez une sélection elliptique à la sélection rectangulaire déjà en place.

Figure 9.10 :
Les quatre
boutons de
modification
de la
sélection de
la barre
d'options.

Nouvelle sélection   Soustraire de la sélection

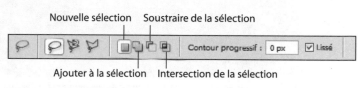

Ajouter à la sélection   Intersection de la sélection

Pour travailler plus vite, utilisez des raccourcis clavier au lieu des boutons de modification de la barre d'options. Ils activent automatiquement le modificateur auquel ils correspondent.

Pour ajouter une zone à la sélection actuelle, appuyez sur la touche Maj et faites glisser un outil de sélection comme le Lasso ou une forme géométrique, ou bien faites Maj+clic si vous utilisez l'outil Baguette magique.

Par exemple, si vous voulez sélectionner le ciel dans une photo comme celle de la Figure 9.11, commencez par sélectionner la partie supérieure du ciel en cliquant dessus avec la Baguette magique (photo du haut). Pour ajouter les autres zones à la sélection, appuyez sur la touche Maj et cliquez sur ces zones également avec la Baguette magique, afin d'obtenir un contour de sélection comme dans l'exemple du bas. Pour supprimer une zone d'une sélection, cliquez-glissez avec la touche Alt enfoncée avec un outil Lasso ou l'outil Rectangle de sélection, ou encore cliquez avec la Baguette magique avec la touche Alt enfoncée.

Quand vous ajoutez à la sélection, un petit signe "+" apparaît à côté de votre pointeur. Quand vous soustrayez, c'est un signe "-" qui fait son apparition. Enfin, quand vous sélectionnez l'intersection, un "x" s'affiche à côté du pointeur.

Figure 9.11 :
Sélection de
l'ensemble
du ciel.

Intersection d'une sélection

Si vous appuyez simultanément sur les touches Maj et Alt tout en
cliquant avec la Baguette magique ou en faisant glisser un autre outil
de sélection, vous conservez l'intersection de la précédente sélection
et de la nouvelle. Jetez un œil sur la Figure 9.12. Si vous commencez
par sélectionner le rectangle noir et qu'ensuite vous appuyez sur
Maj+Alt tout en traçant une sélection autour du rectangle gris, une

intersection apparaît au centre. Elements sélectionne toutes les parties de la seconde marque de sélection qui se trouvent dans la première marque de sélection, et désélectionne tout le reste. Vous obtenez la sélection de l'*intersection*.

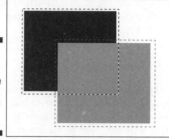 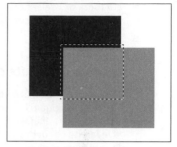

Figure 9.12 : L'image de droite montre l'intersection des deux sélections.

Éviter les incidents de clavier

On peut employer les outils de sélection conjointement à des touches. Ainsi, en appuyant sur Alt tout en utilisant l'outil Lasso, vous accédez temporairement aux autres lassos. En appuyant sur la touche Maj tout en utilisant un outil de sélection géométrique, vous obtenez un carré ou un cercle parfait.

Mais que se passe-t-il quand vous combinez ces raccourcis avec ceux qui permettent d'ajouter, de soustraire et d'obtenir l'intersection de la sélection ? Ce qui suit répond à cette question brûlante :

- ✔ Pour ajouter une zone carrée ou circulaire à une sélection existante, appuyez sur la touche Maj et utilisez l'outil de sélection approprié. Vous obtenez un rectangle ou un ovale. Ensuite, tout en continuant de tracer la sélection, relâchez la touche Maj et appuyez de nouveau dessus. La sélection prend la forme d'un carré ou d'un cercle. Gardez la touche Maj enfoncée jusqu'à ce que vous relâchiez le bouton de la souris pour valider la sélection.

- ✔ Appuyez sur Alt pour passer temporairement à l'outil Lasso polygonal quand le Lasso normal est actif. Mais cela n'est pas sans causer des problèmes. En effet, dans cette hypothèse, vous soustrayez de la sélection. Donc, pour ajouter ou soustraire une sélection à segments de droite, utilisez l'outil Lasso polygonal – n'essayez pas Alt+clic avec le Lasso normal.

Sélection automatique

L'ajout à la sélection est très utile pour sélectionner des détails complexes. Mais ce n'est pas la seule manière de modifier les sélections. Elements propose des fonctions automatiques qui reforment les contours des sélections, les adoucissent, et bien d'autres choses encore. Toutes les commandes traitées dans les prochaines sections se trouvent dans le menu Sélection.

Étendre les effets de la Baguette magique

Deux commandes, Étendre et Généraliser, sont des extensions de la Baguette magique. La commande Étendre augmente la taille de la sélection pour inclure davantage de couleurs continues. Par exemple, si le fait de cliquer avec la Baguette magique ne sélectionne pas toutes les couleurs souhaitées, vous pouvez soit augmenter la valeur de la tolérance, soit choisir Sélection/Étendre.

La commande Généraliser sélectionne toutes les couleurs similaires aux couleurs sélectionnées.

Les commandes Étendre et Généraliser jugent la similarité des couleurs comme le fait la Baguette magique. La précision dépend de la valeur de la tolérance fixée dans la barre d'options. Si vous augmentez la valeur, les commandes sélectionnent moins de couleurs. Par exemple, pour sélectionner toutes les couleurs de l'image qui sont exactement identiques, saisissez **0** dans le champ Tolérance et choisissez Sélection/Généraliser.

Sélectionner l'inverse de ce que vous désirez sélectionner

Parfois, il est plus facile de sélectionner une zone que vous ne désirez pas sélectionner, et d'utiliser Sélection/Intervertir (Ctrl+Maj+I) pour obtenir la sélection finale souhaitée.

Par exemple, vous désirez sélectionner la tour représentée sur la Figure 9.13. Disons-le tout de suite, cela promet d'être fastidieux.

En revanche, sélectionner le ciel est bien plus facile. En cliquant dessus avec la Baguette magique, il ne faudra qu'une fraction de seconde pour le sélectionner. Choisissez ensuite Sélection/Intervertir. Magique ! La tour est sélectionnée ! Pour mieux apprécier la sélection, nous l'avons remplie de blanc sur l'image de droite et nous avons masqué la sélection. Le second exemple de la Figure 9.11 se prête

Figure 9.13 :
Sélectionez
le ciel puis
intervertis-
sez.

également à cette technique ; si nous inversons cette sélection, l'arche sera sélectionnée et le ciel désélectionné.

Créer une sélection atténuée sur les bords

Vous pouvez atténuer les bords d'une sélection que vous allez créer avec les outils Lasso ou avec les outils géométriques en augmentant la valeur du Contour progressif, dans la barre d'options. Dans la plupart des cas, laissez la valeur du Contour progressif sur 0 et appliquez l'atténuation une fois le contour de sélection défini.

Pour atténuer une sélection existante, choisissez Sélection/Contour progressif. Une boîte de dialogue demande de saisir le rayon du contour exprimé en pixels. Tapez ce chiffre et appuyez sur la touche Entrée. La sélection ne changera pas énormément, mais vous constate-rez un effet d'atténuation de son contour quand vous modifierez son contenu – comme nous l'avons déjà mentionné, le contour de sélection ne matérialise jamais la progressivité d'une sélection. Cependant, vous pouvez activer la Forme de sélection et jeter un coup d'œil à la sélection en mode Masque pour voir les résultats.

Le contour progressif peut servir à fondre les contours d'une image avec le fond de l'image. Par exemple, la Figure 9.14 montre une partie de l'image (à gauche) isolée pour produire un cadre estompé (à droite). La première chose à faire, ici, est de tracer une Ellipse de sélection sur l'image. Utilisez ensuite Sélection/Intervertir pour sélectionner l'arrière-plan. Puis, choisissez Sélection/Contour progressif avec un rayon de **15** pixels. Enfin, appuyez sur Ctrl+Retour arrière afin d'obtenir une image semblable à celle de la Figure 9.14 (l'arrière-plan blanc n'apparaît que si cette couleur est bien présente comme couleur d'arrière-plan dans la boîte à outils). Vous obtenez le même effet avec le filtre Vignette circulaire ; il se trouve dans la catégorie Effets d'images, dans la palette Styles et effets.

Figure 9.14 :
Un jeune homme bien habillé (à gauche), auquel on a appliqué un traitement classique de médaillon (à droite).

Extraction magique

Voilà encore une nouveauté magique de Photoshop Elements. Encore un effort, et nous aurons droit au chaudron (quoique le Pot de peinture pourrait en tenir lieu...).

L'outil Extraction magique rappelle quelque peu l'outil Sélection magique, mais il s'en distingue cependant par l'interface, la façon de procéder et par la finalité :

- ✔ Alors qu'avec l'outil Sélection magique vous griffonnez dans la zone à sélectionner, avec l'Extraction magique, vous placez des points.

- ✔ Alors que l'outil Sélection magique produit un contour de sélection, l'outil Extraction magique coupe tout ce qui n'est pas sélectionné en créant un contour de sélection.

L'outil Extraction sert essentiellement à préparer un objet en vue de son insertion dans une autre image. Lorsqu'un objet est simplement coupé et collé, les bords trop nets risquent de donner une impression de "découpage aux ciseaux", bien peu esthétique. En revanche, le contour progressif permet d'intégrer l'objet collé dans le nouvel environnement sans que l'on remarque les bords. Le collage s'effectue alors sans raccord visible.

Un exercice pratique permettra de mieux comprendre la procédure. Nous reprendrons à cette fin la photo des statues que nous avions utilisée pour essayer la Sélection magique.

1. **Ouvrez l'image.**

2. **Choisissez Image/Extraction magique.**

   Eh oui, l'outil Extraction magique ne se trouve pas dans la boîte à outils. Il se présente en réalité sous la forme d'une imposante boîte de dialogue que montre la Figure 9.15.

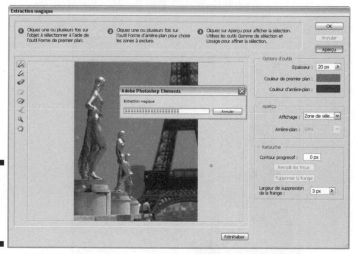

Figure 9.15 :
La statue au premier plan est en cours d'extraction.

3. **Dans le volet de droite, réglez le diamètre de la forme.**

   Il devra bien sûr être approprié au sujet à sélectionner : faible pour des éléments de petite taille, épais pour des éléments plus gros. Ici, la taille par défaut de 20 pixels, dans le champ Epaisseur, convient parfaitement.

Si vous désirez obtenir une sélection à contour estompé, indiquez le nombre de pixels dans le champ Contour progressif.

4. Cliquez plusieurs fois dans le sujet à extraire.

Photoshop Elements utilisera chaque point – en fait, des indicateurs de sélection – pour tenter de déterminer la zone à sélectionner. Ici, nous en avons placé sur la tête, à l'épaule, au coude, à la main, à la hanche, aux genoux ainsi qu'au milieu du voile et en bas, ce qui est plus que suffisant.

5. Cliquez sur le bouton Aperçu.

En se basant sur les indicateurs, Elements calcule la sélection à définir, comme à la Figure 9.15. La Figure 9.16 montre le résultat : à l'instar de la Sélection magique, l'extraction magique a sélectionné trop d'éléments.

Remarquez aussi – bien que ce soit difficilement discernable sur la Figure 9.16 – que quelques points supplémentaires viennent d'apparaître au-dessus de la tête, à droite du genou et près du socle.

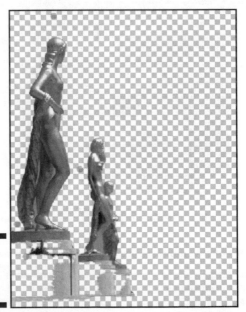

Figure 9.16 :
L'extraction
est trop
vaste.

Plusieurs outils, à gauche de la boîte de dialogue, permettent de limiter la sélection.

Les deux outils supérieurs, Forme de premier plan et Forme d'arrière-plan, fonctionnent exactement comme les commandes Premier plan et Arrière-plan de la barre d'options de l'outil Sélection magique : vous griffonnez dans la ou les zones à ajouter ou, ici, à supprimer.

6. **Activez l'outil Forme d'arrière-plan et griffonnez dans les éléments superflus : les deux statues du fond et les piliers en pierre. Cliquez ensuite sur Aperçu.**

Eléments supprime complètement les statues et les piliers.

Pour bien détourer la statue, nous devons aussi éliminer le ciel qui subsiste entre les jambes et entre une jambe et le voile.

7. **Utilisez les outils Zoom et Main pour travailler avec précision.**

8. **Dans le champ Epaisseur, réduisez le diamètre à 5 pixels puis peignez dans ce qui reste du ciel. Cliquez sur Aperçu.**

Après avoir calculé, la boîte de dialogue Extraction magique affiche une statue détourée, seule sur un fond en damier. Dans Photoshop Elements, ce damier matérialise la transparence : ces zones sont dépourvues de pixels.

9. **Cliquez sur OK pour valider le détourage.**

Si le résultat n'est pas convaincant, vous avez deux possibilités : quitter la boîte de dialogue en cliquant sur Annuler, ou tenter un nouvel essai en cliquant sur le bouton réinitialiser, en bas au milieu du panneau. Dans ce cas, toutes les interventions sont annulées et l'image réapparaît comme à l'ouverture de la boîte de dialogue.

Si vous avez détouré un élément sans définir de contour progressif, et que certaines parties de cet élément présentent un inesthétique effet d'escalier (crénelage), sachez qu'il est possible de le corriger à l'aide de l'outil Lissage. C'est le troisième à partir du bas.

Son utilisation est des plus simples : après voir réglé son diamètre dans le champ Epaisseur, passez-le et repassez-le sur la bordure à lisser.

Utilisation d'un cadre, d'un lissage, et tout le reste

Après avoir examiné les outils de sélections, jetons un coup d'œil au menu Sélection, plus précisément aux commandes du sous-menu Modifier. Elles sont utiles dans les circonstances suivantes :

- La commande Cadre sélectionne une zone autour de la sélection. Vous indiquez à Elements la largeur, en pixels, de la bordure que vous désirez sélectionner. Cette commande est la moins utile de toutes celles qui sont présentes dans ce menu. Si vous désirez colorier le contour d'une sélection, il est plus simple d'utiliser le pinceau (Consultez le Chapitre 16 pour plus d'informations sur la peinture).

- Choisissez Sélection/Modifier/Lisser pour arrondir les angles d'une sélection. Si la sélection est très irrégulière et que vous ne désirez pas conserver ces angles aigus, utilisez la commande Lisser. Elements demande de saisir un rayon de lissage de 1 à 100 pixels. En général, 2 ou 3 suffisent.

- Si vous désirez augmenter la taille d'une sélection de quelques pixels, choisissez Sélection/Modifier/Dilater. Saisissez le nombre de pixels nécessaires à l'augmentation de la taille de la sélection. La valeur maximale est de 100 pixels ; si vous désirez augmenter encore plus cette taille, utilisez plusieurs fois la commande Dilater.

- Sélection/Modifier/Contracter est l'opposé de la commande Dilater. Elle réduit la taille de la zone sélectionnée.

Déplacer un contour de sélection

Pour déplacer un contour de sélection sans bouger l'image, sélectionnez un outil autre que Déplacement ou Recadrage. Ensuite, appuyez sur les touches du pavé directionnel pour déplacer la sélection dans le sens voulu. Chaque pression déplace la sélection de 1 pixel. Pour la déplacer plus rapidement, appuyez sur la touche Maj tout en pressant sur une des flèches. En revanche, si un outil de sélection est actif, placez le pointeur de la souris dans la sélection ; une flèche ornée d'un petit rectangle en pointillé apparaît. Cliquez et faites glisser la sélection à un nouvel emplacement. C'est un moyen idéal pour déplacer une sélection sans perturber un seul pixel de l'image.

Toutefois, cette action ne fonctionne que si, dans la barre d'options de l'outil de sélection, l'icône Nouvelle sélection est active.

Chapitre 10
Les calques

Un des summums de l'art fut sans conteste l'avènement du surréalisme il y a 70 à 80 ans. Des peintres comme Max Ernst, René Magritte ou encore Salvador Dali, ont fait des prouesses. Nous pensons sincèrement que, s'ils étaient toujours vivants, ils apprécieraient Photoshop ou Photoshop Elements. Pourquoi ? À cause des calques, qui permettent de superposer divers éléments sur une seule image et de modifier le contenu de chacun d'entre eux sans porter préjudice aux autres. Un pinceau est un outil génial, mais ce n'est rien comparé à Photoshop Elements, qui est capable de fusionner des photographies, produisant ainsi des effets visuels impossibles à obtenir autrement que par la manipulation numérique des images.

Quel que soit l'appareil photo que vous utilisez, il n'est pas possible d'obtenir, à la prise de vue, des trucages et des effets aussi étonnants que ceux proposés par Photoshop Elements.

Coller des images

Jetez un œil sur la Figure 10.1 : elle montre un poisson à gauche et un sous-bois à droite. Supposons que vous vouliez coller le poisson dans le sous-bois. Voici comment vous procéderez :

Figure 10.1 : Un poisson et quelques fougères, prêts à un rendez-vous dans la palette Calques.

1. **Ouvrez l'image du poisson et sélectionnez-le.**

   Consultez le Chapitre 9 pour en savoir davantage sur les sélections.

2. **Choisissez Édition/Copier ou appuyez sur Ctrl+C.**

   Le fait de copier place l'image sélectionnée dans le Presse-papiers. Il s'agit d'un lieu de stockage temporaire des données d'une image (ou de tout autre fichier). Dès que vous utilisez la commande Copier, le contenu du Presse-papiers est remplacé par les nouveaux éléments ainsi copiés.

3. **Ouvrez l'image contenant le paysage, c'est-à-dire ce magnifique sous-bois illuminé d'une lumière céleste.**

4. **Choisissez Édition/Coller ou appuyez sur Ctrl+V.**

   Cette action colle le contenu du Presse-papiers dans l'image sélectionnée. L'image d'origine, c'est-à-dire le poisson, reste intacte puisque vous utilisez une copie.

Ces étapes ne sont pas le seul moyen de combiner des images. Vous avez d'autres options à votre disposition :

  ✔ Pour couper une sélection, c'est-à-dire enlever une partie d'une image, appuyez sur Ctrl+X. Cela revient à utiliser la commande Édition/Couper. La sélection disparaît de l'image d'origine. Vous pouvez alors la coller dans une nouvelle image.

✔ Vous pouvez cloner une sélection entre deux images. Avec l'outil Déplacement, faites glisser la sélection de l'image 1 dans l'image 2. Il suffit d'appuyer sur la touche Ctrl et de déposer la sélection dans la seconde image.

✔ La commande Copier ne transfère dans le Presse-papiers que le contenu de la sélection du calque actif. Pour copier tous les calques d'une image, choisissez Édition/Copier avec fusion.

✔ Pour des collages plus sophistiqués, utilisez la commande Édition/Coller dedans. Le contenu du Presse-papiers est alors collé dans la sélection de l'image de destination comme cela est décrit dans la prochaine section.

Remplir une sélection avec une sélection

La commande Édition/Coller dedans permet d'insérer une image dans les contours d'une sélection existante. Par exemple, pour coller le poisson derrière la végétation du premier plan du paysage de la Figure 10.1, sélectionnez une zone, puis choisissez Sélection/Contour progressif. Ensuite, choisissez Coller dans la sélection ou appuyez sur le raccourci Ctrl+Maj+V. Le poisson apparaît dans la sélection de la première image comme en témoigne la Figure 10.2. Elements colle la sélection dans le calque actif.

Figure 10.2 : utilisez la commande Coller dedans pour introduire le poisson dans son nouvel habitat.

Redimensionner une image pour sa nouvelle destination

Quand vous assemblez deux images, leur éventuelle différence de taille peut poser problème. Par exemple, le poisson est trop grand pour apparaître entièrement dans la sélection opérée sur l'image du paysage. Voici comment s'assurer que les deux images combinées seront correctement dimensionnées :

1. **Affichez les deux images à la même taille avec le zoom.**

   Pour voir les images côte à côte, définissez un facteur de zoom de 50 %, ou inférieur si nécessaire.

2. **Si l'une des deux images est bien plus grande que l'autre, choisissez Image/Redimensionner/Taille de l'image.**

3. **Combinez les deux images.**

   Copiez et collez, ou opérez un glisser-déposer.

4. **Positionnez l'image.**

5. **Choisissez Image/Redimensionner/Échelle.**

6. **Pour redimensionner l'image, faites glisser une des poignées situées dans un angle.**

   Maintenez la touche Maj enfoncée pour redimensionner l'image proportionnellement, comme le montre la première photo de la Figure 10.3. Dès que vous relâchez le bouton de la souris, Elements affiche un aperçu de l'image redimensionnée. Ne vous inquiétez pas si l'aperçu est un peu approximatif ; l'image redimensionnée sera parfaitement lissée.

   N'agrandissez pas l'image collée ! Sinon Elements est obligé de créer des pixels artificiels, ce qui détériore la qualité de l'image.

7. **Placez le pointeur dans la zone de redimensionnement, et double-cliquez.**

   Après avoir redimensionné une image, placez votre pointeur dans la zone de redimensionnement, c'est-à-dire à l'intérieur du contour orné de poignées. Pour valider le redimensionnement, double-cliquez ou appuyez sur la touche Entrée. Vous pouvez également cliquer sur le bouton Valide la transformation de la barre d'options. L'image redimensionnée apparaît dans toute sa splendeur.

Figure 10.3 :
Utilisez la
commande
Échelle pour
redimensionner
l'image
collée dans
une autre.

Excusez-moi, mais qu'est-ce qu'un calque ?

Pour bien comprendre ce qu'est un calque dans Photoshop Elements, il suffit de l'imaginer sous la forme d'une feuille en plastique transparent que vous placez sur un dessin et sur laquelle vous dessinez avec un feutre. Vous pouvez superposer des feuilles et aussi les décaler les unes par rapport aux autres. Photoshop Elements travaille de la même manière, sauf que ses calques sont numériques, transparents, et autorisent des manipulations jusque-là inconcevables pour l'adepte du pinceau et du crayon.

L'avantage des calques est que vous pouvez en modifier un sans affecter les autres. Cela signifie que vous pouvez appliquer des commandes ou des outils de peinture sur une partie de l'image sans vous préoccuper du reste et sans sélectionner la partie à modifier.

Trouver son chemin dans la palette des calques

La palette des calques, représentée sur la Figure 10.4, est le centre de traitement des calques. C'est ici que vous naviguez d'un calque à l'autre et que vous les gérez :

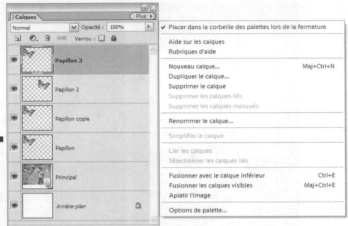

Figure 10.4 :
La palette
des calques
est la clef de
la gestion de
vos calques.

✔ Le calque nommé Arrière-plan est le dernier calque de la palette. Il se situe toujours en bas de la pile. Il est possible de convertir le calque de fond en calque ordinaire, et inversement.

✔ L'ordre des calques correspond à la manière dont ils se superposent dans l'image. Le calque situé en haut de la palette signifie qu'à l'écran, il se trouve devant les autres.

✔ Vous ne pouvez modifier qu'un calque à la fois. Le calque *actif* est celui qui est sélectionné dans la palette des calques, et de ce fait en surbrillance. Pour activer un calque, cliquez dessus.

✔ L'icône d'un œil affichée à gauche du calque indique que son contenu est visible. Pour masquer un calque, cliquez sur l'œil. Pour afficher le contenu d'un calque, cliquez dans le carré vide qui doit afficher l'icône de l'œil. Cette dernière réapparaît simultanément au contenu du calque.

✔ Pour masquer tous les calques sauf un, maintenez la touche Alt enfoncée et cliquez sur l'icône de l'œil du calque à afficher. Pour afficher de nouveau tous les calques, procédez de la même manière.

✔ Si vous masquez le calque d'arrière-plan, un damier s'affiche dans toutes les parties vides des autres calques de l'image. Le damier est la représentation de la transparence dans Photoshop et Photoshop Elements.

✔ Pour personnaliser le damier, c'est-à-dire la représentation de la transparence, choisissez Édition/Préférences/Transparence. Vous y spécifiez la taille et la couleur des carrés utilisés par Elements pour représenter les zones transparentes des calques.

✔ Pour maîtriser les modes de fusion et l'opacité des calques, reportez-vous au Chapitre 14.

✔ Pour créer un nouveau calque vide, cliquez sur l'icône Créer un calque, en haut de la palette des calques (voir la Figure 10.4). Si vous appuyez sur Alt en cliquant, la boîte de dialogue Nouveau calque apparaît. Donnez-lui un nom. Pour dupliquer un calque existant, faites-le glisser sur l'icône Créer un nouveau calque.

Lorsque vous créez un calque par simple clic sur cette icône, Elements le nomme Calque 1, Calque 2, et ainsi de suite. Pour renommer le calque, double-cliquez dessus dans la palette des calques. Saisissez le nouveau nom et validez-le en appuyant sur la touche Entrée.

✔ Pour supprimer un calque, faites-le glisser jusqu'à l'icône de la poubelle. Le fait de supprimer un calque en supprime également le contenu. Vous pouvez supprimer un calque en choisissant Calque/Supprimer le calque, ou en choisissant Supprimer le calque dans le menu Plus de la palette des calques.

✔ Si vous désirez sélectionner un objet sur un calque, maintenez la touche Ctrl enfoncée et cliquez sur l'image du calque dans la palette des calques.

Déplacer et manipuler des calques

Les calques sont des éléments souples. Vous pouvez les déplacer, les organiser et les mélanger comme les cartes d'un jeu. Voici les manipulations les plus fréquemment réalisées avec les calques :

✔ Pour déplacer un calque de 1 pixel, appuyez sur une touche du pavé directionnel. Pour effectuer un déplacement par incrémentation de 10 pixels, maintenez la touche Maj enfoncée et utilisez ces mêmes touches.

✔ Cochez l'option Sélection automatique du calque dans la barre d'options de l'outil Déplacement pour sélectionner un calque quand vous cliquez sur un de ses éléments.

Cette option présente un inconvénient. Vous activez systématiquement le calque, même si vous ne le souhaitez pas.

✔ L'option Afficher le cadre de sélection montre le cadre de sélection entourant l'objet du calque quand l'outil déplacement est actif. Ce cadre permet de transformer un calque sans choisir de commande comme cela est expliqué dans la section "Transformer les calques et les sélections", plus loin dans ce chapitre.

✔ Pour lier un calque à un autre, cliquez dans la deuxième colonne de la palette des calques, juste à droite de l'icône d'œil. L'icône Liée apparaît. Elle ressemble à un maillon, ou *chaînon*. Désormais vous pouvez déplacer, redimensionner et faire pivoter les deux calques en même temps. Pour supprimer ce lien, cliquez sur l'icône de la chaîne. Elle disparaît. Chaque calque retrouve sa liberté.

✔ Pour supprimer des calques liés, sélectionnez l'un d'eux. Maintenez ensuite la touche Ctrl enfoncée et cliquez sur l'icône de la poubelle de la palette des calques.

✔ Si vous cliquez avec le bouton droit sur un objet dans l'image avec l'outil Déplacement, Elements affiche un petit menu déroulant, qui énumère chaque calque contenant des pixels à l'endroit précis où vous avez cliqué. Vous pouvez sélectionner dans ce menu le calque à activer. Vous pouvez également en profiter pour activer l'option Sélection automatique du calque. Avec l'outil Déplacement, cliquez avec le bouton droit, avec la touche Alt enfoncée ; Elements active automatiquement le calque approprié. Ici encore, employez la touche Ctrl lorsque l'outil actif n'est pas l'outil Déplacement (à l'exception des outils Main et Forme personnalisée).

✔ Pour organiser les objets de l'image, il suffit de faire glisser les calques les uns au-dessus ou en dessous des autres. Une ligne noire indique la position du calque. Quand vous relâchez le bouton de la souris, le calque s'affiche à sa nouvelle position, et les objets qu'il contient se trouvent à un nouveau niveau dans l'image globale. Il n'est pas possible de déplacer le calque d'arrière-plan. Comment faire alors ? Convertissez-le en un calque ordinaire en actionnant Calque/Nouveau/Calque à partir de l'arrière-plan. Ou double-cliquez sur le calque d'arrière-plan dans la palette Calques, entrez un nom pour le calque et appuyez sur Entrée. Ou gardez le nom par défaut Calque 0 et appuyez sur Entrée.

✔ Lorsqu'il n'existe pas de calque d'arrière-plan et que vous voulez convertir le calque actif en calque d'arrière-plan, choisissez Calque/Nouveau/Arrière-plan d'après un calque. Elements opère la conversion, déplace le calque sélectionné au bas de la pile s'il ne s'y trouve pas déjà.

✔ Une autre manière de disposer les calques consiste à utiliser les commandes du sous-menu Réorganiser du menu Calque. Dans la palette des calques, cliquez sur le calque à déplacer, puis :

1. Choisissez Calque/Réorganiser/Premier plan pour placer le calque au-dessus des autres. Il apparaît alors en haut de la palette des calques.

2. Choisissez Rapprocher pour déplacer le calque d'un niveau vers le haut.

3. Choisissez Éloigner pour le déplacer d'un niveau vers le bas.

4. Choisissez Arrière-plan pour le placer juste avant le calque d'Arrière-plan.

Aplatir et fusionner des calques

Malheureusement, les calques ne sont pas toujours une partie de plaisir. Leur gestion exige une certaine expérience. Tout d'abord, si une image contient des calques, vous devez l'enregistrer dans un format qui les supporte, c'est-à-dire qui ne va pas les supprimer lors de l'enregistrement de l'image. Le format natif de Photoshop Elements est PSD, mais les calques sont également supportés par les formats PDF et TIFF. Chaque calque ajouté alourdit considérablement l'image finale. Selon la mémoire disponible de l'ordinateur, la présence de trop de calques peut poser problème Il est recommandé d'en utiliser le moins possible.

Quand vous aurez une bonne expérience de Photoshop Elements, vous utiliserez souvent la fusion des calques afin de bien gérer votre image. Voici les options de fusion :

✔ Pour fusionner plusieurs calques en un seul, masquez tous les calques sauf ceux que vous désirez fusionner. En d'autres termes, seules les icônes d'affichage (œil) des calques à fusionner doivent être visibles. Choisissez Fusionner les calques visibles dans le menu de la palette des calques, ou dans le menu Calque de la fenêtre principale de Photoshop Elements. Une autre méthode consiste à appuyer sur Maj+Ctrl+E.

✔ Les calques liés peuvent être fusionnés. Il suffit de choisir la commande Fusionner les calques liés, soit dans le menu de la palette des calques, soit dans le menu Calque. Si aucun calque n'est lié, cette commande est remplacée par Fusionner avec le calque inférieur.

✔ Pour aplatir toute l'image et faire ainsi disparaître tous les calques, choisissez la commande Aplatir l'image du menu de la palette des calques ou du menu Calque.

Verrouiller des calques

Le chapitre précédent traitait des sélections pour limiter la zone de travail active. Par exemple, vous pouvez peindre sans précaution dans une sélection et être certain que la peinture ne va pas s'étaler au-delà des limites imposées par la sélection. Mais, quand vous appliquez une sélection à un calque contenant des zones de transparence, vous peignez sur ces zones. Or, parfois, vous ne souhaitez modifier que l'objet présent sur le calque.

Pour ne pas altérer les zones de transparence d'un calque, cochez la case Verrou de la palette des calques (voir la Figure 10.4). Les zones transparentes autour de l'objet ne sont pas affectées par vos modifications.

L'option Tout verrouiller, identifiée par un cadenas, empêche de peindre, modifier, déplacer ou transformer la totalité d'un calque et pas uniquement ses zones transparentes.

Déplacer et cloner des sélections

Le Chapitre 9 s'intéresse au déplacement des contours de sélection sans toucher au contenu de l'image. Maintenant que vous avez fait connaissance avec les calques, voyons comment déplacer des sélections et les pixels qu'elles contiennent :

✔ Pour déplacer une sélection, choisissez l'outil Déplacement et faites-la glisser. Un cadre apparaît autour de la sélection pour bien voir où et comment vous la déplacez. Quand vous déplacez une sélection sur le calque d'arrière-plan, les pixels qu'elle contient sont remplacés par la couleur d'arrière-plan, comme cela est illustré sur la Figure 10.5.

✔ Avec n'importe quel autre outil (sauf Main et Forme), il est possible d'accéder temporairement à l'outil Déplacement en appuyant sur la touche Ctrl.

✔ Pour déplacer la sélection de 1 pixel, appuyez sur l'une des flèches du pavé directionnel du clavier. Pour un déplacement de 10 pixels, maintenez la touche Maj enfoncée tout en appuyant

Figure 10.5 :
Après avoir
sélectionné
l'obélisque
(en haut),
déplacez-le à
un endroit
plus
approprié (en
bas).

sur une touche du pavé directionnel. Ce déplacement n'est
possible que si l'outil Déplacement est sélectionné.

✔ Pour cloner ou déplacer une sélection, maintenez la touche Alt
enfoncée tout en déplaçant la sélection avec l'outil Déplacement.
Vous obtenez le même résultat en maintenant Ctrl+Alt enfoncés
tout en utilisant un autre outil (excepté Main et Forme).

✔ Pour cloner et créer un effet de trace, maintenez la touche Alt
enfoncée et déplacez la sélection à l'aide des flèches du pavé
directionnel. Maintenez enfoncée la touche Maj pour cloner et

> déplacer la sélection de 10 pixels chaque fois que vous appuyez sur une touche du pavé directionnel.

> ✔ Vous pouvez déplacer et cloner des sélections entre des images comme vous l'avez fait pour les calques des images. Faites simplement glisser la sélection en cours jusqu'à la fenêtre de l'image de destination.

Transformer les calques et les sélections

La fin du Chapitre 4 s'intéresse aux commandes qui permettent de faire pivoter une image et de la retourner. Voyons maintenant ce que nous réserve la transformation proprement dite. Dans Elements, le mot "transformation" doit être pris dans les sens géométrique du terme, c'est-à-dire translations, rotations, étirements et distorsions. Vous pouvez transformer un calque ou une sélection quand son cadre de sélection (ou plutôt de transformation) est visible. Il suffit alors d'agir sur les poignées pour transformer le calque ou la sélection.

Utiliser les commandes du menu Image

Le menu Image propose trois sous-menus contenant des commandes de transformation : Rotation, Transformation et Redimensionner. Le sous-menu Rotation comporte la commande Rotation manuelle du calque/Rotation manuelle de la sélection, ainsi que d'autres commandes équivalentes à celles étudiées au Chapitre 4. En bas du sous-menu Redimensionner se trouve la commande Échelle. Le menu Transformation, quant à lui, dispose de quatre commandes.

Ces commandes fonctionnent avec ou sans sélection. S'il n'y a pas de sélection, les commandes s'appliquent sur la totalité du calque. S'il existe une sélection active, les commandes affectent uniquement la zone sélectionnée. Seule exception : le calque d'arrière-plan. Il a besoin d'une sélection active pour être transformé. Si vous essayez de transformer la totalité du calque d'arrière-plan, vous obtiendrez un message vous demandant si vous désirez d'abord convertir l'arrière-plan en calque ordinaire.

Utiliser l'outil Transformer

Secret depuis la nuit des temps, l'outil Transformer ne se trouve pas dans la boîte à outils de Photoshop Elements. Choisissez une commande de transformation ou faites glisser une poignée du cadre de sélection avec l'outil Déplacement pour voir furtivement apparaître l'outil Transformer. Dès qu'il est actif, la barre d'options prend l'apparence de celle représentée sur la Figure 10.6. Toute transformation peut alors être effectuée avec les champs de cette barre d'options ou avec les commandes disponibles dans les sous-menus du menu Image. Cette possibilité est de loin la meilleure. Voyons les commandes à notre disposition :

- **Rotation manuelle du calque/Rotation manuelle de la sélection :** Placez le pointeur à proximité du bord de la sélection. Il prend la forme d'une double flèche incurvée. Déplacez le pointeur pour faire pivoter la sélection dans le sens voulu. Placez le pointeur dans le cadre de sélection pour la déplacer.

- **Transformation manuelle :** Cette option permet de redimensionner, déplacer et faire pivoter la sélection. La Transformation manuelle peut être invoquée avec le raccourci clavier Ctrl+T.

- **Inclinaison :** Applique une distorsion sur un axe donné.

- **Torsion :** Autorise le déplacement sans contrainte de chacune des poignées..

- **Perspective :** Quand vous tirez la poignée d'un angle, la poignée de l'angle opposé se déplace en conséquence.

- **Échelle :** Faites glisser n'importe quelle poignée pour redimensionner votre sélection. Maintenez la touche Maj enfoncée pendant cette opération pour effectuer un redimensionnement à partir du centre. Cela est bien expliqué au Chapitre 4. Pour effectuer un redimensionnement proportionnel, appuyez sur Alt.

Figure 10.6 :
La barre
d'options de
l'outil
Transformer.

Valider la transformation

La transformation terminée, appuyez sur la touche Entrée, double-cliquez à l'intérieur du cadre de sélection ou cliquez sur le bouton

Valide la transformation de la barre d'options. Pour annuler, appuyez sur Echap ou cliquez sur le bouton Annuler la transformation de la barre d'options.

De nombreuses options sont présentes dans la palette des calques – les modes de fusion, les calques de texte, les calques de réglages, les calques de forme, les calques de remplissage –, mais nous pensons qu'il était important de présenter les bases d'utilisation de la palette des calques. Ne vous inquiétez pas : nous parlerons des autres options dès que nous les rencontrerons dans nos travaux.

Plus vrai que nature

Dans cette partie...

Les photographes immortalisent un bref instant de notre quotidien. Du sourire figé à cette surprenante attitude face à un événement imprévu, tout est fait pour se remémorer, quelques années plus tard, de sympathiques moments de bonheur. La vie paraît d'ailleurs toujours plus belle quand on en regarde les photographies.

Aujourd'hui, vous appréhendez la photo différemment. Pourquoi ? Tout simplement parce que vous êtes l'heureux détenteur de Photoshop Elements. Les clichés surexposés, sous-exposés, mal cadrés, j'en passe et des pires, ne seront plus qu'un mauvais souvenir. Qui n'a pas rêvé de supprimer cet effet "yeux rouges" dont le constructeur de votre appareil photo garantissait pourtant l'absence sur vos portraits ? Malgré de nombreuses précautions et des pré-flashes qui scintillent à outrance, rien n'y fait, certaines personnes ressemblent à des lapins albinos. Vous découvrirez en Photoshop Elements un véritable chirurgien esthétique capable de supprimer de nombreuses imperfections. Des rides ? La belle affaire ! Quelques clics et voici la peau lisse !

Les trois chapitres de cette partie expliquent comment améliorer vos images et les rendre plus vraies que nature. Les photos du passé auront une autre allure. Par exemple, prenez votre appareil photo numérique de 54 mégapixels, visez, appuyez, importez l'image dans votre ordinateur à 50 GHz, lancez la version 36 de Photoshop Elements et comparez avec vos anciennes prises de vues. Certes, nous anticipons un peu... Mais les avancées technologiques permettent de donner un aspect encore plus réaliste.

Chapitre 11

Le Midas
de la retouche

Si vous avez déjà numérisé des images, vous connaissez le problème. Vous placez une bien jolie photographie sur la vitre du scanner. Mais, une fois l'image numérisée, des taches apparaissent çà et là, quand ce ne sont pas des cheveux ou des poils de chat. Parfois une grosse empreinte digitale vient gâcher le superbe visage de votre petit(e) ami(e).

Soit vous nettoyez patiemment la vitre du scanner sachant que l'on ne peut pas ôter toutes les poussières, soit vous avez recours à quelques filtres de Photoshop Elements. Plusieurs outils permettent de retoucher les images, notamment ceux représentés à la Figure 11.1.

Présentation des filtres

Si vous êtes photographe ou avez suivi quelques cours de photographie, vous savez comment fonctionnent les filtres photographiques. Les filtres correcteurs transmettent une partie seulement du rayonnement de la lumière tandis que les filtres d'effets modifient le parcours de la lumière. Ils prennent toutefois de la place dans votre fourre-tout, nécessitent une protection particulière et finissent par se rayer. En plus, il faut savoir quel filtre utiliser avant de prendre la photographie. En d'autres termes, la photo doit être soigneusement préparée à

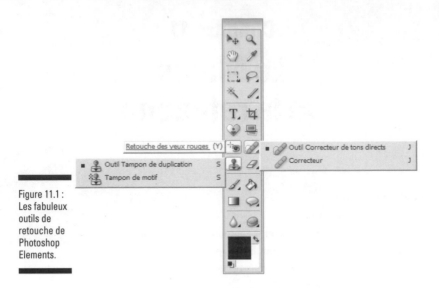

Figure 11.1 :
Les fabuleux
outils de
retouche de
Photoshop
Elements.

l'avance et prise sans la moindre spontanéité. Une fois le filtre choisi, impossible de revenir en arrière, sauf éventuellement au labo.

Il n'en va pas de même avec les filtres de Photoshop Elements :

✔ Tous les filtres se trouvent dans une palette Styles et effets.

✔ Vous pouvez annuler l'effet d'un filtre qui ne produit pas le résultat attendu.

✔ Il est possible de prévisualiser l'effet avant d'appliquer le filtre.

✔ Plusieurs filtres peuvent être appliqués successivement, ou vous pouvez cumuler les effets d'un même filtre.

✔ La plupart des filtres de Photoshop Elements n'ont pas d'équivalent optique. Cela signifie que vous pouvez modifier une image comme ne le permettra jamais un appareil photo, même numérique.

Appliquer des filtres

Les filtres sont utilisables de deux manières : via le menu Filtre ou via la palette Styles et effets. Dans le menu Filtre, ils sont répartis dans des sous-menus thématiques. Dans la palette Styles et effets, vous sélectionnez Filtres dans la liste, puis la catégorie à afficher. La plupart des filtres ainsi appliqués ouvrent une boîte de dialogue servant à paramétrer leurs effets.

Quelques filtres du menu Filtre ne sont pas présents dans la palette Styles et effets. C'est le cas des filtres Égaliser, Courbe de transfert de dégradé, Inverser, Isohélie, Seuil et Filtre photo de la catégorie Réglages. Il en va de même pour le filtre Moyenne (Atténuation), Dispersion (Déformation), Fibres et Texture (Rendu), et Lecture du filigrane (Digimarc).

La palette Styles et effets affiche une représentation miniature de l'effet du filtre. Vous pouvez afficher les filtres par catégorie, comme dans le menu Filtre, ou les garder tous à votre disposition. Les filtres sont classés par ordre alphabétique. Pour les appliquer, soit vous double-cliquez sur la miniature du filtre, soit vous exécutez la commande Appliquer, du menu Plus de la palette, soit vous glissez-déposez la vignette du filtre sur l'image.

Quand un filtre doit être réglé, une petite boîte de dialogue apparaît. Elle dispose d'une fenêtre d'aperçu permettant de mesurer les effets des réglages. C'est le cas, par exemple, du filtre Flou gaussien. Si vous cochez la case Aperçu, vous voyez l'effet du filtre sur le calque sélectionné. Définissez une valeur pour que le filtre altère plus ou moins l'image, et appliquez-le par un clic sur OK. D'autres filtres plus sophistiqués, comme Crayon de couleur, ouvrent la Galerie de filtres. Il s'agit d'une grosse boîte de dialogue pourvue de nombreux paramètres.

Les filtres à boîte de dialogue

De nombreux filtres produisent leur effet par le biais d'une boîte de dialogue. Elle contient des paramètres dont vous définissez les valeurs. En général, les boîtes de dialogue ont une case d'aperçu qui permet de contrôler l'effet directement sur le calque traité. Dans certains cas, la boîte de dialogue est une véritable interface comme vous le constaterez au Chapitre 14 qui traite du filtre Fluidité.

Examinons une boîte de dialogue typique comme celle du filtre Antipoussière. C'est un filtre capable d'éliminer certaines taches. Nous ne sommes pas des fanatiques de ce filtre car il traite la globalité de l'image. Son effet est donc souvent trop radical.

Pour appliquer ce filtre, cliquez sur Filtre/Bruit/Antipoussière, ou choisissez Filtres dans le panneau Styles et effets, puis Bruit, et enfin double-cliquez sur l'icône Antipoussière. Vous ouvrez la boîte de dialogue illustrée à la Figure 11.2.

Curseur de prévisualisation   Zone d'aperçu

Figure 11.2 :
Voici une
boîte de
dialogue
typique d'un
filtre.

Boutons de zoom

Si vous sélectionnez une partie de l'image avant d'invoquer le filtre
Antipoussière, l'effet se limitera à cette zone.

Prévisualiser les effets du filtre

De prime abord, les différentes parties de la boîte de dialogue des
options d'un filtre ne sont pas très évocatrices. Voici comment
fonctionne la prévisualisation, que l'on nomme parfois *aperçu*.

✔ La zone d'aperçu montre vos modifications sur une petite partie
de l'image.

✔ Si vous placez le pointeur de la souris en dehors de la boîte de
dialogue, il prend la forme d'un carré vide. Cliquez alors sur une
partie de l'image pour l'afficher dans la zone d'aperçu.

✔ Vous pouvez faire défiler le contenu de la zone d'aperçu en y
plaçant le pointeur de la souris. Il prend la forme d'une main.
Maintenez le bouton de la souris enfoncé et déplacez le contenu
de la zone d'aperçu. Cette dernière affiche toujours une partie
de l'image sur laquelle va s'appliquer le filtre.

✔ Pour réduire ou grossir la zone d'aperçu, cliquez sur le bouton
"+" ou "-".

✔ Vous pouvez également utiliser l'outil Zoom. Placez le pointeur de la souris dans la zone d'aperçu et appuyez sur la touche Ctrl. Il prend alors la forme d'une loupe. Pour réduire, appuyez sur la touche Alt. La loupe est à présent agrémentée du signe "-".

✔ Si vous ajoutez la touche Maj aux deux touches précitées, le zoom se produit simultanément sur l'image et dans l'aperçu de la boîte de dialogue.

✔ Tant que la case Aperçu est active, la prévisualisation s'effectue dans la boîte de dialogue du filtre ainsi que dans l'image.

✔ Par défaut, une main apparaît quand vous placez le pointeur de la souris dans la zone d'aperçu. Il suffit de cliquer et de glisser pour afficher une autre partie de l'image dans l'aperçu. Pour déplacer simultanément le contenu de la fenêtre de l'image, appuyez sur Maj tout en déplaçant la main.

✔ Si Elements semble ralentir, évitez de prévisualiser l'effet sur l'image elle-même. Pour cela, décochez l'option Aperçu de la boîte de dialogue des options du filtre.

La boîte de dialogue Antipoussière dispose de deux options qui affectent la performance du filtre : Rayon et Seuil. Voici comment ils agissent :

✔ La valeur du Rayon indique la taille des taches de poussière et l'épaisseur des cheveux que vous désirez éliminer. En géométrie, le rayon est égal à la moitié du diamètre. Par conséquent, la valeur du Rayon est égale à la moitié d'une tache de poussière. La valeur minimale est 1. Cela signifie que le filtre supprime toutes les taches et les cheveux dont l'épaisseur est supérieure à 2.

Vous pensez alors qu'il suffit de déterminer un rayon de 100 pour éliminer toute une colonie de poussières. Eh bien non ! Le filtre Antipoussière ne fait pas la différence entre une poussière et les couleurs de l'image. Définir un Rayon de 100 pixels portera inévitablement atteinte aux détails de l'image. On ne distinguera plus rien si le Seuil est lui-même très faible. Un conseil : ne définissez jamais un Rayon supérieur à 2.

✔ La valeur Seuil indique à Elements comment les différentes taches se démarquent des autres couleurs de l'image.

La valeur par défaut est 0. Elements considère alors que les poussières et l'image ont seulement besoin d'un niveau de différence de couleurs de 0 pour être détectées. Comme toutes les couleurs ont au moins une différence de niveau colorimétrique de 0, Elements ignore la valeur du Seuil et ne considère que celle du Rayon.

En augmentant le Seuil, vous demandez à Elements d'être plus sélectif. Avec une valeur de 10, les taches et les couleurs de l'image doivent varier d'au moins 10 niveaux avant qu'Elements n'enlève les taches. Si vous fixez le Seuil à 20, Elements est encore moins pointilleux avec les impuretés.

La Galerie de filtres

Si vous vous demandez pourquoi seuls quelques filtres ont le privilège d'apparaître dans la Galerie de filtres, remontez aux premières heures de Photoshop. En 1990, Adobe avait acquis un ensemble de filtres graphiques édités par Aldus. Devenus Aldus Gallery Effects, Adobe les intégra dans Photoshop. La version CS de Photoshop a vu réapparaître ce concept de représentation de filtres dans une galerie. Il n'est donc guère étonnant qu'Elements en ait également hérité.

Choisissez un des filtres de la catégorie Artistique, Contours, Déformation, Esquisse, Esthétique ou Texture dans la palette Styles et effets. Vous accédez à l'interface Galerie de filtres représentée à la Figure 11.3. Il est également possible d'ouvrir cette galerie par le menu Filtre.

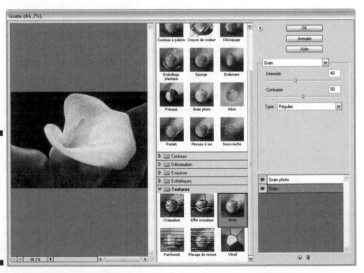

Figure 11.3 :
C'est à partir de la Galerie de filtres que vous appliquez la plupart des filtres artistiques.

Voici une brève description des fonctions de cette galerie :

- ✔ À gauche, une zone d'aperçu montre l'effet des filtres sur l'image. Les touches Ctrl et Alt permettent de zoomer en avant et en arrière.

- ✔ Cliquez sur le triangle situé à gauche du dossier pour afficher les filtres qu'il contient. Puis, cliquez sur la vignette du filtre à appliquer à l'image.

- ✔ Quand vous cliquez sur une vignette, un ensemble de paramètres apparaissent dans la partie droite de la fenêtre. Le nom du filtre sélectionné s'affiche dans la barre de titre de la Galerie de filtres. Le filtre lui-même apparaît dans la partie inférieure droite. Une icône de visibilité (un œil) indique qu'il est actif, c'est-à-dire appliqué à l'aperçu. Cette zone est une sorte de palette de calques d'effets. Vous les superposez et les déplacez pour varier et tester les effets.

À proximité du bouton OK, vous voyez deux chevrons. Cliquez dessus pour masquer la liste des effets et agrandir ainsi l'aperçu de l'image.

- ✔ Dans la zone d'affichage des filtres sélectionnés, vous pouvez en ajouter, en supprimer, les réorganiser et les masquer. Pour appliquer plusieurs filtres, commencez par appliquer un filtre de la catégorie Esthétiques, comme Contour lumineux. Cliquez ensuite sur l'icône Nouveau calque d'effet située en bas de la galerie. Cette action crée une copie du filtre Contour lumineux. Comme la copie est active, cliquez sur un autre filtre, comme Vitrail, dans la catégorie Texture. Désormais, deux filtres sont appliqués simultanément : Vitrail et Contour lumineux.

Supposons que l'effet produit par la combinaison de ces deux filtres ne vous convienne pas. Pas de problème : cliquez sur le calque d'effet Vitrail et glissez-déposez-le sous le calque d'effet Contour lumineux. Vous obtenez un tout autre résultat. Par cette méthode, vous pouvez ajouter et combiner autant de calques d'effet que vous désirez. Quand un calque ne vous convient pas, sélectionnez-le, puis cliquez sur l'icône de la poubelle. Une fois vos filtres définis et organisés, appliquez-les par un clic sur OK.

Les prouesses de l'outil Tampon de duplication

Pour obtenir un dépoussiérage efficace de vos images, il faut utiliser l'outil Tampon de duplication. Il permet de copier une partie de l'image sur une autre.

Tamponner les taches

Procédez comme suit pour utiliser l'outil Tampon de duplication :

1. **Cliquez sur l'outil Tampon de duplication, dans la boîte à outils (voir la Figure 11.4).**

Figure 11.4 :
L'outil
Tampon de
duplication et
sa barre
d'options,
partenaire
incontestable
du clonage
des pixels.

Pour l'activer depuis le clavier, appuyez sur la touche S.

2. **Dans la barre d'options de l'outil, veillez à ce que la case Aligné soit cochée.**

Cette option autorise une duplication relative des pixels de l'image. Vous comprendrez mieux dans un instant.

3. **Commencez par cliquer et puis glissez le pointeur au hasard sur votre image.**

Vous obtenez un message d'erreur ? Évidemment ! Pour utiliser l'outil Tampon de duplication, il faut d'abord, et impérativement, indiquer à Elements la partie de l'image à cloner.

4. **Maintenez la touche Alt enfoncée et cliquez sur la partie de l'image qui servira de référence au clonage.**

Comme le montre la Figure 11.5, nous avons cliqué à proximité d'une énorme tache située dans la partie inférieure et arrière de la comète. Prélever cette valeur de gris permettra de supprimer la tache indésirable sans qu'aucun raccord soit visible.

5. **Maintenant, cliquez dans la tache ou faites glisser l'outil dessus.**

Quand vous cliquez ou faites glisser l'outil Tampon de duplication, Elements affiche un réticule dans la zone où vous prélevez la couleur

La tache cosmique indésirable

Alt+clic avec l'outil Tampon de duplication

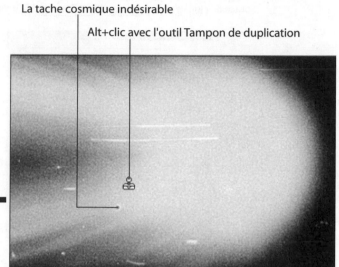

Figure 11.5 :
Détermina-
tion de la
source du
clonage.

de remplacement, comme en témoigne la Figure 11.6. Il représente la
source du clonage, c'est-à-dire la zone que vous dupliquez. Quand
vous déplacez la souris, le réticule se déplace corrélativement,
permettant à l'outil Tampon de duplication d'appliquer les couleurs
qu'il survole. En d'autres termes, vous peignez avec les pixels prélevés
dans l'image.

Si la zone clonée ne se mélange pas bien avec la partie de l'image où se
trouve la tache, cliquez sur le bouton Aller vers l'arrière ou appuyez
sur Ctrl+Z. Ensuite, recommencez l'opération. La touche Alt enfoncée,
cliquez sur l'image avec l'outil Tampon de duplication pour définir une
meilleure source de clonage. Il est souvent nécessaire de choisir
plusieurs zones de clonage successives afin de parfaire le résultat.

Juste pour vous mettre l'eau à la bouche, jetez un œil à la Figure 11.7.
Un quart d'heure a suffi pour obtenir ce résultat.

De vrais tours de magie avec l'outil Tampon de duplication

L'outil Tampon de duplication est parfait pour nettoyer soigneusement
une image, mais il permet de faire des choses bien plus étonnantes :

Source de clonage   Pointeur de l'outil Tampon de duplication

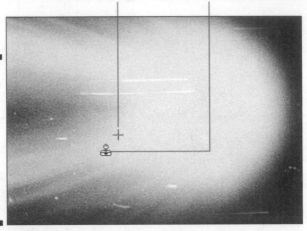

Figure 11.6 :
Quand vous
utilisez l'outil
Tampon de
duplication,
un petit
réticule
indique la
partie de
l'image en
cours de
duplication.

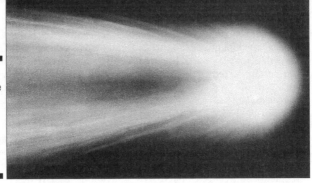

Figure 11.7 :
La comète de
Halley, qui
nous visite
tous les
74 ans,
nettoyée de
ses rayures.

✔ Pour changer la taille ou la forme de la zone clonée, modifiez celle de la forme dans la palette Forme de la barre d'options de l'outil. Pour en savoir davantage sur les formes, consultez le Chapitre 15.

✔ Pour modifier l'opacité de la duplication, réglez le curseur d'opacité, dans la barre d'options de l'outil. A 100%, le clonage est totalement opaque. L'opacité peut être changée en appuyant sur les touches des chiffres ; tapez 5, par exemple, pour obtenir une opacité de 50 %, ou 5 rapidement deux fois de suite pour une opacité de 55 %.

- ✔ Pour supprimer une trace rectiligne, maintenez la touche Alt enfoncée et cliquez pour définir la source du clonage. Ensuite, cliquez sur l'une des extrémités de la trace à effacer, puis en maintenant la touche Maj enfoncée, cliquez à l'autre extrémité.

- ✔ Si la duplication ne correspond pas exactement à ce que vous voulez, modifiez-la plutôt que de recommencer. Diminuez le paramètre d'opacité et clonez à partir d'autres portions de l'image que vous définissez toujours avec Alt+clic. Vous pourrez ainsi mélanger diverses zones de l'image pour obtenir une duplication parfaite, sans raccord.

- ✔ Normalement, l'outil Tampon de duplication effectue un clonage depuis une position relative : quand vous déplacez le pointeur de la souris, la source de clonage change. Que faire pour cloner plusieurs fois à partir d'un même emplacement ? Décochez la case Aligné de la barre d'options de l'outil. Puis, définissez la zone à dupliquer avec Alt+clic. Ensuite, où que vous placiez l'outil, vous dupliquerez toujours à partir du même point.

- ✔ L'outil Tampon de motif, qui se trouve dans le menu local de l'outil Tampon de duplication et dans la barre d'options, clone de manière répétitive. La palette Motif dans la barre d'options donne accès à la bibliothèque de motifs prédéfinis d'Elements. Vous pouvez aussi définir votre motif en sélectionnant une zone rectangulaire, puis en choisissant Édition/Définir le motif d'après la sélection. Donnez-lui un nom, puis sélectionnez votre motif personnalisé en bas de la liste Motif de la barre d'options de l'outil. Faites glisser l'outil sur l'image (c'est-à-dire en maintenant le bouton gauche de la souris enfoncé) et vous verrez apparaître votre motif. Sympa, mais inutile !

- ✔ S'agissant de choses cool mais pas spécialement utiles, une nouvelle option Impressionniste se trouve dans la barre d'options de l'outil Tampon de motif. Elle donne à l'outil Tampon de motif la faculté d'apporter... eh bien... une *impression* de forme impressionniste. Si vous voulez introduire dans votre image des effets de motif tourbillonnant, cet outil est ce qu'il vous faut. Il est de toute façon plaisant à découvrir. Lorsque le Tampon de duplication est actif, vous pouvez permuter vers le Tampon de motif en cliquant sur le bouton Tampon de motif du côté gauche de la barre d'options.

- ✔ Il est possible de réaliser des clonages entre plusieurs images avec l'outil Tampon de duplication. Deux images étant ouvertes dans Photoshop Elements, faites un Alt+clic dans l'une d'elles pour spécifier la source de la duplication. Placez ensuite le pointeur de la souris dans l'autre image et cliquez : les pixels de l'image source sont peints dans l'image de destination.

✔ La Figure 11.8 montre un parfait exemple de clonage entre deux images. À gauche, les deux images ont été mises à la même échelle via Image/Redimensionner/Taille de l'image (voir le Chapitre 4). Nous avons maintenu la touche Alt enfoncée et cliqué dans l'image du haut pour définir la source de la duplication. Ensuite, nous avons appliqué la duplication dans l'image du bas. Les yeux et les rides de la vieille dame ont ainsi été ajoutés au visage du vieux monsieur. Pour maintenir une cohérence de ton, nous avons réglé l'opacité à 50 %. Impressionnant, n'est-ce pas ?

Figure 11.8 :
Le résultat du clonage est d'un réalisme saisissant.

✔ Si l'image contient des calques (voir Chapitre 10), n'oubliez pas que l'outil Tampon de duplication ne clone que le contenu du calque actif. Pour qu'il en soit autrement, cochez l'option Utiliser tous les calques, dans la barre d'options.

✔ L'outil Tampon de duplication est capable de cloner avec un mode d'effet, ce qui permet d'appliquer des effets spéciaux aux pixels. Les modes d'effet sont pour l'essentiel la même chose que les modes de fusion décrits au Chapitre 14. Si vous avez une ou deux heures de libre, amusez-vous à découvrir ces différents modes.

L'outil Tampon de duplication est incontestablement l'un des deux ou trois outils les plus utiles de Photoshop Elements.

Accomplir des miracles avec les formes de correction

Si l'outil Tampon de duplication est l'un des deux ou trois outils essentiels de Photoshop Elements, les correcteurs sont, quant à eux, indispensables. Ils sont déclinés en deux versions : le Correcteur et le Correcteur de ton direct.

Le Correcteur

L'outil Correcteur fonctionne à peu près comme le Tampon de duplication : il faut définir un point source qui servira de base au clonage. Pour cela, il suffit d'appuyer sur la touche Alt puis de passer l'outil sur les zones à corriger. Le gros avantage de ce correcteur par rapport au tampon de duplication est qu'il prend en considération la couleur et le contraste de la zone à corriger. Il n'est donc pas nécessaire de sélectionner une zone source proche de la zone à corriger.

La Figure 11.9 montre comment éliminer une cicatrice. Sur l'image de gauche, nous avons défini la source du clonage sur une partie saine de la peau. Ensuite, il suffit de passer, en une seule fois, sur la cicatrice pour la faire disparaître. Comme l'outil Correcteur parvient à mélanger savamment différentes textures de la source et de la destination, la correction est indécelable. L'image de droite de la Figure 11.9 en est la preuve flagrante.

Voici une brève description des options de l'outil Correcteur :

- ✔ **Taille :** Contrôle le diamètre de la forme. Plus la pointe du Correcteur est grande, plus il utilisera de pixels environnants pour corriger l'imperfection. Pour obtenir un résultat très précis, nous déconseillons une taille trop élevée.

- ✔ **Mode :** Comme pour l'outil Tampon de duplication, il est possible de sélectionner un mode qui déterminera la manière dont les pixels se mélangeront les uns avec les autres.

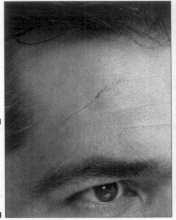

Figure 11.9 :
L'outil
Correcteur a
fait
disparaître la
cicatrice.

✔ **Source :** Si vous optez pour Motif, vous désactivez la fonction initiale du Correcteur. En effet, la source n'a plus aucune importance puisque l'outil appliquera le motif sélectionné dans la liste. Cette faculté peut s'avérer amusante, mais ce n'est pas l'objectif principal de l'outil Correcteur. Pour éliminer les imperfections, vous devez activer l'option Échantillon.

✔ **Aligné :** Activez cette option lorsque vous ne souhaitez pas que l'outil Correcteur se réfère systématiquement à la même source. En d'autres termes, le curseur source s'aligne sur la position du curseur de duplication. Cette option est bien plus utile à l'outil Tampon de duplication qu'à l'outil Correcteur.

✔ **Utiliser tous les calques :** Avec cette option, l'outil Correcteur utilise les pixels de tous les calques d'une image et pas uniquement ceux du calque actif.

Le Correcteur de ton direct

L'outil Correcteur est une amélioration réussie de l'outil Tampon de duplication, dans la mesure où il prend en considération la couleur et le contraste. Par ailleurs, nous pouvons dire que le Correcteur de ton direct est une tentative d'amélioration de l'outil Correcteur plus ou moins bien réussie. Quelle est la différence entre ces deux outils de correction ? Eh bien, le Correcteur de ton direct ne nécessite pas la définition d'une source de clonage en appuyant sur la touche Alt. Faites glisser l'outil sur une imperfection pour la faire disparaître.

Le Correcteur de ton direct ne croule pas sous les options. Bien sûr, vous pouvez définir sa taille, c'est-à-dire son épaisseur. Mais, il dispose d'une option singulière appelée Type. Elle offre le choix entre Similarité des couleurs et Nouvelle texture. L'option Similarité des couleurs permet au Correcteur de ton direct de choisir lui-même le point de source en dehors de la zone sélectionnée. En règle générale, c'est l'option que vous devez choisir. Toutefois, dans certaines circonstances, l'outil fait un peu n'importe quoi. Il pourra arriver que des yeux apparaissent sur le front d'une personne, ou d'autres bizarreries de ce genre. Avec l'option Nouvelle texture, le Correcteur de ton direct analyse la zone située autour du point où vous cliquez. Il résulte de cette analyse une texture très synthétique qui remplace les pixels de la zone à corriger.

Le rouge est mis... enlevons-le !

Les appareils photo grand public sont équipés d'une dispositif d'atténuation de l'effet "yeux rouges" : Pour rétracter les pupilles et réduire la réflexion de la lumière sur la rétine, le flash émet quelques éclairs préliminaires qui provoquent la rétraction des pupilles. Une faible zone de la rétine est alors illuminée, d'où l'atténuation de l'effet de yeux rouges (NdT : ou verts si vous photographiez votre chien ou votre chat).

Cette technique est intelligente, car les "yeux rouges" ne sont pas faciles à éliminer. Mais, encore aujourd'hui, sur certains appareils, ce défaut ne disparaît pas complètement. Elements apporte la solution avec l'outil Retouche des yeux rouges.

L'effet de yeux rouges est désormais automatiquement éliminé lors de l'importation des images dans Eléments, comme le montre la Figure 11.10. Décochez la case Correction automatique des yeux rouges, si vous désirez importer les photos telles qu'elles ont été prises.

Appuyez sur la touche Y pour activer l'outil Retouche des yeux rouges. Ensuite, zoomez sur une des pupilles rouges et cliquez dans la couleur. Répétez l'opération pour l'autre pupille. Vous pouvez également utiliser l'outil en traçant un rectangle de sélection autour d'une pupille affectée. Dans certains cas, cette technique est meilleure que l'autre. Quelle que soit la méthode utilisée, l'outil de retouche des yeux rouges s'avère extrêmement puissant et d'une grande simplicité.

Voici les contrôles disponibles dans la barre d'options de cet outil :

- ✔ **Pupille :** Dans les cas les plus difficiles, le rouge déborde bien au-delà de la pupille. Grâce à cette option, vous pouvez indiquer

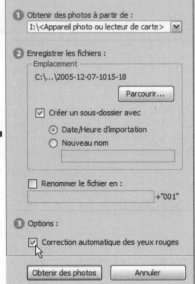

Figure 11.10 :
Par défaut,
Photoshop
Elements
tente de
supprimer
l'effet de
yeux rouges
lors de
l'importation
des images.

que la taille de la pupille est plus importante que celle qu'elle occupe sur l'œil. Mais attention, l'outil Retouche des yeux rouges ne peut pas connaître la couleur de l'iris, qui sera remplacée par la couleur de la pupille par défaut. Vous devrez certainement procéder à une retouche manuelle supplémentaire pour restituer à votre modèle le regard qui est le sien.

✔ **Obscurcissement :** Si vous estimez que le correcteur des yeux rouges risque de rendre les pupilles beaucoup trop noires, diminuez la valeur de ce paramètre. Par défaut, il est fixé à 50 %. Évidemment, si vous pensez que les pupilles risquent d'être trop claires, augmentez cette valeur.

L'outil Retouche des yeux rouges et la fonction de correction automatique des yeux rouges au téléchargement sont incontestablement utiles. Ces commandes portent bien leur nom car ils se limitent à la suppression du rouge. Autrement dit, Médor et Minou ne sont pas concernés par ces outils. De plus, comme nous l'avons précisé dans l'analyse des options, lorsque le rouge déborde sur l'iris, il est impossible de préserver sa couleur. Pour corriger ce type de problème, vous devrez recourir à la commande Remplacement de couleur décrite au Chapitre 13.

Chapitre 12
Quel outil suis-je ?

L a grande force de Photoshop Elements est de pouvoir peindre avec des couleurs spécifiques mais aussi avec celles de l'image. Avec les outils Doigt, Goutte d'eau, Netteté, Densité et Éponge, vous modifiez subtilement l'aspect des pixels en les déplaçant, les étalant, en augmentant leur contraste, ou encore en les éclaircissant ou en les assombrissant. Et, là où les outils Doigt et Netteté sont fastidieux à utiliser, les filtres d'atténuation et de renforcement se rendent fort utiles.

Retouche rapide des images

Photoshop Elements est doté de deux modes d'édition des images : Retouche rapide et Retouche standard. Nous évoquerons succincte-ment le premier, et un peu plus longuement le second.

Pour accéder directement au mode Retouche rapide, il suffit de cliquer sur l'option Retoucher rapidement les photos, dans l'écran de bienvenue du programme. En revanche, si vous êtes dans l'Organiseur ou dans le mode Retouche standard, cliquez sur le bouton Retouche rapide, dans la barre des raccourcis.

Comme le montre la Figure 12.1, le mode Retouche rapide remplace la Corbeille des palettes par une série de palettes fixes : Général, Éclairage, Couleur et Netteté. La barre d'outils elle-même se limite à quatre outils : Zoom, Main, Recadrage et Retouche des yeux rouges.

Vous ne pouvez pas travailler avec des calques. De ce fait, tout ou partie des commandes des menus Édition, Calque et Sélection ont leurs commandes en grisé, c'est-à-dire inutilisables.

Figure 12.1 : Le mode Retouche rapide permet de corriger facilement les images en quelques clics de souris.

Connaissant les limites de ce mode, voyons ce qu'il permet. L'intérêt principal de la Retouche rapide est la vaste zone d'affichage de l'image et une liste de commandes qui permettent de basculer d'un affichage à un autre pour mieux apprécier l'effet de vos corrections :

- **Après seulement :** Cette option d'affichage montre l'aspect qu'aura l'image après la retouche rapide.

- **Avant seulement :** Montre l'aspect de l'image avant la correction.

- **Avant et après (Portrait) :** Affiche deux versions juxtaposées de l'image. À gauche, l'image avant la retouche ; à droite, l'image après la retouche.

- **Avant et après (Paysage) :** Fonction identique à la précédente avec, cette fois, un affichage superposé des versions Avant et Après.

A droite de l'interface, se trouvent quatre palettes dont les réglages servent à corriger rapidement les images. Bien entendu, ces corrections ne sont pas aussi sophistiquées que celles du mode Retouche standard. La palette Général propose des fonctions que vous trouvez normalement dans les menus Image et Accentuation. La palette Éclairage contient des commandes d'amélioration des Niveaux et du Contraste des tons foncés, des tons clairs et des tons moyens, ainsi que la possibilité de demander au programme de définir automatiquement les réglages à appliquer, au travers des deux boutons Auto. La palette Couleur permet de jouer manuellement ou automatiquement (bouton Auto) sur la Saturation, la Teinte, la Température et le Ton, c'est-à-dire des améliorations que l'on trouve habituellement dans le menu Accentuation/Régler la couleur et, pour la température de couleur, dans le filtre Filtre photo (catégorie Réglages).

Approche des outils de retouche

Contrairement à des outils comme le Crayon et le Pinceau, les outils de retouche n'ont pas d'équivalent physique. Par exemple, il est difficile de prétendre que l'outil Doigt de Photoshop Elements équivaut à votre doigt que vous passez sur une photographie. Mis à part y faire de grosses traces, vous ne modifierez pas grand-chose (NdT : en revanche, sur de la peinture fraîche, l'effet digital – dans le seul et vrai sens du terme – est flagrant).

Si nous poussons la comparaison un peu plus loin, nous constatons que même avec les outils de peinture traditionnels de Photoshop Elements, nous n'obtenons pas la même chose que dans la réalité. Essayez de dissimuler cet éclat de peinture dans le salon avec une teinte identique. Si vous ne possédez pas le mélange de couleur d'origine, ce rose pâle ne sera pas le même que celui qui a été étalé la première fois sur vos murs. Et avez-vous pensé à vos tapis ? La moquette doit être protégée avant de repeindre les murs, le plafond, et je ne sais quoi encore.

Dans Photoshop Elements, tous ces travaux s'effectuent facilement et sans bavure. La boîte à outils de la Figure 12.2 contient tout le nécessaire au travail de retouche des images sans risquer l'accident irréparable :

 ✔ Utilisez l'outil Doigt pour étaler les couleurs. Les paramètres permettent de définir l'intensité et la portée de l'étalement. C'est un des outils de retouche que vous utiliserez le plus.

 ✔ Si les transitions entre divers éléments d'une image sont trop tranchées au point d'en déceler l'artificialité, utilisez l'outil

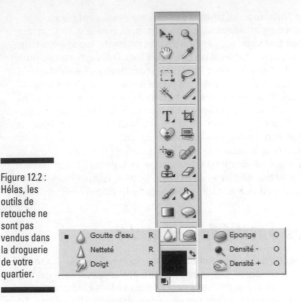

Goutte d'eau. Il atténue les contours des éléments en mélangeant leurs couleurs. Le léger effet de flou qu'il produit crée une unité dans les transitions.

✔ Pour redéfinir correctement des textures, utilisez l'outil Netteté. Bien des utilisateurs commencent par unifier les transitions avec l'outil Goutte d'eau et accentuent certains détails avec l'outil Netteté.

✔ Pour éclaircir une portion de l'image, appliquez-lui l'outil Densité. Il ressemble au cache rond en carton placé sur une fine tige que les photographes utilisent pour retenir la lumière, sous l'agrandisseur. L'autre outil permet d'assombrir l'image. Il a la forme d'une main qui ménage le passage pour la lumière, lorsque le photographe place ses mains sous l'agrandisseur pour délimiter une zone qui sera plus longuement exposée que les autres parties du négatif, et ainsi "faire venir" des détails.

✔ Si une zone de l'image est estompée redonnez-lui de la densité avec l'outil Densité +.

✔ Si les couleurs de l'image sont trop fades ou trop criardes, l'outil Éponge permet de les saturer ou de les désaturer.

Presque tous ces outils sont inspirés des techniques classiques du laboratoire photo. Nous y avons fait allusion pour les outils Densités + et Densité -, mais l'éponge, la goutte d'eau et les techniques de renforcement de la netteté sont aussi utilisées, quoique chimiquement au lieu de numériquement.

Étaler les imperfections jusqu'à disparition

L'outil Doigt pousse les couleurs d'une portion de l'image à une autre. En d'autres termes, vous étalez les couleurs dans la direction où vous faites glisser l'outil.

Le requin de la Figure 12.3 est un sujet idéal pour démontrer la puissance des outils de retouche de Photoshop Elements, et plus particulièrement de l'outil Doigt. La vie d'un requin n'est pas toujours facile et il en porte encore les stigmates sur son visage. Des cicatrices laissent penser qu'un passage chez le chirurgien esthétique s'impose. Pour cela, vous mettrez en œuvre l'outil Doigt afin de parvenir à un résultat splendide qui ravira votre sélacien client.

L'outil Doigt brouille efficacement les imperfections, les rendant indiscernables. Celles du requin ayant disparu, notre animal ressemble maintenant à une statuette en porcelaine.

Tout étaler

Sur la Figure 12.3, vous remarquerez que l'outil Doigt enlève toutes les traces, y compris le grain de la photographie. La retouche ne donne pas un résultat très naturel. On sent bien que ce requin n'est plus véritablement un requin photographié au fond des océans. L'outil Doigt est efficace lorsqu'il est utilisé localement et avec des réglages plus subtils.

Retoucher avec l'outil Doigt demande... du doigté ! Si vous y allez un peu fort, vous obtenez plus un effet de peinture à l'huile qu'une retouche digne de ce nom.

Les contrôles de l'outil Doigt

La barre d'options de l'outil Doigt permet de régler ses effets (voir la Figure 12.4) :

✔ Pour un étalement rectiligne, maintenez la touche Maj enfoncée. Cet étalement peut être vertical ou horizontal.

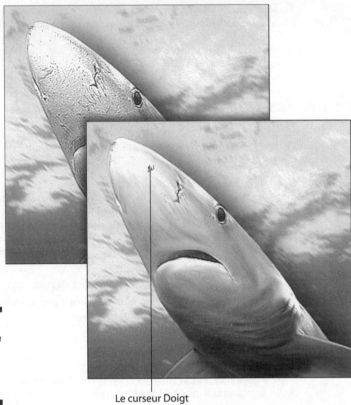

Figure 12.3 :
Une chirurgie
esthétique
simple,
efficace et
pas chère.

Le curseur Doigt

Figure 12.4 :
Les options
de l'outil
Doigt.

> ✔ Pour augmenter ou réduire la taille de la forme de l'outil Doigt, choisissez-en une autre dans le menu local Forme de la barre d'options. N'oubliez pas que vous pouvez changer, de cette manière, la taille de tous les outils de retouche. Pour en savoir

davantage sur la modification des formes d'un outil, reportez-vous au Chapitre 15.

- La barre d'options contient plusieurs paramètres d'étalement. Par exemple, l'intensité est réglable afin d'obtenir une correction plus ou moins prononcée.

- N'oubliez pas que vous pouvez changer la taille de la forme à l'aide du clavier, en appuyant sur * (astérique) pour augmenter la taille, et Maj+* pour la diminuer. Pour modifier l'intensité, tapez directement une valeur à l'aide du pavé numérique. Appuyez sur 5 pour 50 %, 7 pour 70 %, et ainsi de suite. Pour les unités, appuyez rapidement sur les deux chiffres. Ainsi, pour une Intensité de 85 %, appuyez dans la foulée sur 8 et 5.

- La liste Mode de la barre d'options propose notamment les modes de fusion Obscurcir et Éclaircir. Ils permettent de n'étaler que les couleurs plus claires ou plus foncées par rapport aux couleurs originales de l'image. Les autres modes de cet outil sont Teinte, Saturation, Couleur et Luminosité.

- Cochez la case Peinture au doigt pour étaler la couleur de premier plan. Elements applique de la peinture et l'étale dans le sens que vous imprimez à l'outil. C'est un moyen très réaliste de peindre sur des photographies.

- Choisissez l'option Utiliser tous les calques pour étaler les couleurs de tous les calques d'une image.

- Bien que l'outil Doigt soit plaisant, vous disposez de meilleures possibilités. Si vous voulez repousser des pixels pour créer des déformations dans l'image, le filtre Fluidité fait le même travail que l'outil Doigt mais de façon beaucoup plus marquée. On y retrouve la plupart des possibilités de l'outil Doigt, ainsi que d'autres fonctions de déformation. Le filtre Fluidité est décrit au Chapitre 14. Si vous désirez réparer l'image, la débarrasser de ses imperfections, les outils Tampon de duplication et Correcteur donneront sans doute de meilleurs résultats. Ils sont décrits au Chapitre 11.

Les outils Densité

Pour comprendre le fonctionnement des outils Densité, il faut avoir mis les pieds dans un laboratoire photo. Le négatif placé dans le passe-vue de l'agrandisseur est projeté sur le papier. Un photographe expérimenté évalue immédiatement la densité des gris dans les différentes parties de l'image : là où le négatif est clair, beaucoup de lumière passera, au risque de surexposer le papier. A cet endroit, l'image sera quasiment noire. En revanche, si le négatif est très dense, voire presque opaque, il faudra prolonger le temps d'exposition afin que les détails puissent impressionner le papier.

Dans le premier cas (négatif clair), le photographe "retient la lumière" avec un petit cache en carton qu'il interpose entre l'objectif de l'agrandisseur et le papier, et qu'il agite légèrement pour que le bord ne se remarque pas au développement. Dans Photoshop et dans Photoshop Elements, l'outil Densité - simule ce cache.

En revanche, s'il faut prolonger l'exposition dans une partie de l'image, le photographe masque la lumière provenant de l'agrandisseur, ne laissant passer entre ses mains qu'une tache de lumière qui exposera le papier pendant un temps beaucoup plus long. En procédant ainsi, il "fait venir" l'image. Pour que les contours de la tache ne soient pas trop apparents, il bouge légèrement ses mains. Dans Photoshop et dans Photoshop Elements, c'est l'outil Densité + qui simule les mains laissant passer la lumière.

De ce fait :

- L'outil Densité - éclaircit l'image là où il est appliqué.

- L'outil Densité + assombrit l'image là où il est appliqué.

En général, vous paramétrez l'outil Densité comme n'importe quel autre outil de retouche et de peinture. La barre d'options contient quelques réglages supplémentaires :

- Le curseur Exposition est fixé par défaut à 50 %. C'est l'intensité – la puissance de la lampe de l'agrandisseur, en quelque sorte – avec laquelle une zone sera éclaircie ou assombrie. Comme toujours, plus la valeur est faible, plus l'effet de l'outil est faible ; et plus la valeur est élevée, plus il est prononcé.

- La liste Gamme contient trois options : Tons foncés, Tons moyens et Tons clairs. Le paramètre par défaut est Tons moyens. Il se contente d'éclaircir ou d'assombrir les tonalités moyennes d'une image, laissant intactes les teintes les plus claires et les plus foncées. La Figure 12.5 montre le résultat obtenu avec l'outil Densité - sur le requin, avec le réglage par défaut.

- La gamme Tons foncés n'altère que les couleurs les plus sombres de l'image, alors que Tons clairs n'altère que les plus claires. Sur la Figure 12.6, nous avons passé l'outil Densité - sur le requin en choisissant la gamme Tons foncés. Le requin a une

Figure 12.5 :
Le requin est
plus clair,
sans pour
autant
éliminer le
contraste.

Figure 12.6 :
Les zones les
plus sombres
du requin ont
été
exagérément
éclaircies.

allure de ver luisant (à vrai dire, les outils Densité doivent être
utilisés avec beaucoup de délicatesse et l'effet ne doit jamais
être discernable). L'image est uniformément plus claire.

✔ Pour assombrir une image un peu surexposée, choisissez l'outil Densité + et fixez le mode sur Tons clairs.

Jouer avec la couleur

L'outil Éponge est destiné aux images en couleurs. Inutile de l'essayer sur une image en niveaux de gris ou, si vous préférez, en noir et blanc. Sur ce type d'image, l'outil Éponge se contente d'éclaircir ou d'assombrir les pixels comme le font les outils Densité.

Voici comment utiliser l'outil Éponge :

1. **Activez l'outil Éponge.**

   Appuyez sur la touche O. (NdT : cela n'a aucun rapport avec la première lettre du mot Éponge en anglais (*Sponge*), mais que voulez-vous, comme le "S" était déjà pris par les outils Tampon, le "P" par l'outil redressement, il ne restait plus que le "O". Pour une fois, les utilisateurs anglophones et francophones sont logés à la même enseigne). Une fois l'outil activé, sa barre d'options apparaît.

2. **Sélectionnez le Mode de fusion dans la liste adéquate.**

   Choisissez Saturer pour intensifier les couleurs ou Désaturer pour les délaver.

3. **Appuyez sur n'importe quelle touche du pavé numérique pour modifier la valeur Flux.**

   Vous pouvez également faire glisser le curseur de la barre d'options pour définir un pourcentage plus précis.

4. **Passez l'outil dans l'image en couleurs.**

   Observez comment les couleurs changent.

Adoucir les transitions

Même si l'outil Doigt est idéal pour corriger les défauts d'une image, il ne saurait suffire. Par exemple, une transition peut être nette entre deux couleurs. Par exemple, une des dents du requin se démarquera trop ou encore, vous désirez adoucir le bord d'une nageoire. Le problème avec l'outil Doigt est que vous n'obtiendrez jamais une transition invisible, même en déployant d'énormes efforts.

Il suffit alors d'utiliser l'outil Goutte d'eau sur un contour trop net pour en obtenir une superbe atténuation.

Voici d'autres éléments concernant les outils de netteté :

- ✔ Étalez légèrement les couleurs avec l'outil Doigt.

- ✔ Atténuez la transition entre les couleurs avec l'outil Goutte d'eau.

Voici quelques petites précisions sur l'utilisation de ces outils :

- ✔ Contrairement à l'outil Goutte d'eau, l'outil Netteté recrée la transition tranchée.

- ✔ L'outil Netteté produit un pseudo effet de grain sur une image. À utiliser avec parcimonie.

- ✔ L'effet des outils Doigt et Netteté est réglable en agissant sur le paramètre Intensité de la barre d'options. Il est recommandé de ne pas dépasser 60 % avec l'outil Goutte d'eau et 30 % avec l'outil Netteté.

- ✔ Ces outils disposent des mêmes modes de fusion que ceux de l'outil Doigt. Les plus importants sont Obscurcir, Éclaircir et Couleur. Ils peuvent atténuer les effets de l'outil Netteté pour le rendre plus utilisable. Pour en savoir plus sur les modes de fusion, reportez-vous au Chapitre 14.

Accentuer les petits détails

Peu importe qu'une image soit parfaite avant sa numérisation. Elle ne ressemblera pas à l'original une fois que vous l'aurez affichée à l'écran. Pour obtenir une restitution fidèle, il faudrait posséder un équipement autrement plus sophistiqué et onéreux qu'un scanner vendu quelques dizaines d'euros. L'image représentée sur la Figure 12.7 présente un problème fréquent dans le domaine de la retouche d'images.

La solution à ce genre de problème réside dans les filtres de la catégorie Renforcement. Nous allons voir comment ils fonctionnent pour mieux les appliquer.

Netteté immédiate

Les trois premiers filtres de renforcement que nous abordons sont Contours plus nets, Encore plus net et Plus net. Il s'agit de filtres qui

Figure 12.7 :
Une photo
ancienne
trop floue à
notre goût.

appliquent une valeur de netteté par défaut. Aucune option n'est
proposée.

Ces filtres sont faciles à mettre en œuvre, mais ne sont pas d'une
grande subtilité. C'est le "tout ou rien", mais jamais le "c'est exactement ce que je veux". Comme le montre l'application de ces trois
filtres sur la Figure 12.8, l'image est plus nette mais le résultat n'est pas
très satisfaisant.

Sur cette Figure 12.8, vous voyez l'image d'origine, puis le filtre
appliqué une fois, et enfin le même filtre appliqué une seconde fois.
Voici leurs effets :

- ✔ Plus net (première colonne) augmente légèrement la netteté de
  l'image. Ce filtre est parfait pour une photo nette qui a besoin de
  détails un peu plus soutenus. Dans la plupart des cas, vous ne
  l'utiliserez jamais.

- ✔ Le filtre Encore plus net (deuxième colonne) augmente la netteté
  de manière plus radicale. Malheureusement, c'est un peu le filtre
  du tout ou rien. Regardez l'image centrale de la Figure 12.8. Elle
  n'est pas assez nette. En revanche, celle qui se trouve juste en
  dessous est beaucoup trop détaillée, provoquant des effets
  totalement artificiels.

- ✔ Le filtre Contours plus nets (troisième colonne) n'est guère utile.
  Il se contente d'augmenter la netteté des contours en éludant les

Figure 12.8 : Appliqués sans options, les filtres de la catégorie Renforcement ne donnent jamais de très bons résultats.

zones neutres. Sur la Figure 12.8, le filtre renforce le visage de l'homme mais ignore totalement sa veste. Il y a un fort décalage entre les contours et l'image elle-même.

Comme vous pouvez l'imaginer, nous ne recommandons pas ces filtres. Nous leur préférons le filtre Accentuation qui fait l'objet de notre prochaine étude.

Chapitre 13

La correction des couleurs

*V*oici un scénario assez classique : vous donnez vos photographies à développer et, en les récupérant, l'une d'elles vous saute aux yeux. La couleur est superbe, la composition fantastique, tout le monde sourit ; vous la considérez comme l'une des plus réussies. Elle n'est certes pas parfaite à 100 %, mais vous savez qu'il est possible d'éliminer les petits défauts avec Photoshop Elements.

Vous numérisez votre tirage, vous l'ouvrez dans Elements et là, horreur : l'image est sombre, fade et sans attrait. La photo est bien plus belle sur papier qu'elle ne l'est sur l'écran de votre ordinateur.

Dans un monde parfait (NdT : après les toilettes à gauche), ce genre de désagrément n'existe pas. Mais la numérisation est imparfaite par nature. Il n'y a pas de miracle à attendre d'un appareil que vous avez acheté quelques dizaines d'euros dans une grande surface. Ne vous inquiétez cependant pas ! Les premières numérisations sont toujours décevantes jusqu'à ce que l'on sache comment y remédier dans Elements.

Pour ce faire, vous recourrez à deux commandes fondamentales de Photoshop Elements : Niveaux et Variantes de couleurs. Inutile de retoucher au pinceau, sélectionner ou ajouter des couleurs à l'image. Les vôtres existent, il n'y a aucune raison de les ignorer. Il suffit de les raviver.

Elements dispose de plusieurs commandes de correction des couleurs, mais quelques-unes suffiront à votre bonheur. Dans ce chapitre, vous accomplirez des miracles. Vous apprendrez à utiliser des calques de réglage qui permettent de corriger vos couleurs sur un calque indépendant, pour plus de sûreté et de flexibilité.

Corriger rapidement la couleur

Photoshop Elements dispose de diverses commandes de correction rapide des couleurs conçues pour améliorer facilement une image. Elles se trouvent dans le menu Accentuation et sont également disponibles dans le mode Retouche rapide étudié au Chapitre 12. Ces commandes "instantanées" de correction des couleurs méritent votre attention ; elles font parfois du bon travail et, si elles n'apportent rien ou pire, dégradent l'image, il est facile de les annuler.

Niveaux automatiques

La commande Niveaux automatiques permet une première correction de la colorimétrie de l'image en exécutant un travail sommaire sur le spectre. Choisissez Accentuation/Niveaux automatiques ou appuyez sur Ctrl+Maj+L pour corriger automatiquement les contrastes d'une image. Cette commande est également disponible en mode Retouche rapide. Par exemple, la photographie de la Figure 13.1, est manifestement insuffisamment contrastée. Les blancs ne sont pas blancs et les noirs pas noirs ; toute l'image est plongée dans la grisaille. Si la photo était en couleurs, vous constateriez que les couleurs les plus claires manquent de luminosité. Avec la commande Niveaux automatiques, Elements rétablit les teintes claires et les teintes foncées, tout en équilibrant les couleurs moyennes. La Figure 13.2 montre le résultat.

Malheureusement, la commande Niveaux automatiques ne résout pas tous les problèmes. Sur la Figure 13.2, les noirs et les blancs sont encore trop marqués et les gris trop proches du noir (comme le montre le nuancier collé au milieu de cette photo). L'inconvénient de Niveaux automatiques est qu'il produit une dominante de couleur. Cette commande exécute son travail sur chaque couche chromatique, déséquilibrant la balance générale des couleurs de l'image. Résultat :

Figure 13.1 :
Quelle triste
photogra-
phie.

Figure 13.2 :
Celle-ci est
plus
vigoureuse.

une teinte l'emporte sur les autres, d'où la *dominante de couleur*. Bien
que la commande Niveaux permette de corriger chaque couche
séparément, elle agit sur la globalité de l'image. Nous examinerons
cette commande un peu plus loin dans ce chapitre, à la section
"Travailler le contraste".

Autres améliorations d'image

Le menu Accentuation comporte quelques autres commandes de correction des couleurs "rapides et faciles", ainsi que certaines qui flirtent avec l'appellation "lentes et difficiles". Nous étudierons Niveaux et Variantes de couleurs en détail plus loin ce chapitre ; pour l'instant, nous nous consacrerons aux autres.

Retouche optimisée automatique

Cette nouvelle commande de Photoshop Elements 4.0, exécutable via Alt+Ctrl+M, améliore les couleurs, renforce les tons foncés et les détails, en un clic de souris. Comme toute commande de ce type, tantôt elle fonctionne bien, et tantôt mal. Pour améliorer ses performances, exécutez Régler la retouche optimisée. Modifiez la valeur du Facteur de correction. Elle est de 0 par défaut et peut atteindre 200 %.

Une véritable correction ne peut s'obtenir qu'avec les commandes Niveaux et Variantes de couleurs, étudiées un peu plus loin dans ce chapitre.

Contraste automatique

Évitez l'emploi de Contraste automatique (Accentuation/Contraste automatique). Pour corriger le contraste d'une image, tenez-vous-en à la commande Niveaux automatiques ou mieux encore, Niveaux, qui octroie de vraies possibilités de contrôle.

Correction colorimétrique automatique

Cette commande prend en considération les tons moyens de l'image pendant la correction. Dans bien des cas, Correction colorimétrique automatique donne des résultats plus satisfaisants que toute autre commande à un seul clic. Elle mérite de ce fait que nous lui accordions un petit instant ; si le résultat ne vous satisfait pas, annulez, puis essayez Niveaux et Variantes de couleurs.

Tons foncés/Tons clairs

Vous accédez à cette commande via Accentuation/Régler l'éclairage. Elle permet de compenser les nombreux problèmes d'éclairage rencontrés par les photographes, le plus ardu étant le contre-jour indésirable. Le curseur Éclaircir les tons foncés fait ressurgir les détails dans les ombres. Le curseur Obscurcir les tons clairs permet d'atténuer la luminosité des hautes lumières. Lorsque vous obscurcissez les tons clairs et éclaircissez les tons foncés, vous renforcez globalement les tons moyens de l'image. Le curseur Contraste des tons moyens peut augmenter légèrement le contraste.

Luminosité/Contraste

La commande Luminosité/Contraste s'exécute via Accentuation/ Réglage de l'éclairage. À notre sens, elle n'a aucune raison d'être. Si vous ne l'avez jamais utilisée, ne commencez pas aujourd'hui. La commande Niveaux est bien plus précise pour améliorer la luminosité et le contraste d'une image.

Corrections de la dominante de couleur

Elements dispose d'une commande faite pour enlever la couleur dominante. Il suffit de choisir Accentuation/Régler la couleur/Corrections de la dominante couleur. Dans la boîte de dialogue qui apparaît, utilisez la pipette pour cliquer sur une zone qui devrait être blanche ou grise ou noire (bien qu'une dominante soit généralement peu discernable sur un noir pur). La commande Corrections de la dominante couleur détermine l'excès de couleur à cet emplacement, et applique à toute l'image la correction chromatique qui rétablit les couleurs naturelles.

Correction des tons chairs

Les tons chairs sont parmi les plus difficiles à reproduire. Examinez vos photos de vacances et vous constaterez que sur un grand nombre d'entre elles, la peau est trop rouge – un coup de soleil n'en est pas forcément la cause – le bronzage indiscernable ou pire, parcheminé par un rendu inapproprié des couleurs. Même pour un top-model, le photographe doit travailler l'éclairage pour que la peau soit correctement rendue.

Désormais, il est très facile de régler les tons chairs à vue, à l'aide de quelques glissières. Après avoir ouvert la photo, choisissez Accentuation/Régler la couleur/Coloration de la peau. Photoshop affiche la boîte de dialogue de la Figure 13.3.

Il suffit ensuite de cliquer sur la peau avec la pipette, qui est automatiquement activée. Veillez à ce que la case Aperçu soit cochée afin d'observer l'effet des réglages sur le personnage puis cliquez sur la peau. Les trois glissières suivantes sont alors accessibles :

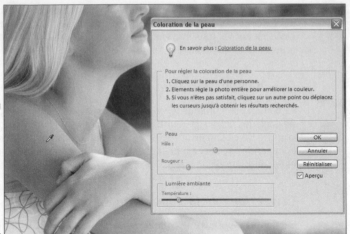

Figure 13.3 :
Si cet
ouvrage était
en couleur,
vous seriez
séduit, oui
séduit par le
bronzage de
ce modèle.

✔ **Hâle :** Augmente ou diminue la quantité de marron. L'effet est relativement modéré et ne remplace pas des séances d'UV dans un solarium. Le hâle est seulement pour donner un peu de consistance à une peau trop blanche.

✔ **Rougeur :** Augmente ou diminue la composante rouge d'un ton chair. Là encore, l'effet est très subtil et ne vise pas à masquer un coup de soleil.

✔ **Température :** Cette commande est la plus intéressante car elle modifie la température de couleur de la lumière qui éclaire le sujet. Sans entrer dans les détails – les photographes avertis comprendront vite l'intérêt de cette fonction – c'est comme si vous aviez placé un éclairage d'appoint équipé d'un filtre de correction à proximité du sujet. Mieux qu'un véritable éclairage, qui décalerait la température de couleur du sujet et de ses vêtements, celui-ci n'agit que sur la peau. Déplacez le curseur vers la droite pour donner une teinte bien chaude à la peau.

Les réglages sont facultatifs car Elements applique une correction dès le premier clic. Ils sont cependant plus que recommandés pour donner à la peau l'aspect que vous désirez. Si l'effet ne vous convient pas, cliquez sur le bouton Réinitialiser puis recommencez. Autrement, cliquez sur OK pour valider la correction de couleur.

Teinte/Saturation

Cette commande (Accentuation/Régler la couleur/Teinte/Saturation) modifie efficacement la couleur et l'intensité de la couleur. Le curseur Teinte parcourt le spectre chromatique (NdT : dans le Sélecteur de couleurs de Photoshop Elements, le spectre est présenté sur un ruban rectiligne. En réalité, ce ruban fait le tour d'un cercle, ce qui explique pourquoi le paramètre Teinte est exprimé sur 360 degrés). Des ajustements minimes sont susceptibles de corriger une dominante de couleur. Gardez un œil sur les barres colorées en bas de la boîte de dialogue ; la barre supérieure représente les couleurs de l'image ; la barre inférieure représente le décalage de teinte. Par exemple, faites glisser le curseur jusqu'à ce que le jaune dans la barre inférieure soit au-dessous du rouge dans la barre supérieure : vous constaterez que les objets rouges de votre image ont pris une couleur jaune. Le curseur Saturation augmente ou diminue l'intensité de couleurs, et le curseur Luminosité change la luminosité d'ensemble. Lorsqu'elle est cochée, la case Redéfinir donne à l'image une tonalité globale utile pour produire des virages, en sépia par exemple.

L'une des fonctions les plus utiles de Teinte/Saturation est de désaturer uniquement certaines couleurs ; par exemple, les photos prises avec certains appareils photo numériques tendent à présenter des rouges sursaturés. C'est là que le menu Modifier, en haut de la boîte de dialogue, entre en jeu. Si vous choisissez Rouges dans le menu Modifier, les changements effectués avec les commandes de Teinte/Saturation n'affectent que les pixels rouges de l'image.

Vous pouvez également régler l'intervalle des couleurs à modifier à l'aide des pipettes et des contrôles de gamme, visibles sur la Figure 13.4. Un clic avec la pipette de gauche dans l'image isole une couleur ; un clic avec la pipette du milieu ajoute une couleur à la gamme ; un clic avec la pipette de droite supprime cette couleur de l'intervalle. Au fur et à mesure de vos opérations, vous verrez les contrôles de gamme et de tolérance (entre les deux barres chromatiques) se déplacer. Vous pouvez aussi les faire glisser pour modifier l'intervalle des couleurs affectées. La zone entre les deux contrôles d'intervalle représente la gamme de couleur que vous isolez. Les zones de part et d'autre de cette gamme, et délimitées par ailleurs par les curseurs triangulaires, représentent la "tolérance", indiquant à quelle distance de l'intervalle des couleurs isolées les changements doivent être appliqués.

Si la lecture de ce paragraphe vous laisse perplexe, sachez que vous n'aurez probablement jamais à employer ces contrôles ; si vous avez besoin d'isoler une gamme de couleurs, un des six choix du menu Modifier devrait suffire.

Contrôle de la gamme

Pipettes

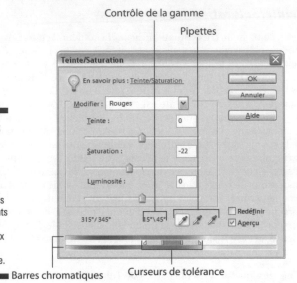

Figure 13.4 :
La commande Teinte/ Saturation permet d'opérer des changements globaux ou sélectifs aux couleurs d'une image.

Barres chromatiques   Curseurs de tolérance

Bien que l'outil Teinte/Saturation soit puissant et utile, il est préférable de ne jamais l'utiliser. Il est en effet disponible par ailleurs sous la forme d'un calque de réglage. Pour les détails sur les calques de réglage, voyez la section "Utiliser les calques de réglage", plus loin dans ce chapitre.

Supprimer la couleur

Cette commande (Accentuation/Régler la couleur/Supprimer la couleur) sert à supprimer la couleur d'un calque ou d'une zone sélectionnée afin d'obtenir des niveaux de gris, autrement dit, la convertir en noir et blanc. Pour ce qui est de convertir l'intégralité d'une image en niveaux de gris, reportez-vous au Chapitre 5.

Remplacer des couleurs

Jusqu'à présent, nous n'avons envisagé que la correction chromatique destinée à améliorer une image. Par ailleurs, la commande Remplacement de couleur aborde la correction des couleurs sous un autre angle : isoler une couleur d'une image pour la remplacer par une autre. C'est de ce fait une proche cousine de Teinte/Saturation.

La commande Remplacement de couleur

Pour utiliser cette commande, choisissez Accentuation/Régler la couleur/Remplacement de couleur. Vous accédez à la boîte de dialogue représentée sur la Figure 13.5. Elle est divisée en deux parties : Sélection et Transformation.

Figure 13.5 :
La commande Remplacement de couleur isole une zone de couleur dans une image.

Voici comment utiliser la commande Remplacement de couleur :

1. **Appliquez Remplacement de couleur à une image ou à une sélection.**

   S'il y a, dans votre image, des zones de couleur semblables à celle que vous désirez remplacer, il est plus judicieux de sélectionner la zone concernée. Pour en savoir plus sur les sélections, consultez le Chapitre 9.

2. **Cliquez sur le bouton d'option Image.**

   L'image ou la partie sélectionnée apparaît dans l'aperçu.

3. **Avec la pipette, cliquez dans la zone cible soit sur l'aperçu, soit sur l'image.**

4. **Activez Sélection.**

Le résultat de la sélection apparaît dans l'aperçu. Les zones noires ne sont pas sélectionnées tandis que les zones blanches le sont. Tout ce qui apparaît en gris est partiellement sélectionné.

5. **Ajustez la sélection avec Pipette + (Ajouter), Pipette - (Retirer) et le curseur Tolérance.**

Les Pipettes + et - parlent d'elles-mêmes. Le curseur Tolérance permet d'étendre ou de réduire la sélection. Plus la valeur de tolérance est élevée, plus le nombre de couleurs remplacées est important. Moins cette valeur est élevée, moins vous sélectionnez de couleurs à remplacer.

Vous pouvez également cliquer sur le nuancier Couleur pour définir la teinte sélectionnée dans le Sélecteur de couleurs.

6. **Dès que la sélection vous satisfait, modifiez la couleur avec les curseurs de la zone Remplacement.**

Vous pouvez ajuster la Teinte, la Saturation et la Luminosité. Le carré Résultat affiche la couleur de remplacement.

7. **Si vous êtes satisfait, cliquez sur OK.**

La couleur des zones sélectionnées a été remplacée par la nouvelle couleur.

La commande Remplacement de couleur est une technique de sélection très sophistiquée dont les résultats égalent ou surpassent ceux de n'importe quel outil de sélection standard. Cette commande est très polyvalente. Comme nous l'avons mentionné au Chapitre 11, c'est une alternative à l'utilisation de l'outil Retouche des yeux rouges. Il suffit de sélectionner la pupille du sujet et d'appliquer Remplacer la couleur en agissant uniquement sur la Saturation et la Luminosité.

L'outil Remplacement de couleur

L'outil Remplacement de couleur (NdT : un sous-outil de Pinceau, dans la boîte à outils) prélève une teinte de référence qui est remplacée dans toutes les zones de l'image par la couleur de premier plan. Si vous l'utilisez pour supprimer les yeux rouges, définissez une couleur de premier plan noire, puis cliquez dans la pupille rouge. Voici les paramètres de sa barre d'options :

✔ **Forme :** Ce menu local permet de définir le diamètre et la dureté de l'outil parmi d'autres options. Ces deux paramètres sont traités en détail au Chapitre 15.

✔ **Mode :** Cette liste contient des modes de fusion qui déterminent la manière dont les pixels peints vont se mélanger aux pixels de l'image. Le mode par défaut, Couleur, est un excellent choix.

✔ **Échantillonnage :** Cette option permet à Photoshop Elements de connaître la couleur à remplacer. Continu autorise le remplacement ininterrompu de la couleur. Une fois, dans la liste des options, modifie uniquement la couleur sur laquelle vous avez cliqué, tandis que Nuancier "fond" remplace la couleur d'arrière-plan désignée. Généralement, les meilleurs résultats sont obtenus avec l'option Une fois.

✔ **Limites :** Supposons que vous ayez choisi le mode Couleur et l'echantillonnage Une fois. Vous cliquez au centre d'un bel œil rouge. Que se passe-t-il si, sans relâcher le bouton de la souris, vous dépassez les limites de cette imperfection à corriger ? Avec l'option Contiguës, l'autre œil rouge ne sera pas corrigé, car il n'est pas adjacent au premier. En revanche, si vous choisissez l'option Discontiguës, l'autre œil sera rectifié.

✔ **Tolérance :** Ce curseur détermine le seuil de remplacement de la couleur. Ainsi, toutes les teintes qui s'y situent seront remplacées. Plus la valeur est faible, plus la valeur des couleurs remplacées devra être proche de la couleur de référence. Plus la valeur de tolérance est élevée, plus la plage de couleur remplacée est importante.

✔ **Lissé :** Cette option adoucit les contours. Activez-la systématiquement.

Comme avec l'outil Retouche des yeux rouges, les performances de l'outil Remplacement de couleur varient d'une image à l'autre. Appliquez-le dans les zones difficiles voire impossibles à corriger avec la commande Remplacement de couleur.

Utiliser les calques de réglage

Les calques de réglage sont semblables aux calques décrits au Chapitre 10, sauf que leur objectif est d'appliquer des commandes de correction de la couleur, et de permettre ultérieurement de modifier leurs paramètres (rappelons que quand une commande a été appliquée directement à un calque, il est impossible de la modifier ultérieurement). Par défaut, un calque de réglage applique la correction de couleur choisie à tous les calques situés dessous. Cependant, vous pouvez toujours désactiver la visibilité d'un calque de réglage ou tout simplement le supprimer, ce qui restaure l'image à son état initial. Les calques de réglage sont dits *non destructifs*, ce qui signifie qu'ils ne changent pas définitivement les pixels de l'image originale ; ils "flottent" au-dessus des pixels sur lesquels ils agissent.

Il est dommage qu'Elements ne mette à disposition, dans les calques de réglage, que deux commandes vraiment utiles : Niveaux et Teinte/Saturation. Les autres choix sont Luminosité/Contraste (bof) et quelques commandes également disponibles dans le sous-menu Filtre/Réglages, certes pratiques lorsqu'elles sont nécessaires, mais qui le sont en fait rarement.

Les calques de réglage partagent leur espace avec les calques de remplissage. Ces derniers servent à ajouter un calque contenant une couleur unie, un dégradé ou un motif. Les calques de remplissage n'ont rien à voir avec la correction de la couleur, mais il est utile de connaître leur usage.

Utilisation des calques de réglage et de remplissage

Les calques de réglage et de remplissage offrent plusieurs avantages sur les calques ordinaires (Figure 13.6) :

- ✔ Les calques de réglage affectent tous les calques situés en dessous. Si vous n'utilisez pas un calque de réglage, la correction des couleurs n'affecte que le calque actif.

- ✔ Vous pouvez créer plusieurs calques de réglage. Il est donc possible qu'un calque de réglage affecte une partie de l'image et un autre, le reste ; créez pour cela deux calques de réglage dont les paramètres de correction sont totalement différents.

- ✔ Comme la correction de la couleur s'effectue sur son propre calque, vous pouvez expérimenter librement les réglages sans nuire à l'image d'origine. Si la correction ne vous satisfait pas, il suffit alors de modifier le calque de réglage, voire le supprimer, pour retrouver l'image d'origine intacte. Vous pouvez également modifier ou supprimer les calques de remplissage.

- ✔ Les calques de réglage et de remplissage peuvent être mélangés avec d'autres calques grâce aux modes de fusion et d'opacité de la palette des calques (Vous en saurez davantage sur les modes de fusion au Chapitre 14). Ces fonctions procurent un meilleur contrôle sur l'aspect de l'image.

Nouveau calque de réglage ou de remplissage

Calque de remplissage

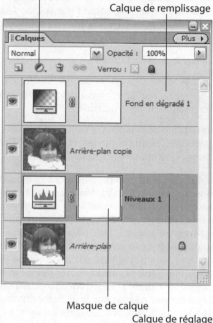

Figure 13.6 :
La palette
des calques
avec des
calques de
réglage et de
remplissage.

Masque de calque

Calque de réglage

Voici comment créer un calque de réglage :

1. **Dans la palette des calques, cliquez sur le calque dont vous désirez corriger la couleur.**

   Quand vous créez un calque de réglage, Elements le place directement au-dessus du calque actif. Ses réglages affectent tous les calques d'en dessous, sauf si vous avez choisi le paramètre Associer au calque précédent, comme cela est décrit à l'Étape 2.

   Si vous sélectionnez une partie de l'image avant de créer un calque de réglage, la correction de la couleur n'affecte que la zone sélectionnée sur tous les calques sous le calque de réglage.

2. **Choisissez Calque/Nouveau calque de réglage et sélectionnez ensuite le type de réglage à appliquer aux calques de l'image.**

   Dans notre exemple, choisissez Niveaux. La boîte de dialogue Nouveau claque apparaît. Vous pouvez donner un nom au calque. Pour le moment, ne vous préoccupez pas des paramètres Mode et Opacité. Vous pourrez les modifier ultérieurement dans la palette Calques. Ne cochez pas la case Associer au calque précédent. Nous verrons, plus tard, la raison d'être de cette option.

3. **Appuyez sur la touche Entrée.**

Elements ajoute le calque de réglage à la palette des calques et affiche la boîte de dialogue Niveaux dont nous expliquons le fonctionnement dans la prochaine section.

La création d'un calque de remplissage est tout aussi facile. Choisissez simplement Calque/Nouveau calque de remplissage. Dans le sous-menu, sélectionnez Couleur unie, Dégradé ou Motif.

La manière la plus simple de peindre sur un calque de masque consiste à maintenir les touches Alt+Maj enfoncées et à cliquer sur la vignette du masque du calque. Si vous avez déjà utilisé la Forme de sélection en mode Masque, cela devrait vous être maintenant très familier. Quand vous peignez sur l'image, vous appliquez dessus un film de protection translucide rouge. Tout ce qui est recouvert par le film de protection ne sera pas affecté par le calque de réglage. Vous pouvez également maintenir la touche Alt enfoncée et cliquer sur la vignette du masque de calque pour ne voir que le masque. Maintenez la touche Maj enfoncée et cliquez sur la vignette du masque de calque afin de désactiver temporairement l'effet du masque. Répétez ces actions pour utiliser de nouveau le masque de calque.

N'oubliez pas qu'un calque de réglage ou de remplissage fonctionne comme n'importe quel autre calque. Vous pouvez varier les effets, donc les réglages, en ajustant l'opacité et en sélectionnant un mode de fusion ; le calque peut être remonté ou descendu dans la pile des calques, dans la palette ; vous pouvez fusionner un calque avec celui d'en dessous pour appliquer définitivement la correction de couleur ou le remplissage à l'image. En revanche, vous ne pouvez pas fusionner un calque de réglage ou de remplissage avec un autre calque de ce type.

Pour modifier le réglage ou la couleur d'un calque, double-cliquez sur son icône dans la palette des calques, ou choisissez Calque/Options de contenu de calque. Elements affiche la boîte de dialogue correspondant aux réglages de correction de couleur ou au type de remplissage. Procédez à vos modifications en agissant sur les options de ces boîtes de dialogue. Pour supprimer un calque de réglage ou de remplissage, faites glisser son icône jusqu'à celle de la poubelle de la palette des calques. Une autre méthode consiste à sélectionner le calque, puis à cliquer sur l'icône de la poubelle.

Pour modifier le type de réglage ou de remplissage d'un calque, choisissez Calque/Modifier le contenu du calque et sélectionnez le nouveau type de réglage ou de remplissage.

Vous pouvez contrôler l'effet du réglage ou du remplissage sur votre image d'origine en cliquant sur l'icône d'affichage (œil) de la palette des calques. Quand l'œil est présent à gauche de la vignette du calque, vous voyez les effets de vos interventions. Quand il est absent, vous voyez l'image d'origine.

Les calques de réglage sont si puissants et souples qu'il est de loin préférable de ne pas appliquer directement les commandes Niveaux et Teinte/Saturation à partir de leurs menus, mais au travers d'un calque de réglage. Certes, la plupart des formats de fichier ne gèrent pas les calques de réglage. Néanmoins, même si vous voulez obtenir finalement une image JPEG aplatie, il est judicieux de conserver un fichier PSD avec les calques, à titre de sauvegarde. Pourquoi appliquer un changement permanent à l'original de votre image alors que vous risquez de devoir le régler de nouveau ultérieurement ?

Les calques de réglage doivent être de règle.

Filtre photo

Le Filtre photo peut être appliqué sous la forme d'un calque de réglage, ou via Filtre/Réglages/Filtre photo. Ce filtre reprend le concept des filtres photographiques que l'on place directement sur l'objectif d'un appareil photo pour corriger la température de couleurs. Lorsque celle de la source lumineuse diffère de celle pour laquelle la surface sensible (pellicule ou capteur) est étalonnée, une dominante de couleur orangée, verte ou bleue apparaît, selon les circonstances. Un filtre compense la dominante au moment de la prise de vue. Le Filtre photo, quant à lui, agit après la prise de vue.

Dans la boîte de dialogue Filtre photo, les deux filtres Réchauffant s'appliquent à des photos présentant une dominante de couleur bleue. Les filtres Refroidissant corrigent une dominante rouge ou orangée. Les autres filtres produisent des effets particuliers que nous vous laissons expérimenter. Vous pouvez activer le bouton d'option Couleur, puis cliquer sur le nuancier pour ouvrir le Sélecteur de couleurs. Là, définissez la teinte du filtre. Le curseur Densité règle la densité du filtre et l'option Conserver la luminosité permet de garder les valeurs de luminosité d'origine de l'image, et cela même après application du filtre.

Si vous possédez une certaine expérience de la photographie (argentique ou numérique), vous maîtriserez rapidement les options du Filtre photo. Comme ils sont utilisables dans les calques de réglage, vous pouvez peaufiner ou supprimer leur effet à n'importe quel moment, ce qui est plus difficile lorsqu'un filtre a été placé sur l'objectif.

Corriger correctement la couleur

Comme nous l'avons mentionné au début de ce chapitre, Niveaux et Variantes de couleurs sont quasiment les seules commandes nécessaires pour les corrections de couleurs des images. Que cela ne vous empêche pas d'essayer les autres. Mais tôt ou tard, vous aurez à faire à une image qui renâcle à se plier aux commandes automatiques faites d'un seul clic. C'est là que les commandes Niveaux et Variantes de couleurs entrent en jeu. Alors que Variantes de couleurs est plutôt intuitive, Niveaux l'est moins.

Travailler le contraste

La commande Niveaux est l'une des fonctions essentielles de Photoshop Elements. Utilisez-la si une image présente l'un des symptômes suivants :

- ✔ L'image est terne, sans zones claires ou sombres affirmées, comme celle de la Figure 13.1.

- ✔ L'image présente une dominante de couleur.

- ✔ L'image est trop claire.

- ✔ L'image est trop sombre.

Faire ami-ami avec la boîte de dialogue Niveaux

Pour appliquer la commande Niveaux, vous pouvez, soit créer un nouveau calque de réglage comme cela est décrit dans la précédente section, soit choisir Accentuation/Régler l'éclairage/Contraste/Niveaux. La boîte de dialogue représentée sur la Figure 13.7 apparaît.

Heureusement, vous n'aurez pas besoin de mettre en œuvre toutes les options de cette boîte de dialogue. Examinons-les :

Histogramme

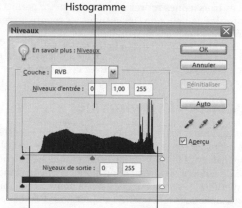

Figure 13.7 :
La boîte de
dialogue
Niveaux sert
à régler le
contraste
d'une image.

Pixels les plus sombres   Pixels les plus clairs

- ✔ Les options de la liste Couche permettent de régler une couleur indépendamment des autres (les couches rouge, vert et bleu sont traitées au Chapitre 5) Vous n'en aurez pas besoin pour les retouches les plus courantes.

- ✔ Les trois champs de la zone Niveaux d'entrée contrôlent les réglages des pixels les plus noirs, moyens et clairs de l'image. Ces options sont si importantes que nous les traiterons spécifiquement dans la prochaine section.

- ✔ Le graphique au centre de la boîte de dialogue est un *histogramme*. Il montre la répartition des couleurs de l'image.

- ✔ Les curseurs sous l'histogramme agissent sur les pixels foncés, moyens et clairs de l'image. Ces trois commandes sont les plus importantes de toutes.

- ✔ Les deux champs de la zone Niveaux de sortie et la barre de dégradé située dessous permettent d'éclaircir les pixels les plus sombres et d'assombrir les pixels les plus clairs de l'image.

- ✔ Les boutons OK et Annuler appliquent vos modifications, ou y renoncent.

- ✔ Le bouton Réinitialiser restaure les valeurs affichées lors de l'ouverture de la boîte de dialogue Niveaux. Très utile !

- ✔ Cliquer sur le bouton Auto revient à utiliser la commande Niveaux automatiques.

✔ Les trois icônes représentant une pipette permettent de cliquer sur des couleurs de l'image pour les rendre noires, gris moyen ou blanches.

✔ Cochez la case Aperçu permet d'apprécier l'effet des réglages directement sur l'image. Activez cette option.

La palette Histogramme

La palette Histogramme, affichée en choisissant Fenêtre/Histogramme, affiche le dosage des trois composants rouge, vert et bleu de l'image. Comme le montre la Figure 13.8, le menu Couche affiche chaque couche de couleur séparément ou alors la couche composite RVB, qui est la synthèse des trois couches. Vous pouvez également afficher l'histogramme de la luminosité ou opter pour Couleur afin d'obtenir l'histogramme de toutes les teintes.

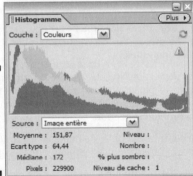

Figure 13.8 :
La palette
Histogramme
révèle le
dosage des
couleurs de
l'image.

La liste Source affiche l'histogramme de toute l'image ou du calque sélectionné. Vous pouvez aussi cliquer sur un calque de réglage dans la palette Calques, et choisir Composite de réglage dans la liste Source pour voir l'histogramme des calques affectés par le calque de réglage. Par défaut, la palette Histogramme affiche une estimation de l'histogramme de manière à le montrer plus rapidement. En revanche, si vous cliquez sur l'icône Actualiser, située dans le coin supérieur droit, l'histogramme sera recalculé pour afficher une représentation exacte des niveaux de votre image.

La luminosité et le contraste comme ils devraient être

L'histogramme de la commande Niveaux, sur la Figure 13.7, est la représentation graphique de la photo à corriger représentée sur la Figure 13.9. Dans l'histogramme, les couleurs les plus sombres sont à gauche, et les plus claires à droite. Les pics et les vallées de l'histogramme montrent la répartition de la couleur. Si les couleurs les plus sombres étaient noires, l'histogramme commencerait au niveau du curseur le plus à gauche. Si les couleurs les plus claires étaient blanches, l'histogramme se poursuivrait jusqu'au curseur de droite. Mais vous constatez que ces deux zones sont parfaitement plates, indiquant que les pixels les plus clairs et les plus foncés ne sont pas aussi clairs et foncés qu'ils devraient l'être.

Figure 13.9 :
Cette scène attend une application de Niveaux.

Si certaines de ces informations vous paraissent un peu ardues, faites un effort pour les assimiler, car il en va de l'aspect final de votre image. L'important est cependant de bien comprendre le rôle des curseurs situés sous l'histogramme.

- ✔ Pour rendre noirs les pixels plus foncés, tirez le curseur de gauche vers la droite, jusqu'au pied de la première colline de l'histogramme. La Figure 13.10 montre la position du curseur et l'effet obtenu sur l'image.

Figure 13.10 :
Faites glisser
le premier
curseur vers
la droite pour
affecter les
pixels les
plus sombres
de l'image.

> ✔ Pour rendre blancs les pixels les plus clairs, faites glisser le curseur de droite vers la gauche pour l'aligner au pied de la dernière colline de l'histogramme, comme le montre la Figure 13.11.

Figure 13.11 :
L'image
s'éclaircit
quand vous
déplacez
vers la
gauche le
curseur le
plus à droite.

✔ Le curseur le plus important est celui du milieu. On l'appelle le *point gamma*. Tirez-le vers la droite pour assombrir les tonalités moyennes. Dans notre exemple, nous l'avons déplacé vers la gauche afin de donner plus de luminosité aux couleurs moyennes, comme en témoigne la Figure 13.12.

Figure 13.12 :
Faites glisser
le curseur du
milieu pour
augmenter
les détails de
l'image.

Gardez à l'esprit que vous pouvez régler ces valeurs séparément pour chaque couche chromatique en la choisissant dans le menu Couche.

Prenez le temps de maîtriser la commande Niveaux car vous y recourrez fréquemment.

 Ne vous inquiétez pas si vous remarquez une perte de couleur après l'application de la commande Niveaux. Vous pouvez la retrouver en utilisant la commande Variantes de couleurs, traitée ci-après.

Variantes de couleurs

L'effet indésirable de la manipulation des niveaux de luminosité d'une image est sa tendance à modifier les couleurs. C'est notamment le cas quand vous éclaircissez des tonalités moyennes en déplaçant vers la gauche le curseur central de la boîte de dialogue Niveaux. Pour retrouver les couleurs d'origine – comme le chante fort justement Alain Souchon dans "L'amour à la machine" –, choisissez Accentuation/Régler la couleur/Variantes de couleurs.

Bien qu'Elements dispose d'une commande pour supprimer la dominante de couleur, la commande Variantes de couleurs est généralement préférable pour s'en débarrasser. Quelle que soit la teinte qui prédomine dans l'image, la commande Variantes de couleurs peut l'atténuer avec élégance et rapidité. Mais avant d'en arriver là, voyons comment cette commande peut accentuer les couleurs d'une image dont les niveaux sont corrects.

Transformer une image délavée en un cliché coloré

Pour augmenter l'intensité des couleurs de votre image, suivez les étapes ci-dessous :

1. **Choisissez Accentuation/Régler la couleur/Variantes de couleurs.**

   La grande fenêtre Variantes de couleurs apparaît, avec diverses versions de l'image.

2. **Activez le paramètre Saturation.**

   La plupart des vignettes disparaissent. Seules quatre images restent visibles, comme en témoigne la Figure 13.13. Les deux prévisualisations en bas de la boîte de dialogue représentent différentes intensités de la couleur. Les deux aperçus plus grands, en haut, montrent l'image telle qu'elle apparaît avant que vous ayez choisi la commande Variantes de couleurs, et telle qu'elle apparaît après sélection d'un mode de saturation.

3. **Tirez vers la gauche le curseur situé dans le coin inférieur gauche de la fenêtre.**

   Ce curseur contrôle l'étendue des modifications faites dans la fenêtre Variantes de couleurs. Si vous le déplacez vers la droite, les modifications sont très accentuées. Vers la gauche, vous travaillez plutôt dans la subtilité. Le résultat est affiché dans les aperçus en bas de la boîte de dialogue.

   L'intensité de la couleur étant une fonction très sensible d'Elements, il est préférable de positionner le curseur assez loin vers la gauche. Vous procéderez ainsi à des changements en douceur.

4. **Pour augmenter l'intensité de la couleur, cliquez sur l'aperçu Plus saturé.**

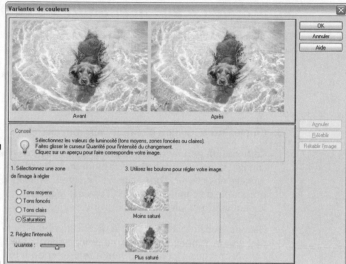

Figure 13.13 :
Cliquez sur l'aperçu Plus saturé pour accentuer l'intensité des couleurs d'une image.

En cliquant une fois, vous appliquez le réglage défini avec le curseur. Pour donner encore plus d'intensité, cliquez de nouveau. Chaque fois que vous cliquez, l'aperçu Après s'actualise, c'est-à-dire qu'il reflète l'application de la modification.

Pour que l'aperçu Après montre l'image d'origine, cliquez sur le bouton Rétablir l'image ou cliquez sur l'aperçu Avant.

5. **Lorsque vous êtes satisfait de l'intensité des couleurs, appuyez sur la touche Entrée.**

   Elements applique les réglages à l'image d'origine. Aucune mauvaise surprise ne vous attend.

Les changements n'affectent que le calque actif. Il n'est pas possible d'appliquer la commande Variantes de couleurs à un calque de réglage. Pour cette raison, Teinte/Saturation est un meilleur choix pour renforcer la saturation d'une image ; vous pouvez l'employer via un calque de réglage, afin que les changements ne soient pas définitifs. Certains utilisateurs préfèrent encore grandement l'approche empirique par "clics et aperçus". Quel que soit le moyen employé, Elements donnera satisfaction.

Suppression d'une dominante de couleur

Pour enlever une dominante de couleur avec la commande Variantes de couleurs :

1. **Choisissez Accentuation/Régler la couleur/Variantes de couleurs.**

   La fenêtre Variantes de couleurs s'ouvre.

2. **Cliquez sur le bouton d'option Tons moyens.**

   Cette option permet de modifier les couleurs moyennes de l'image. Vous pouvez également modifier les couleurs claires et foncées en activant Tons clairs et Tons foncés, mais il est préférable de commencer avec Tons moyens car c'est habituellement la principale source du problème.

   Une fois Tons moyens activé, la partie inférieure de la boîte de dialogue se remplit d'aperçus, comme le montre la Figure 13.14. Les six aperçus à gauche servent à renforcer ou atténuer les trois couleurs de base rouge, vert et bleu. Les deux aperçus à droite servent à éclaircir et assombrir l'image. Cliquez sur l'aperçu Plus de bleu pour ajouter du bleu à l'image. Cliquez sur Moins de rouge pour ôter du rouge.

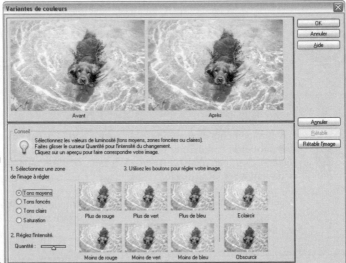

Figure 13.14 : Cliquez sur une vignette pour la visualiser dans la partie supérieure.

3. **Tirez vers la gauche le curseur situé dans l'angle inférieur gauche.**

   Comme auparavant pour la saturation, il est préférable de régler les couleurs par petites touches.

4. **Cliquez sur un des aperçus Plus de ou Moins de, afin de rapprocher ou d'éloigner les couleurs de l'image d'une couleur particulière.**

5. **Si vous vous rapprochez trop d'une couleur, pas de panique.**

   Si ce dernier clic sur Plus de rouge a vraiment tout mis sens dessus dessous, cliquez sur Moins de rouge ou simplement sur le bouton Annulation. Si vous décidez finalement que la correction n'était pas si mauvaise que cela, cliquez de nouveau sur Plus de rouge ou sur le bouton Rétablir. Si vous avez vraiment tout raté, cliquez sur l'aperçu Avant ou sur le bouton Rétablir l'image.

Elements présente les variantes de couleur dans votre image, mais permet également de pallier vos errements chromatiques. Qui n'apprécierait pas une telle application ?

Correction des couleurs d'une image brute (Camera Raw)

Nous allons aborder le sujet de la retouche des couleurs dans la nouvelle boîte de dialogue Camera Raw. Le format RAW (*brut,* en anglais) est particulier : lorsque vous prenez une photo avec un appareil photo numérique, celui-ci effectue un certain nombre d'opérations pour améliorer l'image. C'est un peu comme si un tout petit bonhomme se trouvait dans l'appareil avec un tout petit ordinateur faisant tourner une toute petite version de Photoshop Elements. Mais cette modification n'est pas très appréciée des professionnels de l'image. Ils veulent une image qui soit exactement celle enregistrée par le capteur de leur appareil et non pas bidouillée numériquement par des algorithmes plus ou moins précis.

De ce fait, les appareils photo numériques haut de gamme proposent un format de fichier Camera Raw, en plus du JPEG et du TIFF. Ce format brut préserve toutes les données initiales de l'image, telles qu'elles ont été produites par le capteur photosensible. De ce fait, lorsque vous ouvrez une image Raw dans Photoshop Elements, une grande boîte de dialogue apparaît, semblable à celle la Figure 13.15.

Elle dispose d'une vaste zone de prévisualisation, d'un histogramme et d'une série de contrôles.

Figure 13.15 : Cette boîte de dialogue permet d'améliorer une image au format Raw.

Voici un aperçu des paramètres de l'onglet Réglages :

- ✔ **Profondeur :** En bas de la boîte de dialogue, la liste Profondeur permet de coder les couches sur 8 bits (256 niveaux par couche) ou 16 bits (65 536 niveaux par couche). Choisissez 8 bits pour accéder à tous les outils de Photoshop Elements, car un certain nombre de fonctions et filtres sont inapplicables à des images dont les couches sont codées à la profondeur maximale.

- ✔ **Paramètres :** Sous l'histogramme, choisissez Image sélectionnée si vous avez préalablement ouvert cette photo dans Camera Raw et que vous souhaitiez retrouver les mêmes paramètres. Optez pour Par défaut de l'appareil photo pour appliquer les paramètres de votre appareil, stockés dans la base de données des profils Camera Raw. Conversion précédente applique les paramètres de la dernière image ouverte dans Camera Raw et prise avec le même appareil photo numérique.

- ✔ **Balance du blanc :** Tel quel est le meilleur choix si votre appareil conserve les informations de balance des blancs dans les métadonnées de l'image. Si ce n'est pas le cas, ou si vous l'ignorez, optez pour Auto.

✔ **Température :** Glissez le curseur vers la gauche pour refroidir l'image avec du bleu. Faites-le glisser vers la droite pour la réchauffer avec du jaune.

✔ **Teinte :** Faites glisser le curseur vers la gauche pour décaler l'image vers le vert, à droite pour la décaler vers le rouge.

✔ **Exposition, Tons foncés, Luminosité** et **Contraste :** Les cases à cocher Automatique sont à utiliser comme réglage témoin. S'il ne convient pas, agissez sur les différents curseurs.

✔ **Saturation :** Faites glisser le curseur vers la droite pour intensifier les couleurs.

Sous l'onglet Détails se trouvent les glissières :

✔ **Netteté :** N'y touchez pas et améliorez la netteté avec le filtre Accentuation, quand l'image sera ouverte dans Photoshop Elements.

✔ **Lissage de la luminance :** Sert à réduire le bruit d'une image en niveaux de gris.

✔ **Réduire bruit de la couleur :** Cette commande est censée atténuer le bruit produit notamment lorsque les conditions d'éclairage étaient insuffisantes, lors de la prise de vue. Réglez-la avec parcimonie.

Après avoir cliqué sur OK, Camera Raw calcule les différentes valeurs et ouvre l'image dans Elements. Remarquez qu'il s'agit d'une nouvelle image, car la photo au format RAW ouverte dans Camera Raw ne subit pas de modification.

Si votre appareil photo numérique ne photographie pas au format Raw, vous ne verrez jamais cette boîte de dialogue. En revanche, s'il propose ce format, nul doute que, désormais, vous apprécierez ces fonctions qui permettent de traiter vos images comme s'il s'agissait d'une diapositive, voire d'un négatif.

Quatrième partie
L'art et la manière

Dans cette partie...

C ette partie est la consécration de tous vos talents. Ignoriez-vous que le simple fait de posséder Elements donne du talent et favorise une expression personnelle dont l'efficacité n'a dégale que sa simplicité ? Votre imagination n'a plus de limites. Seule la nécessité de vous familiariser avec de nouveaux outils pourrait entraver vos projets, mais nous allons tout mettre en œuvre pour que ce ne soit pas le cas.

Nous commencerons par distiller quelques informations sur l'utilisation d'outils particulièrement puissants. Il y a beaucoup à lire mais, croyez-moi, le jeu en vaut la chandelle.

Chapitre 14

Une touche de style dans la retouche

*V*os divers essais avec des outils de Photoshop Elements ne vous ont pas encore permis d'exprimer pleinement votre potentiel créatif. Par exemple, vous savez parfaitement utiliser l'outil Tampon de duplication pour supprimer les poussières, les cheveux, et autres petits désagréments qui ne manquent jamais d'apparaître lors de la numérisation d'une photographie. Et d'un seul coup, vous avez une illumination en découvrant que le Tampon de duplication permet, par exemple, de créer votre frère jumeau. Il n'aura fallu que quelques clics de souris pour cloner un être humain, de quoi faire rêver les artistes et faire pâlir les chercheurs.

Vous venez de comprendre un élément essentiel de la créativité en général et de la retouche numérique des images en particulier : le détournement des outils de leur fonction première. Elements présente le gros avantage de donner à ses utilisateurs la possibilité d'exprimer leur propre idée de l'esthétique – peu importe qu'elle soit classique, étrange ou politiquement incorrecte. Les outils que vous mettrez en œuvre ne vous serviront pas quotidiennement. D'autres, comme les modes de fusion, ouvriront la porte aux effets spéciaux en tout genre. Enfin, une dernière catégorie, comme la commande Fluidité, déforme l'image à un haut degré de sophistication.

Ces outils dépassent le simple cadre de la réalité bien terre-à-terre. Vous la transgresserez pour créer un univers personnel, un produit de vos propres sens et styles artistiques.

Utilisation des styles de calque pour l'ombre et la lumière

Les styles de calque sont liés au contenu d'un calque. Si vous modifiez ce contenu, les styles s'actualisent automatiquement, ce qui leur confère une remarquable souplesse. Voici une description étape par étape de l'application d'un style de calque :

1. **Commencez avec un objet du calque actif.**

   Pour certains styles comme les ombres portées ou les lueurs externes, l'objet doit être isolé, c'est-à-dire entouré d'une zone transparente, matérialisée par un damier. En revanche, d'autres styles s'appliquent à la totalité de l'image.

   Remarquez que si le calque actif est le calque Arrière-plan, Elements propose de le convertir en calque normal. Par défaut, ce calque est nommé Calque 0, mais vous pouvez choisir un autre nom.

   Vous avez converti le calque Arrière-plan en calque normal et vous désirez rétablir le calque Arrière-plan ? Rien de plus simple. Sélectionnez un calque puis, dans le menu, choisissez Calque > Nouveau > Arrière-plan depuis un calque. Vous récupérez ainsi un calque Arrière-plan.

2. **Ouvrez la palette Styles et effets et choisissez Styles de calque dans la première liste.**

3. **Dans la zone supérieure de la seconde liste, choisissez une catégorie de styles.**

4. **Cliquez sur un style de calque.**

   Vous verrez le style s'appliquer immédiatement.

Nous décrivons les divers types d'effets et leurs paramètres dans la liste ci-dessous. Mais comme une image vaut n'importe quel discours, examinez la Figure 14.1 pour découvrir des exemples. La palette Styles et effets permet d'appliquer des styles de calque. Ils facilitent la création d'ombres, de halos (lueurs) et d'autres effets spéciaux sur des images et des textes.

Ombres portées

Ombres internes

Lueurs externes

Lueurs internes

Figure 14.1 :
Les effets
obtenus à
partir de la
palette Styles
et effets.

- ✔ **Biseaux :** Créent un effet de biseautage en relief sur les bords de l'objet.

- ✔ **Ombres portées :** Placent une ombre atténuée derrière l'objet, donnant l'illusion que le contenu du calque flotte au-dessus des autres éléments. Des ombres comme Contours ou Néon produisent des effets vraiment étranges.

- ✔ **Lueurs internes :** Projettent une lueur à partir des bords de l'objet vers l'intérieur de l'objet.

- ✔ **Ombres internes :** Appliquent une ombre sur l'objet lui-même, donnant l'impression qu'il se détache du calque sur lequel il repose.

- ✔ **Lueurs externes :** Créent un halo autour de l'objet.

✔ **Visibilité :** Rendent l'objet transparent ou invisible, tout en conservant le style de calque.

✔ **Complexe :** Ces styles prédéfinis sont le résultat de diverses combinaisons de styles de calque, de textures et de couleurs. La création de styles de calque complexes s'obtient en plaçant plusieurs styles les uns sur les autres.

✔ **Boutons de verre :** Aussi simples que leur nom l'indique, tous les styles prédéfinis de cette catégorie permettent de transformer les objets en une multitude de boutons de verre en couleurs.

✔ **Effets d'image :** Ces styles de calque combinent le contenu d'un objet avec divers effets, comme la neige et le brouillard. Probablement plus utiles sur les photographies que sur du texte ou des objets dessinés avec les outils de Forme.

✔ **Motifs :** Remplissent un objet avec diverses textures, comme l'asphalte, le marbre et la boue sèche.

✔ **Effets photographiques :** Ce sont essentiellement des virages, c'est-à-dire des colorations de l'image, en sépia par exemple. Cette catégorie comporte aussi des filtres dégradés et surtout, un mode Négatif fort utile.

✔ **Wow Chrome :** Donnent l'impression que l'objet est recouvert de chrome.

✔ **Wow Néon :** Produit un effet de néon de l'objet.

✔ **Wow Plastique :** Semblables à Boutons de verre, mais souvent avec l'ajout d'une ombre portée et/ou d'une lueur externe.

Pour appliquer un style de calque, il suffit de cliquer dessus. Mais, vous pouvez également :

✔ Glisser-déposer le style depuis la palette Styles et effets sur le calque concerné, dans la palette des calques.

✔ Glisser-déposer le style de la palette Styles et effets sur le calque concerné, dans la fenêtre de l'image.

Il peut arriver qu'une ombre portée soit trop importante. Vous n'êtes pas tenu de conserver les paramètres par défaut des effets. Choisissez Calque/Styles de calque/Paramètres de style, ou double-cliquez sur le "f" qui, dans la palette des calques, apparaît sur le calque ayant reçu un style. Vous accédez dans les deux cas à la boîte de dialogue représentée sur la Figure 14.2.

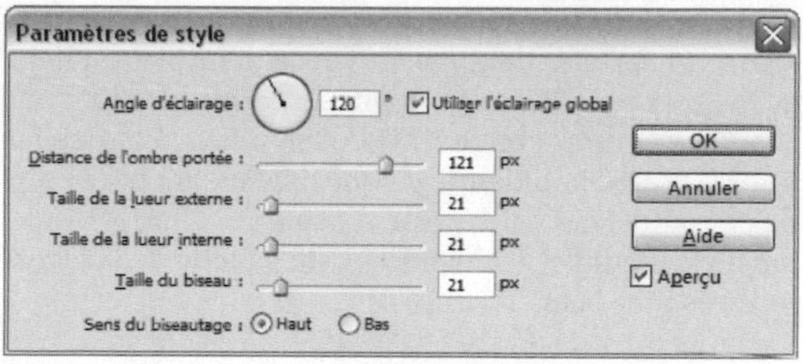

Figure 14.2 :
La boîte de
dialogue
Paramètres
de style.

Voici une explication des paramètres qu'elle contient :

✔ **Angle d'éclairage :** Définit la direction de la source de lumière
pour les Biseaux et les Ombres. Saisissez une valeur exprimée
en degrés, ou contentez-vous de varier l'angle en orientant le
rayon du petit cercle à l'aide de la souris.

✔ **Utiliser l'éclairage global :** Cochez cette option pour conserver
un angle d'éclairage identique sur tous les calques d'une même
image. Ce paramètre est important car il garantit que tous les
objets d'une image, quel que soit le calque où ils se trouvent,
sont éclairés sous le même angle. Modifier l'angle d'éclairage et
la distance de l'ombre portée d'un calque affecte tous les autres.

✔ **Distance de l'ombre portée :** Cette option définit la distance de
l'ombre portée par rapport à l'objet auquel elle est appliquée.
Vous pouvez facilement donner l'illusion que l'objet est plus ou
moins éloigné du fond de l'image ou des autres calques situés
derrière lui. Cette distance est réglable avec le curseur ou en
faisant directement glisser l'ombre sur l'image. Remarquez que
le déplacement de l'ombre portée affecte l'angle d'éclairage pour
chaque calque dont l'option Utiliser l'éclairage global est active.

✔ **Taille de la lueur externe :** Modifie la taille de la lueur externe
appliquée à l'objet.

✔ **Taille de la lueur interne :** Modifie la taille de la lueur interne
appliquée à l'objet.

✔ **Taille du biseau :** Modifie la taille du biseau.

✔ **Sens du biseautage :** Modifie la direction du biseau. Le sens du
biseau sert à définir des surfaces concaves ou convexes.

Un style de calque est *dynamique*. Cela signifie qu'il s'actualise selon le
contenu du calque. Par exemple, l'image de gauche de la Figure 14.3
montre un cercle auquel un Biseau interne a été appliqué. Si, par la

suite, un filtre Onde lui est appliqué, comme à la deuxième illustration de la Figure 14.3, l'effet tient compte de la déformation déjà infligée à l'image. Mais, si vous désirez obtenir un cercle biseauté ondulé, vous devez commencer par convertir l'effet en pixels. Pour ce faire, choisissez Calque/Simplifier le calque. Elements opère un rendu du style de ce calque, qui est à présent *pixellisé :* il n'est dès lors plus possible de le modifier. L'illustration de gauche de la Figure 14.3 montre le résultat final.

Figure 14.3 :
Le premier cercle a été simplifié avant de recevoir le filtre Onde.

Les styles de calque fonctionnent à merveille avec les outils de Forme. Ils peuvent d'ailleurs être directement appliqués depuis la barre d'options de l'outil. Cela est très pratique pour créer des formes simples destinées à des sites Web. Un bouton en est la parfaite illustration. Ces formes géométriques, relevant du vectoriel, peuvent être redimensionnées à volonté sans perte de qualité. Pour en savoir plus sur les outils de Forme, consultez le Chapitre 15.

La tentation des modes de fusion

Le contenu des calques peut être mêlé pour obtenir des effets spéciaux. Ce mélange est effectué par une fonction que vous avez tout intérêt à découvrir : le mode de fusion. Il s'agit en réalité d'une formule mathématique qui combine de diverses manières les pixels présents sur différents calques. Il est alors possible d'obtenir des effets étranges, beaux, surprenants et parfois inattendus.

Jouer avec l'opacité des calques

Le curseur d'opacité, dans la palette des calques, permet de rendre le contenu d'un calque transparent ou translucide. La Figure 14.4 montre une même image à laquelle nous avons appliqué deux valeurs d'opacité différentes au poisson. Pour accéder au curseur du paramètre

Opacité, cliquez dans le champ affichant un pourcentage. Plus vous tirez le curseur vers la gauche, plus le calque actif est transparent.

Opacité : 70 %

Opacité : 30 %

Figure 14.4 : Voici un poisson fantôme dont la faculté à devenir transparent est vraiment sidérante.

TRUC

Pour modifier le paramètre Opacité d'un calque avec le clavier, vérifiez qu'aucun outil disposant d'un paramètre d'opacité n'apparaisse dans la barre d'options de Photoshop Elements. Appuyez ensuite sur une touche du pavé numérique. Ainsi, 9 donnera une valeur de 90 %, 8 de 80 %, et ainsi de suite. Pour rétablir une Opacité de 100 % appuyez sur la touche 0. Des valeurs plus précises peuvent être saisies en appuyant rapidement sur les deux chiffres, comme 7 et 2 pour 72 %.

N'OUBLIEZ PAS

N'oubliez jamais que la valeur d'opacité du calque Arrière-plan ne peut pas être modifiée, car il n'y a rien dessous.

Jouer avec les modes de fusion

La plupart des options de fusion de la liste Mode de la palette des calques figurent également dans la liste Mode de la barre d'options de certains outils d'édition (voir le Chapitre 12). C'est notamment le cas de Produit, Superposition, Incrustation, et j'en passe. De nombreux outils utilisent un nom spécifique pour les modes – le Pinceau emploie le terme modes de peinture, pour l'outil Doigt ce sont des modes d'effet, la Gomme utilise des modes d'effacement –, mais tous réalisent

à peu près le même travail. Dans la palette Calques, on les appelle
"modes de fusion".

Voici une brève description des modes de fusion les plus importants :

- **Produit** et **Superposition** : Produit sous-expose le contenu du
  calque selon ce qui se trouve dessous. Toutes les couleurs
  deviennent plus sombres. Le mode Superposition produit l'effet
  inverse. Les couleurs fusionnées sont plus claires.

- **Différence** : Le mode Différence crée un négatif – ou une
  inversion – des images mélangées en fonction de leurs couleurs
  respectives.

- **Incrustation**, **Lumière tamisée** et **Lumière crue** : Ces modes de
  fusion se ressemblent. Incrustation multiplie les valeurs des
  couleurs sombres et superpose les couleurs claires. Lumière
  tamisée produit un effet plus subtil mais de même facture.
  Lumière crue a un effet plus accentué que les deux autres modes
  de fusion.

- **Couleur** et **Luminosité** : À l'instar de Produit et Superposition,
  les modes de fusion Couleur et Luminosité sont antagonistes. Le
  mode Couleur mélange les couleurs du calque avec les détails
  des images situées en dessous. Luminosité conserve les détails
  du calque et les mélange avec les couleurs des images situées en
  dessous.

- **Densité couleur -**, **Densité couleur +** et **Exclusion** : Pour des
  effets intéressants, faites des essais avec Densité couleur -,
  Densité couleur + et Exclusion. Ils diffèrent chacun subtilement
  des modes Écran, Produit et Différence. Supposons que vous
  ayez deux calques, un calque d'Arrière-plan et un Calque 1.
  Densité couleur - éclaire les pixels sur le calque Arrière-plan et
  les mélange subtilement avec les couleurs du Calque 1. Densité
  couleur + assombrit les couleurs et les mélange. Exclusion
  transforme les pixels noirs en pixels blancs, les pixels blancs en
  pixels noirs, et les teintes moyennes en gris.

- **Obscurcir** : Voici un mode très utile, similaire à Produit.
  Admettons que vous désiriez fusionner sur une image, une lettre
  manuscrite ou une partition numérisée. Vous souhaitez uniquement voir apparaître les lettres ou les notes mais surtout pas le
  papier blanc sur lequel elles sont inscrites. En choisissant
  Obscurcir, seuls les pixels foncés apparaissent. Les zones
  claires deviennent transparentes. Éclaircir fait l'inverse.

Les filtres

Pour l'instant, nous n'avons évoqué les filtres que pour l'amélioration des images, comme leur nettoyage. Mais, ceux de Photoshop Elements sont si nombreux qu'ils dynamiseront votre créativité.

Uniquement présente dans le menu Filtre, la catégorie Réglages propose quelques effets étranges :

- ✔ **Égaliser :** La commande Égaliser prend en compte les pixels les plus clairs et les plus foncés, parmi les trois couches de couleur de l'image, et les transforme en pixels blancs et noirs. Elle tente ensuite de répartir le reste des pixels de façon homogène, en termes de luminosité. Vous obtenez une image plus contrastée bien que l'effet ne soit généralement pas aussi efficace que la commande Niveaux automatiques.

- ✔ **Courbe de transfert de dégradé :** La commande Courbe de transfert de dégradé permet d'associer les couleurs d'un dégradé aux divers niveaux de luminosité de l'image. Il est ainsi possible de produire des effets spéciaux colorés très intéressants.

- ✔ **Inverser :** La commande Inverser convertit la couleur de chaque pixel dans sa couleur opposée. Le blanc devient noir, le bleu devient jaune, etc. L'image qui en résulte est en quelque sorte le négatif de l'original.

- ✔ **Isohélie :** La commande Isohélie limite chaque couche couleur à un nombre spécifié de teintes, produisant des aplats de couleur. L'effet obtenu rappelle la sérigraphie. Il est fréquemment exploité pour les affiches.

- ✔ **Seuil :** La commande Seuil convertit chaque pixel de l'image en blanc ou en noir, selon la valeur de seuil spécifiée. Il en résulte une image faite exclusivement de noir et de blanc, une technique très en vogue dans l'Op'art. La mise en couleur du blanc produit un effet de papier teinté.

Pour en savoir plus sur l'effet Filtre photo, reportez-vous au Chapitre 13.

Créer du mouvement et des puzzles

Tout se passe dans la catégorie Atténuation. Elle contient les filtres Moyenne, Flou, Plus flou, ainsi que trois filtres dévolus aux effets spéciaux : Flou directionnel, Flou radial et Flou optimisé. Ainsi, le filtre

Flou directionnel déplace les pixels, donnant l'illusion d'un flou de mouvement ou d'un filé. Les paramètres Angle et Distance sont réglables, ce qui permet de définir exactement l'orientation de l'effet et son amplitude.

La Figure 14.5 montre une application du filtre Flou directionnel. Pour rendre le petit garçon flou, nous l'avons sélectionné en lui appliquant un contour progressif. Seule la sélection a été modifiée par le filtre Flou directionnel dont les réglages étaient : Angle à 90° – dans une direction parfaitement rectiligne de haut en bas – et une Distance de 30 pixels. Pour donner un effet de bougé au bras de sa sœur – celle qui se trouve le plus près de lui –, nous avons utilisé un Angle de 45° et une Distance de 6 pixels. Comme vous le voyez, plus la distance est élevée, plus l'amplitude du mouvement est importante.

Figure 14.5 : Deux applications différentes du filtre Flou directionnel.

Ajouter du bruit aux images

Logiquement localisé dans la catégorie Bruit, le filtre Ajout de bruit répartit aléatoirement des pixels dans la zone sélectionnée. Le résultat est un calque granuleux.

Lorsque vous appliquez le filtre Ajout de bruit, vous accédez à la boîte de dialogue de la Figure 14.6. Voici comment utiliser ses fonctions :

- Faites glisser le curseur Facteur ou saisissez directement une valeur entre 0,10 % et 400 % afin de régler le bruit de l'image. Les valeurs faibles ajoutent peu de bruit, tandis que les plus élevées modifient considérablement l'image. Toute valeur supérieure à 50 % rend l'image illisible.

- Choisissez un mode de Répartition pour contrôler la couleur du bruit. L'option Uniforme colore les pixels avec des variations aléatoires en fonction des teintes rencontrées ; l'option Gaussienne colorise les pixels en exagérant les teintes claires et foncées. L'option Gaussienne produit un bruit environ deux fois plus important qu'Uniforme.

- Cochez l'option Monochromatique pour ajouter du bruit en niveaux de gris aux images en couleurs. Quand vous désactivez cette option, Elements ajoute toutes les couleurs du bruit. (L'option n'a aucun effet colorimétrique sur les images en niveaux de gris. Elle se contente de répartir différemment les pixels du bruit.)

Figure 14.6 : Ce filtre ajoute du bruit pour donner un aspect granuleux à l'image.

Estampage métallique de votre image

Estampage est un autre filtre intrigant, utile dans certaines circonstances. Vous le trouverez dans la catégorie Esthétique. Ce filtre donne l'impression que l'image est gravée dans une pièce de métal. Les contours de l'image sont en relief et les autres zones deviennent grises.

Quand vous choisissez Estampage, Elements affiche la boîte de dialogue illustrée sur la Figure 14.7. Voici ce qu'il est important de savoir sur ce filtre :

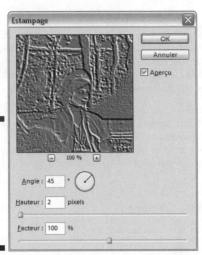

Figure 14.7 : Utilisez le filtre Estampage pour graver des images dans un morceau de métal.

✔ La valeur du paramètre Angle importe peu. Jouez avec si cela vous amuse, mais sachez que vous ne faites que modifier l'angle d'attaque de la lumière sur votre image. Ce n'est pas d'une importance capitale.

✔ Fixez la valeur Hauteur sur 1 ou 2. Toute valeur supérieure a tendance à doubler les détails.

✔ Oui, le paramètre Facteur est important ; saisissez **50 %** pour des effets très subtils, **100 %** pour un effet d'estampage moyen et **200 %** pour une altération dramatique de l'image. Les valeurs très élevées créent un contraste abrupt entre les noirs et les blancs.

Estampage est le type de filtre que vous appliquez à une image entière.

Pour obtenir un effet métallique aussi sophistiqué que celui de la Figure 14.8, commencez par sélectionner les zones sombres de la mère et du fils, puis appliquez un Estampage dont voici les paramètres :

Angle à 45°, Hauteur sur 2 et Facteur sur 200 %. Ensuite, appliquez un Flou gaussien dont le Rayon est de 2 pixels. Vous obtenez l'image du centre (Figure 14.8). Enfin, appliquez le filtre Accentuation en fixant les paramètres Gain sur 500 % et Rayon sur 2.

TRUC

Votre réaction légitime est de dire : "Qu'est-ce que c'est que ces histoires ?! On commence par appliquer un flou, puis une netteté ? C'est complètement illogique !" En fait, tout cela est très logique. Après avoir appliqué le Flou gaussien, l'image devient totalement grise, comme vous le constatez sur la première image de la Figure 14.8. Heureusement, un des paramètres du filtre Accentuation est d'augmenter le contraste entre les pixels clairs et foncés. Donc, pour redonner vie aux noirs et aux blancs, la valeur Rayon de la boîte de dialogue Accentuation est égale à celle de la boîte de dialogue Flou gaussien, en l'occurrence 2,0. Avec cette valeur, vous êtes certain de rétablir les contours flous et d'intensifier le contraste. C'est une technique aussi géniale que fondamentale.

Estampage	Flou gaussien	Accentuation

Figure 14.8 :
La sélection
a été
estampée,
atténuée et
accentuée,
créant un
léger relief.

Fusionner les couleurs des images imprécises

Les deux prochains filtres – Facettes et Médiane – établissent une moyenne des couleurs des pixels juxtaposés les uns aux autres. Cela crée des zones d'aplat. Les détails disparaissent, mais cela atténue largement les imperfections.

Le filtre Facettes se trouve dans la catégorie Pixellisation. Il n'a pas d'option et s'applique donc avec un paramétrage par défaut. Il fait disparaître la différence minime existant entre les pixels contigus pour former des zones constituées d'aplats. La Figure 14.9 montre un des sujets de la Figure 12.7 avant son accentuation. L'exemple du milieu montre cette même jeune fille après application du filtre Facettes, à droite le filtre Accentuation a été appliqué. Vous constatez que les détails des couleurs ont disparu, gommant par là même les imperfections. Pour rendre l'image plus nette, nous avons appliqué le filtre Accentuation avec les paramètres suivants : Gain 250 % et Rayon 0.5.

Original	Facettes	Accentuation

Figure 14.9 :
Le filtre
Facettes a
été appliqué,
puis les
contours ont
été
renforcés.

Dans la catégorie Bruit, vous trouverez le filtre Médiane. Il calcule une moyenne des couleurs de tous les pixels voisins. Pour indiquer à Elements le "nombre de parties" à prendre en considération, fixez un rayon entre 1 et 100.

La Figure 14.10 montre le résultat obtenu en appliquant diverses valeurs de Rayon. La ligne du haut montre les effets de la commande Médiane et, celle du bas, de la commande Accentuation. Plus la valeur est faible, plus l'image est détaillée.

Vous pouvez utiliser les filtres Facettes et Médiane pour atténuer les images de fond, comme nous l'avons fait avec le filtre Flou gaussien. Ou bien, combinez-les avec les filtres Ajout de bruit et Estampage pour créer des effets spéciaux.

N'oubliez pas que la beauté de ces filtres tient dans leur application successive sur tout ou partie de votre image.

Déformer Tatie avec le filtre Fluidité

Vous pensez qu'Elements n'a pas la capacité de sortir des sentiers battus en écartant vos images de toute réalité quotidienne ? Eh bien, prenez votre souris et exécutez le filtre Fluidité.

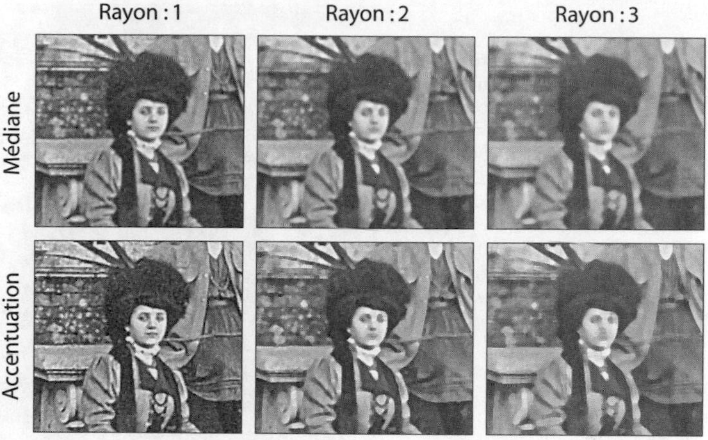

Rayon : 1   Rayon : 2   Rayon : 3

Figure 14.10 :
Le filtre
Médiane
appliqué
avec trois
valeurs de
Rayon
différentes
(ligne
supérieure),
puis
accentué
(ligne
inférieure).

Ce filtre vous laisse déformer, triturer, tortiller, étirer et faire subir bien d'autres sévices encore à vos images.

1. **Ouvrez une image et décidez d'en déformer une partie ou la totalité.**

   Vous pouvez sélectionner une partie de l'image avec un des outils de sélection décrits au Chapitre 9. Ou bien, sélectionnez un seul calque (voir le Chapitre 10). Quand vous sélectionnez une zone, les autres sont protégées contre toute manipulation numérique. Sur la Figure 14.11, le visage de cette femme a été sélectionné.

2. **Choisissez Filtre/Déformation/Fluidité.**

   Vous pouvez également le sélectionner dans la palette Filtres. Cliquez alors sur le filtre Fluidité ou faites glisser son icône jusqu'à l'image. Vous accédez à la boîte de dialogue représentée sur la Figure 14.11.

3. **Sélectionnez la forme de l'outil et définissez son épaisseur, puis sa pression.**

   La valeur Épaisseur contrôle la quantité de pixels affectés à la fois et Pression contrôle la force de trait. Si vous utilisez une tablette graphique, vous pouvez aussi activer Pression du stylet pour qu'Elements ajuste la pression selon la pression que vous exercez sur le stylet.

4. **Réglez votre vue de l'image avec les outils Zoom et Main.**

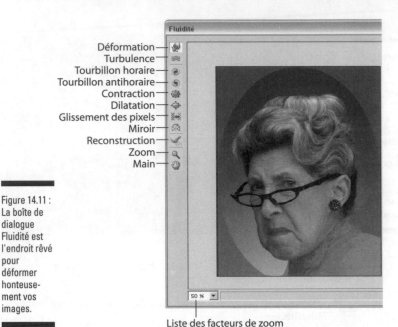

Déformation
Turbulence
Tourbillon horaire
Tourbillon antihoraire
Contraction
Dilatation
Glissement des pixels
Miroir
Reconstruction
Zoom
Main

Liste des facteurs de zoom

Figure 14.11 :
La boîte de
dialogue
Fluidité est
l'endroit rêvé
pour
déformer
honteuse-
ment vos
images.

Notez aussi le menu de facteur de zoom, dans l'angle inférieur gauche de la boîte de dialogue.

5. Et maintenant, voici la partie la plus drôle de l'histoire.

Utilisez un des outils décrits ci-dessous. Reportez-vous à la Figure 14.12 pour apprécier son effet sur l'image.

- **Déformation :** Pousse ou tire les pixels quand vous déplacez le pointeur de la souris. Cet effet déforme l'image au maximum.

- **Turbulence :** Déforme les pixels dans des directions aléatoires au fur et à mesure que vous faites glisser. Lorsque vous sélectionnez cet outil, vous avez accès à l'option Variation de turbulence. Variation de turbulence spécifie la quantité de variation aléatoire. La valeur minimale 1 a pour effet que l'outil Turbulence se comporte de façon très semblable à l'outil Déformation.

- **Tourbillon horaire :** Fait pivoter les pixels dans le sens des aiguilles d'une montre. Soit vous faites glisser le pointeur de la souris, soit vous le placez sur une partie de l'image et vous maintenez le bouton gauche de la souris enfoncé. Regardez l'effet s'appliquer en temps réel.

- **Tourbillon antihoraire :** Fait exactement comme l'outil précédent mais dans le sens inverse des aiguilles d'une montre.

- **Contraction :** Déplace les pixels vers le centre de votre forme soit quand vous déplacez la souris, soit quand vous maintenez le bouton enfoncé sans bouger.

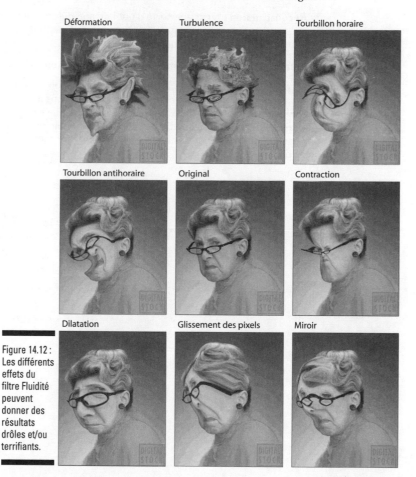

Déformation   Turbulence   Tourbillon horaire

Tourbillon antihoraire   Original   Contraction

Dilatation   Glissement des pixels   Miroir

Figure 14.12 : Les différents effets du filtre Fluidité peuvent donner des résultats drôles et/ou terrifiants.

- **Dilatation :** Effet inverse de l'outil Contraction. Les pixels sont poussés vers l'extérieur, créant une sorte d'effet sphérique.

- **Glissement des pixels :** Fait glisser les pixels perpendiculairement au sens de votre déplacement. (Sur la Figure 14.12, la forme de l'outil a été déplacée vers le haut.)

- **Miroir :** Copie les pixels de la zone perpendiculaire au sens du déplacement de l'outil.

- **Reconstruction :** C'est une sorte d'outil de non-déformation, servant à restaurer des zones sélectionnées de l'image dans leur état d'origine, en peignant dessus.

6. **Cliquez sur OK et admirez votre consternant chef-d'œuvre.**

Le meilleur conseil que nous puissions donner sur l'utilisation du filtre Fluidité est : amusez-vous, amusez-vous, amusez-vous ! Si vous avez un moment à perdre, sautez sur l'occasion (NdT : c'est mieux que sur mine...), ouvrez une image, et laissez libre cours à la spontanéité de vos mouvements pour déformer des images comme ne le permet aucun autre outil.

Si une image vaut mille mots... alors, dessinez !

• •

Dans ce chapitre :

▶ Utiliser le Crayon et le Pinceau.

▶ Tracer des lignes droites avec les outils de peinture.

▶ Sélectionner, créer et enregistrer des formes d'outils.

▶ Supprimer des pixels avec la Gomme.

• •

F aites ce petit test pour savoir à quelle catégorie d'utilisateurs de Photoshop Elements vous appartenez :

✔ Après avoir griffonné sur un bout de papier, le résultat vous horrifie-t-il ?

✔ Lorsqu'on vous demande de dessiner les plans de votre maison, rendez-vous une feuille de papier vierge en essayant de faire croire que vous vivez dans l'Arctique au milieu des ours polaires ?

✔ Faites-vous régulièrement ce cauchemar où vous devez remettre votre projet artistique de fin d'année qui doit valider votre diplôme ? Et tentez-vous de peindre rapidement un modèle nu, pour finalement vous rendre compte que le modèle est habillé et que vous êtes la seule personne à exhiber votre nudité ?

Si vous répondez "oui" à ces questions, vous faites assurément partie du clan des non-artistes. Quel que soit votre niveau d'expérience artistique, vous utiliserez tôt ou tard les outils de peinture de Photoshop Elements. Ne vous inquiétez pas ! En effet, le pinceau impressionniste peut vous donner l'impression d'être le nouveau Van Gogh. De plus, en cas d'erreur, il est très facile de mettre à profit quelques outils qui effaceront votre travail. Par conséquent, respirez bien fort et poursuivez votre lecture.

Dessiner avec le Crayon et le Pinceau

La Figure 15.1 montre les emplacements des outils Crayon et Pinceau dans la boîte à outils. Ils appartiennent à la même catégorie, l'un étant un sous-outil de l'autre. Voici en quoi ils diffèrent :

- ✔ **Crayon :** Il trace des traits nets rectilignes, ou des successions de lignes anguleuses dont l'épaisseur est paramétrable.

- ✔ **Pinceau :** Il dessine des traits nets ou flous à main levée.

Vous pouvez sélectionner les outils de peinture depuis le clavier. Appuyez une ou deux ou trois fois sur B pour le Pinceau et sur N pour le Crayon.

Figure 15.1 :
Les outils de peinture sont réunis dans la même palette.

Si vous le souhaitez, le curseur de l'outil peut ressembler à l'outil lui-même. Ainsi, vous voyez apparaître un petit pinceau ou un petit crayon sur la zone de travail. Pour choisir cette représentation de l'outil, appuyez sur Ctrl+K. Vous accédez à la boîte de dialogue Préférences. Dans la première liste de cette boîte de dialogue, choisissez Affichage et pointeurs. Ensuite, dans la zone Pointeurs outil dessin, cliquez sur le bouton d'option Standard. Appuyez sur la touche Entrée afin de valider votre choix.

Les outils de peinture sont petits, non salissants, et agréables pour les enfants. Pourquoi ne pas leur apprendre à utiliser les outils Pinceau et Crayon pour créer le sympathique M. Soleil illustré sur la Figure 15.3. Pour le dessiner, suivez les étapes ci-dessous :

1. **Cliquez sur l'icône Nouveau de la barre de raccourcis, choisissez Fichier/Nouveau/Fichier vide ou appuyez sur Ctrl+N. Vous créez une nouvelle zone de travail, votre future toile.**

   Elements affiche une boîte de dialogue demandant de définir la taille de la zone de travail. Saisissez les valeurs adéquates dans les champs Largeur, Hauteur et Résolution, comme nous en avons discuté au Chapitre 4.

2. **Créez une zone de travail d'environ 400 pixels de large sur 400 pixels de haut.**

   Puisque nous travaillons sur un écran et que le dessin n'est pas destiné à une impression professionnelle, définissez une Résolution de 72 à 100 ppp (c'est-à-dire *pixels par pouce*). Dans la liste Mode, choisissez RVB et, dans Contenu de l'arrière-plan, sélectionnez Blanc.

3. **Appuyez sur la touche Entrée.**

   Une nouvelle zone de travail – sorte de toile numérique – apparaît dans la nouvelle fenêtre.

4. **Dans la boîte à outils, cliquez sur l'icône Couleurs de premier plan et d'arrière-plan par défaut, ou appuyez sur la touche D. La couleur de premier plan doit être définie sur le noir (ce que vous obtenez immédiatement en appuyant sur D).**

5. **Sélectionnez l'outil Pinceau.**

   Cliquez sur l'icône du Pinceau ou appuyez une, deux ou trois fois sur la touche B. Oui, je sais, vous utilisez un Pinceau et non pas un "Binceau" mais, que voulez-vous, les raccourcis d'accès aux outils n'ont pas été francisés !

6. **Dessinez un cercle au centre de la zone de travail.**

Que ce soit à la souris ou avec le stylet d'une tablette graphique, dessiner un cercle à main levée n'est pas évident. C'est donc un cercle approximatif qui apparaît.

7. **Peignez des rayons autour du cercle.**

8. **Activez l'outil Crayon.**

Il suffit d'appuyer sur la touche N ou de cliquer sur l'icône de l'outil. Là encore "N" n'évoque pas vraiment l'outil Crayon.

9. **Dessinez le visage du soleil.**

L'outil Crayon permet d'obtenir des segments de droite nets, comme l'illustre la Figure 15.2.

Figure 15.2 :
Le visage
d'un soleil
dessiné avec
l'outil Crayon.

10. **Revenez au Pinceau.**

Appuyez une ou plusieurs fois sur la touche B pour activer cet outil ou, ce qui est plus rapide, sélectionnez-le dans la boîte à outils.

11. **Activez les fonctions d'aérographe du Pinceau.**

Cliquez sur l'icône d'activation des fonctions d'aérographe, dans la barre d'options ; elle évoque le stylet qui projette l'encre sur le papier, surmonté d'un petit bouton de réglage du débit et alimenté en air comprimé par le tuyau en forme de "S".

12. **Changez la couleur de premier plan en sélectionnant une teinte orange.**

Cliquez sur l'icône Définir la couleur de premier plan. Dans le Sélecteur de couleurs qui apparaît, utilisez la barre verticale colorée pour sélectionner une teinte orange. Prélevez-la ensuite dans le vaste nuancier situé à gauche de cette barre. Une autre méthode consiste à saisir directement les valeurs RVB dans les champs adéquats du sélecteur. Saisissez **255** pour R, **150** pour V, et laissez B sur 0. Cliquez sur OK pour quitter le Sélecteur de couleurs et revenir à la zone de travail.

13. **Sans déplacer la souris, placez l'outil dans le soleil et cliquez.**

    Vous constatez qu'en mode Aérographe, le Pinceau diffuse constamment la couleur bien que vous ne déplaciez pas la souris. Cela ne se produit jamais avec les outils Pinceau et Crayon. C'est la seule capacité du mode aérographe ; en mode normal du Pinceau et avec le Crayon, l'outil peint uniquement lorsqu'il est déplacé.

14. **Peignez alors une sorte d'ombrage dans la zone inférieure droite du soleil.**

    La Figure 15.3 donne une idée générale de ce que l'on devrait obtenir. Le mode Aérographe est parfait pour créer de beaux dégradés.

Figure 15.3 : Utilisez le Pinceau en mode Aérographe pour peindre un semblant d'ombre irréaliste sur votre soleil.

C'est suffisant pour aujourd'hui. Enregistrez ce magnifique travail dans le but de l'enrichir plus tard. Si vous le perdez à tout jamais faute d'avoir suivi nos conseils, vous savez désormais qu'il est très facile de créer un tel soleil.

Conseils avisés sur les outils de peinture

Faire glisser un outil de peinture dans la fenêtre d'une image est le moyen le plus commun de dessiner dans Elements, mais ce n'est pas le seul :

✔ Pour tracer une ligne droite, cliquez à un endroit de l'image avec le Pinceau ou le Crayon, maintenez la touche Maj enfoncée et cliquez ailleurs dans l'image. Elements trace une ligne droite entre les deux points.

✔ Pour tracer une ligne droite verticale ou horizontale, cliquez avec le Pinceau ou le Crayon, et maintenez la touche Maj enfoncée. Il suffit alors de tracer la droite sans relâcher la touche du clavier pour obtenir la plus parfaite des lignes droites. Dès que vous relâchez la touche Maj, l'outil permet de nouveau de dessiner à main levée.

✔ Appuyez sur la touche Alt pour accéder à la Pipette, puis cliquez dans la zone de travail pour prélever une couleur de l'image. Elle apparaît dans l'indicateur de la couleur de premier plan.

Choisir votre forme

Si les deux précédentes sections traitaient de l'utilisation des trois outils de peinture, il faut savoir qu'un outil peut se paramétrer pour obtenir des effets plus ou moins subtils, adaptés à votre puissance créatrice.

Un changement incontournable concerne la taille de la forme de l'outil. Un peintre dispose d'une grande quantité de pinceaux, de brosses, pour détailler des parties de son œuvre ou appliquer de grosses couches de couleur. Il en va de même dans Photoshop Elements. Une forme d'outil a une épaisseur qu'il faut apprendre à utiliser.

Changer la taille d'une forme

Pour passer d'une forme à une autre, activez l'outil Pinceau et cliquez sur la flèche située à droite de l'aperçu de la forme localisée dans la barre d'options. Elements affiche la palette Formes, reproduite sur la Figure 15.4. La valeur active est Formes par défaut. Vous disposez ici d'un total de soixante-cinq formes.

Le nombre à gauche du trait de pinceau indique le diamètre de la forme, en pixels. Pour le modifier, cliquez sur une icône de trait de

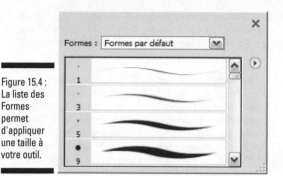

Figure 15.4 : La liste des Formes permet d'appliquer une taille à votre outil.

pinceau. Remarquez que les six premières formes ont des bords plutôt nets, alors que les douze suivantes ont des bords plus flous. On trouve ensuite neuf aérographes prédéfinis, qui ont les bords les plus flous de tous (quand un aérographe prédéfini est sélectionné, l'icône Aérographe est automatiquement sélectionnée dans la barre d'options). Lorsque vous commencez à utiliser la forme, la palette Formes se referme automatiquement pour reprendre sa place. Pour fermer la palette, vous pouvez également appuyer sur Entrée, Echap, ou encore cliquer sur le bouton de fermeture en forme de X.

La palette Formes est affichable de six manières : trait de forme (affichage par défaut), grandes et petites vignettes, texte seulement, ou grande ou petite liste (combinaison de texte et de vignettes). Pour sélectionner une de ces options d'affichage, déployez le menu local de la palette Formes en cliquant sur le cercle avec une flèche pointant vers la droite, dans l'angle supérieur droit de la palette.

En cliquant sur l'image avec le bouton droit de la souris, vous accédez à un menu contextuel où vous pouvez choisir la taille de la forme.

Le Crayon et les outils d'édition, comme les outils Doigt et Éponge, donnent tous accès à la palette Formes. Gardez cependant à l'esprit que l'outil Crayon dessine une ligne dure, dentelée, quelle que soit la forme sélectionnée. Même les aérographes prédéfinis produisent des lignes dentelées lorsqu'ils sont exploités avec le Crayon.

Exploration des autres ensembles de formes

Il existe treize jeux de formes dans Photoshop Elements. Tous ont leur utilité, mais le jeu Effets spéciaux est incontestablement le plus spectaculaire. Pour le découvrir, déroulez la liste Formes en haut de la palette Formes et choisissez Effets spéciaux. Cliquez sur la première forme (Azalée), définissez une couleur de premier plan claire et une couleur d'arrière-plan plus sombre, puis faites glisser le Pinceau à travers l'image.

Le Pinceau répand une variété de fleurs de différentes couleurs, dimensions et formes. Nous verrons tout à l'heure comment personnaliser ces formes. Pour l'instant, passez quelques minutes à les expérimenter et peindre des scènes comme celles de la Figure 15.5. Nous vous accordons que les papillons ne volent habituellement pas de nuit en compagnie de flocons de neige, mais c'est ce que l'on appelle une "licence artistique". L'essentiel est d'avoir compris le principe de cet outil.

Figure 15.5 : Cette scène pastorale a été peinte simplement en cliquant-glissant et en cliquant avec des formes prédéfinies des ensembles Formes par défaut, Formes d'outils variées et Effets spéciaux.

Créer vos propres formes

Trois cent vingt-huit formes prédéfinies figurent parmi les treize jeux de formes fournis avec Elements. En dépit de leur nombre, elles ne sont pas forcément adaptées à votre travail. Par exemple, telle forme s'avérera trop épaisse et telle autre trop fine. Dans ce cas, la seule solution consiste à créer la ou les formes adaptées à vos besoins.

Il est très facile de modifier l'épaisseur d'une forme à l'aide du contrôle Épaisseur, à droite de la palette Formes dans la barre d'options. Vous pouvez placer le curseur sur le mot Épaisseur. Il prend la forme d'une main ornée d'une double flèche. Cliquez et faites-le glisser vers la gauche pour diminuer la valeur, et vers la droite pour l'augmenter.

Pour apporter d'autres modifications, il faut que l'outil Pinceau soit actif. Cliquez sur Autres options à droite de la barre d'options. Elements affiche une boîte de dialogue représentée sur la Figure 15.6.

Voici les paramètres que vous pouvez y modifier :

- ✔ Pour comprendre le paramètre Pas, affichez l'ensemble Formes par défaut et sélectionnez la sixième forme, Rond net 19 pixels. Tirez-la dans une image. Bien que vous ne vous en soyez peut-être pas aperçu avec une forme de ce type, Elements ne peint pas une ligne continue lorsque vous dessinez dans une image. Il dépose en fait une succession de formes. Celles de la forme de base que vous venez d'employer sont des petits cercles. Ils sont cependant si serrés qu'ils produisent une épaisse ligne continue. Ouvrez le menu Autres options et augmentez la valeur Pas à 1 000 %. Vous constatez que les cercles sont maintenant espacés ; d'ailleurs, l'icône de trait de forme dans la barre d'options vient de changer pour refléter le nouveau réglage. En général, vous laisserez la valeur de Pas telle quelle. En revanche, pour des formes comme Azalée, dans l'ensemble de formes Effets spéciaux, vous devrez contrôler plus exactement l'espacement entre les fleurs ou autres formes. C'est à cela que sert le contrôle Pas.

  Les modifications apportées à la forme Rond net 19 pixels ne sont pas définitives. Pour la réutiliser dans son état d'origine, sélectionnez-la de nouveau dans la palette Formes. En revanche, pour sauvegarder une forme modifiée, reportez-vous à la prochaine section "Enregistrer les formes".

- ✔ La glissière Estomper produit un trait de pinceau qui s'estompe progressivement. L'emploi d'Estomper est un peu particulier. La valeur générale par défaut 0 signifie que le trait de pinceau ne s'estompe pas ; tant que vous passez le Pinceau, la peinture est appliquée. La valeur suivante immédiate 1 produit un estompage instantané. Avec une forme ronde standard, vous obtenez juste un cercle. Plus vous poussez le curseur vers la droite, plus le fondu est long. La valeur maximale est 9999. Il faudrait alors peindre en continu pendant près d'une minute avant que le trait soit entièrement estompé.

✔ La glissière Variation de teinte fait fluctuer la couleur du trait de pinceau entre les couleurs de premier plan et d'arrière-plan. La forme Azalée de l'ensemble de formes Effets spéciaux montre parfaitement cet effet.

✔ La glissière Dureté représente les facultés d'atténuation de la taille de la forme. Avec une valeur de 100 %, la forme est nette. Plus vous diminuez ce pourcentage, plus les contours de la brosse sont estompés. La valeur Dureté n'est pas disponible pour toutes les formes.

✔ La glissière Diffusion règle l'écartement entre le pointeur et les formes produites. Pour les formes rondes standard, il est préférable de laisser cette valeur à 0 %. Pour des formes comme Azalée, une Diffusion relativement élevée est recommandée.

✔ Avant de parler de l'option Angle, vous devez comprendre le fonctionnement du paramètre Arrondi. Il permet d'obtenir une forme ovale au lieu de ronde. Une valeur de 100 % donne une forme parfaitement circulaire. Toute valeur inférieure aplatit la forme.

✔ Pour obtenir une forme plus haute que large, il suffit de changer la valeur du paramètre Angle. Sachez que 90 degrés indique un quart de tour, 180 degrés un demi-tour, et des valeurs négatives produisent des rotations dans le sens inverse des aiguilles d'une montre.

✔ Il est plus simple d'utiliser le diagramme présent dans la partie inférieure gauche de la boîte de dialogue pour modifier l'Angle et l'Arrondi. Tirez les poignées pour donner à la forme un aspect ovale, et faites pointer la flèche dans une autre direction pour changer l'angle de la forme. Les légendes de la Figure 15.6 expliquent comment procéder.

✔ L'option Conserver ces paramètres pour toutes les formes, dans le coin inférieur gauche, permet d'appliquer ce réglage temporaire à toutes les autres formes utilisées. Pour employer les formes dans leur état d'origine, décochez cette option.

Si vous utilisez une tablette graphique, les effets du stylet peuvent être configurés via le menu local Options de la table de la barre d'options. Vous agissez ainsi sur la Taille, l'Opacité, la Variation de teinte, la Diffusion et l'Arrondi.

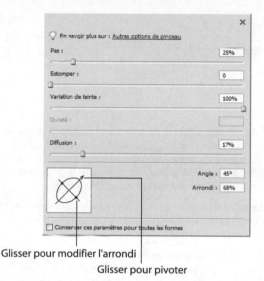

Figure 15.6 :
Les
paramètres
d'une forme.

Glisser pour modifier l'arrondi

Glisser pour pivoter

Enregistrer les formes

Après avoir peaufiné les réglages de votre forme, la première étape
pour l'enregistrer est d'accéder au menu déroulant de la palette
Formes et de choisir Enregistrer la forme. Donnez à la forme un nom
descriptif. Ceci fait, cliquez sur OK. Dès lors, en bas de l'ensemble de
formes actif, vous trouverez votre forme personnalisée.

Une fois la forme ajoutée, vous devez de nouveau ouvrir le menu local
de la palette Formes et cliquer sur Enregistrer les formes. Si vous ne
respectez pas cette procédure, la forme enregistrée sera perdue
lorsque vous fermerez Photoshop Elements. Donnez un nom au
nouveau jeu de formes. Pour utiliser ultérieurement un jeu de formes
contenant des formes enregistrées, cliquez sur le menu local de la
palette Formes, puis sur Charger les formes. Dans la boîte de dialogue,
sélectionnez le jeu de formes à charger et cliquez sur le bouton du
même nom.

Les autres options de peinture

La Figure 15.7 montre la barre d'options lorsque le Pinceau est actif.
Nous avons déjà présenté certaines commandes. Voici les autres :

Figure 15.7 :
La barre
d'options de
l'outil
Pinceau.

✔ La première icône, à gauche, identifie l'outil utilisé, permettant de connaître l'outil actif. Quand vous cliquez sur l'icône, vous accédez à un menu local qui propose deux options : Réinitialiser cet outil et Réinitialiser tous les outils. Ces options rétablissent les paramètres par défaut du ou des outils.

✔ La paire d'icônes suivante sert à permuter entre le Pinceau et la Forme Impressionniste, car ces deux outils partagent la même palette dans la boîte à outils.

✔ Disponible avec les outils Crayon et Pinceau, l'option Opacité contrôle la transparence de la couleur de premier plan. A 100 %, la couleur s'applique sans aucune transparence. Les zones sur lesquelles vous passez l'outil sont totalement recouvertes par la peinture. Plus le pourcentage diminue, plus la couleur appliquée est transparente.

✔ Si vous ne comprenez pas très bien le fonctionnement du paramètre Opacité, jetez un œil sur la Figure 15.8. Quatre coups de pinceau ont été donnés avec des valeurs d'opacité de 100 % et de 40 %, à l'aide de formes standard et progressives.

✔ La valeur Opacité des outils est réglable par pas de 10 %, en appuyant sur une touche du pavé numérique. Si vous appuyez sur 9, vous obtenez une valeur de Pression ou d'Opacité de 90 %. Avec la touche 8, vous obtenez 80 %. En appuyant rapidement sur deux touches, vous affinez la valeur du paramètre. Par exemple, appuyer sur 7 puis 2, produit une valeur de Pression ou d'Opacité de 72 %.

✔ L'option Inversion auto n'apparaît que si l'outil Crayon est sélectionné. Elle sert à dessiner avec la couleur d'arrière-plan chaque fois que vous passez l'outil là où la couleur de premier plan a été appliquée sur l'image. Cela est très utile quand vous désirez faire de petites retouches avec une forme de 1 pixel.

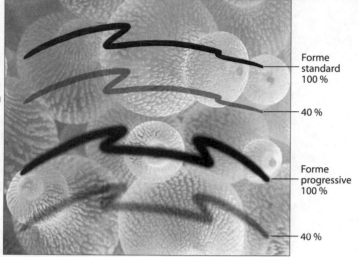

Forme
standard
100 %

40 %

Forme
progressive
100 %

40 %

Figure 15.8 :
Voici ce qui
se passe
quand vous
peignez sur
ces
anémones de
mer avec
différentes
valeurs
d'opacité.

Expérimenter les modes de peinture

Vous avez appris au Chapitre 14 que les modes de fusion combinent
les couleurs des pixels dans les calques. Les modes de peinture
fonctionnent de la même façon, sauf qu'ils combinent la couleur de
premier plan avec ce qui se trouve au-dessous.

Par exemple, revenez à l'image du soleil de la Figure 15.3. Supposons
que vous vouliez colorier le soleil avec du jaune et le ciel avec du bleu.
Le problème est que de telles colorisations risquent d'introduire du
bleu dans le jaune et du jaune dans le bleu. Vous ne résoudrez pas le
problème en abaissant la valeur de l'Opacité. Les couleurs seraient
seulement délavées et vous risqueriez de faire disparaître les détails
du soleil.

La solution consiste à sélectionner un mode de peinture. Choisissez
ensuite le mode de fusion Produit. Vous pourrez ainsi peindre le soleil
et le ciel sans couvrir les rayons et le visage. Le mode Produit fonce en
effet les couleurs lorsque vous passez dessus. L'effet obtenu ressemble à de l'aquarelle.

Voici quelques informations sur les autres modes de peinture utilisés
avec les outils de peinture :

✔ Le mode Superposition est l'opposé de Produit, c'est-à-dire qu'il mélange les pixels en les éclaircissant. Par conséquent, il ne se passe rien quand vous peignez sur des zones blanches.

✔ Le mode Incrustation assombrit les couleurs sombres et éclaircit les couleurs claires. Cela crée un très fort contraste.

✔ Le mode Différence crée un effet de négatif (inversion) en mélangeant les couleurs et en définissant leur opposé.

✔ Vous pouvez également expérimenter Exclusion. Il convertit tous les noirs en blancs, tous les blancs en noirs, et toutes les couleurs moyennes en gris.

✔ Utilisez le mode de fusion Couleur pour coloriser des images en niveaux de gris ou pour changer la couleur des images en mode RVB.

✔ Les modes Densité couleur - et Densité couleur + sont décrits au Chapitre 12. Ils augmentent et diminuent la densité des couleurs sur lesquelles vous passez les outils de peinture. Densité couleur + accentue l'intensité des couleurs, tandis que Densité couleur - la diminue.

✔ Pour peindre sans effets particuliers, sélectionnez le mode de fusion Normal.

"Peindre" avec l'outil Forme Impressionniste

La Forme Impressionniste permet de peindre dans le style impressionniste. Ce courant ne se réduit certes pas à de seuls choix technique. Il est l'aboutissement d'un cheminement esthétique. Mais Photoshop Elements permet de l'évoquer de manière plaisante.

Ouvrez une image. Activez l'outil Forme Impressionniste et commencez à passer l'outil sur votre image. Vous comprendrez rapidement de quoi il retourne.

Les performances de l'outil Forme Impressionniste dépendent des paramètres de la barre d'options que montre la Figure 15.9. Voici une description des options :

✔ **Mode :** Assigne un mode de peinture à l'outil. Consultez la section "Expérimenter les modes de peinture" plus haut dans ce chapitre.

✔ **Opacité :** Plus cette valeur est faible, plus les coups de pinceau sont transparents. Pour définir rapidement une valeur d'opacité, appuyez sur une des touches du pavé numérique.

Figure 15.9 :
La barre
d'options de
l'outil Forme.

Le menu Autres options contient les paramètres supplémentaires suivants :

🖛 **Style :** La Forme Impressionniste peint aléatoirement. Vous pouvez décider de la forme de la spirale en choisissant une option dans la liste Style. Lorsque vous combinez les styles avec diverses tailles de brosses, vous obtenez des effets impressionnistes étonnants.

🖛 **Zone :** Cette valeur définit la zone couverte par un coup de Forme Impressionniste. Plus la valeur est élevée, plus les détails de l'image sont respectés.

🖛 **Tolérance :** Cette valeur accorde une plus ou moins grande tolérance aux zones de l'image sur lesquelles passe l'outil Forme Impressionniste.

La puissance de la Gomme

Aucune boîte à outils de dessinateur ne serait complète sans une bonne gomme. Elements ne faillit pas à la tradition. L'outil Gomme propose la Gomme, la Gomme d'arrière-plan et la Gomme magique.

 Pour passer d'une gomme à l'autre, appuyez répétitivement sur la touche E.

Travailler avec l'outil Gomme

Situé sous les outils Tampon, l'outil Gomme permet d'effacer de deux manières :

🖛 Qaund vous passez la Gomme sur une image contenant uniquement un calque d'arrière-plan, vous effacez en peignant avec la couleur d'arrière-plan. Par défaut, cette couleur est du blanc. Techniquement, cela ressemble à un effacement, mais en réalité vous peignez avec du blanc.

✔ Si l'image comporte plusieurs calques (que nous traitons au Chapitre 10), la Gomme fonctionne différemment et s'avère bien plus utile. Quand vous passez la Gomme sur le calque Arrière-plan, elle ne change pas ses habitudes : elle efface en utilisant la couleur d'arrière-plan (du blanc par défaut). Mais, si vous la passez sur un calque, les pixels deviennent transparents, révélant ceux du ou des calques inférieurs (cela présume que l'option Verrouiller les pixels transparents de la palette Calques n'est pas activée. Si c'est le cas, la Gomme efface avec la couleur d'arrière-plan).

L'outil Gomme peut être utilisé avec trois instruments différents que vous trouverez dans la liste Mode de la barre d'options. Deux de ces gommes sont des outils de peinture – Forme et Crayon – et fonctionnent comme les outils traditionnels auxquels ils se rapportent. Cela signifie que vous pouvez modifier la taille de la forme dans la palette Formes et ajuster le paramètre d'opacité pour donner plus ou moins de puissance à la Gomme.

La troisième option, Carré, transforme la Gomme en carré, avec des angles droits et une taille fixe. Les options de la barre d'options sont alors estompées. Le mode Carré est utile pour supprimer complètement des zones d'une image, mais vous ne l'utiliserez pas souvent.

Travailler avec l'outil Gomme magique

La Gomme magique est la plus simple à utiliser mais aussi la moins performante. Si vous connaissez le fonctionnement de l'outil Baguette magique (voir le Chapitre 9), la Gomme magique s'utilise de la même manière. La grande différence est que la Baguette magique sélectionne tandis que la Gomme magique efface.

Quand vous cliquez sur un pixel avec la Gomme magique, Elements identifie une plage de pixels similaires, comme la Baguette magique. Mais, au lieu de créer une sélection, la Gomme magique les efface, comme l'illustre la Figure 15.10. N'oubliez jamais que dans Elements la transparence ne peut exister que sur un calque. Il n'y a pas de transparence possible sur une image sans calque, c'est-à-dire composée uniquement du calque Arrière-plan. La transparence d'un calque est identifiée par le damier représenté sur la seconde image de la Figure 15.10.

Vous observez sur la Figure 15.10 que la Gomme magique n'a pas effacé tout le ciel. Cela tient à la valeur du paramètre Tolérance de la barre d'options de l'outil. Ce paramètre doit être réglé comme celui de la Baguette magique. Il détermine le nombre de pixels entrant dans la

Figure 15.10 :
Pour
supprimer
des couleurs
homogènes,
comme ce
ciel au-
dessus du
lion, cliquez
dedans avec
l'outil Gomme
magique.

plage des couleurs du pixel sur lequel vous cliquez. Plus la valeur est élevée, plus la tolérance est large, incitant Elements à considérer que les pixels voisins doivent être assimilés à celui que vous désirez effacer. Par conséquent, pour effacer davantage de ciel sur la Figure 15.10, augmentez la valeur de Tolérance, puis cliquez de nouveau.

(le fait de modifier la valeur de Tolérance affecte le nouveau clic, et pas les zones transparentes existantes).

Les autres options de la barre d'options sont :

- **Lissé :** Pour créer une frange douce autour de la zone transparente, activez cette option. Si vous préférez des bords nets, décochez cette option.

- **Contiguë :** Avec cette option, la Gomme magique ne supprime que les couleurs contiguës, c'est-à-dire les couleurs similaires qui se touchent. Si vous préférez éliminer tous les pixels d'une certaine couleur sans vous soucier de leur position dans l'image, décochez l'option Contiguë.

- **Utiliser toutes les couches :** Quand cette option est activée, Elements considère les calques comme invisibles. Ainsi, la Gomme magique supprime tous les pixels de tous les calques, selon la couleur sur laquelle vous cliquez.

- **Opacité :** Diminuez la valeur de ce paramètre pour rendre les pixels supprimés translucides plutôt que transparents. Plus la valeur est faible, plus vous manipulez la Gomme magique avec subtilité.

Pour en savoir plus sur ces options, reportez-vous à la section du Chapitre 9 qui se consacre à la Baguette magique.

Travailler avec la Gomme d'arrière-plan

La Gomme magique est facile à utiliser, mais vous pouvez tout aussi bien recourir à la Baguette magique pour sélectionner une partie de l'image et appuyer ensuite sur la touche Retour arrière pour la supprimer.

La plus utile de toutes les gommes est la Gomme d'arrière-plan. Comme le montre la Figure 15.11, elle supprime les pixels d'arrière-plan sur lesquels elle a passé. L'outil est suffisamment intelligent pour effacer les pixels d'arrière-plan et conserver les pixels de premier plan. Son curseur est constitué d'un cercle et d'une croix. La croix passe sur les pixels à effacer et le cercle englobe les pixels de même couleur devant être supprimés. Il devient alors facile de supprimer des couleurs dans des images particulièrement détaillées comme le démontre la Figure 15.12.

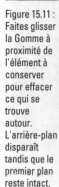

Figure 15.11 :
Faites glisser
la Gomme à
proximité de
l'élément à
conserver
pour effacer
ce qui se
trouve
autour.
L'arrière-plan
disparaît
tandis que le
premier plan
reste intact.

Pour modifier la taille de la Gomme d'arrière-plan, cliquez sur la flèche située à droite de l'épaisseur de la forme dans la barre d'options. Dans le menu local, définissez notamment le diamètre et la dureté. Vous pouvez également accéder à ce menu en cliquant sur l'image avec le bouton droit de la souris.

Vous pouvez aussi modifier les performances de la Gomme en modifiant les paramètres de la barre d'options. Les voici :

✔ **Limites :** Par défaut, la Gomme d'arrière-plan supprime les couleurs qui se trouvent dans le curseur tant qu'elles sont contiguës à la couleur située sous la croix. Pour supprimer toutes les couleurs identiques aux pixels sur lesquels passe la croix, choisissez Discontiguës dans la liste Limites.

✔ **Tolérance :** Augmentez cette valeur pour effacer plus de pixels en même temps. Diminuez cette valeur pour un effacement plus précis et une préservation de détails aussi ténus que des cheveux.

Figure 15.12 :
Maintenez la
croix sur
l'arrière-plan
à effacer (en
haut). Si, par
inadvertance,
vous la
placez sur le
premier plan,
vous
l'effacez (en
bas).

Chapitre 16

Le masque numérique

. . . .

Dans ce chapitre :

▶ Peindre et modifier l'intérieur d'une sélection.

▶ Utiliser l'outil Pot de peinture.

▶ Utiliser la commande Remplir.

▶ Appliquer différents types de dégradés.

▶ Créer un contour.

. . . .

Dans ce chapitre, vous apprendrez toutes les subtilités de la peinture, du remplissage et du traçage des sélections. Tandis qu'au Chapitre 9 nous expliquions comment créer et manipuler les contours des sélections, nous montrerons ici ce qu'il est possible d'en faire.

Peindre dans la sélection

Quand une partie de l'image est sélectionnée, ce qui se trouve hors de la sélection est protégé contre toute intervention. Vous pouvez alors utiliser n'importe quel outil de peinture ou de retouche pour modifier les éléments picturaux qui se trouvent dans la sélection, c'est-à-dire à l'intérieur de son contour.

Ce chapitre s'appuie sur la photo d'un gros récipient qui n'est pas inconnu des cuisinières. On y stocke des aliments baignant dans une préparation qui les conserve au fil des mois, à base d'huile, de vinaigre, et je ne sais quoi encore car je n'ai pas lu *La cuisine pour les Nuls*... et pourtant cet ouvrage est paru aux éditions First. Grâce aux sélections, nous rendrons cet objet bien plus attrayant qu'il ne l'est. Pour cela, il faut l'isoler du reste de l'image, c'est-à-dire le placer au-dessus de l'arrière-plan que nous ne souhaitons pas altérer avec nos diverses modifications. Voici comment procéder :

1. **Sélectionnez le bocal.**

   C'est la seule étape ardue. Commencez par sélectionner la forme du bocal avec l'outil Ellipse de sélection. Comme il n'est pas facile de tracer une ellipse au centre du bocal, faites de votre mieux puis utilisez un autre outil de sélection pour parfaire la forme. Repositionnez le contour de sélection elliptique en le glissant et déplaçant, tout en maintenant le bouton gauche de la souris enfoncé. Maintenant que le corps du bocal est sélectionné, sélectionnez le rebord avec l'outil Lasso. Pour ne pas perdre la première sélection, maintenez la touche Maj enfoncée tout en utilisant le Lasso.

2. **Faites toutes les modifications nécessaires.**

   Dans ce cas, il est essentiel d'estomper les contours de la sélection. Pour cela, choisissez Sélection/Contour progressif, comme expliqué au Chapitre 9.

   Vous serez peut-être tenté d'appuyer sur Ctrl+H pour masquer la sélection après l'avoir créée. Dans ce cas, n'oubliez pas que la sélection sera toujours active. Vous ne ferez que dissimuler temporairement son contour. Masquer un contour permet parfois de travailler plus facilement dans une sélection.

3. **Peignez et modifiez.**

   Utilisez n'importe quel outil. Vous pouvez peindre avec le Pinceau ou le Crayon. Procédez à des retouches avec l'outil Doigt, clonez des éléments avec l'outil Tampon de duplication, etc. Vous êtes sûr que vos manipulations n'altéreront que le contenu de la sélection, laissant intact tout ce qui se trouve à l'extérieur.

Sur la Figure 16.1, le bocal a été peint avec un seul outil, le Pinceau, avec une seule forme et deux couleurs, le noir et le blanc. Nous obtenons une sorte de récipient marbré. En regardant de plus près, vous constatez qu'aucune trace de peinture ne déborde à l'extérieur.

 Les fonctions de sélection sont essentielles. Presque tous les travaux réalisés dans Photoshop Elements nécessitent d'isoler une partie de l'image avant d'appliquer un outil de peinture ou de retouche.

Verser de la peinture avec un pot

Elements permet de remplir une sélection avec la couleur de premier plan, celle d'arrière-plan, un motif ou un dégradé. Mais avant de

Figure 16.1 :
Nous avons
peint le bocal
grâce à une
sélection et à
l'outil
Pinceau.

procéder à ces remplissages aussi étranges qu'exotiques, voyons comment fonctionne l'outil Pot de peinture.

Sur la Figure 16.2, par exemple, l'outil Pot de peinture a été utilisé sur les brocolis. Comme la couleur de premier plan était blanche, les brocolis sont remplacés par du blanc. On dirait du chou-fleur.

Pour ajuster les performances de l'outil Pot de peinture, examinez sa barre d'options, visible sur la Figure 16.2. À l'instar de l'outil Baguette magique, le Pot de peinture est doté d'un paramètre Tolérance qui détermine la plage de pixels affectés par l'outil. La seule différence avec la Baguette magique est que l'outil Pot de peinture applique une couleur au lieu de sélectionner les pixels. Pour une application plus douce de la peinture, activez l'option Lissé. (Sur la Figure 16.2, la Tolérance a été fixée à 32, et le paramètre Lissé est actif par défaut.)

Avec cet outil, il est très difficile de trouver la bonne tolérance pour remplir exactement les pixels voulus. Il faudra procéder à plusieurs essais et ne pas hésiter à cliquer sur le bouton Annuler, dans la barre des raccourcis (ou appuyer sur Ctrl+Z) pour supprimer un remplissage hasardeux puis recommencer. Bien que le Pot de peinture convienne au remplissage de zones sélectionnées, les résultats obtenus, lorsque vous utilisez cet outil pour remplir une zone continue de couleur, vont de corrects à passables. Il est préférable d'employer

Figure 16.2 :
Le Pot de
peinture
remplit une
zone
continue
avec une
couleur
uniforme.

d'abord les outils de sélection, puis de cliquer avec le Pot de peinture ; vous disposez de la sorte de plus de possibilités.

Le Pot de peinture peut être activé en appuyant sur K.

Appliquer une couleur dans une sélection

Bien que le remplissage de contours de sélection soit ce que le Pot de peinture fait le mieux, ce n'est pas forcément le moyen le plus efficace pour remplir un contour de sélection. Par exemple :

- Pour remplir une sélection avec la couleur de premier plan, appuyez sur Alt+Retour arrière.

- Pour remplir une sélection avec la couleur d'arrière-plan, appuyez sur Ctrl+Retour arrière.

- Choisissez Édition/Remplir la sélection pour ouvrir la boîte de dialogue Calque de remplissage qui permet de remplir une sélection avec une couleur translucide ou un motif.

- Tirez l'outil Dégradé pour créer un dégradé de couleurs entre deux teintes ou davantage.

Deux de ces options – Édition/Remplir la sélection et l'outil Dégradé –
exigent quelques explications complémentaires. Nous y reviendrons
plus loin dans ce chapitre.

Je vous demande de remplir !

Choisissez Édition/Remplir la sélection pour ouvrir la boîte de
dialogue de la Figure 16.3. Les diverses listes de cette boîte de
dialogue permettent de spécifier une couleur de remplissage, un motif,
un mode de fusion et une opacité. Nous verrons tout cela en détail
dans cette section. Notez que ce remplissage agit non seulement dans
une sélection mais également sur la totalité d'un calque. S'il n'y a pas
de sélection active et que vous appliquez la commande Remplir la
sélection, la totalité du calque actif sera remplie.

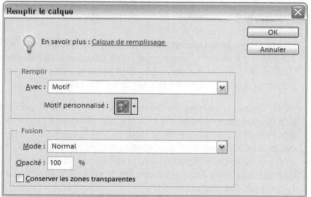

Figure 16.3 :
Spécifiez
comment
remplir une
sélection ou
un calque
avec toutes
les options
de la boîte de
dialogue
Calque de
remplissage.

Vous pouvez également afficher la boîte de dialogue en appuyant sur
Maj+Retour arrière.

Définir les options

La partie la plus importante de la boîte de dialogue Calque de remplissage est la liste Avec. Vous y sélectionnez la nature du remplissage. En
voici les options :

- ✔ Couleur premier plan remplit la sélection avec la couleur de
  premier plan définie dans la boîte à outils d'Elements. De son

côté, Couleur d'arrière-plan remplit la sélection avec la couleur d'arrière-plan.

- Motif remplit avec un motif qui se répète comme une mosaïque. Vous pouvez créer un motif en définissant une zone de sélection rectangulaire, puis en choisissant Édition/Définir le motif d'après la sélection. Si vous ne procédez pas ainsi, Elements crée le motif à partir de la zone de travail intégrale. Vous accédez aux motifs en cliquant sur la flèche de Motif personnalisé. S'ouvre alors un menu local où vous sélectionnez le motif à utiliser.

- Les trois dernières options – Noir, 50 % gris et Blanc – remplissent respectivement avec du noir, un gris moyen et du blanc. L'avantage est que vous n'avez pas à vous soucier des teintes affichées dans les nuanciers de la boîte à outils d'Elements.

Les dégradés

L'outil Dégradé permet de remplir une sélection avec plusieurs couleurs qui passent progressivement de l'une à l'autre par de délicats fondus enchaînés. Par défaut, le dégradé s'effectue entre deux couleurs, celle de premier plan et celle d'arrière-plan.

Mais, Elements permet d'aller bien plus loin. Il est possible de créer des dégradés personnalisés comportant plusieurs couleurs ainsi que des variations d'opacité et de transparence. Elements propose cinq types de dégradés : Linéaire, Radial, Incliné, Réfléchi et Losange. Les options de la barre d'options de cet outil paramètrent les effets du dégradé appliqué. On y retrouve les modes de fusion, l'opacité et l'inversion des couleurs.

Découvrir l'outil Dégradé

Les étapes suivantes sont une introduction à l'outil Dégradé :

1. **Sélectionnez une partie de votre image.**

   Sur la Figure 16.4, nous avons de nouveau sélectionné le bocal.

   Si vous ne sélectionnez pas une partie de l'image avant d'utiliser l'outil Dégradé, Elements remplit toute l'image ou, si vous travaillez sur un calque, comme cela est expliqué au Chapitre 10, la totalité du calque.

2. **Sélectionnez l'outil Dégradé.**

Sélecteur de dégradé

Figure 16.4 :
Les légumes
à l'intérieur
du bocal ont
été
remplacés
par un
dégradé
allant du noir
au blanc.

Faites-le rapidement en appuyant sur la touche G.

3. **Dans la barre d'options, sélectionnez le type de dégradé à appliquer.**

4. **Si nécessaire, sélectionnez l'option Premier plan -> arrière-plan dans la liste des dégradés de la palette des dégradés de la barre d'options.**

   Vous définissez ainsi un dégradé qui commence avec la couleur de premier plan et se termine par la couleur d'arrière-plan.

5. **Définissez les couleurs de premier plan et d'arrière-plan.**

   Vous pouvez utiliser le noir et le blanc ou sélectionner de nouvelles couleurs avec l'outil Pipette du Sélecteur de couleurs. Sur la Figure 16.4, les couleurs sont le blanc et le noir.

6. **Cliquez au point où doit commencer la couleur de premier plan puis tirez dans la direction du dégradé.**

   Sur la Figure 16.4, le dégradé a été tiré depuis la base du bocal jusqu'à la base du col, c'est-à-dire la partie supérieure du contour de sélection.

Notez qu'il n'est pas nécessaire de tirer le dégradé sur la totalité de la sélection. Des effets particuliers sont obtenus en procédant ainsi avec un dégradé linéaire :

- Le tirer sur une courte distance au milieu de la sélection produit une vaste plage de la couleur de premier plan, suivie d'un dégradé étroit qui s'achève par une vaste plage de la couleur d'arrière-plan (des variantes sont évidemment possibles selon le type de dégradé et le nombre de couleurs).

- Tirer le dégradé en commençant avant la sélection et le terminant après n'applique qu'une partie de la plage dégradée. Là encore, des variantes sont possible, comme commencer à l'extérieur du dégradé et finir dedans, ou l'inverse.

7. **Relâchez le pointeur au point où la couleur d'arrière-plan doit apparaître à sa pleine densité.**

Dans notre exemple, il s'agit du haut du bocal. Il en résulte un dégradé vertical s'étendant du blanc au noir.

Modifier la direction du dégradé

Vous pouvez modifier les performances de l'outil Dégradé avec les paramètres de la barre d'options. (Reportez-vous à la Figure 16.4.)

Cette fois encore, nous recommandons d'ignorer l'opacité et les modes de fusion. Pour mélanger un dégradé avec des couleurs existantes dans une sélection, créez le dégradé sur un calque et définissez l'opacité et le mode de fusion dans la palette des calques, comme cela est expliqué au Chapitre 14.

Choisir un des cinq outils de dégradé

Elements propose les cinq dégradés que montre la Figure 16.5 :

- **Linéaire :** Crée un dégradé où les couleurs se mélangent en ligne droite.

- **Radial :** Les couleurs se mélangent en cercles concentriques, du centre vers l'extérieur.

Note : Dans les exemples de la Figure 16.5, la couleur de premier plan est noire et la couleur d'arrière-plan est blanche. Avec le dégradé radial, nous vous suggérons de définir une couleur

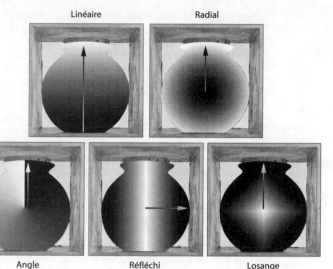

Linéaire · Radial · Angle · Réfléchi · Losange

Figure 16.5 :
Le bocal
rempli avec
cinq types de
dégradés.
Les flèches
indiquent la
direction
dans laquelle
la souris a
été déplacée.

claire comme couleur de premier plan pour créer un effet de halo. Si la couleur de premier plan est plus sombre que la couleur d'arrière-plan, le résultat donne l'impression d'une rupture dans le dégradé.

✓ **Incliné :** Dégradé conique avec application des couleurs dans le sens inverse des aiguilles d'une montre.

✓ **Réfléchi :** Le dégradé s'étend d'un bord à l'autre de la sélection, produisant une sorte de dégradé linéaire avec un effet de miroir.

✓ **Losange :** Comme le dégradé radial, cet outil produit des formes concentriques, en l'occurrence des losanges ou des carrés selon l'orientation.

Les options des dégradés

La barre d'options contient trois cases : Inverser, Simuler et Transparence.

✓ **Inverser :** Quand cette case est cochée, le dégradé commence par la couleur d'arrière-plan et se termine par celle de premier plan. Cette option est utile pour créer des dégradés radiaux sans toucher aux couleurs par défaut.

✔ **Simuler :** L'option Simuler corrige un phénomène appelé "effet de bande" : au lieu d'être parfaitement progressif, le dégradé est divisé en bandes successives de même densité, nettement séparées les unes des autres. Cocher la case Simuler demande à Elements de recalculer le dégradé, quitte à introduire des pixels supplémentaires aux limites des bandes qui, par confusion, donneront l'impression que le dégradé est bien progressif.

✔ **Transparence :** L'option Transparence est plus complexe. Les dégradés peuvent contenir des zones qui sont en tout ou partie transparentes. En d'autres termes, le dégradé part d'une couleur unie et se termine par une couleur transparente. Lorsque cette option est désactivée, le dégradé utilise des couleurs opaques, ignorant les informations de transparence.

Sélectionner vos couleurs

La palette des dégradés permet de sélectionner des types de dégradés prédéfinis. En voici une description :

✔ **Premier plan -> arrière-plan :** Cette option est sélectionnée par défaut. Elle veut bien dire ce qu'elle veut dire. Elle opère un mélange entre les couleurs de premier et d'arrière-plan, comme nous le voyons sur la Figure 16.5.

✔ **Premier plan - Transparent :** Quand vous sélectionnez cette option, le dégradé atténue peu à peu la couleur de premier plan jusqu'à ce qu'elle soit devenue transparente, laissant peu à peu transparaître les pixels sous-jacents. L'exemple de la Figure 16.6 illustre cet effet.

Linéaire   Radial

Figure 16.6 :
Voici le bocal
rempli avec
un dégradé
radial et un
dégradé
linéaire, avec
le type de
dégradé
Premier plan
- transparent.

Premier plan -> Transparent

✔ **Bibliothèque des dégradés :** Elle contient une grande variété de dégradés classés par catégories. Il suffit de cliquer sur le bouton à flèche, en haut à droite de la palette des dégradés, pour accéder à un menu dont la partie inférieure contient le nom de bon nombre de bibliothèques de dégradés. Cliquez sur l'une d'elles pour remplacer les vignettes du sélecteur de dégradés par celles du jeu de dégradés choisi.

Quand vous sélectionnez un dégradé dans la palette, Elements affiche son aperçu dans la barre d'options.

Si aucun des dégradés ne vous convient, vous pouvez créer votre propre dégradé personnalisé. La section suivante explique comment procéder.

Dans le menu déroulant du Sélecteur de dégradé, vous avez le choix entre l'affichage des dégradés sous forme de vignettes, de texte uniquement ou d'une combinaison de texte et de vignettes.

Devenir un alchimiste du dégradé

La création d'un dégradé est très simple pour peu que vous preniez le temps de comprendre les différentes parties de la boîte de dialogue Éditeur de dégradé, représentée sur la Figure 16.7.

La boîte de dialogue Éditeur de dégradé est complexe, et heureusement que vous ne vous en servirez pas beaucoup. Voici une brève présentation de ses paramètres :

✔ **Paramètres prédéfinis :** Palette située en haut de la boîte de dialogue. Elle contient de nombreux dégradés prédéfinis. Sélectionnez celui que vous désirez utiliser comme point de départ d'un dégradé personnalisé.

✔ **Type de dégradé :** Vous pouvez choisir entre des dégradés constitués de couleurs uniformes et du bruit. Le bruit ajoute simplement un aléa dans la constitution des teintes.

✔ **Lissage ou Cassure :** L'option Lissage n'est disponible que si vous choisissez un dégradé Uniforme. Faites glisser le curseur ou saisissez directement une valeur pour déterminer la progressivité du passage d'une couleur à une autre. Ce paramètre devient Cassure quand vous sélectionnez le type Bruit. Il modifie le lissage de la transition des couleurs.

Les options suivantes ne sont disponibles que si vous sélectionnez un type de dégradé Bruit :

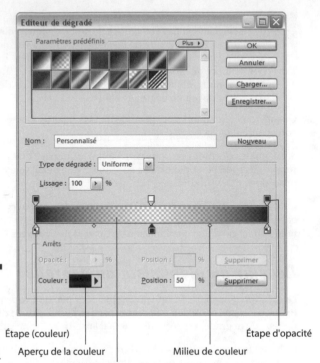

Figure 16.7 :
L'Éditeur de
dégradé
donne un
contrôle
absolu sur
les dégradés.

Étape (couleur)

Aperçu de la couleur

Barre d'aperçu du dégradé

Milieu de couleur

Étape d'opacité

- ✔ **Modèle de couleur :** Permet de changer le modèle de couleur ou de limiter la plage de couleurs en déplaçant les curseurs.

- ✔ **Restreindre les couleurs :** Évite la saturation des couleurs.

- ✔ **Ajouter de la transparence :** Permet d'introduire de la transparence dans votre dégradé de type Bruit.

- ✔ **Phase initiale aléatoire :** Modifie les couleurs d'un dégradé de type bruit. Chaque fois que vous cliquez, un nouveau modèle de couleurs est créé.

Les dégradés peuvent être générés à partir des nuanciers, que nous traitons au Chapitre 5.

Pour ôter un dégradé de la liste, appuyez sur Alt puis cliquez sur le dégradé. Remarquez la paire de ciseaux qui apparaît, symbole de la suppression.

Modifier, ajouter et supprimer des couleurs

Pour modifier une des couleurs d'un dégradé, vérifiez d'abord si son indicateur triangulaire est noir, indiquant que l'étape est active, donc modifiable. Si ce n'est pas le cas, cliquez sur l'étape – l'indicateur carré situé dessous – pour l'activer.

L'étape activée, trois choix sont envisageables : double-cliquer sur l'étape pour ouvrir le Sélecteur de couleurs, cliquer dans la liste Couleur pour ouvrir le Sélecteur de couleurs, ou encore, utiliser la pipette qui apparaît spontanément quand vous placez le pointeur de la souris sur le dégradé ou sur l'image afin de prélever une couleur.

Une dernière méthode consiste à sélectionner une couleur dans le menu local de l'option Couleur. Vous pouvez alors choisir Premier plan ou Arrière-plan. Ces choix agissent immédiatement sur le dégradé en cours d'édition, mais n'affectent aucunement les dégradés déjà dessinés sur l'image. Il est possible de sélectionner une étape, puis l'option Couleur utilisateur de la liste Couleur. Cela ne modifie pas les couleurs de premier et d'arrière-plan affichées dans la boîte à outils de Photoshop Elements.

Voici quelques détails à connaître concernant les couleurs des dégradés :

- Pour ajouter une étape de couleur à un dégradé, cliquez sous la barre d'aperçu. Une nouvelle étape est créée.

- Pour supprimer une couleur du dégradé, faites glisser l'icône de son étape hors de la boîte de dialogue.

- Si vous faites glisser une étape vers la gauche ou la droite, vous modifiez la position des couleurs dans le dégradé. Supposons que le dégradé s'étende du noir au blanc. Si vous désirez que la plage sombre soit plus étendue que la plage claire, rapprochez l'étape de couleur noire de celle de couleur blanche. Notez que la transition est plus étroite et de ce fait plus abrupte.

- Les petits losanges situés au-dessus ou au dessous de la barre d'aperçu du dégradé représentent le point de transition moyen entre deux couleurs ou deux paramètres d'opacité. Si nous reprenons l'exemple du noir et du blanc, le losange marque le point précis où la quantité de noir et de blanc est équivalente. Cette valeur médiane peut être déplacée afin de modifier la pente du dégradé entre deux couleurs.

  Quand une étape de couleur est active, une valeur de 0 % représente le début du dégradé et 100 % représente sa fin.

Les valeurs de couleurs médianes se rapportent aux deux étapes de couleurs situées de part et d'autre. Une valeur de 50 % place le point médian à égale distance des deux couleurs. Les valeurs minimales et maximales sont 5 % et 95 %.

Créer des bordures avec la commande Contour

Le dernier élément que nous aborderons dans ce chapitre est la commande Édition/Contour de la sélection. Elle sert à tracer une bordure autour d'une sélection. Quand vous choisissez cette commande, Elements affiche la boîte de dialogue Contour que montre la Figure 16.8.

Figure 16.8 : Utilisez la boîte de dialogue Contour pour tracer une bordure autour d'une sélection.

Saisissez l'épaisseur de la bordure exprimée en pixels. Elle peut s'étendre de 1 à 250 pixels. D'autres unités de mesure sont acceptées. Par exemple, si vous entrez **0,10 cm**, Elements convertit cette valeur centimétrique en son équivalent en pixels.

Sur la Figure 16.9, une bordure noire de 16 pixels a été appliquée autour du bocal. En utilisant ensuite cette même sélection, nous avons créé une bordure blanche de 8 pixels.

Vous pouvez choisir la couleur de la bordure dans la boîte de dialogue Contour. Cliquez sur l'indicateur de teinte du paramètre Couleur pour accéder au Sélecteur de couleurs. Remarquez que la définition d'une nouvelle couleur dans la boîte de dialogue Contour de la sélection modifie celle affichée dans le nuancier de la couleur de premier plan, en bas de la boîte à outils.

Figure 16.9 :
Effet
classique
d'une double
bordure,
transformant
un bocal en
amphore.

Chapitre 17

Le texte

*E*lements n'est pas un logiciel de traitement de texte. Cependant, il permet de gérer des textes de grande taille susceptibles de recevoir des effets spéciaux. Elements n'est pas conçu pour écrire un roman. Si tel est votre objectif, préférez un programme comme Word ou un logiciel de mise en page comme InDesign ou QuarkXPress.

Travailler avec l'outil Texte

Pour activer l'un des outils de texte, appuyez sur la touche T. Appuyer répétitivement sur cette touche active tour à tour chaque outil de texte. Si ce n'est pas le cas, ouvrez la boîte de dialogue Préférences/ Général et décochez l'option Touche Maj afin de pouvoir changer d'outil. Ceci vaudra aussi pour l'activation de n'importe quel autre outil.

Nous présentons ci-après les différences entre l'outil Texte horizontal (représenté à la Figure 17.1) et l'outil Masque de texte horizontal.

✔ **L'outil Texte horizontal** crée du texte sur un nouveau calque de texte. Les calques sont étudiés en détail au Chapitre 10. Vous modifiez le texte sans altérer les autres calques de l'image.

Pour modifier le contenu et les attributs d'un texte, il suffit de le sélectionner. Bien que vous ne puissiez pas peindre ou retoucher un texte, il est possible de modifier son opacité dans la palette des calques et lui appliquer un mode de fusion.

Figure 17.1 :
L'outil Texte
horizontal et
ses
nombreuses
options. Ici
deux barres
d'options
sont
représen-
tées : au
moment de
l'activation
de l'outil
mais avant la
saisie (en
haut) et en
cours de
rédaction (en
bas).

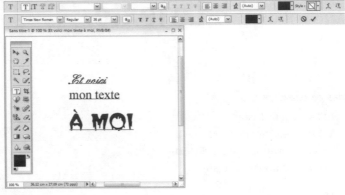

Dans le menu déroulant Police, les polices sont désormais
affichées avec leur typographie, comme le montre la Figure 17.2,
ce qui facilite leur choix. Dans les versions antérieures
d'Elements, les noms des polices étaient tous écrits de la même
manière, comme dans la colonne de gauche de la figure ; il
n'était pas facile, dans ces conditions, de sélectionner une
typographie. La taille de l'aperçu des polices est réglable dans le
menu Edition/Préférences/Texte.

✔ **L'outil Masque de texte horizontal** permet de créer du texte en
forme de contour de sélection. Lorsque vous cliquez avec cet
outil, l'image se remplit d'un film de recouvrement rouge
translucide. Tant que vous ne validez pas le texte, vous pouvez
travailler avec le contour de texte comme vous le feriez avec du
texte ordinaire. Vous pouvez par ailleurs manipuler, modifier,
peindre et appliquer au contour de texte toutes opérations
réalisables avec tout autre contour de sélection. Et puisque
l'outil Masque de texte horizontal travaille comme n'importe
quel autre outil de sélection, vous pouvez l'employer pour
ajouter ou soustraire une partie à un contour de sélection
existant (voir le Chapitre 9). Remarquez qu'après avoir cliqué
sur le bouton Valider, dans la barre Options, vous ne pouvez
plus modifier le contour de texte, ce qui n'est pas le cas du texte
ordinaire créé avec l'outil Texte horizontal.

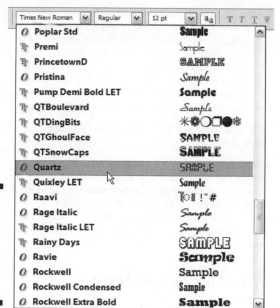

Des mots sur votre écran

L'outil Texte horizontal et l'outil Masque de texte horizontal s'utilisent quasiment de la même manière. Nous étudierons d'abord l'outil Texte horizontal. Si vous voulez créer des contours de sélection d'après du texte, vous devrez néanmoins lire cette section car nous y exposons toutes les options de mise en forme du texte.

Tout commence par la sélection de l'outil Texte horizontal. Ensuite, cliquez dans l'image. Elements crée un nouveau calque spécial appelé *calque de texte* et place le texte à l'endroit précis du clic. Bien entendu, vous pourrez repositionner ce texte après l'avoir créé. Un petit curseur clignotant, appelé *point d'insertion*, apparaît. Les habitués des traitements de texte ne seront pas dépaysés. À partir de cet instant, écrivez ce qui vous passe par la tête.

Saisir le texte à... saisir

Voici une liste de choses à savoir quand vous saisissez du texte sur votre zone de travail. La section "Modifier l'aspect du texte" traite de la mise en forme.

✔ Comment corriger une faute de frappe ? Commencez par vérifier que le calque de texte est actif, puis cliquez juste après la lettre à effacer. Le point d'insertion clignote. Appuyez sur la touche Retour arrière : la lettre est effacée. Saisissez la bonne (rien à voir avec le personnel de maison). Pour ajouter du texte, cliquez à l'endroit où vous désirez l'insérer. Ensuite, retapez le texte. Pour supprimer plusieurs lettres en une seule fois, sélectionnez-les à la souris et appuyez sur la touche Retour arrière.

✔ Pour remplacer du texte, sélectionnez-le, puis saisissez votre nouveau texte.

✔ Elements place tous les mots sur une seule ligne. Pour en créer une nouvelle, il suffit d'appuyer sur la touche Entrée. Le point d'insertion va à la ligne et vous pouvez continuer de saisir le texte. Par exemple, dans le texte de la Figure 17.1, nous avons placé le point d'insertion entre "voici" et "mon" (sans aucun espace entre les deux mots), puis nous avons appuyé sur la touche Entrée.

Modifier l'aspect du texte

La barre d'options dispose de tous les ingrédients pour formater votre texte. Ces options contrôlent le type de police, sa taille, sa couleur, son alignement, et toute autre procédure complexe.

N'oubliez pas ceci concernant les outils Texte :

✔ Les attributs du texte – ses caractéristiques, si vous préférez – ne peuvent être modifiés que si l'outil Texte horizontal est sélectionné. Pour modifier une partie du texte, sélectionnez-la et appliquez-lui les nouveaux attributs. Pour sélectionner tout le texte, activez son calque dans la palette des calques.

✔ Si vous savez exactement ce que vous voulez, définissez les attributs avant de saisir le texte. Choisissez sa police, sa taille, sa couleur, etc. Avec un peu de chance, le texte correspondra exactement à ce que vous souhaitez. Aucune modification supplémentaire ne sera nécessaire. Joli gain de temps !

✔ Choisissez une police dans la liste des familles de police (notez que certaines polices particulières, notamment les alphabets non romains et certains symboles, sont réunies à part en bas de la liste). Sélectionnez un style dans la liste Style. Rien que des choses simples en fait. Les styles (gras, italique, souligné...) sont parfois appelés *enrichissements*.

✔ Définissez la taille du texte dans la liste Définir le corps. La taille – appelée *corps* en typographie – est exprimée en points, en pixels ou en millimètres, selon les paramètres définis dans la boîte de dialogue Préférences. (Édition/Préférences/Unités et règles.)

✔ Pour étirer un texte, activez l'outil Déplacement puis tirez une des poignées du cadre de sélection. Veillez à ne pas agrandir un texte démesurément au risque de le rendre illisible.

✔ Si votre police ne dispose pas des styles gras et italique, les options de texte peuvent les simuler. Cliquez sur ce bouton, et cochez les cases Faux gras, Faux italique, Texte souligné et/ou Texte barré.

✔ La couleur de premier plan est la couleur du texte par défaut. Avant de saisir le texte, modifiez-la en cliquant sur le bouton Définir la couleur du texte. Choisissez une teinte dans le Sélecteur de couleurs. Une autre technique consiste à cliquer directement sur la couleur de premier plan de la boîte à outils et à la définir dans le Sélecteur de couleurs (consultez le Chapitre 5 pour vous rafraîchir la mémoire sur les couleurs).

✔ Sélectionnez une option d'alignement pour déterminer la position d'un texte composé de plusieurs lignes. L'alignement peut se faire à gauche, centré ou à droite.

✔ Vous pouvez appliquer plusieurs attributs de mise en forme sur un même calque. Cela est impossible avec les alignements.

✔ Appuyer sur Entrée ou Retour, permet de créer plusieurs lignes. Il est aussi possible de modifier l'interligne, qui est par défaut en mode automatique. Cela signifie que le programme détermine lui-même l'espace entre les lignes (soit 120 % de la taille de la police, si vous voulez le savoir). Pour augmenter ou diminuer l'interligne, sélectionnez une valeur dans la liste du champ Définir l'interligne, ou saisissez-en une et appuyez sur Entrée pour la valider.

Des options se trouvent dans la barre d'options ainsi que dans le sous-menu Texte du menu Calque :

✔ **Horizontal/Vertical :** Cette orientation du texte permet de basculer les mots verticalement ou horizontalement.

✔ **Lissage activé/désactivé :** Le texte doit être parfait à l'écran et à l'impression. C'est pourquoi, choisissez toujours l'option Lissage activé.

✔ **Déformer le texte :** Cette fonction est décrite ci dessous.

Déformer le texte

Dans Elements, la déformation du texte s'effectue le long d'une trajectoire, d'un tracé, mais d'une manière moins précise que dans Illustrator, Freehand ou CorelDraw. Vous pouvez tordre, dilater, contracter un texte et créer des formes aussi bizarroïdes que surprenantes, comme le montre la Figure 17.3.

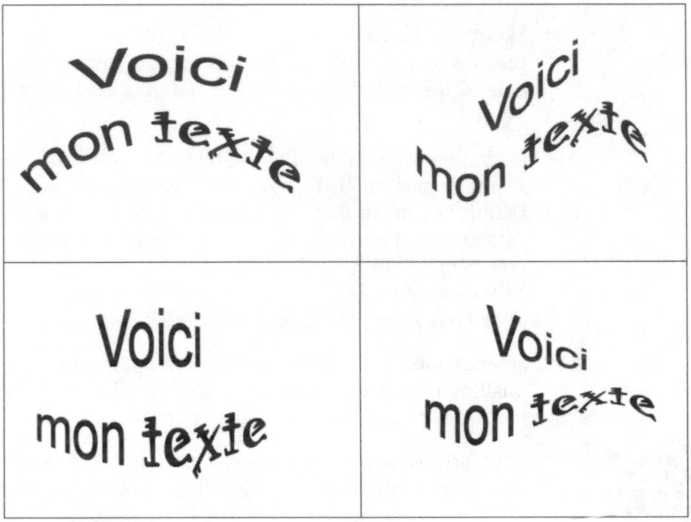

Figure 17.3 : Quelques déformations dansantes d'un texte vague exposé aux divagations d'un esprit tordu.

Suivez ces étapes pour déformer votre texte :

1. **Sélectionnez le calque de texte dans la palette des calques.**

2. **Sélectionnez un outil Texte dans la boîte à outils et cliquez sur l'icône Créer un texte déformé de la barre d'options. Ou alors, choisissez Calque/Texte/Déformer le texte (dans ce cas, n'importe quel outil peut être actif).**

3. **Dans la boîte de dialogue Déformer le texte, sélectionnez le style de la déformation.**

4. **Amusez-vous avec les diverses options.**

   Choisissez une orientation soit Horizontale, soit Verticale. Réglez l'inflexion pour obtenir une déformation plus ou moins prononcée. Les curseurs Déformation appliquent une perspective.

5. **Si la déformation répond à vos espérances, cliquez sur OK.**

Les déformations sont faciles à réaliser dans Elements. En revanche, sa maîtrise et l'originalité des effets imposent l'utilisation avisée des options. Définir le bon style est la décision la plus importante à prendre ; les autres options proposent simplement des variations basées sur le style choisi.

Modifier le calque de texte

Voici ce que vous pouvez faire sur un calque de texte sans perdre la possibilité d'en modifier le contenu :

✔ Vous pouvez réorganiser ou dupliquer le calque de texte dans la palette Calques, comme vous le feriez avec un calque ordinaire. Pour placer le calque au-dessus des autres, faites-le glisser en haut de la pile des calques de la palette des calques. Pour dupliquer le calque, faites glisser son icône sur le bouton Créer un nouveau calque situé en bas de la palette des calques.

✔ Les calques de texte peuvent être verrouillés (consultez le Chapitre 10 pour en savoir plus sur cette fonction).

✔ Déplacez le texte avec l'outil Déplacement. Pour dupliquer le texte, déplacez-le en maintenant la touche Alt enfoncée. Le texte ainsi copié apparaît dans un nouveau calque.

✔ Les commandes du sous-menu Transformation du menu Image permettent d'effectuer des transformations libres, des rotations, des inclinaisons, des torsions et des perspectives. Les commandes Torsion et Perspective ne sont pas disponibles pour tous les calques.

✔ Appliquez des styles de calque (voir le Chapitre 14) au calque de texte. Même après avoir appliqué l'effet, vous pouvez modifier le contenu du texte. Le calque s'actualise comme par magie.

✔ Avec la commande Remplir, remplissez le texte avec la couleur de premier ou d'arrière-plan. Appuyez sur Alt+Barre d'espace pour le remplir directement avec la couleur de premier plan. Appuyez sur Ctrl+Barre d'espace pour remplir avec la couleur d'arrière-plan. Remarquez que la commande Édition/Remplir la sélection est en grisé, c'est-à-dire indisponible. Vous ne pouvez utiliser que le raccourci clavier.

Voici trois actions que vous ne pouvez pas entreprendre tant que le calque n'a pas été simplifié, c'est-à-dire réduit à des pixels (NdT : pour le moment, son contenu est vectoriel) pour en faire un calque ordinaire :

> ✔ Vous ne pouvez pas utiliser des outils de peinture et de retouche. Lorsque vous cliquez avec les outils de peinture et de modification sur le calque de texte, vous obtenez un message erreur signalant que vous devez d'abord simplifier le texte.

> ✔ Vous ne pouvez pas appliquer les filtres de la palette Filtres (palette Styles et effets).

> ✔ Vous ne pouvez pas appliquer d'effets de la palette Effets (palette Styles et effets).

Un calque de texte ne peut pas être créé sur des images en mode Couleurs indexées. Si vous envisagez de créer un graphisme GIF destiné au Web, comportant jusqu'à 256 couleurs numérotées, vous devez d'abord finaliser votre image en mode RVB. Une fois que vous êtes satisfait du texte, procédez à la conversion. Le calque de texte est alors simplifié, autrement dit *pixellisé*. Dès lors, il n'est plus modifiable avec l'outil Texte.

Simplifier un calque de texte

Pour appliquer un filtre, un effet ou de la peinture sur un calque de texte, vous devez préalablement *simplifier* le calque. La simplification consiste à transformer un graphisme vectoriel (représenté par des formules mathématiques) en graphisme point à point (matrice de pixels, comme toutes les images traitées dans Photoshop Elements). Le calque de texte devient ainsi un calque ordinaire. Pour ce faire, choisissez Calque/Simplifier le calque. Le texte n'a subi aucun changement perceptible. Mais, vous ne pouvez plus éditer le texte. Remarquez que le "T" a disparu de la vignette du calque. Un conseil : ne simplifiez un calque que si vous êtes certain de ne plus avoir besoin d'ajouter ou supprimer un mot, corriger l'orthographe ou modifier la typographie. Vous pourriez certes dupliquer le calque de texte en cliquant dessus et en faisant glisser jusqu'à l'icône Créer un nouveau calque dans la palette Calques ; puis désactiver la visibilité d'un des deux en cliquant sur l'œil de ce calque. Vous disposeriez de la sorte d'une sauvegarde, une excellente précaution si vous ne vous sentez pas prêt à valider définitivement vos changements.

Les contours du texte

Comme nous l'avons évoqué plus haut, presque toutes les informations de mise en forme évoquées précédemment s'appliquent aussi au texte créé avec l'outil Masque de texte horizontal. La grande différence est qu'après avoir cliqué sur le bouton de validation, appuyé sur la touche Entrée du pavé numérique ou activé un autre outil, vous ne pouvez plus modifier votre texte.

Dès que vous cliquez dans la zone de travail après avoir activé l'outil Masque de texte horizontal, un film rouge translucide s'applique sur la totalité de l'image. C'est le masque de protection. Il couvre les parties de l'image qui ne seront pas altérées par vos modifications. Quand vous appuyez sur la touche Entrée du pavé numérique, le masque disparaît et une sélection traditionnelle s'affiche dans la zone de travail (consultez le Chapitre 9 pour en savoir plus sur les sélections). Voici ce que l'on peut faire d'une sélection à base de contours de texte :

✔ Pour déplacer le contour de sélection d'un texte, faites-le glisser avec les outils de sélection ou avec les touches du pavé directionnel.

✔ Pour déplacer ou dupliquer la sélection du texte, utilisez les techniques décrites aux Chapitres 9 et 10. Déplacez le texte avec l'outil Déplacement ; maintenez la touche Alt enfoncée et effectuez le déplacement afin de dupliquer le texte.

En d'autres termes, les sélections créées avec un masque de texte se comportent comme n'importe quelle autre sélection.

✔ Vous pouvez peindre dans le texte. Utilisez ensuite les outils d'édition pour saturer les couleurs, les atténuer, les éclaircir, etc.

✔ Vous pouvez remplir le texte avec la couleur de premier plan en appuyant sur Alt+Retour arrière. Appliquez la couleur d'arrière-plan en appuyant sur Ctrl+Retour arrière. Pour remplir le texte avec un ensemble de couleurs, utilisez l'outil Dégradé.

✔ Avant de remplir ou d'appliquer un contour, il est essentiel que le texte soit définitivement positionné dans la zone de travail. Pour cette raison, il est recommandé de créer la sélection du contour du texte dans un autre calque. Vous pourrez ainsi déplacer le texte sans altérer la ou les images situées dessous.

✔ Pour supprimer le texte créé avec l'outil Masque de texte horizontal, vous devez annuler les étapes de réalisation dans la palette Annuler l'historique (voir le Chapitre 8). En revanche, si la sélection repose sur un nouveau calque, déposez-le dans la poubelle, en haut de la palette des calques.

Les étapes suivantes créent un contour autour d'un texte, comme le montre la Figure 17.4. Nous pouvons voir à travers les lettres et créer des bordures. Que demander de plus ?

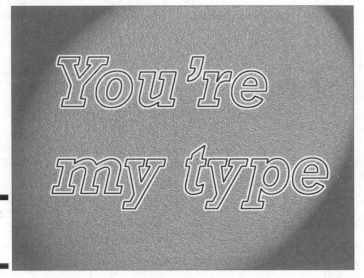

Figure 17.4 :
Un effet de
contour
réussi.

1. **Créez un nouveau calque.**

   Vous n'êtes pas obligé de placer le texte sur son propre calque. Cependant, en procédant de la sorte, l'édition du calque de texte sera plus simple. Pour créer un calque, cliquez sur l'icône Créer un nouveau calque de la palette des calques, comme cela est expliqué au Chapitre 10.

2. **Sélectionnez l'outil Masque de texte horizontal dans la boîte à outils.**

3. **Définissez les attributs de format dans la barre d'options.**

4. **Cliquez sur la zone de travail avec l'outil Texte.**

   Saisissez le texte et validez-le en appuyant sur Entrée (pavé numérique) ou cliquez sur le bouton Validation de la barre d'options. Déplacez le contour de la sélection du texte avec la souris ou les touches du pavé directionnel.

5. **Choisissez le blanc comme couleur de premier plan.**

Appuyez sur D puis sur X pour permuter les couleurs par défaut (noir et blanc).

6. **Si nécessaire, désélectionnez l'option Verrouiller les pixels transparents de la palette des calques.**

Dans le cas contraire, Elements n'autorise pas de peindre sur le calque.

7. **Créez un calque transparent que vous placez entre le calque de texte et le calque d'Arrière-plan. Ensuite, choisissez Édition/Contour de la sélection. Activez l'option Centre, et entrez une Épaisseur de 12 pixels.**

Appuyez sur la touche Entrée. Un liseré blanc de 12 pixels entoure maintenant le texte. Cette valeur doit toujours être adaptée à la taille du texte, et sa couleur au contexte. Un contour blanc sur fond blanc passerait aussi inaperçu qu'un lapin albinos dans la neige.

8. **Choisissez le noir comme couleur de premier plan. (Appuyez sur X.)**

9. **Choisissez Édition/Contour de la sélection, et saisissez une Épaisseur de 4. Laissez le paramètre Position sur Centre.**

Appuyez sur Enter. Bravo ! Vous obtenez un effet similaire à celui de la Figure 17.4. Si le texte est sur son propre calque, positionnez-le correctement sur l'image. Vous pouvez appliquer des modes de fusion et des valeurs d'opacité, à partir de la palette des calques, afin de modifier la manière dont le texte se mêle à l'image située juste en dessous.

Les dix
commandements

"... là c'est moi avec Cindy Crawford, là avec
Madonna, et là avec Céline Dion..."

Dans cette partie...

Avant de nous dire adieu ou au revoir, regardons Elements sous un autre angle : celui des fameux dix commandements, une partie commune à tous les livres de la collection *Pour les Nuls*.

Nous commencerons par répertorier dix catégories de raccourcis clavier qui amélioreront votre productivité dans Photoshop Elements. Ensuite, nous envisagerons dix tâches qu'Elements ne peut pas faire, mais qui sont réalisables avec Photoshop.

Nous sommes certains que, depuis que vous lisez des livres de la collection *Pour les Nuls*, vous vous demandez pourquoi nous donnons dix conseils et astuces en fin d'ouvrage. Pourquoi dix ? Sans doute parce que dix est un chiffre emblématique comme les *dix petits nègres*, les *dix doigts de la main, cinq et cinq égalent dix...* enfin vous voyez le genre de justification !

Dix raccourcis clavier à mémoriser

Dans ce chapitre :

- ▶ Masquer les contours de sélection.
- ▶ Afficher et masquer la Corbeille de palette.
- ▶ Modifier la valeur d'une option.
- ▶ Défiler et zoomer.
- ▶ Créer des lignes droites.
- ▶ Manipuler des contours de sélection.
- ▶ Déplacer, découper et dupliquer.
- ▶ Remplir une sélection.
- ▶ Parcourir les étapes de la palette Annuler l'historique.

C omme chacun le sait, la mémoire est ce qui permet de se demander ce que nous avons oublié. Elle est indispensable dans toutes les circonstances de notre existence, et devient même une priorité en informatique. Ce chapitre vient à votre secours. En feuilletant ces quelques pages, vous réintroduirez dans votre mémoire défaillante tout ce qui permet d'exécuter facilement et rapidement des tâches dans Photoshop Elements.

Les quelques sections suivantes ne prétendent pas regrouper tous les raccourcis disponibles dans Elements, mais uniquement ceux qui font gagner un temps précieux. Ils ne sont utilisables qu'en mode Éditeur.

Masquer les contours de sélection

Ctrl+H

Après avoir sélectionné un élément dans votre image, ce raccourci rend le contour de sélection temporairement invisible, ce qui le rend moins gênant. Ne confondez pas cette action avec la désélection ; lorsque le contour est masqué, vous ne pouvez toujours modifier que la partie sélectionnée de l'image. C'est probablement le raccourci le plus communément utilisé.

Afficher et masquer la Corbeille des palettes

F7

Appuyez sur la touche F7 pour afficher et masquer la Corbeille des palettes.

Changer la valeur d'une option

Flèche haut, flèche bas

Activez les diverses boîtes et champs d'option d'une boîte de dialogue avec la touche Tab, et modifiez la valeur avec les touches flèche haut et flèche bas du pavé directionnel. Vous augmentez ou diminuez ainsi la valeur d'une unité. Appuyez sur Maj+↑ ou sur Maj+↓ pour augmenter ou diminuer la valeur par palier de dix unités. Appuyez sur Entrée pour valider la nouvelle valeur.

Défiler et zoomer

Barre d'espace

Appuyez sur la barre d'espace pour activer temporairement l'outil Main. Tant que vous ne relâchez pas cette barre, l'outil est actif.

Ctrl+Barre d'espace et Alt+Barre d'espace

Deux raccourcis pour activer respectivement le zoom avant et le zoom arrière. Le pointeur prend la forme d'une loupe ornée d'un signe "+" ou d'un signe "-". Cela permet d'agrandir ou de réduire l'affichage d'une zone de l'image sans désactiver l'outil que vous utilisez pour votre retouche. Il devient temporairement l'outil Zoom. Quand vous relâchez les touches de raccourcis, vous récupérez l'outil utilisé jusqu'à présent.

Ctrl++ (plus) et Ctrl+- (moins)

Autre manière d'agrandir et de réduire l'affichage d'une image. Avec ces raccourcis, vous opérez un agrandissement ou une réduction de toute l'image et pas d'une partie spécifique.

Créer des lignes droites

Maj+clic

Pour créer une ligne droite avec des outils de peinture et de retouche, cliquez à l'endroit où doit débuter la ligne. Maintenez la touche Maj enfoncée et cliquez à l'endroit où elle doit se terminer. Elements connecte ces deux points avec une ligne droite.

Cliquez avec le Lasso polygonal et utilisez Alt+clic avec le Lasso et le Lasso magnétique

Le Lasso polygonal crée des sélections sous forme de segments de droite. Cliquez pour définir le point de départ, puis cliquez pour créer des points supplémentaires.

Lorsque vous travaillez avec l'outil Lasso, activez temporairement le Lasso polygonal en maintenant la touche Alt enfoncée. Cliquez alors pour définir le point de départ de la sélection et continuez cette procédure jusqu'à ce que la sélection soit effectuée.

Lorsque vous travaillez avec le Lasso magnétique, appuyez sur la touche Alt et cliquez pour utiliser le Lasso polygonal. Dès que vous relâchez la touche Alt, vous récupérez l'usage du Lasso magnétique.

N'utilisez pas cette méthode pour augmenter ou diminuer la sélection. Quand une sélection est active, le fait d'appuyer sur la touche Alt permet de réduire la sélection en passant l'outil sur les zones à désélectionner. Vous ne basculez pas vers un autre outil Lasso.

Manipuler les contours des sélections

Maj+déplacement et Maj+clic

Pour sélectionner une zone supplémentaire de votre image sans perdre la sélection existante, maintenez la touche Maj enfoncée et déplacez la souris pour sélectionner une nouvelle zone avec l'outil

Lasso ou Forme de sélection. Vous pouvez également utiliser Maj+clic avec la Baguette magique pour ajouter des zones à la sélection.

Alt+déplacement et Alt+clic

Pour désélectionner une partie de la sélection, maintenez la touche Alt enfoncée et faites glisser l'outil Lasso ou Forme de sélection. Utilisez Alt+clic afin d'obtenir le même résultat avec l'outil Baguette magique.

Maj+Alt+déplacement et Alt+Maj+clic

Pour conserver l'intersection d'une sélection existante et d'une nouvelle sélection dessinée au lasso ou avec un outil de forme de sélection, maintenez les touches Maj+Alt enfoncées, tout en traçant la nouvelle sélection. Pour conserver une zone de couleur contiguë dans une sélection, utilisez Maj+Alt+clic avec la Baguette magique.

Ctrl+Maj+D

Pour récupérer la dernière sélection désélectionnée, appuyez sur Ctrl+Maj+D.

Déplacer, découper et dupliquer

Ctrl

Pour déplacer les sélections et les calques, utilisez l'outil Déplacement. Activez-le temporairement en appuyant sur la touche Ctrl. Ce raccourci ne fonctionne pas si l'outil Main ou un des outils de forme est sélectionné.

Flèche

Pour découper une sélection d'un pixel, activez l'outil Déplacement et appuyez sur une des touches du pavé directionnel. Ou bien, appuyez sur Ctrl et sur une des touches, quel que soit l'outil sélectionné à l'exception de la Main et d'un des outils de forme.

Maj+flèche

Pour découper une sélection de dix pixels, activez l'outil Déplacement et appuyez sur Maj+une flèche du pavé directionnel. Ou bien, sélectionnez n'importe quel outil, à l'exception de la Main et d'une forme, et appuyez sur Ctrl+Maj+une flèche du pavé directionnel.

Alt+déplacement, Alt+flèche et Maj+Alt+flèche

Pour dupliquer une sélection et déplacer son clone, activez l'outil Déplacement puis maintenez la touche Alt enfoncée et faites glisser le pointeur de la souris. Vous pouvez également maintenir enfoncée la touche Alt et une flèche du pavé directionnel pour dupliquer la sélection et la déplacer d'un pixel. La sélection s'étale, c'est-à-dire laisse une trace d'elle-même (de l'image) derrière elle. Appuyez sur Maj+Alt+flèche du pavé directionnel pour dupliquer et étaler le clone par pas de dix pixels.

Cette procédure fonctionne quel que soit l'outil sélectionné à l'exception de la Main et d'un outil de forme. Dans ce cas, il faut maintenir enfoncée la touche Ctrl pour activer temporairement l'outil Déplacement.

Déplacer avec un outil de sélection

Pour déplacer les contours d'une sélection avec un outil de sélection, placez le pointeur de la souris dans la sélection. Cliquez et faites glisser la sélection jusqu'à son nouvel emplacement. Vous pouvez également appuyer sur les flèches du pavé directionnel. Vous effectuez alors un déplacement d'un pixel. Si vous maintenez la touche Maj enfoncée, le déplacement se fait par pas de dix pixels. Cette méthode ne fonctionne pas si l'outil Déplacement ou Recadrage est sélectionné.

Ctrl avec un outil de forme

Appuyer sur Ctrl avec n'importe quel outil de forme sélectionné permet de déplacer rapidement des formes et des lignes.

Remplir une sélection

Ctrl+Retour arrière

Pour remplir une sélection avec la couleur d'arrière-plan, appuyez sur Ctrl+Retour arrière. Si vous appuyez sur Retour arrière, vous videz le contenu de la sélection d'un calque.

Alt+Retour arrière

Pour remplir une sélection avec la couleur de premier plan, appuyez sur Alt+Retour arrière.

Maj+Retour arrière

Appuyez sur Maj+Retour arrière pour ouvrir la boîte de dialogue Calque de remplissage. Elle permet de sélectionner toutes sortes d'éléments de remplissage.

Parcourir les étapes de l'Historique

Ctrl+Z et Ctrl+Y

Pour remonter d'une étape dans l'Historique, appuyez sur Ctrl+Z. Pour avancer d'une étape, appuyez sur Ctrl+Y. Vous pouvez modifier ces raccourcis via Édition/Préférences/Général.

Chapitre 19

Dix raisons de passer à Photoshop

. . . .

Dans ce chapitre :

- ▶ La palette Compositions de calques.
- ▶ Afficher les couches.
- ▶ Utiliser le mode colorimétrique CMJN.
- ▶ La palette Formes.
- ▶ Dessiner des tracés.
- ▶ Corriger avec des courbes.
- ▶ Enregistrer des scripts.
- ▶ Peindre avec l'Historique.
- ▶ Ajouter des annotations.
- ▶ Basculer vers ImageReady.

. . . .

*L'*objectif de ce chapitre est de montrer dans quelle mesure les possibilités d'Elements sont autrement plus étendues dans Photoshop. Il ne s'agit pas de vous pousser à acheter Photoshop, un logiciel vendu autour de 1 000 euros. Dans la plupart des cas, Photoshop Elements remplira les fonctions que vous attendez de lui. Mais, Photoshop propose des fonctions impressionnantes, destinées aux professionnels de l'imagerie (photographes, graphistes, maquettistes, imprimeurs...). Bref, voici dix bonnes raisons de franchir le pas qui sépare Elements de Photoshop.

La palette Compositions de calques

N'avez-vous jamais eu envie de sauvegarder le contenu de la palette Historique avec votre image au cas où vous voudriez annuler certaines actions bien après avoir édité ce fichier ? Si la réponse est "oui", vous allez adorer la palette Compositions de calques de Photoshop CS2. Que vous affichiez ou masquiez des calques, appliquiez des styles, modifiiez leur position, la palette Compositions de calques prend régulièrement un "instantané" de l'image. Ainsi, vous pouvez afficher ultérieurement n'importe quel instantané pour comparer plusieurs versions de votre travail. C'est un outil idéal pour présenter différentes versions d'un travail à des clients sans être obligé d'ouvrir des fichiers différents. Un clic de souris suffit : "Préférez-vous le texte ici, ou là ?" "Souhaitez-vous ou non conserver le chapeau sur la tête du chien ?" La palette Compositions de calques ne peut pas garder une trace de toutes vos modifications, mais elle aide considérablement les créateurs confrontés à des clients indécis. Voir la Figure 19.1.

Figure 19.1 :
La palette
Compositions
de calques
de Photoshop
enregistre les
modifications
apportées à
une image
multicalque,
permettant
ainsi de
comparer
plusieurs
versions d'un
même travail.

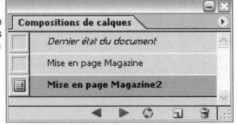

La palette Couches

Nous avons effleuré le sujet des couches chromatiques pour montrer comment elles subissaient l'incidence de commandes telles que Niveaux et Histogramme. Mais, dans Elements, ces couches ne sont pas accessibles. En revanche, Photoshop dispose d'une palette Couches qui permet d'afficher chacune des couches d'une image. Vous pouvez également créer des *couches alpha,* qui sont en fait des couches à niveaux de gris dont chacune contrôle un degré de transparence dans l'image. Cela est très utile pour les trucages vidéo et les montages photo. Vous disposez d'un contrôle précis sur chaque pixel de l'image. La Figure 19.2 montre la palette Couches, une des dix fonctions les plus importantes de Photoshop.

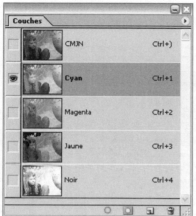

Le mode colorimétrique CMJN

À l'écran, une image est généralement affichée dans l'espace colorimétrique RVB, c'est-à-dire les couleurs primaires Rouge, Vert et Bleu des images vidéo. En revanche, toute image destinée à une impression professionnelle doit être affichée dans l'espace colorimétrique CMJN. Dans ce mode, C signifie cyan (un turquoise clair), M signifie magenta (pourpre), J signifie jaune et N signifie noir. Le noir est important, car le mélange des teintes CMJ produit du marron et non du noir, comme cela devrait théoriquement être le cas. Cette déficience est due à des impuretés dans le pigment des encres. Pour pallier ce défaut, de l'encre noire est ajoutée aux trois couleurs primaires CMJ.

La superposition des couches chromatiques produit une image en couleurs. Dans la mesure où Photoshop est aussi, et surtout à l'origine, un outil de préparation des images pour l'impression, Adobe permet de travailler directement en mode CMJN, comme le montre la Figure 19.2, et de préparer les images qui seront envoyées chez l'imprimeur. Ce mode à visée très professionnelle ne figure pas parmi ceux d'Elements.

La palette Formes

La palette Formes de Photoshop permet de contrôler plus finement encore les formes. La Figure 19.3 révèle que la palette Formes contient des paramètres comme Diffusion, Texture, Variation et Bruit. Elements est certes généreux en ce domaine mais, comme c'est fréquemment le cas, Photoshop le surclasse en termes de puissance et de contrôle.

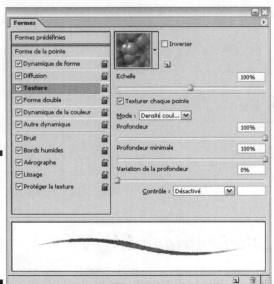

Figure 19.3 : La palette Formes permet de régler des formes personnalisées à votre guise.

Les tracés

Les outils Forme de Photoshop Elements (voir le Chapitre 15) ne sont qu'un aperçu de ce que l'on peut faire avec les outils de dessin vectoriel de Photoshop que vous admirez sur la Figure 19.4. Photoshop utilise des outils à base de *courbes de Bézier* pour dessiner des tracés. Ils permettent de créer des formes vectorielles régies par des points d'ancrage. La forme définitive est alors obtenue en agissant sur les poignées de contrôle. Les outils vectoriels ne sont pas faciles à maîtriser mais, une fois que vous savez les utiliser, vous parvenez à créer de remarquables formes incurvées. Un tracé peut être converti en sélection.

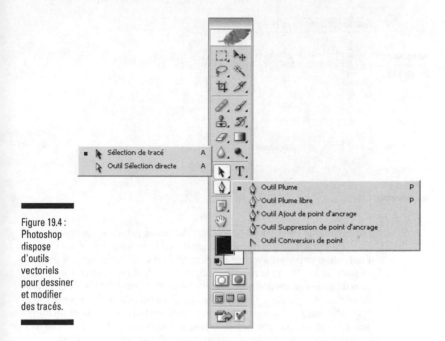

Figure 19.4 :
Photoshop
dispose
d'outils
vectoriels
pour dessiner
et modifier
des tracés.

Régler avec les courbes

Si la commande Niveaux vous impressionne, que dire de la commande Courbes ? Elle permet de gérer plus intuitivement les tonalités que les niveaux, mais elle peut surtout exécuter des tâches impossibles à accomplir avec la commande Niveaux. Cliquez sur la ligne pour ajouter des points d'incurvation, comme le montre la Figure 19.5. Vous disposez alors d'une courbe qui contrôle spécifiquement le niveau tonal de chacune des couches de l'image, pour chaque valeur chromatique. Il est ainsi possible, par exemple, de modifier le contraste dans certaines tonalités de l'image et différemment dans d'autres.

Moteur... ça tourne... annonce... action

Si la fonction de traitement par lots d'Elements vous éblouit, vous serez subjugué par les scripts de Photoshop. Le traitement par lots permet de prendre une série de fichiers pour les convertir dans un autre format en modifiant éventuellement leur taille et leur résolution.

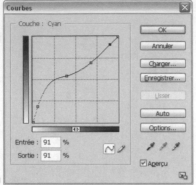

Figure 19.5 : La commande Courbes de Photoshop sert à modifier les niveaux de tonalité d'une image.

Les scripts de Photoshop procèdent du même principe sauf qu'en cliquant sur le bouton d'enregistrement de la palette des scripts, Photoshop enregistre toutes les actions que vous exécutez sur une image (Figure 19.6) : la modification de la taille d'une image, l'application de filtres, la création de sélections et leur remplissage, la création des calques de texte... Tous les menus que vous déroulez, les clics que vous effectuez, les coups de pinceau que vous appliquez sont mémorisés. Les retouches terminées, cliquez sur le bouton Stop et enregistrez le script sous un nom de votre choix afin d'appliquer toutes ces actions à d'autres images. Les scripts sont très appréciés des créateurs vidéo qui doivent souvent traiter les images une à une. Il leur suffit de créer un script pour l'appliquer automatiquement aux centaines, voire aux milliers d'images d'une séquence.

Photoshop dispose d'actions prédéfinies présentes dans la palette Scripts. Ce n'est pas étonnant quand on sait qu'Elements a aussi des actions prédéfinies qui sont stockées dans la palette Effets.

Mêler le passé et le présent

La palette Annuler l'historique d'Elements permet de remonter dans le temps et corriger des erreurs. Celle de Photoshop va plus loin. Elle permet de corriger des parties d'une image. L'outil Forme d'historique (voir la Figure 19.7) permet de peindre à partir d'un état de l'Historique. Par exemple, vous appliquez un filtre à votre image. Ensuite, vous sélectionnez l'état d'historique qui précède l'application du filtre, c'est-à-dire l'état où l'image n'a pas encore subi les effets du filtre. Vous

Figure 19.6 :
Une palette
qui
ressemble
plus à la
façade d'un
magnétos-
cope qu'à un
outil de
création
graphique.
Elle permet
d'enregistrer
des actions
qui seront
appliquées à
une série
d'images.

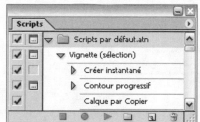

peignez sur cet état, ce qui a pour effet de supprimer les effets du filtre sur les zones où vous passez votre outil de peinture. De son côté, la Forme d'historique artistique est un outil impressionniste capable lui aussi de voyager dans le temps. Votre expressivité artistique n'a plus de limites.

Photoshop parle !

Je sais, c'est difficile à croire. Mais, quand plusieurs personnes collaborent sur une même image, vous pouvez leur laisser des notes du genre "Est-ce que cette police te plaît ?" ou "Puis-je cloner le nez de ce top model sur celui de ce laideron ?" L'outil Note permet d'ajouter des Post-it virtuels sur votre image. Bien sûr, la note n'existe pas réellement sur l'image. C'est une sorte de zone de texte flottante. Vous cliquez sur une icône pour en afficher le contenu (voir la Figure 19.8).

Mais, ces notes ne sont rien comparées aux notes vocales. Avec l'outil Annotation audio, cliquez sur votre image ; vous pouvez alors enregistrer un message qui sera incorporé à l'image. Le message est signalé par l'icône d'un haut-parleur. Double-cliquez dessus pour entendre ce qui est dit. Cette fonction peut avoir un usage multimédia, pour sonoriser un diaporama par exemple, image par image.

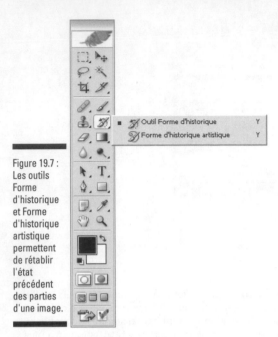

Figure 19.7 :
Les outils
Forme
d'historique
et Forme
d'historique
artistique
permettent
de rétablir
l'état
précédent
des parties
d'une image.

Icône d'une annotation audio

Icône d'annotation

Figure 19.8 :
Les notes et
les
commentai-
res audio
n'ont pas
toujours un
rapport avec
le travail en
cours.

Préparer vos images avec ImageReady

Enfin, le dernier argument pour passer à Photoshop est l'intégration l'ImageReady (voir la Figure 19.9), une application autrefois vendue à part, qui a pour but d'optimiser les images destinées à être publiées sur le Web.

Figure 19.9 : L'interface d'ImageReady ressemble à celles de Photoshop et d'Elements.

ImageReady permet de créer des rollovers (transformation d'un graphisme au passage de la souris) et des zones actives. Ces dernières sont basées sur le découpage d'une image en plusieurs zones auxquelles des liens hypertextes ont été affectés.

Index

G

R

W

Y

Z

Titre	ISBN	Code
3DS Max 5 Poche pour les Nuls	2-84427-516-8	65 3689 0
Access 2002 Poche pour les Nuls	2-84427-253-3	65 3297 2
Access 2003 Poche pour les Nuls	2-84427-583-4	65 3781 5
Apprendre à programmer Poche pour les Nuls	2-84427-651-2	65 4084 3
AutoCAD 2005 Poche pour les Nuls	2-84427-689-X	65 0883 2
AutoCAD 2006 Poche pour les Nuls	2-84427-799-3	65 1047 3
Blogs Poche pour les Nuls	2-84427-763-2	65 1001 0
C# Poche pour les Nuls	2-84427-350-5	65 3410 1
C++ Poche pour les Nuls (2e éd.)	2-84427-649-0	65 4082 7
C++ Trucs et Astuces Poche pour les Nuls	2-84427-787-X	65 1040 8
Combattre les hackers Poche pour les Nuls	2-84427-660-1	65 4093 4
Créez des pages Web Poche pour les Nuls (3e éd.)	2-84427-538-9	65 3760 9
Créer un réseau à domicile Poche pour les Nuls	2-84427-657-1	65 4090 0
Créer un réseau sans fil Poche pour les Nuls	2-84427-533-8	65 3718 7
Créer un site Web Poche pour les Nuls (2e éd.)	2-84427-688-1	65 0882 4
Créer un site Web personnel Poche pour les Nuls	2-84427-765-9	65 1003 6
Dépanner et optimiser Windows Poche pour les Nuls	2-84427-519-2	65 3692 4
DivX Poche pour les Nuls	2-84427-462-5	65 3611 4
Dreamweaver MX 2004 Poche pour les Nuls	2-84427-612-1	65 4060 3
Easy Media Creator 7 Poche Pour les Nuls	2-84427-695-4	65 0889 9
Excel 2002 Poche Pour les Nuls	2-84427-255-X	65 3299 8
Excel 2003 Poche Pour les Nuls	2-84427-582-6	65 3780 7
Excel Trucs et astuces Poche pour les Nuls	2-84427-696-2	65 0890 7
Final Cut Express 2 Poche Pour les Nuls	2-84427-647-4	65 4080 1
Flash MX 2004 Poche pour les Nuls	2-84427-613-X	65 4061 1
Gravure des CD et DVD Poche pour les Nuls (5e éd.)	2-84427- 813-2	65 1056 4
HTML 4 Poche pour les Nuls (2e éd.)	2-84427-731-4	65 0995 4
iMac Poche pour les Nuls (3 éd.)	2-84427-320-3	65 3362 4
InDesign CS2 Poche pour les Nuls	2-84427-819-1	65 1062 2
Internet Poche pour les Nuls (6e éd.)	2-84427-812-4	65 1055 6
iPod & iTunes Poche pour les Nuls	2-84427-762-4	65 1000 2
Java 2 Poche pour les Nuls (2e éd.)	2-84427-687-1	65 0881 6
JavaScript Poche pour les Nuls (2e éd.)	2-84427-716-0	65 0981 4
Linux Poche pour les Nuls (4e éd.)	2-84427-698-9	65 0892 3

Titre	ISBN	Code
Mac Poche pour les Nuls (2ᵉ éd.)	2-84427-319-X	65 3361 6
Mac OS X Poche pour les Nuls	2-84427-264-9	65 3308 7
Mac OS X Panther Poche pour les Nuls	2-84427-611-3	65 4059 5
Mac OS X Panther Trucs et Astuces Poche pour les Nuls	2-84427-662-8	65 4095 9
Mac OS X Tiger Poche pour les Nuls	2-84427-783-7	65 1016 8
Mac OS X v.10.2 Poche pour les Nuls	2-84427-459-5	65 3608 0
Money 2003 Poche pour les Nuls	2-84427-458-7	65 3607 2
Musique sur PC avec Windows XP Poche pour les Nuls	2-84427-764-0	65 1002 8
Nero 6 Reloaded Poche pour les Nuls	2-84427-792-6	65 1045 7
Office 2003 Poche pour les Nuls	2-84427-584-2	65 3782 3
Office 2003 Trucs et Astuces Poche pour les Nuls	2-84427-661-X	65 4094 2
Office 2004 Mac Poche pour les Nuls	2-84427-717-9	65 0982 2
Office XP Poche pour les Nuls	2-84427-266-5	65 3310 3
Outlook 2003 Poche pour les Nuls	2-84427-594-X	65 4051 2
PC Poche pour les Nuls (6ᵉ éd.)	2-84427-811-6	65 1054 9
PC Mise à niveau et dépannage Poche pour les Nuls	2-84427-518-4	65 3691 6
PC portable Poche pour les Nuls (2ᵉ éd.)	2-84427-840-X	65 1073 9
Photo numérique Poche pour les Nuls (6ᵉ éd.)	2-84427-805-1	65 1053 1
Photoshop 7 Poche pour les Nuls	2-84427-394-7	65 3491 1
Photoshop CS Poche pour les Nuls	2-84427-614-8	65 4062 9
Photoshop CS Trucs et Astuces Poche Pour les Nuls	2-84427-648-2	65 4081 9
Photoshop CS2 Poche pour les Nuls	2-84427-798-5	65 1046 5
Photoshop Elements 4 Poche pour les Nuls	2-84427-841-8	65 1074 7
PHP 5 Poche pour les Nuls	2-84427-656-3	65 4089 2
PHP et mySQL Poche pour les Nuls (2ᵉ éd.)	2-84427-591-5	65 3788 0
PowerPoint 3003 Poche pour les Nuls	2-84427-593-1	65 4050 4
Premiere Elements Poche pour les Nuls	2-84427-788-8	65 1041 6
TCP/IP Poche pour les Nuls	2-84427-367-X	65 3443 2
Registre Windows XP Poche pour les Nuls (le)	2-84427-517-6	65 3690 8
Remettre à neuf Windows XP Poche pour les Nuls	2-84427-766-7	65 1004 4
Réseaux Poche pour les Nuls (3è éd.)	2-84427-699-7	65 0893 1
Retouche photo pour les Nuls	2-84427-451-X	65 3577 7
Sécurité Internet Poche pour les Nuls	2-84427-515-X	65 3688 2
SQL Poche pour les nuls (2ᵉ éd.)	2-84427-726-8	65 0990 5
Unix Poche pour les Nuls	2-84427-318-1	65 3360 8

Titre	ISBN	Code
Utiliser un scanner Poche pour les Nuls	2-84427-463-3	65 3612 2
VBA Poche pour les Nuls	2-84427-378-5	65 3463 0
VBA pour Access Poche pour les Nuls	2-84427-703-9	65 0897 2
VBA pour Office Poche pour les Nuls	2-84427-592-3	65 3789 8
VBA pour Excel Poche pour les Nuls	2-84427-725-X	65 0989 7
Vidéo numérique Poche pour les nuls (la) (3e éd.)	2-84427-610-5	65 4058 7
Visual Basic .net Poche pour les Nuls	2-84427-336-X	65 3386 3
Visual Basic 6 Poche pour les Nuls	2-84427-256-8	65 3300 4
Windows 98 Poche pour les Nuls	2-84427-460-9	65 3609 8
Windows Me Poche pour les Nuls	2-84427-937-6	65 3199 0
Windows XP Poche pour les Nuls (5e éd.)	2-84427-803-1	65 1051 5
Windows XP Trucs et Astuces Poche Pour les Nuls (2e éd.)	2-84427-732-2	65 0996 2
Word 2000 Poche pour les Nuls	2-84427-965-1	65 3230 3
Word 2002 Poche Pour les Nuls	2-84427-257-6	65 3301 2
Word 2003 Poche Pour les Nuls	2-84427-581-8	65 3779 9